AURONA
A TALE OF ACTION, ADVENTURE & SUSPENSE

Book One:
THE JOURNEY

Book Two:
THE PLANET

Book Three:
WARPING TIME

Written and Illustrated by BB PRESCOTT
© 2019 All Rights Reserved

Aurona

BB Prescott

Elm Hill
A Division of
HarperCollins Christian Publishing
www.elmhillbooks.com

© 2019 BB Prescott

Aurona

All rights reserved. No portion of this book may be reproduced, stored in a retrieval system, or transmitted in any form or by any means—electronic, mechanical, photocopy, recording, scanning, or other—except for brief quotations in critical reviews or articles, without the prior written permission of the publisher.

Published in Nashville, Tennessee, by Elm Hill, an imprint of Thomas Nelson. Elm Hill and Thomas Nelson are registered trademarks of HarperCollins Christian Publishing, Inc.

Elm Hill titles may be purchased in bulk for educational, business, fund-raising, or sales promotional use. For information, please e-mail SpecialMarkets@ThomasNelson.com.

Publisher's Note: This novel is a work of fiction. Names, characters, places, and incidents are either products of the author's imagination or used fictitiously. All characters are fictional, and any similarity to people living or dead is purely coincidental.

Library of Congress Cataloging-in-Publication Data

Library of Congress Control Number: 2018966975

ISBN 978-0-310103707 (Paperback)
ISBN 978-0-310103714 (eBook)

AURONA
Table of Contents

Book One: THE JOURNEY

Prologue:	vii
Chapter 1: THE GALAXY ROOM	3
Chapter 2: SEEDS	17
Chapter 3: THE ROBE	25
Chapter 4: DECEPTION	33
Chapter 5: DOORS	43
Chapter 6: MAROONED	57
Chapter 7: JOURNEY	71
Chapter 8: THE HOLOSPHERE	83
Chapter 9: INCIDENT IN QUARANTINE	93
Chapter 10: THE PODIUM	107
Chapter 11: THE SHIELD	115
Chapter 12: THE KEY	127

Book Two: THE PLANET

Chapter 13: KIDNAPPED	143
Chapter 14: SOLUMBRA	157
Chapter 15: THE CITY	169
Chapter 16: PLANET OF LIGHTS	181
Chapter 17: PARADISE	195
Chapter 18: AERONAUTAS AND ANCHORPLANKS	205
Chapter 19: RAZAH	215
Chapter 20: SPYRINS	227
Chapter 21: METAMORPHOSIS	241
Chapter 22: THE STORM	253
Chapter 23: PRIMA	267
Chapter 24: MESEO	277

Book Three: WARPING TIME

Chapter 25: CRISIS	287
Chapter 26: THE ISLAND	295
Chapter 27: EVACUATION	309
Chapter 28: THE TOMB	323
Chapter 29: THE POWER	337
Chapter 30: MIND GAMES	349
Chapter 31: THE UNEXPECTED	363
Chapter 32: ZERAN	375
Chapter 33: WARPING TIME	383

PROLOGUE

White ... blinding white. A translucent brilliance of crystals swirled in the air, obliterating the horizons. As daylight washed across the strange landscape, the small planet's hot sun made both temperature and wind rise rapidly. Out in the middle of this vast plain of nothingness, the vague outline of a lone figure stirred and then disappeared under the rapidly accumulating drifts of powder.

A gloved hand lifted weakly. With great effort, a young man rose to one elbow and raised his head. His helmet glinting brightly in the cruel sun, he stared into a blank void: land and sky had merged as one into a total whiteout.

As his consciousness slowly returned he took in a few shallow breaths, wincing at a painful rattle somewhere deep in his chest. His mind swirling, he began to go through the possibilities, trying his best to reason it out: yes, that was it, his rebreather unit was malfunctioning. Struggling to remember the controls, he activated his head-up display with a few muttered commands. A bright schematic lit up, his e-helmet rotating on its axis, the inner workings showing transparently. As the back came into view, he drew in a sharp breath. "Oh no," he scowled. "Where'd that huge *dent* come from?" Just under the surface, the transfer membranes of his life-giving cyborg lungs were laid out in millions of delicate, atom-thin sheets. Looking like a dark bruise in the center, a large section had been mashed out of commission.

With a groan of frustration, he scrolled quickly through a glowing tapestry of readouts. Almost alive and self-aware, the tempered thermoglass auto-darkened to let his eyes focus on the words. "You're kidding," he muttered, "it's way below fifty percent capacity?" He coughed, this time tasting blood. Fighting a wave of panic, he forced himself to take shallower breaths. Suddenly, two lights blinked on. His vision was beginning to swim as he struggled to focus on a pair of small, flashing bar graphs crawling relentlessly up the side of the screen. The temperature was rising at a phenomenal rate and the pedometer revealed that he'd wandered close to seven miles.

"Huh? I-I don't remember walking anywhere...." He shook his head in confusion. "And speaking of *where*, where in blazes am I?" He cleared the display to look outside and recoiled at the overwhelming brilliance. "Whoa! *Way* too much light!" Using the helmet's alternate chin pad sequence, he tapped down the intensity. "Better," he muttered, "but what's all that awful, screeching static in the background?" He cupped a gloved hand over his earpiece and immediately got his answer: the howling storm of silica crystals had been hissing against the audiodomes, amplifying into a deafening roar. Scrolling quickly through a few more menus he found 'Audio,' and then tapping his chin decidedly, he clicked it off. Silence washed over him like a sheltering blanket. "Ahh, thank God. Maybe now I can *think*!" Stiff and sore, he pushed up with his elbows.

Something seemed to be holding him back. "Huh?" He tugged on his arm again, testing. Yes, it was definitely caught on something. Digging with his free hand, his probing, gloved fingertips felt something like a thick steel cable looped tightly around his wrist. His heart hammering, he cleared away the white silica powder to look closer. Frosted with crystals, a sinewy gray-green coil was wrapped tightly around his wrist.

"What in the world is this thing? Some kind of a *snare*?"

He braced his feet and yanked upward with all his might. Nothing moved: the cable felt like steel. "I'm-I'm *trapped?* No way!" He clenched his teeth and pounded on the coil with his free hand, his labored breathing rattling loudly. Suddenly an annoying buzzer sounded and a warning light pulsed a harsh neon yellow, dead center in his head-up display. "Crud!" He panted. "Rebreather's totally maxed out now. Gotta calm down, gotta think rationally...." His head swimming, he paused to catch his breath, his gloved hand resting lightly on the coil.

Unexpectedly, there was a shudder under his fingertips. As he jerked his hand away, the coil started to undulate, tightening, loosening and writhing like a serpent. "It *can't* be!" He gasped, his heart thudding loudly. "Th-this thing's *alive*?"

The buzzer was now howling. He gritted his teeth in the din, the back of his head pounding viciously and his vision swimming from the lack of oxygen. "No, no," he gasped. "Please, not now; I can't black out now! Gotta conserve energy or I'm a goner!"

Steeling himself and gathering his wits, he forced his body to calm down, to lie absolutely still. Shortly, the coil gave a final shudder. It didn't seem to be pulling him under; it just lay there, clamped tightly around his wrist. He exhaled, sweat running down his back in rivers. Waiting a few more scorching minutes, he nervously rechecked the bar graphs again. Both the e-helmet and suit were blistering hot, well within the dreaded red zone: he had to do something, and do it quickly.

In a flash, it came to him. Moving slowly, deliberately, he began to shovel out a deep, body-sized depression in the soft silica. It didn't take long to open up a good-sized pit. He slid down carefully into it, pulling handfuls of the powder over him. Yes, it was definitely cooler in the hole, blissfully cool. With the howling wind assisting, it didn't take long to get completely buried. With a series of voice commands, he sent his rebreather's twin-tubed snorkel snaking up to the surface to scavenge the thin atmosphere's limited oxygen/nitrogen content.

As absolute quiet enveloped him and the pain in his head ebbed away, he began to vent, his eyes tearing up in frustration. "So some kind of creature's got me trapped, but where? Where in blazes *am* I? How'd I *get* here? The gravity's weak, so I gotta be on a fairly small planet, but how...?" There seemed to be an insurmountable wall: no amount of logic or reasoning could cross it. "And what's *wrong* with me? I-I can't remember a *thing*!" He squeezed his eyes shut. "Was it that blow to my head?" He struggled to piece something, anything together, but to no avail. With a shudder of resignation his exhausted, battered body finally gave in.

He slipped away. Distant memories of his childhood poured in like a great wave flooding his mind, followed by visions of a torrid jungle, torrential rain, and swirling mists....

Book One:
THE JOURNEY

Chapter One: THE GALAXY ROOM

Driving sheets of rain were blurring the peaks of the distant mountains. The odd, jagged ring of spires had eroded almost beyond recognition over the eons, but still guarded their hidden world: a lush, flat plain of fertile volcanic soil several miles in diameter. As shadows dimmed, a deep rumbling shook the earth. The chattering jungle creatures grew still, apprehensive.

In a rush, a storm spilled into the caldera of the dormant volcano. Flashes of neon slit the leading edge of the clouds, deafening peals of thunder bellowed out of the darkness, and a moving wall of wind and rain caught the palms broadside, bending them like supple dancers.

The deluge was over in a few hours. With stifled growls, the storm clouds reluctantly slid their long, black cloaks from the distant watercolored peaks. As the eternal tropical sun burned a great hole through the swirling vapors, a sudden, breathtaking shaft of light focused downward onto a muddy stream swollen far over its banks. The skies grew clearer, late morning mist lifted to the jungle canopy and stillness settled in with the heat of the day.

Far away, over the rush of cascading water, the effervescent melody of a child's laughter embellished the thunder's deep, rolling bass. It drew closer, weaving a brightly colored thread of sound through the hushed gray-green tapestry. Vibrant, alive, the cheerful echoes resonated strangely out of place in the lost valley; indeed, man hadn't seen this part of the island continent in centuries.

Strange sounds began to come from the tangled underbrush: an odd, static crackling and a low electrical hum. Puzzled, the creatures listened intently. An apparition slowly materialized in the shadows: silently, furtively, gliding a few feet off the ground, a bullet shape with two figures on it poked around a primeval-looking tangle of cycad palms. The soft, rhythmic staccato sound of wet branches slapped against a sleek, hard surface, and then stopped. The shadowy bullet shape rotated toward a large clearing.

Suddenly a string of blue lights fanned out along its sides. In a whir of motion it veered, accelerated, then darted out into the open. Flashing brilliantly in the sun's spotlight, its vibrant electric blue hull blazed to life with the startling iridescence of a morpho butterfly.

"Ple-e-e-ease!" The excited squeal of a young boy ascended upward into an impossible, stratospheric register. As the sled whipped through another hairpin turn he begged again, this time reaching a high C sharp. The creatures ducked for cover.

"No way-y-y!" The boy was thrilled and chirped in delight as he held on tightly, his wet, tangled hair flying. His eyes watered up in the wind, making the lush, flowered landscape blur even more. "Grandpa," he teased, "where'd you learn to drive?"

The old man chuckled to himself as he sat hunched tightly over the controls, maneuvering intently with a set of small, ultraresponsive thumb steerers. The sled's response rate was far better than he'd ever hoped; it seemed to slice through the jungle's tangle at almost the speed of his thoughts. He glanced over his shoulder at the boy. Roller coasters had always thrilled him: the faster the better. To push the envelope, he hatched up a quick maneuver to feed his grandson's need for speed.

Feigning alarm, he threw his hands up in mock helplessness. "Oh no! Wait, what's this?

There's something wrong with the controls!" The sled stopped, spun 360 degrees, and then quickly resumed its breakneck speed.

Just as he'd hoped, Adam was impressed. "Wow! How'd you do that, Grandpa?"

He chuckled mischievously. "Ever hear of preprogramming? Six seconds to figure out the maneuver, three to lock it in, and one to punch the button!"

The boy's slow, silent ear-to-ear grin was worth the effort. The old man slowed down, leaned back, and scanned the controls with satisfaction: they were floating along on incredibly sophisticated hardware, once unthinkable fantasy confined to the realm of a visionary's dreams or a theorist's tinkering.

"Antigrav, Adam! Who'd have ever figured that an ordinary sphere of polished lead might hold the key? Hey, since our big breakthrough last fall, we've had nothing but fun, fun, fun, right?"

The mop of wet, tousled hair nodded enthusiastically.

"Whoa, hold on! Could that possibly be…?" The man abruptly stopped and stood up in the sled, shading his eyes in the glare. "Yes, there it is, the triple mound, dead ahead! Let's get the coordinates." He glanced into the sky and then back to his wrist programmer to do a few quick calculations. "Perfect! Quick, quick, grab the maps! They'll all be distracted! We're right on time for the release!"

They leaned against each other, peering up into the cloudless sky. Yes, there it was, an unbelievably bright, shining dot, even at this time of day. As the boy dropped to his knees to rummage around for the maps, the old man punched a series of buttons on a small transmitter.

Slowly, majestically, the massive triangular satellite swept by in its endless loop, streaming out a powerful band of encrypted chatter. TriNight had officially been in orbit one year to the minute. Down in Mission Control, its guidance crew was busy celebrating, oblivious to a series of carefully orchestrated, yet stealthy mechanical movements that were starting to show on the monitors behind their backs.

Out on the tips of each of the satellite's three arms, small half-cylinders were slowly rotating open to reveal a set of polished, thumb-sized mirrorlike spheres. At another signal, the MicroSats were silently released from their rubberized magnetic docks to puff a short distance away from the massive structure. Looking like brilliant specks of dust in the unblinking sun, like dancers in perfect synchronization, they puffed outward and upward at a precise angle. Accelerating to a mile's distance from each other, they retrofired their strong propulsion units to park in geostationary orbit, positioned in a precise equilateral triangle somewhere above the western coast of New Guinea. As the enormous wedge shape of the mothership slid over the curve of the horizon, the three stowaways rotated their cameras and sensors downward….

"Yuck!" Adam peeled a pile of wet paper off the floor of the sled. Scowling, he tried his best to smooth it out in his lap. "They're all runny, Grandpa."

"That's okay, I think we got it."

Adam shoved the wad of papers aside to peer over his shoulder. There was a brilliantly glowing screen on the dashboard. "Wow!" He gushed. "Look at that! Your little GPS guys are all cranking out real-time videos!" He pointed, first to the screen then to the humps in front of them. "We must be real close to the…."

Their eyes locked. "The Outpost," they whispered in unison.

"The MicroSats are pointing the way," the old man affirmed. "We had to use 'em to see through this thick jungle. You know, Adam, in spite of the big storm this morning, we've actually covered most of the distance! According to my little spheres, there's less than half a mile to go. Thank God we had our shields up or we would'a gotten soaked."

"Hey!" Adam pointed through a small opening in the trees. "There's the muddy river I just saw on the screen! We might be able to go faster along the shore!"

"Good thinking! A perfect detour, roughly in the same direction," his grandfather grinned, turning the sled toward the water. "But remember, we can fly."

"Huh?"

"We're gonna go right down the middle!"

"No, no! Over the water? It's too wild, Grandpa. W-we can't…."

"Think again! Anything's possible, right! I'll just recalculate our latest coordinates onto the map and we'll make some serious time! Just watch!" He raised the sled a few feet higher and shot straight out over the swollen stream. Hovering rock-steady for a few moments to adjust the controls, he nosed south on the highway of roiling brown water and punched the accelerator. Like some exotic species of flying fish, they soared over the rock-strewn, muddy surface, the sled pulsing powerfully beneath them.

Adam raised his arms high in the air, yelping in delight. "Wow! This is more like it, Grandpa! We're really movin'!

The old man chuckled, squinting his eyes in the spray. "Hey, I'm thinking this would be a perfect time to test our autopilot, don't you?"

Adam rested his chin on the big shoulder, watching intently.

"Here goes," the old man grinned. "Supertechno stuff!" Slowly, deliberately, he slid the delay control up a few notches to let the circle of Doppler radar chips work in closer sync with the side thrusters. With a soft hum, the double row of fine, blue laser locator beams brightened and fanned out around the sled's lateral lines as the big internal neodymium magnet gyro sped up several hundred thousand rpm. Things immediately smoothed out: the sled became alive, anticipatory, and almost human in its reactions.

Adam's sensitive ears picked out another sound: tiny puffs of air were now shooting out all around the perimeter! With short, precise autopulses from a train of valves in the minijet rails, the sled was now a step ahead of the subtlest shifts in wind shear and the ever-changing terrain of the rapids in front of them.

Grandpa chuckled, slipping back quickly into his usual techno jargon. "Man, just look at the schematic! The blue lasers' short wavelengths and the sonar are pinpointing every pebble along the shore!"

The once-roiling stream began to broaden and slow down, and they found themselves in a thicket of odd-looking vegetation. He throttled back, lowered the sled, and reached over the side. At the slightest of touches, a translucent, watery stem broke in his fingers with a decided snap. He raised his bushy brows knowingly. "Aha!" He turned to Adam. "A very exotic strain of the fumitory family, like Dutchmen's breeches: it's only indigenous to marshy ground. We're very close; the runes mentioned a marsh." Their searching eyes quickly spotted a small opening along the shoreline.

A finger to his lips, his head motioning toward the entrance, the old man turned toward the boy with a mysterious air. The tousled head nodded eagerly. He tweaked the sled's antigrav upward half a notch. They entered cautiously, hovering noiselessly above the spongy ground, peering intently into the fascinating web of green. The humid environment was thick, oppressive, yet absolutely thrumming with life. After a long, silent moment, Adam's faint whisper broke the spell, his voice barely audible.

"A-are they watching us, Grandpa?"

"Yes," he shrugged, "Definitely. The animals are watching us."

"Let's hide, then!" Adam interrupted excitedly.

"Hey, all right!" Grandpa whispered, quickly opening up a new a bank of switches on his touchscreen. "Thinking, thinking, always thinking! That's what I like about you, boy! Yes, it's much smarter to watch the critters from cover!"

He programmed a few sequences. With a crackle and hum the sled became surrounded with electrical shields, completely masking their human odor and blotting out the sound of their excited breathing. A cloaking device followed, blossoming from a point somewhere below the sled and spreading slowly upward, simply airbrushing them from view. In a heartbeat they'd become a shimmering mirage, watching life as from another dimension. Many nervous eyes were now blinking in bewilderment from the surrounding jungle.

Suddenly, there was a tremendous crash and SCREAM right next to the sled!

"Yikes!" Adam slid off his seat, rapping his elbow. "Ouch!" Rubbing it furiously, he scrambled to his knees to peer intently through the electronic curtain, straining his utmost to see. "Grandpa!" He hissed. "W-what in the world was that?"

"Hey, we don't exist, remember? You don't have to whisper!"

"Oh, yeah. Right."

Something began to thrash wildly in the branches beside them. Loud screams stabbed unmercifully into the tranquil pulse of life, skewing the droning peace into an instant, shocked war zone. As the horrific din invaded their electronic walls, Grandpa's hands groped blindly toward the controls, his nerves raw, poised on the razor-edge of flight. Without warning, the curtain of leaves whipped apart: a fierce, fire-eyed, demonic apparition burst through, flying directly at them!

Adam squealed in terror, looking up and holding his arms over his head. The silhouette of a struggling brown form was being dragged over their invisible dome, flailing and thumping loudly against the curved shield; it trailed a long stream of blood, the dark red beads sizzling, popping and dancing on the current. In seconds the action resumed on the other side of the sled. As they swiveled in unison, the boy pressed tightly against his grandpa's shoulder, his heart beating nearly out of his chest. "W-what is that thing?"

"Hmm… I've seen a few in documentaries but never in real life. They're an endangered species now. Let's see; lemme do a split screen: the LifeForm Database cross-referenced next to a color-enhanced infrared camera." He twirled a few dials. "Wow, there's your answer, boy," he nodded. "Look at the pictures!"

The database showed the creature's face, with a full description below. Adam's eyes grew wide as he glanced at the infrared image next to it.

A magnificent harpy eagle hovered before them in the sunlit clearing. The infrared was vividly color-enhanced: a hot-red avian shape showed clearly, with powerful, blue-green vortices of wind swirling off the tips of seven-foot, beating wings. It definitely looked like an alien creature with the long, curving feathers of his Medusa's crest flaring wide in alarm. The predator was obviously stunned and surprised.

The enormous wings were powerful, the turbulence pushing the sled away from it. With a sudden loud pop the GPS sensors clicked, initiating an autocorrective maneuver: the port thrusters came on and the whoosh gave them away.

"Oops," Adam whispered. "He's outta here!"

Like a circling halo of snakes, the crest shot out in alarm and he clamped his steely talons down in a viselike death-grip. His prey, a small female monkey, gasped her last and hung limply. As he rose in the air, Adam spotted a subtle movement on the monkey's underbelly. "Uh-oh!" He shook Grandpa's shoulders and pointed emphatically. "Is that what I think it is?"

The man shielded his eyes in the glare, squinting up into the blinding, flickering shafts of light. Shortly, he spotted it. "Yes, yes, there's another one, Adam, there's definitely another monkey.... It's a baby! By gosh, your eyes are sharp!"

A tiny, month-old infant was clinging for its life to its mother's fur. They watched helplessly, speechlessly, as the eagle neared the sunlit hole in the canopy. Suddenly, the little one lost its grip! Plummeting head over heels, it looked like a tumbling speck of dust grasping desperately at the empty air.

"No!" Adam gasped. "He's falling!"

In a quick, deliberate chain of reflexive actions, the man leaped to the rescue. He dropped the shields and cloaking device, sidestepped the sled with a strong blast from the starboard thrusters, and at the last possible second, threw his raincoat wide like a net. The frightened ball of fur bounced once, flew through the air, and beelined into the man's thick hair, looking for something furry and familiar.

Adam was bouncing now, too. "Yeow! Where'd he go? Did he get away?"

A big hand gently cupped over his fluttering lips for silence. "Shhh! Cool your jets," he whispered. "We don't want to frighten him any more than he is!"

A fuzzy head popped up, prompting a stifled squeal. "There he is!"

Somehow he'd managed to squeeze out a few words between the man's thick fingers. Grinning, the old man tried his best to hold the thin, flailing arms to his sides, but the eight-year-old's patience had reached its limit: he could be contained no longer. Slippery as a bar of wet soap, he wrestled his mouth and arms free.

"Is-is he hurt, Grandpa? Is he hurt? Huh?"

The man sighed in resignation and let go. Scowling, he poked around in his thick hair. "All right, let's see..." Oh-so-carefully he plucked at the tiny, clenching fingers with his big mitts, as if they were errant sticky burrs. "Ouch! Ooooch! Darn thing's worse than Velcro!" Resolutely gritting his teeth he yanked hard, pulling out long frazzled strands of salt-and-pepper hair. "Okay, okay! Take him quick, Adam!"

The boy drew back, stunned. "Huh? Me? You're letting me hold him?

All hands and feet, the infant was grabbing at the air. Adam reached out tentatively. It latched onto his thumb, swung down into his lap, and cowered tightly against his chest. Afraid to move his head a fraction of an inch, he lowered just his eyes to study the frail creature. It didn't take long for the bond to form; in a few moments it was as if they were old friends: the boy rocking back and forth on the seat making soothing sounds, the monkey squeaking in response.

As the man watched the two in fascination, he noticed a dark cloud slowly shadowing his grandson's face, erasing his delighted smile. He leaned toward him.

"What is it, boy?" he whispered.

Adam glanced up, his throat tightening. "H-he's just like me, Grandpa," he choked, tears brimming.

"Of course he's just like you. He's got two hands, two ears, a nose…."

"No, no!" he interrupted. "Now, I mean! H-he's just like me now!" The barely contained tears brimmed over, and he began to sob.

As he watched the boy cradling the newly created orphan, he finally understood what had really been conveyed between the lines. A deep wound had just been opened, one that would never go away. Impulsively he reached out and swept the weeping boy to his chest, his heart aching anew. The event that shattered their small family happened only five years ago. As the memories jolted painfully, relentlessly, into place, he began to blink back his own tears. Trembling, he sighed deeply. This little one now in his arms was barely three when his parents died on that distant planet, but he was sharp enough to grasp what had really happened. He glanced down at his grandson again. The boy's eyes were squeezed tightly shut, his tear-streaked face dappled in the sunlight. He drew him tighter to his chest.

After a long moment, the boy began to whisper haltingly, his child's eye recounting the confusion of that awful day. "I-I don't remember too much, Grandpa, except for all those people running by, yelling and crying. And that big nurse lady was squeezing me too tight! Yelling, yelling way too loud!" He lowered his head. "It wasn't until she took me down into the hold to see all those long, black boxes that she finally let me go and handed me…."

"That's right, boy," he whispered. "She gave you to me. I have you now."

They sat quietly in the middle of a green nowhere, lost in reverie for what seemed like an eternity.

Finally, with a scowl and a sigh, the boy forced himself away to sit up a bit straighter. Brightening, he reached down with his free hand to pick up a wad of waterlogged paper. "You know, it must be already way over a year since we drew these maps from your weird old runes! We're the only two people in the whole world that knows about them! But it seems like it's taking forever to get to…."

"Wow, a year's gone by already?" Grandpa interrupted, raising a brow. He was relieved: it was as if the sun had come out again. "Well, it's been way, way longer for me, boy! I've held onto those runes ever since I was a young Planet Hopper!"

"Wow, since the olden days!"

The old man held up an admonishing finger. "Easy! Don't start…!"

Grinning mischievously, Adam slipped off his lap and stood up, looking around intently. "Are we getting closer to the outpost?"

"Yeah, very close, kiddo. But now it's time to watch very carefully, because the next part is gonna get pretty, ah, dangerous."

"Dangerous?" The tear-swollen eyes were suddenly eager.

"Dangerous," he affirmed. "So just do exactly as I say, right?"

"Right!"

He tousled the boy's hair. "Let's go," he whispered.

Two hundred and sixty miles overhead, Grandpa's shiny trio of MicroSats had been silently pinpointing their position. He flipped down a touchpad from the console and began to draw on its surface with a stylus, his hand moving quickly, plotting an intricate overlay on top of the 3D photo terrain. He'd personally developed all this classified tracking technology and hardware for the government, so he'd been right on the scene for the mission's hurried, last-minute preparations. It had been surprisingly easy to stow his personal, multifunctional thumb-sized satellites aboard TriNight.

As the sled glided around a last, tangled thicket of palms into a swampy opening, a fine, scopelike set of crosshairs moved slowly across the screen's real-time overlay. Finally, the crosshairs aligned with the big X on the photomap.

"Bingo!" Grandpa muttered. "There you go, right down to the fraction of an inch! Can't get any better'n that!" He stopped and looked up decisively. "We're here!"

The boy's bright young eyes had been watching every movement, taking it all in. He bounced up and looked around, gently cradling the monkey in his arms. The antigrav sled hovered noiselessly, as steady as a rock, its fine blue laser beams dancing brightly on nearby stationary objects. They were beside a stream with what appeared to be a massive wall on the other side.

"Aha!" Grandpa's booming voice echoed off the hard surface, breaking the silence. "So that's what it looks like!" Shaking with excitement, the boy stowed the monkey into a small specimen cage under his seat. "Grab your backpack!" The old man jumped off nimbly, his boots squishing into the boggy earth. With a clatter and a splash, Adam was quickly beside him. The wall appeared to be seamless, so fine was the fit of each massive stone, revealing just a glimpse of the mastery of the unknown architects. Almost completely overgrown, vines and strange mosses now enveloped an incredibly smooth, mirrorlike surface. They waded slowly across the swollen stream, their eyes fixed on the mysterious ruin.

There was a sudden flash of light stabbing out of the gloom ahead! Grandpa looked down at his grandson's chest. Twin beams were tracing out mysterious patterns!

The boy drew back, his hands flailing to brush them off. "G-Grandpa?"

"Wow! You found them already?" he whispered.

"I found them?" he choked. "I-I think they found me!"

Grandpa stood there like a rock, his eyes darting, analyzing. "Hmm, I'm only guessing here, but I think the beams must be establishing our species."

Adam's chin was quivering, the light dancing on his chest. "Now what?"

"Well, I think it's time you say the word, that's what."

"Huh? There's a word?"

"Think now. The beams found you, and they're waiting for the word! It's gotta come from you…."

"Wait, wait! Don't tell me! Is-is it that funny rune word we talked about?"

"Yes," he answered calmly. "That one."

"But-but I forgot how to pronounce it!"

Grandpa held up a finger. "Listen carefully. We're in a locked pattern here, and there's no getting around it. The rune needs to be spoken to avoid consequences. Big consequences." He looked into the boy's frightened eyes. "Now, remember the keyword, 'Valota'? Try it. You can do it."

The boy took a deep breath. "Val-oh-tah!"

They waited in expectation. Nothing happened.

He tried again, enunciating a different syllable. "Valo-tah!"

Immediately, something snapped upward under his feet! He gasped, his arms flailing for balance. "Grandpa! Under me! There's some kind of underwater cable!"

In a geyser of bubbles, a loud mechanical whir penetrated the surface of the stream in a distressing, high-pitched pulse. The water exploded into motion, a blur of scale, claw, eye, and tooth. Frantic life forms boiled toward the shore, flapping and slithering: lungfish, slithering electric eels, small reptiles, water snakes, frogs, and salamanders, the entire resident amphibian population scrambled wildly away from the source. As the bizarre assortment of cold bodies bumped and twined around his feet, Adam finally lost it. He screamed a high C sharp and jumped into his grandfather's arms. "Wh-what is it, Grandpa?" he quavered.

Keeping his cool, the old man poked at the cable with his toe. "Hmm…. This must be what they called the Hetex, remember? The trigger? How clever! They hid it underwater! We might've been searching all morning!"

A loud scraping sound came from the wall. They both jerked their heads up.

"Stay cool, boy," he hissed. "I think that's the Motaz! Remember that word?"

Adam squinted into the mass of greenery, trying to focus on the source of the sound. "The M-Motaz? What does it do, Grandpa? What…?"

A seam showed up on the wall, appearing from nowhere! With a rending squeal and a loud snapping sound, vines and moss were yanked loose in a huge rectangle. A deep rumbling shook the ground as an enormous rectangular block slid inward into the shadows. The opening was quickly showered with scrambling lizards and falling bromeliad cups; the spiky, hot-pink plants tipped over, spilling and wetting the dry stone.

Grandpa nodded knowingly. "So that's the Motaz! It's what they called the 'moving opening.'" He swung the boy up onto his big shoulders and walked briskly toward the wall. "The runes were spot on, Adam. Now it's time for your job. Make it quick now."

The boy was frightened but knew what to do: they'd rehearsed it a zillion times. As he scrambled up over the edge, an odd odor hit him in the face. Cold wind was rushing up out of the darkness, the swirling eddies blending the odd, sharp smells of hot metal, crushed stone and sap from the bleeding vines. Together, they stunk with an acidic pervasiveness. He crawled a bit further into the darkness on his hands and knees, squinting. A tunnel! All that cold wind was flowing up out of a tunnel! His hand suddenly rested on something warm and smooth. Startled he looked down, his eyes focusing on a faint gleam under the eons of dust. He spun around on his knees, whispering a single word to Grandpa over the edge.

"Rails!"

There was a flash of a smile. The big hands silently motioned for him to hurry. He quickened his pace. Yes, a double set of rails shone beneath the edge of the massive stone plug, now against the far wall. He slid a finger over the slick surface. What kind of metal could this be? Why, it wasn't even rusty! He dug into his backpack and pulled out a knotted climbing rope, locked the grappling end firmly into one of the rails, and tossed it down over the edge. He stopped short. Somewhere in the darkness behind him, he thought he heard a small, metallic clink. What in the world was that?

Grandpa had heard it too, and his head jerked up. Rope in hand, he nimbly scaled the wall with the skill of an acrobat, flipping up over the edge. He landed in a squat, drawing his ion gun. "Down!" he hissed.

As Adam flattened himself, there was a clap of thunder and something massive cleaved through the air, whizzing by the very spot where his head would have been! Their jaws dropped as an enormous stone sphere crashed far out in the jungle, leaving a trail of flying branches and terror-stricken animals in its wake.

It all grew quiet again. Somewhere in the ominous silence, there was a second faint metallic clink, this time followed by an electronic hum. Adam flattened his body and closed his eyes in fearful anticipation. "No, no, Grandpa! Another...."

"Hold on!" the man interrupted, rolling away.

There were several loud pops in rapid succession. Terror pulsing through his veins, Adam cracked his eyes open a slit to see the man lying flat on his back, his ion gun blazing into the shadows. After a loud, electronic screech in the darkness, there was an ominous silence. He watched the old man rise slowly to his feet, hesitate, and then creep inside. His teeth began to chatter. Sweat was now evaporating off his thin body, making him shake uncontrollably in the cold wind from the tunnel. After a moment of indecision, he leapt to his feet, briskly rubbing his arms.

"Grandpa! Where are you grandpa?... Grandpa?"

There was a distant, muffled cough. "Come over and see this, boy!"

He let out a short breath, relieved. He sprinted to his side and knelt down, his eyes taking a moment to adjust to the shadows. His grandfather was bending over a strange-looking, smoldering object fastened low on the wall, the tip of his ion gun gingerly poking at a bunch of smoking gold wires.

Without a word, the boy dropped to his hands and knees, turned, and crawled along the floor into the shadows, tracing another set of gleaming rails to another massive stone sphere! He scrambled to his feet and walked around the back of it, his hand sliding over the surface. This one was way bigger, as big as a truck, and it seemed to be aimed lower, probably to pick off any stragglers. The melted gold wiring gleamed brightly in the darkness.

"They had a giant catapult! You took out the trigger mechanism, Grandpa!" His muffled voice echoed out from the depths. "You zapped the sensor!"

The man peered around the sphere. "Good for you, Adam! Dead on!"

Indeed, a very old and very sophisticated catapult mechanism stood tautly poised, its strange metal alloy still gleaming brightly after eons. "Stand back, boy!" he whispered. "I just want to make sure." A single, well-aimed blast from his ion gun fused the trigger mechanism for good. He gathered up a few slivers of the alloy and stowed them into a specimen bag to analyze later.

Adam looked up fearfully into his grandfather's eyes. "W-we woulda' been squashed, Grandpa!" His teeth chattered. "Like b-bugs!"

"It's okay," he reassured. "Well, the show's over! Let's go! We gotta make time!"

As they lit their powerful Asron gas torches, the stone's highly polished surface bounced the thin pencil beams back into their faces like dazzling mini suns. They turned a dial and widened the focus into a flood. Moving quickly, the man slipped out a small, pressurized vial of strange fluid, cranked open its needle valve a bit, and then clipped it firmly onto his utility belt.

The boy watched in fascination. A thin, glowing stream of phosphorescent vapor wafted into the air, solidified, and settled to the floor in a glowing tracery.

"Wow! Way cool, Grandpa! What's all this shiny stuff for?"

He shrugged. "Just preparing for any eventuality, right? We might have to ditch these heavy torches and come back in the dark. Hey! I kinda like the effect, don't you?"

The boy nodded emphatically, scuffing some of it around with his boots and watching it smear. "We'll just follow the glow back up here, right?"

"Right! Let's go!"

As they entered and the floor began to angle steeply downward, Adam started to slide on the polished surface, losing control. Leaning against the wall, he trained his torch into the depths and squinted down the shaft. Far below, a strangely patterned wall appeared. As they slid closer, picking up speed, he could finally make it out. Bristling ominously at the end of the ramp, great, sharp spikes were sticking out nastily from the surface.

He panicked. "Grandpa! A booby trap! We can't stop! What do we…?"

"Your grippers, Adam!" He snapped. "Do it!"

"Oh! Right!"

Even though they'd spent months preparing for the trip, the foot grippers were thrown in as a last-minute addition, almost an afterthought. The results were instantaneous: at the flip of a switch on their utility belts, a set of small vacuum pumps hummed and their footgear's gripper cups pulled tightly to the polished surface. They skidded to a halt, their feet making popping sounds as they approached the wall of death.

Adam's teeth were chattering. "F-first they t-try to f-flatten us, and then they make a slippery ramp that leads to this?" He played his torch over the glistening needles, and then impulsively reached out to test the spikes' sharpness with a fingertip.

A big hand clamped over his wrist. "Uh-uh, Adam. Poison! Nasty stuff."

He drew back in alarm. "W-why? Why are they trying to keep us out?"

Grandpa shrugged. "Secrets, boy. Great secrets." He motioned silently with his head toward a small opening on the right. "You still game?"

They entered cautiously. A set of meticulously sculpted stairs spiraled downward. Adam slipped off his gloves to run a wondering touch over the curved walls as they descended. His fingertips sensed almost nothing; the white alabaster walls were as smooth as glass and perfectly seamless. After many twists downward, the echoes of their excited breathing began to sound entirely different: more delay, more distant-sounding. They'd reached the bottom.

Hesitantly, they stepped out into a huge, domed vault, their twin torches picking out glittering architectural details on the far wall. What was that? It was an entirely different kind of reflection.... They turned their Asron torches upward.

Gasping, they stared open-mouthed at the distant ceiling. An intricate, heavily embossed fretwork of pure, hammered GOLD covered the entire inner surface of the dome, ending in a magnificent, twenty-foot medallion far over their heads!

Their awestruck gazes locked and then lowered as one to the vast, polished floor. The majestic dome overhead suddenly seemed to pale in comparison to the delicate work of art at their feet.

Glowing softly, spiral galaxies and dustlike groups of stars completely unknown to the Earth had been set into a deep, transparent blue glass background. Hair-thin wires of pure gold had been poured along microscopic grooves, connecting the star systems. Without question, this was obviously the creation of exquisitely sensitive hands and a vastly superior intelligence.

They sharpened the focus of their torches to probe deeply into the three-dimensional universe under them, backing their way up the stairs for a wider view: all around the perimeter of the floor, right up under the surface of the glass, a wide band of intricately embossed, cryptic patterns revealed themselves. Runes!

"H-holy cow, Adam," the old man stuttered, his throat tightening. "This-this is it! We're really here!" His mouth worked noiselessly as he translated, reading random descriptions of this lost section of the universe. In a second, he began to hop in a tight circle, his fist punching the air. "Yes! Yes!" He croaked in loud whispers.

Adam blinked at him, wide-eyed. "What is this place?"

Grandpa couldn't speak; his voice was too full of emotion. Hands shaking, he fell to his knees, rummaging excitedly through the large pockets of his backpack. Finally, he regained his voice.

"All the years," he whispered. "All the searching! This is it! The Galaxy Room!"

"Wow! The Galaxy Room?"

"You'll never know how long I've been dreaming about this moment, Adam!"

After a few minutes of frantic tinkering, he stood up and sent a tiny balloon aloft with a microcamera attached. It bumped and scudded upward along the curved surface of the dome, tracing every contour of the lavish gold embellishment until it reached the medallion, where it stopped dead center. As he triggered the camera remotely, it buzzed to life, faintly whirring and clicking its myriad lenses into place. Wide angles or zooms, every shot seemed to have an endless array of light filters. There was a short pause, followed by a small beep. Autosequence had stopped.

He walked way out to the center of the vault. Taking dead aim, he popped the balloon with his ion gun. Adam flinched at the mini explosion as it echoed sharply around the perimeter of the room. The camera tumbled through the air.

"Grandpa?" His hands fluttered. "How-how are you...?"

A net was already poised. He caught it deftly and impulsively knelt on the spot to examine the images on the bright viewing screen. Adam watched in wonderment. Out in the vastness of this incredible room, his grandfather appeared as a tiny figure out in the center of a colossal blue universe, floating, lost.

"Excellent!" The single, percussive word hung in the air, repeating over and over. He jumped to his feet and scuffled back toward Adam, waving the viewing screen, exuberant and almost uncontainable. "I-I got 'em! The keys to open many doors!" In a rush of impulse, he swept up the boy and swung him around and around. Finally dizzy, they both slumped to the floor in a heap. He lifted the small, swirling screen to Adam's eyes.

The boy tried his best to focus on the confusing, moving images and soon found himself gazing into what appeared to be a deep, endless, nighttime sky. He pulled back with a start. A hologram? Yes, but nothing, absolutely nothing seemed familiar! Not a single star! He studied the image again. All along the edges, running in a band around this fantastic, far-flung capsule of stars and space was a border of golden runic symbols describing the scene in detail.

Giggling at his elbow, Grandpa flipped a lever. "Now watch this," he gushed. He was excited, a boy again. A filter suddenly highlighted something else, something delicate, shiny and weblike: Thin, brightly glowing threads jumped out of the glasslike blue, connecting specific galaxies into ... a Star Map! Adam was stunned.

"Wow! Where'd all those lines come from?" He looked up into Grandpa's face, his forehead wrinkling. Rising slowly to his feet, he handed the camera back, walked out to the center of the floor, and dropped to his knees to examine it more closely. What in the world? Absolutely nothing he'd seen in the viewpiece was visible now! Not one thread! He lay flat on his stomach and put his eye right up against the surface of the cold, transparent glass, peering into it deeply, his sensitive child's fingertips running over the surface.

What was that? He pulled back abruptly, his finger on the exact spot. Heat? Yes, heat! With growing excitement, he traced out an invisible line between two golden starbursts, following the warmth. Infrared! The camera's filters and special heat-sensitive films had picked out the hidden, infrared tracery.

The old man's face beamed as he watched his grandson running back with a grin plastered on his face. The boy had solved the complicated puzzle and was rightly proud. As Adam hugged him tightly around his waist, he pivoted awkwardly on his heels to point at the staircase behind them. "We gotta hurry, now, boy. I wish I'd seen this before we came in. I just read something very troubling in the runes, something we didn't count on. Go over there and push down on those last three steps. Take a second and study them closely. It's very important."

He let go and ran to the staircase, dropping to his knees and skidding the last few feet on the slippery glass floor. Wow! Grandpa was right, there seemed to be tiny gaps along the bottoms of the last three stairs! He pushed down hard on one of them and it moved a fraction of an inch. Maybe it could be…. He looked up, putting the scenario together. "A-another Hetex, Grandpa?"

"You got it, boy! Another trigger! We activated the infrared in the Star Map when we came into the room, and now…."

As Adam caught his implied meaning, a disturbing thought began to rumble through his mind: if this infrared map had lain dormant for eons, waiting for someone to enter the room, now maybe some kind of irreversible sequence had begun? As he stared into the distance, lost in thought, he felt a presence beside him. Grandpa's big hand tugged his reluctant chin upward to gaze intently into his eyes.

"No!" Adam's face fell. "Please say no! All this will be gone? Forever?"

"Yes," the man nodded firmly, with finality. "In the wrong hands, the knowledge contained in this Star Map could upset the balance of power in the universe."

"Aaargh!" He closed his eyes, his hands covering his ears. "No! Don't tell me anymore, Grandpa! It-it's all so beautiful! All this amazing work! You can't be serious!" Suddenly, he felt alone again. There was a distant popping sound.

"Grandpa?"

The man was intently peeling off heavy sheets of gold with his ion gun. "I may be scared, boy, but I'm not stupid! Quick! Take as much as you can carry!" He was rolling up some heavy sheets on the floor and stuffing them into his backpack. "With a few antigrav pods, I know I can carry a bit over a thousand pounds. You should be able to carry about three-fifty! At today's prices, that's a king's ransom!"

It didn't take much coaxing. The boy rolled and stuffed madly, wondering how much 'a king's ransom' was worth. Science he knew. Fairy tales were, well, just fairy tales.

Somewhere, way off in the distance, a small chime sounded, growing rapidly in volume until it became a painful, pulsing cacophony. A thin, angry red line suddenly appeared around the perimeter of the floor!

Adam let out a gasp: his footgear was smoldering! As a hiss of smoke erupted, he danced backward, his eyes wordlessly imploring his grandfather's face.

"Yes, Adam! Now we run!" As a hellish blast rose, he bellowed louder. "Go for it!" They ditched their heavy Asron gas torches and bolted up the spiral staircase, following the bright, phosphorescent trail.

As they reached the ramp and began to pick up speed with their footgrippers, a muffled roar and powerful blast of hot wind propelled them up the slope. Adam felt his feet leaving the ground and looked down. They were! Like a windmill, they were churning emptily in the air! "Grandpa!" he screamed. "What are you…?"

The big man shouted out instructions as he lifted him high, but the boy couldn't hear him over the roar. He finally caught the tail end as they approached daylight.

"And when you hit the ground," he concluded, "roll!"

Without another word, they heaved their knapsacks out into the jungle and dove headlong after them. Side by side they splashed down into a river of mud. The earth was trembling violently as they slipped and scrambled to their feet, pulling mightily on the straps of their weighty knapsacks. Their hearts in their mouths, they spun around in time to see the huge wall buckling, tipping backward into a gaping maw! With a sudden rush, a great wall of water hit their legs and sent them scrambling once again. The stream was diverting its course; in fact, the whole terrain was beginning to tilt alarmingly, with torrents of muddy water beginning to cascade down into the smoking abyss. Speechless, Adam stood riveted, the whites of his eyes rolling. Grandpa pushed him, bellowing.

"Bad news!" he cried. "Steam! Move it!"

Splashing and slipping frantically up the muddy slope, they half-ran, half-swam to the antigrav sled and dove aboard. Grandpa threw up the shields, hit emergency power, and catapulted the sled off the ground at full throttle. They screamed through the air as a cataclysmic explosion rocked the jungle.

The Galaxy Room was no more. Far beneath them, a great circle slumped and disappeared into a stupendous sinkhole. As the swollen river poured over the edge of the abyss, a mammoth, roiling cloud of steam churned upward into the stratosphere. The molten mass tunneled down through the Earth's crust, the crucible's heat mixing untold tons of melted gold, alabaster, and glass with the magma of the depths. On the grand scale, a mere speck of debris was sliding into a bottomless pit.

The volcano had a secret, and they were the only two people on Earth who knew about it. Far more importantly, they had the Star Map in their possession: keys to a whole new chapter in human existence.

Swooping low, they circled the steaming lake for a while, flying free in their shielded bubble, co-conspirators in one of the greatest adventures of their lives. Of course, Grandpa had seen far worse in his youth and began recounting it all now. Adam grinned and rolled his eyes as his endless stories began anew, stories of the years as a young Planet Hopper, stories of the apprenticeship as a deep-space astronomer on the far side of Mars Base. His grandpa had seen worlds colliding, stars exploding, and whole species of alien life forms exterminated on distant planets.

But somehow, deep inside, the boy knew that someday he'd see far more.

Chapter 2: SEEDS

A week passed. As early afternoon sunlight poured through an open window behind his chair, Adam sat enraptured with his grandfather's company. It was just plain fun experiencing him in his natural element, delivering his colorful illustrations. Animated, alive and enthusiastic, he lit up obscure, hard-to-understand concepts with easy word pictures and storyboard scenarios and painted difficult and abstract problems with the brushes and pigments of familiarity.

Now, take a seed, Adam," he mused, raising his brows. "It's an easy concept to understand. If you sow a single seed it'll produce a handful of seeds, right? But then after that handful there'll be bushels of seeds to produce an unimaginable harvest.

"Uh-huh."

"Right. Okay now, wait…." He fished around in his vest pocket a moment and then ever so carefully drew something out. Something tiny. Adam squinted at it, reaching out to pull his big mitt closer. The thick fingers uncurled to reveal a bright, miniscule dot, a mere wedge of gold the size of a fingernail paring. As brilliant blue-green eyes bored into him, the boy's face lit up with sudden understanding.

He glanced up quickly. "A *seed*?"

The old man chuckled, nodding in satisfaction. "You got it, kiddo. Exactly an eighth of an ounce, weighed it myself this morning." He rolled the glinting speck around in his palm, making it flash brightly in the sunlight. "Now imagine this: back in the olden days when I was your age, the price for a whole ounce or eight of these little seeds averaged about two thousand dollars."

Adam whistled in appreciation and eagerly stuck out his hand. Grandpa handed the chip to him. He poked it around in his palm a moment, contemplating. "So eight of these little guys used to go for two thousand? What about today? How much are they asking for these chips right now?"

He leaned forward conspiratorially, lowering his voice. "Gold's become very scarce, boy, *extremely* scarce. Most sources dried up years ago, so there's been a lot of hoarding. Two main reasons: because there are no new mines and because there's lots of demand, the price has shot clean out of sight. That's why banks and governments have been fighting and figuring and refiguring the value in ounces, then quarter ounces, and now eighth-ounces. It's absolutely crazy out there. For that one little blip you have in your hand, we can get, say, ten thousand dollars on this morning's market."

"What?" Startled, Adam fumbled and the chip dropped to the floor. He dove to retrieve it under the sofa and straightened up, carefully blowing off the dust. His eyes suddenly grew wide. "T-that would m-make us…."

"Filthy rich," Grandpa nodded, raising his brows. "But no! Not *ordinary* filthy rich, boy! Way, way above that. After taxes, and just before they stashed the rest into our vault, I asked the bank to weigh our share again."

Adam was beside himself with excitement and anticipation, bouncing in his seat. "How much? How much did our gold weigh?"

"We own a bit over 1,400 pounds. That's a *lot* more than I ever thought would fit into our little knapsacks. Good thing I had a few extra antigrav pods to throw in…. Hey! You do the math. You're good at that."

Adam closed his eyes and eagerly crunched the numbers. "Let's see," he mumbled, "Da-da-daah, and daa-daa … that would equal a total of 128 eighth ounces, times 1,400 pounds, that equals, um, 179,200 eighth ounces. Yikes! At ten thousand dollars apiece…." His eyes popped open wide. "That-that would be close to two *billion* dollars! Wow, we're instant billionaires!"

"And *why* are they hoarding this stuff, again?" Grandpa prompted. "Remember the other reason?"

"Um, it's getting harder to find?"

"Bingo! There's no more where that came from! Our stash doesn't exist anymore! It closed up shop for good! Every speck of the Galaxy Room melted into blobs and slid down the tubes! I mean way, way down! It's probably finished mixing with magma in the core of the Earth by now."

Adam started twisting in his seat. "Yeah, I saw a news report while you were in the shower! It was incredible! Scientists are flying in from everywhere to check it out! They can't figure out why some totally extinct volcano would suddenly cave in and melt its own plug again!"

The old man winked. "And just like a really good novel, there's more to the story, boy, more than anyone's aware of." He lowered his voice to a whisper. "Here's the skinny, the real, behind-the-scenes reason: before we could even begin to explore in New Guinea, I made a deal with their government for exclusive rights to a whole string of my patents relating to CloneBank…."

"No, no! Not that one!" Adam interrupted. "Your reforestation invention?"

"Yup! The culmination of many years and many 'eureka' moments! Well, they loved it. In return, we got unlimited exploration rights. The best part was that whatever we took out, they promised to ask no questions."

"Wow! What a deal! We get two billion, they get trees!"

"Yes. Definitely a win-win."

"Oh, *now* I get it!" Adam's face lit up as he put a few more pieces together. "We did a lot of secret things when we got home last week, didn't we, Grandpa? Like sneaking into your lab and melting all our rolled-up gold? You put on your gloves and poured it into little gray trays," he laughed. "It was just like making superhot cupcakes!"

"Yes, we ended up with bags and bags of those little shapes," he chuckled. "And why do you think we went to all that effort?" he prompted.

Adam shrugged. "Um, so no one could ever guess our gold used to be all carved and fancy, or had those weird runes on them, right?"

"Bingo! We covered our tracks and ultimately protected everybody. Like I said, no questions asked, no questions answered." As the boy nodded, the old man sighed and turned to gaze out the window. "But…."

"But what?"

"I really wish we could have done it all over again."

"What, like a rerun?"

"No, not the same: a *lot* different. Before we accidentally triggered those last five steps when we went into the Galaxy Room, I really wish I'd looked around a bit more. I might have seen the warning in the runes and we could have just…."

"I know. Jumped over the bottom steps. The Galaxy Room was so beautiful," Adam sighed. "I hated to see it…."

"You're right, the room was an amazing work of art. But there's more to it."

"More? What do you mean?"

"The biggest reason of all! Think of it, boy! We might've been able to find out what was *powering* everything down there! There was some kind of great, potential force waiting, for who knows, maybe millions of years for someone to show up. The builders of the outpost discovered how to control that great … force…." His eyes turned to the boy expectantly.

Adam was focusing into the distance, deep in thought. Suddenly, his eyes popped. "Wow!" He whispered. "You-you mean it might have been *fusion*?"

The old man gave him a big thumb's up, beaming in satisfaction.

"But-but we needed fusion, too, as much as our Star Maps!"

"You're right, Adam. And I'm just sick about it." Grandpa sighed. "You know, you might not believe this, but…."

"What's that?"

"I-I didn't have a clue about the gold, or fusion. I just wanted the Star Maps."

"What? Your old runes didn't mention anything about gold?"

"Nope. Not a word. When we stepped into the Galaxy room, there it was. Maybe the aliens thought it was just a pretty metal and something useful to build with. The only reason I brought along those extra pods was in case there might be a few interesting and heavy items. Good hunch, huh?

Adam's eyes had a faraway look. "You know," he whispered, "I was thinking about something else while we were down there."

"What's that?"

"I was thinking that it's incredible that a whole civilization from an unknown galaxy could have set up an Outpost here on Earth long before we were even cavemen."

The old man coughed. "You were thinking about *that*? You're only *eight*!"

Adam tilted his head, his eyes questioning. "So…?"

He raised a brow. "So, *most* eight-year-olds, well, you're not in that category."

"I'm eight-and-a-half now, Grandpa," he corrected. "Almost out of high school."

"Hey! So you skipped a few grades. Hmm. You know, I did too, but never three or four at a time! Well, there are quite a few gifted programs waiting for you out there and then it's on to college in a few years—if they'll have you," he chuckled.

"Grandpa, why is school so boring?"

"Because you have, um, superior genes on your side. You're brilliant!"

Adam reddened. "Come on…."

"No, I really mean it. Just think about it. It might have something to do with the fact that for most your life you've been privilege to the most advanced think tanks and research labs in the world. Maybe, just maybe, huh? We've got some of the brightest minds in the world working with us. On the other hand, it could be partly osmosis. Your brain just sucked in all the lab lingo and obscure theories of physics and math by being immersed in it. The more you figured out, the more you wanted to know! I remember how you used to pepper me with all those questions about our mysterious projects. Blah, blah, blah … what a nudge!"

"Yup." The boy's head bobbed. "We worked side by side. Mostly at night."

"Well, that's a whole 'nother thing. It was quieter then." Grandpa closed his eyes, reminiscing. "Good grief, it seemed like you could run before you could walk. You-you amazed everyone in the lab. I remember watching you toddling down all those long corridors, opening every single unmarked door. Not *one* door was off-limits. Oh, and sometimes that curiosity of yours got us both into hot water, right?"

Adam grimaced. "Yeah, like the debate, for instance. I-I sure do remember."

Grandpa grinned. "Old Doc Fenway, that bag of wind. I can still hear your little squeaky little voice cutting into one of his pompous tirades. "S'kuse me, s'kuse me!""

Adam winced, clamping his hands over his ears. "Stop, stop, Grandpa!"

"You stood up on a *stool* to tug at his sleeve! 'S'kuse me, s'kuse me….'"

"He was a jerk! What can I say?"

"But you trashed him! I can still see you standing there on that stool delivering this incredible monologue, beginning with a startling string of revelations on the latest developments in quantum physics and proton entanglement and backing it all up with the struggles Einstein had in building his unified field theory. Fenway and everyone else in the room looked like they'd been spooked! Where'd you *get* that stuff, anyway?"

"There was an issue of *Science News* in your office," he shrugged.

Grandpa let out a hoot, slapping him on the back. "But you weren't even five! A baby! Whatever happened to Winnie the *Poo*?"

"Who?"

"Never mind. You-you floored everybody in the room, including *me*! There-there was this numbed silence, this-this…." He shook his head in wonder. "You know, somewhere inside that cherub's body of yours there's something else going on, something-something spooky! There's this fearless, rooting spirit, this almost frightening boldness, focus, and intensity…."

"I don't know, Grandpa, I-I just think in pictures. Scenarios."

"Yeah, like Einstein."

The boy winced, reddening even more. "No! No-o-o! Like-like *you*!"

Taken aback, the old man bit his lip and tousled the boy's hair. "Thanks."

His face beet red, Adam made an awkward stab at changing the subject. "Ah, let's get back to your old runes, Grandpa. Where'd they really come from? You never finished telling me the whole story."

A lump in his throat, the old man turned to gaze into the distance as he tried to collect his thoughts. That boy was something else, always trying to divert attention away from himself. He had no concept about his intellect, probably because there were no other kids his own age he could hang with. His mom, Sophie, was shy like that….

Unbidden, the memories flooded back: many, many years before Adam, his wife Annie had died in childbirth, leaving him with an infant son, Ruben. He sighed. Another little one: it seemed like he'd always had a little boy around. Ruben had turned out to be somewhat of a traveler, and by the time he'd reached his early twenties, he always wanted to be away somewhere, doing something crazy in a foreign land. He'd eventually found the girl of his dreams, Sophie: a real Dutch beauty, full of life, her gray-blue eyes brimming with as much excitement and wonder as the North Sea. She'd stubbornly refused to marry him for months until he'd promised to quit piloting those creaky old hypersonic ramjets out of Schipol Spaceport. Good for her … ramjets. How archaic.

After Adam was born, his dad was promoted. Ruben had risen quickly through the ranks to become the bright, promising leader of the very first exploration party to the moon Titan.

He clenched his fists, the scene burning anew in his memory…. Why, *why*? For some reason, he'd wanted Adam's mom to come with him on the expedition that day. As their landing pod descended, something had gone horribly wrong: it became enveloped in a strange, swirling yellow-green aura, then without explanation, burst into flames and streaked out of view!

"Grandpa? Are you okay?"

"Oh, sorry, boy." He wrenched himself out of reverie, turning his head away to hide the tears in his eyes.

Adam laid his small hand on his arm. "Is this about Mom and Dad again?"

He exhaled a long breath and turned back to his grandson. "Yeah. It'll never go away, boy. You're all I have left of my family." He sighed and gave his hand a squeeze. "Let's get back to your question."

"It's okay, Grandpa. I understand."

"Okay, thanks," he smiled. "Now, the runes: It-it was such a long time ago. They were in a cave on Callisto Moon base. I was in my mid twenties when I found them, just before your dad was born. They say most of those impact craters were over four billion years old and it's one of the most heavily cratered planets in our solar system. Just why my group of Planet Hoppers chose to stop there I'll *never* know. Fate, maybe. What a barren place. Well, there they were, those tiny, thin sheets of gold, stamped with odd figures, all bundled together with this long, twisted gold wire. You know, like tie wrap?"

"Expensive tie wrap," Adam grinned.

"Hey! I pawned that skinny wire to pay for your father's college tuition. Well, it took years and years to translate the runes and then I mapped everything out. They pinpointed the location of the Outpost here on Earth! When I knew where it was, I put the bug about my reforestation invention into the ear of the government in New Guinea."

"*That* long ago? Before my dad was born? But, but we just…."

"Hey, the wheels of government turn ver-r-ry sl-l-lowly! Well, I waited a long time for an answer, you came into my life, and then I finally got exploration rights to the peninsula. You know the rest: CloneBank's reforestation has been really working down there and the land's turning back to a pristine wilderness, thank God."

"You can say *that* again. We've even improved the property! There's a new lake out in the middle of the jungle," he offered, brightly. "And I'm glad they're gonna put my baby monkey back into his home after they raise him. A news report said that New Guinea just declared the volcano and its whole peninsula a new national park!"

"Good for them," Grandpa chuckled. "We need more parks." He let out a guffaw and slapped Adam on the back. "And this one has waterfront lots!"

"A theme park!" Adam countered.

"Crocodile rides! Hotels! Casinos!" Grandpa tossed a few more back at him.

"Casinos? Hey, now maybe we can…."

"Whoa, hold on there," he said, chuckling. "Don't get carried away!"

"What do you mean?"

"Even our awesome stash will dwindle away!"

Adam drew back, alarmed. "What? There's so *much*! How could *that* happen?"

"Believe me, it'll sprout little wings. We've gotta take measures right now to make sure it *never* runs out!" The familiar twinkle suddenly gleamed anew in his eyes. "Hey. I-I'm stumped, boy! Whaddaya think we should do with these, ah, seeds?"

Adam caught on in a flash. "Plant, plant, *plant*, Grandpa!" He poked the kernel back into the man's big palm and closed the broad fingers over it. "Plant these little suckers quick, before they fly away!" The old man's blue-green eyes crinkled and his smile broadened to match the youngster's inch for inch. They stared at each other a long moment, nodding in silent, conspiratorial enthusiasm.

The process of plowing began. With the trusted advice of a close friend and financial planner, Adam's grandfather converted a modest amount of the bullion into cash to live on, and then set aside a few sizeable chunks, investing them into a broad, stable financial portfolio with several interest-bearing savings accounts and trusts for Adam. Satisfied, they homed in on the rest: a measured, miniscule amount at a time, they'd sow it into the stock market.

It took some early crop failures to show them this unfamiliar field wasn't to be merely a game of planting roulette. They took their losses gamely. Their advisor hired a few more brilliant analysts, and the new financial team knuckled down to take serious notes. There'd be no more waste. This was war: a focused, exhausting, all-consuming effort. They began to watch live, streaming global market coverage on the Internet while several ancient twenty-teraflop computers hummed in the background, spewing out condensed timetables and spreadsheets that blanketed the kitchen table. Grandpa's apartment quickly resembled a top-secret, undercover situation room.

Shortly, the numbing number fog thinned a bit, just enough to see unexpected things in unlikely places. It was as if everyone's financial eyes were opening for the first time. Camouflaged inside all that cipher chaos were a few subtly stable numerical repetitions and promising trends revealing themselves in neat, orderly rows.

Harvest fields! Excited, the team redoubled their efforts. With computer enhancement, they quickly extracted the good soil from the mediocre, then sifted out the excellent from the good. As a subprogram dusted off the results, Grandpa leaned back and pointed to the screen. "Finally! I think we've plowed a bit of fertile land here, boys! Whaddaya think?"

There was a matching glint in Adam's eye. "Let's *plant*! Big time!"

"Yeah," they chorused. "Let's *do* it!" A group high five sealed the deal.

Grandpa punched in their broker's e-mail address. With their fingers side by side on the "enter" button, he and Adam transmitted an unheard-of sum.

The financial world was abuzz the next morning, watching in shock as a young, seemingly vulnerable investment partnership called G&A dumped an embarrassing amount of capital into a handful of dark horses on the market. Speculation on the mysterious duo, both of their motives and targets, loosened the tongues of even the most liberal. A short week later, to everyone's total surprise and embarrassment, G&A had made a stupendous killing. After the inscrutable duo reaped a fortune in earnings, their daunting logo began to appear daily, veering wildly around the charts. It seemed this G&A had a Midas touch; whatever the pair breathed on suddenly came to life and spewed out profits!... Had they really discovered the secret to a self-perpetuating money machine?

Chapter 3: **THE ROBE**

A neglected historical landmark stood in the heart of the city, a soaring, Gothic-inspired skyscraper the locals had aptly dubbed "the Aerie." Indeed, a few nests of Peregrine Falcons did inhabit the upper crags. Adam spotted a photo of the slim, needlelike structure as he was flipping through the financial pages and quickly shoved the paper toward his grandpa.

"What have you got here, boy?"

"Quick! Quick! Just read it, Grandpa. You'll see!"

"Hmm." The old man buried his nose in the article. "Wow, she's a beauty! But what's *this*? It says that 'to the dismay of historical groups and the public alike, this abandoned structure is slated for demolition this afternoon.'" He looked up with a start. "*This* afternoon?" He bent back to the paper immediately. "Hey! It says that it can still be purchased for a song, but the buyer has to deal directly with cash in hand!"

"A *song*, Grandpa! A song! We've got that!"

He spun to his financial team and raised a questioning brow. "Guys, six months have flown by and we've grown *way* too big for my kitchen. Waddaya think? We got about a billion to play with, and two more in reserve. Can we pull this thing off?"

There was no hesitation. They all finished reading the article on the fly. One trip up the Aerie's express elevator and a spectacular view from the once-posh penthouse roof garden convinced the group to buy the building on the spot. With the sale quickly out of the way, they decided to spare no expense on the much-needed renovations. Garnering enthusiastic nods from a small army of historical experts, the common areas would once again see only the thickest carpet and finest marble, with gold and crystal appointments. After the team got permission to totally rewire the soaring edifice and bring it into the information age, tiny, precisely aimed 3DSat and FarNet receptors were concealed on top of every stone outcropping and behind every gargoyle.

G&A's new home base proved to be a winner right from the ribbon cutting. The contractors had hardly finished refurbishing the lower hundred and twenty floors when the big-name tenants began to pour in. The prestigious location, superior amenities, and unparalleled accessibility to the world all justified the sky-high leases.

Things really began to hum when a popular, savvy headhunter website put out the word: G&A's fledgling empire would pay top dollar to a select group of financial whizzes and they'd be privilege to the Aerie's six most coveted floors below the penthouse. Soon, the army of eager number crunchers were intensely schooled in the superior financial system and began to pull in incredible amounts of profit. In six more months, with seemingly unstoppable momentum, G&A had leaped from simple stock market whizzes into the ranks of one of the top ten venture capital firms in the world. G&A's foot was securely in the door. Two incredible, dizzying years later, they pulled away from the pack as number one. Their lives had been turned totally upside down.

Grandpa breathed a sigh of relief: manipulating money and figures was never his forté; his real passion and skills were focused entirely on inventing. He promoted his trusted friend to CEO with total responsibility to run the show. All he wanted was to sit secretly on the board, erase his name from the roster, and pull a few strings from the shadows. In capable hands, G&A's seeds started to produce that unimaginable, self-replicating harvest that he and his grandson had dreamed about.

Far more valuable than any kind of wealth, the old man had finally gained the precious, elusive commodity of time: now there'd be time for exploration, time for discovery, time for all the research and inventing he'd ever want … all with unlimited funding. Gradually, he pulled himself further and further back into the shadows.

Meanwhile, Adam swept through the finest gifted programs, prep schools, and universities in the world, causing a commotion as he attracted top honors like a superconducting magnet. In a coup, he astounded academic circles when he received the equivalent of his third doctorate at sixteen, a true prodigy. Amazingly, no one was aware of his vast wealth; both he and his grandfather had gone to great lengths to help him "blend in" and be just one of the guys.

His exciting years of education began to ring hollow. Living abroad at boarding schools most of the time, he was away far too long from his beloved grandpa and adventure. With no roots, there was no meaning to his lonely life. Nobody at college understood his crazy talk or the inventions he was constantly dreaming up.

Stopping by the Aerie on a rare visit, the old man filled him in on his latest exciting progress with the Star Map. Sensing a disturbing shift to the boy's mood, he quickly made up a game of translating and memorizing the mysterious runes they'd photographed in the Galaxy Room. After he left, he sent off a salvo of encrypted messages, bombarding his grandson with their new secret code. It seemed to work for a while, but Adam's keen mind soon mastered the symbols. The newness wore thin; mere words could never substitute for just hanging with his best pal.

The times of utter, grinding isolation crept in: long, lonely days staring at clouds from the Aerie's penthouse and longer, lonelier nights fending off waves of disturbing dreams with alien-filled invasions and amazing, shape-shifting saucers. The dreams became relentless, so real and so vivid they began to frighten him. Was he going crazy? He woke up sweating and confused, trying desperately to separate fact from fantasy. As his life's foundation crumbled, his fearless, rooting spirit began to wither. Once inquisitive and full of life, he grew quieter and more withdrawn. His voicemails and texts to Grandpa were starting to go unanswered. The old man was increasingly unreachable, busy on all consuming "projects" at undisclosed locations. He'd never experienced this degree of isolation before and started to grow angry and jealous; he and his grandpa had always been a team, right in the thick of everything.

Eventually, to his total dismay, his grandfather's cherished notes and cheerfully illustrated runic letters stopped coming. It seemed that he'd simply dropped off the face of the Earth. Adam suddenly realized the chilling truth: only seventeen, he was now completely on his own. Any more postgrad college was out of the question; he'd garnered all the post and post-post grad degrees he'd ever want or need. It was time to move on, to take command of real matters … like his future. He loathed the very concept of just sponging around and living off his fortune. He knew he had a lot to give, and was way too adventurous to turn into a house cat.

He knuckled down and scanned the Internet for employment ideas. There was a promising job offer, a ground floor position at the Interplanetary Flight Academy, an exciting new offshoot of his all-time favorite, Space-X. He moved fast and was immediately accepted at IFA; it seemed his education and reputation spoke for itself.

On a short introductory visit, he was astounded to find the fledgling institution clumsily flapping along on outdated ideas and obsolete equipment that he and his grandfather had discarded as ballast when he was a kid. Taking a gamble, he tactfully suggested a short list of radical changes to get IFA airborne. When his rambling conversation began to focus in exclusively onto R&D, he casually dropped his grandfather's name and O&A's philosophy of distributing venture capital. Maybe they could use some help?

The shop foreman stopped dead in his tracks. Keeping his voice low, he turned to Adam to explain something that he didn't know: it was O&A's generous grants that had funded the formation of their secretive, radically new R&D department: Adam's own investment firm had already been working behind the scenes!

The shocked board of directors pulled a late-night emergency meeting. Suddenly, sitting right in their laps was this genius, their main investor's teenage grandson, with a list of astounding suggestions and ideas. Things began to rumble. Wasting no time, they shook off the dust of bureaucracy and took a leap of faith. In a unanimous decision, they gave the boy an unprecedented promotion, catapulting him from the lowly ground floor position he'd sought to a coveted spot within the lofty senior ranks in their Space Lab Division. He'd be involved in research, pure research ... and flying as a test pilot as well! He was astounded. Just like his grandpa, now he could actually think! His future assured, he knuckled down and began to put in long, exciting hours. The hectic, rewarding, yet tiring days turned to weeks, and then years.

Then it happened. One night, barely a week before his twentieth birthday, his fragile, scholarly world came crashing down. A mysterious messenger showed up at his penthouse door with the news he'd secretly dreaded for years. Grandpa had died.

Numb with shock, he slumped against the door listening with only half an ear. The nervous messenger would only identify himself as a government employee and, as such, was courteous and to the point. He'd be divulging classified information, so Adam would be expected to remain close-mouthed about it. It seemed there had been a disturbing... incident.

The story unfolded: a few weeks ago, on a routine flight through the asteroid belt, planetary patrol had spotted a nimble, ultrafast spacecraft of unknown origin streaking toward the Earth, decelerating rapidly and ignoring all efforts at communication. After a wild chase, interceptors forced it to land at Mars Base 7. The moment it touched down, all hatches had popped. The space-suited boarding parties had found grandpa's frozen body strapped tightly into the pilot's seat, his last will and testament recorded in the craft's flight log.

As the messenger leaned toward Adam, his eyes darted curiously around the Aerie's slick 50's style penthouse. He lowered his voice still more. Per his grandfather's recorded instructions, they'd pulled both him and his strongly crated, incredibly heavy cargo off the silver craft. Suddenly, unexplainably, the mysterious vessel had burst to life. Despite all they could do, it blasted away at an incredible rate of acceleration. Within moments, it had reached sublight speed and disappeared without a trace. The press had been given a severely laundered version of the unsettling rendezvous: after all, international panic had to be suppressed. His grandfather had been revealed as the mysterious founder of G&A, and had become an icon even in the intrasolar planetary circles. The abbreviated, edited news of his untimely death was being broadcast at that very moment. Without another word the caller nodded curtly, turned on his heel, and quietly slipped out the door.

Absently thanking him, Adam sagged back into a chair, his head reeling in confusion. "How cold," he muttered. "H-how absolutely unfeeling. Was that mole of a man a robot? Did he actually say the news was being broadcast? But Grandpa loved to work from behind the scenes! He *hated* the spotlight!" Trembling with hesitation for a moment, he cleared his throat to activate the apartment's voice-remote. A single word followed by a spoken numerical code turned on the huge, 10-foot wall screen. One by one he called out the news channels, scrolling through them in astonishment and throwing them up in multiple split-screen arrangements.

"Wow! He wasn't kidding!" he gasped. "They're *all* covering the event!"

Despite himself, he was sucked into the frenzy. A great funeral was planned, running for the next few days! With true-to-form sensationalistic fervor, the wild-eyed journalists all portrayed Grandpa as the elusive, secretive cloak-and-dagger figurehead behind G&A. The old man was an eccentric hermit and supposedly the wealthiest man ever to have lived!

As they spewed on effusively, Adam's jaw sagged. "What *is* all this crud?" He had to back his chair way back from the big screen to take it all in. Multiple cameras were panning ever so slowly over a sea of famous faces as a sequence of prerecorded well-known voice-over personalities droned with their testimonies of Grandpa's generosity. 'Philanthropy' seemed to be the catchword of the hour. He sat there numbly, shaking his head in disbelief. Apparently, it seemed that no one could calculate the actual total of this mysterious man's lavish gifts, but they dwarfed that of all charitable organizations, relief funds, philanthropies, scholarships, and Nobel prizes combined!

His eyes popped. "Grandpa, you've been *busy*! I never dreamed you helped so many people in so many countries!" The 3DTV camera unexpectedly cut back to America, to Washington, DC, then to the Capitol building.

"Wow! You even helped out *our* crazy government??"

It zoomed inside the entrance toward a dazzling, blurry gleam in the center of the huge screen. Adam caught his breath as the camera pulled in for a close-up of the old man's face. Grandpa! Yes, there he was, hands folded, lying in state in the Capitol Rotunda like a king! What in the world was going on?

Shaking in his gut, he turned down the volume and slumped in his chair. He squeezed his eyes shut. "Why hadn't he...? Where'd he...?" It was all happening too fast. As the raw, underlying truth struck with an icy sword, he fought valiantly to keep the tears from coming. He'd just seen everything with his own eyes: his only real friend was dead and he was indeed alone now. Suddenly life itself had become impossible, unbearable. The torrents broke loose and he cried himself into a fitful, exhausted sleep in the chair.

Too early the next morning, the phone rang. After a round of seemingly endless incoming calls and condolences, a long black limo appeared to sweep him away. A quick flight to Reagan Airport in Washington, DC, produced an even longer limo waiting out on the tarmac. He raised a brow. This one was enormous: a disproportioned, ugly land yacht sporting twelve flags and a motorcycle escort to boot. But it was smooth. As they glided silently up to the Capitol building, he was amazed at the pandemonium outside. It looked like there were thousands of important people outside awaiting his arrival. Presidents of nations, kings, ambassadors, everyone jostled for space to see him, elbowing into each other's way. His heart began to pound painfully in his chest.

"Yikes! They're all waiting for *me*?"

Teeth and fists clenched, he glanced up nervously over his head, peering out through the full-length electrically darkened roof panel. Swooping low over the Capitol's dome and jostling dangerously for the restricted airspace, a swarm of blunt-looking Notar jetchopper drones sounded like angry bees. Their undersides literally bristled with antennas and domes concealing state-of-the-art 3D radar cameras panning the dramatic scene.

Suddenly, the door of the limo was jerked open and a wafting of bad body odor assailed his nostrils. Eclipsing the sun, a wall of sweating bodyguards bent toward him as a unit, yanked him out of the car, and closed ranks behind him. Through chinks in the armor of black-suited muscles, he caught a few glimpses of the curious crowd. His stomach flopped in fear and revulsion. Pressing closely around the rapidly moving wedge of bodies, a mass of new, hopeful "friends" seemed to be all smiles and teeth, attempting to catch a glimpse or perhaps win a favor. Blinking in confusion, he felt like a young wildebeest circled by a herd of protective, bad-tempered adults.

Abruptly, like a cork buoyed along in the rapids, he was literally lifted by his elbows and whisked above the throng. Grunting and sweating profusely, the group carried him up the stairs and through a set of open doors. Hemmed in tightly by a sea of broad, damp backs, he felt like screaming. Who *were* these people? Who assigned these brawny, Kevlar-lined brutes to him anyway? Why, he was a nobody, a nothing! He didn't even *exist* until last night, when the press named him as the only surviving next-of-kin! Forget the spotlight; in a heartbeat, he'd been thrown center stage!

As the circle parted, he made a Herculean effort to compose himself. Pulling down his rumpled sleeves and straightening his hair, he peered inside. As his eyes slowly adjusted to the dim light, he noticed a smallish, specially constructed room with an ornately gilded doorway out in the center of the hushed rotunda. There seemed to be an endless, looping line of silent, black-clad figures disappearing into it and coming out somewhere on the far side.

He jerked involuntarily as someone tapped him on the arm. He glanced over his shoulder. Seeing nobody, he turned back to the spectacle. There was an insistent tug on his sleeve. His eyes traveled downward. It was Senator Caulfield, literally at his elbow. She smiled sweetly and motioned ever so discreetly for him to bend to her diminutive level. He bent his head awkwardly; she stood on her toes to whisper in his ear. She'd been appointed acting executrix of Grandpa's will and, as such, informed him of his last recorded request.

He listened, blinking in astonishment. Incredibly, most of these elaborate provisions had been made for *him*! He squinted in the bright lights. Well, whoever was in charge of carrying out his grandfather's last requests had *run* with the theme. Too much fake gold, everywhere! It looked like a gaudy, recycled movie set. She continued smoothly. That fancy, guarded room was created for him, exclusively, and it was a way to be completely alone with his grandfather in the middle of this blatantly public spectacle. No strangers would be inside weeping on his arm, no cameras spying down his neck. He listened incredulously, but inwardly breathed a silent sigh of relief. Whispering a heartfelt thanks to Senator Caulfield, he gathered his courage.

The crowd melted away as he slowly walked up to the heavily guarded privacy chamber. He entered, the pneumatic doors closing behind him with a soft whuff. For a long silent moment he stood there trembling, his eyes closed. Exhaling slowly, he turned to face the open casket in the corner.

"*Holy cow!*" He gasped. "What in...?" His hands flew to his mouth in shock, his eyes popping out of their sockets.

Grandpa was lying there in an ornately gilded alabaster coffin, decked out in a resplendent golden ROBE! It covered him from hooded head to slippered foot, blazing and glittering garishly under the bright Asron minispots!

He inched closer and leaned over the icy, gold-encrusted rim, quavering in his gut. "This-this is unbelievable, Grandpa," he whispered. "What have they *done* to you?" He studied the unfamiliar features. The person in the coffin looked just plain awful: the coroner's makeup hadn't quite covered all the flat, bluish veins under the skin and the forehead seemed grotesquely swollen. He turned to study the robe in the reflected glare, his eyes aching painfully in the spotlights. It was woven of the purest spun-gold threads, a scintillating tapestry, polished and buffed to an almost blinding sheen. Despite himself, he reached out to touch the cool, slippery fabric, admiring the delicate workmanship. Suddenly, almost involuntarily, his eyes narrowed.

Column after column of stylized, brilliantly burnished golden shapes stood out in bas-relief against a pebbly matte background, seeming to repeat and repeat in a hypnotic, interwoven pattern. Drawing in his breath sharply, his eyes and fingers traveled down the column. "EROBEADA," he read, his heart pounding. "MKEYSINSID...."

It hit him like a thunderclap. He was reading his own name! He blinked hard and read it again. "ADAM," it said plainly, "KEYS INSIDE ROBE."

Jolted, he gripped the casket. *Runes*! The message was meant for him only, yet it was written boldly, openly, from head to foot! He started sputtering in a coarse whisper. "*Grandpa*! W-what incredible nerve! I-I take back everything I ever thought! Th-the robe's *fabulous*!"

He acted quickly and obeyed the message. Feeling along the inner lining of the impossibly heavy garment, he carefully explored for any abnormality, any kind of lump. Could it be? Sure enough, there it was! Under one arm, a few knotted threads were out of place!

"Yes!" he whispered excitedly. Suddenly remembering where he was, he glanced suspiciously around the room. "There'd *better* be no cameras, Grandpa...." As the seam unraveled, he slid out a small, featherweight, plain-looking package.

"This is *it*?" He turned the tiny bundle over in the light. "This is *all*?" Plain, brown wrapping paper crinkled softly in his hands, tied with a whisper-thin gold wire.

He chuckled. "Expensive tie wrap." With a sudden chill, he realized that in a way he'd just been spoken to from beyond the grave. Spooked, he smoothed out the robe and steadied himself.

Flipping the slim package over and over in his fingers, he pondered his next move: the hordes would be waiting outside, scrutinizing him in the minutest detail! His heart started to pound painfully.

"W-what do I do now, Grandpa?" he stuttered. "I've got this thing in my hands, but how do I get it outta here w-without anybody knowing?... Wait, wait, I *got* it! Yes! The shielded box for my security pass at IFA!"

Fumbling inside his suit coat, he removed the metaceramic sleeve from an inner, zippered pocket. His hands trembled violently as he tucked the slim brown package in next to his ID card. He quickly zipped the thin box back into his pocket, paused, and took a deep breath. Yes, he understood completely: some kind of important keys now lay in his possession and Grandpa had entrusted them with him alone. He knelt next to the old man one last time to squeeze the icy, cold hands.

"H-how do I say goodbye?" He gritted his teeth, trying to hold back the inevitable flood. "We were the best pals in the whole world, weren't we, Grandpa? Pals to the end." It was no use. The torrent burst and he wept bitterly. After a long moment, he shuddered as reality jolted him once again. The crowds outside would be watching his every step! IntraSolar television would be revealing the new heir to an inestimable fortune!

"I'll do you proud," he vowed softly. He rose slowly to his feet and turned resolutely toward the door. Steeling himself, he summoned the guard with a small transponder. As the panels opened with a pneumatic puff, his face appeared, bowed in grief.

Chapter 4: DECEPTION

Acting important and flashing official-looking badges, a group of men were pushing determinedly through the crowd and rudely elbowing their way up to the ropes in the receiving line. In their midst, a darkly-clad person directed their movements with subtle signals of hand and eye. Many murmurs of annoyance arose, but quickly subsided as the young heir appeared in the doorway.

Adam's steps faltered. Somewhere out there he'd heard an echoing wave of protest, the sound amplified by the shape of the circular room. His mind started reeling. "Uh-oh! What was *that* all about?" he mused, peering around the marble pillars. "I sure hope security's taking care of it...." Awkwardly attempting to hide his reaction, he stopped and turned on his heel to appear as if he were taking in a long, last last look at the dazzling spectacle in the vaultlike chamber.

The day was becoming almost too much to bear. With great reluctance, he turned to face the crowd and begin his endless obligatory walk down the receiving line. He felt trapped, like a bug under a microscope, dissected and scrutinized in the minutest detail. He inched along with his face red and his knees shaking. Shortly, some of his grandfather's old buddies reached over the ropes to warmly thump him on his back, press his hands, and dole out some reassuring hugs. Despite himself, he found that he was actually smiling. Yes, they'd come to express genuine sympathy.

But the rest ... he was sure they'd all shown up out of pure curiosity, clueless about this skinny kid or that mysterious, awful-looking codger in the coffin. As he pressed on down the ropes, he began to feel a lot of heartfelt warmth and genuine sympathy being conveyed. It was quite obvious that his grandfather had helped and was loved by a ton of people, from kings and presidents to common folks! The sea of smiling faces and skin of all colors peppered an amazing tapestry of colorful traditional national costumes. Shortly, his confidence crept back and he began to feel a bit different: calmer, even encouraged.

As he paused to wipe his eyes, a subtle movement caught his attention out of the corner of a lowered lid. Something flashed and fluttered, followed by a strange, excited whispering. A chill swept over him, a sense of foreboding. He put his tissue away, smiled bravely, and looked up. An odd group was facing him. Summoning all his courage, he reached over the ropes to shake their hands.

Poorly disguised in a thin veneer of formality, their toothy smiles, shifting eyes, sly winks, and sweaty palms revealed all the signs of deceit. They stood out in the throng, flashing like warning lights: mourners who came, but not to mourn. Hard, scrutinizing eyes bored into him, their pointed gaze telling him plainly that they knew something very interesting must have gone on behind those heavily-guarded doors. As they acknowledged him with grunts and frozen smiles, he turned and quickened his pace down the line, his mind awash with gruesome scenarios.

Suddenly, his brows went up. Was that *heat* he felt against his chest? Discreetly he slipped his hand under his suit coat. Yes! His shielded security pass had suddenly grown blistering hot! He glanced around, searching for an exit. Somehow he had to get away quickly, out of range of those ever-present cameras. But where?

Standing on his toes, he spotted a small sign on the far wall. In a flash of pure inspiration, a solution hit him. Excusing himself politely, he slipped away. Immediately, two security guards were on his tail. Off in the distance, another one spun on his heels and sprinted toward him, holding onto his earpiece with pointed fingers as he called for more backups.

"Hey, guys, guys!" he whispered. "I-I just have to use the bathroom!"

Trotting alongside, the group glanced at him questioningly, then shrugged and nodded in unison. As he entered, they crowded in closely behind him, leaving one to guard the hallway. "Hey! Just-just give me a minute, man." He sidestepped quickly into a stall and slammed the door shut. The thud of their bodies rattled the hinges. Rolling his eyes, he sat down and took a deep breath.

As quietly as he could, he unzipped the inner pocket of his suit coat with trembling fingers and slid out the shielded ceramic security box. Wow, it *still* felt hot! As he flipped it over gingerly, his eyes popped. *Scanned*! He bit his lip. The magnetic recorder didn't lie! As the security guards yammered loudly outside his door, joking and swapping stories, he counted the bars. His precautions had served him well: the long row of dark stripes proved that he'd been scanned no less than thirty times! "Holy cow," he muttered, "it-it looks like a UPC Code!!" He looked up in dismay. "So I'm a target now?"

Taking a moment to compose himself, he flushed the toilet and stepped out. Seven security goons were staring at him. He squeezed toward the sink, dried his hands, and made his way toward the door. They tailed him into the hallway in lock step, a neat, suit-encrusted row.

His heart fell. There they were again, that same odd group loitering outside the men's room! An involuntary, stifled gasp escaped his lips. As his steps faltered, their eyes widened; they elbowed each other sharply, exchanging knowing glances. With a chill, he realized that he'd just given himself away! He'd better do something, and fast!

Waving off a forest of microphones and obnoxious television interviewers outside, he quickly formed his brute squad into a protective wedge and rushed down the steps into the waiting limo. As they sped away, he spun on his knees to peer out the blackened rear window. The sinister group receded into the distance, their arms gesturing and pointing excitedly, and then the scenery flashed by in a dizzying blur, just like the frightening thoughts reeling through his mind.

In moments, the group was back at the plane. He sank exhausted into a soft VIP seat in the upper lounge as the powerful thruster jets vectored the Metroliner upward in a steep sixty-degree angle above the Potomac. While his clueless brute squad settled in around him, he devoted his short, precious time to think. He knew that the weird group intensely coveted the package in his pocket, enough to kill for it. There was murder in their eyes.

Muttering quietly, he rhythmically tap-tapped his armrest in deep concentration. "A place, a place, a place to hide the package. "A place, a place. Hey! Maybe...?" He glanced at his watch and groaned. "Dogs! That idea's out, it's already past three; the banks are closed."

A new wave of panic gripped him and he peered out of the Metroliner's huge windows, searching the ground. "Good grief! I hope they don't *shoot* us down!"

His fingers drummed with renewed urgency. "Yikes, I-I don't know, m-maybe I can *hide* it somewhere in my apartment until tomorrow? I've got that big meeting later this afternoon with all those lawyers. Yeah, t-that'll have to do for now... I guess." He visualized his familiar floor plan room by room, checking off a long list of weird possibilities. "Hide the package, hide the package...." Finally, it came to him in a flash of pure inspiration. He raised a brow, shrugging. "Hey," he whispered. "That's a unique spot, for sure! They'd never think of looking *there*!"

As the plane taxied toward yet another waiting limo, he put a new three-step plan into action. Taking out his checkbook, he enticed the security guards into a bit of four-figure overtime. No problem: they knew he was good for it. Hastily checking their ordinance, they piled into the big car with him.

Halfway home, he had the driver make an unexpected stop at a hardware store. Exchanging puzzled glances, the heavily armed entourage hopped out with him. They walked as a unit, facing outward and keeping the circle tight. He smiled politely at the shuddering cashier, made a small purchase, and left.

Home at last. Discreetly stationing six men down in the busy lobby, he selected the beefiest specimen for the most lucrative post: the door right outside his penthouse. He rushed inside, drew the curtains, and dug out his toolbox. In minutes, there was a rasping sound of hollow metal being sawed and the vinegary-smelling odor of acetic acid permeating the air. He hummed quietly to himself as he worked. "There you go. A little silicone cement here, a little twist there, then a Ziploc baggie...." The package was concealed. It took a half hour for the glue to cure. Its extremely light weight adapted perfectly to the odd location, just like he'd thought.

"Well, so much for step one." He sighed nervously, glancing at his watch. "Yike! It's a quarter to six! The *lawyers*!" he groaned. "Now I gotta make it through all *tonight's* garbage!" He threw on his overcoat and dashed out the door, signaling to two of his bodyguards. A block away, endless rounds of paperwork were awaiting his signature: wills, trusts, memberships, stocks, bonds, bulging bank accounts, deeds; they were all his now.

The time crawled by. He began to pace nervously between the flurries of nervous lawyers and gales of flying documents, glancing repeatedly out of the darkening window. His pen had run out of ink and writer's cramp had set in. The whole thing was too hard to believe; he'd never dreamed Grandpa owned so much!

Two hours later, the circling crowd of lawyers thinned a bit, seeming to pause and catch a collective breath. As they readied more stacks of paper for another round, he threw up his hands in exasperation. "Yo! Guys!" They looked up in surprise. "So stop already! It's been a long day! Can't we just use a rubber stamp, or something?" Backing toward the door, he excused himself effusively. "I-I gotta *go*! Really!" Without another word he raced out into the dark city streets, the two bodyguards puffing along behind him.

Squad Cars! The strobing lights electrified his senses. Nervously showing his ID to the cops, he sprinted into the Aerie's lobby. Nobody was there! It was *empty*! Where was all that security he'd paid for?

The three bolted into his private elevator and raced up to the penthouse. Sure enough, the other four were there, red-faced and shouting at each other and the cops. The beefy guard lay unconscious next to his penthouse door. As they spotted Adam, they started to fidget nervously, avoiding eye contact.

"So." He kept his voice level. "What's up? Or, should I say … down?"

One of the cops looked up. "Simple: the goons jimmied open a back door, came up the stairs, and then climbed through the ceiling of your elevator on the second floor. When they got to the top, there were just too *many* of 'em pourin' outta the elevator for this big guy. He didn't even have a chance to draw his piece before they clubbed him. He's gonna have a whopper of a headache tomorrow!"

"I see." Adam took a deep breath, turned resolutely on his heel, and walked in. Just as he'd expected, Grandpa's pride, his comfortably furnished penthouse in the late 50's style, had been thoroughly ransacked, turned upside down, and methodically smashed to bits! He groaned, righteous anger rising in hot waves.

A flock of detectives appeared, descending on the splintered piles. He grit his teeth anxiously, watching their gel tape lifting fingerprints, scanners beeping for clues and tweezers nipping tidbits of DNA. Waiting until everyone's back turned for a split second, he discreetly checked out the package's hiding place. A sigh of relief escaped his lips in a short breath. It seemed undisturbed.

Kicking away a small clearing in the center of the room, he paced back and forth, thinking half-aloud as he groped for answers. "What am I gonna do now with those jerks on the loose?" he muttered. "Th-there's no telling when they'll show up again! There's gotta be a way to throw them off my back for good!" Suddenly a spark kindled way back in his mind, rushing forward almost as a full-blown vision. His eyes widened. "Yes, that's it! A bit of red herring across the trail; an interesting, ah, sidestep!" He shrugged his shoulders. "Hey, why not," he muttered quietly, "it works in the movies."

"What's that?" One of the cops jerked his head up.

He had to think quickly. "I, um, ah … I was just saying, 'm-move! I hope I don't have to *move* out of here! In any case, I gotta see if a few friends could come over and help me straighten out this junk. It's gonna be a lotta work to…."

"Hey," the chubby cop interrupted good-naturedly. "Me 'n my buddies are off duty in a coupl'a minutes. Soon as we grab the info we need, we'll all stay a few and help ya straighten out—won't we, guys?" He paused and repeated the question a little louder. "*Won't we, guys?*"

A sea of eyes rolled and heads nodded reluctantly. They'd gathered all the information they needed, so after a minute of banter everyone bent to work making a semblance of order, plowing paths through the debris.

"Gee, thanks, guys!"

"Don' mention it. Hey, wanna Twinkie?"

"No, please." Adam sighed, his arms crossed. "Well, at least they didn't completely destroy my computer. I'll just plug in the hard drive back in and…."

"Hey!" the cop interrupted again, chuckling and waving his Twinkie in the air. "You mean at least they didn't break your stupid *neck*!"

As the elevator closed a final time, he wedged a bent chrome-and-vinyl dining chair under the doorknob, gathered some blankets, and settled wearily to the floor. It was midnight and there was no recognizable bed, just feathers … everywhere. Hundreds of them. Feathers sticking to everything. He sighed wearily. "Just *look* at this place! All my memories mashed into mincemeat!"

His exhausted gaze rested on the bathroom's open door. Aside from the ripped shower curtain and broken glass on the medicine cabinet, nothing else seemed to be touched; the crooks probably realized they were running out of time. "Whoa, I'm way too wiped out to even *think* about digging out the package now!" A lopsided grin spread over his face. "If the cops had seen me looking in *there*, they'd think I flipped *my* lid! Well, the Aerie's totally surrounded and security's on every floor, so I-I'll just have to wait 'till after my errand tomorrow."

The floor was way too hard. Why had Grandpa insisted on feather beds? He flopped back and forth awhile then lifted his head in exasperation. "Hey! Here I am, without a doubt the richest person in the world—no, maybe in the solar system—and-and I'm sleeping on the floor like a pauper?" He leaned back in disgust. "Not for long, you dummy," he vowed, "not for long." His heavy lids started to close. "One more day," he mumbled. "I-I really don't think they'll come back *here* a second time. Yeah, my next step's *gotta* work tomorrow! One more day, that's all I ask. Gotta buy some time."

He was up early, his mind reeling. After a few minutes of tinkering and reconnecting, he rushed to work on his computer, burying himself on the Internet with downloads of galaxy records, star discs, and volumes of early explorations. In few hours, his research was done and he was ready to commence. Cracking his knuckles and flexing his fingers, he hunched low over the keyboard and began hacking away, snarking softly to himself. Star-Cad had always been one of his favorites. "Now let's see: this newly discovered globular cluster near Orion's belt looks like a good reference point." Carefully, he set the bearing. "Hmm," he mused, coding in instructions, "fourteen months' of travel should fit in nicely right about here; a real trip along well-known pathways. Okay. That's it! Now let's veer off into the unknown...."

About one o'clock he printed out the pile of bogus star maps, burned the rest of the phony information onto a minuscule flash drive, and slipped everything into a large, important-looking envelope. "Rats, that took a lot longer than I thought! Gotta hurry now, the bank closes at three! Hmmm," he thought, hefting the package. "Needs a little *weight*...."

He unzipped his jacket pocket with a sigh. "Well, there's a time for everything." He contemplated for a minute, turning it over: the little three-inch piece of stamped golden runes had been his last remembrance of the Galaxy Room; he'd held onto it for years, carrying it around with him almost like a good luck charm. He swiftly reconsidered. "Nope, sorry little guy. Not this time. Gotta keep you."

He switched gears and quickly yanked out his bottom desk drawer onto the floor. "I hope they missed my stash...." Yes, they were still there, wedged under the back runners: the first two experimental slugs of gold that he and Grandpa had melted. Smiling, he dropped them into the envelope for good measure. "Bye-bye."

He stood up decisively. "There! step two done, and the results *do* look convincing, if I say so myself!" He slipped on his overcoat, grabbed the heavy, bulging envelope, and rushed downstairs. After dismissing all his puzzled security guards, he made a real show of stealth as he left. "Here we go, now, step three ... the bait!"

Popping his head out one of the Aerie's side entrances, he slipped through an alley, dashed across the street, and slunk along storefronts. "Come *get* me," he taunted, "your skinny little target's on the move; I've got what you *want!*"

A brisk walk in the open quickly flushed out a long, gray vehicle trailing him. "*Yes!*" His heart in his mouth, he quickened his pace. Ahead, to the right, a lone figure slunk backward into the shadows. "Wow, you're not wasting any time, are you!" Sure enough, excited followers were beginning to close in from all directions; from the looks of it, about three or four sets of them, cellphones pressed tightly to their ears. "Hmm, *lots* of interest!" He quickly realized that the groups were trying to keep out of each other's way. "Even… competition, maybe? Man, the word's sure gotten around! This is gonna be a real thug slugfest," he smirked, getting into the role. "Thank God I'm finally at the bank or I'd be roadkill by now."

Pausing outside the big bronze doors he leaned way out, looking up and down the sidewalk, checking and double-checking several times. He stopped short. "Oh, come *on*, Adam. A bad, *bad* job of overacting!" Shrugging, he turned and strode into the lobby of the marble and velvet mausoleum, the picture of blithe, youthful innocence. An oily clerk recognized his face immediately and rushed up, fawning.

"Good morning, Master Adam," he drooled. "Coming back so soon to make another, ah, *deposit?*" His eyes had an eager, expectant look.

Adam settled comfortably into a plush, burgundy velvet chair in the man's cubicle, looking absently over the thick oak railing. "Um, not a deposit, really…." He turned back to the man, deadpanning in a loud stage whisper. "Just some *important records* my grandfather left me in his *will*! I-I can't make out hide or hair of them, though. I've searched everywhere but I couldn't find these *star maps* anywhere on the Internet!"

The clerk's eyes grew wide.

Adam continued to set the bait. "Maybe the *planet* that he's describing on the flash drive could be the place where… um, the place he went to…." Feigning alarm, Adam craned his neck to look around the room and spun back to the clerk. "Hey," he whispered a bit louder, "you guys'd better lock up this mess real tight! These maps were obviously very important to my grandfather! Oh yeah, and there's some good-sized chunks of *gold* in that envelope, too!"

The words *"important records," "star maps," "planet,"* and *"gold'* hung suspended in the air, charged and full of electricity. As he glanced around discreetly, many eyes, ears and microphones probed.

A jittery security guard bustled out with a safety deposit box and handed it to the clerk, who was now sweating noticeably. As the man's eyes darted uncomfortably around the crowded room, Adam hammed it up and dropped the heavy envelope.

"Oops! Sorry," he fumbled. Out of the corner of his eye he spotted several excited half-steps in its direction. The clerk lunged for the envelope, the metal box rattling loudly on his knees.

"Hey, it's okay, man," Adam soothed, "don't have a heart attack! The stuff's probably worth … nothing!" He was doing a superb job of keeping a straight face.

Blinking the sweat out of his eyes, the clerk licked his lips and reverently placed the envelope inside the box. "It'll be safe with us," he cooed, his mouth twitching only a bit. He closed the lid with a loud snap.

"Famous last words, pal," Adam muttered. The tension in the room had become unbearable. Smiling and nodding politely, he signed the papers and took the key. Ever so slowly he ambled toward the door, his heart in his mouth.

Moving swiftly across the street, he slipped into a busy storefront to watch through the plate glass. No one followed! A tremendous weight was slowly lifting from his shoulders. He peered out through the glass again, his finger in the air, counting off the seconds on the big clock in front of the bank. "Any time now."

A shot rang out! There was a siren, then another, then more shots! In minutes, an entire squadron was converging on the bank! "Well, there you go! Step three right on schedule!" The safety deposit key was still in his hand: contemplating it a moment, he tossed it into a trash can. A loud pulsing suddenly vibrated the air. He looked up. "And helicopters, too! This town is getting to be dangerous!"

Grandpa's vintage phone was ringing off the hook when he got back.

"They got it, sir, they *got* it! There were too many of them!" It was the clerk, blubbering. "They were shooting each *other* to get it!"

"What do you mean?" Adam huffed.

"The *envelope*! They got your envelope before we could put it in the vault," he quavered wetly. "The one you just gave us!"

"What? I don't *believe* this!" Adam shouted, pacing and rolling up his sleeves.

"And when all the shooting stopped, there were just *two* of them left standing! I-I had to give it to them, I *had* to! I'm so sorry!" The clerk was sobbing openly now.

Adam's eyes suddenly widened: Grandpa's old landline phone might be *bugged*! He held it out at arm's length, his mind racing. Well, if so, this would be a golden opportunity to set his hooks in a little deeper. He paused a moment for effect, then delivered his showstopper. "Well, try this on for size, you bonehead! I-I lied to you! That stuff was *priceless*! The knowledge revealed by those star maps could upset the very balance of power in the *universe*!" his voice thundered, shaking with emotion. Wow, he was even convincing himself! Oscar material, without a doubt.

There was a loud thud on the other end of the line.

"Hello?" Adam waited a minute, listening, and then slammed the phone down with a bang. With a loud whoop he punched the air with his fist. "*Yes*! They took my *bait*!" He bent low to the table to yell at the bugged phone. "And to whoever else was just listening out there in cyberland, good luck and bon voyage!"

Spinning around the room, he threw up the shades and opened the tall windows wide. A fresh breeze hit his face. Humming softly, he scooted into the bathroom. "Wow, I don't know why Grandpa loved these temperamental old fixtures so much." He sat backwards on the avocado-colored toilet seat, facing the wall. "Well, they worked, somehow," he shrugged. Reaching under the tank, he closed the shutoff valve and carefully removed the lid. With a few quick twists of the wrist, he unscrewed the copper float ball from the rod and pried it open with a screwdriver. It separated reluctantly; the cured silicone was very tenacious. In moments, a Ziploc baggie fell into his hand, containing the dry, featherweight package. "That," he concluded, quickly unwrapping the brown paper, "is that!"

Three tiny holodiscs and two thin, glowing alloy bars lay in his hands!

Trembling, he turned the strangely-lit metal objects over and over, scrutinizing them in detail. Slowly, it dawned on him: only from his years working as a test pilot for IFA's experimental spacecraft could he venture to calculate their possible function. He shook with excitement, his heart pounding. "C-could it *be*?"

He sprinted back into the living room to rummage wildly through the piled-up contents of another desk drawer. "Please, please, please don't be broken, or missing, or … yes!" He yanked out a small black object and tested the battery level. "Wow! Still good after two years? Last time I used this thing was…." He ran back to the bathroom, this time locking the door behind him: although security guards were swarming all over the building, he still wanted to play it safe. He drew back the torn shower curtain, balanced the holographic viewer carefully on the edge of the tub, popped in the first holodisk, and turned it on.

His jaw dropped. A spectacular shape materialized, suspended in midair and rotating slowly on its axis. He quickly checked the scale markers. "Wow, *immense*," he gasped. He knew state-of-the-art when he saw it, but this apparition was that unknown factor, that quantum leap into the future that could only come from another world. A starship, a big one, was waiting for him somewhere, and the glowing bars were the keys to it! He could hardly wait to see the other discs. Next to this gleaming, flawless vision, all the starcraft he knew looked like DaVinci's clunky wooden flying boats! This seamless wonder surely wasn't from this galaxy!

His hands shook as he removed the tiny, wireless earplugs from the back of the viewer. As he cranked up the volume, he heard a robotic voice narrating loudly, and a parade of the starship's incredible functions began to pass before his startled eyes, a panoply of slick, self-demonstrating computer generated models. Hatches popped open where there was once a seamless surface. There was an internal gravity system, fully adjustable for tempering frail human bodies to different pulls on different worlds; flying through hyperspace, the crew could walk around the ship normally. There was a Super Grav gym on level six, to get the crew beefed up for the rigors of exploration. A semiconscious netherworld awaited on level eight: the Dream Library. Sleeping in padded contour chairs, volumes of information could be absorbed via electrodes woven into a soft cloth and worn simply like a ski mask.

The starship dissolved and the robotic voice faded away. Shrugging, he popped in the second disc. Oddly, there was nothing to see except the shadow of someone's head against a wall. As he recognized the narrator's voice, he drew in his breath.

"Grandpa?" he whispered. "What…?"

"*Adam,*" the tired rasp of a voice began. "*I trust this package has reached your hands and that you've taken the utmost care to guard its secrecy!*"

He glanced around the bathroom and shrugged his shoulders. "Yes, Grandpa, the utmost care. T-the bathroom door *is* locked…."

"*I'm talking to you from the ultimate destination revealed by those holographic Star Maps* we got in the Galaxy Room. Remember, Adam? I'm so sorry about all those years I was away—so sorry!"

Adam's mind was racing. "So *that's* it! That's where you disappeared! But why aren't you showing me your face? Why are you…?"

"*I finally deciphered some really important runes around the edges of the glass floor and made another quick trip back to New Guinea. I found 'em, boy! They had a couple 'a pretty slick starships stashed in the jungle a few miles from the Galaxy Room! They were there all along, just beyond that ring of mountains, hidden with a cloaking device! Mine was an ultrafast, one-man job. I called it a Time Warper. I figured that since you were about twelve at the time, you still had your education to take care of. That was far more important than any galaxy-hopping.*"

He groaned. "I would've *loved* to have gone with you, Grandpa."

"*I've been here for a long time now, Adam, but not time as you know it. I've gotten old and quite sick. I really, really want you to come here in the other starship, the big saucer-shaped job you just saw in the holodisc. It's a lot slower than my little Time Warper, but you'll make it. By the way, I parked it close to the Aerie.*"

Adam blinked. "*What*? Grandpa, where in the world could you have hidden that monster in *this* crowded neighborhood? By the scale in the hologram, it's gotta be at least a thousand feet in diameter and a hundred feet high!"

"*I'm a rich man, Adam! I don't need a thing! No, it's not money I'm talking about, and it's not even what money can buy! I've found utopia here! Pristine wilderness! A fantastic, primitive, yet highly evolved planet.*"

A *planet*! Yes! He was getting excited now.

"*But like I told you before, I could care less about the gold. It's everywhere here on Aurona, lying around like rocks. It's infused into the whole ecosystem, the atmosphere, everything! It's the rest I'm talking about! I want to stay here forever!*"

He shook his head. "You didn't make it to the forever part, Grandpa," he whispered. "Whatever 'forever' is."

"*But you know, Adam,*" he mused, "*it's like a knockout sunrise here. You know what I mean? It's no good unless you share it with someone!*"

He nodded affirmatively: Of *course* he was right. Suddenly, the barest glimpse of his face showed in profile at the edge of the screen, then disappeared. He quickly backed up the viewer and squinted at the hologram. The veins on his swollen forehead seemed to be pulsing strangely. Wow, his grandpa *did* look a lot like that man in the coffin, but somehow….

"*Please come home, my dearest friend. Oh, and by the way, bring a crew, you'll need it to fly the ship!*" He was chuckling now, in his old, familiar way. "*Grab about three or four hundred good ones, Adam. Check 'em out just like I taught you. Only the best! Oh, and give 'em all one of those new super-encrypted wrist communicators. You know, those bendy jobs with the fancy displays my pal Marlon's been working on over at ComEx? Have him add about 10 terabytes of programmable memory, though. That's extremely important.*"

Adam nodded. "Yeah, I know, Grandpa. Those rubbery, flexible guys with the OLED screens finally made it out of prototype. Super, super comfortable…"

"Seriously, I know you've got what it takes to pull all this together, my boy. Oh, and another thing: if a coupl'a bad apples sneak into your pile, don't worry about 'em; you can root 'em out when you get here. Don't ask me how, you wouldn't understand right now. So now, listen closely. Here are the details of your mission...."

"Huh? Apples? How will *I* root them out, Grandpa?" Shaking his head in confusion, Adam shifted around on the hard toilet seat. He finally got semicomfortable by sitting on a few folded towels, then ran certain sections over and over to memorize the contents. Two-and-a-half hours later, as the message closed with a farewell, he staggered to his feet rubbing his rear end. Yanking out the earplugs, he filled the sink and splashed cold water on his face. It felt good. Suddenly, he noticed his bleary red eyes in the shattered mirror. He backed away, posing and studying himself, his hand on his chin. "Grandpa, come on, you can't be serious! Me? A crew captain?" he whispered. "Hey, I'm barely twenty! There's no way! I-I can't...."

There was a loud thump outside. The hair coming up on the back of his neck, he cracked the bathroom door open to scan the living room. It was dark, cold, and windy out there. His computer stared back at him with a blank, gray face and beside it, fluttering in the breeze, stacks of paper were starting to fly across the room. The staple gun that had been weighing them down lay on the floor. Ah, so *that* was the noise! He breathed a sigh of relief, shivering and rubbing his arms forlornly.

"Oh, man, how am I gonna *do* this?" Scowling, he raised the thermostat. "Utopia, huh?" He paced around the living room, his mind racing with possibilities yet filled with doubt and an overwhelming feeling of inadequacy. "But, Grandpa, *you* believe in me and that's gotta be enough!" He set his jaw. "I'm *going*!"

As he closed the tall penthouse windows with a decisive bang, the curtains brushed the backs of his hands. He grabbed a corner of the material and stared at it, a pleasant slate blue. His head jerked up. "*Uniforms*! That's right! I gotta get uniforms for my crew! And-and provisions, and...." He looked around. "Yes, that's it, I'll change this mess of a place into an *office*! A desk over there, a couple of chairs, a plant or two, and *people*! People are gonna come into my apartment for interviews, and...."

Suddenly he felt immensely better. Grinning from ear to ear, he settled in front of his computer. "It's magic time! Let's see: an updated list of Star Flyers and maybe an ad on Global Net. But first, I think I'll call that gorgeous bio-genius I read about in Earthtime's eMagazine, what's-her-name, Serena or Elena something? She and her team of genetic wizards at Biozyne have been digging into some *really* exciting stuff," he mused. The screen flashed as his fingers flew over the keyboard typing out lists and phone numbers. "The uniforms! I'll design them *myself* and have Grandpa's friend Max knock 'em off! That's right, Fabri Tech was one of Grandpa's.... No, Fabri Tech is one of *my* companies now. I'll use that new material that Max showed me a while ago, that Bio Steel spider-silk stuff that's been ion bombarded with Kevlar or something! I think it comes in colors now!" Working busily into the night, he flipped up a CAD program, drew a quick schematic of his apartment, and began arranging his new executive suite.

Chapter 5: **DOORS**

> OPPORTUNITY
> Of a lifetime. Travel beyond
> the limits of your imagination.
> Crew needed. Call T3379

Adam's small classified appeared on every available feed to Global Net. Attention-getting, yet with a deliberately ambiguous air of mystery, he'd crafted it to lure that unique type of nomad-adventurer: those who were willing to drop everything, do anything, and go anywhere.

He'd upgraded his grandpa's ancient five-petaflop stock market computer to handle the preliminary screening. Soon, clicking and flashing around the clock, the tireless machine began to weed out and summarize the answers to his carefully worded sequence of preprogrammed questions. Although he was asking for simple "yes" or "no" responses, the timing, order, degree of difficulty, and increasing depth of thought each question provoked was carefully crafted: he wanted to intentionally force the unseen responders to wake up and face the reality of their decision. The closing question was indeed a superclincher: "Would you be willing to leave the Earth *forever*, never to see your family again?" On this last soul-searcher, the AI detected some extremely long pauses and a very high percentage of callers ended their idealistic infatuation with a reluctant, "No."

A few weeks of computer winnowing yielded his intended quota: six hundred of the most promising responders. Although the chaff had been separated, the most arduous part of the process now lay ahead: the personal interviews. He figured on three weeks of at least ten-to-twelve-hour days to skim off the cream of the crop.

An army of well-paid security guards and a forest of cameras would watch for the inevitable crackpots. The plainclothes agents were posted outside his penthouse door, in all the elevators, discreetly lining the downstairs marble foyer and blending in with the crowds outside in the street. Everyone was scanned for weapons before they entered his private elevator and were confronted at the slightest suspicion. Young and hopeful, they soon filled the waiting room of his newly renovated penthouse suite.

Attitude, aptitude, and heart: he carefully made his decisions. Along with a lot of genuine surprises, a few diamonds-in-the-rough and two polished gems lay at the bottom of his winnowing screen, people of exceptional character. Three hundred and fifty people would make up his team. It was a nice, round, manageable number, and nearly the limit the big starship could accommodate. Reading between the lines, it was quite obvious that Grandpa wanted him to start a colony. With this in mind, he carefully balanced out the genders with a slight advantage to the number of men. He knew firsthand the rigors and dangers of exploration from his years of working with the Star Flyers and explorers at IFA.

After a warm handshake, each new crewmember stepped onto the slow turntable inside Fabri Tech's total body scanner. Sensors penetrated their clothing and recorded their actual body contours to measure them for a precisely fitting uniform. Adam issued each crewmember a wrist programmer, and just before they slipped on the flexible, rubbery strap, he programmed it with an individually coded and encrypted number. Secrecy was top priority. At a certain time at the end of the week, they'd be alerted to the location of their final rendezvous with a silent, running display on their screens.

As for Adam, although the arduous selection process was over, an even more trying time lay ahead. He had to settle all his own Earthly affairs in just five days.

Friday night. The long-anticipated hour had finally come. All over town, in hotels, movies and restaurants, a sudden, urgent series of wrist vibrations sent the crew scuttling into corners to shield their softly glowing screens from prying eyes.

The moving, encrypted words scrolled by: *"Congratulations and welcome aboard,"* Adam's message began. *"Say your good-byes.... Get some sleep if you can.... Final instructions to rendezvous will come ... at precisely four in morning ... on these wrist screens.... Come in secret and cover your trail.... Adam.*

He was up at two. Everything was ready. The keys to his empty penthouse were in an envelope and he dropped it at the security guard's station as he went by. That was it. The skyscraper "the Aerie" had been donated to G&A and everything he'd inherited was now in capable and extremely grateful hands. He'd carefully saved the small hip pack he was wearing since he was a child and it contained only a few treasured items: the three discs and holo-viewer, the two keys to the starship, a photo of himself with his parents and Grandpa, his favorite diploma, and a toothbrush.

Alone on the windswept street, he paused outside the Aerie to take in the beautiful building. Tears suddenly brimmed in his eyes. It had been a bittersweet time in his life, full of excitement and learning, yet marred with long empty holes of loneliness. He squared his shoulders and took a long, cleansing breath.

Public transportation was predictably sporadic at that hour and he ended up running the last three blocks to an abandoned warehouse near the docks. He glanced nervously at his programmer as he ducked inside. "Quarter to four," he puffed. "Still have a minute or two to get into uniform before I send out the final signal." As he flipped on the lights, he had to smile. "Max, Max, *Max*! Wow, an excellent job! The uniforms look *great* and they're *exactly* what I asked for!" The crew from Fabri Tech had all the uniforms labeled and arranged alphabetically, hanging neatly on long racks. He brushed down a row, feeling the incredibly slippery slate blue material.

Finding his name, he impulsively stripped naked on the spot, pulled up the internal underwear, and zipped on the one-piece garment. The low-rise boots felt like he was walking on air. "Lookin' good, man," he strutted. "Fits like I was *born* in it!" As he glanced around the room for a mirror, he nodded in satisfaction at the hundreds of boxes of provisions now filling the warehouse and cramming the huge, portable walk-in superfridge: quite a change from a few days ago. No matter, plenty of help would arrive shortly to load it all into the starship. He held up his transmitter watch and counted down the seconds.

"Precisely *four*!" He punched out the signal. "There! No backing out now!!"

A few blocks away, a pair of scarred, trembling hands held up one of Adam's rubbery wrist screens. A single bulb dangled from the ceiling over the man's head, swinging slowly back and forth in the predawn darkness. The sound of the small beep summoned four figures out of the shadows to squint at the moving words. They rudely jostled each other to see.

"Well, well, transmission received," a gravelly voice sneered. "And it's a lot closer than we thought."

"But-but how could it be in *there*?" a higher voice interrupted, sounding incredulous. "That dump's been condemned for years!"

"Shut up, you boob!" another voice answered. "This guy's smart. Too smart! You guys'll hafta be smarter, hear me? We'll bide our time, and when his guard is down we move! Now grab your stuff and let's get going!"

Adam looked down, shaking his head. At his feet, looking like relics from the past, lay his rumpled, discarded clothes and threadbare hip pack. "Hmm," he mused, "this'll *never* do, not now! I gotta *look* the part!" Walking up and down the long aisles of supplies, he selected a slim attaché case and carefully laid his few personal belongings into it. Gathering up his old clothes and hip pack, he impulsively stuffed them into the warehouse's ancient furnace. He slammed it shut with a decidedly loud bang.

"Helloooo!" A voice echoed behind him. "Anybody *here*?"

He collected himself and sauntered casually around the corner just as another figure entered and then another. "Hi," he called out. "Wow, *that* was quick! Where do you guys live, down the hall?" He chuckled along with the trio. "Hey, since you're the first ones here, help me tell the others what to do as they arrive." He pointed down the aisles. "Tell them the uniforms are over *there*, arranged alphabetically, the forklifts and dollies are parked over *there*, and they're to be all loaded immediately with the supplies that are located over *there*. Once everyone's in uniform and the trucks are loaded, including what's in the super fridge, we'll open those big doors over *there* to get into the inner courtyard. Got it?"

Grinning, they nodded and eagerly flew to work. Within twenty minutes, the place was swarming with people climbing into uniforms in every available corner. At Adam's request and surprisingly without a single exception, they all eagerly tossed their old clothes into the furnace, sending the flames high. This final act was cathartic and symbolic, but also practical: there'd be absolutely no trace of their rendezvous.

Adam directed the progress, carefully orchestrating their movements with smiles and hand signals, lining up the heavily laden supply trucks near the warehouse doors. Fighting a sudden wave of nausea, he stopped dead in his tracks.

"*Doors*," he mused. He found his heart was suddenly pounding. He stood quietly to the side, contemplating, his hand on his chin. "In ten minutes these rickety old warehouse doors should open to reveal…." He stood on his toes to clean a spot on the dirty glass. "T-to reveal *what*? It's too dark yet. Grandpa, all I can say is that the ship had *better* be out there in the courtyard! If it isn't, my name is *mud*!"

Almost time to leave. He took a breath, turned around, and raised his hands. "Okay, all of you," he called out. "Let's see: line up fourteen deep in twenty-five rows." As they scuffed around, laughing and sorting themselves out, he stepped onto a box. "That's right, you guessed it. There should be three hundred and fifty of you geniuses!"

When they'd settled down to a murmur, a small voice called out hesitantly from the back of the crowd. "Ah, sir. T-there's three hundred and fifty-*one*, sir."

Silence fell. A tall figure walked hesitantly toward the front, holding onto someone else's hand. Adam squinted. Who was *this*? Someone he *hadn't* interviewed? He leaned way out to the side to see a young boy coming toward him. A pert face smiled back warmly.

"Please explain yourself? Your name?"

The man looked apologetic, but spoke firmly. "My name's Jon, sir, and this is Todd. He's, ah, very friendly," he offered lamely. "He's my little brother, sir, and he's got Down syndrome."

"Yes, I can see that. Please continue?"

"Um, well, I'm his guardian. Our mom died in childbirth, Dad took off for parts unknown, and we've got no other relatives. We'd both like to come on this mission, but if you say no we'll … we'll understand."

The crew leaned toward each other whispering in hushed tones. Nobody had counted on *this* development!

"Jon," Adam murmured, trying to think. "Jon, Jon…*yes*, I remember you now. You really know your *code*! One of the best programmers in the business!" He hesitated a moment; the man was to play a vital role in the mission and couldn't be replaced. He was smart, too. He'd played his cards right and had waited until the last second to drop his bombshell. He smiled, sighed, then dropped to one knee and held out his arms. "Okay," he said softly. "Help the kid up here onto the box next to me. He's too short. He won't be able to see."

The crowd broke into enthusiastic applause as he rested a hand on the boy's shoulder. Todd's eager, pixyish eyes seemed to be mirroring his own. Yes, he was an explorer, too! Not a person objected to Todd's presence; they were all taken in by his cheerful spontaneous ways.

"I've chosen *well*," Adam began, and meant it. A murmur of approval riffled through the crowd and smiles broke out everywhere. "Inside the right pockets of your immaculately tailored uniforms you'll find your specific tailored orders. Your position and rank have been determined by me on the basis of your aptitude." He turned to Todd, giving him a snappy salute. "Todd, there are two very petite young ladies in the back who would be delighted to share one of their three extra uniforms with you. Their size two should translate well. As for *your* specific, tailored orders, Todd? You're to be Jon's shadow. Stick to him like *glue*! Understand?"

The boy laughed delightedly, nodding his head vehemently.

"Okay! On my signal, we'll take exactly fifteen minutes to load the cargo, get inside, and strap in!"

Light had begun to filter weakly through the dirty, broken windows behind him, silhouetting his rangy young form. He checked his watch and then delivered his own calculated bombshell. "As you see, dawn's coming and we've gotta be out of here, pronto!" He took a long breath and began. "According to our flight schedule, about fifteen minutes after takeoff we'll be outside the moon's orbit and accelerating… hard! Next, Mars! For you number crunchers out there, I'll give you a few simple math problems: right now, Mars is at its perihelion, or about 34 million miles from the Earth. Shortly, this ship will have reached about a 16th of light speed, or about 40 million miles an hour. Hmm, think hard now: Mars is 34 million miles away, so it should take a bit over an hour to get there. Right? Had enough math yet? Well, Jupiter's next, about 450 million miles from Mars! We'll have ramped up to a bit more than 1/3 of light speed by then, or over 250 million miles an hour."

"Whoa!" A hand shot up amidst the sea of shocked faces.

He nodded, curtly. "Yes?"

"Sir!" The voice sounded incredulous. "That's *impossible*! Those numbers don't make any sense! Plus, we'd be crushed to *bits*!"

He smiled and continued resolutely. "In less than a month, at 9 billion miles from the Earth, we'll be leaving the solar system! Still accelerating, mind you, and approaching light speed!" He was beginning to sound deranged. Another hand shot up.

"In *what*, sir?" A woman quavered. "*Nothing* can travel that fast, not to mention the forces of…."

Smiling, he cut her off politely with a finger to his lips. The crowd fell to an expectant silence. "You'll be sleeping by that time," he answered quietly. "The combined forces of impenetrable shields, a powerful internal antigrav system, and massive thrust from nuclear fusion will be whisking your suspended atoms through a wormhole and out of this galaxy in just six months."

Eyes blinked. Jaws dropped. Heads shook. Their leader had spoken firmly, with authority. Adam checked his watch once again. "Ready?"

"Y-yes, sir?" they answered shakily.

On his signal, two men slid the wide doors open to the inner courtyard. Except for a few old tires, tons of rubbish and a few startled rats, the immense field was….

EMPTY!

He grimaced, then glanced furtively over his shoulder at the crew. Their necks were craning as they intently searched the big courtyard. A murmur of unrest swept the room: this was *too much*! Todd was looking, too, and slid off the box to run out into the field, his short legs churning up puffs of dirt. Apologizing profusely, Jon broke ranks and chased his brother out into the soft morning light.

Adam turned slowly to face the crew. "Anyone want to back out?" he challenged, reaching slowly into his attaché case. "It's now or never…."

No one dared to move or speak; uncertain, they played along.

His heart was pounding loudly in his ears. "Grandpa," he breathed, "Please, Grandpa...." Doing his best to keep his emotions in check, he braced his feet on the box and raised the two glowing keys over his head, twisting them in the air in a memorized sequence of moves. There, the remote signal had been sent. He puffed out his cheeks with a short breath and waited trembling, staring at the empty courtyard.

There was a faint sound of machinery, like a distant turbine winding up. An eerie fog appeared, beginning to swirl and coalesce into a titanic, amorphous shape. Suddenly, out of nowhere, a starship like no other began to solidify, slowly darkening the field like an immense eclipse, blotting out the first bright rays of dawn!

Out in the middle of the field, Jon and Todd fell to their knees and bent way back, their jaws gaping as they looked over their heads. In the warehouse, most of the crew leaned on each other for support.

Soft spheres of light started to glow under the colossal, smooth disc, bathing the field with an intensifying brilliance. Out of nowhere, an outline suddenly traced a hatch and a cargo hold appeared, lowering from an apparently seamless hull! The body of the ship seemed to have almost a SKIN that healed over, concealing its openings!

That was the final straw: with a loud cry, Todd cowered behind Jon's back. Was that enormous thing an *animal*? Was it *alive*? The boy's terrified whimpers shook Adam out of his trance and he came to, shouting out instructions.

"Okay! The dawn's coming! Cargo in! People in! Doors shut! Ship gone! That's it! That's all!" He clapped his hands. "Move it! And don't worry about tying any of the cargo down, the internal artificial gravity system's fully automatic!"

Three men stopped cold, rope in hand and mid-lash, glancing at him in astonishment. He grinned disarmingly and shrugged, returning the incredulous stares of his three new resident physicists. "Hey, I don't get it either!" he yelled. "This thing doesn't have 'Made on Earth' stamped on the bottom! On the other hand, it *did* come with tons of instructions, and you'll get to see them all later. Anything happening *inside* the shell of the ship is supposed to be completely independent of the *outside*, and vice versa!"

They glowered at him speechlessly, screwing up their faces.

"Hey, I got the equivalent of three doctorates before I was fourteen! I can't figure it out *either*!"

They rolled their eyes at each other for a fleeting moment, then shrugged and joined the running throng, their immaculate white lab coats flapping along behind them, their uniformed, slate blue legs churning. Todd fell in right at their heels, busily shooing them along, with Jon in turn chasing him. Laughing to himself, Adam watched them all go. Who was supposed to be whose shadow, anyway?

His stomach growled loudly and reminded him of a last, important note. He looked up, shouting out a final order. "Hey! *Food*! Don't forget all the fridge stuff! It's super-frozen in those big Cryotanks over there!"

Huddled in a dark corner of the warehouse, a small group conversed in hushed tones. Although four of them were wearing official uniforms and were handpicked by Adam as crew-members, the fifth was nearly undistinguishable in the shadows; a long, black cloak with a floppy, hooded cowl covered his features. They helped him scramble into a crate, then lowered the lid and picked up the box. Nodding to each other, they trotted out into the dawn, blending in seamlessly with the running crew.

It was amazing. Nothing was left behind. Not a trace. The trucks and forklifts were driven back inside the warehouse, the doors shut and locked and in just forty-five minutes they were sitting nervously in their assigned seats with every buckle secure. Adam settled into his commander's chair, listening closely to some synthe-voiced instructions coming in through his ear inserts. He knew the entire journey had been preprogrammed into the grand craft's incredible memory; he'd watched the demo on the holodiscs. The saucer's entire trillion-petaflop assembly of amorphous chips was about the size of his body, including both the compact, supercooled optical cubes and miniature holo-relays.

The two alloy keys began to blink rapidly in his hand, prompting him. As he inserted them into their slots and twisted out another memorized sequence, all around him a neon jungle of holographic screens blazed to life.

"*Wow!*" he gasped, craning his neck around, thrilled and amazed. The largest display over his head was phenomenally crisp, pinpointing their stellar position at the center of a three-dimensional grid of galaxies. Yes, there they were, he could see the Milky Way in miniature, from a three-quarter view! Incredible!

Another light prompted him. "Engage cloaking device," the runes flashed. Moving quickly, he turned the keys one last time. As a green internal guidance light blinked on near his elbow, the cloaking device smoothly engaged and silently, and the starship disappeared in a shimmering mirage. Autosequence had begun and would now take over for the entire journey. He pulled his hands away, watching carefully.

Now totally undetectable, the immense saucer levitated silently upward, early morning mists swirling in the invisible disturbance. It was surreal: no sensation of movement, no vibration, no pulsing, no sound, just a slight static lifting of the hair on his head and arms. They climbed vertically and paused at about six thousand feet over the warehouse. Off to his left, a detailed holo-schematic of the Earth's solar system showed the starship as a tiny blip near the surface of the third planet from the sun. An oddly curving schematic line extended out from that point, plotting their course through the dustlike asteroid belts, and then … beyond. For a few minutes the starship didn't budge. It seemed to Adam as if it was timing itself for the run, waiting for exactly the right moment to start. It didn't take long. Abruptly changing climbing modes, the ship rotated ninety degrees on its axis and began to accelerate straight upward, slicing cleanly through the atmosphere at a tremendous rate!

He watched his screen, instinctively bracing himself, but any push he might have felt had been immediately neutralized by the ship's artificial gravity system. "This is *impossible*!" He gasped. "Those three physicist guys must be having a *bird*! W-what about all those supposedly unbendable laws of physics we learned? Maybe there *is* a fifth force, or a sixth we don't know about?" He leaned back in his seat, trembling in his gut, pondering over his now seemingly meager education.

He left the control room to join the crew at their stations, explaining and reassuring as he went. The ever-present external monitors showed a rapidly shrinking Earth, and a shocking fifteen minutes later they indeed streaked past the moon. A small chime sounded. Beginning in an unknown tongue and quickly switching to English, a soothing female synthe-voice wafted out of hidden speakers to invade everyone's thoughts.

"Good morning," it lulled, modulating in an amazingly warm fashion, full and rich. "Based on your collective body mass and the weight of cargo, the acceleration rate has been established in autosequence. Everyone is now to adjourn to the pod rooms on level three to prepare their bodies for sleep mode. We will be leaving this solar system in less than twenty-six days. The trip will be relatively short for this class of vessel, a mere seven hundred Earth years."

Adam blinked in alarm. "S-seven *hundred* years?" He gulped. "I didn't remember *that* part! We'll all *die*!" The warm voice oozed on, unhurried, like a rich, sugary confection.

"You will slip into form-fitting electrostimulator suits, which in turn are to be worn over a thin layer of AmnioGel. There are specialized throat inserts and catheters to feed you, respire you, and take away your wastes and a dedicated body and blood-cooling system to gradually lower your metabolism to just above the threshold of life. You will then enter the realm of suspended animation, where the aging of your human bodies and therefore the subjective conception of time itself will slow to the approximate ratio of one human year per century of travel. Have a safe and pleasant journey and thank you."

"*What?*" a loud, distraught male voice came from somewhere behind Adam.
Startled, he jerked his head up.
"Is that *time travel* we just heard?" the voice wailed. "Where'd this ship *come* from, anyway?"
Unbuckling his belt he turned around, a finger to his lips. "Sssh," he grinned. "I'm sorry, your name again? Is it Trevor?"
"Close." The man was short and round, with a pudgy face. "It's Tola, sir."
"Sorry. I'm usually much better at remembering names. Well, Tola, we've got approximately ten hours to go before we all, um...."
"Lapse into seven years of suspended animation," the man concluded wryly.
"That's true. We *will* be seven years older when we wake up. Hmm, let's see, that'll make me a little over twenty-eight when we get there. Wherever 'there' is."
"A trifle, sir. A mere tidbit of time," Tola said, grinning. "But that's still seven hundred years of time travel to this la-la land, in that language-lady's book."

Adam suppressed a chuckle. "She's just a synthe-voice, Tola. Someone's computer keystrokes."

The man shrugged hopelessly. "Is *anything* real here?"

As they unbuckled their restraining belts and walked slowly toward the elevator, Adam prodded a little deeper. He remembered from the interview that this little guy was an interesting character with a unique gift for words.

"So, ah, you were a writer, huh?"

"That's correct. Space Odyssey, Popular Science…."

"*That* old e-rag's still around?" he interrupted. "Wow! I devoured every *issue* when I was a kid! They've gotten more and more into holograms now, haven't they?"

"Yeah. It's incredible how fast things change, huh? Way, way more detail than those old flat photos, especially when you look down into the close-ups of Smoky Joe's great-grandson ripping ion propulsion engines apart! As they say, 'Easier to see in 3-D!' Oh, by the way, at the exact moment I was online checking out the editing on one of my articles, I happened to glance up and see your ad on Global Net."

"Hey, Tola. I-I meant to ask you something. Ah, may I?"

"Sure, go ahead."

"I purposely didn't pursue something during your interview because I had a gut feeling you were the genuine article. I noticed that you had a master's in social work among your other degrees and if I remember correctly, there were about ten years in your resume that you didn't account for. Ten years is a long time, man. What'd you do *then*?"

There was an awkward silence. The elevator door noiselessly slid open on level three, revealing a long, curving corridor separating the men's and women's pod rooms. Tola was cornered, and he knew it. He threw up his chubby hands, grinning. "Hey, ya *got* me! You've got a sharp memory. I don't know how you rooted it out, but I might as well, ah, as we say … confess? I was, um, a-a minister."

"What, *you*?" Adam laughed. "A *preacher*? I don't believe it."

"It's the gospel truth."

"This is getting interesting," Adam mused. "I used to go to church once in a while with my grandfather, but then I was, um, alone for a few years. My grandfather just seemed to disappear and I was a real emotional mess. I missed him like you wouldn't believe! There was this-this social worker lady where I worked at IFA; I talked to her a lot and she helped pull me through those empty years, but I always felt like I'd missed something. The church stuff sounded intriguing, but, whoa! It was the *people* who didn't hit me quite right. They tilted my 'truth-o-meter' the wrong way."

As they walked slowly down the corridor, Adam's hand went to his chin, contemplating. "So listen. I'm going to float an idea. Just hear me out, Tola. You don't have to answer right away. On this, ah, shall we say … mission, there's an unfilled opening, an important position."

The round man caught his drift. "*Mission*?" He grinned.

Adam shrugged. "Yeah, mission."

"C'mon, are you serious? Are you thinking…?"

"Yes, as a matter of fact, I *am* thinking what you're thinking I'm thinking."

"You want me to...?"

"Yes. Exactly. Every detail."

"It's tough, ya know," Tola scowled. "When you get right down to the nitty and gritty, the real teachings are hard line, nothing like all that commercial, puffed-up fake stuff on TV." He paused a minute, thinking. "Well, from what I see, this crew is wild and young and from *all* walks of life, if ya know what I mean. The Blueprint of Life offers *no* compromises. None. That's a concept that's hard to swallow."

Adam glanced at the round man out of the corner of his eye. "Oh, um, by the way there are no robes, hats, or special collars with the deal. Sorry."

"Hey! Who *needs* 'em? I got a *mouth*!"

"Are you game or what? I have to tell you that there are two other recruits aboard with theological backgrounds, a man and a woman."

"Nah. To me, that's somewhat of a handicap, sir. What counts is heart."

"Well, I only want the truth. Period. And teach me some of the hard stuff, too."

Tola stuck out his hand. "I'm your man."

They pumped enthusiastically. "Wow, a ten-year veteran!" Adam gushed. "So why'd you *leave*, anyway?"

His innocent question seemed to throw a bucket of ice water in the little man's face. He took a deep breath. "Ah, it's a long, long story, sir. I'll-I'll tell you later...."

Adam probed tenaciously. "Lemme guess. Hypocrisy?"

Tola sighed. "Okay, okay, ya got me there. Yeah, doctrinal issues. I spoke out big time and made national headlines. Walked out on the whole money-grubbing lot of them with their fancy glass cathedrals and jets and limos. Got tons of job offers, but refused 'em all."

"Till now, you mean, right?"

"Right." Tola looked up at him and smiled warmly. "Till now."

Chuckling, they opened the door to the men's pod room.

They were all indeed quite young, and now looked scared and vulnerable. They were standing near their assigned pods trying to decipher the instructions on the glowing tech tablets. A few were half undressed, poking at the impressive-looking sleep equipment.

Adam nudged Tola in the ribs, motioning with his head. "*Sic 'em.*"

"Huh?"

"Do your *stuff*! Y-you know...." He made a shooing motion, glancing at the men.

"Oh, oh! Right," Tola whispered. "Gotcha." He scurried into their midst, gesturing animatedly.

The young crew's wide-eyed expressions said it all. Nothing had made sense so far, not a thing. For beginners, the tremendous acceleration versus the lack of movement within the ship flew smack in the face of reality, and seven hundred years of travel was totally unthinkable. As the technical questions confronted Adam everywhere, he tried his best to reassure them scientifically, but most of the other issues were beyond his ability: they were pure, gut-level emotional issues. Tola's territory.

He stood back and smiled as he watched the pudgy man make his rounds. His instincts had been right on track. Tola appeared to be doing an excellent job, easing back into his element just as if he'd never left. His years of training and experience as spiritual counselor gave him a rock-solid presence, an inner peace and confidence the crew sorely needed. These were frightening, indecisive moments. He felt it too, that weakening, gut-wrenching fear of the unknown.

There was a tug on his sleeve. Todd was looking up at him, hero-worship crinkling his almond eyes. He took a deep breath and sighed, tousling the boy's hair. Suddenly he felt inadequate. What had he gotten all these people *into*? He noticed the three physicists standing in a tight little knot in the back row, deeply engrossed in a hushed, emotional debate. They glared over their shoulders from time to time, throwing him subtly disapproving looks and shaking their heads.

What to *do*, what to *say*? He found himself floundering in indecision, bogged down by his own doubts. Suddenly, a movement caught his eye. He checked his wrist programmer. Yes! There it *was*, irrefutable *proof*! He raised a finger, pointing silently to the large monitor over their heads. Another finger shot up. Todd was pointing, too, mimicking his motion. One by one the men stopped talking and looked upward, watching the screen. *Mars streaked by at an incredible speed!*

The three med spun back to him speechless, their eyes as round as the mysterious saucer they were on. Absolutely, positively, no way could this *be*! As Adam shrugged his shoulders, Todd shrugged too, his innocent smile an eager mirror of his moods. Impossible? In a contagion of sheepish grins they followed Todd's eloquent, mute example. Impossible? The boy didn't know the word existed. What they saw and what they knew had been immovably stuck on either side of a deep chasm; the universal bridge, the only missing ingredient, was a simple, childlike acceptance. Shrugging in acceptance, they took this final, blind leap of faith.

The time swiftly drew near to sleep mode and most of the crew had finally finished strapping in and had begun breathing moist air through their triple-tubed throat inserts. Suddenly, a pudgy finger pointed emphatically at the big screen. Todd let out a whoop. *Jupiter streaked by, a mighty, watercolored blur on their screens! Right on schedule!*

A muffled cheer went up. Yes, indeed, a blind leap of faith. Adam walked up and down the rows, shaking outstretched hands, reassuring and helping the stragglers finish their prepping. Todd had put up no fuss. He was tired, ready for his nap, and was already in his pod. All around the soft pneumatic hiss of closing pods signaled an end to conversation. Silence crept in, blotting out the hum of life. Returning to the front of the room, he stood there quietly tracing the smooth contours of his own sleep pod. It was quite a bit different from the others: more tubes, more tanks, a different shape entirely, truly a work of art.

"Well, here goes!" He undressed and then sighed resignedly, his heart in his throat. "Time to die for seven hundred years!" He rubbed a mysteriously soothing salve all over his naked body. "Hmm, AmnioGel, huh?" Shivering a bit, he quickly zipped on the plush electrostimulator suit. The catheters hurt a bit as they entered, as did the multitubed throat insert, but a numbing jelly quickly took the pain away. As he settled back gingerly into his sumptuous, ergonomically shaped sleeping table, it moved subtly, enveloping him like a nurturing womb. The AI had sensed his weight and triggered a whole sequence of reactive motions.

A captive audience now, he watched in amazement as a set of wide straps slipped around him and self-adjusted comfortably. With a click, a hidden catch released and the pod smoothly hissed shut. A pleasant-smelling gas began to seep down his nose plugs, invading his senses. His mind began to swim, his core temperature dropped, a black tunnel closed in, and he was gone.

"Now! They're all in!" In the swiftly darkening pod room, four jostling shadows unclamped one of the sleep pods from the last row and rolled it into a freight elevator for their stowaway waiting down in the warehouse. As the hooded figure began his prep routine, they scurried back up into the pod room, dashed into the last empty row, tearing off their uniforms and prepping their bodies in frenzy. Shortly, the last buckle was secured and the last pod closed. They all slipped away, time evaporated into a cold, dark eternal void, and the starship left the galaxy far behind.

Four, long centuries slowly passed. Fragile human bodies lay suspended and frozen in Amnio Gel coating, the tenuous silver cord of life stretched beyond all known limits. As they slowed down to change course in a preprogrammed maneuver, a sudden, unscheduled event unfolded. A shudder passed through the great starship and a yellow warning light came on in the dead, flat blackness.

A small, errant planet was directly in their path, an unusual planet with a massive, memory-blanking electrical field that reached out like tentacles millions of miles into the surrounding void!

The seemingly invincible craft suddenly found itself unable to change course. After a battery of failed autocorrective maneuvers, it began to decelerate at full power. As another shudder passed through the ship, the navigation holograms turned on in a blaze of light around the captain's console in the command center. The starship's emergency thrusters began to fire one by one, and the synthe-voice crackled to life. "Attention! Possible collision! Attention! Possible collision…!"

Somewhere far, far away, the sound pushed against Adam's senses. Suddenly, he writhed in agony as a long needle punched into his chest below the sternum. It slid in deeply: adrenaline was being pumped directly into his heart, burning like molten fire! He thought he was having a nightmare, but the pain was too incredible, too real! The distant voice was more urgent, nearer this time, right in his ear! "Off trajectory! Collision course! Off trajectory! Collision course…."

His eyes flew open, his heart thudding loudly in his chest. "What?" He coughed, gagging on something. The throat insert had begun to slide out of his mouth as oxygen poured into his pod. A small monitor over his head revealed a strange sight: A fuzzy-looking ball filled the view! He squinted at it, trying to comprehend. "It's snowing?" he rasped. "No, no! It's a *planet,* dead ahead! No time to…!"

All went blank as they plunged deeply beneath the surface. Nothing moved. As the synthe-voice rasped back to life, Adam shook his head groggily, trying to understand the words. There it was, clearer now. *"No damage! Shields down! No damage! Shields down!"*

"What?" He broke into a spasm of coughing. His throat felt like it had just been ripped out. "No damage? *That* doesn't make sense!" The straps popped open and his pod swiftly regulated its temperature to the outside. He sat up and felt his damp skin. It was strangely cold, yet his body was seething inside. His fists clenched.

"T-the ship's *crashed*? How could that have happened? E-everything was going so well!" The pod finished its opening sequence and he staggered out weakly, feeling like an antigrav barge had just flattened him. Something was tugging at him. He looked down impatiently.

The catheters were stretched tight. No sensation, they were just... stretched tight. Rolling his eyes and feeling foolish, he pulled them out. "Numbing jelly," he remembered. Red-faced, he glanced over his shoulder toward the crew, then scowled. What kind of protocol was *this*? Why hadn't anyone *else* been awakened? The lights shining out of his pod revealed the chronometer on the wall. He squinted. The Earth-time was just a bit past four hundred years! They were only *halfway there*!

Dumfounded, he tried his best to reason things out, but had to give up quickly. The emergency resuscitation hadn't been gentle by any means. There was a long trickle of blood running down his chest where the needle had gone in just below the sternum. He blotted it off with a towel and yanked on his uniform.

Well, it was quite evident that it was up to him to get everyone out of this mess. He ran his hands over the surface of their pods. They were smooth, unmarred by a single dial, switch or visible opening; in fact, they seemed to have the same unblemished skin as the hull of the starship! How could he possibly get anyone out to help him? Feeling drugged, he staggered into the elevator, rode it up to the control room, and lurched drunkenly into his commander's seat. Maybe there was a menu to open a few pods and get some help? The ship's external attitude display was showing the blinking red outline of the saucer. He shook his head in disbelief.

The starship had plunged straight in, cutting into the planet like a knife! "We're-we're standing on *edge*? No way! How can I still walk around? What's holding me up?" Another short search revealed the answer. A small light pulsed near the monitor. "*Artificial Gravity - On*," it read. He shrugged. "My head isn't together yet, I guess." He slapped his palms, trying to get rid of the pins and needles. "So let's see now: maybe I can pull up out of the ground with some manual thrust...." As he slid the levers gently forward, the mighty antigrav engines labored. Nothing moved!

Breathing a quick prayer, he opened all twelve channels to the external display monitors and scanned them one by one. Every camera was blank except one. Alpha D was still protruding from the surface, but the ground was quickly rising under it!

"Holy moley, I gotta *move*!" He leaped out of his seat and lurched through a maze of corridors to the airlock. Suiting up into explorer's gear and survival knapsack, he threw the ship's tiny, oval transponder into a zippered pocket. Seconds before he opened the inner hatch, he suddenly remembered the artificial gravity.

"*Stop*, Adam! No more mistakes now!" He reasoned it out then entered, shut the inner hatch, held on tightly to the ladder, and pressed a button with his elbow. Sure enough, as the outer hatch opened, he felt gravity shifting quickly around him.

He gazed out into a nightmare world. An unknown substance blasted against his face shield in a gale force wind and all around in a great circle, strange, tall objects were waving eerily.

Something stuck onto his gloves, a white, powdery substance. Before he had time to react, a torrent of the white particles poured into the airlock!

As he shoveled frantically against the tide, he had a sudden, sinking feeling. "What've I *done?*" he agonized. "I can't shut the outer airlock now! He looked down behind him. "That means there's no way I can open the *inner* airlock either, because this stuff'll spill into the ship around the seals and prop it open! We'll depressurize! I gotta get outside right *now* or get buried alive!" He frantically checked his equipment one last time. "Man," he lamented, "I really blew it big time!" At the last possible second, he dove out of the shrinking opening and clawed his way up a steep slope, grabbing some weird, sinewy objects.

There was a loud crack. Something big toppled over and swung up behind Adam in an arc, whistling through the air. A stunning blow to the back of his helmet sent his body spinning out of the crater. He blacked out as the ship disappeared under a relentless tide of moving ground.

Chapter 6: MAROONED

The small planet's scorching sun rose over a strange, desert landscape. As the temperature climbed, the wind followed suit and picked up to a gale force. A shadowless, translucent brilliance of flying silica crystals quickly filled the air in a swirling maelstrom, obliterating the horizons. Land and sky merged as one into a total whiteout.

Out in the middle of the vast plain of nothingness, a small geyser of crystals erupted as a fist punched through the surface. Adam awoke with a start, gasping for air. Total darkness enveloped him, as close and stifling as death. He pushed hard with his feet. They met resistance; something seemed to be enveloping his body and restricting his movements. Fear rose in waves. Taking quick, deep breaths, he fought valiantly to calm himself, his mind reeling with dire scenarios. His wrist was throbbing painfully beneath him, as if it were caught in some kind of a tourniquet. He pulled. No go.

Fighting panic, he turned on a low level of light inside his helmet and dropped down some menus to check his stats. As his eyes adjusted to the light, he spotted the pedometer and time graph. "What?" he gasped. "Seven *miles*? I walked seven miles? He blinked in disbelief. "And then I passed out for fourteen hours after that?" He slumped back. "Wow, I didn't pass out, I watched my whole life whizzing by in some kind of a rerun! It seemed like an eternity! Was it a dream?" He struggled to figure it out, but to no avail; his recent memory simply refused to come back. He grimaced in pain, pulling at his wrist.

"I can't breathe!" He choked. "Why's it so hard to *breathe*? And where in blazes is this, some kind of a hole? How'd I get in here?" Something was moving. He looked up. A 3D schematic of his e-helmet was spinning in split-screen up in the corner of his face shield. As it rotated, he could plainly see the back of his helmet. The rebreather unit was badly dented, probably from a massive blow to his head. "Whoa! My helmet's crushed? *Definitely* not good news!" He looked at it again, scowling.

"Wait: I didn't call up this function; I must've been checking this schematic *before* I passed out!" He studied the timeline. Sure enough, the twin tubes of his rebreather's emergency snorkel had been deployed fourteen hours ago, and were now just barely poking through a rising surface. "How much did I do? Is there more?" Dazed and confused, he reeled in the tubes and pushed upward with his free hand. Fortunately, the silica was light.

He tugged his wrist again. Yes, it was definitely caught on something. He dug quickly, piles of crystals flying, working in an ever-widening circle. In moments the stabbing, blinding sunlight took over. "Whoa!" He turned away from it quickly, squinting into the shadows. Taking a breath, he finished digging. His eyes widened. A cable? Yes, some kind of *snare* was wrapped around his wrist, grayish green and frosted with crystals! As he finished clearing off the slick surface, he felt a shudder. He paused, his fingers resting lightly on the surface. The coil started to squirm at his touch! He yanked his hand away, his heart pounding. "Holy cow! Th-this thing's *alive*??"

Tentatively, he pushed at it again. It shook violently, writhing in spasms. "Woah, this bad boy *hates* that!"

He leaned back, thinking."Well, it moved, and that's a whole lot better than shutting off my circulation." A sudden idea crossed his mind. "Hey, lemme push the envelope!" Determinedly, he wrapped his gloved hand around the cable and held on. It shuddered, writhed, then stretched out like an uncoiling spring and ... *let go*! He snatched his arm away and scrambled out of the hole, watching in mixed fear and wonderment.

Hissing through the thin atmosphere, a huge gray-green coil rose gracefully out of the shallow crater, unfolding like a steel fern. The glistening trunk undulated like a tentacle into the sky and, in seconds, a long, tapering whip was towering fifty feet over his head!

Staring open-mouthed, he quickly scooted away on his butt. Something was happening near the top. He squinted at it suspiciously, shielding his eyes. The long whip was starting to transform, the diameter subtly swelling and splitting along tiny vertical grooves. With a series of popping noises, it fanned open into a web of ever-increasing complexity, each successive strand splitting and resplitting in a highly ordered sequence. Within a few breaths, he found himself sitting at the base of a fantastic, flat, two-dimensional webbed tree of mammoth proportions!

As it started to sway back and forth, he took no chances and sprang to his feet. The giant frond simply rotated on its axis and stopped, presenting itself broadside to the howling wind. Instantly, it trapped millions of the flying, glittering crystal shards in its delicate web. With this final transformation, it became a vision of ethereal beauty.

He gasped, blinking in a daze, turning in a slow circle. The wind had subsided a bit and the horizon now stretched all around him, flat and unbroken. "W-where *am* I? How'd I *get* to this God-forsaken, whiteout planet? This sure isn't Aurona!" Rubbing his head and neck, he tried desperately to remember something, anything.

A spark lit up. "My *ship*!" He looked around. "Yes, where's my ship? I-I don't remember any landing sequence! Where'd it go?" The strange surface kept giving away as he turned in a circle; it seemed to be loosely packed under his feet. He bounced up and down, kicking up chunks of the powdery ground and testing his weight in the superlight gravity. As the breeze swirled the clumps of crystals into the air, his eyes followed the wafting stream back up to the tree. It glittered like spun sugar—no, like diamonds dazzling brilliantly in the light! He gasped, overcome, exhilarated.

He was an accidental traveler on an alien world, alive, but living in a dream!

Feeling a bit bolder and keeping a wary eye on the webbed top, he sidled up to the trunk and poked it. Nothing moved. Slowly, carefully, he wrapped his gloved hands around the thick stem and gave it a squeeze. Immediately, a great tremor shook the plant! He stared at it in shock. "What *is* this thing, a plant or an animal?" He knit his brow, figuring, then flexed his fingers, studying his biofeedback gloves. "Hmm, could there be an electrical field? I know my whole suit's internally microwired with electronic systems...."

The specs reeled out: the gloves were a masterpiece of technology with a fantastically complex neural network that could amplify his fingertip's delicate sense of touch and monitor his skin temperature, moisture, and grip pressure. The engineers had even added sophisticated shape recognition for working in the dark, and they…. He stopped short. "Whoa, whoa! Why can I remember all this complicated tech stuff verbatim, but I can't remember the simple, *vital* things, like how'd I get here and where'd my *ship* disappear to?" Unbidden, a disturbing thought percolated through his mind.

"No! It *can't* be!" he gasped. "I've got … *amnesia*? Did that blow to the back of my head give me some kind of short-term memory loss?" Frowning he dismissed the thought, denying it could have possibly happened to him.

After a moment of denial and self-examination, he reconsidered, then bit his lip as he faced the truth: he'd been winged. Hopefully, prayerfully, his memory would return or he'd be stuck here for good. No food, no water, no ship, no Adam. It wouldn't take long.

He let out a sigh. "Well, I just gotta be patient. This is memory stuff is a bit dicey. I've heard that some people's memory returns right away, but others take a lot longer."

Glancing down at his gloves again, the list of specs resumed right where it left off, reeling effortlessly through his mind. Suddenly, his brows rose. Yes! A thought clicked into place, something his grandfather mentioned on the holodisc. There was something the glove's engineers hadn't been able to filter out: almost as a by-product, the gloves emitted a strong electrical force of their own, amplifying his body's Kirlian effect!

He looked up excitedly. "Amplifying? Maybe I've got all this Kirlian electricity shooting out of my fingertips, only *megastrong*?" A ray of hope washed over him. "Wow! I-I might be able to control this weird plant electronically! Let's see, I know sunflowers follow the sun using cell turgidity and relaxation, so maybe, just maybe…." Impulsively, he reached out to test his theory: wrapping both gloved hands tightly around the stem, he circled to the other side of the frond and then let go.

It followed! Unbelievably, majestically, the huge, flat network over his head followed his path, twisting completely around! It stopped when he stopped, disgorging itself of the wind-whipped, flying crystals. Immediately, it caught them on the backside, and in seconds the web was full again, like nothing had happened.

"Good night, it's *true*!" he gasped. "I-I *can* control it!"

As he pondered his new discovery, he sensed a distant rumble. He jerked his head up suspiciously. Tapping out his e-helmet's radar function, he scanned the horizon. At one point a single, vertical line ran halfway up his face screen. Puzzled, he leaned to one side and then the other, but it remained in the same spot. "Hmm." He eyed it suspiciously. "Could be just a glitch … I-I hope." The tapering outline was soon broken up by a storm of crystals and it disappeared.

Suddenly, he felt a stab of pain. As he rubbed his temples, a sliver of recent memory slipped out. "The *transponder*!" he gasped. "The ship's wireless transponder! I *have* it! I-I remember! It'll show me where the ship is!" He fumbled through his pockets excitedly. "Where *is* that little sucker? Crud! Too many stupid zippers!" He fished around for a few minutes but gave up abruptly as the shadow of the plant crossed his feet.

He looked up. It was moving again, trembling and opening even further. Intrigued, he stretched up on his toes to pull down a section of the frond. The resilience surprised him; it felt like tempered steel. He tugged it down closer to his face. "Huh? What's this? The crystals on the surface are *moving*?" As he tapped out the code for microvision on his chin pad, a sharp world of giant crystals and colossal webs filled the screen. "Wow," he gushed, "what *fantastic* equipment!" His eyes swept in wonder across a glittering, virtual 3D panorama. "Grandpa said an alien race called the Bitrons invented these helmets. I'd sure like to meet them some day."

The jagged crystals seemed to be covered with tiny crumbs of organic material, and were carried along by tiny filaments on the webs. Millions of them, like cilia, were cleaning and turning each irregular shard to every facet. Suddenly, it came to him.

"*Food*! This plant's eating the food that's stuck all over the crystals, just like a whale feeding on plankton!" He looked closer. Sure enough, at every fork in the web, a mouthlike opening was engulfing food particles, then several longer, specialized cilia were flicking away the empty crystals. He scowled. Something just didn't add up. He let go of the frond and watched it whip away. "So if that's food, where does it all *come* from?"

He studied the ground, pushing the soft crystal strata around with his toe. It broke up easily, like powdered snow. Kneeling on the spot, he rummaged through his backpack and pulled out a lightweight carbon fiber folding shovel and snapped it onto a set of matching brackets on his forearm. He dug deeply around the base of the tree, moved outward slightly in a widening circle, and then dug several shallow trenches. In fifteen minutes, he'd revealed what he wanted to know: the trunk had one deep taproot, bulging and apparently full of food, and then with almost geometric precision, the root sent out runners in every direction under the surface. Each runner ended in another coil, poised and ready to spring upward. As he folded up his shovel, his eyes widened at the possibilities. The entire planet could be connected with an underground web of these things!

As sweat from the exertion began to run into his eyes, an annoying, imperative yellow light flashed dead center in his face shield. He looked up in alarm. Shade! He needed to find shade; the suit's power supply and rebreather unit simply couldn't be overtaxed much longer! He scanned the blazing horizon again, this time switching to a color-enhanced infrared temperature mode. Wait, was that a cooler-looking crescent of deep blue-black sky in the distance? Was night and relief from the heat coming?

He stopped suddenly, listening, the hair rising on the back of his neck. An eerie, low wail was coming from behind him. He turned around slowly, every sense on alert.

"No!" he gasped. His once-majestic frond was disintegrating, blackening, and falling apart with huge holes in its delicate webbing! He leaned closer. The sound was whistling through the dying plant's thousands of mouths as it withered and shrank, expelling the planet's nitrogenous atmosphere. It recoiled to the ground, swiftly turning brittle and drying up in the blistering heat. Suddenly, he felt responsible. "Wow! I-I opened you up in the daytime and upset your natural biorhythm? You come up... at *night*?"

As if in direct answer, the root jerked spasmodically and sent the top flying. His jaw dropped.

Like tumbleweed, the dry, coiled frond rolled toward the distant shimmering horizon and the eerie wailing faded away. Soon only the sound of the wind remained.

After a moment, humor finally got the better of him. "So," he grinned lopsidedly, "the, ah, *net*work expelled a nonfunctioning member, hmm? Just like *real* life! Cut and dried!" He chortled, feeling better. His fierce headache was finally abating.

The wind was lessening, too. Gazing at the dark nighttime horizon, he tapped out scope vision on his chin pad. As it snapped toward him, he involuntarily fell backward onto the drifts of silica. He got up, brushing himself off. "Man! Talk about weird and spooky! That horizon's sure got a strange, fuzzy, moving edge to it!" He squinted at it again, trying to understand what he was seeing. Was his vision deteriorating from the lack of oxygen? "Wow, it looks … *alive*! Could it be my eyes? Is the scope vision damaged? Holy cow, this whole *planet's* a nightmare!"

He gritted his teeth in frustration, fumbling through his pockets. "And where's that stupid transponder?" Gathering his wits, he forced himself to calm down. Sweat was now pouring down his back, and the annoying buzzers and flashing readouts were warning that the temperature inside his suit had finally risen to the peak of the dreaded red zone. He shrugged and gave in to the inevitable. Yes, thank goodness he remembered *this* trick! Kneeling, he shoveled out a shallow body-sized depression in the soft silica and settled into it, pulling handfuls of the stuff over him.

Nearly two hours passed. Darkness had fallen as he'd rested and the wind had subsided dramatically to a steady, gentle breeze. He snapped awake, his senses overriding his dreams. Was the ground stirring around him? He sat bolt upright, the silica flying off his body. "A *quake*!" he gasped. "It's gotta be, the ground's *definitely* moving!"

He scrambled out of the hole, clearing his face shield. Right at his feet, a spurt of crystals flicked from the surface and wafted upward in a long, silvery ribbon. A bit further away there was another flick, and then another. Suddenly, an explosion of crystals erupted all around him! Jostled, he thrust out his arms in alarm. Something big just slithered under his feet, throwing him off balance! Showering crystals into the air, a huge coil suddenly erupted. As it snaked by his shoulder, it hit him with a glancing blow and shoved him squarely onto yet another erupting projectile. In a heartbeat, his body was whipped into a melee of titans springing out of the ground. Airborne, he tumbled head over heels onto something soft and springy, bounced, and then slid down a trunk to the crystal surface.

Breathing hard, he spun his head around in amazement. "A *forest*? The desert just turned into … a forest?" All around him were enormous trees, all exactly the same, all turned precisely in the same direction and functioning as a unit. It came to him in a flash: his theory was true, but on a monumental scale!

"So *that's* why the planet's a desert in the daytime: all the fronds are hiding from the heat, just like *me*! And-and now that it's cooler, they're shooting up to filter food out of the breeze!" Shaking his head in wonder, he watched the great tidal wave of erupting fronds recede into the distance, timed precisely to the rotation of the planet.

His mind was a lot clearer now. He looked up at the steely web over his head. "Maybe I could climb up there…. Yes!" he blurted impulsively. I gotta get *higher!* I-I gotta see what's going on!" He paused to think things out. "Woah, that's right, these biofeedback gloves are gonna make the plant move!" he scowled. "Wait a sec: I gotta go outside the box, here. I really don't think this thin atmosphere would hurt my skin…." Shrugging, he yanked off his Kirlian gloves and shoved them into a back pocket. Rubbing his sweaty palms together, he shinnied up the smooth trunk, then holding his arms wide for balance, he scrambled across the trampolinelike web and settled into a fold at the top.

"There!" He scanned the horizon excitedly. "*Definitely* a great vantage point! Now I gotta find that stupid transponder," he muttered. This time he poked around in his pockets in earnest, carefully squeezing every fold of his suit with his bare hands. Shortly, he felt a tiny lump wedged into the corner of a zippered sleeve pocket. "*Yes!*" He yanked out the miniscule oval device and turned it on.

Immediately, a faint signal came back, heavily distorted and broken up in the silica-laced atmosphere. As he scanned in a slow circle, it grew louder. "Come on, it's *behind* me? That's where I came from?"

He shifted around in the webbing and gazed into the distance: the fronds, all precisely the same height, waved like a sea of grass in the brilliant starlight. Suddenly, he drew in a sharp breath. He squinted, struggling to focus.

Something else, something massive, was looming far above the fronds! As he snapped on scope vision, his eyes popped. Wreathed in clouds of crystals was the silhouette of a massive spire, tapering upward like the shape of an obelisk!

"Holy cow! There *is* another life form, and it's *monstrous!*" His heart thudding loudly, he flipped on a computer-enhanced radar mode, then gaped in awe at the obelisk's colossal size. "W-what in the world could it *be?*" Triangulating, he did a quick chin pad calculation. "No way! It's almost a thousand feet high? B-but that's impossible, nothing alive could reach that height!" Suddenly, his eyes narrowed. "Hold on! Is it moving?" He checked the obelisk in Doppler mode, studying its trajectory.

There was doubt about it, the monster was indeed moving steadily, coming directly toward him! Somewhere between, the signal was coming from his ship!

"*No!!*" he shouted. "If these readings are correct, it should reach my ship in about five hours!" As he stood riveted in fear, a brilliant flash of green flickered at the top of his face shield, followed by a pinging, resonant tone. Right in the same spot as the yellow warning light, an automenu dropped down dead center, blocking his vision. Distractedly, he read it aloud. "Auxiliary Rebreather on Standby: Enable/Disable?"

He drew back with a start. "Huh? Did that function get jammed when I was whacked? Well, duh!" His chin dove for the button. Immediately, there was a labored whirring sound, followed by fresh air and an enveloping, cool mist. Something like curtains parted. He remembered everything. Every detail. He took a deep breath.

"That's *it*," he exclaimed, excitedly. "I-I climbed out of a huge *crater*! And something big hit me on the back of the head when I was scrambling up the slope! My ship had the shields up and it got *buried* when we crashed!" His eyes widened with fresh understanding. "So *that's* why I couldn't see it when I came to," he groaned. "All the while it might've been right *under* me! Then I wandered for hours and hours?" He stopped short. "I-I shouldn't be so hard on myself. I was dazed and confused from lack of oxygen. How was I to…?" He swallowed his words as his throat constricted.

Angrily, he threw himself forward, slid down the trunk, and landed up to his knees in the loosely packed strata. He stood there a moment, thinking. The silica seemed to resist packing, probably because of its oddly shaped crystalline structure. Suddenly, it dawned on him. "That's *it*! My ship cut into the surface, just like this! With the shields up, it sliced right into this soft stuff like a knife through butter!" He drew in a breath. "And-and my crew's still aboard, in sleep mode! That Obelisk monster's gonna *crush* them!"

Suddenly, over the soft hiss of the wind, his sensitive audiodomes picked up a different sound: some kind of weird, guttural vibration was wafting out of the forest beside him. He heard a low rumble, a twang, and then a loud wail!

He jerked his head up to see tall thin shape toppling toward him in an arc, crashing through the trunks! He dove behind a stem, landing in a tuck and roll. Shaking uncontrollably, he whispered the e-helmet's code for full alert. In enhanced mode, the audiodomes and flat panel sensors filtered out a low, choking roar accompanied by a strange series of gusts buffeting the air. An *animal*? He crawled stealthily toward the sound and looked out into what appeared to be a small clearing.

In the strangely glittering starlight, there was a shallow path receding into the distance: broken fronds were still tipping over, their torn underground webbing hanging limply from the rim. Hundreds of them had just been flattened in an even, mown-down trail. As he glanced down at an exposed taproot, he let out a gasp. Buds! Root buds were already forming along the underground webbing near the breaks, probably to close the gap across the trench. These fronds seemed to have tremendous regenerative power! Summoning courage, he got up on his feet and stepped out into the clearing.

Lying in the trench, an immense trumpet-shaped mouth huffed, pulling in clouds of luminous, flying crystals.

His body alternately freezing and surging with adrenaline, he angled his feet to run, poised on the razor edge of flight. "I-I really don't have time to…." He studied it warily. "Well, it-it's not moving," he whispered. A sudden thought flashed through his mind. *"Know your enemy."* He bit his lip. "Yeah, you're right, Grandpa, I gotta do this. Thanks," he breathed. "You taught me well." He held up his hands. "I know, I know; I gotta *see* what I'm getting into…." Emboldened, he turned up the e-helmet's bright searchlight to full power. As the beam played over the shape, he could see the outline clearly.

"Yes, it's *definitely* one of those obelisk creatures, but this is definitely a young one." He calculated quickly. "Wow, this guy looks like he's about twelve feet in diameter here at the bottom and about thirty feet high." The creature was huffing weakly, breathing its last. Its lungs must have been torn from the fall, crushed under their own tremendous weight. Gravity was suffocating it like a beached whale.

A sudden realization swept over him. "Yikes! This sneaky little guy probably sensed my body, and-and he was creeping up on me while I was underground!" He tried to dismiss the thought as he edged closer to the creature's shell, his searchlight sweeping over the rough surface. "Wow, he must be able to skitter over surface pretty fast; I-I *know* I didn't see him before I lay down!" He checked his wrist programmer and let out an impatient breath. "Five hours? I gotta go seven miles in five hours? Hmm. I got time…."

Something snagged his toe. Wincing, he stopped short and looked down. A thin strip of gray-green was glistening under the edge of the shell, stretched taut like a guitar string. "Aha! So *that's* what tripped you!" He dropped to his knees near the trumpet mouth and opened his explorer's pack. His hands trembling, he took out a syringe, drew a sample of grayish obelisk blood, grabbed some fragments of shell, root, and frond and then sealed the pieces tightly in small quarantine jars. That was it. He'd seen enough.

He shouldered his pack, locked in a bearing to the ship and picked up his pace to make up for lost time. Zigzagging through the trunks, he followed a faint green line he'd plotted inside his face shield. "Gotta hurry," he puffed. "I've got a long trip ahead of me through this forest." Suddenly feeling famished, he pulled a meal out of a pocket, slipped it through a small feeder airlock in his helmet, and ate greedily.

He thought about the young obelisk creature as he trudged along. The trumpet shape had flared at the bottom, thinning out to a razor-sharp, saw-toothed edge. A scenario quickly fell into place: the obelisks must swirl along, spinning and cutting a few feet below the surface, mowing down fronds and devouring taproots. In the process they plowed up crystals, leaving a trench behind with their immense weight. The shape of the shell was incredible. The saw teeth blended into great, spiral ridges that ran up the outside, twisting upward and inward like a unicorn's horn. Not far from the top, several vertical slits blended into the grooves between the spiral ridges. Probably nostrils.

Getting into it, he started talking to himself loudly. "And then, the crystals get sucked into the bottom of the obelisk and spew out of the top. The obelisks feed on the frond's taproots like huge vacuum cleaners!" He paused, breathing hard. "Wait! That also means the fronds are eating pieces of … *themselves*! They're cannibals!" He picked up his pace, his legs churning.

The rumbling of the big obelisk suddenly felt a lot closer. He looked up. The top of the tremendous creature was now showing over the fronds. Clouds of crystals were erupting from the top, making it look like a giant, spiral smokestack. That young one behind him was a mere speck compared to this behemoth! It was probably just learning to feed by itself when it got knocked over. Unbidden, the scenario popped into his mind. "Yes!" He nodded. "I bet the young ones follow along behind the old-timers and feed on leftovers in the trenches. When they get older and heavier, they can knock over fronds by themselves!" Somewhere deep within, he tapped his failing reserves of energy and began to dodge and weave through the evenly spaced fronds like a quarterback.

As he drew closer to the big granddaddy, he began to feel the ground vibrating in a deep, rhythmic pulse. "Wow, this old guy's booking! I-I'm sure he's curious about what *real* meat tastes like!" He grimaced at the scenario of his broken starship and mashed, bloody bodies. Puffing in exertion, he bent his head way back, trying to see the dark, belching top through the swirling clouds of crystals. "Holy cow, this thing's *immense*!"

Struggling to see, he stopped short. "Wait a sec! My scope vision and searchlight will definitely help here...." He turned them on. A set of colossal spiral air valves started at about eight hundred feet. He gaped, watching the slow, sequential opening and closing, then scanned on upward. A blast of crystals was pouring out of the top into the planet's thin stratosphere, where it was carried by strong winds toward the distant horizon. He played the spotlight down over the shell. The individual ridges near the bottom were immense, probably twenty feet thick. "Wow," he whispered, awestruck. "This obelisk must be ancient! I bet he's one of the oldest and largest living species in existence!"

By the crunching and snapping sounds pouring through his audiodomes, he knew it was cutting an extremely deep swath through the fronds. Checking its speed, he quickly calculated the time of contact. "Oh, no! Less than two hours left? All my friends will die and I'll be stuck here forever? *No way*!"

With a burst of speed, he zigzagged through the trunks and staggered out into a large clearing. His heart hammering, he turned on his ship's transponder. "Yes, yes! This is *it*! I'm here! My ship plowed in right in the middle!"

Gasping, he ran out to the center of the immense circle, kicking at pieces of broken frond in frustration. "So I'm *over* my ship now? I-I know I can't dig this thing out by myself!" He slowed himself down, trying to think rationally and fighting panic. "I wish I could *see* better! I've gotta see!"

Out of nowhere, a familiar voice flashed through his mind. *"Adam, you gotta get a good vantage point!"* He stopped dead in his tracks, his arms dropping to his sides.

"Grandpa! Those are *your* words again! All those years of working with you taught me well: in order to see any kind of problem clearly, I had to stop, step away, and look at it from a completely different angle. The solution will just... pop up!" He jabbed a fist into the air. "Yes! A vantage point! Grandpa, you did it again!"

Staring at the big obelisk, he reasoned it out objectively: the actual, living creature lived inside that thick shell like a snail and couldn't get to him. Suddenly, he knew what to do. Opening his knapsack, he yanked out a pile of equipment: gripper gloves, toe and knee spikes, and an antigrav belt. In minutes, he was dressed and ready, suited for a climb. Taking a deep breath and breathing a prayer, he sprinted across the clearing at full tilt toward the towering creature, then began to dodge through the last trunks to get closer.

A great, circular ridge of crystals and broken fronds greeted him, churning and tumbling like a moving waterfall. Turning up his antigrav belt to three-quarter strength, he jumped high over the debris and landed squarely on a spinning ridge of rough, callused shell. He began to half-climb, half-fly upward and quickly reached the bottom of the enormous, sequential air valves. He wedged himself between the deep ridges; there was a deafening, pulsing roar and blasts of wind were buffeting him with a gale force. He knew he couldn't go any higher or he'd surely get sucked in. Turning off his audiodomes for silence, he held on tightly and surveyed the slowly turning panorama below. Yes, this was an *excellent* vantage point!

What was that in the distance? Daylight was approaching like a moving crescent of blinding white! Ducking under the surface, the fronds were folding into the ground in front of it like a receding wave!

He looked beyond the approaching crescent of light. "Holy mackerel!" He drew a sharp breath. "*More* obelisks! *Hundreds* of 'em!" He quickly looked down behind the ancient one. "Wow, and there's those little suckers, feeding on the scraps!" As the slowly moving tower of death turned, he spotted the big, round clearing way out in front him. On a sudden hunch, he tapped out the helmet's infrared vision.

"Yes, there it *is*! My *ship*! It's still radiating tons of warmth from reentry!" In perfect silhouette, the glowing saucer form of his ship sat on edge; it had plowed straight into the planet, cutting like a surgical blade through the fronds!

The panorama rotated back toward the approaching daylight. As his face shield autodarkened, he watched the fronds diving beneath the surface. He blinked in wonder. An instant, endless desert stretched out behind them and great great eddies of windswept crystals swirled into the air, looking like dust devils spinning along the surface. Already, he could feel the wind rising.

Suddenly, something clicked. His eyes widened. Something about the fantastic scene below him struck a deep chord, and his artist's visual mind kicked into overdrive. "Dust devils…. Dust devils spinning like mini tornadoes…. *Hey*, that's *it*!" He gripped the rough shell in excitement, a daring plan unfolding in his mind. Would it *work*? It would be a *huge* gamble, but taking a calculated risk was far better than taking *no* action! There was no time to lose! He had his three-step plan formulated on the fly.

He steeled himself and leaped fearlessly out into the air. Looking like a speck of dust floating down the face of the obelisk, he plummeted headfirst in a skydiver's posture.

No time to waste! He dialed up his antigrav belt to a full climb near the bottom and stopped, hovering in midair. Reaching out with the toe of his boot, he landed on the crest of a massive saw-toothed ridge. Taking a quick breath, he half-ran, half-hopped to the leading edge and dove off, landing in a tuck and roll. He staggered to his feet, letting out a shout of relief. "There! Step one!"

Sprinting for all he was worth, he reached the middle of the clearing, now less than a half-mile in front of the obelisk. "Now for step two!" With a series of voice commands, he initiated a CAD program and threw up a schematic of a galaxy-like spiral inside his face shield. Three arms would do…. No, *six*! Satisfied, he enlarged the elegant shape inside a circle, tipped it into an ellipse, and then carefully shaped it in perspective to match the terrain. Carefully fine-tuning, he plotted the glowing, dotted lines of the six arms to spiral away from the central, buried starship. Another tap locked the shape into virtual memory. Holding his breath tentatively, he stepped inside it.

It stayed in place. With a glowing, phantom blueprint traced out around him, he began to dig frantically with his shovel. This thing *had* to be precise or it wouldn't work. Besides, the wind was rising and the fronds wouldn't last long under the intense heat. As he grabbed a wiry coil it stirred sluggishly. "Huh? What's the *matter* with you? You worked *before*!"

Glancing at his hands, he groaned and shook his head sheepishly. "Try *again*, you dummy!" Impatiently, he yanked off his insulated gripper gloves and pulled the Kirlian gloves out of his back pocket. Scowling, he slipped them on and squeezed the stem. "Come on, baby, come on! Step three's gotta work!" The coiled knob burst to life. He had to duck aside quickly as it shot upward like a spring. "*Yes*! *That's* what we're talkin' about!" He twisted the fat trunk with his hands, fine-tuning its direction. As the top turned diagonally to the wind, a gust immediately blasted at a shallow angle off the face toward the center of the phantom spiral. "Yeah, way to *go*!" Scrambling wildly, he followed his phantom schematic and uncovered another frond, turned it, and let it go. Two *doubled* the effect! Enthusiastically, he worked inward along the dotted line toward the buried starship.

As the first arm of open fronds neared completion, the wind spiral was already sending a gale whipping across the center. He squinted. What was this? On the other side, the bumpy tops of coiled fronds were being uncovered! "Hey, I can really move now! No more digging!" He tossed the shovel, sprinting to the other side. Scurrying along on all fours, he started resolutely on the second arm. These fronds were *far* easier to resurrect, their tightly coiled knobs were well above the surface and scoured clean by the wind. With his back to a rising gale, he followed his virtual, curving paths and finished the remaining arms of his pattern. He backed away. The blast was intense and the inner fronds were getting shredded, but the wind spiral was holding its own!

It was working! With nowhere to go but up, the crystals rose in a dense, violently twisting column and were carried away. In seconds, the sharp edge of his starship was exposed. The hull gleamed brightly in the intense sunlight, undamaged!

He leaped exuberantly, his fists in the air. "My *ship*! *My ship*!"

Suddenly, the ground started to slump. He scuttled backward, frantically kicking himself away from the edge of his widening crater. His groping hands quickly found a section of exposed webbing and he held on for all he was worth, watching the swift process in amazement. "Wow! This is flat *incredible*! Far better than I could have hoped for!"

Autogyros running, the saucer was standing on edge, squarely in the center of a great, wind-blasted bowl of crystals. Shredded and tattered, the fronds were hanging limply over the rim and the howl of the wind was subsiding. Shaking his head, he took a deep breath. "I only hope to God that this beautiful bucket of bolts still works."

Phrasing carefully, he spoke a precise series of codes. Deep in the core of the starship, the great antigrav machinery responded. It rose majestically, leaving a clean, knife-edged groove in the bottom of the crater. Holding tightly to a trunk, he leaned out precariously over the rim. Way down in the bottom, relentlessly trickling in through the crystal strata, he caught a glimpse of liquid. His eyebrows rose. "Water?" He blinked in surprise as the proportional bars on his elemental analyzer spelled it out for him. "Yes, it's *definitely* a chloride of sodium. There might have been a huge sea here at one time!" At a sudden rumbling sound, he quickly cleared his face shield and looked up.

The far wall was collapsing! The obelisk was breaking through!

It fed noisily, shaking the ground with subterranean rumbles of satisfaction. As the tautly stretched webs snapped with loud twangs, he could see a mammoth tongue of greedy, grayish obelisk flesh licking up the ruptured taproots. Suddenly, his body shook in the blast of a deep, subsonic bellow. The saw-toothed edge picked up speed, singing a new note!

"Oh, no," he gasped, "He's closing in!" The wind off the spinning trumpet shell was starting to buffet the hull of the starship as if it were a paper cutout suspended on a string. He sprinted around the rim of the crater toward the obelisk. The spinning, saw-toothed edge appeared to be clogged, wet and shiny with the ruptured shreds of fronds. He looked up, checking. The open hatch of the starship was way at the top, too far to jump. Dialing up his antigrav belt to max, he leaped fearlessly, jumping nearly thirty feet through the air to land squarely on the obelisk's moving ridges. Checking over his head again, he sped up the starship's outer gyro. As the moving ridges carried his small body toward the point of contact, he commanded his e-helmet to take over and fine-tune the ship's rotation. They drew nearer, the autoprogram timing and synchronizing the two paths. "Closer, closer…." As the open hatch swung down, he watched it flop open, pouring out crystals! He dug in his heels and tensed. "*Now*!"

Like a tiny mote between two behemoths, he flung his body through the air and dove head-first into the hatch just as the saw-toothed points clacked loudly against the ship. He had to duck great shards of broken shell tumbling through the open hatch behind him. Operating on pure adrenaline, he grabbed the ladder inside the airlock and held on tightly, pulling down menus and tapping madly with his chin. In command of his ship once more, he rotated it up into a horizontal plane. As the floor tipped, the crystals and pieces of shell fell to the floor of the airlock in a torrent. Breathing a prayer, he reached out and closed the hatch with his free hand. It locked with a loud click. The artificial gravity light came on, blinking softly.

"*Bingo*!" he whooped. "I'm *in*!" Quickly decontaminating both himself and the airlock, he opened the inside door, then flinging off his backpack and gloves, he slammed it shut behind him and sprinted through the corridors to the command center.

Breathing hard, he dove into his chair, yanked off his helmet, and strapped in. "Okay baby, do your stuff!" Locking in a rapid climb, he punched the appropriate buttons and waited for a response.... *Nothing happened!*

"Huh? What's the *matter*?" he shouted in frustration, clenching his fists. "This *can't* be happening! This planet's a *nightmare*!" Although his body was exhausted, his mind flew into overdrive, trained by years of schooling in 'what if' scenarios. He calmed himself down, fighting hard to remain objective.

"So what if the creature *is* intelligent," he panted, "and it doesn't *want* me to leave? What if this big Obelisk, or *all* of them for that matter, figured out a way to jam the ship's controls? Hey! That might be why we *crashed* into this stinking planet in the first place! Anything's possible!" He reached down to retrieve his e-helmet. "Well, I know *this* thing worked a few minutes ago." As he yanked it down over his head, he could see a brilliant flash on the helmet's screen.

Jagged, angry bolts of LIGHTNING were lighting up a wide panorama! He blinked his eyes in shock. They were coming from somewhere inside the obelisk!

He cleared his face shield and shouted, half-crazed, at the ship's flashing holographic views in front of him. "*Electricity*? Of course! That's *it*! You generate electricity! You've got huge, built-up static charges from moving around in the crystals!" He wasted no more time. Switching the ship's flight controls entirely to his e-helmet, he pulled down the appropriate menus and punched out a rapid climb.

Like a slave suddenly freed from its master, the ship took flight and rose high above the crater. As the spiral openings appeared in front of him, a sudden tornado blast began to pull the starship relentlessly toward the obelisk like a great vacuum! What was *this*? The intelligent creature had already figured out that there was a new source of commands, and he couldn't pull away! He worked the helmet's controls frantically, gripping the arms of his chair. "So you're not done *yet*, huh?" He set his jaw. "You think you've outsmarted me, huh? Well, if you *want* me, you *got* me! I'm not resisting anymore, so try *this* on for size!" Simultaneously he threw up the shields, banked the starship sharply onto its edge, and blasted toward the vertical openings at full thrust.

"*Into the fire*!!" he screamed.

A great storm of electrical charge greeted the ship as it disappeared into a cloud of crystals, there was a loud, cracking noise, then an explosion of shattered, flying shell. As ship climbed over the ragged top, there was a loud wail and the electrical resistance immediately stopped.

His primal instincts were now on full alert. Instinctively, he threw on the cloaking device and hid inside the obelisk's dense column of crystals, following it toward the horizon. His ship had become an invisible, invincible quarry. He looked back one last time, shaking his head in wonder.

The entire *planet* was lighting up in a dazzling spectacle! Helplessly consumed with rage, all the wind obelisks were blazing to life, thundering and bellowing in anger! He grimaced. So this *had* been a collective effort! Now, each suspecting the others of stealing the prize, they were sending great, arcing bolts through the air! He gaped at the screen, enthralled.

Like a spiny sea urchin being zapped in a shimmering aurora, the spiky ball of a planet writhed in agony. Smaller spires weaved and toppled, cleaved in two by the old giant's massive bolts.

"So they *tricked* us," he growled. "This planet was positioned directly in our path, right at some interstellar crossroads! When we slowed down to change direction, they scrambled our controls and made us crash! Well, I'm sure they didn't count on my new Bitron e-helmet." He held it up, admiring it, and then pushed away from the counter, shaking with exhaustion and relief. "Enough, already!" he breathed. "I've *had* it with this place!"

A green light blinked to life. He looked down to see the main controls engaging: autosequence had resumed! "Well, whaddaya know! We're out of range!" As he stared at the steady green light, the shaking in his gut subsided.

Totally exhausted, he threw up his hands in resignation, threw his hemet aside, and staggered back through the corridors to the pod room. The cool salve felt delicious on his hot skin as he stumbled through the prep routine. "Just a few more minutes," he whispered groggily. "Just a few more...." He swallowed hard: the throat insert made him gag. "I'm almost there...." He closed his eyes, the pleasant gas seeping in.

The tunnel beckoned. A deep sigh of victory escaped from his lips as he loosened his grip. Finally! On to the goal! Good riddance and sweet dreams.

Chapter 7: JOURNEY

Blackness.... Dead, cold blackness. The saucer's great, dark silhouette hurtled through space like a fleeting shadow, its silent rows of pupalike pods nourishing their fragile life forms within. After seven impossibly long centuries, a chronometer in the starship's mainframe sounded with a small, final click.

The crew's frozen bodies had depended on mechanical devices to keep them on the threshold of life for an unthinkably long time. Now at the end of their sleep, a battery of far-infrared heaters began to glow inside their contour tables. As the temperature rose, thousands of nano pumps awoke in a carefully timed sequence, nudging and coaxing their blood to trickle through elaborate, fluidic switching devices. Inside the great battery of capillarylike tubes, their sluggish hemoglobin cells lined up in single file to be oxygenated. As micro doses of adrenalin were injected into their arteries and small electronic surges stimulated their hearts to beat, their blood pressure rose in response to balloon their newly flexible arteries.

Somewhere out there, somewhere at that fleeting time and place on reality's nebulous fringe, it was Adam's turn. He felt a tiny prick on his skin and turned slowly, drifting with sudden purpose through his vast, dark emptiness. There was a faint suggestion of light in the distance and then a quickening, tortuous pull. Frightened, he resisted with all his might, but felt his comforting veil of darkness relentlessly slipping away behind him. Gathering momentum, his body began to careen recklessly toward an odd, bright, translucent membrane, that frightening, uncertain threshold where the past and future merge into the elusive moment of 'now.'

He broke through in a rush of awareness, a newborn once again, a helpless child forced from his fabulous, fetal limbo. As an electronic jolt awakened his heart to beat and his diaphragm to breathe, his sleep pod opened like an unfolding flower.

There was a sound of voices. Yes, faint voices were out there somewhere, coming from far, far away. Many people were murmuring in the distance, sounding concerned. Suddenly a mask was slipped over his face and moist, fresh air poured into his cold lungs. He summoned all his will and forced his eyes to open a slit. Amorphous shapes floated around him in a thick fog, then slowly resolved into focus. As the distant voices spoke again, this time they were a lot clearer. He understood.

"What in blazes happened to you, sir?" someone spoke out of his range of vision. "You look awf...." There was a sharp nudge to the man's ribs from his companion and a deeper voice interrupted.

"Ah, not awful, just a bit, um, older. Not much."

Adam jerked as a needle pricked his skin. "M-m-m-mph!"

"Sorry, sir. Just hair and nail growth activator. The manual says on page twelve to give you this shot when you wake up. Gotta start those cells dividing again!"

"Um-hmm," he agreed, with a slight nod. His vocabulary was improving.

A female voice intervened, sounding motherly. "Everyone, please! Give him a minute or two!"

"Sorry, sir. Ah, the manual said we got microdoses of some kind of growth retardant serum while we slept! It makes sense, doesn't it? If we hadn't gotten them, our masks wouldn't fit tightly to our faces. We'd all have seven year old beards...."

"Hey!" the female voice interrupted. "Not *all* of us!" As she rubbed her chin in mock horror, the room echoed with laughter. "On the other hand, so to speak...." She held up her fingers, studying them. "I wouldn't mind the nails a bit!"

There was more laughter and then the sound of rapid footsteps. Another voice filled the room, sounding out of breath. "Th-there's a lot of strange debris in the hallways, guys," he wheezed. "I traced it back to an airlock!"

Adam stretched his aching arms. There was a strange, deep chill in his bones. Was *this* what it was like to be twenty-eight? His swollen eyes swept the Pod Room and came to rest on the man's startled face.

"Oh, ah ... hi, sir," the man coughed nervously, "I-I wasn't aware you were back with us yet. Sorry!"

Adam nodded, letting his questioning gaze fall to the man's hands.

"Oh, yeah! Look!" He awkwardly stuck out his hand. "This is the strangest stuff. These powdery crystals were sticking to everything in the airlock!"

Crystals? Adam squinted at them falling in clumps and floating eerily in the bright lights. As he opened his mouth to speak there was a rough, sliding movement against his tender, wet skin. He looked down, momentarily distracted. The towel they'd draped over his naked body had slipped to the floor. Someone snatched it and threw it back over him. Suddenly embarrassed, a vein pounded in his neck. After a long pause, he tried to talk, readjusting the shape of his tongue and mouth to unfamiliar speech. "Re... mem ... ber...," he croaked.

As they waited expectantly, he studied their faces. Funny they all looked the same, yet somehow different. Older versions of themselves? He finally rasped it out, this time a lot more coherently. "R-remember the rules of quarantine!"

Quarantine? Why quarantine? As they stared blankly at each other, someone produced a jar and the now-suspect crystals were unceremoniously dumped into it. Chagrined , the man who'd found them slipped away to disinfect.

Another man bent toward him, pointing. "Ah, sir? What's that thing in your hair?" He leaned closer to study the object. As Adam reached up, he felt something spiky, almost metallic. The man pulled out a pair of nippers from his tool bag and commenced to awkwardly poke and cut at it.

"Gloves!" Adam rasped, suddenly alarmed. "And-and get a toxicity reading!"

"Right again, sir! Sorry!"

A flurry of white gloves seemed to float through the air like January snow, blanketing all the upraised hands. The man yanked out the object in a flash, then gingerly holding it up with just the tips of his nippers, he turned on his hand-held toxicity meter. As the gadget beeped, the incoming data began to be analyzed.

Adam squinted, trying see the thing with his blurry vision. The man's white-gloved fingers were absently folding and unfolding the small gray-green object like an accordion. As it swam into focus, an unforgettable image jarred in his memory.

A *frond*? Could that wiry thing be a piece of the net? Then all that white stuff in the jar must be the *crystals*! He slumped backward, his mind whirling. The scorching sun! The obelisks! His endless searching for the ship, the terrible wind! A loud beeping snapped him out of his turmoil.

The man held up the net. "Wow! All green, sir! Toxicity readings negative!"

Adam looked relieved, then confused. "Ah, what if those readings had been positive? Some-some kind of killer microbe could've invaded the ship … by now…," his voice trailed off as he wrestled with the gray areas of protocol.

Chastened and chagrined but totally confused, the small group glanced furtively at each other, shrugging.

He winced, feeling the sudden, uncomfortable wall of silence. "Listen, guys, I'm sorry," he mumbled. "I need to confess how this weird stuff got into our ship in the first place. It-it was all from *my* bungling."

"Sir?"

"That's right," he affirmed, then paused once more, a slow smile spreading across his face. "But wait! Actually … I didn't bungle at all, in fact I saved you from certain death! Yes! You have two undeniable items of proof, right in your hands!" He swung his legs to the floor with purpose, tying the towel tightly around his waist.

They stepped back warily, bewildered by his rapidly shifting emotions.

"Those weird items? You want answers? I'll *give* you answers!" He scanned the floor, his mind razor-sharp at last. "Where's my explorer's pack?" No one answered. "Elke! Sahir! Joelle! All of you! Find it!"

A feeling of relief swept through the crew as he snapped out commands. Their leader was back. They'd been waiting for orders, any orders, direction of any kind, and were jubilant upon receiving them. They leaped into action.

Down in the hold, a faint yellow light was pulsing. Looming behind a pile of crates in Warehouse F, a lone sleep pod sat unmoving and quiet. Although the main power was connected, a small data plug dangled loosely, forgotten in the frantic, last-minute move. Separated from the ship's mainframe, its internal backup chronometer flashed, searching for commands. In a frozen state, the stowaway slept on.

It was a completely different story in the brightly-lit Pod Room; the same phenomenon of Adam's rebirth had started to echo behind him on a grand scale. Softly blooming, bank upon bank of sleek cocoons were whirring open with precise timing to expose their naked, wet, and still quite fragile occupants.

Spotting an open manual lying next to him, Adam leafed through it. The sequence became clear on page four: a small, select contingent of medical personnel had emerged from their pods in a precisely-timed resuscitation schedule. Prompted by the ever-present synthe-voice, they read their manuals. Following its procedures and directives to the letter, they'd gathered next to his large pod to wait.

He chuckled at the thought. Like workers helping a queen bee from her royal cell, they'd swarmed around him to assist his emergence. "Man," he muttered, "they were all helping *me*? Wow, that sure beats that first emergency round, when I was *hammered* awake!" He glanced down at his chest, probing with his fingers. Sure enough, the scab from the puncture wound was still there, right below his sternum.

A rapidly growing group was searching excitedly for his equipment, running up and down the hallways, their questions hanging thickly in the air. What had really happened while they slept, and what were all those strange crystal particles? And that net-thing that was stuck in Adam's hair looked like nothing they'd ever seen! The riddle was about to take on a new twist.

With a shout, Elke ran past them down the corridor. "*Found* it!" he shouted.

They were on his heels immediately. He burst into the Pod Room, the group piling in behind him. Flashing a broad grin, he handed the explorer's pack to Adam.

"Thanks, Elke," he nodded, heaving it onto a table. It was heavy—heavier than he'd remembered. Maybe his muscles weren't up to it yet? As he ripped open the straps, piles of crystals spilled out in a torrent, pouring out of every fold. They seemed to have infiltrated everywhere! He dug deeply, carefully lined up the four quarantine jars on a counter, and then turned to face the crew. Their wondering eyes searched his own for answers.

"Oh!" He held up a finger with a start, suddenly remembering a final piece of evidence. "My-my, ah, helmet," he mumbled, bending over to look under his pod. "Where's my e-helmet?"

Sahir answered with a question. "Your Explorer's model, sir?"

"Yes, yes!" he replied quickly. "The big, oversized one." He raised a brow. "How'd you know its name?"

She shrugged. "A diagram right here on page twenty-six explains them in detail, sir." She leafed through it quickly and held up a picture. "Read it yourselves, guys! These e-helmets are fantastic! The chin-codes are there as an alternate to voice commands! The codes are more accurate, though…."

Adam cut in, echoing her enthusiasm. "Yes, Sahir, you're right; they're *way* more accurate! In fact, they're almost extensions of your brains! You read system menus on heads-up displays inside your face shields, then either speak or tap out simple three or four-digit function codes on your chin bars."

They murmured in excitement. The mood was swiftly becoming contagious.

"Um, you'll recognize my e-helmet when you see it…." He paused for the effect. "It's got a big *dent* on the back where something, um, something *hit* me!" Reluctant to tell all, he let the riddle unravel a skein or two to tantalize them.

It worked. They scattered like leaves in a fall wind. Sprinting between the airlock and control room, they searched with competitive zeal. "Oof! Hey, outta my way…." Their voices trailed off, echoing as they vanished down the halls.

He chuckled as he trotted after them. His deliberate hedging had resulted in the desired effect: a student of human nature, he knew that a precisely timed, provocative suggestion was far more powerful than an outright statement.

A sharp cry brought everyone down a side corridor. Elena was there, her arms outstretched, turning the badly dented helmet over and over.

Adam careened around the corner and stopped short. Elena? *The* Elena from Biozyne? When did *she* wake up? How did *she* know about his helmet? The word must have passed through the ship at light-speed! He pulled his towel closer.

"Wow," she gasped, honest concern in her voice. "This is *really* bad! You're lucky your neck wasn't broken, sir!"

"Y-yes…. *No*! Um, thanks, Elena!" His heart was racing strangely. As she smiled sweetly, he grimaced awkwardly, finding himself gawking deeply into her eyes. They seemed to be unfathomable. He snapped back to reality and turned his battered helmet over, suddenly embarrassed at its condition. "Ah, t-thanks again. Thanks." Smiling a bit too much in the tooth, he backed oafishly into an elevator. As the door slid shut with a muffled thump, his fist shot into the air.

"*Yes*!" he hissed excitedly, hopping in a tight circle. "Yes! Yes!" Suddenly, he saw his multiple reflections in the polished bronze panels all around him.

"*No*!" he gasped, shocked at his appearance. His eyes rolled heavenward. "No! No!" Awkwardly slicking down his wild-looking hair, he muttered angrily. "What a specimen! No wonder she was worried that I almost cracked my knuckehead!" As the elevator neared the starship's control center, he forced himself to calm down and think objectively. "But wait, if this knucklehead had wimped out and stayed inside the ship, everyone would've been dinner!" He gulped. "Including … *her*!"

A sudden flash of inspiration came to him, an answer to his inner turmoil. "An *assembly*? Why not! I'll get everyone together and I'll tell my story! The whole thing, warts and all! They're all dying to know what happened, so why hide anything?" Holding his helmet and towel tightly and pacing in a circle, he pieced a plan together. "Yes, I'll show them how quick thinking and resourcefulness can be a vital link to their own survival!"

The elevator door opened and he slowly walked out into an upper corridor, his hand on his chin. It was a gamble. Would they take it the right way? Maybe. He'd inspire them how to use their brains instead of panicking…. He stopped short, his eyes widening at another sudden flash of inspiration. "Hold on! There's that *other* amazing message, my gift out of the blue!"

The gift was really different, even in the way it was delivered. A few days before his departure, he happened to glance outside his penthouse windows to see a small brown cardboard box lying on the balcony. Initially afraid to touch it and pondering how it could have possibly gotten there, he noticed some sketchy runes penciled along one edge. He bent down and translated them: 'Special Delivery.'

Deliberating a moment, he shrugged and opened it. There was a holo-recording inside with a runic note explaining that it was from some friends of his grandfather. As he brought it inside and watched it with his little holo-viewer, the story drew him in and blew his socks off. He grinned. "Perfect! I'll show that to the crew right after my speech. It'll have much more impact! Now if I remember the Observatory's floor plan correctly, it's connected overhead to the…."

He paused outside his control room, startled. Someone was standing there in full dress uniform! His back was to him, intently studying his wrist programmer. He caught a glimpse of the man's face reflecting in a monitor. "Ah, that's right, my runner…." Straightening his shoulders, he entered, composed and in charge.

"Ensign Rico!" he barked.

Rico turned sharply on his heel and stood at attention.

"Thanks for waiting. How long have you been up here?"

"A bit over an hour, sir. That robot-voice told me where to look in the manual for my first assignment, then I got dressed and came right up…. I mean, after I spent a while studying the ship's layout to even find this room."

"Great initiative, man. Hey, I've got a job for you. Think you're up to it?"

"Ready and raring to go!"

"Okay, I want you to coordinate a general assembly. That means everyone."

The man's eyes widened wordlessly.

"There'll be absolutely *no* exceptions. The rest of the crew should be out of sleep mode by now. I expect them to regain full possession of their faculties, clean up in their quarters, and then meet up in the Observatory Room in full dress uniform!" He held up his wrist programmer. "That's two hours from … *now*!" He tapped the button. "You're dismissed!"

Rico spun nervously on his heel and trotted toward the door. Suddenly remembering his station, he turned with a snappy salute. "*Sir*!" He grinned.

Adam stumbled into his quarters, showered, shaved off a fine layer of peach fuzz, and suited up. His new captain's rig looked sharp. Sitting at his desk, he drafted an outline of the assembly and memorized it, then satisfied, he gathered the items he needed and stuffed them into a shoulder valise. Seven minutes to go. Great timing.

His private elevator rose to the Observatory floor. As he stepped off into a long, curving hallway surrounding the central room, the crew was dashing by in various states of undress. Spotting him, they slowed down to a stately walk, tucking in their shirttails. He entered the cavernous hall, stifling his smile and picking his way through the throng to the far wall. Catching Rico's eye, he waved him over.

"Good job," he whispered. "Everyone accounted for?"

"Yes, sir!" the man said, nodding. "No stragglers."

"Good…. Oh, wait!" He slipped off his shoulder valise. "Here, you're in charge of this. Just, ah, conceal it somewhere over there, maybe behind that panel. Don't look inside. I'll tell you when to unzip it."

Again, Rico's eyes questioned.

"It's alright, man, just wait for my sign. All you have to do is unzip it. Let's just say it's a surprise," he teased. "You'll see soon enough, along with everyone else."

Rico saluted and left, doing his best not to bump the oddly heavy, bulging bag.

Adam punched a numbered sequence on his wrist programmer, then watched a remote mike telescoping out on the end of a boom on the far side of the room. It swiveled, searched, and then locked onto him. A small ping alerted everyone.

"Your attention, please!" As his voice rose over the din, an excited silence fell. The focusing mike worked great, following his every movement. "First, would everyone please step back behind that blue line on the floor?" They looked down and backed away from him in an obedient wave, like the outgoing tide.

"Thanks! Very nicely done," he chuckled. "Second, there's some really comfortable memory-foamish, squishy floor cushions behind those tall panels all around the room. We'll be in here a while, so when you're ready to sit, git 'em!"

As they turned to study the panels, he raised a finger. "Oh, by the way…."

They spun back to him. "I'm sure of this one: what you really, really, *really* want is behind those two wider panels on either side of the bronze entrance doors."

They spun back toward the entrance again.

"Our robo-chefs and bot-baristas have been awake for several hours, and they've masterfully whipped together some hot, gourmet coffee and fluffy, gooey pastry stuff. It's behind those doors; just push on the skinny bars and they'll open!"

The crew stood poised in eager expectation, but a polite, obedient restraint seemed to be holding them back. Did he mean … *now*? Suddenly, someone's stomach growled, echoing in the big room like rolling thunder.

He roared heartily along with the crew. "Oh, go *on*! Get 'em! Be back in twenty minutes!" Their tongues hanging out, they surged as one toward the goodies. He'd nailed it: they were ravenous after their long sleep mode.

"Now, where's that function?" he mumbled, flipped through menus and submenus on his wrist screen. "Ah, there it is! Hope it works…." As he tapped out the sequence, there was a faint mechanical rumbling under his feet. He shuffled backward quickly. The blue line on the floor had outlined the edge of a great, semicircular stage. As it rose in silence, the startled crew drifted back toward him juggling cushions, drinks, and food.

Sahir reached up over the edge of the stage, handing him a cup. "Smells mighty good, sir," she smiled, her dark eyes shining with the mystery of Arabian dunes.

He winked a big thank-you, sipped a moment, and then signaled for silence. When they'd settled, he got right into his story. He told it simply, from the beginning, exactly as it unfolded.

"Here's the facts, guys: our ship crashed halfway to Aurona. I was awakened by emergency resuscitation with a massive dose of adrenaline directly into my heart. The ship wasn't responding, and I looked outside. It was getting buried in a crater."

He'd just barely begun, but his tale was already far beyond the crew's wildest conjecture. their food was forgotten as they elbowed each other in amazement.

"I had to get out at the last possible second before the top airlock went under, then I got knocked out cold," he continued. "Something big whacked me from behind. I didn't remember getting up, wandering several miles, and then passing out."

They were dumfounded. All this had happened while they'd slept?

He continued relentlessly, recounting the twists, turns, surprises, and amazing sights he'd come across. Reaching into his pockets, he yanked out his sketch pad, fragments of fronds and chunks of obelisk shell, offering them as undeniable proof. In a surprise to everyone, he passed them all down into the crowd. As their wondering hands touched, squeezed, and folded the specimens, his quick pencil sketches in the pad gave them an accurate visual.

He was far from over; the incredible tale continued to unravel. Their eyes widened when he told them how he'd thrown his own fears aside to climb the fearsome Obelisk creature, and then jumped eight hundred feet from the top like a skydiver. Their jaws dropped in disbelief when he revealed how he'd constructed a mathematical spiral inside his face shield and then tilted it in perspective to match the terrain. Was that feature really possible with their e-helmets?

When he revealed the ultimate goal of his far-reaching resourcefulness and used the force of the wind itself to dig out their ship, they sat in awe of their young leader's sparkling ingenuity, calculated risk-taking, and raw courage. This was crazy stuff! Their interest quickly budded into respect, then blossomed into admiration.

As he described the final scenes, many were clenching their fists in fear and excitement: megawatts of electricity were jamming the ship's main controls and stopping it from pulling away! He confessed that he was totally frustrated, then suddenly remembered that his e-helmet had navigation controls, too!

Abruptly reversing thrust, he dove toward the massive, towering Obelisk, crashed the ship into its very nostrils, and then shrouded in a cloud of crystals, streaked toward the horizon. In a quiet voice, he summed it up: he'd lost his memory, he was traumatized and exhausted, but his long ordeal was over. They were all free.

They leaped to their feet in a wild, standing ovation. He'd given no apologies, no puffery, just truth. They all felt it now, that elusive bond of unity, gratitude, and trust. Why, they owed their very *lives* to him!

His face beaming, Adam leaned over the edge of the stage to return a forest of eager high fives. As he'd hoped, the 'moment' was here. Perfect. Time for part two. He raised his voice.

"I want all of you to display *similar* initiative!" he shouted over the din. "Use *your* gifts!" The tumult slowly died down and they settled back onto their cushions. "For instance!" As everyone looked up expectantly, he looked out over the sea of faces, searching. "*You*, there!" he pointed.

A set of started eyes blinked.

"Well, stand up!"

A young man rose and stood, his feet slightly apart, his arms folded. He had the appearance of a coiled spring, superb in musculature and keenly alive.

"Come up here!" As he gestured to a spot next to him, he touched a virtual button on his wrist programmer's screen. A set of panels along the edge of the stage slid away smoothly to reveal a hidden set of stairs. The man lithely picked his way through the crowd and bounded toward him.

He continued. "Now, way back! And I'm talking way, *way* back, before we embarked on this epic journey seven hundred years ago. Remember your interviews? I know that most of you had doubts about yourselves on that day. Of course you did. How and why *you* were chosen, what hidden qualities did *you* have beyond thousands of others that helped me select you as one of my crew?"

Tentative, reflective smiles of agreement lit up. He was right.

He paused, raising a loosely packed sheaf of paper high over his head. "This mess represents someone's résumé! True, it did play a minor role in my decision, but...." He released it in a blizzard and let it flutter to the floor. "It wasn't so much what you accomplished or who you were...." Looks of incredulity greeted him: Where was he going with this train of thought? "It is, and always will be...," intrigued, they leaned forward as one, "who you *are*!" he concluded.

There. They were in the palm of his hand. "This guy," he pointed, "came to my attention as he was leaving his first interview with me! *Leaving*, mind you! He was actually walking out of the room! He simply stopped to pick up...," he stooped to the floor and retrieved one of the fallen sheaves, "a piece of paper!" He wadded it into a ball and tossed it into a nearby basket. "Big deal, you say? No, not to me: twenty-six others before him just walked over it!"

The young man stood riveted, his face flushed in embarrassment. "Kron!" As he stopped short in front of him, the man looked up in surprise. "Yes, *of course* I know your name," he chuckled, then turned aside to the crew. "Don't hold me to it, guys, but I think I know *all* your names. As your captain and leader, I need to to count on each of you for your unique abilities."

He bent toward them, lowering his voice and speaking confidentially. "Hey, listen guys. Although this journey is still a mission of mystery, I promise I'll do my best to make it an unprecedented time of fun and true exploration."

As they began to stir excitedly, he held up his hands in admonition. "Remember, I'm not complete. We need each other to survive, right? Your job is to be my hands, eyes and ears, and yes, in many circumstances, extensions of my brain!"

He laughed along with them and then concluded, his voice steady and sure. "I have something to show you now, something marvelous. We're all on the same great quest! We all want to know what's out... *there*!" He turned to the curving wall behind him and pressed a thin bar at the center. Simultaneously, the stage dropped and the panels slid back to reveal a huge, curving panorama.

Gasps of awe escaped. A magnificent spiral galaxy filled the view, dead ahead! Stars, trillions of them, washed across a great black velvet canvas of nothingness, amazingly compact star systems within systems swirled inside stupendous bands of light in a mind-boggling aggregation. All clustered toward a glowing orb of light at the center. Out on the fringes, thousands of other pinwheels glowed softly, with spectacular nebulae and impossibly dense globular clusters studding an endless, galaxy-filled cosmos.

A deep silence fell as they valiantly tried to comprehend the vastness and scale, overwhelmed by the crystal clarity of the immense forty-foot screen. Several long, breathless minutes passed before a mellow, hushed voice rose near the front of the room. It was mature, and familiar with the Knowledge of the Ages.

"*'In my Father's house,'*" Tola spoke quietly, "*'there are many mansions. If it were not so, I would have told you.'*" He rose to his feet and turned to face the crew. "As a preacher, I feel compelled to share these timeless words with you. Even as a kid back in Oklahoma, that scripture popped into my mind every time I drank in the stars on a clear night. Just *look* at those countless mansions! Have you ever *seen* such perfect specimens of creation?"

Quiet murmurs of agreement riffled through the crowd.

The round man glanced at Adam. "And now, sir, I'm just, plain curious, and I believe I'm speaking for everyone here.... Um, where in blazes are we *going*?"

Adam walked across the view, his lanky young form darkly silhouetted against the blazing star field. "Right about *there*," he pointed. "That big globular cluster. As to where we are at this very moment, it's anybody's guess," he shrugged. "Our starship is slowing and turning toward that point; everything's been preprogrammed into the internal guidance computers. This section of the universe is far beyond the range of our most powerful and sophisticated space scopes."

Tola smiled mischievously. "Ah, we're nearly 'there,' despite...."

Adam beat him to the punch. "Despite our short sabbatical on the Obelisk Planet, you mean?"

A wave of nervous laughter swept the room.

"Sorry, Tola. Didn't mean to be rude. I meant that despite our unexpected crash landing and subsequent three-day delay, the ship's computers and gravity wave sensors quickly found a nearby wormhole, an 'open line' so to speak." He turned to the crew. "Believe it or not, guys, we're more than a month *ahead* of schedule!"

On the far side of the room, Dexor's eyes flew open. He elbowed his companions, whispering nervously. "Oh, no! D'ya hear that, pinheads? A whole month ahead of schedule?" He let out an oath. "Damn! I hope that doesn't mess with our pod! A month is a lotta time!"

As murmurs of surprise riffled through the crowd, Adam turned to the big screen, busily punching out another code on his wrist programmer. "Let's get right down to business." He watched the screen light up. "This ... is our *journey*!"

Overlaying the enormous window to the stars, bold, graphic highlights suddenly flickered to life: curving arrows and pulsing, dotted lines pointed the way inward to an obscure globular cluster, a little to the right of center, where a tiny blip began to pulse steadily.

Adam pointed at it, shrugging. "Aurona," he stated simply. Wonder was in his voice, too. "That shiny ball represents her solar system, still quite a distance away even at our present rate of deceleration. Absolutely nothing is known about the planet, except that it was of great importance to my grandfather. He called it his 'utopia.'" He looked up. "And speaking of my grandfather," he added softly, "he's been to Aurona and back, although he, um ... he died during his return to Earth. He had a little speed job that he called a TimeWarper. I'm sure that if we'd all been able to fit into it, we'd have been there already." He held up his hands. "Don't ask me how that's even possible. Who knows, he may have hit direct wormholes both ways. I still can't figure it all out...."

He collected his thoughts. "So. Seeing that there's still a whole month to go, we'll spend our time wisely. We've been in sleep mode so long we'll have to get used to our muscles again. Build them up! And we can't forget our *minds*, either!

As they nodded in studied agreement, he tantalized them with a little bait.

"How can we *do* this, you ask?"

They shrugged. Was he implying there was more?

"Aha!" He grinned. "We'll work out downstairs in our big, SuperGrav gym and Olympic-sized pool, then enrich our minds in the Dream Library!"

Startled, they stared excitedly at each other and broke into a buzz of anticipation. A Dream Library? A gym? *A pool*? This ship was getting interesting!

"A little over and hour from now, we'll start briefing sessions to familiarize ourselves with a lot of radical exploration equipment! We're a large group here; exactly three hundred and fifty-*one* noble characters!"

Todd jumped up with a shout, bobbing up and down like a buoyant cork in a pool. His chubby arms waved in the air, his beaming face sending out a spontaneous, concentric circle of laughter.

"Okay! I'm almost ready for part two!" Adam held up a finger, chuckling. "Just like I assigned Todd to be Jon's shadow, I'll need to have *my* shadow!" He spun around, pointing. "Kron!"

Stunned, the muscular man shifted his feet and stepped hesitantly out of the shadows. All eyes turned to him, scrutinizing.

"In Kron's remaining three interviews, I found out all I needed to know about him. This man has real character, guys! Guts! Unknown to all of you, and surprisingly even to him, I have a holo-recording of quite a memorable day in his life."

Kron glanced at him in surprise, his face quickly turning beet red.

"Believe me, in a few moments it'll be delivered to you in a spectacular fashion! I have a holo-recording that was, ah, *mailed* to me by some close friends of my grandfather's, some of the prime benefactors of this journey. They urged me to present this slice of time to you sometime before we reached our goal. While I've seen it with a mini-viewer, you'll be experiencing it in a whole, different way. It's amazing!"

They squirmed excitedly on their cushions, elbowing each other.

"As your leader," he continued, "I want to share this vision and hope with you. I'm sure we'll all benefit greatly from this unforgettable, graphic example." He nodded to someone waiting eagerly in the front row.

"Okay, Rico. It's time."

As the crew whispered questioningly to each other, the young ensign pulled out Adam's valise. There was the faint, unmistakable sound of zipping.

Motioning for Kron to wait, Adam walked up to the front of the room busily punching codes on his wrist programmer. Turning toward Rico, he held one hand high in the air, his palm outstretched. "Remember!" He shrugged. "*Anything's* possible!"

A large black sphere rose out of the valise and flew toward him. As the crew watched in astonishment, it hovered rock-steady over his head, and then lowered slowly into his hand. Holding the gleaming orb at eye level, he traced out a few codes on the glassy surface. Mysterious, hidden lights flashed a response.

Chapter 8: THE HOLOSPHERE

A colorful graphic quickly flooded the enormous screen behind Adam. Not quite comprehending what they were seeing, the crew stared at the display in total confusion. He went quickly through the steps, animatedly waving his arms and giving them a short summary of what was about to happen. Holding up a finger, he turned and made his way back into their midst. The crew gawked at the graphic. No way, this was totally impossible; he'd just dreamed this all up! Smiling enigmatically, he held the sphere high over his head and punched in another command.

In rapid sequence, the galaxy wall slid shut, the lights dimmed, and there was a faint sliding noise somewhere overhead. Startled, the crew looked up. The ceiling was moving! Their jaws dropped: it was true! The graphic had just shown them! What had been masquerading as a series of decorative spiral overlays now revealed themselves to be part of a great lenslike eye. It dilated open from the center and the panels quickly vanished into a thin slit along the circular wall.

There was a faint vibration under their cushions. No, it just couldn't be happening! They glanced nervously at each other and then down at the floor. With a mechanical whirr, the huge, circular disc they were sitting on parted along a blue line about two feet from the wall. With startled exclamations, they scuttled toward the center on their cushions. The entire *room* was transforming!

As the floor rose slowly on a great central piston, they peered over their heads, craning their necks and trying to focus on something, anything. It appeared to be just a huge, empty, black hole up there. Soon a soft glow fanned out from the edges of the disc. They could now see each other, but still couldn't focus on a single thing beyond the perimeter. Murmurs of unease grew, especially near the edges. Was there really a force field to keep them from falling? One by one they turned their eyes to Adam for answers.

"No, your world isn't flat," he chuckled mischievously. "There *is* something out there beyond that wild, blue horizon.... Oh, sorry, I meant that blue line."

The floor stopped smoothly and they waited in expectant silence.

"You are now in a visual void," he began, stretching out his palms, "created specifically for the viewing of holo-recordings. Essentially, you're inside a big empty sphere at the top of the starship." He paused and looked down, studying the floor near his feet. Quickly finding what he was looking for, he tapped out another sequence on the ball and stepped backward. A slim, black metal rod rose in front of him, stopping at shoulder height. Lifting the sphere above his head for everyone to see, he explained further.

"This round object I'm holding is what we're going to call a holocamera, for lack of a better term. In a moment, this skinny rod will raise it up to the precise height that it originally filmed the action you're about to see. Now, ready for this one? Here's a mind-bending twist: the upcoming scenes are now actually seven hundred and four Earth-years old. In other words, this 3D cyber-slice of time happened four years before I received this holo-recording.... Get it?"

He glanced discreetly at Kron. The man's eyes suddenly widened, his hand flying up over his mouth. He chuckled. Just as he thought, he didn't have a clue. He glanced back at the crew. There was a lot of whispering going on; they were clueless, too, doing their best to piece everything together. He smiled encouragingly and continued.

"Okay, down to business. The ensuing action was originally shot, um, I mean 'imaged' from a *very* unique perspective. In this case, you'll actually see the location of the camera, although it was masterfully disguised. You're about to experience the ultimate in VR, far surpassing our feeble, earthly stabs at this incredibly complicated technology. You'll actually believe you're 'there,' so get ready, because some pretty intense action will pass over, around, and yes, even through you!"

He paused, sensing their uneasiness. "And don't worry, guys, that glow you saw *is* a force field around the edge of the platform. It's an invisible barrier, almost like a safety net about two feet wide. Don't worry about falling!"

They smiled, but still edged nervously away from the drop-off: there were no shadows or movement out there; the ambiguous light was revealing absolutely nothing. Their slim disc of a platform appeared to be floating, suspended in space.

He snapped them all back to reality. "Remember to watch this black holocamera! The minute the action begins, the sphere will transform into a very familiar object! Kron here will supply the narrative."

Kron's jaw dropped. "*Huh? Me?*"

Adam laughed along with the crew. "Yes, you! And believe me, Kron, you'll know *exactly* what to say as soon as the scene opens. This event, I'm sure, is burning in your memory as it will be in ours!"

He motioned outward with his palms, urging the crew to form an opening in the center. Nervously, they complied and slid backward on their cushions. Glancing apprehensively over their shoulders, they refused to go any further and lined up a few feet from the edge. As Adam twisted the tip of the black rod, it snapped open and flared out into a trumpet shape. The sphere neatly fit into the resulting cup on top. In moments, it rose high above their heads. "Remember one word, everyone!" he called. "Initiative!"

Slowly the ball started to spin, gathering speed. Emanating from the surface in glowing ribbons, strange, wispy lights began to drift outward in undulating auroras. The surface of the sphere transformed quickly, shading from a jet, obsidian black to a tarnished-looking, metallic gold. They stared at it, thinking, then their eyes lit up. Could that be the ball on top of…. They grinned. Yes, it was! They were looking up at the ball-shaped finial on top of a flagpole! What a disguise!

More images were starting to appear in the distance, but they were blurry, as if seen through a heavy fog. As they resolved into focus, a tinny sound, at once familiar, rattled and clanged nearby. They cocked their ears, listening. What, could that be a trash can? Surely not. But … If so, who, or what, was making the noise?

Suddenly, incredibly, they were there, totally immersed in incredibly sharp virtual reality! Their jaws dropped as they looked around. A phantom breeze sprung up, riffling their hair and clanking a pair of empty pulleys against the flagpole's chipped surface.

There was a sudden, loud yowl off to the side. Startled, they turned to see a small brown streak hurtling toward them! With a shout, a few scooted aside to let it through. An alley cat! The lid from a trashcan rolled out after it, tipped into a spiral landing pattern, and settled onto the middle of the floor with a clatter, flutter and flourish. As the horrific din died away, they became acutely aware of their location.

They were outside, it was late afternoon, and they were sitting in a large circle in the middle of a park! They craned their necks, spinning around on their cushions, seeing but not believing. Where *was* this, somewhere in the slums? As far as a human arm could reach, graffiti covered every square inch of every vertical surface. Once-proud buildings surrounded them, but the structures were now dilapidated, neglected, scarred and kicked into shame. Nearby, the entire roof was gone from one building: it gaped open to the sky, blackened from a recent fire.

In the shocked silence, there was another movement in their midst, this time a real one. Kron rose slowly to his feet and cleared his throat. He gestured at the mess, looking apologetic.

"My home," he shrugged.

They were stunned. How could such a sharp-looking specimen be the spawn of such decay?

The man lowered his head, his face reddening. "This is really hard, guys," he murmured. "It was a really tough time in my life." He paused, thought a moment, then took a resolute breath and turned to Adam. "Sorry about not mentioning this during my interview, sir. I-I thought you might chalk me off as a crackpot, or a lunatic. When I found out what you were up to, I really, really wanted to come along on this mission."

Adam smiled. "It's all right, man; you made it. Now go on...."

Kron turned back to the crew. "Something amazing happened to me on this day, guys, and it changed my life forever! First, I hafta' clue you in on some details before things start happening: I was, ah … different. I was a punk. I was washed out and being flushed into the sewer along with the rest of my gang. We lived on the streets. You know, literally, the *streets*? We got our bread from pickin' pockets, rollin' drunks, breakin' into condos or whatever else we could do to survive. Some of us had seen more bars than a gorilla at the zoo!" He was clearly doing his best to make light of his embarrassing situation, and the crew began to chuckle along with him. They understood.

There was a loud rustle of crinkly paper down one of the alleys. In unison, everybody turned their heads to see an old bag lady wander out, finishing off whatever was staining the dirty food wrapper in her hand. Suddenly she paused, wrinkling her nose. Evidently, something had displeased her palate. Taking a deep breath, she spit out a big wad of goo and sent it flying through the air.

With a loud cry a man jumped up, turning green and madly slapping at his chin and neck. He stopped short, suddenly remembering the goo was actually a *virtual* moldy, wet crust of bread. Changing from a sickly green to an embarrassed red, he joined along with the crew's hooting and laughter.

"That's Fanny!" Kron shouted over the din. "Our resident bag lady! This was her prime pickin' territory!" He felt more at ease now and started loosening up, offering a simple, yet eloquent running commentary. "Ya know," he said, shaking his head, "now that I'm seein' all this again, it's funny but sad at the same time? This dump was actually where I *lived*! I-I had to belong, to have friends like anyone else, so I changed what I *looked* like, ya' know? I had to look 'bad' in this turf or I'd get ripped to shreds! I had to beef out and learn how to fight, be strong in order to *survive*!" He turned, pointing at the bag lady. "On the other hand, some people just accepted what life doled out to them."

Fanny wandered about, doddering aimlessly, poking and searching. She was soon forgotten as they heard a loud rustling and thumping near the center of the room. What could *that* be? It was far too loud to be an animal. They turned toward the source. Something was moving at the foot of the flagpole. They watched and waited in expectant silence.

Debris rolling off his back, a weird-looking old man staggered to his feet from under a pile of trash! His face was deeply creased and dirty; his wet clothes were in deplorable condition.

Kron pointed excitedly. "There he *is*! That's him! So *that's* where he was hiding!" As he edged slowly toward him, the man lurched drunkenly and fell. Picking himself up, he stood there rocking on his heels. Tentatively, Kron stepped a bit closer and started to poke at the man's clothes. "This is unbelievable, guys," he muttered, "this VR image looks as solid as a rock!" He bent closer to peer deeply into the man's face, eyeball to eyeball, as if he were searching for something inside, then with a sudden thrust, pushed his arm through the man's chest! The crew gasped in shock. To them, the two figures looked equally real!

The phantom sun was dipping lower in the sky, as real as "now" could possibly be. The slice of time was fleeting, too, and Kron spun around as he suddenly remembered the important sequence of events to follow. He looked apprehensive. "Sorry, guys, I-I got carried away, ya know?" he paused, listening. "Yeah, there it is! That sound's the cops chasing us!"

The crew strained to hear. Sure enough, there was the faint wail of a siren in the distance... the police! Kron wasn't kidding! As they focused in the direction of his pointing finger, they heard the faint sound of frantic, running feet and labored breathing echoing in one of the narrow alleys. It grew louder.

Suddenly, five young punks streaked out in single file! In a quick reflexive reaction, the crew opened up a path for them, scuttling back on their cushions as the group careened out into the center of the circle. Gasping for breath, the punks bent over with their hands on their knees, their sides heaving. The crew stared in astonishment at their crazy getup. Their leader was the worst of the lot, absolutely bristling with menacing, spiked collars on his neck, wrists, and ankles. His spiked hair matched the metal, pulled into sharp peaks and sticking out in all directions like a pincushion. To complete the intentionally discordant ensemble, a skimpy vest showed off his truly massive chest and biceps, and a pair of wild geometric pants were printed in bold black-and-white zigzags and explosions.

Kron looked calmly back and forth, first at the punk and then at the crew. With a shrug of his shoulders, he explained everything in a single word.

"Me."

Their mouths flew open when they saw the resemblance. Yes, it *was* him! A few sprang to their feet to look a little closer, but Adam quickly waved them down. "Hold on, guys! I believe this is the point where everything starts to happen pretty fast. Right, Kron? Let's pull away from the action!" He scooted backward, sliding on his cushion. Picking up on his cue, others quickly followed suit. Just as he'd predicted, one of the punks let out a loud expletive and yelled at the top of his lungs.

"Hey! A boozer!" he pointed. He'd spotted the cowering drunk and started to swagger toward him. A brightly painted Day-Glo design covered his taut ebony skin, so bright it seemed to be yelling in contrast. War paint? With a bounce in his step, he started to stalk his prey. Approaching by a circuitous route, he feinted back and forth, taunting, intimidating and frightening the old man.

The drunk began to blubber. "Hey! I-I ain' got no money!"

"I'm gonna clip you up, scum," the Day-Glo punk snarled.

"Leav' me 'lone! I was jisht pashin' thru!" he wailed.

The mood grew ugly. The other punks strolled out arrogantly and formed a tight circle, surrounding him. Suddenly, the old man panicked. Lurching toward an opening, his arms flailed wildly. Debris flew. Muffled grunts and pitiful, drunken wails set everyone's nerves on edge. One of the gang quickly had him pinned, a set of strong young hands mercilessly throttling him.

"Hey, wino! Time you learn sompin," one of the punks hissed, out of breath.

"Yeah! We ax you a question, big man!" a greasy-haired punk with a bad case of acne sneered, lifting a pipe over his head. "Where yo' money?"

Gasping for breath, the drunk suddenly wrestled an arm free and smashed him in the pimply jaw. The youth's head snapped back, sweat and hair flying. He started to scream, bleeding from his mouth.

"*Waste* him! Scum!"

The pipe came crashing down hard. The drunk groaned, thrashing weakly. All reason seemed to fly as the group closed in like jackals, intent on their quarry and anticipating the kill.

The spiked Kron slowly pulled away, shaking his head.

A knife flashed! The crew had become totally involved now: incensed and horrified, they forgot themselves completely and started yelling.

"*Watch out! Stop him!*" a woman screamed.

The situation spiraled completely out of control. The long blade rose in the air and paused, seconds ticking away. A voice rasped out viciously.

"Say goodbye, boozer!" It plunged downward in a blur.

Suddenly, unbelievably, a hand shot out. The sharp blade sliced cleanly through a muscular palm and out the other side, stopping just as it touched the old man's skin. Everyone stared in shock, wide-eyed.

Kron's face was a frozen mask. "*Enough!*" he spoke quietly, powerfully. He'd taken on a strange new look, his body tense and consumed by a seething, inner rage. Slowly, deliberately, he withdrew the knife from his hand and wiped it on his pants, letting it drop with a clatter to his feet. As the punk rose unsteadily, Kron glared into his pale, cowering face. Wordlessly, he grabbed the punk's dirty, torn shirtsleeve and yanked down hard, ripping it off. Eye to eye, turn after turn, he wrapped it slowly around his bloodied hand. As the old one stirred near his feet and began to retch in dry heaves, he glanced down for a fleeting moment.

At the same moment, eight furtive eyes motioned to each other. Once more, the pipe rose slowly in the air, this time behind their leader's back. They took a half step toward him, preparing to pin him down.

Kron's head snapped up, his eyes blazing. On the attack now, he spun around, his foot striking out with tremendous force to bury itself deeply in the greasy youth's soft belly. The pipe clattered to the ground and the punk doubled over, out of commission. Enraged, the rest converged on Kron, three on one. Whirling, lashing out powerfully, he became a blurred fighting machine, his supple body flying through the air in a dazzling display of acrobatic skill. Badly outclassed, the punks retreated into a tight knot, whimpering to each other. This time, it was Kron's turn to be enraged.

"That's *it*! This is the *end!*" he roared. "I'm *leaving* this crud!"

Suddenly, a new voice rumbled in a deep, rolling bass. "He's so right!"

Everyone's eyes widened. They looked around, searching. Who could *that* be? The punks looked equally puzzled. Shortly, the strange voice boomed again.

"I was waiting for SOME sign of intelligence here!"

As the old man slowly unbuttoned his coat and studied his four assailants, the crew stared at each other in astonishment. It was the drunk!

One of the gang spoke up, his fragile ego challenged. "Hey, wise man, stop blabbin' yo mouth!" he sputtered, bleeding profusely from his nose.

Silence fell. Every eye was riveted on the old man. He stopped mid-button, then slowly raised his fist and pointed an ominous, gnarled finger at the punk. Partially concealed in his palm was a small, smooth object.

Kron was beside himself now: literally. As he stood next to his spiked phantom version, he let out a loud, excited stage whisper. "Watch this!"

The punk was babbling weakly. "You don' scare me, you...."

A tiny, glowing ball streaked through the air and smacked him on the chest. His eyes rolled back in his head and his voice trailed off, ending in a wheeze!

"What the...?" As the Day-Glo punk tensed to run, the other two caught his panic and began to claw over each other in terror, scrambling toward an alley.

Once more the gnarled hand waved the smooth object in an arc. Three more balls of fire hissed through the air! Their bodies stopped mid-stride, their mouths open in a yell, but no sound coming out. As their eyes rolled back inside their paralyzed bodies, their feet dangled loosely off the ground, suspended in midair.

Darkness had crept into the park and a few lights flickered on in nearby windows. Silhouettes of curious heads appeared behind dirty, torn curtains, and small groups gawked from the narrow, rat-infested alleys. The crew had begun to cluster into small, tightly knotted groups for security.

Warily, everyone studied the old man as he stepped out of his dirty clothes. He began to grimace, his face taking on a strange, rubbery look. Smoothing out, his features transformed. What they saw in the twilight transfixed them all.

A tall, sleek-skinned alien with luminous eyes was now standing next to the ring of floating punks! His rotten clothes, wet with booze, were piled at his feet and a form-fitting, electric blue uniform was now stretched over his lanky figure.

A *disguise*! Some kind of plasmorphic alien had evidently been lying in wait! But for what? As a buzz of speculation rose, Kron raised his voice to explain.

"Believe me, guys, I had no idea my encounter was being recorded. Honestly, I didn't even know a holocamera *existed*!" Excitedly, he pointed at the alien. That's Jeban! He turned out to be my best friend ever, one of the Bitrons I ended up living with for nearly a year. They're a technologically advanced race and he's one of their special agents."

Everyone began to study Kron in a new light. Why, he'd never given a hint of his past and had blended seamlessly into their midst, just 'one of the guys'! Their eyes questioning, they glanced back at Adam. He acknowledged them with a shrug and a wink, and then quickly redirected their focus back to the action.

As the plasmorphic Bitron swiveled to face the outrageously dressed, spiked Kron, he stepped back warily, his hands raised in defense. "Yes, we know you, Kron," he began in his deep, rolling bass, "and have seen that your life, up to now, has been a tragedy. But your great act of heroism in sparing the life of this useless drunkard has greatly impressed my people.

You've held on to principles that most, including your friends here, have lost!" He smiled, and then turned to speak directly to the curious throngs gathering in the alleys. Fanny was there, too, shaking in the shadows.

"After visiting many places for many years, we have singled out this gash, this scar of a city to rescue the few remaining humans with a purpose. We're seekers. We're reclaimers of responsible, reliable humans." He gestured in a circle with a broad, sweeping motion, his deep voice permeating. "Look around you!"

Unexpectedly, a gray blur scurried into the open followed closely by a brown streak. With a scuffle and squeal, a rat breathed its last.

Shaking his head with a sigh, the Bitron continued. "We have been monitoring this incredible, blue-green planet for centuries. They say there are marble columns lying unseen beneath your Atlantic waters. Great cities are cloaked under the last of your once-vast rainforests. Your primitive satellites have picked out the remains of great civilizations, forever lost under the dunes of your Sahara Desert. Look around you! Look, and see *today's* neglect and discord face to face!"

No one had to look. Ruin was everywhere.

"These were once proud homes, built by dreamers. This was a delightful park, an oasis of green with fountains and magnolia trees. Can you believe it? They're gone now. This ruin started from the *inside*. Like fruit rotting from the core, it spread outward as the dreamers died or left, one by one. Their only hope, their children, once played where you now stand. When the time was right and decay had reached its peak, the wolves came, lurking in the alleys. The wolves? You all know of the wolves! They're the beasts who destroy the mind for profit. Yes, and once the mind is lost, the soul is lost. Once the soul is lost, the life is lost."

His strong voice faltered, falling to almost a whisper. "This-this we cannot understand. How can your lives, your future, go on with no one to build? How can you prosper with no one to dream? We see your civilization to be now in reversal, turning backward as if it were a black hole consuming itself in the great scheme of creation! For decades, we've followed this irreversible, growing trend with great dismay and have finally decided to step in and take action. So today, in front of your eyes, we've thrown ourselves into the midst of this pack of wolves, seeking survivors."

His hand rested on Kron's shoulder. "Survivors. You, Kron, are a true survivor! From our starship cloaked in orbit, we've watched you for many years. You never knew your father, and for that matter, neither did your mother. As a child, she was enticed by those wolves. The mind-killer was introduced into her body, coursing through her veins, destroying all the delicate and wonderful machinery. We saw it all happening, Kron. She died when you were four, correct?"

A faint gasp swept through both assemblies, human and phantom.

He continued resolutely. "You lived off and on with different families for a while, didn't you? But at fourteen, you were back out on the streets fighting for your life, a mere child fighting off the wolves against overwhelming odds."

Kron was trembling now, along with many of the crew. The truth stabbed deeply. They'd all been living the pain of his hard life for a mere twenty minutes, but it seemed like an eternity.

The wise man continued, lifting his voice with a new hope. "But you've overcome! Yes, you've won!"

The spiked Kron muttered, wavering. "I-I've won? What…?" A steady rivulet of blood had been oozing from the dirty cloth and gathering in a pool at his feet.

"Yes, you've *got* it! You've got what we seek! We're here now to claim this elusive prize, then to refine and polish it!"

"Prize?" Kron whispered weakly, grasping for comprehension.

The Bitron sighed. "It's simple, Kron. This prize is your integrity. It's a rare commodity anymore, a jewel, and you've got it. The privilege of claiming it has become our group's obsession and destiny. We seek the last of the dreamers."

Kron was visibly slumping. "I used to dream…," he whispered.

The Bitron bent low to reassure him, speaking in soothing tones. "Yes, we know, my boy. But you're to come with us now. We'll help you rekindle that spark! Your struggle on this hard world is over and you've got nobody left to hold you here!" Turning to look upward, he raised his arms.

A low pulse became quite evident in the still air, growing into a powerful beat. As great banks of clouds roiled over their heads, the pulse pushed physically against everyone's body, a deep rumble shaking the floor beneath their feet. The holosphere was duplicating this unforgettable slice of time with breathtaking realism!

Trembling, soaked in blood, the spiked Kron slumped to his knees the dirt, his pale face signaling approaching shock. The Bitron quickly knelt next to him to peel the dripping, dirty sleeve from his clenched fist. Drawing a flexible rod from a slit in his utility belt and deftly bending it into a ring, he passed it over the wound. After he'd daubed a clear fluid on both sides, he pricked the back of Kron's neck with a double-pronged instrument. Immediately, color rushed back to his face. He became intense, excited, sputtering out questions. "W-what? How did they… how did you…?"

"These are the products of dreams, Kron!" the Bitron interrupted, chuckling. "Your people *have* none of these wonderful things because they've killed off most of their dreamers!" He paused to glance distastefully at Kron's wild appearance. "It's almost time to go," he sighed, "but first…." He pulled a sleek, multiforked instrument from his utility belt and ran it through his spiked hair. In a flash and puff of smoke, the layers of goo dissolved, evaporating in a sizzle. Kron's real hair, a thick, golden mane, bounced into place! Pulling out a small, tightly folded package, he opened it by simply turning it inside out. An incredibly thin, electric-blue, one-piece uniform unfolded. Smiling, he shook out the origami masterpiece and held it up to Kron for size. "Perfect! If you're going to *be* one of us, you've got to *look* like one of us, right?"

Suddenly, out of nowhere, a blast of neon light blew Kron's clothes away in shreds! The cuffed spikes, the vest, the chains, the pants, everything!

He stood there in shock, covering his naked form with the skimpy blue uniform, the only thing available. The Bitron roared with laughter, pointing upward. "Hey, I'm so sorry, Kron! My *friends* did this, not me! That's their way of saying, 'Hurry up!'" He held up a finger. "Wait a minute...."

He quickly shook out a folded origami blanket, shielding him from the gawking eyes in the alleys. In a colorful spectacle, a red-faced Kron scrambled into the electric blue uniform, his tousled blonde hair bouncing up and down. Chuckling, the Bitron dropped the blanket and held out an arm. "Here! Don't forget your utility belt!" He burst into laughter again, the rippling, musical sound bouncing off phantom buildings in fantastically real echoes.

In moments, a transformed Kron stood there, casual, handsome, and hopeful. The spark in his eyes had begun to glimmer once more. Standing arm in arm and laughing, they slowly dematerialized in a purple light as the four totally confused punks dropped to the dirt with muffled thuds.

The scene began to shift. Fading, wavering, the park, buildings, lights, and people lifted, transforming back into glittering, nebulous ribbons. Flowing toward the center, they streamed into the top of the flagpole. The sphere changed from tarnished gold to black, the lights came on and the illusion was gone. They were back.

A tumultuous cheer broke out. The unforgettable holo-recording had visually delivered a difficult, gut-level message, extremely personal and very hard to put into words: a message of renewed hope, a spark that had rekindled and burst into flame. They were *all* dreamers now! Adam bounded into the center, ecstatic. An arm draped over Kron's shoulder, he motioned for silence. The crew beamed, confident in his choice of leadership and accepting him wholeheartedly.

"I, for one, am sure that this man would lay down his *life* for me! Remember, guys, just like me, *he* was in an impossible situation! Just like me, he saw the only way out and *did* something about it! He *acted*! As the saying goes, 'It's a wise man who keeps himself under control.'"

Adam's carefully planned presentation had worked: his powerful, double-barreled message hit its target dead center. First, they'd learned about their narrow escape from the Obelisk Planet, and then they'd seen Kron's courageous escape from personal ruin. Neither man had panicked under stress. They'd both kept their cool and displayed a level of maturity and responsibility far beyond their years.

He held up his hands. "In conclusion, let me remind you of one thing: the Truth never changes. It's us knuckleheads who need to change to conform to the Truth. All Kron needed to change his whole life's situation was a sense of urgency, the right motivation, and a bit of help to steer him in the right direction. He's fortunate, guys! A note attached to my recording said that all four of his pals died a few years later from the same cause. The wolves devoured them!"

He turned to Kron and held something up, something that glittered brightly. "This small token visually represents what we already feel is right in our gut." Without further ado, he pinned it on his chest. "There. You are who this pin says you are. The symbol is pure gold, hammered out by someone in an unknown civilization."

Kron glanced down, surprised. "What does it say, sir?"

"It's a Runic word," he answered. "It means 'Leader.'"

As one, the crew stood to honor them both with a prolonged, heartfelt, standing ovation.

Chapter 9: INCIDENT IN QUARANTINE

Adam used his wrist programmer to retract the long black stalk, then lifted off the holocamera. As he tapped out a numbered sequence on the sensitive surface, the crew felt an immediate, physical response: the massive floor began its descent.

"I have an assignment," he announced. "I need a few strong, beefy, volunteers to go downstairs and get something for us."

Immediately, there was a buzz of anticipation.

"When this big disc reaches the bottom, they can hop on a freight elevator down the hall and zip down to a warehouse on Level E. According to the ship's inventory, they should find four large crates stenciled with the word 'Bitron.' Load 'em onto some antigrav barges and shoot 'em back up here." As the excited buzz grew louder, a few hands rose in the air. He turned slowly on his heel, contemplating.

A short distance from the crowd, four men quickly slid their cushions together. Whispering in hushed, nervous tones, they bent their heads low, keeping a wary eye on the crew and Adam's back.

"Hey! Level E? That's right above our pod on Level F!"

A beefy one interrupted. "Yeah, an' what if he's awake?"

The other two broke in, talking over each other in haste. "Worse still, what if he's walkin' around down there? That's bad news. Real bad news!"

The first one scowled. "I think it's about time you knuckleheads check in on him, huh? Just go down one more floor, take a look, and then go get the crates!"

They pulled back, alarmed. "But boss, boss, we dunno…."

The first one interrupted, glowered darkly. "This is important!! Quick! Raise your hands, dummies! Look eager! It's a perfect opportunity! You'll be alone!"

"Ah, okay, boss!" they whispered. Glancing nervously at each other, they scrambled to their feet.

Adam noticed the men immediately and let out a laugh. They were almost comical in their enthusiasm, jumping up and down and jabbing their hands into the air. He gave them a thumb's-up. "Okay, okay, guys! You three just got the job!"

They plopped back down on their cushions, giving each other high fives.

"Wow, that's what I like to see," Adam chortled. "Excitement! Enthusiasm!" He held up his hands for quiet. "Okay, guys, we've got short time to talk before the floor stops and our three friends over there bring those crates up. There's a huge collection of Bitron goodies to rummage through and it's gonna take a while take to explain them! For instance…." He raised the black sphere above his head. "Let's talk about *this* gem! You already know that this holocamera is a prime example of Bitron manufacturing! What you didn't know is that the ship's log says that we've got *four hundred* of 'em downstairs in the hold. That means there's one apiece with a bunch of backups. Here! Take a look at it!" Unexpectedly, he tossed the ball out into the middle of the crowd.

A woman jumped up and snatched it deftly from the air, landing lightly on her feet. Holding it at eye level, she squinted deeply into it. "How's it work, sir?"

Kron elbowed Adam appreciatively in the ribs. She was an extremely pretty blonde with long, flowing hair. "Wow!" he whispered. "That woman sure can catch!"

Winking at Kron, Adam turned back to the woman. "Joelle, is it?"

"Yes, sir!" She brightened, surprised that he remembered her name.

"Oh, I-I'm sorry, I meant *Doctor* Joelle. You got your MD from Harvard, top honors, summa cum laude, valedictorian, and then on to Emory for postgrad, right?"

She reddened as the crew studied her with sudden surprise and admiration.

"Ah, how does it actually work?" he repeated. "Well, first of all…."

A strobing flash interrupted him. Joelle almost dropped the sphere, astonishment written plainly on her face. It was inevitable: with all her poking, she'd accidentally triggered the holo-camera's menu function and the choices were scrolling by at a rapid clip. "Wow!" she gushed. "It can do all *this*?"

Adam walked over to her and retrieved the sphere. "That's right," he said, smiling. "All this and tons more. We're gonna make very good use of these amazing instruments. Hey, speaking of good use, we've got about five minutes before the floor's down all the way, so let's make good use of our time!"

As they got comfortable on their cushions, he waved a hand over the sphere with a mysterious air. "As I gaze into my crystal ball, I look ahead to our mission on Aurona…." Egged on by the laughter, he silently contemplated the depths of the mysterious orb, turning it over and over in his hands. "Ah! I see exploration parties," he exclaimed. "I see groups going out into the mountains, desert, or jungle with one or more of these small, black dots hovering over their heads, documenting everything in 3D. The camera can beam everything back up into this room in real time, or just keep a record of up to a month of action. At our convenience, we get together from time to time to review and edit the most interesting footage. But there's far more here than meets the eye. This little eight-inch wonder's not just a 3D camera!"

"He's right!" Joelle bounced on her cushion excitedly. "It does a *zillion* other things!"

He held up a finger. "For instance!" Chuckling, he tapped out a few sequences on the smooth surface. "Sssh! Wait, wait," he mumbled, his voice barely audible. As the mysterious lights blinked to life, he released the sphere and it shot up ten feet over his head. "Watch me now! You all have remotes on your wrists! You can control the altitude and direction of your own spheres by using your wrist programmers!" He rocked a few virtual buttons back and forth to make it jiggle up and down. "See? Follow the bouncing ball, everyone!"

They got the connection, studying their wrist programmers and chuckling.

"That leads up to the next function, and it's an extremely important one: it's called '*SEEK*,' where the sphere actually homes in on someone's PIL signal!" Stifling a smile, he glanced around the room. There was a sea of blank stares. "Oops!" he teased. Poker-faced, he reached into his pocket. "Oh, the PIL? I didn't mention *this*?" He slowly drew out a small, round object.

They squinted at the speck, craning their necks to peer over each other's shoulders. He held it high in the air, pivoting slowly around on his heel. "This little red dot is called a Personal ID Locator, or PIL! You might call it an RFID chip on steroids! Everyone's getting one—it's vital, and some day it may save your life!"

A hand shot up. "Ah, what does it *do*, sir?"

"Good question. It emits a specific, powerful frequency in a radius of three hundred and fifty miles assigned to your name, to *you* only!"

Ensign Rico raised his hand. "This sound like an obvious question, sir, but where will this PIL thingy be, ah … located?"

Laughter rang out. Nearly everyone joined in, shouting out answers and grinning from ear to ear. Several imaginative places were suggested.

Adam hooted, waving them all down. "My, what a raucous group! Yeah, you got it," he chuckled, nodding. "You're gonna *swallow* it!"

A contagion of grimaces passed through the crowd. They'd suspected as much.

"Hey! They're totally safe, guys, don't worry. These PILs have a unique structure of advanced biomaterials and your immune systems won't recognize them as foreign objects. They've got millions of noninvasive nanohooks that lock securely onto the wall of your stomach, and then for about three months they stimulate tissue to grow around them." He looked up. A man in the back row had his hand raised to speak. "Yes?" As Adam nodded, the man stood up slowly.

"Sir…."

"Yes?"

"Is this all, ah, *voluntary*?"

"Sorry, I've forgotten your name. It's been seven hundred years."

As the crew chuckled, the man grinned. "Dexor, sir."

"Thanks, Dexor. Well, I must say I did a lot of thinking about this when I reviewed the specs on the PIL, but the answer's quite straightforward: it's a 'No.'"

"Huh? How so, sir?" The man's voice faltered ever so slightly.

"Well," he shrugged, "the PIL's *only* function, its only reason for existing is for your safety." He noticed a few green faces. "Hmm … think of it as an internal GPS. There's no equipment to carry, it's *inside* you." He turned back to Dexor, grinning disarmingly. "Thanks again," he said, smiling. "I was hoping someone would bring this up."

Speechless, the man shrugged and raised a brow at his three companions.

"Hey, look, perfect timing! We're nearly down!" Walking to the edge of the circular platform, Adam parked the sphere in midair, turned off the platform's force field, and hopped down over the edge. Grinning mischievously, he poured himself another cup of coffee. "Now watch carefully, everyone: here's a demo. I'm punching out 'SEEK ADAM' on my wrist programmer and then adding my own PIL frequency. In a few seconds I'll punch the 'Enter' button."

The crew was doing their best to piece everything together. They glanced at their leader's poker face, and then the sphere. Both remained emotionless, masklike and enigmatic.

Adam put his coffee aside and lightly tapped the 'Enter' button.

A brilliant green laser beam sizzled out of the sphere's interior. There was a collective gasp as it swept the room, searching. Brightening, it focused intensely on Adam's chest. Hurtling through the air at a blinding speed, it stopped impossibly fast and hovered motionless over his head. Unruffled, he calmly reached up and retrieved the holocamera from the air.

"Oh, and one more thing!"

They exhaled as one, their eyes wide.

"All PILs are to be ingested within at least two hours!"

A groan went up. "I think I've lost my appetite," someone griped from the back of the room.

"Okay, the stage is down! It's crate time! Go for it, guys!"

The three beefy men hopped to their feet, picked their way through the crowd, and sprinted through the bronze doorway, their slate-blue uniforms a blur.

He turned back to the group with a twinkle in his eye. "Now as for the rest of us, how about *breakfast*? I could go for some real *food* now! How 'bout you?" The words hung in the air, their tantalizing echoes repeating in the round room. The crew's answer came roaring back, rivaling the impressive sound system in the holosphere.

"Food! Food! Foooood!" the gleeful, ravenous chant went up.

He'd pegged it; their small, carefully crafted biosnack didn't cut the mustard after seven years in sleep mode. "Be back up here in an hour!" he yelled over the din.

Delicious odors were starting to waft through the open bronze doors; an automeal, yes, but it sure smelled good! The hungry horde streamed out, pulled by irresistible magnetic waves emanating from the cafeteria.

Down in Warehouse F, the three men stood shoulder to shoulder, their faces pressed tightly against the pod's darkened glass. Its monitor's chronograph clearly showed that it was working, but the sleep mode's timetable remained blank.

"Where's the switch? Damn! Is there a switch anywhere?"

Their hands flew, sliding over the smooth surface.

"What? No openings anywhere? This-this thing's like Fort Knox!"

They searched earnestly, frantically. Finally, way down low on the back of the pod, someone's hand bumped into a small computer connection hanging limply from its cord. He twisted it toward the light to read the label. "Crud!" He slapped the cord away in frustration. "The plug's been crushed! One of the pod's wheels musta run over it! This mother never got plugged into the ship's mainframe! We BLEW it!!!"

Their panic rose to a peak as they realized their mistake. Their eyes met.

"Dexor's gonna kill us!" The three chorused.

"Well, he helped push this thing down here, didn't he? He can't finger us for...."

One of them held up a cautionary hand. "Forget Dexor, he's the least of our worries!" He glanced at the pod. "We sure don't want to be anywhere near this room when HE wakes up!"

The crew was in high spirits as they ate, filling the cafeteria with laughter. Off to the side Joelle sat by herself, finishing off the last of a hasty meal. She wasn't especially hungry, just ravenously curious. The lengthy menus inside that black sphere had really sparked her overactive imagination. She got up determinedly.

Elena had been watching her wolf her food down and swiveled on her seat. "Hey! Where 'ya going, Joelle?"

She turned in surprise. "Ah, ah, I just wanted to, um, walk around a little, do some exploring? You know … *snoop?*"

Elena chuckled. This lively one seemed to share her own basic instincts. "Have a good time, kid," she winked, her eyes scanning the room discreetly. "Just be careful."

Joelle melted away. She'd already spotted a back door to the kitchen, shielded by a row of auto-ovens, and slipped out unnoticed. Stepping over pipes and cables, she followed a long, curving corridor past several similar doorways. As she rounded a sharp corner, a formidable door suddenly stood in front of her, closed tightly with a large wheel and several clamps. There was a small panel on the wall next to it at eye level.

"QUARANTINE ROOM," it read. She shuddered, then read on. "ENTER ONLY WHEN GREEN LIGHT FLASHES."

Wow, this was great stuff! Her eager eyes scanned downward. Below the printed warning was a red and a green lens, underscored by a small bar marked "PUSH." She hesitated only a millisecond before tapping the bar. As the corridor became flooded with pulsing green light, her hand shot to her mouth. She leaned way back to peer down the hall toward the kitchen and paused, composing herself. In a burst of determination, she twirled the big wheel and unfastened the latches. The door gave a slight, hermetically sealed puff, then swung open.

It smelled clean. Antiseptic-clean. White counters and cabinets lined the walls as far as she could see and stacks of enormous cages filled the center of the cavernous room. She walked over and eyed them suspiciously, rattling the doors. "Good grief," she whispered, "what could possibly go in *these?*"

True to her nature, she began to snoop. Cabinets were peeked into, jars were opened and the contents sniffed, drawers of ominous dissecting tools were gingerly poked through, syringes were squirted and reams of empty plastic bags ruffled. Suddenly she stopped dead in her tracks, almost falling over in her haste.

An odd cabinet particularly intrigued her. It was really different from the rest, being up on wheels and sitting at an angle behind wide restraining straps. This time there was no hesitation whatsoever. She unfastened the straps and wheeled the whole thing over to a counter. The cabinet opened from the top with a hinge. Straining, she raised the heavy lid and peered inside. Immediately, there was a faint scratching sound emanating from a large, translucent five-gallon bucket in the bottom.

"Hello?" Her heart began to pound. "M-maybe I shouldn't…." Her hands shaking, she reached inside and grabbed the handle, testing the weight. "Hmm, not too bad, I think I can…." Taking a deep breath, she hefted it out and set it precariously on the edge of the counter next to her. "There!" She exhaled. A thin booklet was lying on top of the lid. As she turned on a light bar under the cabinet to read the cover, the odd scratching intensified, growing louder.

Suddenly, right behind her, the heavy lid of the wheeled cabinet slammed shut with a tremendous crash! She spun around, her heart in her mouth. Too late, she felt her elbow whack the bucket. "Oh, *noooo*!" she wailed. As it hit the floor, both the lid and booklet flew off, sailing across the room. She jumped back, gasping in horror.

Hundreds of black, alien insects boiled out of the bucket! With audible snaps of their pincers and loud pings, they flicked themselves impossibly far into the air and proceeded to scurry up every vertical plane within reach. In less than a heartbeat, thousands of wriggling legs were swarming up and over her, digging under her clothing, scratching her skin and twisting her long hair into knots. She clenched her fists, drew in a long, deep breath, and let loose.

Down the corridor, all conversation stopped midsentence: about twenty men flew to the kitchen's back door with drawn Stiflers. Clustered in a tight knot, they peered down the corridor. Suddenly they backed away in a rush. Some kind of screaming apparition was hurtling toward them!

A path opened wide as something resembling a human burst through the doorway and stumbled out into the cafeteria. Covered from head to toe with a roiling, glittering black mass of insectlike creatures, the silhouette of a female body was thrashing at herself in panic, yanking off handfuls of the bugs and flinging them everywhere. It was only when the hard black bodies started to bounce off the crew's uniforms that they came to their senses. They sprang into action, stomping and squashing the bugs in oddly loud crunches.

One scurried across the floor toward Adam. Thinking quickly, he grabbed a potholder and dropped to his knees, pinning it down. Suddenly, a purplish puff of smoke squirted out, followed by a horrible odor! A defense mechanism? He gagged, backing away. Here and there, more insects began to rise up and let loose with stink-clouds of their own! The stench quickly became overwhelming, sending waves of people staggering out into the halls. Fighting his heaving stomach, he pinched the strangely quiet form with his potholder and turned it over. Suddenly, his eyes widened, his jaw dropped, and he got up shouting.

"*Stop*! Stop right now!" He ran out into the midst of the throng, waving the potholder over his head. "It's all right!"

Joelle tagged closely behind him, sobbing and shuddering uncontrollably. In turn, an entourage of women surrounded her, swatting the insects off her shoulders and doing their level best to comfort each other. They winced in revulsion as Adam threw his potholder away and held the wriggling form in his bare hand.

"They're *ours*!" he shouted. "They have writing on the bottom!"

The scrunching stopped. What did he say?

"These blasted things are *man-made*!!" he affirmed. "They're *robots*!"

The crew kept a wary distance, watching him as he oh-so-carefully turned over what appeared to be a shiny black marble with legs, studying it in minute detail. He looked up. "I dunno. Not a thing was mentioned in my holo-recordings about these little guys. I can see that they're definitely mechanical. I don't know what they *are* yet, or what they *do*, but I assure you we're gonna get to the bottom of this!"

Joelle pulled away from her clinging, weeping circle. She looked beat. There were hundreds of tiny, round, red suction marks all over her face. "I'm sorry, sir," she sniffed. "I-I didn't mean to…."

"Where'd you find these?" he interrupted. "Show me."

They retraced her fateful route through the kitchen, stepping gingerly over piles of squashed, metallic rubble. Kron motioned hurriedly for a small group to follow. Along the back corridor, the creeping forms had invaded everywhere. Apparently, the geckolike suction cups on the tips of their feet enabled them to climb anything, so they skulked around seeking darkness, anchoring their feet with a wiggle as they settled into crevices.

The bucket lay on the floor just as she'd left it, with the thin booklet spread-eagled off to the side. As Adam pushed at it with his toe, a lone, black form skittered out. He caught the robotoid quickly, handed it to Kron, and then grabbed the book.

As he flipped through the manual with growing excitement, Joelle hugged her chest protectively, shuddering from the core of her being. Her eyes swept suspiciously around the darkened room. Her disheveled hair was still moving, now hopelessly knotted with dark, struggling shapes.

"Holy cow!" he burst. The men crowded around his elbow to see, but he pulled the book away, mischievously covering the title with his hand. "You're not gonna believe this, guys! The black glass bubble over the center shields an advanced nano-holocamera, an improved, miniaturized version of the black sphere. It says here that these things are used mainly for surveillance!"

"Surveillance?" Kron interrupted. "What *are* they?"

He pulled his hand away and pointed at the title. The single, capitalized word in bold face type prompted a round of laughter all around. Even Joelle stifled a smirk.

"*Spyders*!" They tossed the name back and forth. "Get it? *Spy*?"

Adam eagerly turned his eyes back to the text. "Wait! Wait! There's more!"

Kron shouted back, grinning. "Tell us, sir!"

"Listen to this, guys! The name's an acronym, and states the robotoid's purpose! Think hard now and spell out all the letters: S-P-Y-D-E-R! The room fell to a puzzled silence. "Any clues? Ready?" he teased. "It's a whopper! All six letters, now!"

They made hurrying motions with their hands.

"Sophisticated Photo-Yielding Devices for Extraterrestrial Reconnaissance!"

An appreciative round of whistles, hoots, laughter, and applause swept the room. One of the crew sprinted down the corridor to the kitchen with the update, and immediately there was a distant cheer. Joelle snatched the book away from Adam in a huff to read the title, her mouth a tight, hard line. "*Men*!" she snipped, and flounced out of the room, recoiling at the icky arachnoids covering the doorway.

Adam looked up with a start. "G-get her!" he wheezed, stifling his laughter. "We need that book! We gotta find out more about these, ah…."

"*Bugs*!" Tola cut in and guffawed loudly. The men lost it again. Bumping into each other in haste, they crowded out of the narrow doorway.

It was now an amazingly different group in the mess hall. Everyone was totally over their fear and had scooped up handfuls of the robotoids. Even a few women were gingerly passing the bugs around, holding them by the tips of their legs. As Adam reclaimed the book, a noisy group huddled around him to get briefed.

Off to the side, Joelle's entourage clustered tightly around her, whispering condolences. It was evident that the Spyders were hopelessly tangled in her long hair, so she gave permission to one of the women to cut it closer to her head in a short, pixy style. Her long, frazzled blonde locks fell in moving clumps to the floor.

Elena pulled up a chair, holding her hand. "You seem to have the regulation arachnophobia, Joelle," she probed. "Bad experience, or something?"

Joelle shuddered as a deeply imbedded memory flooded back.

"C'mon, hon, you can tell us," someone soothed. "What happened?"

She closed her eyes and sighed. "Well, it all started because of those cats."

Their eyes blinked. "Cats?"

"Yeah, when I was a little girl my mom used to raise show cats, mostly chinchilla Persians and Himalayas. Well, anyway, one day one of her prize kittens got away and ran into the neighbor's yard. The people next door were real slobs; you know the kind: hoarders? They collected old cars and piles of junk, never mowed their lawn...." Her big blue eyes opened impossibly wide as her story unfolded. "I'm talking *forest* here. I got lost in all that stuff when I ran after the kitten! Well, all of a sudden I tripped over a tangle of wires and fell into this huge mud puddle, and...," she shuddered deeply, from her toes.

"And?" they prompted, all concerned.

"And there I was, flat on my back, absolutely covered with brownish, greenish goo, and this humongous spider's web!" She cringed in revulsion. "His-his TV dinners were all *over* me!!

Someone snorted nearby. The men's backs had been turned and they were poking each other, holding their sides in silent laughter.

Joelle shot them a disdainful look and continued, unperturbed. "Well, when I finally realized *what* could've made a web *that* size, I screamed, and...."

"And?" they all prompted nervously.

"'*He* came out! I screamed, my mom came flying out the back door...."

"He?" they chorused.

"*Mega* 'he'! *Colossal* 'he'! You know, the kind that have those icky, hairy yellow legs and the big knapsacks?"

They all grimaced. Yes, they knew. Knapsacks: the ultimate gross-out.

Joelle seemed almost possessed, wringing her hands in revulsion and picking imaginary bits off her sleeves. Teary-eyed, the women hugged her.

Adam held up his hands. "Okay, okay! Show's over, everyone! We've had intermission, and now it's time for Act II! Everybody back up to the Observatory Room!" He checked his wrist programmer. "Those crates should be there!"

They trooped out of the cafeteria in excitement, their hands full of Spyders. The elevators were quickly filled to capacity so most took to the spiral stairs, looking like a swarm of slate blue ants as they corkscrewed upward. Adam beat them all. As they began to arrive he was already standing in front of the big screen with his face buried in the Spyder manual, boning up on the specs. Tola nudged him out of his concentration.

"Holy cow! How'd you get up here so quickly, sir? Did you *fly?*"

He looked up, distracted. "Oh, um, no. Private speed elevator." The book pulled his nose back downward, almost like a magnet. "Ah, gimme a minute," he mumbled. "This is great stuff, Tola!"

Chuckling, the round man slipped away to talk with Kron. They quickly formed a team and took charge, settling the crew down as they arrived, shushing them and waving them onto their cushions.

Adam stood riveted to the spot, deeply engrossed and oblivious to all the activity around him. Only when the noise level had finally subsided to a whisper did he look up. His eyes gave him away. Their look of wonder and unbridled excitement spread like a silent wildfire through the great round room.

"Wow." He let out a long breath. "It says that these, ah, bugs, are miniature versions of our holocameras. They send out the same digitized, coded signals, but the main difference is that your Explorer's Helmets can project the signals inside your face shields in *real time!* Think about it! These Spyders are miniature, mobile 3D TV holocameras! What *they* see, *you* see, as it happens!"

A whistle of appreciation escaped from their lips, echoing his enthusiasm. Joelle's incident in quarantine was behind them now, left somewhere far away. They zeroed in on Adam as he turned a page in the manual.

"Wow! According to this inventory, we should have thousands of these Spyders in storage! They've been mass-produced on nano-robotoid assembly lines and they're to be considered as expendable. That small bucket of Spyders Joelle, ah, 'found' in the quarantine room had been prepped and cleaned for introduction into an alien environment!"

He started reading. "The Spyder's locomotion is threefold: it can walk, hop, or fly." He looked up with a start. "*Fly?*" He pulled a featherweight Spyder out of his pocket and tossed it into the air. Incredibly, the black marble shape seemed to hang motionless for a moment, then begin to slowly descend. Pulling his eyes away, he read on excitedly. "'The smooth airfoil shape is actually an ultralight lifting body, flat on the bottom and rounded on the top. When sensors on the tips of the legs signal it's airborne, an internal mini gyroscope is activated. The guidance computer stiffens all the bimetallic strips, straightening the legs out to steer with their flattened and enlarged suction tips.'"

They were all watching the speck descend gracefully, like a piece of feather from a down pillow. Suddenly it flipped over, the big holo-eye pointing downward. The crew's eyes darted back to Adam.

"I-I dunno," he shrugged, "the book doesn't tell me *everything*. Maybe its logic circuits are looking for a place to land?" Upside down, the Spyder steered purposefully toward him, tilting its flattened suction cups at minute angles and using them as both air brakes and rudders. It got to a few inches from his bare arm, flipped over, and landed gracefully. He tried to pry it loose, but the strong, strangely moist suction tips gripped tenaciously. Suddenly, there was a cool puff against his hand. He looked up at the crew, aghast.

That odor again!! Scrambling over each other in haste, the people in the front rows scooted away on their cushions. Adam leaped out of the purple cloud flapping his arms and holding his breath, reading the manual in desperation.

"*Aha*!" His finger jabbed at an illustration. "Here it *is*! The stink! There's a cross-sectional diagram of the Spyder under 'Defense Mechanisms'! The putrid, purple stink is the Spyder's first line of defense!" He fanned the air with the book. "I'd say it's more like *offense*! Enough said about *that*!"

They laughed only with their eyes; their hands were clamped tightly over their mouths.

"Jumping?" Someone offered weakly. "How about 'jumping'?

"Yes, yes, let's press on," Adam agreed, stifling his persistent smile. "Jumping. They walk, hop, or fly. Let's see: evidently these little fuzzy logic creatures can sense danger approaching. Remember I mentioned bimetallic strips? Their legs are constructed with.... Oh, just listen to the jargon, it's way too technical to paraphrase."

Concentrating, he bent to read. "'Their legs are constructed with a closely integrated combination of micromotors and layered bimetallic strips, fired in a variety of programmed sequences in direct reaction to input from biofeedback sensors and logic circuits. Jumping, therefore, is the simplest of functions: all legs are fired at once, in effect flicking the Spyder into the air. In an Earth-gravity situation, Spyders can jump over seventy times their own diameter,'" he stopped, amazed. "Wow! That's about twelve feet!"

The crew was duly impressed. While it was true that most of these concepts had existed for decades and if taken separately each idea was relatively simple, the total product formed a true synergism, serendipitously conceived by the minds and hands of brilliant artisans and engineers. Like their starship, these jumping Spyders seemed to have taken a quantum leap of their own into the future.

He bent back eagerly to the text, now paraphrasing in haste. "Their power is entirely solar, with a retentive storage capacity of well over fifty years." He looked up with a start. "The *light*! That's it! They sprang back to life when Joelle tipped over their bucket and the room lights hit them!"

"*Ta-da-a-ah*!" Joelle leapt to her feet triumphantly, gamely waving a Spyder in each hand.

As the laughter died down, a loud clunking greeted their ears. They spun around to see the bronze doors to the Observatory Room thumping and swinging open, signaling an end to the subject. Three sweating men backed in, pulling a line of floating barges. One of them turned around, red faced. "Ah, sorry, sir, we-we got lost! This is a huge ship!"

Adam shrugged. "That's fine, we were all, ah, distracted! You can park the barges right where you are. If you want some food, take a trip back downstairs to the cafeteria and get a quick bite, or just grab some snacks over there."

They glanced at each other. "Just snacks, sir," the first man affirmed. "We're, ah, dyin' to know what's in these crates, too!" They scanned the crowd nervously.

Out in the center of the room, Dexor's smoldering eyes caught theirs. As he raised a single, questioning brow, one of the three discreetly shook his head and shrugged, then glanced pleadingly at his companions for support. Dexor's jaw dropped in disbelief.

As Adam stood in front of the big screen waiting for silence, he used his wrist programmer to do a quick roll call, counting their PIL signals. After a moment, it flashed in a steady pulse and started to beep loudly. "NOT FOUND: TODD. NOT FOUND…." As the crew turned to him in surprise, he glanced up.

"Jon, have you seen your brother lately?"

"No, sir. I looked everywhere for him and then ran up here, thinking he might have followed the crowd. I was just about to sneak out and go look for him."

Wow, Todd was missing! An anxious buzz went up.

"Oh, by the way, guys, thanks for swallowing your PILs. It made this demonstration easy." The bleeping suddenly increased in tempo and volume, and his grin widened. "Well, whaddaya know, Todd's coming … and on the run, I might add! His PIL signal just entered a twenty-yard radius I set on my 'LOCATE' function."

An anxious Todd slipped into the room, wiping the last of his breakfast from his face. Most likely he'd wandered off somewhere along the way to look for stars on a big flatscreen monitor. Red-faced, Jon sat him down to explain everything, whispering in his ear. Todd looked downcast, squirming uneasily on his pillow.

"Thank you, Todd!" Adam smiled. "Yes, thanks for this opportunity to demonstrate a vital function to all your friends! And Jon, will you now please lock your wrist programmer onto your brother's PIL frequency and set it to a ten-yard radius?" His gaze caught the boy's anxious eyes. "Yes, Todd, Jon's helping you to be an even *better* shadow now!" The boy smiled, visibly relieved.

Adam turned back to the crew. "You know, guys, I do want to see what's in those crates as much as you do, but first I feel it's more important for us to nail the operation of these wrist programmers. They're quite unique: I purchased them back on Earth from a company my grandfather used to own. He left instructions for me to buy only these specific models and add about 10 terabytes of programmable memory. Why these specific models and why so much memory? I found out that as we slept in our pods, they connected themselves to the ship's mainframe with some sort of Bluetooth and were completely reprogrammed from their original purpose."

Almost involuntarily, nearly everyone held out their arms, checking out their wrist programmer in this new light. As they started to poke at them in earnest, they quickly discovered many menus they were unaware of.

Adam continued. "These things are a cinch to learn. In reality, they're just simple transceivers with a series of menus, submenus, and codes for their functions. They're all exactly the same, but mine's way larger, with about 50 terabytes and one additional function…." He slipped his programmer off his wrist and held it up. "Direct control of this starship. So let's make it fast! I'll demonstrate the most important features in five minutes, tops."

Dexor squirmed, nervously squishing his pocket to make sure his PIL was there. Yes, there it was, he could feel the lump. Wow, direct control of the starship! He flipped his collar up furtively, adjusting a switch to transmit Adam's message more clearly into a tiny, hidden recorder.

After Adam's short class in programming, the large chests were opened. A group of excited volunteers passed around stacks of strange-looking medical equipment, mini transporters, communicators, and radical, special-use clothing. Soon, except for the flat, featureless rectangle under each crate, they were totally empty.

He stood up. "Okay. At this point, I hereby turn over complete explanation of all these strange items to the only human in the universe, with the possible exception of my grandfather, who could possibly know more than me how they work!" He turned and nodded to his second in command.

Smiling, Kron stood there quietly, holding up a finger. "Wait a sec," he announced, looking over the equipment. "Yes, these seem to be duplicates of my Bitron models." He looked up. "Would you three guys please lift the last of the empty crates off the antigrav slabs? Just carry them out into the hallway for now." As they jumped to his bidding, he explained. "Since you guys now know how your programmer's 'LOCATE' function works, I'm going to give you a practical demo…."

He began tapping furiously. "Okay, everything's set. These slabs each have codes. I punched in their four respective sets of transport code numbers, followed by the command 'CLIMB/5FT.,' then finally 'RADIUS 20 FT./ LOCATE KRON.'"

He studied the crew's puzzled faces intently. Obviously, nobody had a clue. "Follow me yet?" he said, grinning mischievously, picking up on Adam's clowning. "Nothing happens until I tap the 'Enter' button on my programmer…."

The four thin, flat slabs seemed to be nearly featureless. Floating about six inches off the floor, they were simple, elegantly proportioned rectangles with rounded corners and some kind of a rubberized, nonslip finish.

"Here goes!" Shrugging, he pressed 'Enter.'

Silently they rose to eye level and, almost on cue, turned and began to circle the perimeter of the room entirely on their own. As the astonished crew scooted toward the center to watch, he pressed out another series of codes. "I'm locking in their paths and setting their radar spacing distances," he explained. "Okay now, give me some room." As a path opened through the crowd, he got a running start and hopped up nimbly onto one of the floating transporters. His blonde hair flying, he stood there casually, confidently, his legs far apart and his hands on his hips. Astonished faces followed him as he flew around the room.

"You can do the same!" he shouted. "Almost anything that's mobile on this ship—SpeedSleds, barges, and so on—have a code and frequency number assigned to them! These slabs may look plain, but they're extremely sophisticated: they have radar, sonar, infrared, terrain mapping, and laser guidance systems along their lateral lines, just like the SpeedSleds! So dig, guys! You have exactly the same menus as me, with an almost infinite list of submenus. The codes are all there, right at your fingertips!"

Adam walked out to the center of the room. "I just thought of something important here. I'm going to throw a scenario at you. Imagine this: if Kron were injured somewhere, this slab could fly out to him all by itself, homing in on his PIL frequency. The slab has a 'SEEK' function, too! Right, Kron?"

"Yes. And it also has some manual controls as a backup, built into the front bumper." Grinning, the taut, muscular man flicked a hidden panel open with his toe. As it unfolded and raised from the surface, it lit up brightly. The crew watched, enthralled. "And as if *that* weren't enough, in emergencies it's possible to run all this equipment remotely with voice commands or chin codes from your e-helmets! They repeat every function on your wrist programmers… everything's connected!"

Joelle raised her voice as the sled breezed by, her short hair ruffling. "Why don't the e-helmets just use voice commands, Kron? I don't like the chin codes. Everything electronic has been using voice commands for decades! They're so *easy*!"

He explained from the other side of the room. "If it's really quiet, yes, but sometimes there's too much background noise," he shouted, smiling. "It might 'hear' the wrong thing and do something unexpected or dangerous. The human voice is, as best, an unreliable source for intricate commands and subcommands. A keystroke is always more exact than a sneeze or stutter when moving such sophisticated objects!"

Adam held up his hands. "Thanks, Kron!" he concluded. "Great job! There's tons more to learn, guys, we can all be sure of that! But we're done for the day. We'll just leave all the rest of the equipment piled up right here and come back to it."

As a disappointed moan went up, Adam held up his hands. "I'm sure a lot of you have reached your saturation point. You've just woken up and I'm sure you'd like some time to yourselves to work the kinks out. Really. We've just scratched the surface, here. We'll have to form learning teams on this long, last leg of our journey to dig deeply and know all this stuff cold."

Kron lowered the circling barges, slowed them to a stop, and nimbly hopped off. Suddenly, he caught Joelle's admiring eye and turned away, reddening. A few others had caught the subtle exchange and elbowed each other with knowing looks.

Adam had caught it too and continued smoothly. "There's a last important key to the success of this mission—in fact, *the* most important one. Although we don't really know each other yet, I feel it's starting to happen already…. Even though we've been, um, shall we say, sleeping together for seven hundred years."

An explosion of laughter swept the room, along with a few reddening faces.

Adam held up a finger. "Thank you so much, Joelle. After our, ah, 'adventure' downstairs in the kitchen, I think we *know* the key I'm talking about: the forging of deep and lasting *friendships*!"

The crew jumped to their feet with a wave of applause, hugs, and laughter. It had indeed been a long, tiring, yet extremely enlightening first day. Gathering their belongings, they put away their cushions and filed out through the big bronze doors.

There was another enlightened face in the center of the room. Dexor stood up stiffly, stretching out his limbs, nodding and smiling at the crewmembers as they filed out of the room. He took his time, trailing along behind everyone. Safely down the hallway, he glanced furtively over his shoulder and slipped into a freight elevator.

Chapter 10: THE PODIUM

The days flew by and their bodies and minds strengthened rapidly. Some of the crew became almost addicted to the Galaxy Wall's huge screen, reclining on piles of memory foam cushions and immersing themselves in the unforgettable panorama for hours at a time. As they pushed deep inside one of the spiraling arms and drew closer to Aurona's solar system, the starship began a programmed sequence of deceleration maneuvers, streaking impossibly close to some large dying suns and using their massive gravities to slow down. Swirling, zigzagging, the schematic of their path looked like the track of a pinball machine.

Finally, as Aurona's solar system centered itself on the big screen, a new display popped up along one side: some ornate numbers began to count off the days until they arrived. The info served its purpose, calming the crew and giving them a time frame to anticipate and plan until they reached their goal. As they entered the system, they found it to be immense, with great, gaseous giants and hundreds of rocky planets surrounded by clouds of tiny moons. The starship almost seemed to linger as it slipped past some watercolored Jupiter-like beauties, treating the crew to some spectacular close-ups.

Finally, one evening as Adam was standing by himself in front of the big screen, they slowly rounded a large planet. A long, straight stretch opened up toward a small, shining dot. He drew in his breath sharply.

Aurona! Even from millions of miles away, the planet was spectacular!

He sprang to action. As he sounded the tone for general assembly, they came on the run just as they were, midway in their prep for bed. Everyone had been anticipating this moment, and there was a loud buzz of excitement as they entered the room: this couldn't be Aurona already—they weren't expecting to see it for a few more days! They settled onto their floor cushions in nervous anticipation.

"It's late, so I'm keeping this short and simple, guys: five minutes, tops." He pointed at the display. "See that tiny, bright metallic blip in the center? It looks like a star, doesn't it? Well, it fooled me too! Just like you, I thought we'd have to wait awhile, but we can actually *see* the planet from this tremendous distance!" He turned around to face a sea of uncomprehending stares.

"Why does it do that, sir?" Kron asked. "What makes it glow like that?"

He shrugged. "I don't have a clue. It's a complete mystery…." His voice dropped off as his wrist started to vibrate. "Wait a sec." As he read a message on his programmer, his eyes widened. "Wow, speaking of mystery, it's a mystery how anyone's going to get to get any sleep tonight! According to this latest latest update, our starship just began to accelerate to close the gap! We should be establishing orbit by early tomorrow morning!"

A collective gasp went up, the crew staring at him in disbelief.

"Okay, that's it!" He shrugged. "I *did* say that I'd keep you here five minutes, didn't I? Get back to bed, so you can get up early! We've got a planet to explore!"

They rose reluctantly, putting their pillows away and glancing repeatedly over their shoulders as they filed out of the room.

Adam lingered in front of the screen to study the dot in minutest detail. It looked totally different, more like a shimmering ball of gold foil than a planet. After a moment, he shrugged his shoulders, closed the screen, and turned off the lights.

He couldn't sleep. Something wasn't right; something just didn't wash. Suddenly a train of disturbing thoughts started to rumble around a track inside his mind, along with a vision of flashing yellow warning lights. A short phrase lit up: *'Anticipate your problems.'* He sat bolt upright: Grandpa! Always solution-oriented, he'd drilled the concept of red, yellow, and green lights into his head as a child. Mumbling to himself, he began to mull it over. "Hmm … so, if potential problems are yellow lights, loosely translated, that means I gotta know what I'm getting into! Friend or foe, I gotta figure out this mystery planet!"

He jumped out of bed and finished dressing on the run. Pacing inside his private speed elevator, his mind was filled with a blur of scenarios. "What if there's dinosaurs or swamps or poisonous bacteria in the air? Is that why Grandpa looked so sick?" He gripped the railing. "Yow, I'm responsible for the lives of a lot of people here!"

As the Observatory's big bronze doors opened, he flew across the room and opened the screen. Yes, there it was: the tiny ball had a distinctly warm, golden hue around its edges. Aurona looked foreign and out of place, almost as if it were suspended on a string in the middle of a cold, dark panorama. Shivering in the cool semidarkness, he fumbled through his pockets for his wrist programmer. "Oh, come *on* now," he sputtered in frustration. "Give me a break! Don't tell me I left it back in my *room*! Crud!" he scowled. "I really don't want to go back to … wait!" He paused a moment, thinking. "Yes, there should be a set of *manual* controls hidden somewhere." He explored a row of identical-looking panels, poking with his fingertips. One felt a bit spongier, as if it were on hidden springs. Shrugging, he pushed hard. A door flipped open.

"Aha!" In front of him, plainly marked, was the Observatory Room's master programmer! A small button blinked expectantly: 'PODIUM.' Shrugging, he pressed it.

In the dead silence, he heard a faint, low hum coming from somewhere near the blue line of separation at the center of the stage. Cocking his head aside, he followed his ears to the source and knelt down, feeling with his palms. Yes, there was a definite vibration underneath the floor. He expelled a long breath, shaking his head in wonder. Just like the holocamera, there was far more than met the eye inside this starship!

Suddenly, an impossibly thin, masterfully fit, circular outline appeared under his fingertips! Shocked, he pulled away from it just in time: nearly catching him on the chin, an odd-looking, cylindrical form extruded itself rapidly out of the floor. He watched it warily. A finely ribbed, flat-topped tube nearly three feet in diameter was oozing up out of nowhere! He started to sputter. "Huh? What the…? I walked over this spot hundreds of times! I never *dreamed* this thing was here!"

The Podium

Stopping about chest height, the podium began to transform, swelling slightly and splitting down its backside along a thin line. He watched it guardedly: the thing looked like a giant chrysalis splitting open and something was *definitely* emerging! With a whoosh and a thump, the top simply flipped over to reveal an impressive array of controls, lit brightly from within.

"That's it?" He edged closer, amazed. "Well, I'll be...."

A button was flashing. PIVOT, it read. Tentatively he reached out, touched it, and quickly jerked his hand back. With a hum, the podium simply swiveled around to face the screen. "Wow!" He walked around the cylinder, his hand on his chin. "Good night," he gasped, "there must be fifty or sixty *extra* buttons on top of this thing! None of *these* are on my wrist programmer!"

One button stood out from the rest. MAGNIFY, it read, in a soft red glow.

"Magnify? I wonder if that could mean...?" His fist shot into the air. "Yes!" There was no hesitation this time. He punched the button emphatically. The screen jumped forward, with Aurona enlarging from a pinpoint to about the size of a quarter! With a racing heart, he proceeded to tap out a series of magnifications, his eyes widening as each one doubled the planet's diameter! In moments, he stood there open-mouthed.

Aurona now filled the screen! Mountains and rivers, jungles and deserts, continents and oceans—they all stood out in breathtaking crystal clarity! But where was that golden hue they'd all seen from the distance? Could it be that pencil-thin, metallic shimmer around the edges? Odder still, there were thousands of densely packed vertical columns of light striating the narrow band of twilight along the day/night boundary! What could they be?

He blinked his eyes, squinting closely at the fantastic columns of light. His mind racing with possibilities, he turned to the controls and scanned them with renewed intensity. Another promising-looking button stood out from the rest. PHOTO, it read. He pressed it emphatically.

Somewhere in the darkness behind him, there was a muffled click, followed by a whir. Spinning on his heels, he spotted a tall, narrow panel swinging open near the bronze entrance doors. "What's *that*?" he sputtered. "I-I thought that skinny panel was just a decorative filler next to the door! This-this is incredible!" He sprinted across the room. "I don't remember seeing *any* of this stuff on the holo-disc's demo. Could this starship be an enhanced version, maybe a-a newer model?"

As he reached the door, a machine slid out on rollers, spitting out a large, shimmering sheet of paper. It floated through the air and dropped into a wire basket. He hesitated a moment, then bent over to retrieve it. The plasticized material still felt wet, probably a little damp from processing. "Perfect! Now I have *proof*!" As he turned it over in excitement, he drew in a sharp breath. It was a photo, all right, but *what* a photo!

A *hologram*! Nearly three feet in diameter and circled by a thin shimmer of metallic gold, the bulging sphere of a planet looked as if it were literally floating off the paper! He held it out at arm's length to stare at it, bug-eyed. How could this *be*? It was a hologram of crystal clarity and perfection, taken from millions of miles away! What kind of lenses could.... He turned around, his gut quaking. Why, the possibilities of this new equipment were incredible! He sprinted back to the controls, the big sheet of paper fluttering behind him.

Just as he suspected! Right under the PHOTO button were several smaller sub-buttons! INTERVAL, one read, then next to that, MAP. And what was this? An interesting one read SECTION. He hesitated, surmised wildly, then tapped it and held his breath.

An electric blue line sizzled down the center of the huge screen, bisecting the planet through its poles! He drew in a sharp breath. "Good grief!" he intoned. "That's what I'd call a *section*, all right!" He studied it a moment, then bent back eagerly to the controls. There was a small trackball in the center. Hmm, could it be? Purely by intuition, he rolled it a bit with his thumb and watched the screen. Yes, the blue line warped to the right in a big arc, still connected to the poles on the ends! It was now running down a mountain range. He let go. It stayed there, locked in position.

"Whaddaya know!" he whispered. "Let's see if this does what I think it'll do...." He tapped the PHOTO button. As the now-familiar whir immediately sounded behind him, he trotted back to the basket. This time, a very different photo was spewing out of a thin slot near the top, not so much a photo but a four-foot ribbon of paper, about six inches wide.

"Huh? What in the world?" He held it up by the ends and squinted at it, studying it from different angles. Suddenly he looked up with a start, his mind boggling with the answer. There was no mistake about it: The photo-strip was a silhouette, a perfect cross-section of the planet's crust, running along a thin blue line from pole to pole! Even the sea floor showed in minute detail below a dotted line representing the surface!

Rolling it up, he flew back to the podium, beside himself with excitement. The ergonomically placed controls seemed to be laid out by a sensitive, intuitive mind. It only took a few minutes of brainstorming to come up with a sizeable list of logical conclusions. Without delay, he pressed a small blue control marked AREA.

A flashing blue rectangle appeared in the center of the screen! Wow, maybe the trackball could.... He nudged it a little with his thumb. As he'd anticipated, the rectangle slid smoothly in response! Grinning from ear to ear, he moved it around the screen, playing with the feel of it. In a moment, he placed it decisively over a very interesting spot, a large lake in the southern hemisphere.

"Hmm. Should I try to MAGNIFY?" He shrugged and pressed the button. A true geek, he'd always been one to push the envelope and drive any given machine to its limit. Why fight it now? He waited in eager anticipation. After a short spasm of fluttering, the screen faded to black, then snapped back into focus.

"*Wow!*" He stood on his toes. An aerial shot appeared, as if the ship were hovering only a few miles above the surface! Transfixed, he edged around the podium and walked right up to close the screen to study the surface. "This is amazing! Truly amazing!" he babbled in excitement, and then spun back around on his heels. He was totally hooked. The envelope had only been nudged; no blue smoke was coming out of the podium yet. He wrung his hands in excitement.

"Maybe, just maybe I can zoom in *closer*?" He studied the controls, his eyebrows raised in lock position. "Sure, why not? What the heck, anything's possible!" He jabbed the AREA button again and carefully rolled the blue rectangle to a spot on the shore of the lake. "Now,

MAGNIFY!" As before the screen faded to black, but this time it seemed to take much longer to display the results.

He gritted his teeth. "C'mon, baby, you can do it!" As an image finally crackled into view, he let out a gasp.

What was that? Something was moving! Way down near the bottom corner, almost off the screen, something was definitely coming up out of the water!

Oh-so-carefully, he nudged the AREA button and rolled the rectangle over the object. Shaking in anticipation, he tapped the MAGNIFY button a final time. A strange, yellow light flickered to life. He read it, trying to understand.

COMPUTER ENHANCEMENT – ON.

He found himself biting his nails and listening to his heart thudding loudly in the silent room. It seemed like an eternity before tiny blocks, bits and bytes of subtly shaded color started to clump together and build out slowly from the center of the screen. "What's going on?" he breathed. "Am I really at the limit of the computer's range?" He slipped closer, watching and waiting, his sweating hands balled tightly into fists. With seemingly great effort an image appeared, a little grainy, but filling the view completely.

An animal! Adam scurried away from the screen to see it clearer. As a great set of stripes moved across the view, his heart began to hammer. The top of a wrinkled, wet head paused, then slowly tilted upward toward the starship. Glaring venomously, a set of yellow cat eyes seemed to scan the interior of the room, searching intensely from left to right. In a heartbeat, they snapped to dead center, focusing directly on *him*!

"*Wh-what*??" He recoiled in horror, groping behind him for the podium. The eyes followed his movement, the vertical, slitlike pupils dilating. "No!" He shook his head and ducked behind the podium, clutching his chest.

Suddenly there was a *scream* in the darkness! He spun around, his heart pounding. Elena was in the doorway, her hand clamped over her mouth. She was pointing emphatically at the screen. He spun back. An incredibly oversized set of bared, ivory fangs filled the view! The creature was enraged! The yellow eyes were clenched shut as it silently roared, long strands of saliva dripping like venom from its teeth.

It was too much for Elena. She ran toward him crying and shaking uncontrollably. He grabbed her and pulled her close. After a long moment, they leaned hesitantly around the edge of the podium like frightened children confronting the unknown. Drawing in a sharp breath, they pulled back quickly. The creature's sharp eyes had just spotted them! They were like mice caught in a trap! They were his … prey!

"Adam!" Elena quavered in his ear. "How can this *be*? How can that beast see us? We're millions of miles away! This is impossible!"

A loud, electronic-sounding hum suddenly invaded the room. He rolled his eyes. "Oh, no, what now?" he groaned and hesitantly looked back at the screen. With a shout, he sprang to his feet. "Elena, look! The image is starting to break up!"

She peered over the top of the podium. "W-what can we *do*?"

As they both watched, a golden haze started to fog the edges. It was definitely happening, all right. He held up a shaking finger. "We need a record! Pictures! We gotta document this!" His eyes flew to the PHOTO button, hastily scanning the row of subcategories beneath it. He drummed his fingers on the podium, trying to keep his cool. "There! SEQUENCE looks great, the fifth button down!" He punched it. The camera behind them started to click at precisely timed intervals as the glittering fog filtered in relentlessly. "What *is* that stuff?"

Elena sounded far away, her voice trembling. "I-I don't know! It looks like some kind of metallic haze in the atmosphere! Try backing away a little!"

He scanned the rows of subcategories under the MAGNIFY button. "Yes! Here it is, MINUS! It's *gotta* be the right one!" He punched it, waiting nervously. Nothing happened. He pushed harder, then tried holding it down. Nothing again. He found himself sweating and wringing his hands in agitation.... Could it be broken?

"Um, Adam?" Elena was suddenly at his side. As her hand brushed softly by, her eyes caught his own. "Try this," she whispered with a wink. She simply pushed both buttons at the same time. The screen flickered, gearing up for a big shift.

"Ah, thanks," He grinned sheepishly.

The computer enhancement light winked out and the fuzzy close-up was immediately replaced by a sharper image. He noticed a faint flicker of blue around the edges of the screen. What was *that*? They were definitely further away. A grotesquely fat, striped creature was pacing back and forth, snapping the tip of its long tail in agitation as he glared upward at them. From their new perspective, they could see it had a massive, bulbous head, grossly oversized in proportion to an obviously well-fed body.

Once more, his eyes caught the same subtle flash of blue around the edges of the screen. He pointed emphatically at the set of closely spaced blue lines.

"Hey, *that's* what those lines are! They're scale markings!"

"How do you know?"

"They just *changed*! I saw them flicker, and then different numbers came up when we backed away! According to this reading, we're exactly a hundred and forty two feet above the surface. Wow! That means that striped creature must be nearly twenty feet long!"

Elena's jaw dropped slightly. "He looks...." Her voice trailed off, shuddering.

"You're right," he whispered. "Fat. And his head looks deformed, or something."

She turned to him, her eyes questioning. "He scares me! We should...."

"Right again," he whispered. "Time to climb."

He backed the view away until the planet filled the screen and then accelerated the SEQUENCE to about three seconds apart. They stepped back to watch Aurona undergo a startling transformation. In a rush, a bright, glittering halo relentlessly filled in toward the center, blotting out the surface. The very atmosphere was changing into an opaque, metallic golden shell! He whispered quietly, breaking the awed silence. "Honestly, Elena, I-I don't know what's happening! But I gotta tell you I'm plenty scared, too." Somehow it seemed all right to be vulnerable with her: he knew from experience that truth and humility bred respect. He could see it now, reflecting back to him, shining in her eyes. They stood gazing at each other for what seemed like an eternal moment. She leaned softly against him. As they turned back to the big screen, their mouths gaped in awe.

Aurona was now a planet of mystery. A magnificent, highly polished sphere of gold hung suspended in the blackness of space, reflecting its two moons. The surrounding stars and galaxies played across its surface in a spectacular light show. Somewhere within that shell of gold, an intelligent, hostile life form lay in wait, expecting their arrival.

Chapter 11: THE SHIELD

It was a long, sleepless night, and Adam's throbbing head felt like it was floating off his shoulders. The answers just weren't coming! He got up, got dressed, and went back to the Observatory. Turning the podium lights down low, he began to ponder, pace, and prepare notes. After half an hour, he switched gears and took out a small hand lens. One by one he propped up the fantastic sequence of holograms to scrutinize their surface in minutest detail. He marveled at their glittering, iridescent beauty; the depth and clarity of focus was unbelievable; the resolution just seemed to go on forever!

Checking his wrist programmer, he sounded the chime for general assembly. Quickly shuffling through the photos, he chose seven of the most outstanding images, propped them up in sequential order, and turned them around to face the wall. Within minutes, there were noises coming from the hallway. Looking over his shoulder, he hastily threw a large cloth over the stack of holograms. Wow! They were here already!

The crew filed in, yawning and rubbing the ill-gotten sleep from their eyes. Almost in a zombielike trance, they trudged to the wall cabinets, got their cushions, and settled onto the floor. With the big screen shut tightly behind him, Adam stood at the new podium waiting patiently for silence. He'd found a small throat mike inside one of the podium's many drawers, and at the appropriate moment, activated it with a small ping.

"Good morning! If you're not awake yet, I'm sure you will be in a few seconds! This is a historic day, one that I'm sure we'll be talking about for generations to come!" He rolled up his sleeves. "Let's get right to the point! The planet has thrown up some kind of shield! In defense? I don't know yet, but I watched it happening last night!"

They were definitely awake now, and sat bolt upright in rapt attention.

"Okay! I need seven people up here quickly, volunteers." As hands shot up, he chose them at random. "Okay, now face me and line up across the stage about a shoulder's width apart." As he passed out the holograms to the volunteers, they each drew in an astonished breath as they looked down.

"Okay, guys, now turn around!"

A collective gasp went up. Seven magnificent spheres now floated on the stage! Each person looked like they were holding onto a clear glass box with a three-dimensional sphere trapped inside it! From zero to full closure, only the borders of the paper confined Aurona's breathtaking transformation! Outshining them all, the last hologram was truly spectacular. At the shield's full closure, the three-foot planet dazzled like a blob of polished, molten gold in the Observatory's mini spots. Adam walked over and knelt down in front of it. "Yes, this one's the prize. It's absolutely incredible. But there's more! When I examined it with a hand lens, I found out that it's not just a visual shield! There's an *electrical* field running through it!" His finger traced along a faint, red line. "There's a massive disturbance down here in the southern hemisphere, possibly a meteor penetration."

An electrical field? They leaned forward as one, straining to see it.

He stood up. "I wasn't alone last night when I took these holophotos; someone else joined me only minutes before this event occurred!"

As necks craned around the room, Elena's startled eyes grew wide, pleading in mute volumes. He shrugged apologetically. "I-I'm really sorry, Elena, but I do need you up here to help me verify this sighting and establish the facts."

She rose reluctantly and picked her way through the startled crowd to his side. He whispered into her ear. "It's important that we skip the part about the creature right now. Call it 'security,' but we don't want to start a panic, do we?" Once more, she answered only with her eyes. He reached under the podium and handed her a throat mike.

She put it on and began nervously, her voice trembling, her eyes lowered. "I-I couldn't sleep last night, either. I had a terrible time." She noticed a wave of bleary-eyed agreement sweep through the crowd: yes, most of them had suffered the same symptoms of major anticipation. "I just couldn't stand it anymore, so I got up, got dressed, and sneaked up here in the dark. Now, I know we *all* know how to open the screen."

Adam glanced at her in surprise. Her face turned red. "Ah, I just wanted to open it just a teeny, weeny bit!" She held up her hands about six inches apart. People shifted nervously on their cushions, grimacing; yes, most of them were guilty of a prolonged peek or two during the off-hours. Curiosity knows no bounds.

"But I found the screen already open! Adam was here looking at…," she paused, glancing at him with impossibly wide eyes. Taking a deep breath, she collected herself and leaned forward to point to the first hologram. "Looking at this first view on the screen. It-it was gorgeous, guys! As I joined him watching it, suddenly…." She raised her arms, wiggling her fingers in the air, and drew her hands slowly together. "These … what would you call them, these little flecks of gold foil seemed to come out of nowhere, and then … zap! Nothing! The whole planet was encased in a shell of gold!" The sea of heads turned back and forth to study the incredible sequence. "After I went back to my room, it got even worse. It was impossible to sleep! Those gold flecks bothered me. Where did they come from?"

A buzz arose: yes, that was *exactly* what everybody had been thinking! Assuming she was finished, Adam took a breath and started to speak.

She held up a finger politely. "So!"

He turned back to her in surprise. "So? There's more?"

She nodded. "At precisely four thirty-three this morning, two things happened: at that exact moment, when I was looking at the time readout on my OLED wrist programmer, I suddenly remembered my grandmother's old wrist watch, one of those with an LCD display. A quick vision of something like miniature venetian blinds went through my mind." She paused and looked around the room. "Voila? Don't you get it?" The crew stared back blankly. "The flecks were there all the time, guys, dispersed throughout the atmosphere! They just rose up into the stratosphere to form a thin sheet, then turned on their axis to block the view like an LCD display!"

Adam was stunned. Wow! Who *was* this woman? Why, she was brilliant! As she handed her throat mike back to him and picked her way back through the cushions, he meekly returned to the podium. His prepared speech was in shambles.

Suddenly, his grandfather's voice flashed into his consciousness; he'd mentioned something about this in the holodiscs: *"But, like I told you before, I couldn't care less about the gold. It's everywhere here on Aurona, lying around like rocks. It infuses the whole ecosystem, the atmosphere, everything!"*

His gut was shaking and it took a moment to reassimilate his thoughts. "That's-that's flat incredible, Elena!" he stuttered. "Thank you! We now have a solid theory to build on, and I have to say it ties in perfectly with what I'm about to reveal to all of you."

The room quickly fell back to silence.

"Last night, after many sleepless hours of my own, I decided to take action. We're now a lot closer to the, ah, problem than you'd think. I've taken the starship totally out of our journey's programmed autosequence. Yes, we're finally on our own. At this moment, we're hovering in antigrav mode near the equator, about half a mile over the shield's surface!" He spun the podium around to face the wall screen. As he punched a button, it swept back silently to reveal a brilliant, curving horizon. *Gold*! Polished, mirrored, molten *gold* as far as the eye could see!

In the back of the room, Dexor sat straight up, his eyes bugging out. He jabbed his companions sharply in the ribs. Why, this was far, far beyond their expectations! With shaking hands, he discreetly lifted the lapel of his uniform's jacket to uncover the lens of a microcamcorder. He penned a few notes on a receptor pad and tapped a switch. The annotated, subtitled visual account was instantly transmitted to a receiver in the depths of the starship.

After a moment, Adam resumed. "With Elena's theory in mind, I think it's time to look at this flaky stuff a bit closer. I'm going to zoom in closer to the shield," he exclaimed. He carefully nudged the trackball on the podium, but unexplainably he'd pushed it a bit too hard. Without warning, the horizon tipped up and down in a crazy rising and falling wave, then in a gut-wrenching rush, disappeared entirely off the top of the screen!

The illusion was way too real. The crew panicked. The starship was tipping and they were all going to slide across the shiny, polished floor into that paper thin screen on their butt-cushions and crash into space! There was a frenzied thumping. They braced themselves with their feet, leaning back and desperately grabbing for each other.

"Whoa!" someone wheezed. "Hold on!"

Adam hunched his shoulders. "Ooops?" Grimacing, he slowly turned around to apologize lamely. "Ah, I'm really sorry, guys!" Muffled whimpers answered. They were all struggling to sit back upright. "My bad! I-I *promise* I'll announce my intentions before I touch one more button! Oh, um, by the way we're, ah, looking straight down, now?" As he glanced at them out of the corner of his eye, he saw a sea of blanched white faces, a few shading toward green. He groped quickly for another button, smiling brightly. "Ah, next you'll see a blue rectangle," he soothed. "It's a visual border, or a frame that you can move over any area you want enlarged! In this case, I'm going to place it over that dot."

"D-dot?" a reply squeaked out. "W-what *is* that dot, sir?"

"It's our reflection," he shrugged. "It's *us*! Now get ready, everyone. I'm going to press the 'MAGNIFY' button!" They braced themselves for another visual onslaught.

Suddenly, a detailed view of the underside of their sleek starship snapped forward, a perfect circle dancing in a shimmering, golden cast! As hoots and cheers of appreciation burst out around the room, he breathed a sigh of relief. Thank God they were finally back with him. He carefully announced a few more magnifications and the reflected ship jumped toward them in steps.

"Now!" He turned around. "I'm really gonna test Elena's theory!" Without another word, he got busy. First, the AREA button lit up the screen in a blue rectangle, outlining a shadowy portion of the starship's reflected rim. He zoomed closer and the same thing appeared, only more spangly looking. He kept closing the distance tighter and tighter. "Okay. Ready? Remember, we're hovering over half a mile above the shield, but the blue scale markers you see around the edges of the screen say that we're only a virtual sixteenth-inch from the surface!" Rubbing his palms together, he punched MAGNIFY. The screen faded to black, then exploded to life.

Yes, there they were! Millions of minute, overlapping, discs of gold appeared before them, suspended in droplets of clear fluid! They were looking straight down at the shield and it was filling the entire wall with droplets in extreme magnification!

"Bingo!" someone yelled. "Elena was right!"

As they gazed in mixed wonder and awe into the untold depths between the glittering, closely-spaced bubbles, they marveled at the sharpness of the holographic resolution: it was as if they could slide a finger between each wet sphere and pluck it right out of the screen! Someone whistled appreciatively.

"Let's take a look at a SECTION of this, ah, Elenosphere," Adam said, chuckling.

As a round of laughter swept the room, she joined in, her face reddening.

"Here goes...." Adam punched the button and a thin, electric blue line sizzled across the screen. "Ah, this stuff should show up in cross section, so get ready. I'm going to press DISPLAY!" As he punched the button, an incredible visual effect immediately took over. Rippling in thin, luminous dashes and reflecting brightly out of the tops of their clear bubbles, the impossibly thin foil discs were now seen from their *edges*! Packed tightly together like glowing, living cells, the shimmering pattern of bubbles ran off the bottom of the screen. A curious voice piped up.

"Ah, how deep do these flakes go, sir? I-I mean just how thick *is* the shield?"

"Excellent question!" he replied. "You know, believe it or not, there *is* a way to find out! Gimme a second...." His voice trailed off. Backing the view away several stops, a more solid-looking metallic band suddenly ran across the center of the screen, remarkably straight and uniform. He walked up to the screen, pointing at the scale markers around the edges. "There you go, guys. Human estimates are out of the question here. Whatever this stuff is that we're looking at is *exactly* ninety-five feet, three inches thick! My guess? I think we'll find the same, uniform answer around the entire planet!" He silently pondered a few moments, then turned and walked back to the podium, pivoting it to face the crew.

"Okay, this is it. In view of all these facts, I'm going to take action. I've just made a few tactical decisions. Kron, I want you to take a group with you down to Launch Bay A-5. When you get there, prepare both a metallic and a ceramic-hulled probe. That's right, we're gonna use one of each."

He nodded. "Signal when you're ready, pal!"

His second in command sprang to his feet and wheeled into action, tapping several shoulders as he sprinted toward the bronze doors.

"Now as for the rest of you, please repair to your flight stations at once and strap in! For purposes of safety, we'll need to conduct this experiment from a much higher orbit. You're dismissed!"

He nodded to them curtly, and then to Elena graciously. Her warm, returning smile sent his heart soaring. As the crew dashed out of the room in excitement, she saluted him with an overly exaggerated snap, a mischievous twinkle in her eye. "C'mon, you," he grinned, teasing. "Double time!" Clapping his hands, he shooed her out of the room. Taking a quick breath, he pivoted on his heel to grab the holograms and beat a hasty retreat down the elevator.

A small chime sounded. Adam glanced up momentarily and went back to his programming. Good. Kron and his men were ready. Locking in a steep climb, he piloted the starship into a higher orbit, then flattened out and circled the planet to the other side.

As they crossed the sharply contrasting day/night boundary in a brilliant flash of light, everyone did a double take. What just happened? Did the shield *disappear*? It took a few moments to figure it out: the surface was so polished that it was now reflecting the black, starry cosmos in a curving mirror image!

Adam slowed the craft, got a fix on his position, and recorded the time precisely. As they stopped, he whispered into the intercom. "Okay. I'm sure you're wondering what's going on. We've diverted their attention to this side of the planet, but I've got a trick up my sleeve: I'm gonna use the old 'shell game.' You know, the one magicians use? We'll disappear with the shields and cloaking device, I'll zip back to the other side of the planet to do some quick experiments, and then come back here. I wanna poke at the shield with some tests. Ready, everyone?"

The crew glanced at each other, questioning. Why was he *whispering*?

As he punched the buttons, the huge starship was blotted from the sky. His urgent answer immediately filtered into their ear inserts. "Yes, I'm whispering. I'm deliberately keeping my voice low because I'm sure we're being watched. Now, these are the facts: One, we just disappeared. Two, they know we're up to something. Three, and most likely, they may retaliate! We're cloaked and shielded, so we have full advantage at the moment. We'll just have to sit here and watch out monitors to see what happens...."

Even as he spoke, the smooth reflection below them started to break up.

Wow," he whispered, "*that* didn't take long; my hunch was right! Take a look at your screens!"

Below them, the tranquil surface was crackling to life! Luminous red veins of electricity bulged upward like huge solar flares, then great arcs of light began to snap toward them! Sure enough, they *had* been watched!

"Ready to roll?" Their instantaneous answer came back cloaked in heavy static, barely audible. "Untold gigawatts of electricity, remember?" he hissed. "Hold on!"

The day/night boundary flashed beneath them once more and in moments they approached their original spot, this time cloaked and totally undetected. As the starship slowed to a stop, he was ready with his preplanned orders, not missing a beat.

"Okay, Kron! First probe! Cloak the metallic one! Ready, *launch*!" he hissed.

The probe shot out of a tube in a long trajectory to the east, invisible to the eye but showing up as a plotted course on everyone's screens. Finally, coming straight down, it hit two thousand miles away.

A bright flash of electrical luminescence erupted from the spot! The angry red surface bulged upward in a towering circular wall, converging on the hapless probe. It disintegrated immediately.

He bent low to the microphone, whispering intently. "Just as I thought. Okay! Second probe! Cloak the ceramic one! This time rotate 180 degrees! Ready, *launch*!"

The dotted line of its plotted trajectory traveled in the opposite direction in a long arc, nosed over, and then hit the shield straight down.

Nothing happened. Absolutely nothing. Not a wrinkle or a bulge, just a neatly punched hole. Completely undetected, the probe continued to streak toward the planet's surface. The edges of the hole started to waver and fill in behind it.

What was happening? They were still getting transmission from the probe through the shrinking opening! The crew leaned toward their monitors to watch the tiny vehicle's drogue chute open, slowing it down into a darkened, nearly featureless atmosphere. Suddenly, they all saw movement! Neon lights? A flash of wings? Puzzled, they squinted intently through the amber mists at a vague, bright fluttering. Suddenly, the steep side of a mountain was directly below them! Gripping the arms of their chairs, they watched the craggy rocks come up. As the last vestiges of the hole in the shield closed, their screens went blank in a buzzing gray static.

Adam's crude, two-step shell game was nearly complete. Swiftly accelerating, he slipped the cloaked, invisible craft back to the dark side of the planet and slowed, triangulating his position and speed carefully.

"Everyone, listen! This is important! We're going to reappear, but we're gonna be a little further ahead of where we were a few minutes ago," he whispered. "It's got to be the *exact* spot and look good on *their* screens. I hope it works. They've gotta think their equipment glitched or something!" He scanned the instruments nervously, fine-tuning his timing. "Okay, steady. We're on track … cloaking device and shields … *off*!" The ship popped back into view, assuming orbit exactly where it should have been. They all held their breaths, their eyes glued to their monitors.

Beneath them the rough, fiery looking surface flickered, smoothed slightly, and then slowly regained its glassy appearance. In moments, it was serene once again.

Cheers resounded all over the ship, sending Adam quickly to his throat mike. "Guys, guys! Cool it!" He grinned. "Ah, nothing happened here, right? At least they've got to *think* so. We're gonna park right here in orbit awhile and figure out this new development. One thing's for certain. There's no way that this ship, with its metal-alloy hull, can penetrate that death trap under us. We gotta find some *other* way to get in. We need to think as a team and put our heads together. We gotta do whatever we need to do to come up with answers or this mission's a bust!"

Like a nervous swarm of army ants, they disbanded from their stations and spread throughout the ship. Some formed loud, fiery brainstorming groups, others ran up to the Dream Library to research, but they all dug deeply for hours. Gradually, group after group, they gravitated back toward the Observatory Room to settle in front of the big screen. The noise level began to rise sharply as they swapped ideas and debated the mysteries of the enigmatic shell beneath them.

Adam walked into the room and stopped short in surprise. "*Well!*" he exclaimed, his finger poised over his wrist programmer. "I guess I don't have to sound the tone for general assembly, do I?"

They glanced over their shoulders at him, grinning uneasily. The absentees arrived in a run, and in minutes the room was packed.

He raised his voice to speak. "Okay. Thoughts ready? Practical ideas now!"

About twenty hands shot up.

"Yes?" he pointed.

Elke stood up nervously. "Ah, how about punching a whole slew of holes in the shield to make a *big* opening!" He held his arms wide. "Then we could dive into the hole at warp speed... or something?"

The crew wouldn't let him finish: a chorus of hoots and jeers brought him down.

"Warp speed?" Adam tried his best to keep a straight face. "What kind of reruns have *you* been watching in the Dream Library? Okay, thanks, Elke. Hey, don't feel intimidated, guys. We're all in this together and need any kind of input we can get." They sat there chagrined and thoughtful. A hand rose.

"Peter? Yes, you. Stand up, please."

He stood slowly. "I don't know," he shrugged. "Maybe a negative static charge around our ship, or something? We know our shields have a positive charge."

Adam nodded. "Hmm, that's better. It sounds good, but we're up against a tremendous amount of electricity here. An unknown factor. We only get *one* chance."

Peter smiled, shrugged, and sat down. Another hand rose tentatively.

"Yes, Elena? I-I noticed your hand was up the first time. Go ahead."

She looked at him in surprise and stood. "Well, I'm just thinking of a way we might be able to, ah, '*see*' through the shield. It's not exactly the same as going *through* it with our bodies or the starship yet; we can figure that out later. It's a way for all of us to virtually go through without exactly ... being there...?"

As her voice trailed off, a perplexed silence fell over the assembly.

"Please explain?" Adam probed gently. "Wait, wait, here's a throat mike."

Her hands trembling, she put it on and turned to face the crew. "Okay, here goes." Putting her hands together, she formed a small O with her fingers. "Suppose, just suppose, we could actually open up a little hole in the shield, a small hole, poking through it with something like a tube over a hundred feet long. If I remember right, the shield's uniformly a bit over 95 feet thick, so anything longer than that should be able to go completely through, right?" She paused to look around. Most were nodding hesitantly.

"Now, this is my idea," she continued, a bit more confidently. "I-I found a huge coil of clear, flexible plastic pipe about five inches in diameter down in the cargo hold. I remembered reading in the manual that the pipe is supposed to be used for siphoning drinking water from lakes into our storage tanks. So this is it." She paused, flattening out her palms and bringing them closer together. "We go down real close to the shield, almost touching it, and poke the plastic pipe through. It *is* nonmetallic, so nothing should happen, right?" She glanced at Adam.

He shrugged and raised his brows expectantly.

Encouraged, she continued. "The next part's a lot more interesting. We get a big funnel, also in the cargo hold, stick it into the end of the pipe and pour a few thousand of our Spyders through it, right into Aurona's atmosphere. I found out that you can program them to go into 'transport' mode, where they tuck in all their legs to protect them. They'll look like marbles. When they hit the air, they'll sense they're flying, open up, and float down to the surface, beaming back what they see through the hole that's been opened." Her hands were very expressive, making funnel shapes, Spyder motions and beams. They understood. Adam understood.

"Finally, we clamp a small, ceramic antigrav ring...."

"Also in the cargo hold?" he interrupted respectfully.

"Yes, I've located all these parts on board," she smiled. "We clamp the ring around the neck of the pipe that's sticking out of the shield, holding it in place and making it float. Finally, we cut the pipe and snake an antenna wire down through it to pick up all the Spyder transmissions. A relay transmitter mounted on the rim of the antigrav ring should amplify the signals and send them back to the ship. Of course, we'd be parked in a wider orbit for ... safety...." She trailed off, realizing there was dead silence in the big, round room.

Everyone, including Adam, was staring at her open-mouthed.

He broke the spell. "*Yes!*" His fist shot into the air. "That's *it*! We'll *do* it!"

The crew leaped to their feet, breaking into spontaneous, noisy applause. He picked his way to her side, beaming proudly. "So tell me, girl, how do you *do* it?"

She was overwhelmed and a bit frightened, but her blue eyes rose to meet his confidently. "I guess I think in pictures," she shrugged. "Then I combine all of my images into an idea."

Bending down, he whispered in her ear. She whispered back her answer, shaking her head. Laughing, he looked up and motioned for silence. "Listen to this, guys: she just informed me she didn't *write* our manual, she merely *memorized* it cover to cover. Hmmm! In any case, Elena, I'm appointing you the project leader of Operation Spyder!" As the crew cheered, he held up his hands for silence. "Think about it! It's only logical to use these robotoids in the very function they were designed for! They *are* photo-yielding devices for extraterrestrial reconnaissance, right? In any case, I think Elena might consent to run through the manual page by page, summing it all up for you."

Laughing along with the crew, Elena seemed more at ease and nodded graciously. "Thanks, guys. Well, I guess it's 'down to business'! As project leader, here are my thoughts: first and foremost, you control your own Spyder's movements. The controls are inside each of your e-helmets. Although your chin pads have joystick capability and can control a few of the simpler movements, your biofeedback gloves are the real stars of the show: they're the vital link, the integral part, real nano-engineering wonders. Once you put them on, they're locked onto you, and only you. Their Bluetooth receptors see and respond to your entire body's movements, then transmit them to your Spyders."

Adam quickly slipped away to sit down on the floor in the front row, deep in thought. When did she have time to read all the manuals, much less memorize them? She was absolutely amazing and a knockout, too! He listened, enraptured. Her expressive hands were busy again, making everything crystal clear.

"This will be an intuitive, easy function to learn. First, your chin pads get things going: you pull down the 'Explore' menu and scan through the images streaming in from many Spyder frequencies. Lock onto a maximum of three that interest you. They'll be displayed in triple split-screen inside your face shields, in living color and real time. Remember, out of the three, you can only control one at a time. That image automatically centers itself, larger than the other two. Then begin your mission. Act out what you want your Spyder do with your arms and body: flee, climb, go closer, grab and pull with its manipulator arms, fly or whatever."

Adam tilted his head, questioning. "Huh? You, um … *act* it out?"

She chuckled. "Yes, when you spread your arms, your biofeedback gloves spread your Spyder's arms. Paddle with your wrists to steer your Spyder in the air. Spread your fingers and your suction pads flare. Kick with your legs in many different ways and your Spyder jumps, runs, or turns, and so on. In theory, we should be able to carry out an entire mini mission from the safety and comfort of our ship!"

As a murmur of amazement shot through the crowd, a hand rose in the back.

"Ah, yes, Dexor?"

The man jumped to his feet. "Can you pick things *up* with the manipulator arms?"

"Of course! Think about VR: this is all old, but new technology, refined and in miniature scale. Get this! With your biofeedback gloves, you can actually feel textures of surfaces and test weights! Whatever you can do with your thumb and four fingers in a mitten position, the Spyder's claws can do. Their manipulator arms are extremely strong and can lift *many* times their own weight!"

Dexor sat down smugly, satisfied with his answer.

She pressed on. "So there you go. It'll be exactly like learning how to ride a bike. It'll take a lot of practice to learn how to maneuver these little guys. I think it would be a good idea for everyone to get used to their own e-helmets, chin pads, and biofeedback gloves and learn to put them through their paces." She spoke with authority, seeming to offer no alternative with the exquisite logic of her reasoning.

Adam stood up, totally mesmerized, edging toward her as she drew to a close. Suddenly her bright smile flashed, dazzling him. Embarrassed, he spun away, pretending to adjust the volume on his throat mike. "Well," he coughed, "y-you've got your orders, guys. Ah, like she says, practice makes perfect. I think the ones who learn the fastest should tutor the slower ones, right?"

A few sharp eyes had caught the subtle exchange. As Kron and Tola raised their brows and elbowed each other, Sahir and Joelle nodded knowingly at each other.

"So it all boils down to this, guys," Adam shrugged. "Everyone's ultimately responsible for his or her own mini mission!"

A wave of laughter and spontaneous applause swept the room. Everyone was genuinely excited about the possibilities of these extraordinary robot-creatures.

He concluded. "The more info we gather, the sooner we crack the mystery of the shield! So let's go! We gotta open the Elenosphere and get this big baby down!"

He turned to playfully salute Elena. As she slyly stole a wink, a lot of sharp eyes in the audience caught the exchange. Adam's ears grew hot, the flames spreading like a crowning forest fire, raising in intensity in direct proportion to the redness of his face. She'd felt it too; the deep, mutual admiration was real, like a meteor falling: the rush, impending, inevitable. Her hand shot up to her mouth. They paused, smiled uncertainly, and parted.

The ensuing hours were filled with surprises and excitement for everyone. The crew soon had Spyders sneaking around on the ceiling and lining up for competitive sports. Jumping contests led the way in popularity, followed by mini-pulling and lifting events. To top it off, no place seemed to be safe from actual spying, by far the robotoids' main talent. Adam had to step in quickly and establish a set of ground rules. The eyes of the Spyders yielded three-dimensional views in full color, from some pretty unique perspectives.

Some people just preferred to sit back and do some serious "people-watching." The sight was hilarious: droves of grasping, thickly-gloved people walking around like puppets, their arms waving, their bodies twisting and oversize helmets bouncing up and down on their heads. Focusing intently on their Spyder's viewpoints inside their private video chambers, they groped awkwardly along the walls, doing their best to keep up with their scurrying squadrons. Collisions were inevitable, so it didn't take long to figure it out. Just park in place, kick around and grab at the air, and let the Spyder do all the moving.

Soon, forming long Spyder trains, they had the robotoids digging in with their suction feet to pull some surprisingly heavy objects. Others had them flying down airshafts in star-shaped formations like mini skydivers, their suction feet glued together. There seemed to be no limit to what they could do.

Adam suddenly spotted an entire pie sneaking by with several Spyder legs sticking out under it. He dropped to his hands and knees and crawled after it quickly, following it to a corner. As a hand reached out, he grabbed a chubby wrist.

"*What* the…?" A muffled voice sounded hollowly from beneath an e-helmet.

He peered around the corner. "Tola! *You?*" He grinned.

"Ah, ah, we'll put it back, sir. We-we were just seeing if our team could…."

"*We?* Our?"

Red faced, the round man slipped his helmet off. "Yeah: Jon, Todd, and me. They're waiting down in their room for their share."

He laughed heartily. "Enough, enough! I think everyone's got the hang of this thing, don't you?" He turned on his throat mike and gave the order through everyone's ear inserts. "All Spyders to Alpha Quarantine Room on the double, and I mean *all*! And yes, there *is* a numerical list! You'll have to sign off on your individual Spyder frequencies as you return them to the Quarantine's prep area!"

He sent out a search signal and called in the stragglers. They shuffled in dejectedly: in a surprisingly short time, their Spyders had become a virtual part of their own bodies! Reluctantly, they held out their personal robotoids, surrendering their alter egos.

Soon, except for a few squashed specimens, they were all back, cleaned and prepped for their trip through the shield. Like a guarantee, even if this big group of Spyders was lost, there were thousands more in storage for another attempt.

It was time. The cloaked starship eased out of orbit, gliding down like a silent ghost toward the burnished shield. As the excited crew manned their stations, Adam piloted the craft with true expertise, honed from his years as a test pilot for IFA. They were soon hovering a few scary feet above their reflection on a seemingly endless golden plain. Elena and a small group had suited up in the hold near the big water siphon reel to guide the plastic pipe. As it snaked out and tentatively touched the surface, they held a collective breath.

There was no response, just as the ceramic probe had shown them! It unreeled, penetrating the shield, with Elena carefully measuring out the length. Knowing there were two more reels in storage as backups, she motioned for the men to spool out an extra twenty feet for good measure. Moving carefully, she clamped the ceramic antigrav ring and solar-powered transmitter onto the neck and adjusted the whole assembly for neutral buoyancy. Satisfied, the men cut the pipe and snaked in a long, thin antenna wire.

Taking a nervous breath, she dropped a single Spyder down the tube and waited. It soon poked its holo-eye out of the open end and beamed back a breathtaking, dark panorama into her helmet. She gasped, cleared the view, and nodded affirmatively. They unceremoniously dumped the hoard of balled-up Spyders into the funnel. They rolled down the long pipe in 'transport' mode, looking like black marbles.

Adam piloted the starship far above the surface, the cobbled-together assembly hovering steadily in place, the small transmitter flashing and the antenna wire bumping softly inside the rubbery pipe. The tiny ring was soon out of sight. As he established a higher geostationary orbit, the crew waited patiently in their seats, whispering excitedly.

"It won't be long now," someone breathed.

Chapter 12: **THE KEY**

Shadowy, moving images suddenly burst into view on everyone's face shield. They were falling!

As a breathtaking 3D panorama swung up into view, Adam gripped the arms of his commander's chair, visually overwhelmed. Trailing far above him like a long smudge of inky vapor, the sky was seeded with nearly two thousand tumbling black specks. He spread out his suction cups to slow down. As a few other Spyders tumbled past his face shield, some looked like empty pinwheels, but others were definitely manned and moving about on their own. He flipped his robotoid's body over to look downward.

He let out a gasp. Through a break in the glittering amber mist, he spotted the shore of a great lake coming up swiftly below him. Nervously, he checked the direction of the wind, studying the ripples on the surface. "Good," he intoned, "I might make it. The breeze is blowing toward the land." He exhaled slowly, deftly steering his robotoid with his gloved fingertips. "Now for two more backups … just in case." Scanning quickly, he locked onto some unmanned Spyder frequencies and threw them up in split-screen on his left and right. The big gold shield overhead was dramatically darkening the landscape; clicking on ENHANCE mode, he brightened the images as much as possible.

Suddenly, out of the corner of his eye, he caught a glimpse of slender, snapping beaks diving at him! "What?" Alarmed, he sat bolt upright in his chair. "Beaks? Where'd *they* come from?" Immediately, in a shower of flying body parts, his Spyder was crunched out of commission. "Oh no, number one's down *already*?" The screen instantly autocentered on number two, while number three's scene spun along in a small rectangle off to the side. He scanned the horizon warily. Wait, there they were again! The distant sky was filled with strange, flying silhouettes! Out of nowhere, there was a brilliant flash of phosphorescent color, then without warning, a gaping beak engulfed his tumbling number two! "Come on," he wailed, "gimme a break! Not already!"

All around his station he could hear whirrs, clicks, and muffled shouts echoing his own private drama. His mini mission was turning into a robo-massacre! There were no options left, unless…. Wait! He pulled down a menu to enable one last evasive tactic. Tapping out the code, he squirted a purple cloud of noxious odor out of his stink-jets. In a flash of light, the glittering sky immediately swirled back into view. The winged creature had spit him *out*! He was tumbling through the air, free again! Spreading his gloved fingers and twisting his wrists, he carefully ruddered his robotiod's suction feet to angle the body around and catch a glimpse of his attacker.

"Wow!" he gasped. Like a bright, glowing meteor, a birdlike form was diving toward him, his incredibly long pennant wings folded tightly against its body. "What? That-that thing *can't* be lit up!!" He looked again. The creature was indeed awash with a brilliant, multicolored luminescence, its incredible body smearing a watercolored streak of phosphorescence against the dark, glittering dome of the sky. As he desperately tried to think, the gap was closed. "Oh, no-o-o-o!!" He grimaced and hunched his shoulders, anticipating the worst. After a moment of silence, he dared to open his eyes a slit.

The fantastic creature was hovering in front of him, descending in slow motion! Eye to eye, inches away, the spectacular apparition was studying Adam's *Spyder* body in bewilderment. Equally baffled, Adam stared back through his face shield.

"Holy Pokemon!" he whispered excitedly under his breath. "What *are* you? How can you *be*? H-how do your feathers light up?"

His questions went unanswered. Rapidly closing in from both sides, long streamers of neon color streaked in for the kill! He clicked madly in a flurry of evasive tactics, his face shield turning into a flashing, roiling rectangle of glowing abstract shapes. Suddenly, with an electrical zap and spark of light, number two was dismembered in a fluorescent feeding frenzy. Only one Spyder now! He let out a wail of disappointment and cleared his face shield to look around at the crew.

They were all kicking out wildly with their feet, grunting, ducking their heads and snapping at the air with their gloves. He shouted words of encouragement into their earbuds. "Use your *stink gas*, guys! They don't *like* it! It's bad news!" As a chorus of muffled affirmative grunts answered him, he flipped back excitedly to his last scene.

Suddenly, the air around him was dyed with a crazy, swirling, purplish hue! Good! The entire Spyder crew was squirting their stink clouds into the blur of wings! Almost on signal, the flock stopped their attack and wheeled away. As they spit out the last of the distasteful bugs, the dark cloud of Spyders tumbled madly in the turbulent wake of a thousand pennant wings.

Stabilizing with his mini gyro, he caught another glimpse of the lake below. "Flip over, guys, flip over and watch the ground!" he shouted into his throat mike. "Watch your trajectory! Flare your suction pads out just before you hit, and then dive for cover! Climb anything that doesn't move! If it moves, just hold on tight!" As he blinked, a sudden tangle of greenery swept up in front of him.

"Whoa!" He flipped, flared, and landed gracefully in front of ... a big *snout*! His eyes widened. The snout quivered in anticipation, paused, then descended. "Crud! Not again!" he squeaked. "Gimme a break! No, wait...." He tapped his chin, let out a short stink blast, then peered through the purple cloud.

The snout jerked away in horror, recoiling tightly into a loop under a billowy, fragile body. Surrounding his Spyder, more of the same pale creatures were eyeing him suspiciously. Edging away, they let go of their branches and began to float upwards.

"What in the world? Where did I *land*?" Reaching down with his fingertips, he unlocked his chair's restraining latches to swivel around and take in a sweeping view of his virtual panorama. The purplish haze from his stink cloud was rapidly dispersing in a puff of wind. "Wow! It looks like I'm near the top of a tree," he whispered, "surrounded by ... surrounded by *gas bag* creatures?"

He studied them closely. Through their milky, transparent skins, he could see rather smallish hearts beating rapidly in fear, with a network of bluish veins pulsing around the skin of their taut, distended bubbles. "Timid," he mused. "Probably harmless vegetarians, with an occasional bug or two for protein." He lifted a manipulator arm above his head in defense and snapped its mandible loudly. That was it. They'd seen enough. Wheeling, they pulsed away in rapid bursts, twin-tubed orifices puffing underneath their bodies.

"*Hey*," he yelled into his mike, "they're all *leaving*! I-I've got some kind of air-squids up here!"

"I see them *too*, sir!"

He jumped at the proximity of the loud voice, his heart in his mouth.

"I'm right behind you," the voice chuckled. "No, wait. Let me amend that. I-I should say the smaller part of me has landed on a big leaf, sir! Where's your alter ego?"

"Near the top of a tree," Adam gasped. "Is-is that you, Tola?"

"Yes, sir," the familiar, liquid voice filtered back. "My husky little body's parked right behind you, remember? From my Spydey-hero's perspective, your air-squids look like clouds up there! Hey, look! They're starting to, what…? Coalesce? They look like separate bubbles zipping together with Velcro!"

Adam scampered to the tip of a nearby leaf and angled his Spyder eye around excitedly.

"You're right! He answered excitedly. "They're joining together into huge rafts up there!" His jaw dropped in amazement. With their larger surface area, the cloud of white bubbles began to gather speed in the wind and recede swiftly into the distance. "Wow, look at those little suckers *go*, Tola! The bigger the area they form, the faster they move!"

"Sailing on the wind!" the voice quipped, poetically.

"Huh? Whazzat?"

"Like Clipper Ships, sir." Tola paused, contemplated, and then offered a suggestion. "H-how about this? Why don't we just call them … Aeronautas?"

Adam cleared his shield and turned around. The little man's round form fit his mellow voice perfectly, just like the newly coined name. "You got it, man! Sailing on the wind? I *like* it! Aeronautas they are!!"

"Ah, wait a sec, sir…." Muffled under his helmet, Tola's voice suddenly took on an urgent tone. "There seems to be an injured, um, Aeronauta toward the top of the tree. Could he be closer to you? I'm looking at the side of the tree that's toward the lake."

"Toward the lake?" Adam restored his screen and angled around on his Spyder legs, surveying the jungle of leaves beneath him. "Yes! I see the lake! We must have landed in the same tree!" He held out one leg, testing, spreading its suction pad. There was a slight updraft, not much of a wind, but in his favor. "Thanks, Tola! Sorry, but I gotta fly!"

"Huh?" the voice came back. "You don't mean…."

"Yup!" His suction cups spread wide, he hopped far out into the air and soared upward. Suddenly, he saw it: a whitish shape, hanging limply from a branch far above him, fluttering in the breeze like an empty plastic shopping bag. "There he *is*, Tola!" Maneuvering his suction pads expertly, he landed quietly and peered over the edge of a leaf at the forlorn creature. No doubt about it, he was caught. Protruding from the shadows, a huge, sharp pinscher was latched onto him! The Aeronauta was rolling his bright peacock eyes around in helpless terror, his empty, wrinkled gasbag looking especially pale. He'd evidently given up his long struggle and was now hanging exhausted, breathing in shallow puffs and anticipating his demise.

A plan formulated quickly in Adam's mind. "I've *got* it!" he breathed.

"What, sir?"

"Ah, I'll fill you in in a minute, Tola. Gotta move! My Gas Guy is about to be dinner for Mystery Claw!"

"Huh?"

There was no time to lose. Brazenly, he hopped right onto the Aeronauta and hunkered down between his eyes. As he latched tightly with his suction feet, the startled Aeronauta began to thrash his body around, coiling and uncoiling his snout in panic.

"Good," he breathed. "Now try *this* on for size!" He wriggled his Spyder body as hard as he could, nipping the skin painfully with his manipulator pinschers. As his gloved fingers closed, he could feel the texture and resistance of the creature's elastic skin with the biofeedback sensors. "Wow!" he gushed. "This is way, *way* beyond amazing!"

Terrified, the Aeronauta flew into a frenzy and struggled frantically, swelling his bag-body with gas. "Excellent! Come on, fight baby, *fight*!" As the bubble started to lift them, he caught a movement in the shadows. He looked up with a start. "Yikes!" In front of him, two enormous eyes were focusing on his Spyder body! A great, parrotlike mouth was opening as Mystery Claw drew him closer. Wasting no time, he aimed carefully and emptied the last of his stink tank. "Take that, and that, and *that*!"

With an audible snap of rubbery skin, they were free! As they tumbled away, somewhere out there he thought he heard a faint shriek! His eyes widened. "What in the world?" he whispered. "Sound? I-I can *hear*?" Excitedly, he fiddled with his chin pad controls and threw up a series of menus. On the third pass, he spotted AUDIO. "Hmm, I must've accidentally whacked this button...." Impulsively, he turned up the volume.

Sound! Incredible, living, three-dimensional stereoscopic *sound* greeted his ears! Right beneath him he could hear a frantic puffing, and over his head, the wind whistled by as they rose over the tree. Turning his head, he listened in different directions. A squealing cloud of Aeronautas appeared, dispersing to feed on top of the tree. Their soft pulsing sounded like motorboats.

"Excuse me." An urgent nudge, then an insistent tapping on his shoulder brought him quickly back to reality, back to his chair and back to the ship.

"Yes, *yes*! What in *blazes*?" He locked his Spyder in a holding pattern and cleared his screen. Elena was standing there with a small group of men. His face reddened. Everyone seemed to be carrying something and they seemed excited. He shrugged apologetically. "I-I was, ah, *busy*. You see, there was this...."

Kron shoved a handful of sleek boxes toward him. "Recorders, sir!" he interrupted. "We've got holographic quantum-disc *sound* recorders!"

Adam took one, turning it over in his hand. "Wow! There seems to be a whole bunch of equipment that wasn't mentioned on my holodiscs!" A single-pronged mini coax plug protruded from the center of its slightly concave side. "So were does it *go*?"

"It just snaps onto the left side of your face shield, sir." he boomed excitedly. "There's a small shielded jack on both sides. Feel them? The recorder snaps into the left one as you're looking out."

Adam fumbled around awkwardly with his gloved hands, trying to plug it in.

"That's it, sir, stage left. We don't know what the right-hand jack is for yet."

He still had trouble finding the hole, fumbling with the tiny recorder.

"Let me help you, sir," a softer voice intervened, and a pair of gentle hands slipped over his. He let go of the recorder quickly, his pulse racing. Elena plugged it in.

"How...?" he began, and then swallowed hard as she interrupted.

"This is the P-Y part of the word Spyder, sir. Photo-Yielding?"

He smiled, gawking at her face through his face shield. She seemed like an excited child with a new toy. Yes, she had a recorder on, too. The smooth, sculpted shape looked like a small bump fitting snugly to the edge of her curving face shield.

She bent closer, one hand pointing through his face shield, the other resting on his arm. "And see that thin, black rubber bar running up the inside left of your helmet? It's not just a decoration."

He nodded mutely. Her red-hot hands were burning through the thin, slate blue fabric of his uniform.

"The bar activates the recorder and then it's pretty easy to use voice commands or tap out chin codes. You can take unlimited still shots in 3D and beam them back to the ship's mainframe. From there, you can direct your shots up to the holosphere for some really big three-dimensional panoramas!"

He stared at her, speechless. She blushed inside her helmet and then held up a big black holocamera. "Remember this, sir? The sphere that floats in the air?"

"Yes," he gulped, "I remember ... floating in the air...."

She reddened and giggled, taking his hand. "You can also plug your still recorder onto this thing! The prong goes into this shallow depression on top! See? Together, they make an assembly! A unit! The holocamera and recorder act as transmitters up in the Holosphere! What do you think?"

He couldn't think, couldn't breathe, couldn't look up, couldn't focus on anything except her hands. He was her pawn and is heart was pounding helplessly.

"Yeah...," he squeaked, limply.

"Sir?"

"*You'rerightitsgreatequipmentElena*!" he blurted.

Stifling his smile, Kron caught the other men's eyes, then motioned with a slight toss of his head toward the door. As they left discreetly, Tola sat down and quickly yanked his e-helmet back over his head.

Elena looked up with a start. "Oh, should I...?"

He turned to her in a rush. "No! No! Don't go!"

Her eyes widened. "Sir?"

His heart was thudding. He glanced over his shoulder at Tola. The round man was back in action, snapping at the air, his helmet bobbing. "Ah, sit right there that seat next to me, where you belong!" he whispered. "And-and I-I ... my name is Adam, Elena! Adam! I've mentioned this to Kron and he agrees. He thinks it's a great idea!"

"He agrees I should call you by your name?" she teased.

"*No*!" he caught himself, then softened his tone. "I mean, no. About your new position, I mean! Kron's my left hand and now you're, ah, to be my right. I-I *need* you!" His face burned. "Up here, I mean," he concluded, lamely gesturing at her seat.

"I-I don't know what to *say*, sir. I mean Adam!... Adam. Sorry."

"Please, sit!" He smiled warmly, gesturing awkwardly. "This is your commander speaking!" She brushed off the empty chair and snuggled in, adjusting the contour controls. He turned to face her. "Now I just have to know something, Elena. H-how'd you find all these 3D recorders?"

She grew contemplative, then let out a short sigh and turned to him. "I'm...I'm afraid of heights," she confessed, lowering her eyes. "I just *had* to turn off my face shield when we started to fall inside those Spyder bodies! It-it was like a roller coaster!" She shuddered, her hands waving emphatically. "No stomach, nohow, no way, no siree! I just sat quietly in my seat for a while with all that thrashing and shouting around me, and then got to thinking about the photo-yielding part."

He prompted her. "Yes, the P-Y part. So?"

"So," she grinned, picking up his cue, "I scanned through the Spyder manual in my mind, knowing I'd missed something. Honestly, I didn't remember reading a thing about still photos, and really didn't have a clue as to how they fit in."

"So?"

"So I-I went down into the warehouse, *snooping*! Did you know that everything down there is arranged alphabetically? Under R, I found a huge case of these recorders! There was a page to the manual, an addendum, stapled on top of the box! How was I to know? It contained all the information we needed to run these holo-recorders! Oh, and they described a new, enhanced *audio* part, too. None of us knew!"

"So?" His hands made a quick motion for her to continue.

"So I, ah, hurried," she laughed. "I really ran! I figured I had to bring the recorders up here fast. Everyone needed them to...keep a valuable...."

"To keep a valuable photo record of the mission as well," Adam concluded, his voice speaking the words as her lips formed the syllables. He paused, staring intently into her eyes. Incredible. This excited, exciting woman with a childlike innocence was always thinking about the good of all, the success of the mission. Thinking? No, she actually *did* something about it! She *acted*! Yes, she *was* a leader. His decision was firm.

"There's *no way*!" he blurted, shaking out of reverie.

She looked up, surprised. "What's that, Adam?"

"There's no way this mission can fail now! We've got the brains. You and me."

"I'll try to be a good second mate, Captain," she flirted.

He raised his brows. "Okay, we'll see about *that* right now! Let's go back to Exhibit A! Your first assignment, Number Two, is to put your e-helmet and bio-gloves back on and *help* me! I-I was left high and dry, literally up in the air riding around on top of this squiddy thing. Tola called it an Aeronauta! Right, Tola?" He turned around.

No answer. Tola was hopping for his Spyder's life, his audiodomes blaring, knees jerking, fingers snapping and chin bobbing madly. Judging from the sound of it, there was a major battle blasting inside his helmet. He definitely wasn't with them.

Elena laughed. "Great! He just got a recorder from Kron! Looks exciting, too!"

"Man! Look at those chubby feet go! If he doesn't slow down pretty soon, he's gonna pass out!"

As he turned to resume his own battle, he felt another round of insistent tapping on his shoulder. He looked up, fighting annoyance. It felt urgent. "Yes?" He cleared his screen.

"What *is* this room, anyway? Crossroads at Titan Moonbase?"

One of the nurses stood there, looking stern. "I'm sorry, sir. You mentioned something about passing out, sir?"

"I *did*?" He softened his tone. "Yes, I did. Go on...?"

"We have *five* in sick bay right now, sir!" She was doing her level best to focus her attention straight ahead, somewhere on the far wall.

An eyebrow went up. "Five?"

"Two women and, ah, three *men*, sir," she smirked.

Elena snorted. The nurse's hand shot to her mouth. She composed herself and then continued with a straight face. "Motion sickness mostly, sir, except for one! How can I say this? He, ah, fell off his chair and broke his wrist."

"Broke his... well!" Adam exclaimed. "Looks like this mission is a bit more, um, dangerous than we thought! Please make your rounds and see that everyone's securely strapped in. Jenny, is it?" he offered politely.

"Yes, sir. Jenny. Thank you, sir! You remembered my name! Thank you!" She let out a snark and scooted out of the door, her hand clamped tightly over her mouth.

Elena glanced at him, her nose quivering. "Dangerous?"

"Dangerous," he affirmed, nodding. With a slight tic, the corner of his mouth gave him away. Throwing up his hands, he let out a belly laugh inside his helmet.

She leaned toward him. "Stop! Stop! You'll fog up your Spyder scene! We gotta get moving!"

"You're right," he nodded, slipping on his gloves. "I'm glad you brought all your equipment up here with you. See if you can lock onto a few unmanned Spyder frequencies and let's get going!"

As he cranked up his audio once more, a loud chorus of squeals and grunts greeted his ears. He flipped on the view. There had been a growing circle of intensely curious Aeronautas packing in tightly around him, peering closely at his alien form. His Spyder body hadn't moved for a long time and their snouts were nervously twining with each other for moral support. He had the chance now and studied them right up close. Tiny, vestigial, hooked legs protruded from their sides. The tips of the fingers seemed fleshy and blunt, most likely to keep them from tearing into each other's fragile bag-bodies.

"Aha! So *that's* how they link together," he mumbled. "Little Velcro zippers! Tola was right!"

"Hmm?" Elena looked up momentarily and quickly went back to scanning.

He thought a moment. So the finger-links *were* important, playing a vital role in their survival and social life. Social life? Yes, they were definitely talking about him right now, and having quite a lively conversation at that! His own transparent mount was holding tightly onto a branch with its snout, squealing with a rising and falling pitch and his companions were answering in short, clipped, piglike grunts. Their enormous, jeweled eyes were really expressive, a peacock's iridescent rainbow of blues, greens, and purples. A large cranial swelling hinted at real intelligence. Suddenly, somewhere below them, there was a loud exclamation. Their jeweled eyes rolled around, looking at each other.

"Squeee! Pop-pop-pop. Squeee!" One of them was alarmed, backing away from an odd shadow on the bottom of a sunlit leaf! They unlinked their fingers and wheeled away, descending rapidly and letting out volumes of their mysterious lighter-than-air gas with a loud hiss. His

Aeronauta found himself suddenly alone, then squealed and dove after his companions. As they drew closer, he recognized a familiar silhouette.

"Hey! I see another Spyder!" he exclaimed.

"Of course," Elena answered, right at his elbow. "They're peppered all over the place! Wait! Wow! Over *there*! Quick!"

"Tell me what you're looking at. Where are you?"

"I'm on a tall blade of grass! I can see something chasing a herd of weird animals of some sort, Adam! It-it has stripes…. Wait! I think it's our monster!"

"Can you get pictures?"

"Nope, too far! No telephoto! Too bad we couldn't have stuffed a couple of our big spheres down the pipe!"

"Maybe a panorama?" he interrupted. "We could blow up the shot."

"Too late, they're all gone, Adam. There's nothing again."

"So switch bugs! Grab another frequency!"

She tapped madly. "Okay, I'm inside another Spyder. Hey, wow! Adam!"

"What?"

"There are three or four empty ones near me!"

"*Empty*?" He chuckled. "What do you mean?"

"Well, nobody's moved into them yet! They must've all floated down with their suction feet stuck together!" She started bouncing up and down in her chair. "Hey, switch out of yours and get one! They're just *sitting* here…."

"Okay, I'm scanning. Nope! Nope!"

Suddenly she inhaled sharply. "Adam! There's something moving in the field!"

He shook his head in frustration. "This is harder than I thought, Elena! Way too many frequencies! I'm getting nowhere! Hold on! I just got an idea!"

"Make it fast, because it's coming this way! I think it sees me!"

"Listen, Elena. Could you turn over the, ah, empty Spyder nearest to you and read me the transmission code on the bottom?"

"Got it!" Her gloved hands grasped in the air, manipulating her Spyder arms. "Oof! This thing's heavier than I thought! Wait, here it is! Trans Code: 9330."

"Okay, got it!" he shouted, "Here goes!"

He took in a sharp breath as an unforgettable scene unfolded before him. Standing there was a two-legged creature! A-a man? It sure looked like one, but what an enormous head! A pair of long, graceful fingers suddenly reached out and plucked one of the empty Spyders off the bark of the tree next to them.

"*Wow*! Who or what is *that*?" Elena whispered. "What do you think?"

"Why are you whispering?" he hissed. "He can't hear you!" As he found himself whispering, he reddened and shut up nervously. Unexpectedly, the scene in his face shield shifted and bounced up and down in a blur. "W-what's he doing?" He gulped, gripping the arms of his chair.

"He's picking you *up*! He's *collecting* you like-like a specimen, or a bug!"

The humanoid delicately flexed one of his manipulator arms. Adam didn't dare move his Spyder body and held its legs out stiffly, feigning death. As the agile fingertips pried open a tiny mandible, he reacted with a start. One of his gloved hands gaped open! The biofeedback coming through was amazingly strong! Suddenly thinking better of his tactics, he came to life and hunkered down, holding on tightly to the branch. Startled, the humanoid's thin fingers slipped under his hard body and lifted, pulling gently and testing the suction pads to their limit. Finally, with a string of tiny staccato pops, they let go.

"Oh, *no*!" he yelled, flailing wildly with his Spyder arms.

The fingers placed him onto a broad palm and carried him up through the air to a smooth face. As a pair of amazingly dark, intelligent eyes began to scan him, the back of his skull suddenly felt weird and tingly!

"Elena," he gasped. "There's this… *pressure*! A-a probing inside my brain!"

"Huh? What do you mean?"

"It's a pushing, driving force inside my head. It-it doesn't *hurt*, exactly, but I think I kind of hear something! It's really faint, though…."

"Can you make it out?"

"No, it sounds like gibberish. Huh? Now he's bowing his head to me! Nodding, sort of. Wait a sec, lemme try something different…."

He awakened his Spyder from its resting position. Rising slowly on the humanoid's smooth palm, he tipped his whole body forward in response. Tentatively, a slender finger reached out and dipped up and down. Adam raised a manipulator arm and dipped it in response. The enormous, dark eyes widened with a startled look.

"I think I'm, ah, '*talking*' to him," he whispered. "In-in body language!"

"Adam, I'm coming down! I want to *be* there!"

"Well come on, then!" He angled his Spyder body around to see hers and then waved a manipulator arm in the air. The big eyes darted quickly in the direction he was pointing and immediately spotted Elena.

"He *sees* me!" she squeaked, her heart hammering.

"Well, c'mon," he beckoned, "I don't think he'll hurt you!" He was surprised to find himself manipulating his Spyder naturally, like it was his own body. The big eyes looked back and forth, fascinated, putting the relationship together. Adam hammed it up. Tipping up onto six of his eight legs, he stood as high as he could. Folding one manipulator arm on his hip, he waved her down with the other. The dark eyes crinkled and shot back up to her.

"Adam!" She giggled. "You're crazy! This is no time to fool around!" She'd caught on, though, and made a rejecting motion with both manipulator arms, as if she were waving him away. The eyes snapped back to Adam expectantly.

He jumped up and down and pouted, crossing his arms.

The creature exploded into gales of laughter! Jouncing around, Adam gripped the palm tightly with his suction pads. Well, *that* was certainly communication!

The humanoid suddenly turned and beckoned to Elena, his long finger curling and pointing to a spot on his palm next to Adam. The eyes were crinkled in a smile. He tapped on the spot again, impatiently.

"*Go* for it, kid!" Adam whispered.

"All right, all right! Lemme figure this thing out…. Okay. Got it."

She jumped into the air, twirled like a ballerina, then flipped over in a triple somersault and landed with a flourish. The creature jerked his finger away, stunned.

"All *right*!" Adam shouted, raising his manipulator arm. "Gimme five!" They slapped manipulator palms and turned to the creature, bowing grandly.

It was too much. His thin sides were now heaving in spasms of laughter. After a moment, he collected himself. The surprise on his face had turned into respectful admiration. He pointed at them urgently and then to the sky, looking up.

"What does he *mean*, Adam?" she whispered.

"Truthfully? I-I'm pretty sure he's asking if we come from the starship. He knows, Elena, he *knows*! His kind probably put the shield up!"

The humanoid emphatically repeated his pointing action, speaking with unmistakably clear body language now. He lowered his hand to his side with finality, awaiting their answer.

"W-what should we *do*?" Her voice was quavering.

"Okay, Number Two! Just watch and do what I do. Ready?"

"I-I'm afraid, but okay."

First Adam, then Elena, pointed to the sky with their manipulator arms, then nodded their whole bodies up and down. The creature's eyes widened. They did it once more, confirming their whereabouts. It was done. They held their breaths.

A flash beneath them caught Adam's holo-eye. What was *that*? He angled his Spyder body to look over the edge of the palm. Gleaming in a wide border all along the rim of the humanoid's robe were heavily embossed symbols of *gold*!

He drew in his breath sharply. "Runes?" He coughed. "Yes! I-I see *runes*!"

Elena angled her Spyder around. "Where, where? Can you read them?"

Suddenly, his vision clouded as the pressure in his head returned with a blast of intensity…. *Telepathy*? No doubt about it, he was being *scanned*! He rubbed the back of his neck in pain. "*Yow-w-wch*! This guy's mind is *powerful*, Elena! I'm sure he wants to know our intentions, but…. Wait. I think I just figured out a way to, ah, talk to him, but–but I'm stumped! I don't know what to *say*! Isn't that stupid?"

She thought quickly. "Adam, this may sound odd, but a short phrase can be really powerful. How about, 'We come as friends'?"

"Perfect!" he blurted. "You're a genius! I'll *do* it!" Closing his eyes, he translated the phrase into runes and then concentrated deeply on the symbols.

"We come as friends." The shapes of the runes seemed to stand up in a row in his mind, blazing as if they were on fire. Suddenly they dissipated as another, simpler runic word formed in their place. His eyes widened.

"Welcome," it translated, simply.

He let out a whoop. "*Bingo*!" he shouted. "We're *in*!"

Their playful games and offbeat sense of humor hadn't been wasted on this intelligent creature. All of it had been deeply appreciated. He gazed up into the smooth face and bowed his Spyder body diplomatically. The creature bowed back, a slender palm slowly closed over them and all went black.

Slowly, almost immeasurably at first and then with gathering speed, the skies began to lighten. Suddenly, in a blinding flash, it was broad daylight! The entire crew stopped in mid-Spyder action, breaking into wild cheers.

Adam stripped off his gear and breathed a deep sigh of relief. He turned to face Elena. She blinked back at him, her eyes glistening.

"It was so easy," she whispered.

"Thanks for the show, kid," he said, grinning. "Wow! What was that amazing Flying Spydette number? Where'd you pick *that* up? The swirls! The swoops! The flourish! I'm impressed!"

"You're not so bad yourself," she laughed, drying her eyes. "Adam? The creature couldn't help it … laughing at us, I mean?"

"Well, that's what we *wanted* him to do, right? The whole thing just, ah, happened! Improv! We were in the moment! We *winged* it!"

A round of applause erupted from the open doorway. As a group of women descended upon Elena in a pack, all teary-eyed and squealing, Kron and several men pushed by them and grabbed Adam, thumping him roughly on the back.

"Boy, that was the weirdest thing I ever experienced!" Tola whooped, pulling off his e-helmet.

Still more people spilled into the room, all in high spirits. "It's *down*! The shield's down, guys! C'mon, let's go see!"

Kron winked at the pair. "Can you *believe* it? There's already an impromptu party forming in the Observatory Room, sir. Everybody's running up there to look at the surface of the planet! It's amazingly beautiful!"

"So let's go up and talk later," Adam interrupted, grinning. "C'mon!"

As they blended smoothly into the throng running down the corridor, he suddenly grabbed Kron and Elena by their utility belts and pulled them aside into his private elevator. They bumped in after him, puzzled. The door slid shut.

"What?" he asked innocently, looking back and forth.

"Ah... *this*?" she pointed to the elevator. Kron nodded.

He straightened his back and stuck out his chest. "This is a bronze elevator," he puffed, "and it's reserved for my commanding officers. Plural. Officers-s-s, get it? You two and myself are they ... them! Whatever! We're it!" He gave them a lopsided salute.

Ever so solemnly, Kron turned to Elena, his eyes darting nervously at their leader. "Is he *always* like this?" he whispered gently.

"Love dust," she confirmed, flatly.

Stifling a smile, Kron drew back, feigning alarm. "Is it contagious?"

"In small doses."

"No kidding! What about larger ones?"

She wrinkled her nose distastefully. "Then it's *really* sickening!"

Adam hammed it up, staggering and grasping weakly for the bronze railing.

"Wow, he must really have it bad!!" Kron chuckled.

"I do! I *do*!" Adam interrupted, a dazed, starry look in his eyes.

"Poor Captain," she lulled, mopping his brow. "You'll get over...."

The elevator door opened silently. Somehow, they sensed they were no longer alone. They turned their heads as one. No one moved, no one breathed. About fifty startled eyes were staring at them. Adam let go of the railing and stood up straight. The three leaned against each other for moral support.

Elena thought quickly. "Um, he had ... motion sickness," she fibbed.

Kron caught on. "Yeah, motion sickness. First the Spyders, now the elevator," he expounded. "You know, up, down. It happens every time." He glanced at Adam out of the corner of his eye, nudging him discreetly for some kind of response.

Adam went with the moment and raised a shaking hand. "I-I'm okay," he reassured. "Just a little...," he puffed out his cheeks, "*q-queasy*!"

The group backed away. After a moment of uncertainty, Joelle found her tongue. "Congratulations?" she offered weakly.

Hesitant grins, then broad smiles broke through all around. Adam took a deep breath and stepped triumphantly from the elevator on the arms of his two new best friends. A wide, cheering path opened in front of them all the way to the big screen in the Observatory Room. They turned, silhouetted in front of the spectacular planet, acknowledging the thunderous ovation.

Aurona filled the view in pristine, untouched beauty. Under a gossamer, gold-spangled veil of mist, rainforest encircled the equator in a wide belt, thickly blanketing all the continents. Far to the north and south, narrow ribbons of deciduous and coniferous forests leveled out to tundra, then to small polar caps. The planet looked warm. Its vast oceans were dotted with thousands of tropical islands that gleamed brightly with Earthlike rings of coral. Deep blue clearwater lakes lay at the foot of spectacular, white-capped mountain ranges and everywhere, mighty rivers were cutting their way to the sea. They became lost in the tremendous scale of the planet.

Tola edged up to the screen, studying it intently. "I-I don't see a single sign of *civilization*, sir!" he whispered. "Just wilderness. Beautiful, unspoiled *wilderness*!"

Adam shrugged. "I don't know what to say, Tola, but I'm afraid the odds are that some of us are going to get hurt down there in that wilderness, perhaps even killed." As Elena pressed to his side, he slipped her gently under his arm.

She sighed. "No matter what," she whispered, "I'm with you all the way."

Book Two:
THE PLANET

Chapter 13: KIDNAPPED

"We're down to fifteen hundred feet, sir."

"Let's *do* it."

"Are you absolutely sure?"

"Positively."

"But, sir...."

"It'll fit, Kron! Trust me!" Adam walked slowly around the huge floor-to-ceiling hologram being projected in the center of the room, then paused on the other side to check out a skeletal-looking schematic on a nearby monitor.

Dwarfing the starship, a colossal column of green loomed far over them, the top lost in clouds of amber mist. Of gargantuan proportions and an unthinkable age, it was to all appearances a single, living structure. Riveted to their individual monitors at their flight stations, the entire crew gawked in silence at the mysterious wall.

Kron shook his head in disbelief at the schematic's scale markers. "What could this thing be, sir?" He turned around and dropped to one knee, peering under the edge of the sharply detailed holographic image. "It sure looks like a tree, but...."

"But a tree couldn't possibly grow this big, right?" Adam interrupted. He nudged the controls. "Let's look a bit closer."

As the craft touched the tree, there was a sudden, unexpected flurry of activity near the center of the hologram. "Hold on!" Tola exclaimed. "What's this?" He bent closer to the hologram to squint at group of minute dots and then waved excitedly. "Hey, can you magnify this spot, sir? It looks like a tidal wave of *aphids*, or something!" The round man's eyes riveted on the movement. As Adam punched the 'MAGNIFY' button, a blaze of bold colors, patterns, and textures filled the view.

"Whoa!! Tola jumped back. "Definitely not aphids! They're *animals*! *Hundreds* of them!"

Completely fearless and obviously fascinated, a bizarre range of species swarmed over the immense saw-toothed leaves toward the starship. A hoard of outstretched hands, a forest of tentacles, a bewildering array of stripes, spots, wings, fur and scales all strained their utmost to touch the smooth hull.

The three men gaped at the menagerie in silence, dumbfounded. After a moment, Kron cleared his throat. "Ah, there's an uncanny resemblance...."

"Huh? What's that?" Adam looked up distractedly. There was a slight pause.

"Looks like my old neighborhood."

The three let out a whoop. "No contest, pal!" Adam grinned. "But your spikes put 'em all to shame, hands down!"

He turned back to the controls, trying to focus. "Okay, let's get back to, ah, reality? Whatever *that* is?" He scanned further. "Ah! There you go, guys: I found an opening! A way into the core of this, ah, neighborhood! Ready? I've turned on Artificial Gravity, Kron, and I'm in a holding pattern. Go ahead and rotate the hull."

With a low pulsing, the starship's disc upended slowly 90 degrees on its axis. Nudging sideways, the sleek saucer parted the fan-shaped leaves and slipped in like quicksilver toward the center. Soon, the green wall was far behind, replaced by gargantuan, sun-dappled branches.

Kron did a double take at the hologram. "Well whaddaya know! This *is* a tree, sir! The radar shows a wide, flat area directly under us! Look at it! All the branches seem to fork out horizontally, curve upward, and then disappear into those clouds of haze up there. I-I don't know," he hedged, raising his brows. "Soft landing?"

Adam nodded emphatically. "*Go* for it!"

Kron started the sequence. He'd been meticulously trained on similar starships for the entire year he lived with the Bitrons. As he leveled the hull again, five-foot sacs filled with gel telescoped out, the tips widening and becoming cup-shaped. The massive craft slowly settled its weight onto the broad cushions.

Suddenly, a tremor passed through beneath their feet!

"*Hold on*!" Adam exclaimed, grabbing the arms of his chair. "Oops! There's *another* one!" Holding up a tentative finger he waited, listening intently through his ear inserts. In a moment, it was still again. He shook his head, scowling.

"W-what was *that*, sir," Tola gulped nervously, "an *earthquake*?"

"Auronaquake," Adam deadpanned. "You're on Aurona now."

"Right. Auronaquake. Got it." He rolled his eyes at Kron, grinning.

Kron checked the seismic readings, concern in his eyes. "Hey, whatever you two wanna call it, that mystery quake wasn't up here on the surface. It came from directly beneath us, about five thousand feet down!"

"Any aftershocks?"

The group listened intently for a moment, hearing nothing. Adam stood up decisively, flipping a few switches. "Okay, Kron! Are all your atmospheric sampling gizmos and element thingys ready?"

"Yessir!" He chuckled. "All my, ah, doodads are on standby!"

"Good. Atmospheric first. Broad spectrum: temperature, humidity, CO2 level, presence of harmful gases, pollen counts, fungal counts…," he went down the list.

"Check! Check! *Check*!" One by one, Kron gathered the results, brightening as he went. "Sir," he gulped, "can you believe this? Every reading is absolutely pure! Wow! I'd even say that Aurona's atmosphere is in *far* better shape than the Earth's! It's got a significantly higher oxygen and ozone content, too!"

Adam grabbed the printout, nodded thoughtfully, and then sighed, his feelings of anxiety ebbing away. "So let's not mess it up, guys? We've been invited down here in good faith, as honored guests."

Tola's eyes grew round. "Huh? We're *guests*? Of whom? And where? When did *this* happen? We haven't detected a single sign of civilization, sir!"

"They're *out* there," Adam whispered. "Elena and I, ah, met one of them. We don't know where they *live* yet, but they're definitely here, somewhere." He climbed out of his chair, yanked the glowing keys out of their slots, and locked up the command center. Zipping them into an inner pocket, he motioned with a toss of his head toward his private speed elevator. "Hey, *move it!* You guys coming or what?"

A small, hand-picked landing party of six joked nervously in the quarantine room, casting suspicious looks at the imposing rows of decontamination equipment.

"Okay! Ready to run the gauntlet?" Adam taunted.

Kron peered apprehensively over the top of his manual. "You first," he offered brightly. "Show us all how it's done!"

"Amateurs!" Adam scoffed. Steeling himself, he turned and sauntered calmly through the shimmering curtain of blue light. Fingerlike projections gently traced the contours of his body, zapping unseen, minute particles with static charges, popping them into puffs of smoke. As he reached the airlock to the suit room, he spun around to wave them on. "See? Nuttin' to it! C'mon, you wimps!"

Shortly they were all in the locker. Congratulating each other in high spirits, they thumped their feet and watched fine particles of ash fall from their bodies to the floor. An array of thin biosuits had been prepped thoroughly and hung in rows along the walls; the peripheral equipment was stacked neatly on shelves above them.

"Tell me, sir," Joelle probed quietly, "why'd you *ever* want to land way up here in this huge tree, anyway?" She bent back to her prep routine, studying him nervously out of the corner of her eye. As the rest listened in silence, they slipped on their suits, busily adjusting the various straps and buckles.

Adam looked blank for a moment, then shrugged. "I dunno, I thought maybe it would be safer up here. Um, let's just say I had a 'gut feeling' about it?"

Tola jumped awkwardly to his defense. "I know! You were thinking of, like, Swiss Family Robinson or something, right? This tree's like a fortress!" He glanced at Adam nervously. "Ah, actually, how far is it down to the ground, and how…?"

"Nope, we're not going down, guys." Adam zipped up a last pocket and turned around, making a hovering motion in the air with his hand. "We're going *up!*"

They all stared at him, stopped in midprep.

He grinned broadly. "Anybody ever hear of antigrav SpeedSleds?"

"Wow! Cool! You *got* it!" they chorused.

"And let's not forget a black holocamera! We need it for the record!"

Kron immediately pulled one of the black spheres from a shelf above his head, set it to home in on his PIL signal, and sent it aloft. As Adam opened the airlock, a broad platform slid away from them, jutting out beneath the starship's immense hull. They hesitated a moment, then walked out as a tight unit, gaping in awe at the tree's eighty-foot leaves and massive, skyscraper-sized branches. Somewhere in the distance, a faint sound filtered in through the audiodomes of their e-helmets. The noise was steady, powerful, like rushing water.

"Wow, what's that hissing sound?" Sahir whispered. She edged behind an equally cautious Joelle. "B-bugs? Or-or snakes?"

They gazed up into the branches, listening intently and scanning the mists in growing apprehension. Yes, the sound was *definitely* coming from somewhere above them. Adam walked determinedly to the platform's thick, curved railing and brushed off a small lizardlike flying creature. Quickly locating a narrow slit along its inner edge, he lifted the hinged top to reveal a built-in control panel.

Elena sidled up behind him, warily watching the scuttling animal out of the corner of her eye. "How'd you *know* about all this," she whispered, "was there a manual or something?"

"Holo-discs," he winked. "I memorized 'em all…. Well, at least all the information available to me when they were made. We've stumbled onto quite a few surprises and additions since then, haven't we? I'll show you the discs later."

There was a thumb-sized joystick down inside the well. As he maneuvered it, a trio of SpeedSleds silently appeared from a cargo bay somewhere beneath them, rising in single file. In moments, Adam had the sleek bullets docked against the side of the platform. "Okay, guys, we gotta stay in pairs and stay within the safety of the tree," he breathed excitedly into his throat mike. "Keep your antigrav belts on standby, and no cowboys! It's a long way to the ground!"

Inside a warehouse on Level F, four men stared at the flashing chronograph in their stowaway's pod. Cursing, Dexor bent down and swatted at the broken computer connection dangling under it. His men were right: the plug must have been crushed when one of the pod's rollers ran over it during their hasty move. The machine hadn't been connected to the ship's mainframe for the entire trip and was relying on its internal backup for the timing. He groaned: a whole month off, and with limited knowledge of electronics, nobody had a clue what to do about it.

After a round of shouting, blame-shifting and hateful glaring, they stole back out into the bright corridor. As the light penetrated the pod's dark glass, the features of its gel-suited occupant were revealed: the profile of a man of hideous countenance.

Tola looked sweaty and uncomfortable, pulling at his collar. The group was hovering in a tight formation, awaiting further orders. "What about these e-helmets, sir? It's stifling, they're quite heavy, and the air *is* pure."

Joelle's head popped out from behind Kron, her eyes studying the branches suspiciously. "I'm keeping mine *on*," she shuddered, revulsion tingeing her voice. "I don't want any of those lizardy things scratching down *my* neck!"

Adam considered a moment. "Well, don't get me wrong, guys; I'm open to the idea, but there *is* a catch to it: who wants to be the first volunteer? The, ah, king's official taster, shall we say?"

Kron stood up, his hands flying to his helmet release. "Sir!" he shouted, eagerly. "I, for one, would die for you and request the honor of breathing the first real Auronian atmosphere…."

"Stuff it, Kron."

As they hooted in laughter, the muscular man released his catch and lowered his helmet to his side. Sniffing tentatively, he broke into a broad grin. "Wow!" His eyes widened in euphoria. "It smells fantastic out here! C'mon, guys!"

As they slipped off their helmets, a look of startled surprise gripped them all. Elena threw her head back and sighed deeply, closing her eyes. "Man, what a *perfume*! Where's it *coming* from?"

Adam shrugged, jerking his thumb toward the sky. "Up there, most likely. Okay, guys, time to *climb*! Lock in your radar and side lasers and set your sleds to power level six! We'll rendezvous at the top in about twenty minutes!"

Their spirits rose along with the buoyant sleds. As the three teams and small black ball climbed into the heavy amber haze, a wash of brilliant blue locator beams danced over the branches, sending sparks of amber-encased gold sizzling in their wake. In a few minutes they separated, each team going in a different direction, the holocamera following Kron like a clinging speck of dust.

Adam and Elena finally noticed the mists had started to thin, dissipating into bright, cool sunlight. The strange hissing had grown louder, too, and now seemed to be coming from all directions. They stopped, hovering over a massive eighty-foot leaf. His knees shaking, Adam stood up carefully on his sled to scan the horizon. The panorama took his breath away.

Suddenly he stopped, squinting and trying to focus. What was *that*? A faint, watercolored silhouette caught his eye. Could it another…? Excited, he slipped his e-helmet back on and enhanced the view.

Yes, it was! Another gargantuan tree loomed in the distance, perhaps fifty miles away! He tapped out scope vision. Beyond it, there was another tree, then still another! As he filtered the view with various lenses, scores of faint silhouettes revealed themselves, all evenly distributed and receding into the distance as far as he could see! A regular pattern soon emerged: Why, they looked like they'd been *planted* there in a colossal gridwork of some kind! Amazing! Who could have….

Suddenly, there was an insistent tapping on his shoulder.

"Um, Adam?"

It was Elena. "Yes?" he answered distractedly, his eyes darting excitedly along the horizon. "What is it?"

She sounded nervous. "Adam. I-I *hear* something."

He slipped off his e-helmet and turned around. "*Holy mackerel*!"

Towering behind her, an odd creature sat perched on the back of their sled licking its long, supple fingers with an impossibly longer tongue. It blinked momentarily at his outburst and then returned to its grooming ritual.

She stiffened, not daring to look. "Do I hear *slurping*?" she asked, in a steady tone. "Tell me. What *is* it, Adam?"

He groped behind his back for the cool barrel of his Stifler. "Um, a nectar-eater?" he ventured, lamely. "It's got a good-sized tongue…."

"Adam!" she interjected, her voice cracking thinly and her teeth clenched. "Get it *off*, Adam!"

"Why? He's not even *looking* at you!"

Her brows lowered, her eyes glaring. "I don't *care*! I'll *scream*! You've never heard me scream before. It's not pleasant!"

As her voice teetered on the edge of hysteria, Adam clenched his fists with uncertainty. The creature rose up on all six legs, arching its back and yawning, lazily coiling and uncoiling its long tongue. Absently, it leaned toward them and peered down over Elena's shoulder. As his shadow crossed her lap, she jerked her head up.

Their eyes locked.

Far, far away, great clouds of Aeronautas took flight, squealing in panic. As the jungle canopy echoed and reverberated in the distance, terrified life forms scattered. The big nectar-eater dove under the sled, flailing and thumping, his gangly legs akimbo. Adam gritted his teeth. It was endless. Trembling, he cupped his hand over her mouth. There, it was gone. The noise was gone. He squeezed out a thin smile.

Her eyes smoldered.

"Ah, sweetie?" Taking a calculated risk, he lifted a finger.

Muffled under his hand, she uttered something unprintable.

He clamped again, waiting a long, uncertain moment. There, her breathing seemed to be more even. Slowly lifting his hand away, he studied her out of the corner of his eye.

"Gross! Yuck! Poo!" She began to spit vehemently, her hands trembling. "Slimy, *ugly*! It-it-it *drooled* on me!"

His mind was racing. Maybe a fatherly, protective image might work? Gently slipping an arm around her shoulders, he whispered in her ear. "Most of these animals appear to be harmless," he lulled. "Look! They live up here in the clouds, eating nectar all day! They're our friends! Hey, they're all coming back! We scared them away!"

She slowly pulled away, studying him with a wary eye.

"Wait a sec...." He stifled a smile. "I've got a collar and leash under my seat."

There was a sudden elbow to his ribs. "That's *it*! You're *history*!"

They wrestled in the seats, giggling and jostling, Adam getting the worst of the punishment. With a final round of pummeling, they settled back.

Elena freshened her lipstick. "Feel better?"

"Yeah."

"No more pet jokes?"

"No more pet jokes."

"Protect me?" she batted her eyes, coyly.

Silence. She looked at Adam's face. His pupils seemed to be involuntarily constricting and dilating, focusing somewhere behind her. She spun around and let out a muffled exclamation.

Advancing toward the sled were eyes. Eyes of all descriptions, attached to creatures of all descriptions hovered in the air, twined in the branches, slithered, rolled and hopped toward them.

Slowly, stiffly, she twisted her body back to face him, clenching her fists whitely in her lap. "Okay-y-y, Adam," she muttered. "It's decision ti-m-m-me!"

In a swift motion, he threw up the shields. There was a sudden sizzling sound, followed by a loud, anguished honk. He rolled his eyes. "*Now* what?" The nectar-eater shot out from under the sled and scurried back into the mob, his fur singed and smoking. "Wow, so *that's* where that bad boy disappeared to!"

"Adam!" she squeaked, latching onto his wrists. "You don't have to *remind* me! That slimy creature was *huge*!" Her voice grew tighter as her fingernails dug in. "And to think he was nearly on-on-on *top* of me!"

"He was just curious! I'm sure he's never *seen* a person!"

"Are you *sure* that ugly thing is harmless?"

"Well, yes!"

"Positive?"

"Yes. In fact, I'm sure *all* those guys are harmless," he offered lamely. "Lemme see...." Awkwardly pushing a button with his elbow, he dropped the shields.

"Adam!" she hissed, frightened.

"Hey! Don't worry!" He unlatched her nails from his wrists and slowly, resolutely stepped off the sled. Scooching down, he reached out into the thickest part of the menagerie. A long-legged ball sniffed his hand and let loose with a primal, satisfied grunt, followed by series of clicking noises. The ice was broken. They converged on him, tongues tasting, noses twitching, sensitive finger pads probing with gusto. Catlike, one walked up to him, briefly rubbed against his legs, and then turned away, disinterested.

He shrugged. "See?"

She glanced into the air. "A-and now what's *that* thing coming at you, Adam?" She shielded her eyes, pointing nervously. "Is that one of your Aero, Aero...."

"*Aeronautas*!" He stood up too quickly, sending a balloonlike form bouncing off his head. Squealing in alarm, it pulsed a short distance away, its peacock-blue eyes rolling. "Oh, c'mon off the sled, Elena," he urged. "It's *okay*! Really!"

After an agonizing moment of deliberation, she stepped off and gingerly picked her way through the upraised snouts, tongues, and tentacles. Reaching his side, she latched back onto his arm, her fingernails digging in deeply.

"*Aaargh*," he coughed, "you got quite a *grip* there, hon!" His eyes pleaded. "Could you, ah, lighten up a bit?"

Silence. Her brows were knit, her eyes darting around uncomfortably.

"They're our friends...."

"Don't start!" she snapped, cutting him off.

He popped out his eyes in mock fright. "Oooo! They might *lick* me to death!"

A smile teased at the corners of her mouth.

Encouraged, he hammed it up. Pulling away, he mimicked the nectar-eater's loping, awkward gait, finally squeezing out a chuckle.

"That's better. You okay now?"

"Yeah, sorry." She smiled. "Just a little stage fright, I guess."

"Hey, we're just a passing *fancy* to them," he said, laughing. Holding his arms out for balance and placing his steps carefully, he traced a path along the leaf's saw-toothed edge. "Look! They're gone and we've been totally forgotten! Let's go over there and explore a bit!" He turned and started off.

"Wait, wait!"

He stopped dead in his tracks and turned around expectantly.

She was pointing over his head. "Look, Adam! *Fruit*!"

Something stirred deeply in his ancestral memory. Fruit? He looked up. Yes, there it was, hanging tightly against a branch, a shriveled, raisinlike fig about five inches long. He glanced over his shoulder, his eyes questioning.

She shrugged, her hands making hurrying motions. "Well, *get it*!"

He pulled. The stem was tough. Rummaging, she pulled a knife out of her bag and handed it to him. He sawed slowly, twisting the sticky fruit off the branch. Unceremoniously, he plopped it into a quarantine jar, screwed the lid down tightly, and stowed it under his seat. That strange ancestral memory, that persistent feeling of déjà vu refused to go away. He knit his brows, perplexed.

She held out her hand expectantly, wiggling her fingers. "Ah … my *knife*?"

"Oh!" He fumbled in his pocket, reddening. "Wait a sec. Crud! Now everything's stuck together!"

"Be careful," she cautioned, "that scalpel's surgical steel…."

"*Ouch*!!" Even as she spoke, the sharp point pricked him. In a quick reflex, he jerked his hand away and stuck his finger into his mouth.

"Adam, *no*!" She grabbed for his arm, but not quickly enough.

Suddenly his air passages constricted. "*E-Elena*?" he rasped. A nasty, bitter coating enveloped his throat and an odd pressure grabbed the base of his skull. He shook his head, fighting it off. In a few moments he looked up, a bit dizzy. "Wow," he croaked. Bad *stuff*! Sorry. I-I wasn't thinking. Hey, I'm um, *almost* okay now, really."

She shook her head. "That might have been *old* fruit? See, there's more over there, and they're a lot bigger!"

He looked. She was right. Clusters of fruit in varying stages of maturity were hanging all around them. "I don't know," he rasped. "Do you think this stuff goes bad when it gets ripe? At least it seems to get denser, like… a raisin…."

Without warning, molten fire spread down his backbone. As his heart started to thud strangely inside his chest, he gasped for air, sucking in several deep breaths. His body became tingly, jumpy and alive, his nerves dancing on razor's edge. The sounds around them became amplified to an incredible degree! He glanced at Elena as if through a shimmering curtain. Totally unaware, she slipped her slender arm through his and looked up, smiling. In a moment, everything ebbed away. He blinked in confusion. The strange symptoms had left as quickly as they'd come.

"Look over there, Adam," she pointed. "It looks like a floor!"

Several enormous leaves seemed to be overlapping, their great sawtoothed edges entwining like a zipper to form an enormous flat area. As they peered around a large stem, they stopped short. In the center of the big clearing was an odd circle of animals. The jostling menagerie faced inward shoulder to shoulder, looking like animals gathering around an African waterhole.

Elena squeezed his arm with uncertainty. "Adam," she whispered, "what in the world are they, ah ... *doing*?" Startled by the sound of her voice, a few of the animals backed away. A broad wash of brilliant red opened up between them.

He squinted. "Huh? What's that big red thing?"

Suddenly, there was a loud snap over their heads, followed by a prolonged hissing. The heady odor of perfume quickly became overwhelming. They jerked their heads up, their eyes traveling along a stemlike projection to a cluster of pollen-laden pistils. Towering far above them, a surreal fountain of glittering, golden spray was audibly jetting into the atmosphere from the stamen of a huge, sticky red flower!

Adam's eyes popped. "Yes!" His fist jabbed the air. "This is where it all *comes* from! It's just, flat incredible!"

"All *what* comes from? And that huge red thing couldn't really be a-a *flower*...."

"Yes! It's one blossom, thirty feet in diameter! A-and there's probably a zillion of 'em all over the planet! Get it? This is where all the atmospheric gold comes from! The shields, Elena, the *shields*!"

She definitely got it. Her eyes were now huge, reflecting the glittering spray. The bizarre animals were hesitantly returning to the great, velvet-textured petals to resume feeding in the great bowl of nectar. She tore their eyes away and knelt down, poking at what seemed to be a viscous, amber resin settling in scattered pools.

"Wow, just *look* at this stuff!" Long snouts and tongues appeared from under the petals, lapping it up as fast as it congealed. As Adam pushed them away to scoop some up, she grabbed his wrist.

"Maybe we shouldn't touch it," she warned. "How about a syringe?"

"Sure, got one?"

"Of course," she chided, handing it to him. "I *am* a doctor, right?"

He chuckled, sucking up copious amounts of the fluid and squirting it into a quarantine jar. His eyes suddenly brightened. "Hey, I just thought of something!"

"Hmm?" She was shielding her eyes in the glare, studying the horizon.

"This syringe just gave me an idea! The tree's capillary system might be liquefying this stuff and drawing it up out of the soil!"

"Hmm? Sol?" she murmured distractedly. "It's not a lyophobic sol, Adam. Most likely it's a suspensoid," she corrected.

"Huh? No, no, I said *soil*, Elena. Soil."

She turned around. "Do you think all those other trees out there are doing the same thing? I mean, pumping out gold droplets into the air?"

"Definitely! Look at the pattern! It's obvious they've been planted in a grid for that purpose! This planet's one big garden and someone takes care of all these trees!" They stood arm in arm, gazing into the distance.

"*Ambrosia*!" A loud voice suddenly boomed behind them. "That's what *I* call it! Somewhere between passion fruit and honey, with overtones of coconut! Try it!"

They spun on their heels. Tola! Nectar was smeared on his lips and several creatures were trailing him, licking his fingers. A ball of fuzz suddenly floated up in the breeze and perched on his shoulder, eyeing the shiny buttons on his chest. Sahir watched from the safety of their SpeedSled, looking around apprehensively.

Adam hefted a plastic container, sloshing it triumphantly. "Look! We got some liquid gold! Think about it! This tree actually draws gold up out of the ground!"

Tola put his hand on his chin. "Gold? Out of the ground? So why don't you just call this thing a Motherlode Tree?"

"Hey, perfect!" Adam's fist punched the air. "You've chalked up *another* great name! You're batting one for one!" He gave Tola a sticky high five. "I hereby designate you our mission's creator of names, our official lexicographer!

"Why thank you, thank you, lady and gentleman. I'm honored."

"I've got a request, too," Elena prompted. "What about all this perfume?" She took a deep breath. "It's like gardenias, or maybe jasmine. Whaddaya think?"

"Yeah," Adam chimed in, "take a good whiff, man!" He grinned. "There's millions of these, ah, Motherlodes pumping this stuff out! Got a name yet? Come on, the clock's ticking...."

"Of course!" Tola winked. "That's simple! Eau de Motherlode!" He held up a hand. "No extra charge, sir, just doing my job."

As they laughed uproariously, a cloud suddenly seemed to pass over Tola's face. He looked around, his mellow voice taking on a more serious tone. "I-I'm sorry, guys. Before we got distracted, I really wanted to tell you something else. I-it's not quite as idyllic up here as you might think."

"Huh?"

"Your gut feeling was *right* about parking the ship up this tree, sir. About fifteen minutes ago, Sahir and I were down near the base of the tree checking things out, and we-we saw...."

Suddenly, like a bolt of lightning, a disturbing vision flashed through Adam's mind. He squeezed one eye shut, the pounding in his head almost unbearable. He took a quick breath and interrupted, the words escaping involuntarily from his lips.

"Y-you saw flashing teeth and buzzing wings, right?"

Tola jumped like he was spooked. "How did y...." He blinked.

"I don't know," he interjected, shrugging, "but I'll tell you the *rest*, too. You saw long, sharp spikes pointing downward, looking like they were growing right out of the trunk, and below that, lots of bones piled up around the base of the tree. There were a lot of strange species impaled on the spikes and it looked as if they'd been *poisoned*!" As Elena drew in a sharp breath, he continued, relentlessly. "The flashing teeth were on a big, striped, catlike creature with a funny, bulbous head and the buzzing wings belonged to a persistent, black hornet-creature with a brilliant phosphorescent glow on its head and tail." He caught Tola's eye. "Do I have it right?"

The round man nodded slowly, staring at him in mute, shocked silence.

Adam closed his eyes and pressed on, seeming to be describing the scene from his own memory. "They were fighting! The cat-creature was impaled on the spikes and couldn't get away and the hornet kept attacking it with his sharp, six-inch, barbed stinger. Oh! One more thing," he added, holding up a finger. "There was a *lot* of noise down there. The hornet's wings were about eight feet across and it was buzzing really loud in this deep base note. The cat was roaring and Sahir was under her seat, screaming at the...."

"But y-you weren't *there*, sir," Tola interrupted, ashen-faced. "You were up here at the top! You couldn't *possibly* know! And yes, she *was* screaming at the top of her lungs, so I threw up the shields for protection. We backed away and threw the shields up to watch the battle. The tiger-creature died real fast...." His voice trailed off in midsentence as he pondered, waiting in uncertain silence.

Adam swallowed hard. The bitterness was still there, way back on his tongue. He suddenly jerked his head up, disturbed. "No, I'm *not* possessed!"

Tola answered, softly. "I-I didn't *say* that, sir." He held up a finger. "But I confess the word *did* cross ... my mind..." As his voice trailed off again, he paused, thinking. "Hey! L-let me try an experiment, here: a pop quiz, if you will. Quick, close your eyes and tell me what you see."

"Huh?"

"Please. This is really important. Trust me."

"Okay, I guess," he shrugged. "I'm game."

As Adam concentrated, the heavy pressure returned full blast. There were visions of clouds scudding across an azure blue sky and then a farmhouse with a windmill. A fat lady was sitting on the front porch with a white cat in her lap.

He opened his eyes in shock. "I know, Tola, I *know*! You were thinking about *home*! You were born in Oklahoma, right? Wow, that old place must have been one of the last farms in that region!"

Tola was surprised, yet cautious and skeptical. "Y-you might be guessing, sir. Most of that information was on my resume...."

Adam dove into the breach. "I've only started, man," he interjected. "There was this fat, um, heavyset lady on the front porch with a white cat in her lap. She got up from a rocking chair. It looked carved, with lots of spools and a blue cushion. The floorboard creaked, second step. You were down in the yard eating a handful of dirt with worms in it! She pulled it out of your hand and wiped your runny nose! She called you...," he squinted one eye, looking skeptically at him, "*Packy*?"

Tola staggered, looking around for support. "No *way*!" he gasped. "You *nailed* it, sir! Yes, my mother was husky, like me! I couldn't pronounce my middle name, Patrick, and yes, the second step did creak! We fixed it years and years later, but...."

"But the farm was sold and torn down by that housing developer who built those sterile-looking high-rises. Your father *hated* them, right? He called it 'Slab City'!"

There was an extremely long and very uncertain pause. As the two stared at him in awkward silence, he suddenly felt like an outcast, a leper.

"Adam?" Elena offered softly, "I-I think you've become slightly...."

"Telepathic." he finished. "And not slightly." There, it was out. He'd said it. He turned his head away, suddenly not wanting to face them. After a moment, he sighed. "It was easy, Tola. You practically beamed what was on your mind and I picked it up!"

The round man shrugged. "Well, I guess everything is weird 'til you get used to it, right?" He motioned with his thumb. "Like this piece of fuzz on my shoulder? That's what I call weird!" A nose, and then a long tongue appeared from somewhere within the featherweight ball of fluff. He reached up and gently lifted the creature, handing it to Elena.

"You're right," Adam agreed. "Who knows? Maybe we're *all* hallucinating on something. This whole *planet* is weird!"

"Do you think it was anything you ate, sir?"

"Yes, I'm positive. There was this fruit...."

"Dried fruit," Elena corrected.

"Yes, dried fruit. I only *tasted* it, though. Hey, that's right, we *have* a piece of it!" He stooped down. "Wanna see?" He opened the quarantine jar, holding it out.

Tola took a sniff and drew back quickly, wrinkling his nose. "Arf! Woof! That's...," he shook his head, "that's definitely not gourmet fare!"

"Well, if it does what I *think* it does, we have a priceless commodity in this jar! Hey, mister official lexicographer," he challenged, "see if you can think up a name for this, ah, mind-fruit. C'mon! I *know* you can do it!"

Tola quickly got over his shock. "Hmm, do I sense another challenge?" He scowled. "Let's see, ah, Fruitbeam. No, no. Omnipote! No, no, how about Telefruit? Wait, wait! Dried raisins, boiled down to the essence? Telessence?"

"Almost there," the group prompted, laughing. "Keep going!"

Tola eagerly continued his game of free association. Closing his eyes and concentrating hard, he began to combine, switch, accept, and discard words in amazing, rapid-fire succession. "Videotel, Televid, TreeSee, Eat'NTell, Cephalocast, Mindview, Mother...hmm!" He opened his eyes, questioning. "Mothermind?"

Adam was laughing uproariously. "I'd say *never* mind, for now anyway! Most likely our unseen guests have a name for this stuff already."

"Um, maybe they call it the Forbidden Fruit?"

There was a stunned silence.

"Whoa!" Adam inhaled sharply. "I-I do remember some of that church stuff, Tola, even though I was maybe five or six when my grandfather stopped taking me...."

"Coincidence," Tola interrupted. "It can't be what you're, ah, thinking."

Adam made a concerted effort to change the mood. "Hey, our names are *almost* right, right?" He leered apishly at Elena. "Me Adam, you Eve!" As she swatted him off, he began to mimic one of the odd creatures loping by, bending forward and letting his arms dangle loosely by his sides. The creature glanced at him in alarm and quickened his pace. He hammed it up and followed closely behind, loose-limbed and limber, glancing repeatedly over his shoulder at his friends. As the creature scuttled faster, Adam stepped up the pursuit. Nervously, a few of the other animals had started to run away. He quickly had a herd in front of him and began to shoo the howling, honking menagerie around the back of the flower and out the font again.

Their cautious smiles soon gave way to laughter. It looked like fun. Sahir slipped away from the safety of her SpeedSled and walked over to the group. She glanced at Tola and Elena. Shrugging, the three merged into the chase.

Kron and Joelle suddenly showed up, waving. "Hey! Whassup, guys?"

Laughing, Adam turned to wave at them and quickly rejoined the mob.

There was no hesitation. Kron jumped off and shouldered his way into the pursuit, the pinging holocamera and his own yelping adding to the confusion. A grand chase ensued, round and round the big red flower, with the humans first acting as the frightened, screaming quarry and then as the puffing, eager pursuers.

Joelle finally had had enough. She'd been watching the idiocy unfolding and couldn't contain herself any longer. Running into the meleé with her arms flailing, she merged into the rotary and added her coloratura's high C to the chorus.

The universal sense of play knows no barrier among species. At first baffled, the watching creatures finally caught onto the mood and bounded out of hiding in a great, enthusiastic wave. In a sea of tails and tentacles, they joined the mad chase. Swooping in from the air, flying creatures joined the free-for-all, belting out their own brand of excited honks, buzzes, and trills. The somber mood had been completely blasted away. As the broad platform of entwining eighty-foot leaves bounced up and down with thumping and scuffling, the top of the tree resounded with assorted brands of laughter. Six apparently mindless human intruders were now running in a senseless circle, screaming at the top of their lungs. Adam's innocent romp had escalated into a cacophonous clash of careening, undefinable biological classification.

He screeched to a halt, his eyes focusing on his wrist programmer. "Holy cow! We're *late*!" he wheezed, out of breath.

"You're right," Kron puffed, bumping into him, "the crew's probably looking for us right now, down on the platform!"

Tola, Sahir, and then Joelle reeled out from behind the flower, winded and laughing, gingerly picking their way through upraised snouts and excited, flapping wings.

Adam smiled, glancing at his wrist programmer once more. "Elena," he called, "come on out! The animals are tired! It's time to go!"

The loud buzzing of a few insects rasped near them.

"Elena," Joelle called, "hurry *up*, hon! We're all *waiting*!"

Silence. As their eyes searched intently, waiting for a reply, the creatures quietly resumed feeding, disinterested. Adam ran to the far side of the flower, his heart racing,. Exchanging shocked glances, the group joined in the search. Shortly, the awful truth sunk in. They blinked, stunned, their jaws hanging open.

She was gone!

Suddenly, involuntarily, bolts of pain shot up Adam's spine. He jerked in an intense neural spasm, dropping to his knees and clutching his head. A massive *pressure* was searing his brain! The horizon was tilting, upending itself and flipping upside down! As his eyes rolled back in his head, his mind suddenly saw a vision of cloudy sky, then a forest of branches whizzing by, followed by a fleeting glimpse of white robes fluttering in the distance.

"*Robes?*" he gasped. "What am I *seeing*? What's happening?" A cruel hand suddenly clamped down on his throat and shut off his breathing. Gasping for air, he fell forward on his face. "Please," he choked. "Help me…." A deep, pervading chill crept through his body, his hands flailed weakly, and darkness closed in.

Chapter 14: SOLUMBRA

The searching holographic eye floated silently through the shadowy rainforest with sweeping, urgent motions. Its brilliant emerald-green lasers pierced intently through the vaporous mists, catching and recording every falling drop, every grasping tendril, every nuance of palette in the somber gray-green fog. SEEK ELENA... SEEK ELENA... SEEK ELENA.... The black holocamera was single-minded in its purpose, driving on relentlessly toward its distant, unseen goal.

Thinking quickly, Kron had snatched the black sphere from the air over his head and reprogrammed it to home in on Elena's PIL signal. The small landing party watched in shock as it took off like a shot and disappeared into the distant rainforest. There was absolutely no doubt about it, someone, or something had taken Elena! Strapping Adam's unconscious body onto the backseat of his sled, they dove down recklessly through the massive branches toward the starship. As they landed on a loading dock, he began to stir weakly.

The entire crew was waiting for them up in the Observatory Room, concern etched on their faces and an air of electrical anticipation charging the atmosphere: this was for real, the first acid test of the holocamera in action. As the rising disc of the floor stopped under the great dome, Adam was well enough to resume command. He signaled weakly for the unforgettable three-dimensional story to unfold. Acting as a transceiver, a second holocamera began to ride up and down over their heads. Long ribbons of light streamed out, coalescing into an amazing, fast-moving virtual terrain.

They were there! Wet and dripping, the jungle burst upon them, rolling over, around and through the crew. They became phantoms, flying without form or substance, penetrating effortlessly through the hearts of ghostly trees in an amorphous netherworld. The urgency and reality of the mission quickly hammered home: Elena was gone, *really* gone, lost somewhere in this endless, tangled labyrinth! She'd become everyone's favorite.

Now and then, their eyes stole away from the rushing scene to glance at Adam. They were truly concerned about him. He'd propped himself up on his knees like an unmovable stone in the rushing current of trees, completely unaware of his appearance. His eyes were squeezed shut, his fists were clenched in his lap, and the veins on his neck were standing out alarmingly from the collar of his uniform.

The mind-fruit had been powerful. Adam shook his head, desperately trying to focus his scattered thoughts. There was an entirely new problem: his brain was throbbing with a cacophony of vague, fuzzy mind-messages from the crew! He fought through the clattering, clamoring turmoil, straining his utmost to hear Elena's faint PIL signal. Yes, there it was, he could just barely make it out through the mind-din.

As he began to reflect on the past few hours, his eyes welled up with tears. Scowling, he clenched his jaw in frustration. "What a *jerk* I was, letting my top commanders *play* on top of a two thousand-foot tree! And-and I was the one who initiated all that horseplay?" He paused, pondered a moment, and came at it from a different angle. "Well, it *is* true: we all had cabin fever and we were just blowing off a little steam. We finally had a chance to...."

Abruptly, he snapped out of reverie. "What's *that*?" He sprang nimbly to his feet, his senses razor sharp. "Everyone!" he rasped, his finger pointing into the distance. They spun toward him in rapt attention. "Listen! Could it be…?" They bent their heads, straining to hear. Yes, there was a faint pinging noise!

The scene around them began to accelerate, zigzagging through the dense undergrowth at a phenomenal speed! His body coursing with adrenaline, Adam braced his feet and leaned forward, ducking instinctively under the phantom branches and banking into the hard turns. "Elena!" he groaned. "Please, *Elena*!"

There was a faint, metallic gleam dead ahead! What in the world was *that*?? Everyone rose to their feet, trying to see over each other's shoulders. The room had turned into a blur of motion, and adding to all the confusion, the pinging noise of the signal crescendoed into a shrill, deafening whistle.

Suddenly, the holographic eye snapped to a dead stop, hovering motionless. The visual effect was overwhelming. The crew staggered and fell backward, grabbing each other for support.

An incredible, shimmering golden DOME stood in the center of the floor!

There was a stunned, collective gasp. They backed away from it warily. Except for the strange calls of distant animals and the steady, sporadic pattering of raindrops in the canopy, deep silence reigned. Fifteen feet high, the dome stood like an enigma, mysteriously reflecting everything except the large crowd surrounding it. A gleam of light showed all around its base, interrupted by an occasional zap of blue sparks as water dripped off the rim. There were no paths. The forest litter appeared to be carefully tended, yet at the same time somehow completely undisturbed.

Slowly, tentatively, Tola reached out and poked at it, his finger passing through the phantom image. "So, ah, she's in … *there*?" he whispered.

"Apparently," Adam mumbled. "It looks like the signal's blocked. The holocamera is just hovering, clicking, searching…."

"What *is* this dome thing, sir?" Kron interrupted quietly.

"I dunno," Adam shrugged. "I don't have a clue. But for the sake of time, I think the question's more like *where* is it? We gotta hurry!" His eyes glanced at his wrist. "Hey! Wait a sec!" Tapping madly, he searched for the holocamera's locator function on his wrist programmer. "Ah, here it is! Hmm, the readout says two-and-a-half miles…."

A hand shot up. "Sir? Where are our reflections?"

He raised a finger, adjusting the volume on his throat mike. "This dome is approximately two-and-a-half miles due west of the ship, guys. And we can't see our reflections simply because we're not out there with the holocamera!" His eyes followed the tangle of vines upward until they were obscured by mist in the steamiest heights. "This mystery dome looks like it's completely covered by rainforest canopy, so we couldn't possibly spot it from the air!" His hand on his chin, he began to pace off the perimeter of the glittering hemisphere, calculating its size, composition, and function. The crew watched in respectful silence, awaiting his verdict.

"As to its purpose," he postulated, "I'd say this dome is covering…. Yes, that's *it*! There's some kind of entrance to the underground and this is a force field or a *shield* protecting it! This thing looks just like the big shield around the planet!"

Kron spun on his heel. "Of *course*, sir!" His eyes dropped to the forest litter. "But-but there seem to be no paths leading into it. How do they get in?"

Adam closed his eyes in pain. The mind-pressure had just returned in force. A scene suddenly unfolded: a haunting vision, those same white, fluttering robes that he'd seen at the top of the tree were waving in the distance, taunting him. Struggling, he forced himself back to reality. He let out a breath, thought a moment, then put it together quickly. "That's right," he concluded. "There are no paths, because…," he glanced over his shoulder at the crew, "I think they can fly."

"*Fly*, sir?" Joelle piped up incredulously.

"Yes! I believe a group of aliens kidnapped Elena wearing antigrav belts."

Stunned, they turned toward each other speculating in hushed tones.

Adam grabbed Tola by his elbow and whispered confidentially into his ear. "Listen, man, this is extremely important: the crew can't even get a whiff of my, ah, telepathic abilities. No one knows about them except you, Sahir, and Elena. If they did, they'd put me away. They'd-they'd think I was crazy or something, right?"

The round man agreed. "Definitely, sir. A screwball. Demented. Wacko."

"Easy…." Adam chuckled. "So you wouldn't betray this trust, would you?"

Tola yanked in his chin indignantly. "Absolutely, positively *not*!" His eyebrows rose to a little peak in the middle of his forehead. "We took a solemn oath not to tell a soul! It-it definitely wouldn't be in the best interest of the mission, and…."

"Whoa! That's good enough!" Adam speculated a moment, his jumpy mind racing ahead. "Oh, by the way, could you keep working on a name for that disgusting mind-fruit? Who knows? I might have to take another bite of it before too long."

"Why, sir?"

"I might have to, shall we say, *communicate* with whomever, or whatever, took Elena down this God-forsaken rabbit hole."

Tola shrugged uncertainly. "Okay-y-y … Roger. I-I think."

He spun back to the crew. "Okay! Were going *out* there!" They looked up expectantly. "Listen, guys, I've been working on a crazy idea. Since this shield appears to be exactly like the one surrounding Aurona, we should be able to penetrate it in a similar way, right? In other words, why can't we use a big, *man*-sized tube to poke through it? Think about it: since our Spyders penetrated the big shield with a *small* tube, why couldn't us humans go through this small shield with a *big* tube?"

An excited buzz arose: he was right!

"So let's get down to the brass tacks: Do we actually *have* something like ductwork aboard? If anyone has seen a large, nonmetallic tube or anything like it, please let me know. This might be a crazy spin-off of Elena's brilliant deductive reasoning, but if we have the pieces, it should work! We-we just need to figure out the blips. You know, the minor details?"

Logic prevailed. They huddled excitedly. In a few minutes, Adam's impromptu exercise in problem solving began to bear fruit. They gathered the facts, fleshed out his unique plan of attack, and summed up their proposal.

Adam listened, nodding. "That'll work, but there's a tiny blip: for mobility, you'll need to limit this rescue mission to a group of twelve." He studied the sea of disappointed faces. "Well, we can't get in each other's way, right?"

Reluctantly, they agreed. Everybody wanted to get into the act.

"Now! That large section of ductwork is where? Level B?"

"*Yo!*" a voice yelled from the perimeter. Dexor was standing on his toes, waving. "*I'll* get it! I know *exactly* where it is!"

Adam gave him a thumbs-up. "Okay, perfect. You're in charge, man!"

"Yes, sir!"

"Bring it out onto a cargo dock on one of our antigrav barges."

"Yes, *sir*!" A snappy salute returned.

That's what I like, *enthusiasm*!" Adam beamed. "Take note, guys!"

Like a bolt of lightning, his head and spinal cord began to throb once more with the effects of the mind-fruit. Masking his pain and forcing a smile, he nodded to Kron. "Okay, second in command, you're in charge. Take it from here...."

"So," Kron blended in seamlessly, "we've got the duct taken care of. Thanks, Dexor! Once we've arrived on the scene, we'll slide a couple of antigrav pods into the tube, then insert it carefully through the dome. Then we'll turn up our antigrav belts to neutral buoyancy and float in through the duct in single file. Follow me so far?"

It all sounded solid, far more than just speculation. They nodded excitedly.

"Once inside," Kron continued, "we'll dial our belts down to a slight negative buoyancy and drop down into the entrance hole ... if there is one...," his voice tailed off. "Hey, this might be just theory at this point, guys," he shrugged. "But as Adam said, anything's possible on this crazy planet!"

The crew rolled their eyes, throwing each other knowing looks.

He resumed. "This is important: the last guy in line needs to pull the duct into the shield behind him. Remember, the shield's there for a purpose. It keeps stuff from falling in, but mostly it's there to protect whoever's living downstairs. That duct had better be waiting for us when we leave; we gotta use it to get back *out*!"

Adam listened in satisfaction, rubbing the back of his head. Kron was doing a superb job, leading with logic and authority. He had a thorough knowledge of the equipment and was demonstrating a multilayered, insightful grasp of the situation.

Kron's eyes scanned the room. "Now! I need twelve volunteers!"

Two hundred hands shot up. Smiling, he chose the qualified few and thanked the rest. "Okay, the floor's down! Dex, its duct time. Grab your three buddies to help you tie it onto the barge," he said, smiling. "Make sure you lash it down real tight. We're counting on that duct; it's our vital link! Oh yeah, and don't forget to send it through one of the bigger quarantine airlocks!"

He spun around. "Rescue team! Remember, we gotta zap everything, including ourselves, before we get into full explorer's gear! E-helmets, too!"

Adam caught his eye, giving him an enthusiastic thumb's up.

The early afternoon was balmy after a passing sun shower, but they knew that the night and the unknown would be closing in. They couldn't waste a moment. Feeling awkward and encumbered in their fully rigged suits, utility belts, and e-helmets, the small party passed through the quarantine room and stepped outside onto a docking platform in the misty atmosphere. A few of the crew assisted them, freer and more relaxed in their shirtsleeves.

They pulled away, six SpeedSleds, two men on each. Following the group, a seventh barge-like utility sled carried the big section of ductwork. Adam set close radar distances, nose to tail, then programmed the lead sled's autopilot to home in on the distant holocamera. On his signal, the shields and cloaking devices engaged, the flying string of men and machines vanished, and the phantom train flowed silently into the rainforest's perpetual twilight.

As the twelve craned their necks, gawking and marveling at the fantastic diversity of species, they heard a distant, bell-like chime. They squinted through the shields, scanning the jungle. There was a flash of light, and then a strange cascade of glowing ribbons began to float toward them through the branches.

Tola turned to Adam."What in the world?"

Calling noisily to each other, a pair of luminous flying creatures suddenly swept alongside them on brilliant pennant-wings of fluorescent color!

Adam drew in his breath. "Wow, there they are, men! The same birds that attacked our Spyders!"

The blurred pennant wings and impossibly long, flowing tails were leaving a glowing, phosphorescent wake behind them, creating an undulating ribbon of light in the dark jungle. As the birds bobbed closer, the crew gaped in wonder. Thousands of tiny, glittering pinpoints of light were glowing on the tips their feathers. The overall effect was spectacular against the somber gray-green of the jungle.

"Good heavens, now we have lights?" Tola whispered into the intercom. "How's it possible for birds to have *lights*?"

"I'm goin' in closer, guys." As Adam tapped out his scope vision, glowing dots danced across his face shield. Hmm," he murmured, "maybe it's…. Yes, it is! I-I believe it's luciferase!"

"Lucifer *what*?" Tola recoiled. "How'd *he* get into this?"

"Luciferase. You know, the stuff that glows on the end of a firefly's tail?"

"Hmm," Tola mused. "But really, sir, in *colors*?"

"Ya got me there," Adam chuckled mischievously. "Hey! Like they say, the devil's in the details!"

Tola winced. "Come on, that's not exactly what…."

Adam interrupted excitedly. "Quick, quick! Take pictures, everybody! Tap out scope vision and use your recorders! We gotta grab some videos and stop-action stills before these guys disappear!"

As their helmets bobbed madly, a voice rose excitedly from the rear.

"Hey, I see *iridescence*, too! See how the clear filaments on their feathers are diffracting the light? They're biological prisms! The barbules are forming iridescent colors! These creatures go *way* beyond iridescence, guys, they have fluorescent, phosphorescent, and neon colors, too!"

Adam glanced at their holocamera. It had been bobbing and weaving over their heads, transmitting the entire mission back to the starship in real time. "Boy, that black ball sure looks busy! The crew up in the Holosphere must be getting an eyeful! It's funny, but the only thing missing from their picture is *us*! We're flying right underneath them, but they can't see us with our cloaking devices on."

A voice piped up from the back. "Hah! Neither can the birds! These SpeedSleds are ultimate hunting blinds; even our *scent* can't be detected!"

Tola chuckled. "I'm glad we all took showers before we left."

As the men guffawed, there was a loud squeal, followed by a frenzied thrashing in the forest ahead! Startled, they spun on their seats toward the sound.

About fifty feet away, two enormous, buzzing hornetlike insects had just ambushed something fat and furry. Vastly overpowered, their victim was thrashing in agony as powerful mandibles throttled its windpipe and rapierlike stingers skewered deeply into its flesh. Slowly, it stiffened out in rigor mortis.... Poison!

Adam recoiled in horror. "Yike!" he gasped. "That might've been *Elena*!"

He was right! They readied their Stiflers, watching in shocked silence.

Setting their foot hooks into the plump body, the insects rose heavily into the air, their black wings beating laboriously in a mighty, deep-throated basso profundo duet. They paused as they entered the shadows and touched their antennae together. Suddenly, unbelievably, a glow appeared on their foreheads! Flickering, it intensified quickly. Two brilliant *searchlights* suddenly cut through the darkness! The hornets swept their dazzling beams around, got a bearing, and disappeared.

It grew silent once again. Everyone's gut was shaking.

"Holy Laser Beam!!" Adam gasped. "What in the world did we just see?"

"Ah...." Tola let out a breath. "Now I *know* we're not in Kansas anymore!"

A voice erupted from the back. "Wow! Did you get a load of those incredible searchlights? I had my scope vision on when they lit up! I-I was nearly *blinded*!"

Tola leaned toward Adam, whispering. "Should I tell them? You know...."

Adam caught on immediately. "Oh yeah, what you saw this morning. Yes, yes definitely. Go ahead; I'm sure it'll give us some valuable insight."

Tola raised his voice. "Guys! Listen! Sahir and I saw one of those bad boys right up close this morning, out in broad daylight! There was this big, parabolic depression on his forehead with some kind of shiny, mirrored substance inside. Maybe some of that, ah, Lucifer light stuff could reflect down into it?"

Kron's eyes widened. "Hey, that's *right*! Think about it! If birds have feathers that light up, why can't bugs have biological sealed beams?"

An anonymous voice stuttered from the back of the train. "N-now we have giant h-hornets with headlights? I'm not comin' out *here* in the dark! No *way*!"

"That's for sure," Adam affirmed. "We'll have to cloak and shield our SpeedSleds on all future trips into the jungle. And set our Stiflers to 'Kill'!"

Deep in thought, they traveled in silence for the remainder of the journey. Soon, someone caught a glimpse something shiny and metallic in the distance, looking like a beacon piercing the gloom. The team rose in their seats, straining to see.

Tola began to concentrate. "Ventlock, Electrodome, Goldenshield…."

"What's that, my friend?" Adam leaned toward him. "Workin' on another tag?"

"Wait, wait! I *have* it! It shines like the sun, doesn't it?"

"Um, yes, it does. Kind of…." He raised a brow expectantly.

"Well, how about *Solumbra*? It shields like an umbrella and…."

Adam winced. "Shines like the sun?" He thought a minute, then tried out the word. "Hmm…. Sol-*um*-bra!" It seemed to roll nicely off the tongue.

Grinning, the men repeated the new word in a chorus. "Sol-*um*-bra!"

The name was confirmed. They slipped quietly into the big clearing and formed a loose circle around the glittering shield. On Adam's signal, they dropped their shields, drew their Stiflers, and slid off their sleds as a tight unit. As they approached the curved golden surface, it distorted their heavily-suited images way out of proportion like a fun house mirror. Stifling a contagion of chuckles, they glanced up at the holocamera. It hovered motionless over the center of the dome, clicking and whirring futilely. Yes, the signal was definitely blocked.

Adam bent down, looking at the ground. "I'm gonna try something here. This thing should have an electrical field, right? Wait a sec…." Picking up a pebble, he tossed it at the glassy surface. It just punched a clean hole and disappeared. The shield filled in behind it. "See?" he shrugged. "Nothing."

"Wait, wait! Grinning mischievously, Peter tossed a twig at the Solumbra.

"*Craaaccckkk*!" There was a brilliant flash. They jumped back in shock as the branch was consumed in a great arc of electronic firepower! The shield swiftly closed in, but the air was smoking. They sniffed: there was a familiar odor of ozone.

"W-why'd it do *that*, sir?" Peter stuttered. "A-a *leaf* isn't metallic, is it?"

"Not the leaves I know!" Adam picked up another branch and held it close to his face shield. "It *seems* to be normal," he mumbled. "Here, Kron. We gotta speed things up, here. Try an elemental reading with all your gizmos and flashy thingys while I go over there and help those guys unload the duct."

The blonde man swung out a small compartment on his sled. As he placed the branch on a tray and closed the lid, a summary began to flash by on its tiny screen. "Well, everything appears to be normal, except…." His eyes widened. "Wait, could that be…? No, no, it can't. Lemme try a different filter."

The analysis was unmistakable: there was gold inside. Huddling, Kron's small group pulled out a surgical knife, dissected the branch, and peered at it closely under microvision. Just under the edge of the bark, thousands upon thousands of capillary wires were drawn out to an impossible degree of thinness, floating in the air. As Kron snipped off a minute section of fluff with a pair of tweezers, it mashed down readily to almost nothing. The branch was *wired*! They stared at each other, trying to grasp the scope of their discovery.

Adam dropped the last of the duct's restraining straps and hurried back to the group. They filled him in. Speculating, he knelt and began to dig under the leaf mold. Exposing a shallow root, he cut it off, examined it, and rose to his feet. "Just as I thought! Wires! Some kind of liquefied gold must grow along with the plants and mature into solid wires. That means when the roots die, the ground must be left with…." He knelt again, this time digging with purpose.

Layers upon layers of dead roots had compacted tightly over the eons, rotting along with the fallen leaves, leaving behind the imperishable prize they once contained: tons of matted gold wiring now lay there, just waiting to be scooped up!

He grabbed a handful, wrenching it free. A delicate filigree hung from his fist, riffling in the breeze; decomposed vegetation was coating its surface a deep amber color. As the clump dried in the air, he gave it a quick tap on his knee. Fine brown powder blew away and bright, pure gold remained! He slowly turned to the men. "If you're thinking what I'm thinking…."

His postulation went unanswered. There was a sudden wrenching and grunting behind them. Spooked, they spun on their heels, stiflers drawn, and stared into the woods. Twenty feet away, one of the crew was digging in the litter.

"Dexor!" Adam exclaimed.

"Huh?" The man stood up, holding a mass of roots. Thinking quickly, he nodded his head in excitement. "Yes! Ah … wow! The same wires are over here, too, sir!" He sprinted to another spot. In moments, dirt flying, the same answer came ringing back. "*Gold*, sir! There's gold *everywhere*!"

Tola's cheeks puffed as he let out a long, unsteady breath. "Well, it looks like the *real* motherlode is just lying on the ground, sir!"

Adam dropped the glittering web to his feet. "Okay. No more distractions. This stuff is all flat-out amazing, but we've gotta focus on our mission!" He waved Dexor back.

"Anybody can come out here at any time to dig, but right now, Elena's infinitely more valuable than *this* stuff!"

The section of duct slipped easily through the shell, revealing a strong source of light inside. They floated through eagerly, boot to helmet, an unbroken string descending into the depths. First in line, Adam programmed their holocamera to begin to scan for Elena's PIL transmission. Disappointingly, the orb clicked a few times, then fell dark and silent.

The shaft was incredibly smooth and seamless. Slowly the light grew brighter around them, and then the shaft abruptly widened into a trumped-shaped opening. One by one they floated out into a great void. Straining their eyes mightily, they still couldn't see a thing under their feet; the space was immense and a roof of earth and stone stretched out into the distance, lost in a strange mist.

The moment was almost upon them and again, Adam's mind started racing ahead. He'd been feeling strange, jumpy and wired ever since he'd tasted the bitter fruit. He knew the watchers below must be keenly aware of their presence: after all, they'd thrown the shields up around the planet when the starship was still millions of miles away. Somehow, he had to communicate with them and let them know….

"Yes! That's *it*!!" He yanked a small sketchpad out of his pocket.

"Huh?" Kron glanced down between his feet. Adam was drawing something.

He looked up, distracted. "Ah, wait a sec, Kron…." Making a few simple, cryptic markings, he passed the pad over his head.

"Ah, what's *this*, sir?" Kron asked. "I mean, does this *say* something?"

"Yes. But for now just pass it to the guys over your head and bear with me." He opened up his e-helmet's intercom. "Can you all hear me? I know these marks may look weird, but I want you to study the shapes closely. They're, um … a message."

"Huh?" they chorused. They obviously didn't have a clue what he meant.

"Sorry, let me rephrase that: it may sound crazy, but I'd like us to try to form our bodies into these shapes on the paper. Don't laugh, just answer yes or no. Do you think it's possible for us to, ah, 'spell out' this word? I know five people can form the central part and the rest should be able to link yourselves together and form the outer sections.…"

"Of *what*, sir?" a voice interrupted. "What *are* these chicken scratches?"

"Runes," Adam answered. "It's their language. These shapes are some of their oldest forms, so they're quite simple. With any luck they'll be able to read our message—I mean, read *us* as we descend. They're smart. I'm sure they'll catch on."

Tola asked the obvious question. "Just what is it we'll be spelling out, sir?"

He shrugged. "It's one word," he whispered. "Peace."

It became brilliantly clear. As the hushed group dropped through the air, they lined up their bodies the best they could to form the runic symbols. Tola's excited whispering filtered into their headsets. "Man, I couldn't think of a better way to bring greetings than this great flash of inspiration, sir," he gushed. "You have a formidable sense of capturing the moment then forming it into an indelible impression. This simplest of gestures should ease their anxiety, making them feel right about us, and.…"

"Stuff it, man! Thanks for the compliment. Let's just wait and see."

The runic word "*PEACE*" now floated down from the sky. Completing the illusion, Adam set their holographic camera off to the lower right like a period. As he turned on his scope vision, he drew in his breath. There was a glimmer of odd needle shapes in the distance!

"Guys, guys!" he hissed. "Get a load of what's *under* us!"

There was a muffled collection of clicks, then gasps of awe. Beneath them, a vast metropolis filled the view, fading off toward the horizons. Overwhelmed at the sheer grandeur they floated silently downward, their bodies locked together in their simple, silhouetted message of hope.

There was movement! Out of nowhere, a huge vehicle swiftly drew near, appearing to be nothing more than an enormous flat disc. Pale-looking humanoids were thickly covering the top surface, gesturing at Adam's group. Hundreds of dark eyes were turned upward and long, slender fingers were pointing excitedly at the floating crew.

"Wow, this is *it*!" Adam whispered nervously.

Wide-eyed, their hearts pounding, the men reshuffled back into an orderly line. As the disc moved swiftly up under them and pressed lightly against their feet, they turned off their antigrav belts.

"Who's got my sketchpad?" Adam hissed. He found his voice quavering.

It was down at the end of the line. Twenty-two shaking hands passed it back to him. Glancing up nervously and fumbling with his pen, he scrawled out a short runic message of greeting.

Diplomatically imitating their mannerisms, he approached their apparent leader in a floating, graceful walk. Smiling awkwardly, he bowed, offering his simple scrawl.

As a pair of surprisingly anxious hands reached out with an easy spontaneity, quiet, sibilant-sounding gibberish hissed from hundreds of slit-mouths.

He whispered into the crew's ear inserts. "I-I just wrote, 'Greetings from the Earth'! What else could I say?"

The alien's dark eyes widened as he read the message aloud to his companions. He spun around and looked squarely at Adam, firmly holding out his hand for the pen.

"Wow!" Tola gasped. "Apparently, sir, the pen *is* mightier than the sword!"

Adam winced, glancing over his shoulder. As he retrieved the pad, the writing immediately caught his attention: the alien's flowery script was amazing, even beautiful. He studied the author's sensitive hands. The fingers were slender and nimble, well adapted to turn out such a superior product, and the gracious words, warm with feeling, seemed to flow freely from the ornate piece of artwork. Although he found it harder to read, he translated the runes and read them aloud to his crew.

"I, Fendor, extend greetings from Aurona! Your message of peace coming down from our skies has finally dissuaded the few who have opposed your presence on our planet. First, we dropped our shields and now we have put away our great guns. Some, including myself, have anticipated your arrival for hundreds of years, Adam."

He blinked with a start. "This guy knows my *name*? How…?"

Tola's eyes urgently motioned him back down to the message.

Collecting himself, Adam continued translating. "Your grandfather simply appeared in a small craft one day. Although we initially opposed his presence, we finally reconsidered. Since then, his lively presence on our planet has been acknowledged by all as a true gift. Although we no longer know of his whereabouts, we welcome his progeny with open arms."

Adam blinked back sudden, unbidden tears and bowed courteously, thanking them. He fired off a rapid reply on the pad. "I'm extremely sorry to inform you of my grandfather's untimely death. He was my best friend."

A terse, shocked conversation rapidly ensued. They passed the notepad back and forth, each reading the other's reply aloud to their respective parties. Their host began to look even more pale as he wrote.

"But he simply cannot be dead! We talked with our minds a mere six hundred and twenty Earth-years ago! He, like us, was looking forward to your arrival with great eagerness!"

Adam couldn't stop his hands from shaking. "That couldn't be possible. I'm sorry to report that he died a few months before we embarked on this journey. I simply do not understand your concept of time. It is unthinkable. Did you know of his whereabouts while he lived on Aurona?"

"No, he was very secretive. Some say it may have been in the jungle, in a surface dwelling that he invented."

"A surface dwelling?"

The alien tilted his head, perplexed. "Yes, the concept is repulsive to us as well." Fendor visibly shuddered. "We do not understand how anyone could possibly live 'up there' on the surface. But he died so young! Could you please explain?"

Trying to remain unemotional and diplomatic, Adam pressed on. "Forgive me, but I simply don't have any answers. The issue at the moment is not of my grandfather's untimely passing, but of one of my crew. She is very special to me. Her name is Elena; she is missing and we think she has been taken down here."

Truly surprised, the humanoids gaped at each other, their slit-mouths wide.

"If this female Elena is in our city," Fendor answered, "then it is not by our knowledge. Perhaps she has been taken by force? We confess that we, as you, are not perfect. We have outlaws in our midst."

Grimacing, Adam narrated the reply. Wow, this definitely wasn't what he wanted to hear. Trying to keep the anguish out of his words, he forced himself to remain objective. "Elena is very dear to me. Perhaps you could help me find her?"

There was no hesitation. "Most definitely, my friend. You appear to be as genuine as your grandfather said you would be. We will help."

Kron whispered into his ear inserts. "Ah, something just doesn't wash, sir. Ask him why, if they were expecting us, did they have their shields up."

Adam nodded. "Wow, that's an excellent observation, Kron! Thanks!" He turned back to their host, scribbled rapidly, and handed him the question. Fendor's dark eyes bored into him as he translated the answer.

"Some sensed opposition."

"Yet you let us in?" he wrote nervously.

"Yes," he read. "We trust you, Adam." Suddenly, one symbol further, he noticed a larger, unmistakable runic marking, written in a heavier hand. "Secret."

He glanced up in surprise at Fendor's face. The dark eyes caught his own, then quickly motioned his attention back to the paper. Suddenly, he understood completely. He read on silently to himself, his eyes darting over the symbols. "Since you have tasted of the Rasheen, or mind-fruit, Adam, you should soon be able to see things clearly. We must protect our planet. Again, some sensed opposition within your crew. Watch your men closely." His words carried great weight and were obviously meant to be answered immediately.

Pretending to have a simple problem in translation, Adam turned to the crew, hoping they hadn't caught on. "Um, ah, I think these runes said that since we've tasted of the, ah, *hospitality* of the planet, they hope we find it to our liking."

The explanation seemed plausible. The men shrugged their shoulders, smiling acceptance. Out of his peripheral vision, he studied his small team with his host's new perspective. They all looked innocent enough as they stood there whispering to each other. His mind was reeling: obviously there were two sides to this thorny issue, so all future conversation would have to be continued in absolute privacy. But how? He glanced up. His host's eyes were now boring deeply into him.

Suddenly he felt a familiar, uncomfortable pressure returning full force to the back of his skull. His eyes widened. Could this be ... *telepathy*? Thinking quickly, he constructed some runes into a short, visual sentence. Concentrating, he beamed out the floating mind-message.

"Please help me."

Immediately, thousands of startled eyes snapped toward him. There was a soft buffeting in his mind, a weird probing, and then as he'd hoped, an answer to his plea.

"Congratulations."

Telepathy! And it was effortless! He translated his host's blazing runic reply in his mind, the symbols scrolling by in a rapid clip.

"You have passed your first test, Adam. The rest is quite easy. Yes, we WILL help you. From afar we sensed a pressure of opposition within your crew, but as we cannot yet understand your difficult language, we could not read their actual thoughts. That task is up to you, but remember this: the ability to read another's mind is a sacred privilege and not to be taken lightly. You will learn, with our tutoring, how to turn your new telepathic ability on and off, how to focus, and how to shield your thoughts."

The symbols abruptly stopped. He looked up in surprise. His host looked nervous. *"Excuse me, Adam, but you must turn back to your men immediately. We have been staring at each other far too long."*

He was stunned. The eleven were beginning to throw each other nervous glances. He grinned at them, waving awkwardly. His host nodded politely, turned on his heel, and walked back to his group.

Suddenly, another runic message flashed back to him! *"And do not think that we cannot continue our mind-conversation because we no longer FACE each other!"* He watched Fendor's back in disbelief as he continued to walk away. This was flat out incredible! What kind of door had just been opened?

It was like drinking from a fire hose: the runes continued to flood his mind. *"You will soon be able to send and receive mind-messages as we do, over great distances. I must close my thoughts for now, as we both have pressing formalities to attend to. I, for one, will be introducing you to our Supreme Leader. But remember, Adam, we are here, millions of us at your aid. You will not be alone. Good-bye."*

As the craft continued its descent, Adam rejoined his nervous group. Suddenly, he felt like he was a thousand years old. The unfamiliar pangs of etiquette and mind-manners were hammering relentlessly in his brain, and the intense cranial concentration was sapping his energy. He grimaced, his head pounding.

Kron broke the spell, nudging him. "Ah, you all right, sir? I hope I'm not speaking out of turn here, but what in the world just went *on* between you two? You were making faces like crazy, but that humanoid seemed calm enough."

"Oh … *that*!" Groping for answers, he shook his drumming head. "Do you find it hard to adjust to the barometric pressure down here, Kron? I've always been hypersensitive! My ears pop like crazy! We must be nearly a mile below sea level!"

"Really? *That* far?" Satisfied, Kron quickly turned and explained it to the men. They nodded in sympathy, smiling back at him and pointing to their own painful ears.

As the craft neared the ground, preparations were frantic below them. The twelve huddled together, peering uneasily over the edge of the disc.

Chapter 15: **THE CITY**

Like thousands of glittering needles, a forest of sharply sculpted buildings soared up toward the transporter disc. The airy structures were of incredible workmanship, with cathedral-like spires and translucent white alabaster buttresses inlaid with fine filigree borders. Everywhere there were architectural embellishments of pure gold.

The large disc landed. Craning their necks around and gawking like tourists, the small party disembarked and scampered after their nimble, long-legged hosts. The black sphere hovered over Adam's head, intently combing the horizon for Elena's PIL signal, but it remained disappointingly silent. Everyone was moving fast. It seemed that Elena's disappearance had spurred them all into a common sense of urgency.

They sprinted toward what appeared to be the on-ramp to a series of rapidly moving sidewalks. Anchored to the center of each rubbery moving belt were forward-facing seats and gleaming handrails. In single file, they edged nervously onto ever-faster traffic lanes, successively crossing them until they were at the center of a wide sidewalk superhighway.

Adam gripped a handrail tightly as they sped along, using his e-helmet's infrared and radar to scan through the misty atmosphere. No vehicles seemed to be in evidence except for a few strange, flying wedge shapes and discs near the incredibly sharp points of the buildings. Evidently, the Auronians didn't need surface transportation with this sidewalk speedway to take them everywhere! He sampled a quick air quality reading on his face screen. Just as he thought: absolutely pure! With a series of taps, he opened an outside port to take a whiff. Warm air poured in, clean, fresh and moist, but somehow with an undeniable tinge of perfume from … Motherlode Trees? He blinked in surprise. How could that odor make it down here into the depths of Aurona? Vents to the outside? Under low-power scope vision, he scanned the peaks of the distant buildings and then looked up, sharpening his focus. Thunderstruck, he gripped the rail.

"Holy cow!" he gasped. "I didn't notice *those* on the way down!"

The men turned toward him in surprise, then followed his gaze upward. Showing faintly through the heavy, low-lying clouds, a widespread pattern of colossal stalactitelike *cones* covered the distant, vaulted ceiling!

Adam gripped the handrail and planted his feet apart for better balance. High power snapped one of the mammoth shapes up close. "Wow, *incredible*! Are they machines? But there's hundreds of them, all exactly the same and spaced out over the ceiling!"

Suddenly, his headache returned in a rush of pressure. *"Adam!"* a blazing runic message scrolled by in his mind. *"Please forgive my apparent lack of manners, but as you know, I cannot look toward you as I mind-speak. Your men simply would not understand our strange, silent conversation."*

He replied. *"You mean I'm not supposed to look at you, either?"*

"Yes, but not all the time. This is called the art of 'separation.' You must learn to separate your thoughts and actions in order to avoid disturbing those who have not yet eaten of the

Rasheen. Now, I see you have just noticed our cones. How observant! I will try to answer your questions before we reach our rendezvous. Do not worry: the entire planet is now aware your Elena is missing."

Adam gasped in surprise, then glanced nervously at the men behind him. Kron caught his eye, smiling. Thinking quickly, he returned to his tourist mode and smiled back, gesturing excitedly at the ceiling. Kron nodded enthusiastically.

"That is better, Adam, but still not perfect. Keep practicing."

He noticed his host was slowly turning to face forward again. Evidently, his feeble attempt at separation had just been observed. His ears grew red. Chagrined, he quickly beamed a reply. *"Thank you. I'll try harder. Now, please tell me about those machines. I'm really curious!"*

"The largest cone you see in the center is an antigrav support in the trillion-ton range. It aligns precisely on the surface with what you call a 'Motherlode Tree.' The smaller cones are laid out between them in a regular half-mile gridwork and are wired directly into each other. As a unit, they are multifunctional, but essentially they form our life support. All the gold and electrical fields that shield our planet are processed by the Motherlodes, which in turn are central portals for the electricity generated by photosynthesis. Yes, Adam, all our trees generate electricity: our genetic engineers discovered and enhanced this phenomenon. We observed your group an hour ago as they discovered our live bioelectric wiring. Your powers of experimentation and swift deductive reasoning were thrilling and exciting to experience!"

He grimaced. So they *had* been watched! He had a feeling that thousands of eyes had been boring down his neck.

His host continued. *"For millions of years, all surface vegetation has been linked by their roots into what is now a huge web of production. We have power in abundance, with emergency backup storage for thousands of Auronian years. What you call Motherlodes are both our pride and our prize. Although we regularly eat of their fruit and nectar for its superior nutritive value, we eat of their Rasheen, or mind-fruit, in monthly rituals. We were extremely thankful that you only tasted it, Adam. In concentrations of more than one Earth-milligram, it is quite deadly!"*

He gulped, grimacing. *"Good thing I didn't take a bigger bite! I want to, though."*

"Oh, no! I repeat: do not be tempted to ingest any more for now! A fragile human body cannot assimilate the Rasheen's toxin at the rate of more than one gram per month! Unfortunately, our ancestors had to prove this fact through trial and error and have evolved through the millennia into our present body shape. Oh, speaking of shape, Adam, please take note of this: the softening of your cranium to accommodate a larger telepathic frontal brainmass has already begun and will soon be obvious to your crew."

His eyes widened in shock. *"What?"*

"Do not worry, the cranial swelling is gradual and painless. The skull will grow outwardly from its fissures like a seafloor ridge expanding beneath the oceans."

Adam was doing his best at practicing his new split personality. Desperately assimilating and translating the incoming reams of preposterous-sounding information, he was simultaneously acting out a totally different body language for his crew. Fendor turned to stare at him pointedly, making eye contact.

"Very good, Adam! You are learning 'separation' extremely fast! Hmm, actually much faster than your grandfather, probably because of your age. Well, no matter. Age is no longer that much of a consideration to you."

He suddenly felt overwhelmed. *"What-what did you mean by that? I meant the age part? I don't understand."*

His host seemed to anticipate his question. *"A twofold series of neurological and physiological events have already been triggered within your body, Adam,"* he answered calmly. *"Besides the fact that your neurons have begun to grow much faster than any time during your short human gestation, the mechanism of aging within each of your body's cells has begun to enter a most critical phase. The Bandor element within the Rasheen has begun to slow down all of your cell's internal clocks by securely tying together the ends of what your grandfather called 'telomeres.' Do you understand me thus far? What I am saying is that time and aging have now begun to be distorted far beyond your present comprehension."*

Adam found himself nodding vehemently inside his helmet. He glanced around, hoping the men didn't see. *"Ah, does that mean I'm not getting any older?"*

"No. You ARE getting older, but at a vastly slower rate. Let me see: speaking in Earth terms, I am estimating that your next one-year anniversary of birth should occur in approximately fifty Auronian years...."

He interjected excitedly. *"What? That means I can now multiply my expected Earthly life span of eighty-five years by a factor of fifty?"* He did the math quickly. *"No way! That computes to 3,825 years! Impossible! That I cannot believe!"*

The answer was adamant. *"Believe it, Adam. And with your extreme youth, there is even a chance that this rate of aging turns out to be an exponential factor, but...."*

"But? But what?" Adam was truly overwhelmed.

"There is one aspect, however, of which I have not yet told you. There is a price for this longevity."

"A catch! I knew there had to be one somewhere!"

Turning around, his gentle host caught his eye and nodded silently. *"Excuse me, Adam, but we are nearly there. Follow me as I move across to the slower-moving ramps."* For the benefit of the crew, Fendor lifted his slender arm and pointed animatedly to their destination. *"Are you ready, Adam? I am sure that in turn your crew will follow you. Once we have all disembarked, I will continue."*

Ahead of them, a large, multilevel park with cascading waterfalls opened up a breathtaking vista all the way to the horizon. Low clouds scudded over the broad, refreshing band of green and overhead, many of the creatures they'd seen on the surface flew freely about. The men followed their host in a tight cluster, entering through a strangely tingling boundary into the open green space. They couldn't help but notice that the animals seemed to turn aside sharply when they reached some kind of invisible boundary. Adam picked up his sketchpad once again and translated his message aloud to the crew as he wrote.

"A force field?" he translated, pointing.

"Yes," their host smiled as he wrote, glancing up into the air. "It keeps the specimens from wandering. We entered through what we call a Force Gate."

Adam asked the obvious question. "What happens now?" The men nodded.

His host penned a quick reply. "First, you may discard your helmets. The air quality is optimum here. Second, our leader approaches the city even as we speak. He has assumed all responsibility for Elena's rescue operation and will be its director. His intelligence surpasses us all."

As Adam pulled off his e-helmet, a mind-message flooded his consciousness. *"I did not forget our previous conversation, Adam, regarding your question about the price, or consequences of longevity."*

His eyes widened. *"Yes? I'm sorry, please continue."*

"Once you have started eating of the Rasheen, you must continue to eat of it sparingly, joining us in our monthly rituals. To stop at any point after the inception of your program would be dangerous and unstable for your rapidly changing metabolism. There is even the possibility of death."

He thought it out. "Yes, I see. It's my decision: stop eating and die at eighty-five, or nibble and live for centuries?"

A slight smile teased at the corners of Fendor's slit mouth. "Centuries? No. Millennia, Adam," he corrected. "We consider the small, ripe, superconcentrated Rasheen to be a priceless commodity, worth far more than all the gold you see lying about. Incidentally, as you may have already guessed, some have tried to steal this Rasheen in the past, but their attempts have always failed."

"Why?"

"Simply because it spoils rapidly and dies once it has been separated from the Motherlode. Nothing, absolutely nothing can preserve it." His host paused. "Excuse me, Adam, but it is time to return your attention back to your men. You must remember to obey the few, simple rules of mind-etiquette."

He grimaced, suddenly realizing that he'd indeed been standing with his back to everyone for too long, pretending to watch the scenery. His face grew hot as he heard Kron's footsteps approaching.

"Ah ... sir?" The man's tone sounded like he was feeling a bit isolated.

"Yes?" Adam smiled, rubbing his neck. "I'm sorry, go ahead."

"The men are starting to wonder why you've been acting so, um, strange. You'd better speak to them."

"Thanks, buddy." He thumped him on the shoulder. "I'll take care of it." He walked back to the group, determined to perfect the difficult art of separation. "Sorry I appear to be so distracted, guys. I-I guess I've been expecting a quick answer to Elena's whereabouts. It seems to be taking forever to get things rolling down here."

"I see, sir," Tola piped up, "It's been bugging me, too!"

The men nodded and gave each other knowing looks. Good. Their suspicions had turned to sympathy with a few, carefully chosen words. Concentrating, he sent out a runic message.

"How's that? Did I separate my thoughts and actions to your satisfaction?" He exhaled slowly. This multitasking and juggling of two conversations was extremely challenging!

"Excellent, Adam! I have been holding off telling you this, but I must now inform you that this delicate art of balance is one of the hardest levels to achieve, and normally comes only after years of training! But what we all found far more difficult to believe is that while you were still inside your starship, you demonstrated that you had a natural aptitude for telepathy. And you had not even tasted of the Rasheen!"

"What did you say? You, ah, saw me inside the starship??"

"Yes, we caught your image in our minds when you sent your first runic mind-message! That alone was a surprise. But now, with only the smallest taste of our Rasheen, your mind seems to have a superior power unknown to us! You are not only constructing your thoughts into visual runic sentences, but also translating them while you are simultaneously conversing on an entirely different plane with your men! We have no idea how far you can take your abilities once you have started our ritual! Yes, we have been deliberately testing you, Adam, and are now in awe of your youthful mind's tremendous flexibility. You are an unknown factor, a true prodigy! Please, can you stay with us so we may learn of these wonders together?"

Adam's answer erupted almost spontaneously from his mind. *"Yes! I'll stay! Indefinitely! I'm fascinated by these inner workings of the mind as well!"*

His host was beaming. *"Excellent! For now, though, we will give your mind a rest and write back and forth openly in front of your crew. Perhaps a better time can be arranged to continue our mind-conversation, such as this evening, when you are alone?"*

Adam jumped at the chance. *"Yes! A great idea! Tonight!"* He turned to Tola. "Ah, could you just give me a nudge if my mind seems to be wandering?"

"Yes, sir. By the way, have you asked these people what they call themselves? Names. I'm curious about names. I mean, do they call themselves Auronians, or what?"

He raised a brow. "Wow. Never *thought* about that! Lemme find out!"

The scribbled question went out and the answer was passed back quickly. He read it aloud. "We call ourselves Bandors, a name that has been passed down through the ages. Our Supreme Leader is nearly up to the Force Gate. He will explain further."

As his crew turned away to catch a glimpse, Adam smiled to himself. *"Bandors?"* he asked his host.

"Yes, Adam. After the Bandor element within the Rasheen."

"Ah hah! You knew I'd ask for the connection, but you kept your answer simple for the men's sake. I'm beginning to understand your concept of 'separation.'"

Standing a short distance away from the others, two of the crew were watching intently. The beefier one had already proven his abilities by supplying some real muscle power when they'd needed it, so he'd been chosen once more to help load the barges and insert the duct through the Solumbra. Dexor nudged his friend with his elbow.

"Glad you came along, Nastix?" he whispered. "You looked 'eager' enough."

"Yeah, what a sap! He picked me again?"

"So whassup with that guy, anyway? He's been starin' around all googly eyed and actin' like a stuck-up jerk ever since we got down here! Well, the tables are gonna turn real soon, 'cause his days are numbered."

"The clock's ticking," Nastix nodded. "That pod's gonna open, and…."

"End of the line!" Dexor's face darkened. He discreetly ground his fist into his open palm, his lips forming a tight, hard line. They both shuddered.

Nastix's brow furrowed. "How'd we ever manage to cram so much ammo into that big box with our, ah, 'guest'? And that capey thing he wears was hangin' outta the side! I-I tried as hard as I could ta stuff it back in. I was breakin' a serious sweat! It took all *four* of us to lift it, and then we were runnin' with it, too!"

Dexor rolled his eyes. "I know, I know. I almost got a hernia! Yes, we packed some serious firepower into that crate."

"Too bad these skinny bald-headed wimpos put their big guns away when they saw us floatin' down. I wanted to get a look at the guns, you know, see what we're up against?"

Dexor's eyes suddenly blazed. "Peace?" He curled his lip in revulsion. "He made us spell out the word 'peace' with our bodies? C'mon! How lame!"

Nastix snarked quietly. "Yeah, that creep must take us for saps!"

The lanky one scowled. "Hey, come on, people; let's get movin'! What's holdin' things up? I've had just about enough of this ant farm."

Adam looked around uneasily, rubbing the back of his neck. There was an undistinguishable, angry muttering in his head … side effects his host hadn't mentioned?

He felt an insistent tapping on his shoulder. His body tensing, his hand poised over his Stifler, he slowly turned around. A tall, elegant Bandor was standing there, his great, dark eyes glowing warmly from under the shadow of a tremendous, bulbous forehead. Overall, he looked much more wrinkled than the others and was dressed completely differently. He glanced at the Bandor's pale face. His mouth looked somewhat odd, like an awkward, upwardly curving … slit.

Kron nudged him, whispering. "That's the leader! He's the one!"

Adam returned the old one's gracious bow, surreptitiously stealing a closer look at his oddly contorted lips. It finally hit him. "Of course," he mused, "he's *smiling*! He's trying his best to copy *my* smile!" He looked down hastily, reading the Bandor's written message to the crew.

"Ah, he says, 'As a proclaimed Elder and Supreme Leader of the Bandors, I officially welcome your people to Aurona.'"

Bowing profusely, Adam smiled a bit wider. Immediately, the leader stretched his mouth-slit further. Smiles frozen in place, they began to converse, each reading their messages aloud. "I-I just wrote," Adam strained, "Thank you. On behalf of my crew, I accept your hospitality." His mouth was starting to feel tired, stuck in this position. Resolutely, he continued reading. "Could you please tell us your name? Mine is Adam."

"Yes, my name is Duron. For now, we will forget the rest of my names, as they stretch far back into my ancestry. They have simply assigned me a number in the Official Registry. We all call ourselves by one single name, followed by a number. For example, I am Duron 44235. My journey is well advanced, even for a Bandor; I have achieved almost six thousand Earth-years in this failing body."

As the men whistled softly and shook their heads in appreciation, Adam scribbled a quick reply. "Have others surpassed you in achieving these remarkable years?"

"Yes. Only one: a female, Roson. She has just marked her nine-and-a-half thousandth anniversary of birth. She is very wise and knew your grandfather well before he disappeared. They were extremely close friends. She is temperamental, though, and for the past hundred years or so seems to be showing more signs of the collapse of her mind. Elderly Bandors suffer greatly from this sickness, which is usually followed by death."

Adam glanced up from the note, exchanging surprised looks with his crew. This Duron was being quite candid about his people! He quickly bent back to his pad and continued reading. "But with new medicines being developed, there seems to be no limit to achieving years now."

Duron slit-smiled at the men, held up a finger, and then motioned for Adam to follow him a short distance away. As he walked, a telepathic message came back, the runes blazing hotly. *"I have a question for you, Adam. It cannot wait any longer!"* The old one stopped and looked around secretively, then reached into an inner pocket of his cloak.

His slit-smile seemed almost mysterious. *"Tell me about these strange, mechanical insects."* As his slender fingers uncurled, Adam's eyes popped.

"Spyders!" he gasped. *"Five of them!"*

The old Bandor studied his surprised reaction. *"Yes, I was the one who went up to the surface. I just had to find the remote operators of these wonderful surveillance tools! I laughed inwardly for hours after I experienced your antics. Humor is extremely rare on our planet. We have become so dulled by our intellect that there are few words left in our vocabulary to describe the phenomenon. And yes, I was the one who opened the shields. I alone made the final decision to let your ship through. I just had to see who else could be so fresh and exciting! Your grandfather was very much like you, Adam."*

As the old one slipped his cherished Spyders back beneath his cloak, Adam bent down, pretending to be writing something on his notepad. The big, dark eyes tried to follow the meaningless scribbles, questioning with a tilt of his big head. Adam explained his odd actions. *"No, I'm not writing anything, Duron. The men can't read these cryptic scratches anyway. Not a word. We've got to keep up appearances while we talk with our minds. It's a lot quicker, right?"*

Duron nodded with his whole body, his slit-smile impossibly wide.

A loud pinging signal brought their mind conversation to an abrupt halt. The sphere! Duron reached up quickly and plucked the black ball out of the air over Adam's head. Raising his scant, wispy brows, he punched out a quick code and handed the loudly vibrating object back to Adam. His dark eyes were gleaming.

Adam squinted into the surface. A new, altered display was scrolling by!

"Enhanced search mode… SEEK ELENA… Enhanced search mode… SEEK ELENA…."

He let out a loud whoop, punching the air. "*Elena*! We have a reading, men! We've located her!" As the crew cheered and gave each other high fives, he pretended to scribble a quick note to Duron.

"This is a surprise! You knew about this enhancement?"

"Yes, although weak, her frequency still resonates within the metallic haze you see all around you. We must hurry! It has not been long since she passed this way!"

Adam shook his head in disbelief. *"I'm sorry, Duron. We're not familiar with every function of these Bitronian holographic cameras. They're still new to us. Now may I ask yet another favor from you?"*

Slit-smiling, Duron took the pad and scribbled some more nonsense onto it. *"It has already been taken care of, Adam,"* he beamed. *"Your rescue craft approaches swiftly, even as we mind-speak. But we still have a moment; tell me more about these insects."*

Adam grinned. Wow, this one was really persistent! *"Thank you for anticipating my question, Duron! Well first, the letters in the Earth-name 'SPYDER' spells out their purpose! They're miniature holographic cameras on legs!"*

Duron's face brightened. *"Really, Adam!"*

There seemed to be an instant bond forming between the two, almost as if they were kindred spirits. Side by side they walked slowly back toward the men, deep in mind conversation. The notepad had now become meaningless and irrelevant, and Adam slipped it back into his pocket. The Bandor stifled his slit-smile, but a twinkle remained in his eye.

Adam turned to his men. "Ah, we just wrote out a long conversation, guys. Among many other things, Duron told me they'll be giving us a means of transport, as it's an absolute necessity when we track the sphere in enhanced search mode."

As if to back up his words, a sleek, silent craft appeared at the Force Gate. The glassy, teardrop-shaped bubble opened and a lone operator anxiously motioned for them to sit down and strap in. They shrugged, filing obediently into their seats. Adam sent the sphere aloft, and as the canopy closed it took off like a shot, its green lasers sweeping urgently toward the horizon. Hot on its trail, the ship hurtled after the disappearing speck with a tremendous, unexpected acceleration! It seemed to be flung into the air as if released from a catapult! Their bodies sunk deeply into the soft gel cushions, and the needle buildings turned into a blur around them.

In moments, the twelve sensed deceleration and looked up. There seemed to be a lot of construction going on. Ahead of them, a great, gold-streaked vertical wall seemed to define the western boundary of the continuously excavated metropolis.

Kron pointed excitedly. "There it *is*, sir! The sphere!"

They stopped, hovering alongside the holocamera. It was making whirring and clicking sounds, floating over a trio of metallic tubes sticking up out of the ground.

There was a low moan. Duron appeared to be in distress. He took a deep breath and closed his eyes, holding out his slender hand for the notepad. *"Please, Adam."*

Pretending to read his scribbles to the crew, the spark of hope ebbed from Adam's body. "He said, 'what you see, my friends, is one of the newest entrances to a labyrinth of supercooled vacuum speed-tubes that penetrate our planet. The tubes link this city to the other side, passing close to the core. In other words, Elena could be anywhere *in*, or anywhere *on* Aurona right now. We are truly sorry. Do you wish to continue your search?'"

Scribbling, Adam translated for the men as he beamed out his mind-message and handed Duron the reply. "Yes! Most definitely! Please lower us to the surface!" Resolutely, he reached out, retrieved the sphere, and stuffed it into his backpack.

As the craft touched down in front of the tubes, Adam looked around desperately. He noticed some Bandor workmen off to the side tinkering with a compact, sophisticated system of air supply and exhaust valves. An sudden idea flashed through his mind and he beamed another request to Duron. *"May I ask those Bandors workers a few questions?"*

Duron nodded, beaming out a hasty mind-message to the wary workers.

Adam hopped out and walked over to them, scrawling a quick note. "Greetings. We are guests of your Supreme Leader, Duron, and are searching for one of our party who is missing." As he handed the note to them, he beamed out a simultaneous runic mind-message of his own.

"Do not be afraid. I can read your runic reply with my mind, as I've tasted of the Rasheen. Please pretend to physically write, however, for the sake of appearance in front of my men. Conversation comes more rapidly with our minds and there is little time."

Without missing a beat and exhibiting true mastery of separation, they disguised their reactions. *"What do you wish to know?"* The shorter one made a show of scribbling a reply, studying Adam warily out of the corner of his eye.

"Very recently, have either of you noticed any suspicious-looking Bandors carrying someone ... or something?"

The taller one's eyes brightened subtly. *"Yes. I pretended not to look at them, because they obviously had their mind-shields up."*

His friend agreed. *"I saw them, too. They took a capsule into the center tube."*

"A capsule?"

"Yes, one of our larger shipping capsules. It is sized to fit only the center tube. Although it is slower, that tube follows a direct freight link to the other side of the planet, to the continent of Arrix. We have construction going on there as well. The right tube goes to the undersea city of Meseo and the left one connects to a speed station."

A spark kindled. *"A speed station? Can it get to Arrix faster than the freight capsule and be waiting outside when the larger center tube opens?"*

The Bandors glanced at each other and shrugged. The shorter one replied. *"It might be possible. I do not know the newest schedules, but let me converse with my friend Tunek 44366 in Arrix. He is the master controller and he should know."*

A powerful wave suddenly blasted underneath Adam's body. He tensed his shoulders, his eyes widening in alarm. *"Holy cow! What was that?"*

"Cow? I do not understand, sir. Please excuse my friend's small breach of mind-etiquette," the taller Bandor apologized. *"He was trying to reach Tunek quickly."*

"But in Arrix? You said the continent was on the other side of the planet!"

"Why yes, it is, but that is not so surprising! We have mining colonies on both of our moons and converse with them the same way." The workers glanced at each other.

Adam tried hard to keep the surprise from his face. *"I'm sorry, I just didn't know the extent of your people's telepathic abilities. Your range is phenomenal!"*

The short Bandor interrupted. "*Pardon, but Tunek 44366 just said your request is possible, but only if you leave immediately and make the right connections at the speed station. There is one important consideration though: the smaller speed tube can hold no more than six. You must divide your group and hurry.*"

Thanking them profusely with his mind, Adam turned and sprinted back to his crew, an impromptu plan formulating. His orders spilled out as soon as he reached them.

"Listen!" he puffed. "We may be able to *overtake* them!"

Kron's eyes widened in surprise. "Really, sir!"

"Yes! I'm sorry, Kron, but I'm going to need you and six men to remain here and guard this entrance until either we or they come out! I'll ask Duron for additional Bandor reinforcements at both terminals!" As he handed the notepad to Duron, he waved the others back toward the tubes. "Okay, you four come with me!"

Shocked, Dexor and Nastix followed eagerly, sprinting to catch up to Adam. "The *guns!*" Dexor puffed in a loud whisper. "We got a chance! Waddaya think?"

Nastix nodded vehemently. "They might be down in the middle of the planet!"

Running side by side, they discreetly punched the air with their fists.

In moments, the five humans and a short Bandor guide squeezed into a tiny speed tube, standing uncomfortably close. As the hermetic seals hissed shut a bell chimed, and they followed the Bandor's eyes upward. Above them, a flat panel displayed a schematic outline of the planet, with hundreds of lines passing through it in a jumbled morass. A long, slender finger reached up to touch the screen twice: first the source, then the destination. All but two lines disappeared. He nodded to the men. Immediately, they felt a slight sensation of movement. Barely thirty seconds passed before the Bandor was tugging at Adam's sleeve and motioning toward the exit in unmistakable body language.

"What? The seals are opening?" Adam glanced over his head. "It-it *can't* be!"

A red blip on the display showed them to be almost three thousand miles into the core of the planet: they'd arrived at a mammoth, supercooled underground station. The Bandor guide urged them to switch to another, larger speed-tube. With the hollow sound of running feet, they sprinted toward it and piled in, a small detachment of armed Bandor warriors crowding in after them. Duron had evidently sent the urgent mind-message ahead and things were *really* moving!

Again, a slight sensation of movement tugged at their bodies, feeling strangely familiar. "Of course!" he whispered to the men. "It-it all makes *sense* now! They have artificial gravity inside these pressurized speed tubes! The underground stations must be sealed, insulated, and the pressure adjusted to surface tolerance, or we'd have been crushed to death!" The five turned their eyes back to the ceiling to check their progress. Unbelievably, the red blip was almost to the other side! The Bandor soldiers were stirring, unobtrusively checking their weapons as they anticipated departure. His heart in his mouth, Adam activated the electrochemical charge in his Stifler, turning up the dial to full stun.

As the speed tube's seal opened, they spilled out quickly into the early dawn and dove for cover. Suddenly, there was a great whoosh of air behind them! Startled, they slipped into the shadows to watch anxiously. Their timing was incredible! The vacuum seals were opening on the central freight tube!

After a short pause, there was a subtle movement in the entrance. Motioning behind him, a lone figure warily stepped into the open. A sinister-looking group appeared behind him, weapons drawn, an antigrav pod floating in their midst.

Adam's fists suddenly clenched. Out of the blue, a crazy idea had flashed through his mind. He knew *exactly* what to do. His heart racing, he stealthily pulled the holocamera out of his backpack, tapped out a code, and sent it aloft.

"Seek ELENA!... Seek ELENA! ...Seek ELENA!" An enhanced, shrill scream announced its presence. Its screen flashing imperatively, its green lasers blazing brilliantly in the morning light, the sphere hurtled toward the kidnappers at a tremendous velocity!

The kidnappers recoiled in total confusion. Ducking and covering their heads, they fired their weapons randomly into the air, not knowing which way to turn.

An odd, cold adrenaline was pouring through Adam's veins. He snapped his head toward the crew. Why wasn't anyone *moving*? He blinked in confusion. Everyone seemed to be frozen solid, their movements locked in midair! No matter, Elena was there. Shrugging his shoulders, he grabbed the initiative and stepped coolly out into the open.

Just like a shooting gallery, he picked off the captors in rapid-fire, one by one. Had time itself *stopped*? He gawked in disbelief. They just hung there, impossibly suspended in mid-action, frozen as they were hit! Ever so slowly, their twitching, paralyzed bodies floated to the ground, a single, smoking hole marking the exact center of each robe.

Adam glanced over his shoulder at his companions. Everyone seemed to be swiveling their heads toward him in ultraslow motion. Suddenly, the odd surging that had distended his arteries flew away as swiftly as it had arrived. He drooped, his arms falling to his sides.

"What in the…?" Tola walked over to him, astonishment written all over his face. "D-do you realize what you just *did*, sir? We were all just getting into position when it was *over*! How in blazes did you move so fast?" His finger jabbed emphatically at the stunned bodies on the ground. "Twelve! Count 'em! You got all *twelve*! They dropped like flies!"

As the Bandor warriors cheered, Dexor's jaw sagged. He yanked Nastix aside, whispering in confusion. "I-I couldn't follow his movements! What *is* he, superhuman?"

"And a *dead shot*, too!" Nastix affirmed. "Man! We'd better watch out for *him*!"

Adam was sagging, leaning on Tola's arm. They watched as the Bandor warriors picked up the paralyzed bodies and slowly, carefully, slipped them into some kind of straightjacket, locking an equally strange helmet onto their bulbous heads. The flashing holocamera was hovering steadily over the pod, recording every movement.

"*Elena!*" Blinking to his senses, Adam stumbled toward her. "The *pod*!" he shouted. "The pod! Help me get this stupid thing open, guys! We don't know how long she's been *in* there!" Dropping to his knees, he twiddled helplessly with the dials and straps. Accidentally, he touched something he shouldn't and the pod fell heavily to the ground with a loud thud. Its antigrav function had just been disabled.

As a Bandor warrior reached out to restrain Adam's wrists before he could do any real damage, another warrior tapped a memorized sequence on a control pad. With a sharp hiss, a seam parted along the hermetic seal on the side of the pod. It opened slowly, revealing Elena's damp, sweat-soaked form. Pushing everyone aside, a Bandor checked her with a battery of strange instruments, then gave her a small injection.

As she began to stir, Adam scooted closer on his knees, watching the color reenter her face. Trembling, he reached out to hold her hands and wait for signs of recognition.

She coughed. "A-Adam?" Her eyes blinked, trying to focus.

A dark tunnel closed in. The sense of urgency gone, a viselike grip invaded, grabbing Adam at the base of his skull and choking off his windpipe. Vainly, he tried to swallow. The Rasheen! With great effort, he staggered to his feet. "Oh, no, not *again*!" he gasped. "I-I'm gonna...." He blacked out, collapsing backwards into the arms of his men.

Chapter 16: **PLANET OF LIGHTS**

Out in the rim of the great starship, the long, curving hospital bay was humming with activity far into the night. Even the most sensitive Bitron diagnostic equipment couldn't identify Adam's odd condition. With great reluctance, the last of the baffled Bandor attendants gave up and left around three in the morning. Kron and Tola remained at Adam's bedside, their bleary eyes glued to his monitors. Suddenly, at precisely five-thirty, every gauge unexplainably leveled out to normal. His brain had relaxed out of neural spasm. They watched the gauges a few more minutes, let out a breath of relief, then gave each other silent high fives and quietly slipped out the door.

Adam began to dream. Deeply troubled, he became soaked in a pool of sweat, stirring and groaning in his sleep. All the day's events were jumbled together: somehow, he found himself back in the jungle carrying Elena, who was hanging limply over his shoulder. As he slashed frantically through the dense, steamy undergrowth with a laser cutter and battled endless waves of thundering winged creatures, Solumbras suddenly swelled up out of the ground and popped open all around him. Packed together like sardines, armies of large-headed humanoids began to swarm out. He was exhausted, his arms felt like they were falling off, vines were twining around his feet and ranging searchlights kept spotting him as he ran. There was nowhere left to hide.

Suddenly, there was and odd twist in the jungle path. Slashing through one last thicket, he broke free and stumbled into the open! Elena stirred, woke up, and jumped off his shoulder. Somehow, as dreams go, there just happened to be two antigrav belts lying on the ground. They strapped them on quickly and jumped into the air. Flying side by side, they skimmed over sand, ocean, and clouds, gaining altitude and getting stronger. He felt like screaming for joy; at the mere snap of a finger their circumstances had been totally reversed! They glanced over their shoulders: far behind them, a roiling, flashing, black cloud receded into the distance.

Reveling in his new powers, he took a long, deep breath, smiling in his sleep. His mind was transforming rapidly, becoming sharper and extraordinarily different, his body was becoming more taut and keenly alive than he could ever remember. As they accelerated into the blue, he actually began to feel a cool wind on his face.

Out of nowhere, there was a gentle pressure on his shoulder and a soft hand caressing his forehead. An even softer voice whispered into his ear.

"Um, are you okay, Adam?"

The curtains of sleep parted. "Whazzat?" He opened his eyes a slit. The clammy hospital sheets were wringing wet under his back and his eyes were aching from an impossibly bright fiber optic diffuser over his head. Somehow, the same cool, lavishly perfumed breeze in his dream had woven its way through a hidden ventilation shaft. As his wandering eyes came to rest on Elena's face, he drew in a sharp breath. He reached up impulsively, pulling her close. The nightmare was over.

She sighed, trembling in his arms. "Bad dream?"

"A-and how," he muttered. "H-how long was I, um, z-zonked?"

"You couldn't have gotten much quality time," she muttered. "Kron said he couldn't sleep and came back. In fact, he's still sitting outside the door. He told me you were thrashing around half the morning, and, ah, you just made a loud whoop."

"I whooped?" He grinned. "Yeah, that's right. I-I was in sort of a race."

"Did you win?"

"You bet," he chuckled. "I got the jackpot!"

She snuggled closer. "I really shouldn't *be* here, Adam." She looked around furtively. "But I *grabbed* the chance and sneaked in. You can't imagine how many times I wanted to check on you, but I figured it was best to leave you alone. I left my room real early and wandered down to the dining hall with Joelle. We've been talking for hours! She told me all about how you went down into that city after me and knocked out those Bandor outlaws. I'm so proud! You-you really must…."

"Love you?" he interjected quietly, finishing her sentence. "Yes I do, more than anything in this world, or any other."

She drew in a quick breath. Her whispered words were lost, muffled against his cheek. After an eternal moment she leaned back, pulling her damp hair off his face. "So what happened? They said you got a horrible pain, right about here!" She reached behind him and rubbed a spot on the back of his head. "After you made sure *I* was okay, *you* collapsed and blacked out!"

"I know," he shrugged. "It was embarrassing. Ah, how'd we get back?"

She ran her fingers through his sleep-matted hair. "Tola and Peter carried you out. Those Bandor people were so kind to us, Adam, so polite and civilized. They escorted our group back through the speed tubes into the city, then up out of the hole."

Her cheery countenance darkened. "Speaking of nightmares," she whispered, "it *really* got scary when Duron turned off that gold shield. Those horrible, gigantic bees with the lights on their heads attacked us!"

"Are you *sure* I was unconscious? I swear I saw…."

She laid a finger across his lips. "You were out cold, Adam. First you, and then the bees. The men killed them all, but not before Peter got a horrible bite on his arm. He didn't get stung, thank God. We flew out of the rainforest in total darkness with our shields up." Suddenly she gripped his arm tightly, her blue eyes wide. "And, ooh, ooh! Adam!"

He raised a brow. "What? *What* ooh?"

"*This* ooh!" She giggled. "It was beautiful! The trees were all shimmering with this-this phosphorescent glow!" Her eyes had a misty, faraway look. "Just the growing tips of the branches were lit up like stars, millions of them! And then…." Her eyes popped. "We spotted this huge light through the treetops, kind of a tall, vertical beacon. When we broke through into our Motherlode's clearing…." She slid off the bed and threw her arms far apart to form a big tubular shape. "Our tree was bathed in this-this *intense* column of light, coming straight down from somewhere *above*!" She pointed upward, wonder in her eyes. "The-the whole clearing was lit up! It was *really* spectacular!"

He struggled to sit up. "Was it just *our* Motherlode we're, ah, parked in?"

"No, Adam, *all* of them. Every last one of them."

He drew back, studying her eyes. "How'd you find *that* out?"

"Well," she hedged, "while the doctors were trying to resuscitate you, a bunch of us flew up to the top again…"

"No! To the top? In the dark? But the hornets, the animals!"

"Don't worry," she assured quickly. "We had our shields up. But listen, it was *so* intense." She stared into the distance as if in a trance. "As far as we could see, hundreds of Motherlodes were lit up, marching toward the horizon as if they'd stepped into brilliant columns of light! Even though it was late, their flowers were still active. They were sending out these long, spangly washes of gold confetti, streaming up inside the columns!"

He was struggling to piece it together. "Columns of light, huh?"

"Hundreds!" she breathed. "Huge! Miles and *miles* high!"

A memory suddenly jolted his consciousness. "Hey, wow!!" He sat bolt upright. "Just before the shields closed, I remember *seeing* those columns of light from space! They were all along the day/night boundary, making the horizon look like a pincushion of full of needles from that angle. I've got a few holo-photos of them! He leaned back, reflecting. "But it figures. Listen. I think the Bandors have given the Motherlodes a few extra hours of daylight to keep up the production."

Her head tilted questioningly. "Production? You're moving too fast for me. Of, what, the mind-fruit?"

"Rasheen," he corrected, gently. "Bandors call their mind-fruit Rasheen. No, believe it or not, it's *electricity*, made through *photosynthesis*!"

"No *way*!" she exclaimed. "You've gone too far with that one, you screwball!"

"But it's true!" He shrugged. "The Bandors told me. Every leaf, every vine, every tree on Aurona manufactures it, and it's all routed into the Motherlodes! Ah, and there's something else, hon." He looked deeply into her eyes. "Something big. Huge. I-I don't know how to say this…."

She found her voice. "What is it?"

"Um, the Bandors told me all this incredible stuff by, um, telepathy." He turned away quickly, checking her reaction out of the corner of his eye. "We-we had a whole a mind-conversation going on in their runic language."

Her mouth flew open. "You *speak* in runes now?"

"No, not exactly." He pointed to his head. "I-I…."

"Oh," she nodded. "You write it in your head and they pick it up?"

"Bingo!" He grinned. "Just think of it, Elena! I-I'm *telepathic*!"

She squinted at him. "Don't go pulling any of that spooky stuff on *me*!"

His hands went up, his face a mask of innocence. "Promise, Elena! Hey, hey," he soothed. "I think it's time to change the subject here. Got any of your famous theories about where the light might be coming from?"

She paused, changed gears, and contemplated a moment. "Well, I-I *think* I do." She looked down into her lap and began to form a small o with her fingers. "Don't laugh. This idea came to me last night while I was staring at the light show." She raised her arms, her imaginary circle growing larger. "Maybe, just maybe, way above each tree, the Bandors have figured out how to clump a big, dish-shaped section of gold particles together and tilt it at an angle to the sun." She glanced at him out of the corner of her eye.

"You're saying it's done with *mirrors*?"

She gave him a shove. "Yes, you goofball! But *gold* mirrors," she said, giggling. Her fingers returned to their circle. "You know, slightly warped, fine-tuned parabolic dishes of gold up in the sky? Theoretically, they should catch the sunlight and focus it … downward.…" She tipped her o section slowly toward the bed.

He laughed, jerking his hand away from the imaginary hot spot. "I'm getting jealous, Ms. Einstein! So it's mirrors now?"

"Yes. There's a separate reflector. One for each tree."

"Think you've got it pegged again as usual, huh? Huh?"

She batted her lashes, then flopped against his chest. "Wanna know what I *really* think?" As she stared dreamily into the distance, there was a long silence. "Adam?" She raised a brow, slowly lifting her head.

Two bugged-out eyes were boring deeply into her.

"You-you *beast*!" She pummeled him on the arm. "Don't *ever* pull that spooky mind-stuff on *me*!" She yanked a pillow over her head, glaring at him from the shadow.

He squinted hesitantly into her cave. "Aw, sugar plum! I'd *never*!"

She scowled darkly.

He shrugged. "All right, I give up! I couldn't possibly penetrate *that* mind-shield!"

There was a muffled giggle.

"I gotta obey *all* the rules of mind-etiquette, or those selfish Bandors won't let me taste any more of their yummy Rasheen!"

She sat back, dumping the pillow to the floor. "You're kidding. Tell me you're kidding. *Mind*-etiquette?"

His heart raced. She was irresistible, impossibly beautiful with her face flushed and her hair tousled. Impulsively, he pulled her to his chest. In a moment he found his voice.

"Ah," he croaked, hoarsely, "wanna honeymoon?"

"Y-yeah," she echoed, then looked up mischievously. "But it's honeymoons-s-s-s, Adam. Plural. There are *two* moons on Aurona, remember?"

He pushed her head back down onto his chest.

"Tonight," he vowed. "Tonight you'll be mine. Promise."

"Okay." She buried her face into his neck. "But we'll do it right.… Right?"

He drew back. "Is there any other way? Yes, the wedding is *definitely* first. We're leading the way by example. Besides, everybody *knows* we belong together!

The dining hall was packed with the anxious crew when they entered. Spinning around in surprise, they erupted into sudden noisy cheers. Way off to the side, an unexpected visitor turned around, startled. He hesitated briefly at the commotion but then put on his best, curved slit-smile.

"Duron!" Adam towed Elena through the throng to the skinny Bandor's side.

"He's been waiting for you all *morning*, sir!" someone shouted. "We finally enticed him to come in here and try a little Earth food!"

As Adam returned the old one's gracious bow, Tola eagerly shoved his notebook and pen toward him. Smiling warmly, Elena offered her hand to Duron. There was a puzzled tilting of his big head. In a rush, runes formulated quickly inside Adam's mind.

"What does this mean, Adam? The extended hand? What custom is this?"

Diplomatically, he lifted the pad and wrote. "We welcome you, Duron," he paraphrased loudly. "The offered right hand is meant to be taken and grasped in friendship. This Earthly custom originated as a means to show that the one offering an open palm had no concealed weapons, so as we originally stated to you, we do indeed come in peace."

Duron drafted a quick reply. As he returned the notebook and pen, he turned to Elena and bowed, grasping her hand firmly.

Adam read his message. "We, the Bandor people, are as anxious to learn your language as you learn ours." How nice. Pausing for the barest second, he studied Duron's wrinkled face. There seemed to be a strange twinkle he hadn't noticed before. He glanced back down and continued. "But until then, your leader, Adam, and myself will be distributing these translator buttons."

He stopped abruptly, mid-message, turning slowly to face the crowd. His mouth silently formed the words: "Translator buttons?" In the silence of a near-perfect comedic pause, he heard a snicker. Ah, there it was, his cue. Shrugging, he tossed the notebook aside and stuck out his hands. "So *gimme* one already," he hammed, "I've *had* it with all this writing!"

As the crew hooted in appreciation at their leader's unexpected clowning, there was a rustle of fabric. With his slit-smile now stretched impossibly far, Duron produced a small box from the voluminous folds of his cloak.

"Boy, *that* was fast … and you *deliver*!" Over a round of renewed laughter, he read the label. "Hmm, this is fortunate. It's marked in both runes and English! 'Three gross: Bandor/English Trans.' Enough for everyone, huh?"

At the back of the room, Dexor urgently motioned his pals out into the corridor. The three followed him tightly on his heels. As he twirled to face them, they piled into each other like a derailed freight train.

"Oof! Hey, slow down!" he hissed. "Did'ya hear that, pinheads? Translator buttons! A breakthrough!"

Senn nodded back enthusiastically, pulling down his rumpled sleeves. "Yeah, boss! We'll be able to talk to anybody on the planet now!"

As the four gave each other a round of fist bumps, Dexor muscled the beefy man into a headlock, rumpling his sleeves again. "So let's go back in and see how those little suckers work!" His eyes were as cold as ice. "A little sweet-talk, darlin,' and we'll find out where they hid ALL the guns!"

The crew watched the tall Bandor opening a crinkly, cellophanelike material. He held up a bright red, nickel-sized button, then peeled off a backing and stuck it low on his throat, just above his chest. Tapping it once, he turned to them. "This little device is heat-activated," he began, "and it is powered by slight temperature differentials with what Adam's grandfather called a nano-Sterling engine."

He was talking! In English! They stared at him, not really believing what they were hearing. While his small slit-mouth made hissing Bandorese sounds, the tiny red button was broadcasting an excellent English translation, complete with proper inflection!

"As you might guess," he continued, "these translator buttons can only be a temporary measure. To really *learn* our Bandor language, translator cubes are also available for you to install in your Dream Library! It has been a long journey. Our scholars toiled for many decades in close association with Adam's grandfather to produce these buttons. He said they are vastly superior to the Earthly prototypes he arrived with: there is almost no lag time between the spoken and the resulting broadcast word."

In a few short sentences, he'd earned their respect and captured their imagination. Yes, he was no longer just a hissing, babbling foreigner but one of *them*! Their eyes turned to Adam. He already had one stuck on his neck. Following Duron's example, he tapped it once, lightly.

"Hsst ssmshh…," he whispered hesitantly. It was Bandorese, but sounded awful.

The crew stifled their smiles, glancing questioningly at Duron. Maybe it wasn't working? Maybe he'd picked out a reject?

Adam took a deep breath and put everything into it, enunciating the words carefully this time. "Hsst ssmshh tbl Z*Zoossh*!"

Amidst a wave of nervous chuckles, Duron raised a slender finger for attention. "What is the problem? Adam just said, 'I am trying to speak' in Bandorese, and I understood him perfectly!" He turned, slit-smiling, and offered a button to Elena. "Try one! You will find it even transmits in a higher register to match your female voice!" Nimble fingers flying, he peeled off the backing and stuck it on her neck.

"Zeeeeeee!" It squeaked to life. "Zee, hee hee!" She was laughing! In Bandorese! It translated roughly the same. As the crowd began to lose control, Adam chimed in, his shoulders heaving spasmodically.

"Ooo! Zoo, hoo hoo!" he rumbled. "Zooo, hoo hoo!"

Elena squeaked louder in response. "*Zeeeeeeee!*"

"*Zoo! Zoo, hoo, hoo*!!" he roared.

The crew was teetering on the razor edge of composure.

Elena drew in a sharp breath, trying to regain her composure. "*Snarrrkkk*!!" it translated, as the air went in.

That was it. Pandemonium reigned. Her face turning red, she broke away, sprinting toward the door with her hand clamped over her mouth. "Zeeeeeeeeeeee-e-e-e…." The muffled squeal trailed away down the corridor.

Suddenly, it was all the rage. Red buttons flew among the crew and soon, amidst the loud crinkling of wrappers, everyone had one stuck on their neck giving them a run for their money. Duron had to turn away from the wild, boisterous crowd, his narrow shoulders jiggling, his big head bobbing. Adam was helpless with laughter, twisting his button futilely. He tried to eke out something, *anything* recognizable. "Ssshoo! Hmeeesh!" No good. One more try. He took a deep breath and shouted at the top of his lungs. "*Hronnnnnk*!!" he honked.

Beet-red faces slid under the cafeteria tables. The crew had lost it completely, quacking and mooing in an alien barnyard gone amuck. After what seemed an eternity, someone shouted over the din.

"Th-the translators, sir!" a man gasped. He'd peeled his button off his neck and was waving it in the air. "A-ask Duron how to *d-deactivate* them!"

Adam turned around. The old one was holding onto his stomach, standing a little stooped over. "Hurt?" he asked in perfect Bandorese.

"Yes, Adam."

"Oh, thank God you can understand me!"

"The unused musculature in my face and abdomen have been greatly strained, Adam," he interrupted. "We are a sedentary, scholarly people, not at all familiar with the phenomenon of humor. But you have brought *life* to our planet! We did not know what we were missing!"

Adam was inspired. "Hey, how's this idea? We got fifty extra bunks downstairs. Your people are more than welcome to stay up here with us! You'll be safe! Once everybody's settled in, we'll get together and form exploration parties! You guys show us the planet and I'll crack jokes!"

Duron slit-smiled, holding his sides. "Thank you for your kind offer, but I really need to change the subject, Adam. I have to calm myself. I really want to tell you the story of our planet, but first," he held up a cautionary finger, "I'd strongly suggest that you remove your starship from this, ah, Motherlode Tree? When you settled into its branches, you caused a small tremor along the Eastern wall of our capital city of Azimos. The sudden, colossal weight of your ship caused our force field to activate. We were afraid we'd lose both you and our ceiling."

"Oh, no," he breathed, rubbing his sore stomach. "I'm so sorry, Duron! Ah, we did notice a tremor but we were all set to take off at a moment's notice, I swear!"

"For obvious reasons, Adam, we never build under a large body of water."

He grinned nervously. "Well, moving on... I'll scoot the ship down to the shore of the lake as soon as possible. Howzat?"

"Thank you, Adam. Ah, 'howzat'? I-I do appreciate the rich variations within your language," he chuckled. "We do want to get to know you better, so your suggestion about providing guides and tours sounds timely. Yes, we will *do* it. You can all visit all our great cities under different circumstances now!"

"Super!" Adam pumped the old one's skinny hand enthusiastically, then lowered his voice to a more serious tone. "Ah, tell me. This may be personal, so please don't be offended. Why'd your people move underground anyway?"

The old one glanced around the noisy room. About twenty of the crew had pulled up chairs to listen to their intense, lively conversation. More were gathering on the outskirts of the growing circle, filling in the gaps and pulling up chairs. He shrugged. "Well, as I promised, it looks like now would the right time to deliver the story of my planet, right?"

The room quickly fell to silence, save for the scraping of chairs on the floor.

He began hesitantly. "Well, initially it was only in small groups, but our earliest ancestors had to dig simple caves to escape from the dreaded Razah. It roamed around feeding freely on our people...."

"Excuse me," Adam interrupted, "but before we start, was this Razah a huge, striped creature with a bulbous forehead?"

The frail leader drew back, alarmed. "You have already *seen* one?"

"Um, yes!" Adam was genuinely surprised at Duron's reaction. "Tola and Sahir were right up close to it yesterday. One of those bad boys was impaled on those weird, long spikes sticking out around the base of our tree!"

Duron's slit mouth formed a small, round o. "No, no! Your crew was *much* too close, Adam! The Razahs are *deadly*! They can throw out their mind-stuns for *extraordinary* distances now! One's body becomes instantly paralyzed!"

Tola's eyes bugged out. "Wow, we weren't aware of that, Duron! Ah, don't you guys have any guns?" he asked incredulously. "Any defenses?"

Duron shrugged. "We choose not to kill, Tola. It is our way."

"Oh," the round one nodded, "I understand."

"Listen, all of you!" Duron raised his voice, holding up his skinny arms for attention. "This is *very* important! Your lives may depend on this information! The Razah has learned to cast out a low-impulse signal, a sort of mind-net, if you will. He senses, locates, and then stuns his prey with it. With our active minds, higher organisms like us are extremely easy to find. When one of us wanders too far from the others, the Razah actually 'hears' our thoughts of separation!"

He glanced at Adam pointedly and beamed a quick, simultaneous mind-message: *"Adam, I believe the Razah was after YOU yesterday! If the beast hadn't become impaled on the Dazeen spikes, your awakening telepathic mind would've been stunned and you'd have fallen paralyzed from the top of the tree!"*

Elena returned quietly to the room and slipped her arms tightly around Adam's waist. He pulled her closer. "Wow, Duron! Thanks for filling us in! So why don't you just *trap* them all? Yes! Just trap all the Razahs and those big hornets and put them into protected reserves using force fields, or something."

Duron looked startled. "Hornets? Explain those creatures to me, please."

Elena spoke up. "Remember, Duron? They were waiting at the entrance to your city last night. Those gigantic insect creatures with the bright searchlights?" she shuddered.

The dark eyes grew large. "Oh, you mean the Spyrins!"

The crew glanced at each other, whispering and mouthing the new word.

Sahir had pulled up tightly against Joelle's side. "They have big stingers, too, guys! I was with Tola yesterday and we saw a Spyrin attacking that Razah right under this tree!"

Duron spun to her in alarm. "What? You saw one out in *daylight*?" he gasped. "They have always stalked their prey in total darkness, blinding them with their searchlights!" His mouth turned into a tight, hard line. "So, they have evolved far beyond our expectations. I am sorry to admit this, but they are our fault."

Sahir pressed for an explanation. "Huh? How could that be?"

Duron shrugged. "We created them. They are an early genetic experiment gone terribly awry.

Eons ago, they were much smaller insects and had only vestigial stingers. Our genetic engineers enhanced their natural bioluminescence for enjoyment in the nighttime sky, just like they created the lights on the Arren trees and the plumage of the Dazzor birds."

Adam exchanged knowing glances with the crowd. Their ears had quickly learned to filter out the unknown language for the known, and from their expressions, it was obvious they understood both sides of the hissing, confusing conversation. With Duron's string of fascinating revelations, more pieces of Aurona's complicated puzzle were falling rapidly into place. Without exception, the old one had captured everyone's attention. Even Dexor and his cronies had stopped sneering from the back of the room.

Duron continued, "With the unexpected phenomenon of the Spyrins, our engineers hadn't counted on what we now call 'the Razah factor.'"

Adam pressed, gently. "Ah, was this some kind of food chain?"

"Yes, a good comparison, Adam. We Bandors are right at the top of the chain, as we occasionally eat the fruit of the Motherlode, which we call the Rasheen. No living creature except us can withstand the direct effects of Rasheen toxins. Next, you'll have to remember," he shuddered, "that the Razahs occasionally feed on us…."

There was a sudden scraping of chairs. Several of the women were starting to draw into tight clusters for support.

Duron continued. "I must explain the 'Razah factor': the Spyrins learned to feed on dead Razahs for protein and quickly developed a special fondness for the delicate flavor of its marbleized, fatty flesh. The diluted Rasheen toxin in the Razahs invaded their insect bodies and triggered an abnormal growth spurt. Disturbing, sporadic sightings of ever-larger Spyrins began to trickle in."

Adam sent the old one a quick mind-message. *"I'm sorry, Duron, but this crew is a handpicked collection of extremely bright young people. Someone will undoubtedly ask you about the Rasheen: since it's so toxic, why you Bandors ingest it? I'd prefer if you offered them a simple explanation for now. It's better that they don't know anything about the telepathy part."*

Duron didn't miss a beat and continued smoothly. "We have found that small, extremely diluted amounts of this highly toxic substance helps our thoughts to be clearer and more focused in order to create and invent more intuitively."

Adam acknowledged his immediate response. *"Wow! That's pretty darn good, Duron! And the 'thinking clearer' part IS true. You didn't have to make up a thing!"*

He turned to the crew, deftly finishing Duron's cover-up. "So I think we've got it. A simple food chain: Motherlode to Rasheen to Bandor to Razah to Spyrin, right?"

"Correct, Adam. And I would further recommend that none of you go near the source of all this trouble, the Rasheen. It has taken us centuries to unravel the amazing, complex mysteries within its genome. As far as we know, Spyrins are the only known predators of the Razah. They sometimes even kill them for sport. They are social insects and live underground in large colonies, filling the abandoned caves of our ancestors."

Elena shuddered. "In *hives*? Ugh!"

Duron looked at her pointedly. "Yes, yes, Elena! We share your feelings completely! We *never* venture out of our cities at night anymore, at least not us older Bandors! Our youths are far more daring. No, we decided long ago to devote as much of the planet's surface area as we could to the direct production of electricity through photosynthesis. That meant moving totally underground."

She put it together quickly. "Oh, that's it! And the larger your cities grew, the more power you needed to hold up your ceilings, right?"

"Yes," he nodded. "Our billion-ton antigrav machines were soon replaced by trillion-ton models, and so on. It is still growing. We older Bandors occasionally miss the outdoors, but our underground parks...."

"Duron," Tola interrupted, "I'm sorry, but why don't you just live outdoors and corral the pests with a Force Field?"

"What you call 'pests' are the apex of Aurona's food chain. Without them, the planet would soon be overrun with lesser creatures, including the numerous species that devour our vital plant life. By eliminating them, we'd upset the natural balance."

Adam nodded. "Elena has a bit of experience on this subject," he smiled warmly. "She was the head engineer at Biozyne, a multibillion-dollar conglomerate that always seemed to make international headlines! I'm still baffled why she left to join us."

As the startled crew studied her with new respect, she attempted to explain, red-faced. "I-I was just part of a team, guys! Back on Earth in the mid-twenty-first century, we had to resort to some pretty drastic measures. We were abandoning international treaties left and right and the last of our breeding zoos were dwindling down to mere handfuls of endangered species. The genetic engineers in my team finally perfected how to reproduce healthy offspring using artificial wombs, and repopulated our small wildlife preserves to capacity! Unfortunately," she shrugged, "the real problem remained: their original habitats were almost gone. Rainforests were turning into dead, windblown Sahara...."

Adam chimed in. "Hey, on the other hand, New Guinea's back on track! They've restored all their rainforests into pristine condition! Right after I was born, my grandfather sold them exclusive rights to an invention he called CloneBank...."

"Huh?" Startled, Elena spun to him. "Not *the* CloneBank? You're kidding! My company invested heavily into it and it's become the gold standard!"

He looked surprised. "Wow, that means New Guinea finally released their patent rights! Good for them!"

"Yes, that *is* very encouraging," Duron interjected. "Your grandfather did mention something about his CloneBank years ago and was wondering if it helped. He was pleased to learn that we had also developed a technology to reclaim vast stretches of useless desert back into verdant, productive rainforest. Our reflectant cloud canopies of gold are an integral part. You may find this hard to believe, people, but our planet Aurona was once dry, cold and arid, almost entirely desert!" He beamed proudly, slit-smiling back at everyone's incredulous stares. "Millenniums passed and our technology flourished, but eventually the deserts stopped shrinking. Aurona had shifted slightly into a more regular orbit around our sun and slowed its axial wobble. The planet became warmer."

Adam scooted to the edge of his chair. "You stopped having seasons?"

"Yes. As the icecaps melted, the oceans rose. There was eventually a short time of terrible flooding when we lost irreplaceable records of our earliest voyages to distant star systems. Many of our ancient coastal caves are inundated to this day." He paused, his eyes focusing somewhere in the distance. "Our people will never visit them," he whispered. "We consider those vaults to be sacred tombs."

Adam shifted uneasily. "Ah, how long ago did all this happen, Duron?"

"Just before the discovery of what you call the 'Motherlode Tree.' Although our records were lost and our memories were insufficient, our oral tradition remained. We estimate that the two events coincided over two million Earth years ago."

"Two *mill*...?" Adam caught himself, then toned down his voice a notch "Wow! Two million years? You had scientists and underground cities way back *then*?"

Duron continued, unhurried. "Why, yes! And it was only by purest chance—no, a miracle—that our scientists obtained that first tree. Up to then, they'd spent many frustrating years combining countless plant species through genetic engineering. One day, a large shipment of exotic plant and animal species arrived from a distant galaxy. As I have said, we lost all the records of that particular voyage during the coastal flooding. They noticed something unusual about one of the saplings: a tiny, rooted cutting, apparently taken from a colossal parent tree."

"The Motherlode!" someone whispered.

He glanced up. "Yes, the Motherlode. It was a truly momentous discovery that day. They found that the cutting manufactured a strange enzyme in its sap that could dissolve gold, an abundant mineral, and pull the resulting liquid in through its root system. They planted it over a healthy surface vein. As the cutting matured into a small tree, its flowers began to send out small quantities of gold vapor into the atmosphere!"

Adam edged closer. "You mean that all your Motherlodes came from that *one* original cutting and it didn't even come from Aurona?"

"Why yes," Duron nodded. "But why is that so strange? The Motherlode is an alien species, as are nearly all of our flora and fauna. Remember, Aurona was once almost entirely desert!"

The skinny one shifted uncomfortably on his hard cafeteria-issue chair, gathering his long robe under his bony frame for padding. "So in our never-ending quest for greening, that one cutting quickly became many and matured at a phenomenal rate. Our people propagated millions of the vigorous cuttings, eventually blanketing vast acres of our desert planet. But something else began to happen, something totally unexpected. In only a few short centuries, the skies grew darker as the golden flakes blocked out Aurona's sunlight."

"Wow! Your planet must have been cooling down real fast!"

"Yes, Adam," Duron said slit-smiling. "Then we remembered an old Bandor saying: 'To learn, you must dig deeply.' So our people dug, literally, and found two things. First, the abundant underground wiring you have seen had spread beyond imagining! The Motherlodes were forcibly inducing all the greenery to provide additional food for them! That is partially why they are so colossal. But second and more importantly, another strange thing was happening. Aurona's weather patterns were changing. It was getting balmy for hundreds of miles around the trees!"

Elena was shaking her head in disbelief. "The Motherlodes were actually changing the weather to suit their needs? What kind of supertrees are they?"

The old one contemplated. "We still do not know their full potential, but back then it was a paradox. Although our ancestors saw that the global network of underground wiring was stabilizing the enormous static differential between planet and atmosphere, thus abating the most severe storms, the trees seemed destined to eventually destroy the planet as the skies continued to darken! To make matters worse, one day news came that a Razah had stalked and eaten our last truly knowledgeable elder-scientist as he worked outside. A great sense of foreboding fell that evening, crippling initiative and destroying hope. That very night, an unknown youth performed an unlikely experiment down in one of our underground dwellings."

As the crew leaned forward expectantly, his slit-smile appeared to be almost mischievous. "It was Duron 229, my distant ancestor! A mere child of eighty-six years! He sent up a polarized charge of electricity through the tap root of a Motherlode!" His slender palms rose excitedly in the air. "Immediately, a great hole opened in the sky as a circle of flakes turned on their axes!"

As Elena nudged Adam pointedly, the crew smiled. Her fingers were discreetly forming an o in her lap. Duron continued his eloquent roll.

"The answer had been within our grasp all the time! Within a few years, Duron 229 discovered and refined the phenomenon of electricity manufactured through photosynthesis. With unlimited quantities of this new power at our disposal, we began to electrify the entire planetary network of Motherlodes!" His dark eyes were sparkling. "*We* controlled the weather! By turning flakes selectively, heating some landmasses with light and cooling others with darkness, we moved clouds and made rain! A few years after his death we began to reclaim the desert, fifty square Earth-miles at a time. But then…." A dark cloud of painful reminiscence suddenly passed over his face. He lifted his eyes upward. "The invasion," he sighed.

There was a stunned silence. No one dared to ask the obvious. Adam took the bull by the horns and probed gently. "Ah, another civilization found out you had gold?"

Duron spun toward him. "*Yes!*" he sputtered. "C-can you imagine? Such an *abundant* mineral!" The gentle leader had caught everyone off-guard. They drew back, surprised; they hadn't as yet seen such a display of emotion coming from him.

The old one stood up indignantly, smoothing out his cloak. "True, it has been calculated that a tremendous percentage of our planet is made up of this-this gold," he sputtered, shaking his big head in disgust. "When they attacked us, we threw up all our electrical shields at once. Collectively, it-it *vaporized* them! *We* were more surprised than *they* could ever have been!"

Duron's pointed gaze fell on Adam. "In the two million years hence, we've had to repeat this defensive action only two more times. As you may have guessed, the first was for the arrival of your grandfather and the second was for you. Frightening? Not so much when you put it into perspective. In comparison, the shields are just a puny, defensive weapon. There is another, a far greater offensive weapon at our disposal. We have tested it once and put it away, confident of its power."

Cautiously, Adam stepped into the breach once again. "How did you test it?" He glanced around the room, shrugging. "I mean, what did you do?"

Duron turned to him. "Our astronomers warned of an impending collision with one of our three moons."

"*Three* moons? B-but we've seen only two!"

As a true leader, Duron knew that diplomacy was useless without a powerful deterrent to back it up. The old one turned and directed his weighted words toward the back of the room. "We used the power of the Big Guns to blast the planet out of orbit!"

As shocked whispers hung thickly in the air, Dexor formed a quick huddle, muttering into his cronies' ears.

"*C'mon! C'mon, bean-brain! Tell Dexy where they are so we can all go home!*"

Senn agreed, nodding vehemently. "*Yah,*" *he echoed,* "*tell us where dey are!*"

Dexor's eyes glinted as he focused intently on the old Bandor. "*So whaddaya waitin' for, mushroom-head? A shakedown? A little blood?*" *he muttered, his teeth clenching.* "*Don't tell usss it'sss a sssecret now!*"

The old one talked softly to the group, like a father. "I'm sure you are wondering where they are kept, but I am afraid that is a matter of planetary security," he concluded. "While the Big Guns were originally used as a defensive weapon, they are now considered offensive. You are our invited guests, our friends. Thank you for now," he bowed.

Dexor elbowed Senn painfully in the ribs. "*A secret!*" *he hissed.* "*I KNEW it! That mutant SCUM! We're gonna hafta....*" *He drew his mouth into a tight line. With another hard elbow into the man's beefy ribs, he nodded discreetly toward the doorway.*

As Duron acknowledged the crew's spontaneous applause, Adam leaned toward him. "Thanks. I must say that you've stretched our imagination to the limit this morning. All of us keep saying that anything's possible on this planet, and you've just proven it. I'm sure there's a lot more to come!"

It had been a hard, first night and an overwhelming second morning. The crew drifted off into small groups, chattering excitedly about the new information.

"Adam?" The old eyes looked tired. "Thank you for welcoming me. I never did get to tell your crew something important about the translator buttons."

"I understand. They've been a breakthrough, but they're very exhausting. When you want to revert back to your own language, how do you turn them off? D'ya just peel these little red suckers off your neck, or what?"

"That is the very feature I neglected to explain. It is easier than you think." He slit-smiled, shrugged, and then tapped his button in a quick code: two short taps followed by a harder one. It clicked off. "Bzzz stylph zzor runnnch?" he asked in Bandorese. With a single tap, it sprang to life again. "Does *that* answer your question?"

Adam tapped the code. "Huh! It works!" he sampled quietly, in English.

"Of course! Your grandfather helped invent it!" Duron nodded. "His data disks provided *all* the English translations!"

As they shook hands warmly and Duron headed for the doorway, Elena slipped her small hand into Adam's open palm. "D'ya think we could get in a little sightseeing today?" she whispered.

"I'd love to, hon, but first I promised to move our ship outta this big tree. We're way too heavy for their, ah, roof!"

Duron popped his big head back into the cafeteria doorway. "Oh, I forgot one more detail, Adam. See you up in the control room in a few minutes," he pointed.

"Yeah," Elena shrugged wanly. "That's true. You *did* promise."

He squeezed her gently. "Maybe when we get down to the ground we could take out a three-man sled? Duron said he'd show us around."

"You're saying you, me, and ah … him?"

"Uh, huh."

She drooped dejectedly. "I-I was hoping for just you and me."

"That's later," he whispered. "After our wedding and after all the lights on this incredible planet are out."

Chapter 17: PARADISE

The Motherlode's great branches creaked loudly as Adam raised the starship. Their eyes glued to the proceedings, Duron and several of the crew had gathered around the big holographic display fanning down from the ceiling, watching it slip toward the open sky through a tall, narrow corridor of green. As Kron flipped on the external cameras, they glanced over their shoulders at the curved monitors. Sure enough, the animals were back in force, straining their utmost to touch the smooth, silent hull as it slid by. In moments, clear sky surrounded them. They were free.

"Yes!" Adam let out a whoop, punching the air. He settled the mighty craft on the shoreline, the gleaming knife-edge of the hull protruding fifty feet over the surface and crystal-clear water lapping against the gel feet.

The old Bandor was nodding with his whole body. "Very, *very* good, Adam! I watched the seismic readings," he exclaimed, "No tremors!"

"Thanks," Adam replied, grinning, yanking the glowing keys out of their slots. "So! D'ya think it's safe to get out and take a stroll, or maybe do a little swimming? That water sure looks inviting!"

"Perhaps, but remember, you have predators to contend with, primarily Razahs."

Adam pointed at the large, circular clearing around the Motherlode. "So what's up with all that grass? Did you guys plant it?"

Duron shrugged. "No, the sap in the Motherlode's root systems created it. That was a completely unforeseen phenomenon. The resulting circles are indeed quite large, about two Earth-miles in diameter. Fortunately, Razahs are creatures of stealth and rarely come out into them." He thought a moment. "Unless there is a *reason* to."

Grimacing, Adam glanced over his shoulder at the men. "Ah, I think we should go somewhere and talk about a few things in private. I'm bursting with questions, Duron." He walked around to the far side of the big hologram, whispered his intentions in Kron's ear and returned, smiling. "It's all set. I told him that you and I needed to go 'strategize.' C'mon, I have an office right down the hall."

Adam looked up and down the corridor and shut the door. "First things first," he began. "Our Stiflers might have the range to handle the Razahs," he exclaimed, "but-but of course that depends entirely on one detail: what's the Razah's range?

Duron thought a moment. "I would say one thousand Earth-feet on the average, but larger specimens occasionally throw stuns over twice that distance."

Adam whistled. "No kidding! That's incredible! Nearly half a mile? Sorry to say, but that's the limit of our Stifler's range, too! Ah, what would happen if one of us actually got stunned?"

The old one grimaced. "Temporary paralysis and neural spasm, for about two Earth-hours. I-I really don't think he would bother a large group of people, though. He is way too smart for that."

"Just paralysis? You mean you don't die?"

"I did not say that. The closer the Razah is to his prey, the greater the neural spasm. If he is less than ten feet away, irreparable brain damage occurs. Total destruction. And do not forget, Adam, when he reaches you he begins to feed immediately."

"Hmm." Adam deliberated a minute. "I've got an idea, Duron. Here's what I'm gonna do: I'll park three unmanned SpeedSleds along the perimeter of the rainforest, set their external sensors to scan 360 degrees, then shield and cloak them. If any of them spots one of those bad boys, it'll send out an alarm in plenty of time."

"Excellent!" Once more, Duron nodded with his whole body. After a moment, his tone grew more serious. "Adam, ah, I really need to discuss something I have been struggling with all morning."

"Whazzat?"

"I sensed a great, negative aura among some of your crew."

Adam grimaced. "You noticed, too? I thought I was feeling some kind of a barrier. I tried and tried, but just couldn't push through it. I'm just plain stumped, Duron."

"Stumped? What is…?"

"I'm sorry. What I meant was, I really don't know *who* they are."

"Nor do I."

Adam scowled. "My gut tells me it's Dexor. He and his three buddies are quite stand off-ish. Believe it or not, I've tried to capture their thought pictures the same way I did with Tola yesterday morning, when we were all up in the tree. Couldn't do it, though. It was as if there were this-this impenetrable wall. It was totally the opposite with Tola. He practically spoon-fed me his thoughts…"

Duron was visibly stunned. "Adam!" he gasped, his dark eyes round. "You did not tell me you could capture thought pictures from your own people! That is amazing, especially since you have not as yet ingested a full dose of the Rasheen. Your youthful mind is fascinating!"

"Really?" He shrugged. "But I keep blacking out under stress! I really *hate* that part. Is-is it normal?"

"No, no, Adam, quite to the contrary! A normal first reaction for our youths would be a two-week neural spasm, or as in your grandfather's case, a month-long coma nearly ending in death."

"Oh, no! He went into a…. Wow! I guess I got off pretty easy, didn't I?"

"Yes. To the extreme, Adam. Your case continues to break all known precedents. We do not know what to think anymore. Your mention of a 'wall' is bothersome, though. It sounds very much like our defensive mechanism called 'mind-shields.' Perhaps your people have a natural affinity for this, especially if they have something to, ah, hide?" His wispy brows knit together in the middle of his forehead. "Unfortunately, you can't arrest anyone for what you *think* they are thinking. Perhaps their PIL frequency could…?"

"I'm sorry, Duron," he interrupted. "If they're *really* up to no good, those foxes just stuffed those little suckers into their pockets right after they got 'em. Even more, I've got a gut feeling they might just do something even more deceitful, like parking their PILs out in the rainforest as red herrings so they can go around and snoop!"

The big head was tilting quizzically. "Red … *herrings*? Please explain. Some of us older Bandors have a rudimentary knowledge of the complexities within your language, but unfortunately, not I. Perhaps I could assign a few scholars to interpret for me? I could also assign some of our police force keep your outlaw group under surveillance."

Adam stopped short. "Surveillance! That's it! We have the *Spyders*!"

Again, Duron squinted at him questioningly. "What do you mean?"

"Our little robotiods aren't exclusively a *video* tool, Duron! I tinkered with a broken one a while ago. The eye just sort of unscrewed and the ring of legs…."

"Show me!" The old one pulled out one of his cherished insects from his cloak.

"You don't mind?"

"Please. I understand you have plenty," he reassured.

Adam sat down at his desk and bent to work with a pair of tweezers. As the nano-parts fell away like specks, Duron grabbed one of the legs and held it up to the fiberoptic light diffuser over his head. "What are those miniature hooks near the suction tips, Adam? I did not notice them before." He lowered his gaze to the mound of parts lying on the control panel. "And those three miniature canisters, as well? There is a purple one and two white ones that seem to be joined together at their outlet. Look."

Adam poked at them gingerly. "Ah, I dunno," he shrugged. "Maybe two backups for the stink gas? Gotta be careful with those! Ah, maybe the hooks are for climbing? We'll look at 'em later. Anyway, wait a sec…." More parts flew, and in moments he was left with a thin, flat recording assembly: a mike, recorder, and power pack, all weighing practically nothing.

"Bingo!" He perched it on the tip of his finger, winking. "This little speck is the *audio* system! Sorry, there's no remote; we'll have to retrieve it afterward to listen. It looks like it might have two hundred and fifty layers of rewriteable nano-flash memory! Maybe five terabytes of RAM!"

The old one was left in the dust. "Bingo…?"

"Slang, Duron, slang," he chuckled. "It means 'right on the money,' or, 'you *got* it!' Um, ah…."

The big head tilted further. "You mean the disc unit is very small and light in weight and can easily be hidden inside the suspect's clothing. Therefore it should serve well in its specialized, abbreviated function as a purely audio recording surveillance tool and then deliver the contents when recoupled to your nano-laser sound reading equipment inside your e-helmets? It's worth a try, Adam."

Adam let out a low whistle. "Wow! Couldn't have said it better myself! C'mon, white boy, let's catch a ride up to the Observatory. I wanna sneak a peek at the lake! I'm cravin' the waves!"

The old one trotted closely on his heels, shaking his head in confusion.

Down in Warehouse F, Dexor and his companions were pressing their faces to their pod's dark glass, their hearts racing. The chronometer inside was blinking unsteadily. The light would came on strongly for a minute, fade, and then repeat the sequence. Suddenly a different display scrolled by. They read it quickly.

"Internal autosequence commencing… bypass mainframe… internal autosequ…."

As the words abruptly cut off, they glanced at each other in confusion.

Trennic raised his voice in exasperation. "See? It's been tryin' to say somethin'. It's been goin' back and forth like that for the past two hours! On, off, on, off...."

Senn cut in. "Yeah, boss. I saw it first!" His chest puffed out. "There was this little blue light and then a bigger blue light and then an even bigger...."

Dexor sighed. "And then a big, BIG blue light. Right?"

Senn's eyes popped. "You saw it too?"

The men rolled their eyes at each other.

Dexor tapped on the glass. "Well, something's finally happening in there, but we still don't have clue about a timeframe. We gotta stay sharp," he scowled. "Every day, pinheads. You'll hafta come down here every day and look. At the first sign of opening, we all gotta be ready or...."

Their eyes met. Expelling a collective breath, they slipped out of the room.

As Adam and Duron entered the Observatory, they spotted a large group clustered in front of the screen, surveying the wide vista. Tola glanced over his shoulder. "Boy, that water sure looks cool, sir," he breathed wistfully. "Real cool."

Adam elbowed his way to the front and stared a moment. "I was thinking," he toyed. "Nah." He spun around. "You guys wouldn't go for it. Too radical."

They took the bait, nudging each other. "*What*, sir?" someone prompted.

"Maybe, just maybe, a loading dock, say, way up on level R might make a good high diving platform?" As they whooped enthusiastically, he held up a finger. "Whoa, now! There's just one tiny problem, a small glitch, really."

They stopped, freeze-frame. A glitch?

"Don't concern yourselves, but remember what Duron told us. The jungle seems to be chock full of predators, particularly the Razah. Remember that stealthy, demented Sabretooth upwards of fourteen feet long capable of sending out telepathic mind-stuns for half a mile? Small things like that," he shrugged. "You know. Blips. Tiny ones."

Someone coughed and then spoke up hesitantly. "G-got anything in mind, sir?"

They formed a huddle, he filled them in with the details and in minutes they were with him all the way. "Remember," he concluded, "even if all else fails, you've got the shields on your SpeedSleds, its blazing acceleration, and your wrist communicators...."

"No, *no*, Adam!!"

They all turned toward the old one. Totally out of character, Duron had interrupted, breaking his silence. His dark eyes were blazing with excitement.

"No?" Adam questioned. "But I don't understand! We just...."

"Go ahead and *stun* the Razahs!" he said firmly.

"What? Stun them? But you...."

"Stun them! Definitely! After our revealing group discussion in the kitchen this morning, I have been thinking and have come to a conclusion. As Supreme Leader, I have decided to repeal our strict policy of noninterference: Both the Razahs and Spyrins are indeed mutant species and should be restored to their original state. You have my full permission to start a program of trapping and relocating. And your amazing Elena is my obvious choice to initiate and lead this new series."

Adam was flabbergasted. "Wow! I don't know what to say… ah, thanks? I can assure you we'll use utmost care and the beasts will be well-sedated." He spun back to the crew. "Well, there you have it. Now vamoose! You should be able to get in a few hours of R&R before lunch. And remember to contact Kron about how to park those three empty SpeedSleds out in the jungle."

They stared at him blankly. Things were moving way too fast.

"So whaddaya waitin' for, Christmas? Take a hike!" he shooed them off.

The old one's head had tilted to an impossible angle. Adam thumped him on his bony shoulders. "You too, water boy! It's time you learned a few strokes yourself!"

The water was exhilarating as he broke the surface in a clean dive. Adam swam lazily underwater, his eyes wide open in amazement at the crystal clarity and purity of the water and the teeming abundance of freshwater life forms skittering by inches from his face. The bizarre surface dwellers they'd seen so far suddenly seemed ordinary in comparison to these pulsing, glowing, hyperextended expressions of someone's imagination gone berserk. He floated in place, paddling and turning slowly around.

This was a totally different world: an *aquatic* planet of lights! The incredible, lit-up creatures amplified the extremes of the spectrum: In shocking, metallic, glowing infrareds and neon yellows they burst from every spangling, gold-festooned grotto; in heavy-lidded blues and glowing ultraviolets they skulked under every shadowed rock; in squid-like schools they swept by in alarmingly long strings of bioluminescence before disappearing in a flash into the unfathomable depths.

Totally unnerved, he popped his head out of the soothing bath to glance around for a reality check. Duron stood awkwardly on the shore, looking painfully thin in a borrowed bathing suit. His bony ribs were clearly outlined and his flat, fluttering abdomen revealed his excited breathing. Adam chuckled. "Yike, a reality check? Hmm … definitely not a pretty sight out here in broad daylight." He raised his voice. "Hey, c'mon in, man!" he waved gleefully. "Chicken!"

The pale Bandor leader stuck in a long slender toe, then gathering courage, waded quickly toward him. His big, dark eyes darted around fearfully, scanning for danger.

Adam bit his lip, stifling his urge to laugh. "Don't worry, Iron Man, we've got a whole battery of underwater probes hooked up! Nothing bigger'n a tadpole can come within a mile of the ship!"

His thin lips were drawn back, his small, even teeth exposed in a grimace. "T-the water is very c-cold, Adam, b-b-but somehow soothing to the s-skin," he quavered. "Fortunately, these t-translator buttons have been manufactured as sealed units. We Bandors are extremely s-sensitive to electrical s-shock." He waded in a step further, then suddenly sunk over his head. He popped up sputtering, his thin, fuzzlike hair plastered against his great domed head. "Watch *out*, Adam! The shoreline descends rapidly beyond this point!" He squinted into the depths. "But-but your feet … your feet are not touching! How can you hover in the water like that?"

Adam let out a belly laugh. "Its called 'swimming'! I'm *swimming*, Duron!"

A shadow crossed the water. They both looked up to see a muscular form leap far out into the air, spin in a showy triple somersault, then knife vertically through the still surface without a ripple. No sooner had Dexor entered the water than Senn, Nastix, and Trennic followed with noisy, spirited cannonballs.

Adam watched quietly, treading water at Duron's side. "There they go," he muttered, squinting in the glare. "See what I mean? They stick together like glue. I talked to Elena and she agrees. Do you think she...?"

A runic message interrupted his consciousness. *"Yes, Adam. As soon as all of Dexor's men jumped, I saw movement up there. Elena just removed Senn's uniform."*

"Hey!" He turned in surprise. Duron was staring innocently the other way. Chagrined, he beamed back a message in silence. *"Sorry. I keep forgetting about this telepathy thing.... So it's Senn, huh?"*

"Yes, the heavyset, muscular one."

"Well, it's only a matter of time now. I sure wish we could read their minds, though. It would be so much easier."

Duron shrugged. *"That may come eventually. Be patient. Right now Elena should have no trouble hiding the disc. We will just have to wait for another opportunity to recover it. She showed me her abilities as a seamstress, Adam. She is very adept at forming garments. Her closet contained an odd, colorful, robelike uniform."*

Adam let out a loud guffaw, breaking their silent conversation. "A dress! It's called a dress, Duron! I-I haven't seen her in one yet," he sighed, "or out of one, for that matter." He heard a faint chuckle over his shoulder. The old one was sharp; he'd caught the implied meaning loud and clear. He reddened. "Um, by the way, I've asked her to marry me, Duron. Tonight."

A lone brow raised in profile. "So *soon*? You have just arrived!"

"I can't wait another *minute*! Oh, yeah. Um, there *is* one small detail. My crew doesn't know about it yet."

"Another, ah, blip, Adam?"

"Yeah, we thought we'd make our announcement before lunch and then have the afternoon to prepare for a ceremony this evening. You're invited, of course. Bring as many of your friends as you want."

The pale mushroom-shaped head protruded a bit further from the water as the old one stepped up onto a rock. He turned toward him. "You move fast, Adam," he slit-smiled. "You make decisions, good ones, then act on them immediately. I admire you and agree wholeheartedly with your choice of a mate. Congratulations!"

There was a humming noise behind them. They turned to see a bargelike utility sled skimming over the surface, picking up a load of divers. Duron watched, fascinated. Packed to the limit, their bare legs were dangling over the edge, their toes skimming the surface. It rose quickly through the air to one of the many loading docks now jutting out over the water to empty its excited throng. In varying degrees of expertise, they flung themselves into the air with complete abandon, yelling raucously at the top of their lungs.

The old one spun toward Adam fiercely, his eyes flashing. "What fools! Fools!"

"Huh? It's okay! They're safe!"

"No! It's us Bandors! *We* are the fools! For centuries we have been wasting our lives living in *caves*!" he sputtered. "There is absolutely *nothing* like this in our boring underground cities, Adam! Nothing! Up here on the surface there is a joy, a freedom that few have seen save for the bravest of our youths! As chosen leaders, we elders have been foolish and prideful, thinking we could handle all the answers. In truth, we have been driven purely by a misplaced, ungrounded fear of the unknown!"

"So, why don't you just compromise, Duron?" he offered quietly. "*Keep* your cities! Live in them, but turn the outdoors into a huge park! Have your people work and sleep underground and then come out to explore! Even … *play*! We'll protect you!"

His skinny body bobbed up and down in the water. "Excellent idea! The best of both worlds!" Suddenly he stopped short, looking at the noisy scene. "This," he gestured, "is what you just called … play?"

"Yes."

"We will *do* it!" The bulbous head nodded emphatically. "My people *need* this! Oh, um, there is one small blip. They do not know they need it yet!"

Adam let out a hearty laugh. "Whoa, whoa! There's an even smaller blip. First we gotta rid your planet of mutants," he reminded. "We'll set up Elena's capture station about half a mile down the shore," he pointed. "We've got plenty of huge cages in the quarantine rooms and all the equipment we'd ever need for collecting specimens."

Duron suddenly brightened. "I just thought of something! My people can *make* living enclosures for you," he interjected. "Plenty of them!"

"Huh? You mean you can build buildings?"

"Absolutely. Your grandfather left elaborate plans for surface dwellings. He called it his AnchorPlank System, covered in something called FlexFoam. He wanted to put his dwellings out in the rainforest, to be as close as he could to his beloved nature." The old one shuddered, gingerly rubbing his thin arms.

Adam smiled wanly. "Okay, it's time to get you back to shore," he sighed. "You're beginning to show a little color around your shoulders … *blue*!"

Duron slit-smiled, his small teeth chattering.

"Hey! C'mon! You'll catch a *cold* just standing there! Move it, buddy! Lemme show you how to, ah, hover in the water! Just cup your hands like this and paddle! That's it! You've got the hang of it!"

The Auronian sun climbed higher in the sky. Everyone had switched gears and was now beachcombing along the scintillating, nugget-strewn shore of the lake, their blankets sagging with fabulous specimens of gold. Everywhere they looked, something either glittered or was alive. The air hummed with odd-looking insects, clouds of Aeronautas gathered near the top of the Motherlode Tree, and herds of spotted, hopping creatures fed in the distant grassy plain.

Adam and Elena had wandered, poking around way down the shoreline, nearly at the limit of the hidden SpeedSled's sensors. Suddenly, some kind of orange pulp squished under Adam's foot. He peeled it off. "Yuck! What *is* this stuff? I-I *hope* it's fruit." As he scraped intently, there was a great whoosh of wings over his head. A large bird of paradise floated down onto the grass nearby.

Elena gasped excitedly. "Good God, Adam, *look* at him! He's fabulous! Look at the length of his tail ... and those colors!"

Adam bent down to one knee. "Hey, whaddaya know, a Dazzor bird! C'mon, buddy, we meet again. Third time's always the charm!" He glanced at Elena over his shoulder. "I got a glimpse of him from inside my SPYDER, then with the guys out in the rainforest and now face to face, right out on Duron's front lawn!"

"You know him?"

He glanced at the bird. "Yeah, we're pals!" He held out a piece of mashed fruit. "I really think he's just hungry; he's sure interested in *this* stuff!" The bird approached boldly, strutting proudly. As it reached out with its slender, hooked bill, Adam pulled the morsel back a few inches and offered his arm as a perch. A great, multihued crest fanned out. After a short hesitation, the elegant bird hopped on his arm and began to feed. Adam stood up slowly. "Wow! Look at this bad boy, will you? His tail must be twenty feet long!"

Elena's wondering eyes traveled downward. Indeed, he was magnificent; his luxuriant, iridescent plumage sparkled and cascaded over the lake's smooth stones in an ever-changing palette of colors with trailing tendrils of.... With a cry, she knelt quickly in Adam's shadow to examine them closer.

"What? Am I actually looking at *lights*, Adam?" She held up a feather, shading it with her hand. "Wow! It's actually quite bright! Blues, greens, and purples?"

The Dazzor turned, pulling his tail feathers out of her hand. He'd finished the fruit and was lingering on Adam's arm to study them. Taking a chance, Elena slowly reached out and scratched him gently behind one eye. Enraptured, the bird tilted his big crested head toward her. His cheek feathers puffed out, luxuriating in her touch.

"I think we've got a friend, Adam," she whispered. "What is he, some kind of parrot? He's got a crest like a cockatoo and a tail like a quetzal. His bill's different, though. Straighter, and softer."

"Probably adapted to eating fruit," he ventured. "With all this abundance, they apparently don't have to crack anything open like ordinary nuts or seeds...."

The bird's eyes popped open. "*Seeee? Seeeeeeeeee??*"

He laughed and mimicked the sound, piping in a high falsetto. "Seee? Seeee?"

"Adam," she chuckled. "Please! Is that your mating call, too?"

Once more, the bird ruffled and bobbed his head in recognition. "Oooo? Oooo? See-ooo!! See-ooo!" It answered excitedly, flapping its wings. "See-ooooooo!"

Elena joined in. "I see you, too!"

Whatever they'd said apparently meant something in this bird's language. He cocked his head, looked intently at them, and then crouching, took off in a thrilling blaze of color. "See-ooooo!! See-ooooo!!" He spiraled upward, his tail feathers tracing his path in long, flowing ribbons. Faint, hollow, bell-like chimes answered from the distant rainforest. He bobbed toward the sound, his tail following like an undulating pennant. After an impossibly long, magical moment, the metallic melody died away. "Bells?" She turned slowly toward Adam, squeezing his arm. "Did I actually hear *bells*? How in the world can the Bandors live underground with such an exotic garden up here? This is *paradise*!"

"Hey, you're right!" He grinned, fanning his arms. "Look! No mosquitoes! No gnats! No greenheads! It *must* be paradise!"

Chapter 18: AERONAUTAS AND ANCHORPLANKS

There were sudden loud exclamations and the sound of running footsteps in the distance. Adam and Elena turned to see three women sprinting toward them at full tilt, their arms flailing over their heads. Seeming to have lost the last traces of their characteristic timidity, a cloud of hungry--looking Aeronautas were puffing after them in hot pursuit.

Adam cupped his hands, yelling. "Hey, kids! Whazzup?"

Joelle reached him first, totally out of breath. "Get them *away*!" she gasped. "They're trying to get our *food*!" She hid her sandwich protectively behind her back.

"Gimme a piece," he laughed, "and try to keep quiet a second, all of you!"

The Aeronautas approached him cautiously, their trunks snuffling about. As he held up a crumb, their iridescent peacock eyes turned to focus on the morsel, glinting in the sunlight. Protectively linking their stubby hooked feet and twining their trunks together, they edged toward him in a nervous cluster. He placed the bread in his open palm, waiting patiently. The last bonds of restraint broke. Bodies bumping and blunt, hooked toes flailing, their trunks converged. They picked away hungrily.

"See? They're *piglets*!" Joelle whispered in exasperation. "Just plain swine! We were having a peaceful picnic, minding our own business when they sneaked up behind us and tried to steal our sandwiches! Sahir thought it was funny."

"I only gave them a few crumbs, sir," Sahir explained, "and then more and more came over...."

"And it got out of control," Adam concluded. "I see. Well, we certainly don't want to *scare* them away; they're normally quite timid and may learn to start avoiding us. They're also extremely smart. That's what makes them so interesting."

His eyes brightened. "Hey, I just got an idea! Joelle, see if you can lure them away with a piece of bread. That's right, just break it up and scatter it on the ground." As the Aeronautas jostled for position and followed her eagerly, Adam reached into his backpack and pulled out a small trash bag. "Voila!" He grinned. "Some things haven't changed in seven hundred years!"

Joelle's mouth flew open indignantly. "You'd *never!*"

He grinned. "Sssh! Just keep 'em busy, girl. *Promise* I won't hurt 'em!"

Slipping up nonchalantly behind a lone straggler, he bagged it. Instantly, the dark plastic burst into a cacophony of pathetic, heart-rending squeals and thrashing bumps. Abandoning their crumbs in haste, the flock scooted toward the bag and circled it, bumping against Adam's face as they probed the plastic with their snouts. He had to stretch his arm to the limit and turn his head away. They'd forgotten completely about *him*, the *bag* was the villain: it had just *eaten* one of them! As the squealing in the bag died down, the Aeronautas drew back into a cluster, plainly stumped. Twining their trunks in agitation, they began to converse with high-pitched, sensitive pops and whirring motorboat sounds.

"Awww, let him out, Adam," Elena urged.

The women nodded vehemently, hugging each other and scowling.

"Nope. Gotta see what makes him tick."

Sahir drew in a quick breath. "Y-you're not going to … you're not going to cut him *up* are you? D-dissect him?"

"*No!* Of course not," he scowled. "Never!"

Joelle pursed her lips. "You must have been a horrible child," she scolded. "Did you pull the wings off flies? Pop ants with a magnifying glass?" She glanced knowingly at the other women. "*All* men are like that, right?"

"Vulgar! Disgusting! Nasty!" They chorused.

Elena squinted at him. "Look me in the eye, Adam. Do you *swear* this pig-napping is purely in the interest of science?"

At a sudden, affirmative grunt from the bag, they all burst out laughing.

"C'mon," he chuckled, "you *know* I'd never cut up this little guy! Let's go show him to the others over there and then finish our lunch!"

With the late morning heat approaching eighty degrees, most of the crew was sunbathing on the shore. They stretched out, basking luxuriantly and turning their pale bodies to drink deeply of the warmth and sunlight after seven hundred years in darkness. As Adam's group approached, several people rose to their feet, curious about the floating bag. He gave it a squeeze and it promptly squealed in response.

"Wanna buy a pig in a poke?"

They burst into laughter, prompting heads to turn in their direction. The trailing cloud of Aeronautas scooted toward the bag and surrounded it once more, puffing and bumping into everyone's faces in their haste. Surprised at their uncharacteristic boldness, the crew backed away quickly, holding their arms protectively over their heads.

"See? We don't *exist!*" Elena grinned. "They're after the Bag Monster!"

"That's right; to these guys, we're just trees or something!" Adam added.

Abruptly, the Aeronautas ceased their actions. Their bright peacock eyes rolling toward the sky, they disbanded in a flurry of excitement and shot upward. The startled crew looked up to see an enormous, mysterious shadow sweeping in over the lake.

Suddenly, a voice yelled in distress. Another took up the cry, and then another.

Adam flinched. Something wet and gooey had just hit him on the head. "What the…?" Another glop hit the trash bag, splashing into his face. He jerked his head away, wiping his eyes.

With a loud roar, a curtain of wet, jelly-like slime poured out of the sky and swept over the beach, smacking onto everyone's bare bodies. The women leaped to their feet, screeching in revulsion and dashing for the overhanging shelter of the ship.

Elena stood riveted to the spot, turning green. "*Gross*!" She shuddered. "Dis-*gus*-tingggg!! Yucky, ucky, messy! What is it, Adam?"

"Gack!" He recoiled. "I dunno… frog eggs?"

Someone heard him and echoed immediately. "Yeah, *frog eggs*!"

"*Frog eggs*! *Frog eggs*!!" The name spread like wildfire. They covered their heads with their blankets, clawed at their hair, and scraped the stuff off their bodies. It seemed like the heavens had opened up.

"Run for it! We're getting a *slime storm*!!"

Shortly, everyone was under the the ship, watching long strings of bubbly goo falling out of the sky. With loud calls, ravenous flocks of birds swept in to feed among the discarded blankets, gobbling down the stuff with relish. Their crops soon bulged alarmingly. Attracted by all the commotion, great herds of spotted hopping creatures bounded in from the field, looking almost like tumbleweed rolling toward the shore.

Suddenly, Joelle gasped, pointing into the sky. "Hey! Look up *there* everyone!"

A momentary clearing had appeared in the apparent overcast. Darkening the sky from horizon to horizon, an excited mega-colony of breeding Aeronautas wheeled in an endless, roiling mass, skirting the shoreline of the lake. Their eggs dropped into the shallow water like sheets of rain.

Kron squinted, shading his eyes. "Hey, those aren't *clouds*…."

"Bingo!" Adam interrupted. "And this glop ain't *rain*, either!" He raised his voice and shouted. "Hey, everyone! It's Aeronauta eggs!"

The crew was divided right down the gender line in their reactions: the men saw the whole thing as hilarious while the women glowered from the shadows, shuddering in revulsion. A few of them were still retching behind the leg pods.

The egg shower abated as unexpectedly as it had begun, prompting a few men to step out cautiously into the open. The vast majority of slime had made it into the water, sinking slowly toward the bottom. There was a sudden frenzied thrashing in the shallows.

Adam's eyes narrowed. Wasting no time, he started running.

"*Fish*!" he yelled over his shoulder. "*Get* 'em!"

About fifty of the crew sprinted into the water with him and began to scoop up fat, silvery aquatic creatures with their blankets, throwing them in heaps onto the shore. The supply seemed endless: the more they scooped, the more rushed in to feed. As they labored, Kron commandeered a small group to fetch some antigrav barges. Shortly, they flew out of a cargo hold with stacks of empty bins. In twenty minutes, every container was filled to the brim. Exhausted, the sweating crew waded out into deep water to cool off.

Adam looked up, panting. "That's all? No more empties?"

Sahir's voice was muffled behind her towel. "Yeah, that's it, sir. We haven't eaten much of our food yet." She blotted her wet hair. "The guys looked everywhere for more bins: in the cryotanks, the walk-in superfrige, everywhere!"

"Ladies and gents," Adam announced, "you're now looking at dinner! In fact, *many* dinners, probably enough for the next six months! Let's get to work!"

Most of the haul went immediately into the superfridge, but some appetizing-looking specimens were cleaned and prepped for an impromptu noontime feast. The enthusiastic crew brought out pots and pans and dug pits in the sand for a barbecue. With a wary eye on sky and jungle, they ate.

Down by the water, Kron was gazing transfixed into a large, cylindrical specimen tank. Elena and her bio team had put a few of the more interesting creatures into it, and he was watching them swim around in the clear lake water. Suddenly, a grotesque apparition appeared, distorted and out of shape. "*Yike*!!" He jumped away, stumbling in haste.

Peter was on the other side, his eyes bugged out, his nose squashed against the polymer. "What's *that* one?" He jabbed his finger, pointing. "It looks familiar, somehow," he grinned. "The way it moves, I mean." He cupped his hands and made jerky, trailing motions in the air, his tongue hanging out. "You know, kinda squiddy?"

Kron scowled through the acrylic. "Hey, you goofball! How'd you get out of your tank? You-you scared me out of my wits!"

Wait, wait!" Peter held up a finger. "I-I think I know what that thing *is*!"

Adam trotted over and joined them. As the three made nose-prints on the polymer, Peter pointed out the creature again. "Yeah, *there* he is, sir, right there! Whaddaya think?"

Adam shrugged. "Ah, some species of freshwater squid?"

Peter nudged him. "Think again. Look closer: the loose membrane forming on its back? The eyes? Peacock? Think! They're unmistakable!"

Adam let out a gasp. "Wow! It's an *Aeronauta*?"

"Yeah! Their eggs land in the water and hatch, the young live as aquatic nymphs, and then they emerge as air-breathing, floating bubbles of gas…. Right?"

Kron elbowed Adam, motioning at Peter's grinning face. "So whaddaya think this specimen will evolve into?"

Obligingly, Peter crossed his eyes, letting his tongue hang out.

"See? It's already a bag of hot air!"

"Hmm," Adam deadpanned. "Nope. Still a mono-browed knuckle dragger."

"Hey, listen, you two," Peter piped up. "There's no telling what I might turn into," he drooled.

"On Earth we had dragonfly nymphs, mosquito larvae, tadpoles and caterpillars, and we all know what *they* turned into!"

Kron thumped him on the back. "Yeah! *Pests*!"

The three laughed uproariously. "No, you're absolutely right, Peter," he said, grinning. "This is a great find. Thanks for spotting this little guy. Why couldn't these squiddy-looking Aeronauta nymphs turn into those banks of clouds up there?"

In the tall grass, a bizarre assortment of creatures was devouring the last scraps of fish from the morning feast. Surprisingly, Elena was sitting bravely on the ground, right in their midst. She lifted a spotted, featherweight ball of fur into her lap. The creature sat docilely, its long, sticky tongue snaking out and licking crumbs from the ground. "Hey, guys!" She waved them over. "Take a look at this weird poof ball!"

The three men trotted toward her.

"I think he's the same creature that was sitting on Tola's shoulder. I'm going to call him Fandango! Whaddaya think?"

Adam shrugged. "Me? What do I think? Sorry, Elena, but honestly I think he's kinda' stupid-looking." His hand went to his chin. "Make a good hat, though."

Joelle jerked her head up. "See?" she hissed. "Just like I told you!" Her circle of friends bent into a tight huddle, whispering and swapping horror stories.

Ah, his cue. Adam had been waiting for the opportunity since lunchtime. Winking broadly at Kron and Peter, he slid his hand into his pocket and pulled out a plastic baggie, revealing the collection of garbanzo beans he'd saved from his Earth-salad. Making a hovering motion, he pointed at the Aeronautas. They glanced at him questioningly. He made snipping, cutting motions, then pointed down at the beans. They got the idea immediately and turned away to stifle their smiles.

Putting on his best poker face, Adam turned to confront the sea of disapproving female eyes. "Hey kids, I got something to show you! Wait a sec…," he whispered, glancing around furtively. "Look at these!" He dumped out the small baggie into his palm and rolled the wet beans around, letting the women catch just the barest glimpse of the wet, pinkish-beige color. As they strained to see, his prank unfolded. He squashed one and held it up. They coughed, swallowing hard. Suddenly, Joelle's eyes widened.

"You *didn't*!" Her jaw worked, trying to form the words. "They're not…."

"Yup, Aeronauta brains!" he confirmed. Bright eyed, he popped one into his mouth. "Mmmmm, tasty, too! Here, try one!" he offered.

As they gagged, Kron and Peter let out a snort, scurrying away. Adam's shoulders shook in silent laughter, the beans dancing on his palm. They'd been duped, in spades.

"*Get* him!" Joelle hissed. Eyes narrowed and mouths stretched into thin, hard lines, they stepped forward as a single-minded unit.

Suddenly, there was a sound of rapid footsteps in the tall grass, approaching with purposeful strides. They stopped in freeze-frame, their heads turning.

Tola paused, holding up a tentative finger. "Ah…." His voice faltered.

"Hey, big guy!" Adam ducked the beans. "Whassup?"

Tola studied the group. "Um, I-I came to tell you that Duron's waiting for everyone down on the shore, sir. He and his Bandor crew have brought a lot of strange-looking building material with him. None of us have ever seen anything like this stuff."

Adam shrugged and smiled, all teeth, offering him a garbanzo bean. As the women scowled darkly, Elena caught his eye and gave him a discreet thumb's up. Chuckling, he popped another bean into his mouth and trotted eagerly after Tola.

Many pale Bandor workers were toiling in the sun, unloading a long string of antigrav barges. Stacks of strange-looking supplies were being laid onto the beach in neat, orderly rows. They gibbered loudly to each other in their native tongue as they kept a wary eye on the jungle. Duron glanced up and waved the crew over.

"Oh, hello, people!"

As they focused on the old one, Adam's prank was quickly forgotten.

"As promised, it is now time to introduce you to a new form of construction," Duron explained brightly. "Let us go down closer to the shore of the lake so I can demonstrate this remarkable material to everyone at the same time. Adam's grandfather invented what he called his AnchorPlank System for future surface dwellings! I will guide you in the individual phases of construction. It is really quite simple to set up a large complex of buildings, completely interconnected with passageways."

His workers nodded enthusiastically: they could plainly hear their own Bandorese language over the translator button's simulcast English translation.

"First!" He lifted up a long, quivering pole. "This is a Flexrod. It links inseparably to other Flexrods to make up any length you choose. The laminated material is a nearly indestructible alloy of Bitron origin, adapted for manufacture in our underground plants."

They shrugged, looking at each other. Simple, so far.

"Second! This is an Anchorplank! As a mixed group gathered, Duron raised what appeared to be a thick, yet lightweight polymer board over his head. "They come in many lengths and shapes and connect to each other in modular sequence."

They looked closer. Dotted lines of preformed holes were molded into the ends, a dovetailed groove ran down one long edge and a matching tongue down the other. The crew glanced at each other, shrugging. Okay, still simple enough.

Duron raised his hand. "Let me demonstrate the system thus far...." He directed his workers to slide a few Anchorplanks together on a patch of level ground. As another worker took several long Flexrods and joined them together, Duron dropped small capsules into the preformed holes on both ends of an Anchorplank. Gathering his robes, he knelt down on his knee, gesturing at the point of connection.

"The capsules contain what Adam's grandfather called epoxy. The sharp ends of the Flexrods rupture them and the epoxy sets immediately, melding rod and plank as one." His workers flexed a long, quivering rod into an arch and inserted the ends into the holes. Duron swept his arm in a radius over his head. "This large arch represents a profile, say a passageway between two buildings. Do you follow me thus far?"

Adam nodded. "Absolutely, Duron. It's all amazing and quite intuitive."

There was the sound of running footsteps. The rest of the crew joined them, tapping the translator buttons on their necks to listen. There was a mood of growing excitement.

"Third! These are Linkrods," he continued. "They are also modular and come in many lengths, but these have small, connecting clips on their ends, see? They join horizontally, arch to arch. I think I will frame out a window with a few of these." As his workers scampered ahead of him sliding Anchorplanks together and arching Flexrods into their holes, he proceeded to make an opening for a window, and then a door.

Walking a little further, he stooped down to pick up a short, rolled up section of netlike material. The group followed in a tight cluster.

"Fourth!" he continued, "Flexnet! This material diagonally stabilizes the modular sections of Flexrods and Linkrods and also serves as a scaffold, or base, for the finishing material to adhere to. This final bonding layer is a miraculous substance that Adam's grandfather formulated, and it is the key to the whole system. Now watch as my workers demonstrate how fast this Flexnet ties the whole structure together."

In ten minutes, an open-ended twenty-by-fifty-foot passageway was ready and leveled on the ground, with framed-out spaces for working doors on the ends. Sliding windows with built-in awnings were stacked nearby. They clicked a few into place on the sloped sides. The Bandor workers were noisily pointing at the piles and mouthing the odd-sounding English words: "Anchorplanks, Flexrods, Linkrods, Flexnets...."

Adam pushed at the taut web. "*Wow*, this stuff is *super*strong! Really rigid! And all this prep work is just a base for the last, ah, miracle layer? What's it called?"

Duron raised his arms. "Flexfoam! Yes, Adam, we are now ready!" He stepped aside to allow his workers to clip a pair of electrical cables to the skeletal structure. "We practiced this last step down in our city early this morning," he explained. "There are thin, golden threads woven into the Flexnet to carry the current. Following your grandfather's instructions, we are now going to apply a slight static charge to the whole unit." On his signal, a large sled rose and hovered toward them. With its manipulator arms, tanks and hoses waving, it seemed almost alive. An electrical sizzle filled the air as the sled sprayed on a rubbery, epoxy-based material.

Adam was nodding enthusiastically. "Wow! This is *way* cool! I wish we had this stuff back on Earth for housing, especially for emergency situations! Poorer countries would *love* them! Are they inexpensive?"

Duron raised a wispy brow. "That is odd; your grandfather mentioned this as well. You two seem to think very much alike. Yes, he said they were, ah, 'dirt cheap.'"

Adam chuckled. "Yup, that sounds like my grandpa all right."

The static charge attracted the foam. As it flew through the air, it penetrated right through the mesh and covered the net-tunnel on both sides in one step. The froth swelled up, drying almost immediately to a grainy, light beige surface. There seemed to be no odor, no dripping, and no toxic-smelling residue. The workers adjusted the windows and doors, then squirted a thin line of Flexfoam around their perimeters.

The sample was complete. Duron stepped inside a doorway to finish his presentation. "Adam's grandfather wrote that these units can be laid out in any modular configuration and in any height. They are completely waterproof and quiet. Additionally, they are rot- and vermin-proof, organically based, and nontoxic. Chewing jaws, burrowing animals, weapons, nothing seems to harm this dried foam. It is an *ideal* building material! Oh, and one more thing." He picked up a small piece of Flexnet and shook it out. "With the addition of an optional outside layer of this same netting, the dwellings quickly become camouflaged in the jungle. Within a month, some species of our vines will completely overgrow a structure. You can easily cool the air inside and dry it out with a system of airlocks to ensure air temperature and quality...."

"Whoa!" Adam cut in, chuckling. "You sound like an *infomercial*, Duron!"

Tola picked up a blob of Flexfoam from the ground, stretching and testing it. "You're right, Duron, a cooling system would *really* be efficient with this insulation!"

Duron pointed over their heads toward the lake, a faraway look in his dark eyes. "It even floats, people! Adam's grandfather said it has a totally closed-cell formula. Conceivably, your crew could construct a floating city with bridges to link those islands out there...."

Abruptly, his tone changed completely. He turned to face the crowd,. "Listen to me, all of you! Adam and his grandfather have awakened our planet from a long, Dark Age of sleep into a great future! Up to now, we had been content and complacent with our underground existence, but *no more*! As of one hour ago, the expansion of our cities has come to an abrupt *halt*!"

"What? Adam stepped back, startled. "I ... we really didn't mean to...."

The old one seemed unstoppable. "Speculation is ablaze below with this new hope, this dream of a *safe* surface existence inside these dwellings!" His bony fist thumped on the hard, rubbery surface. "This has been a test for *us*, too, Adam! I will confirm the completion of this sample habitat to our people *immediately*!"

"Huh? Right now?"

"Yes. Like you, Adam, I waste no time. I will transmit the results of your grandfather's building plans, as well as your intentions to capture our Razah and Spyrin populations without delay!"

He stepped out of the building, planted his feet firmly in the tall grass, and closed his eyes. Out of nowhere, a series of strong waves pulsed through everyone's bodies. They cringed, looking down at their feet in alarm.

Duron slowly raised his head. "There. It is done."

Everyone was confused. "Done?" Tola coughed. "*W-what's* done?"

"I have just updated the news. The entire planet knows."

As the crew shook their heads in disbelief, Adam seized the opportunity. He beamed out a mind-question of his own, one that he'd only postulated before. *"Duron, is planetary communication really possible? Why didn't you tell me sooner? You should warn all your people not to disclose the location of the big guns!"*

That is amusing, Adam," came the cryptic answer. *"Of course you are referring to Dexor and his men. Do not worry, the secret is safe; it lies within each of us. If one knows, we all know. That is all I can say about this subject for now. I have already informed my people to avoid his group and ignore their questioning. They are quite easy to spot. Unlike us, your people are very different in their physical appearance."*

"Wow, that's for sure," he answered. *"Sometimes it's only by your special robes that I can tell it's you, Duron. Well, thanks. You've answered my question."*

Out of the corner of his eye, he saw Duron giving him a subtle, affirmative slit-smile and nod.

True to his nature, Adam immediately took action. Half a mile from the ship, he hammered a stake in the ground, proposing an ambitious, sprawling, twelve-acre complex. With a long rope in his hands, he walked in a circle, plotting out a large, mysterious circular area halfway between the jungle and the lake. Bandor and human, they all elbowed each other, exchanging questioning looks.

"Do I have everyone's full attention?" He chuckled. Bending down with a Linkrod in his hand, he scratched out a strange-looking silhouette in the dirt. "There. That's our first project: a tapering, three hundred-foot vertical tube."

A *tube*? There was a sea of raised eyebrows and murmurs of bewilderment.

He explained, patiently. "This tube is important: It's gonna be the anchor point for our whole complex: There'll be a wide platform with a railing at the top' and a simple antigrav barge will become a dedicated elevator up the center, shuttling people and equipment. Although it'll serve primarily as a cooling system and watchtower, there'll also be a battery of communications gizmos at the top. You know, various antennae and sensors mounted along the balcony's rim?"

Their questioning murmurs were quickly transforming into genuine excitement.

Kron spoke for the group. "Ah, when do we start?"

Adam shrugged, glancing at his wrist programmer. "How about now? I say there's no time like the present!"

They stared at him in shock.

"Well," he hedged, "we'll lay out the materials, plan it out, and start at one o'clock! Are you guys ready for a *real* challenge? I say we can build this tower in *six* hours!"

Their shock turned into gasps of disbelief.

"Let's go! Let's put these piles of building material through their paces!"

"B-but *sir*!" Tola stammered.

"No, think about it! Duron's sample took only thirty minutes from start to finish, and he did the whole thing with only twelve workers. He kept stopping to explain as he went along, too!"

Kron was busily tapping on his wrist programmer. He looked up. "If that's the case, sir, why don't we *up* the ante? With our huge crew, I'd say we could knock out this tower in, say, *four* hours, tops!"

There was no hesitation. Behind him, the crew's answer came back in the form of a raucous cheer. They sprang to work, running toward the site with bundles of Flexrods, Linkrods, and Anchorplanks bouncing on their shoulders.

The Auronian sun had dipped lower in the sky. At the top of the tower, a group of exhausted crew members, men and women, leaned against a smooth Flexfoam railing around a broad, circular platform. Their bodies soaked in sweat, they surveyed the sweeping panorama below. Some clustered around the big hole in the center, spreading their arms wide, luxuriating in the upward rush of strong breezes already being generated.

Adam mopped his brow, turning excitedly to Kron and Duron. "Ha! *Instant tower*! Some thought it was impossible, but here we are at the top!"

Kron glanced at his programmer. "Well, we came close. It's five-thirty. It took four and a half hours, start to finish!"

Tola was leaning against the railing, a faraway look in his eyes. He'd spotted a large group of islands offshore, barely visible through the gathering mists. "Wow, I sure like the looks of those islands out there." He turned to Duron. "Do you get many storms here on Aurona? I was thinking of, you know, possibly making a little, ah, hideaway cabin out there in a floating Flexfoam job?"

The elder gathered his fluttering robes tightly to his chest. "The Motherlodes have dampened out the worst of the storms and they do allow occasional wind," he hedged. "But a great storm does happen about once in every thirty to fifty Earth-years. We are well within that time frame now." He paused, sensing everyone's apprehension. "Yes, we are due. The wind serves many purposes, such as carrying seeds and pruning deadwood. We do not seek to dominate nature, but conversely we do not let nature dominate us. We protect what we have. For instance, I am sure you have seen that our Motherlodes are bathed in light for six additional hours each daytime sector." He nodded toward the big tree looming behind them. "Three in the morning, three in the evening. Yes, we pamper our providers."

Adam had been listening quietly, his hand on his chin. Suddenly his head popped up. "Holy *cow*!" he exclaimed, staring at his programmer. "F-five-thirty? I've got a *wedding* to go to tonight!"

Kron spun toward him in shock. "Ah … whose?" he asked tentatively.

Duron's slit-smile seemed to stretch halfway around his face.

"Yeah, *whose*, sir?" Peter echoed.

The old Bandor answered for them, sliding his thin arm around Adam's shoulders. "*This* one," he pointed. "This one is getting married!" His slit-smile had reached impossible limits. "I must say it is about time! Elena is an excellent choice for a mate!"

As the top of the tower resounded with jubilant shouts, a matching chorus of squeals answered from below. It seemed that Elena had just made the same announcement.

Duron beamed, drawing Adam close. "You and your women are no longer guests but family, our brothers and sisters. Your motives are transparent, honest, and exciting! Our paradise is your paradise, so please stay and as you say … *colonize*!"

Chapter 19: **RAZAH**

They met breathlessly inside the base of the new tower, their footsteps muffled by the rubbery, textured surface of the round room. Adam made a discreet shooing motion, and the last of the crew slipped away to give them a few moments of privacy. He pulled Elena close, his face flushed in exhilaration.

"Ready?"

"I've been ready all my life."

"Well, it *has* been a long time, about seven hundred years…."

"Really, Adam? That long, huh?"

"Yup! We were destined for each other. It-it just took a while to *get* here!"

As they embraced, Elena's eyes traveled up the walls of the empty tube. At the top, a few lingering shafts of sunlight were gilding a semicircle.

"Speaking of here," she breathed, "Where are we?"

"Huh?" His mind had been racing.

"What *is* this thing we're in, a giant chess piece or something?"

"Hey, you're right!" he exclaimed. "It does look like a huge castle! Well, this chess piece is just the beginning. See all those stakes we pounded into the ground outside? They mark off the rest of our city…."

"*City*?" she interrupted. "I thought you guys were just going to build a small research lab, a few holding pens…."

"Hey," he shrugged, "we got carried away!!"

"Well, what *is* it?" she persisted. "This thing looks like a tall Bandor with his robes flaring out at the bottom. All it needs to complete the illusion is a big head!"

"That's coming later," he nodded, straight-faced. "The radome. You know, a big weatherproof bubble to cover all the equipment?"

She raised a brow. "You're actually building a giant Bandor? That's scary, Adam. For your information, some people have even weirder ideas about it. For one, Tola says it looks like a modern-day Tower of Babel on the Plain of Shinar."

He let out a belly laugh. "He did, did he? Well, you can tell that little round exclamation point that he's dead on! It *will* be a tower of 'Babble'! We purposely built the structure this high to house our communications equipment, among other important things."

Her eyes crinkled. "'Babble?' Really, Adam. You're as bad as Tola. But why don't you let us know all this stuff beforehand? Wait, wait, don't answer; you *like* to keep us guessing, right?" She thought a minute. "Well, personally, I don't care. I think the shape is elegant. It's an elegant solution and an extremely resourceful use of a brand-new material! I'm proud of you!" She clung to him for a long, silent moment, listening to the muffled buzz of the crew's voices outside the wide cargo door.

Kron poked his head in, glancing at his programmer. "Almost time, guys."

"I'm nervous, Adam." She rubbed her arms, shivering. "And why's it so *cold* in here, anyway? Where's all that wind coming from?"

"I like to keep you guessing, remember?" he winked. "C'mon. I'll tell you later. They're all waiting outside with our, ah, limo."

In high spirits, they hurried over to one of the numerous arched doorways. Kron was standing in the waning sunlight, his hands on his hips. As Adam coughed discreetly, he spun on his heel.

"Oh, *there* you are!" He summoned them excitedly. "Time for your long ride!" He really liked them, and especially together; there was a rare chemistry between the two, an exquisite blending of personalities.

Outside the door, two men were holding up a tall curtain stretched between a pair of Flexrod poles. Elena glanced at Kron, her eyes questioning: they seemed to be hiding something. As the curtains parted, she squealed in delight.

Looking like a mini Rose Bowl parade float, a once-plain cargo sled was festooned with flowers. The crew had labored for almost two hours with the wedding preparations, covering the top of the flat slab with Anchorplanks and arching several Flexrods over it for the women to decorate. Joelle and her crew had made many trips to the edge of the rainforest, picking exotic species of orchids and bromeliad-like flowers, and a circle of heavily armed men had surrounded them on SpeedSleds.

Someone gave the cue: drifting down from speakers somewhere on top of the tower, soft music fell on the wedding party like an ethereal blanket. Adam stepped aboard the float, extended a hand to his bride, and circled to the front of the tower. The jungle reverberated with raucous cheers. On impulse, Elena leaned against her man with a big, satisfied smile, winking broadly at the crew. There was an immediate, renewed response.

A mischievous glint in his eye, Adam raised his hands to speak. The tumult died to a hush, with a few lingering catcalls. "As you can plainly see," he shouted, "the shields around this planet have come down, just like Elena's defenses!" As a round of hoots and whistles filled the air, he felt Elena's nails dig into his arm. He bent low and whispered into her ear, smirking. "Top that one if you can, hon."

Smiling confidently, she raised her small hand. "I'd say *everybody's* defenses have come down on this planet, both Bandors and humans...," she paused for the effect, and the crew leaned forward expectantly, "with the power of *love*!" She looked up at Adam with blatant self-assurance, batting her eyes.

He grimaced. "Ya got me! I've met my match, Ms. Einstein."

Tola cleared his throat. "Ah, knowing Elena, sir, I'd say *your* resistance melted like wax over a flame!" Once more, the crowd applauded their approval.

The round man had decided to waste no time dallying in the spotlight. This was to be their day, their hour, a moment that they'd never forget. He slipped his tiny e-Bible from his utility belt and opened it discreetly to perform his first meaningful ministerial assignment on Aurona. "As Elena said," he began, "it really *does* start with the power of love. There's no better place to find a description of this amazing power than in First Corinthians, Chapter 13." His voice rang out, clear and strong. 'If I speak with the tongues of men and of Angels, but have not love....'"

It was nearly dark. Slowly, the Motherlode's great column of light began to bloom into existence, backlighting the unforgettable scene with a growing wall of brilliance. Something else was happening. Rushing in toward the warm column of light, long, trailing strands of gold-spangled vapor rose inside the shaft toward the sky. Within a breath, the Motherlode had become a spectacular, glittering beacon.

Awestruck, trembling, the young couple faced an equally stunned preacher. It had almost seemed preordained that they should meet and marry at this hour. The ethereal wall of light seemed to be coming down from Heaven itself, as if it were a stamp of approval. Impossibly far from home on an unknown planet, the crew looked like tiny specks in front of an enormous, glittering beacon. With no one realizing it, Aurona's history was being forever altered; time was being forever marked with this insignificant, impromptu ceremony.

They kissed for the first time as husband and wife and then an impossibly long, heart-stopping moment later, parted. It was done. They drank in the spectacle a few more minutes, then bolted for their wedding suite on the ship.

A week had passed and it was early evening. The tower and starship were both lit starkly from the side, bathed in the now-familiar column of light enveloping the Motherlode. The broad platform on top of the tower and the curved dome of the starship were both crowded with nervous knots of people. One of the crew had found a hatch over the Holosphere's bulbous dome and quickly told the others. A group climbed out, gathering on the slippery surface with their footgrippers turned to max.

It was Razah time, the inauguration of Elena's capture and restocking program. Everyone gazed out into the distant jungle canopy, armed and confident with the protection of his or her weapon; even at a quarter strength, the Stiflers had proven themselves to be powerful weapons.

As the sun began to set earlier in the evening, Kron and a small group of men had picked off one of the first Spyrins to appear. They quickly sedated and caged it down in a cargo hold, and his men had nervously stared at the huge insect from a doorway. Without warning, it had roared to life. Spotting them, it had whipped itself into an enraged, thrashing frenzy. With loud wails, it began to strobe furiously with its searchlight, squirting poison from its jabbing stinger and clicking viciously on the alloy bars with its saw-toothed mandibles. Tola finally stepped in to restore order. Turning off the lights, he shooed everyone away from the room and closed the door.

Everyone was back outside now, swapping Spyrin horror stories and shivering in the breezy, cool night air. All around them, a trillion pinpoints of light were winking to life on the Arren trees. In the distance, they could see the columns of light from the other Motherlodes, row upon row of them marching toward the sunset.

Elena raised the suction on her footgrippers. It was scary on top of the starship and she was shivering in excitement. "See? Isn't it just like I told you?" she pointed. "The darker it gets, the brighter those spangly columns around the trees get! From here, it looks like they're holding up a canopy of stars!"

"Hey, you're right," Joelle agreed. "And the Arren trees look like they're reflecting that blanket of stars down on the ground."

"Wow! Shooting stars, too!" Adam interrupted, pointing. "Look over there! I see three moving lights a the edge of the jungle!" As everyone's head turned, three spotlights burst into the grassy clearing, flying in formation. "*Spyrins*! Holy cow! I hope someone gets them before…." Even as he spoke, the electrical snap of a Stifler echoed loudly.

"*Craaaaaack*!!"

It had came from the other direction! They all turned toward the source.

"*Wow*!" someone yelled. "That was super loud! Three-quarter strength! Definitely not a Spyrin! Maybe … a *Razah*?"

With the buzz of distant thunder, the three flying searchlights banked, turning toward the sound. Adam watched, dumbfounded. "Wow, that's intense! How'd they know a Razah just got hit? They must be going after his body!"

"Crack, crack, *craack*!"

Three more Stifler blasts sounded almost simultaneously, this time at quarter strength. As the living searchlights dropped and faded, a brighter group of mechanical ones appeared stealthily at the edge of the jungle. It was over. About twenty speeding sleds converged on the scene, throwing their blinding beams on a pile of smoking, paralyzed bodies.

Adam cranked up the volume on his wrist intercom. "Cages ready?" he breathed. "Got your time-release tranquilizer serum?"

Startled, the men at the scene turned toward the source of the transmission. Standing off by himself, Adam waved, a tiny, backlit figure on top of the starship.

A voice drifted back. "Holy cow! Is it *safe* up there, sir?"

"Absolutely," he affirmed. "We've all got our footgrippers on and we're armed; what else could we need? Hey, can you guys *lift* that beast, or what?"

"No problem! There's twelve of us down here!"

One of the men chimed in. "Good God, what a monster! This Razah's way over twenty feet, sir! Our estimates were *way* off! Tell Kron to bring a bigger cage!"

Adam signaled to his second in command down in the quarantine room. Kron had already heard them and was halfway out the door, on the fly. He grabbed Elena's hand. "C'mon hon, you're way better at this medical stuff than us novices. They've got all the help they need with those beasts, so we'll just wait for them downstairs."

Out in the jungle, Elke had been watching the action. He was sure he'd seen Dexor and Senn looking around furtively and then concealing themselves with their sled's cloaking device. The two were up to no good, and he knew it: Adam would be pleased at his report. Up ahead, a tunnel of leaves was still moving in a path straight away from him. Suddenly, there was movement to his left, deep in the undergrowth.

"Aha!" He concentrated on it, his finger poised over his Stifler's trigger. "I see you, creeps," he muttered. He hopped off his one-man SpeedSled and ducked behind a softly glowing Arren branch. "Thought you'd give me the slip, huh?"

"*Snaaaap*!!" He spun around, his eyes wide in shock. "What the…?"

Behind him, his tiny SpeedSled rocked in the air as a visible, moving wave of energy smashed into it broadside. The little speedster let out a puff of smoke and dropped to the forest litter. The shields hadn't been up and some kind of massive electronic disturbance had just shorted everything out!

A branch rustled. Elke's primal senses took over, the hair rising on the back of his neck. Wafting in over the smell of burnt wires, his nostrils picked up a faint, rank odor. His heart began to hammer.

Two dilating, glowing eyes had been watching him from deep cover. Sensing fear, the beast flattened to the ground and slunk excitedly toward him.

In spite of all his efforts at self-control, Elke panicked, dove headfirst into the jungle, and got up sprinting at top speed. Spooked out of his wits and fighting his way through the tangle, he screamed for help at the top of his lungs. Suddenly, there were bright lights ahead! He burst into a clearing, yanking off the clinging vines.

Startled, Peter rotated his SpeedSled toward him. He dropped his shields and jumped out, yelling. "E-Elke! You-you shouldn't be *out* here like this! Where's your sled, man?"

Mid-yank, Elke paused a minute. "W-well, that's another story. You see, I thought I saw Dexor, and...."

There was a loud electrical snap from the jungle's cover, followed by a sizzling sound. Buffeted by an unseen wind, Elke's clothing fluttered and his eyes rolled back into his head, the whites glowing eerily in the sleds' headlights.

"Elke?" Peter leaped off his sled in horror. "*Elke*? Someone! Anyone! *Help* us!" With an abrupt thrashing of branches, a permeating, rank odor filled the air. He spun on his heels.

A Razah! He jumped aside as the great, frightening shape hurtled toward him. The beast was at the throat of his prey in seconds, his hateful eyes glowing in the headlights. His tail lashing in fury, he straddled Elke's small body, poised for the kill. Curling back his lips, he hyper-extended his great jaw to reveal a colossal set of sabertooth fangs.

Suddenly, with a flash and roar, a sea of headlights burst into the clearing. The Razah froze, his tail snapping in agitation. The sleds circled him, their riders screaming at the top of their lungs. On signal, they dropped their shields and aimed their Stiflers.

Peter screamed the order. "*Waste him*!!"

At full power, fourteen simultaneous electrochemical blasts cleaved the air. As the blinding bolts sizzled deeply into his flesh, the Razah expelled a great gasp of putrid air. With his jaw locked in open position, he jerked in convulsive death throes and fell heavily, squarely on top of Elke. The massive sabers impaled themselves deeply into the ground, bridging the man's neck.

Elke's lips turned blue. Peter lunged and pushed at the Razah, his eyes wide in desperation. "Quick! Get him *off*, guys!"

They threw their backs into it, straining mightily at the smoking, scorched carcass. Clods of dirt flew. "What's this fat cow made of, *lead*?" Peter wailed. "Why can't we budge him? We've got more than a dozen men here!" Elke's lips fluttered as the last ounces of breath were squeezed from his lungs. The ponderous beast was crushing him! It couldn't be moved!

There was a distant hum. A lone SpeedSled appeared, its headlight probing the jungle. Kron sat at the controls, red-faced and shaking with anger. There seemed to be an odd set to his jaw. Suddenly, he veered and surged toward them. A wide path quickly opened.

Thrusters on full blast, he mercilessly rammed his sturdy two-man SpeedSled into the Razah's body. As the smoking beast rolled off, the sled hovered momentarily over Elke's still form and then backed away. The small group was speechless.

Kron jumped off and straddled the body. After a frantic moment of CPR, the man began to choke in shallow gasps, trickles of blood running from the corners of his mouth. Kron stood up slowly, wiping his hands on his uniform. Hot tears of anger welled up in his eyes. "What in…? What were you guys thinking," he choked. "Why-why didn't you…." His voice trailed off.

Peter was mortified. Stone-faced, he bent down and helped the men lift Elke onto the back of Kron's sled. "I'm sorry," he muttered. "Go. Quickly."

A phalanx of doctors was ready with the Bitron's diagnostic instruments as Kron flew into the cargo door and quickly converged around their fallen comrade. Retreating to the back of the room, a chagrined Peter and a furious Elena paced back and forth, avoiding each other's eyes as they awaited the outcome. Finally, Peter couldn't stand the silent, unspoken charade. As she passed, he gently touched her on her sleeve. She wheeled toward him, her eyes flashing.

"*You*!" she snapped, her voice razor-sharp. At the doctors' startled glances, she nodded grimly toward the exit. "Outside," she hissed.

Their voices echoed in the long, curving hallway.

"Didn't you *see* the Razah coming?"

"No! Man, I'm so sorry. I saw Elke running and screaming out of the forest, and then, bam! It happened! The Razah...."

"Came out of nowhere!" she finished. Taking a deep breath, she softened her tone. "And what was Elke doing out there alone, anyway?"

"He-he mentioned something about following Dexor."

"What? *He* was out there, too?"

"Apparently."

Her eyes widened. "Oh ... so *that's* it!"

The tensions of the past hour finally took their toll. Breaking down, Elena slumped. "So Elke was spying for us," she muttered, hot tears welling up. "He *must* have been! But he shouldn't have been out there alone!"

"We all let down our guards, Elena. I'm sorry."

She shuddered. "Remember what Duron told us, the part about the Razah's mind-net? That beast must've been out there casting his net to locate prey."

Peter's hand went to his chin, pondering. "Hmm, maybe we could put up a force field, or even something old-fashioned, like a big electric fence around the jungle?" He paused, mulling it over. "But-but we shouldn't interfere, really ... should we?"

Kron had been noticeably eavesdropping. Elena motioned him over, drying her eyes. Suddenly she brightened as a spark of inspiration hit. "Hey, that's right! In the broader sense, force fields can be extremely selective. Listen to this, you two!"

As she whispered in their ears they listened incredulously, then broke into broad grins, their eyes sparkling. They nodded in enthusiastic agreement. Feeling vastly better, the three slipped back into the emergency bay.

As Elena stood on her toes to peer intently over the doctor's shoulders, a set of bright eyes met her own on the other side of the circle.

"Adam!" Her arms flew into the air, the wall of attendants parted, and she descended on him like a cresting wave. "Where have you *been*? With all the confusion, I thought you'd be right behind me! I had to move fast!"

He pulled her tight. "Too fast for me, sweetpea; you took off like a shot!

There was a groan behind them. Elke grimaced, his ribs tightly bandaged. "W-what happened?" he wheezed. "Everything went blank...."

She bit her lip. "Shhh, quiet, you! A Razah almost had you for dinner! You got mind-stunned!"

Wincing in pain, Elke glanced apologetically at Kron and Peter. "Wow, intense! Everything just ... Poof! Went blank! Sorry, guys."

Kron caught Elena's eye and they exchanged winks. "Listen everyone," he offered enthusiastically, "Elena's got a dynamite proposal!"

She shrugged. "Well, I don't even know if it'll work but if it does, the Bandors should never have to live in fear again." She lifted her gaze to study the reaction of each white-coated person in the room. "And as doctors, my plan directly concerns *you*! I'm going to need a top surgical team to make it work!"

The medical staff stared at her, waiting in suspense.

"There'll be two steps. Two operations, really," she began. "The first one would involve a fitting and the second, a set of implants. We'll practice our surgical technique on this dead Razah."

Someone snorted. "What? On an ... *animal*? We're not veterinarians!"

"Hey," Adam chided. "A body's a body, right?"

Elena continued. "He's right. We're not that much different. So this is my plan: tomorrow I'm going to ask some Bandor metalworkers to work on a prototype. I know they can hammer a large, custom-formed helmet out of gold."

"Huh?" Adam spun to her, uncomprehending. "A gold h-helmet?"

"Then it'll be up to you doctors," she continued, unhurried. "You guys will lift away a triangular, eight-inch flap of skin from the Razah's forehead and then fit an ultra thin, ferrous metal plate to the surface of their skull, using that new bio-epoxy. It will remain there permanently, as an implant under the skin of their foreheads."

Adam stared at her, his jaw hanging open. "Why all the elaborate prep?"

She continued smoothly. "I'm almost there. Now as we all know, gold is impervious to the elements, it's abundant on Aurona, and therefore perfect for the job. The gold helmet will have three permanent supermagnets precisely aligned on its inner surface, set to 'hover' at two inches. Once in place, the Razah will never be able to pry it off."

"It's permanent?" Tola was incredulous. "But why a helmet, of all things?"

She smiled, glancing at the round man. "In theory, this large metallic skull plate should both reflect and short out the Razah's forward-thrown mind-stun." She explained. "In effect, they'd be giving themselves a zap of their own medicine!"

Her plan bordered on the preposterous, yet smacked of boldness and innovative daring. Still, the very idea of Razahs running around with gold helmets on their heads brought out a contagion of backhanded smirks.

She raised her voice confidently. "Come on, honestly. Think about it," she chided. "After a few self-inflicted knockout drops, the Razahs should learn very quickly *not* to use their mind-stuns!"

She'd finally captured their imaginations: the more her radical plan unfolded, the more plausible it sounded. The initial shock and resistance was quickly evaporating in the face of flawless logic. They started to nod in studied agreement.

Sensing the shift in mood, she continued, greatly encouraged. "Look. Over the centuries, these big cats have gotten just plain fat and lazy, using this easy method of bringing down prey! Now, like it or not, they'll have to completely relearn the forgotten art of stealth!"

Kron chimed in helpfully. "And Elena's even got a 'Step Two' to her plan, guys. I think it'll be a lot easier than the surgical part."

"More? There's *more*? What else could there be?" Tola asked.

"Since you asked, oh small round one, we're implanting a PIL transmitter."

He grimaced. "Yikes. You mean like, ah ... down the hatch?"

"Yup," Kron laughed. "And I hereby delegate *you* to push it down his throat!"

The tension finally broke. As the small group laughed, Elena explained. "After the Razahs receive their specially modified PILs, all of us should be able to monitor them and follow their movements, learning their habits. It's important to know where they are at all times, day or night. Why, we'll eventually be able to run a continuous living census, if you will!"

"In other words," Tola concluded, "we'll be 'tying the bell on the cat's tail'?"

Adam let out a hoot. "Bingo! But, on the other hand...," he suddenly paused, his voice faltering, "they'll really gonna *hate* us for that." He ended quietly, his voice choking off. With a chill, he exchanged startled, knowing glances with Elena.

Her eyes grew round and she turned away quickly. Had they just stumbled on something far larger in scope than they could ever dream? They shuddered at their unexpected, rekindled memories: the big cat had pointedly, furiously stared at them from millions of miles in space.

Adam finally found his voice. "Um, Elena's right," he continued, trying to sound controlled. "The Razahs should be, in effect, telepathically neutralized once they get their helmets, right?"

As the two purposely avoided each other's eyes, Elena took a deep breath and embellished his thought. "Yes!" she cut in. "Think of it, everyone: telepathically neutralized! Let's take it even further! For their young ones, we'll make small helmets with overlapping gold plates that spread out on their foreheads as they mature. Are you with me? Bandors, and therefore the Rasheen toxin, will no longer be a part of their diets! That means that over the years, the Rasheen will naturally filter out of their reproductive systems, resulting in only nonmutant, healthy offspring. This is a humane method and it should permit all the existing Razahs to live out their lives in the rainforests. They'd still be holding onto their role as the number one predators, but forced to teach their young the forgotten art of stealth!"

Someone applauded, then the rest quickly followed suit. They were finally with her wholeheartedly and began to gesture and talk excitedly.

Adam caught Elena's attention, rolling his eyes. She shrugged discreetly, looking around. The group hadn't picked up on their silent exchange.

Suddenly Elke moaned behind them, rubbing his head. "Ouch!" he mumbled. "I think I've got a brain cramp!"

As the group hooted, Adam slipped his arm around his wife's small waist. "I think *all* our brains got cramped! It's been like drinking from a fire hose around this gorgeous little fountain!" He rubbed his palms together. "So okay, now. Three things, in ascending order of importance: First, aside from a few bruised ribs and a badly winged brain, Elke's fine. We've all leaned some valuable lessons tonight. Second...," he paused, looking pointedly at his wrist programmer, "Duron will be here at precisely seven tomorrow morning to review our capture and release program."

"Third...." As they waited expectantly, he winked and his brows rose silently. Elena blushed. No explanation was needed.

Adam was up at six. He'd lain awake for quite a while, itching to go down and study the Razah in the daylight. He slipped Elena's arm off his chest and snuck out of bed, dressing quickly in the corridor.

As he entered the cargo hold, his flaring nostrils were instantly assailed by the strong, now-familiar rank odor. While the larger cat lay cold, stiff and scorched, the smaller one languished in a deep stupor. The beast was frightening, even grotesque: he had a huge, bulbous forehead, his fur was badly kept, and his rough cat tongue dangled loosely as he exhaled a terrible breath. Behind one ear there was a small, singed patch of fur, about the size of a fist.

A paw twitched. Taking no chances, Adam slid his Stifler from its holster. After a moment's hesitation, he poked through the bars with the barrel of the gun and lifted a loose cheek, exposing the full set of great, curved ivory fangs.

"Whoeee! Man, look at those choppers!" he gasped. "Eighteen, twenty inches long?" Suddenly, they snapped together with a loud crunch. "Yike!" He grimaced. "This bad boy's startin' to come around! "

The door slid open behind him. Spooked, he slowly turned around. Elena was standing there, holding out a full syringe. "I watched you leave our room, and suddenly I remembered it was almost time for the sedative to wear off." She pushed the needle toward him. "I just can't. I'm too scared," she shivered. "You do it."

He slipped up behind the creature and quickly emptied a full slug of time-release serum into a muscular shoulder. The stripes jerked, quivered, then lay still.

She peered over the Razah's head. "The respirator, Adam." She smiled sweetly, holding it at arm's length. "It goes down his throat."

As he shoved it in, they heard a loud conversation in the hallway. The rest of the party was arriving, dragging the caged and drugged Spyrins from a cargo hold next door. They busied themselves jabbing long needles between the armor plates to sedate them for the day, and soon the small collection of creatures was safely out.

Duron entered the bay, looking around. "I must say, I am impressed! One night, Adam, and already your crew has caught four Spyrins and *two* Razahs?"

"It was easy, Duron. They, ah, came to *us*! You know, there's something really odd about these Razahs. Cats are usually fastidious, right? These blimps have gotten fat and lazy and lax in their hygiene. They're-they're just plain slobs!"

"Slobs?" Duron was stumped. "Blimps? What is…?"

"Oh. Sorry. Slang again."

"Your lexicon is astounding, Adam," he mused. "There seems to be no end to your variation on a single theme." He looked around with sudden purpose. "What I really came to tell you is that our production facilities are running at full capacity. In a few days you will have all the material you need for your new city."

"Wow, thanks, Duron! You know, that watchtower we built yesterday is already generating cold air at an amazing rate! As soon as we install the baffles and recirculating membranes under the top rim, we should be able to cool off all the other buildings in…."

"So *that's* it!" Elena interrupted. "A *cooling* tower! That's why you shaped it like that: wide at the bottom and tapering to the top?"

Adam grinned. "Also, why it has so many open 'doors' around the bottom."

Duron slit-smiled. "Yes, Adam, I like your tower very much! It has an elegant shape and the view from the top is quite wonderful!"

"Yeah! I can hardly wait to get cracking on the lab and holding pens!"

"Cracking...?" Duron winced, then turned to Elena. "The men have told me of your newest plan for the Razahs. It sounds like it could work, but..." He looked around, then bent low to their ears. "I am afraid there is something else I have to discuss with both of you. We really do not know what we are dealing with; there is another factor involved, a big one." As they glanced at each other questioningly, he pulled them onto the loading dock, glancing nervously over his shoulder at the jungle.

"Listen," he whispered. "The Razah has evolved into a creature *far* more complex than you realize. His phenomenal mind-stun is only one facet of a many-sided intelligence. He has become a sentient creature with powers more highly evolved than either you or I could ever imagine!"

"I, ah...," Elena stuttered, fear creeping into her voice. She fought it, trying her best to sound composed. "I'm sorry, but I-I think we both need to confess something." She turned to look at Adam pointedly.

He shrugged, motioning for her to continue. "You tell him, sweetpea."

She took a deep breath. "Well, both Adam and I have already experienced this power, long before we landed on Aurona."

"*Before* you landed?" Duron drew back, astonished. "How could that *be*?"

Adam filled him in, relating the unforgettable incident exactly as it happened. Elena clung tightly to his arm, watching the old one's expression fall in rapid stages, first from wonder, then to alarm and fear.

He clutched his chest. "You said 'nobody is the wiser,' Adam? I am afraid you are in error! We have long suspected this creature to have psychic abilities, but not to the extent you have just described! Judging from what you have revealed, the Razah knew of your arrival and your intentions *before* you conceived this morning's intricate plans for his containment in your minds! He could 'see' your plans for the gold helmets, the PIL signals to trace him, the...."

"No *way*!" Adam shook his head in disbelief. "Get outta here! You *can't* be telling me that this ugly beast is *clairvoyant*!!"

The old one looked at them levelly. "Yes. Believe me, I have always thought it might be so, but now confirm it as fact. Listen. Other facets have begun to display themselves, too: We have seen that they can actually move objects with the physical waves of their mind-stuns; they 'talk' with others of their species over long distances; they can...."

Elena's voice was quavering. "Y-you're saying that Razahs have evolved into an intelligent species and they're *aware* of their existence and their place in the order of things? Why, these helmets are going to stifle their potential, reducing them back to mere animals again!"

"As I said," Adam grimaced, "they're gonna *hate* us for that!"

The three stared at each other in shock, overcome by the wide-ranging implications.

Duron finally recovered his voice. "So," he breathed, whispering solemnly, "let it be. Go ahead with your plan. Who knows how our *own* self-awareness came about? In any case, the

Razah remains our prime enemy and so must suffer this dark period of transition to his former state. Let us go now."

He turned purposefully toward the doorway and strode into the cargo bay, pausing to look at the sedated insects lying in a neat row. "Yes, yes," he nodded quietly, lifting a stiff, hooked leg to examine it. "Again, Adam, I have changed my mind. Total elimination would be acceptable for these Spyrins. They are destroying too many very desirable species with their aggressive, and I must admit, very successful hunting techniques. Unfortunately, I cannot help you locate the caves. They were abandoned millenniums ago and have become completely overgrown."

Adam contemplated a moment. "Well, how about this? We'll *follow* them! We'll get up early tomorrow morning, attach transmitters to these bad boys, and let 'em go!"

"At dawn?" Duron stopped short, his eyes wide. "Why, that is an excellent time! They sleep during the day and should go straight back to their hive!"

"What?" Elena groaned. "You two can find more ways to get yourselves into...."

Adam held up a finger. "Duron isn't going, hon. It's just me and the boys. We'll be okay, I promise! We're just gonna follow 'em back to their nest, cloaked and shielded on our antigrav sleds."

"Are you *sure* that's all?" She crossed her arms suspiciously.

"Well, I *have* been toying with another plan of attack once we're there.... You know, kind of putting things together on the fly? I think it might work, but I need more input. Listen...," he pulled them both closer, lowering his voice to a barely audible whisper.

Duron beamed. "All at once? A great idea!"

Elena tried to keep the anguish out of her voice. "Use your shields, Adam? Please? All the time? For me?"

"Done," he vowed. "All the time. Now let's get to work on these Razahs. Tomorrow's another day. A big one."

Chapter 20: SPYRINS

Looking like dark specks out in the middle of a crazy, swirling, spun-glass sea, Adam and nineteen of his most trusted men gathered in an excited knot. Although they were about a half-mile from the trunk of the Motherlode, they found it to be unexpectedly windy in the big circular clearing. Like the mighty engine driving a hurricane, the warm air rising inside the immense column of light was pulling strong breezes from the perimeter, flattening the grass into a spiral pattern. Dancing in the current, long, undulating ribbons of gold spiraled upward, the blizzard of flecks nearly blotting the tree from view.

Dawn approached. Washing away with the silken bloom of morning, the immense colonnade of light began to fade, the breeze died down, and the field soon lay cool and still. As the first rays of sunlight gilded the top of the Motherlode, a Dazzor bird chimed its bell tones from the rainforest

Tola raised a finger, counting down. In ten seconds, the column was totally gone. "There ya go, guys. Badda boom: sun's up, light's out, end of story."

"Wow!" Peter breathed. "That's all I can say."

"And the sunlight controls it all," Adam exclaimed. "That's incredible. Let's try to figure out the timing here. Aurona's much bigger than the Earth, about a third larger."

"And it turns much slower, too," Kron added. "Duron did mention it was something in the order of thirty-two Earth-hours. That makes sixteen hours of daylight, right?"

Adam shrugged. "Eh, close enough for jazz. So let's see: on top of that, there are three bonus hours of light in the morning and three more at night."

Tola looked up. "Ah, that makes twenty-two hours … and?"

Kron brightened. "Remember what *else* Duron said? 'We pamper our providers'? These Motherlodes have gotten twenty-two hours of sunlight for what, millions of years? Plus, they've roped the whole rainforest into their feeding frenzy!"

"Hey, that's right!" Peter chimed in. "These big trees are gluttons and their root networks are covering the whole planet! No wonder they're so colossal!"

Tola covered his ears. "Tilt! Tilt!" His voice had a robotic twang. "Information overload! Too many numbers! Words, I know; numbers, eh…," he shrugged. He pointed at his newly calibrated wrist programmer. "And all this extra Aurona time is making my screen look cluttered. It's just plain messy!"

Adam chuckled. "Well, no matter how you slice up the old dial, it's almost five-thirty in the morning, Earth time. We're leaving." He checked out the equipment and then trotted back to the excited group. "Generators ready?"

They answered eagerly. "Check!"

He went down the list. "Flexfoam pumps operational? Remote cage releases working? PIL transmitters activated?"

"Check. Check. *Check*!" They sprinted toward their SpeedSleds, answering on the fly. In moments, they were strapped in.

"Okay now, three things, on my signal: activate your cloaking devices, throw up your shields, and open the Spyrin cages! Got it?"

"Yes, *sir*!" they chorused.

He dropped his hand. "*Now*!"

The SpeedSleds disappeared like a mirage, the cage doors flew open, and the four raging Spyrins streaked out. Getting their bearings, they banked like a fighter squadron toward the dark rainforest, turning on their searchlights as they approached.

"Holy Pokemon, can they ever *move*!" Tola yelled. "Daylight's a-comin' an' they wanna go *home*!"

Adam laughed. "Hey, Kron! Got four PIL signals showing on your screen?"

"Yes!" Kron yelled into the intercom. "And-and they're already a half mile away!"

"*Sick* 'em!" he pointed.

They flashed across the dewy field in hot pursuit, fourteen mysterious trails of slick, moving grass the only clue to their movement. As they approached the rainforest, Adam switched to Amplified Autopilot and lined up the sleds in close single file. Abruptly, they were in the thick of things, whipping sinuously through dense undergrowth, bobbing and weaving in a neck-snapping, tortuous trail. Homing in on the Spyrins' PIL signals, the sleds took on a mind of their own; the only thing the group could do was to strap in, hunker down, and hold tight. Nose to tail with only inches of radar distance separating them, the speeding bullet train created a great vacuum-tunnel of wind in its wake.

A voice wailed over the intercom. "Owwwwch! Crud! W-what are we p-playing here, sir, c-crack the whip?"

Adam shouted above the roar. "Think about it, if *w-we* were trying to steer, we would'a lost 'em in t-the first five seconds! Just t-thank the inventors for AAP!"

"What'd you say, s-sir? Can't hear you!"

"Ooooch!" Adam rapped his elbow as the sleds snapped through a particularly tight turn. "Amplified Autopilot! J-just sit b-back and r-relax," he gritted through his teeth. "P-put your f-feet up! En-j-joy the s-scenery!"

A faint voice returned. "*W-what* scenery?"

About twenty blurred miles into the rainforest the Spyrin's PIL signals slowed, forcing the sleds to auto-decelerate. Soft morning light was filtering through the palms ahead. Releasing their belts, they leaned forward and craned their necks to see.

With a deep, ear-slitting roar, the four Spyrins were suddenly beside them! The men recoiled in their seats, their hearts hammering. The basso profundo quartet gathered in a circle, flashed their blinding searchlights in some kind of strange code, then banked in formation toward the clearing to merge into an enormous black cloud of glistening wings.

The men slipped out of the forest into a swampy clearing, then stopped a short distance away to watch, nervously rechecking their cloaking devices. As they turned up their audio, they could hear the roar: echoing with hollow-sounding thunder, the last of the great, venomous cloud of Spyrins were disappearing into a huge, rectangular opening about nine feet above the ground.

Adam began to feel weird, his mind racing. Had he seen this before? The sleds were hovering rock-steady, their fine blue laser locator beams focusing on nearby stationary objects. He shrugged it off. On his whispered cue they settled to the ground on their runners, squishing into the soft muck to wait. All of a sudden, a powerful feeling of déjà vu swept over him. Yes! He'd *been* here before: the jungle, the swamp, *everything* fit! Excitedly, he slid to the edge of his seat and looked around, still not believing his eyes.

They were beside a boggy stream, with what appeared to be a huge wall on the other side. He slumped back, his gut quaking, staring intently at the huge, precisely fit stones. "The G-galaxy Room!" he stammered. "The-the Outpost!"

Tola laid a hand on his shoulder. "Ah, what's that, sir?"

Holding up a finger, he opened the audio channels and began to whisper excitedly into his mike. "Okay, now listen, guys. You may not believe this, but I'm pretty sure I know what to expect here! As you enter that big rectangular opening, you should find a tunnel to the left, sloping down into a long, slippery ramp. There's a wall at the end with, ah, Dazeen spikes sticking out of it," he paused, realizing what he'd just said. "Dazeen spikes?" he mumbled. "But that's impossible! How'd they get *them* back to the Earth?" As the men exchanged uneasy looks, he continued, almost in a daze. "Then you turn to the right when you get to the wall. Yes, to the right! Follow me so far?

"Ah … sir?" Tola asked hesitantly, pulling his hand away.

"Next!" Adam held up a finger. "A spiral staircase should be at the end, going way, way down into this humongous domed vault. Hey, come to think of it, the environment down there should be *perfect* for a nest. Yes! And the Spyrins shouldn't be able to get *out* any other way, because there are no other exits, just a bunch of small ventilation shafts going up to the surface! The shafts are probably out in the woods on the other side of the wall!" His voice was shaking in excitement. "Yes! Yes! Our plan should work flawlessly!"

After a long silence, Kron probed gently. "Sir? Ah, how…?"

"Intuition," he interjected quickly. "Ah, let's just say I've seen it all before."

Another silence. Their minds were racing.

"Hey! I'll fill you in later!" he blurted. "Let's go!"

They men glanced nervously over their shoulders.

"C'mon, c'mon, we're wasting time!" Adam shouted impatiently. "Crank up those generators! Unlatch your safeties and set your Stiflers to 'kill'!"

They leaped into action, raising the four generator barges into the air and maneuvering them carefully to fit tightly across the rectangular opening. After snipping small, flat sections of Flexnet into various sizes, they plugged the spaces around the edges and sprayed Flexfoam over them. In minutes they had an airtight seal.

Without warning, a deep buzz thundered behind them! A chill ran down their spines and they spun around, their hearts in their mouths.

A Spyrin! The lone straggler was furiously strobing his light, clacking his jaws, and jabbing his stinger. The shredded, partially eaten body of a Dazzor bird was dangling limply from the hooks on his feet, trailing along the ground like a battered, blood-streaked pennant. A single, glowing feather fell into the stream and slowly drifted away.

Adam's hands were shaking in anger. "Steady, men…." They aimed their Stiflers, awaiting his command.

"*Waste* that mutant scum!"

They fired in unison. As twenty blazing arcs bored into their target, the Spyrin's body immediately hissed and swelled, the abdomen ballooning grotesquely. With a loud retort, the insect exploded violently in a ball of superheated steam and smoking body parts!

"Yes!" They ducked, slapping high fives and jabbing their fists into the air.

Amidst the steaming clumps of wings, claws, legs and guts, the Dazzor's small body dropped in a crumpled heap. Impulsively, Adam vaulted off the generator barge and dashed out into the clearing, picking his way through the swampy muck.

The bird's body was still warm when he picked it up. He turned it over gently, his hands shaking. "Damn!" He snapped his head up, his finger pointing emphatically at the generators. "Let's *do* this thing!"

They bent into action with renewed purpose: the four generators roared to life, pumping clouds of billowing, suffocating smoke down the passageways. It didn't take long to reach the first hornets. There was a faint, questioning wail, followed by a pencil beam of light stabbing up into the dark forest canopy.

Kron spotted the bright, moving line on the other side of the wall. "Huh?" He stood on his toes on top of a barge. "Wow!" he gasped. "Look at *that*!"

The men scrambled over the top. Looking like mute exclamation points, ten tightly focused beams were flashing in alarm, stabbing up through the ventilation shafts into the morning fog. In a gathering light-storm of fury, mist and shadow began to strobe in a maelstrom of insanity.

A great roar began. Somewhere beneath their feet, hundreds of black wings thundered, making the ground vibrate. Wide-eyed, their nerves on edge, the men could only imagine the flying forms under them, colliding and thrashing in a terrifying, hollow-sounding roar of death and confusion. They watched and listened, their fists clenched tightly at their sides. The ventilation shafts were only revealing a telltale light-glimpse, a screeching sound bite of the writhing, subterranean agony. A cracking sound took over. Doomed, asphyxiating, the wailing Spyrins were crunching into each other's exoskeletons with their powerful mandibles and frantically stinging anything that moved.

Adam's heart was pounding. "Good grief," he breathed. "This smoke is more powerful than I thought! Hey, I just thought of something. We don't want to choke the whole jungle with it! As soon as we see it shooting out those shafts, we'll cut off the generators and wait for stuff to finish its work down there."

The lights flickered and the faint wails continued for an endless, adrenaline-pumping span. Suddenly, ten vertical puffs of smoke shot out! They silenced the generators immediately and waited, listening to the quiet pulse of life returning to the jungle.

It was done. Tilting his head back, Adam let out a long, tremulous sigh. "Hallelujah," he whispered, shaking his head. "Okay, guys. Ready for recontainment?"

Regaining his composure, Kron gave him a thumb's up and twirled a few dials. As the four freewheeling generator pumps began to inhale deeply, ten swirling vacuum currents materialized over the air shafts: graphically revealed by the the smoke and mists, they looked like mini tornadoes. The pumps sucked the smoke back up through the passageways and into the hoses, filtering it through a series of fine, wet, vibrating screens. Something like concentrated slurry began to plop down into small, clear jars.

"Wait a sec...." Adam vaulted nimbly over the top of the wall and sprinted over to the nearest shaft. Bending down, he plugged the hole with his hand, gauging the strength of the suction. "Wow! *Very* powerful!" He yelled over the noise of the machines. "Four generators *are* a bit of overkill," he shrugged. "Well, it won't be long now!"

Shortly, all the air quality indicator dials read optimum: fresh air was now being sucked out of the nest. They eagerly hit the switches and ripped the sticky Flexfoam off the stone. As the barges backed away, a heap of Spyrin bodies tumbled out. They hopped into the opening, kicking the last of them over the edge with their muddy boots.

"Vengeance is ours!" Adam's voice echoed, already halfway down the ramp. "Hey! Footgrippers turned up? Stiflers ready?" Spooked, the men entered the tunnel behind him, climbing over piles of stiff, spiky bodies.

Every detail was exactly where Adam had predicted: the ramp, the wall, the spiral staircase, everything. With Asron torches blazing, they filed silently down the spiral staircase and stepped out into the vault, lining up against the great, curving wall of gold. As Tola swept his torch upward, he let out an involuntary gasp. "L-look!"

Far above their heads, an enormous nest was swinging back and forth, hanging precariously from the center of a deeply embossed gold medallion. A few Spyrins were still hanging from it, twitching weakly. As their flickering searchlights blackened with a lingering hiss, they released their tenacious hooks and fell, tumbling through the air onto a mountain of black bodies.

"Wow!" Adam shook his head. "*Look* at this mess! Well, we've got our work cut out for us! Anyone remember to bring the rope and antigrav grapplers?"

They stared silently at each other, overwhelmed.

"No? Okay, two of you, upstairs on the double! Hup! Hup!"

They returned with the equipment clattering down the stairway behind them and everyone whipped into action. Handling the spiky bodies with thickly gloved hands, they clamped small, humming antigrav grapplers onto the thorax of each insect and turned up the power to lift the heavy carcass about a foot off the floor. As the men tethered them onto the rope and packed them tightly together, the monumental task finally began to make sense. In no time at all, they had a long line of Spyrin bodies ascending the stairway, looking like a string of floating, burnt-out lightbulbs.

At the entrance, another group released the black carcasses from the grapplers' hooks and tossed them over the edge. Adam snatched the loose end of the rope and pulled it back down into the vault, a string of empty grapplers floating along behind him. At the bottom, he quickly tied the loose ends of the rope together and formed a continuous loop.

At the top, the men quickly realized his scheme.

"Well, waddaya know! A conveyer belt! I swear, that man's a genius."

"Would *you* have thought of this, bean-brain?"

"Ah, no. I'd still be doing a ton of grunt work, you know, sweating, schlepping these bad boys up the stairs one at a time?"

"You're right. Me too. Well, we should be glad we got Adam in charge, because we'd all be *dead* by now. Remember how he saved us on the Obelisk planet?"

"Yeah, but then again, how'd he seem to know the *exact* layout of this hive? We all *know* he's never been here before! It's creepy, if you ask me! Creepy!"

They heard a chuckle in the shadows. Adam jumped out, popping his eyes.

Startled, they grinned nervously and dumped Spyrin bodies a bit faster.

"How'd I know? This Bandor cave is an original model of the Outpost I explored back on the Earth! I was just a kid then, and we were in New Guinea.... Oh, I'll tell you the rest later," he teased. "Maybe."

The taller one squinted at him in the bright morning light. "Ah, you said that this cave is the same as one you went into on the *Earth*?"

"Yes. Exactly. Apparently, it's only one of thousands throughout the universe."

"The Bandors came to the Earth?" he persisted.

"Eons ago. They called their Earth-cave an Outpost."

"Oh." They glanced at each other, shrugging undecidedly. "I think we get it?"

He smiled, saluted, and turned on his heel, purposely leaving them with their mouths hanging open. Downstairs, the pile was nearly gone. As the last of the Spyrins were untangled, a great bulging lump lay exposed near the center of the room.

Kron instantly recognized the hulking form. "The queen!" he pointed. The wingless body was several times longer than her workers; reduced to nothing more than an egg-laying machine, her swollen abdomen looked like a water balloon about to burst. He poked at the taught-looking membrane with the toe of his boot, letting out a low whistle.

Whooee! Gotta be *extremely* careful with this one, sir! Maybe use some extra *wide* body slings? Whaddaya think? We don't wanna be, ah, shall we say…mopping up, do we?"

Adam grimaced. "*Perish* the thought!"

Suddenly, a shout echoed down the spiral stairs, and then one of the men burst excitedly into the round room, skidding across the glass floor. "*Animals*! Hundreds of them! They're swarming out of the jungle and carrying away all the Spyrin bodies!

With a loud whoop, Adam jabbed his fist in the air. "*Yes!*" He spun to his men. "The *ultimate* in poetic justice! Let's go watch the great feast of revenge!"

"Hold on, guys," Tola smiled mischievously, "got your black ties on? There's Smoked Spyrin on the menu!"

Laughing, they maneuvered the queen's bulky, floating body up the spiral staircase. As the excited group crowded the entrance, Tola jumped up and down, trying to see over their shoulders. No go. He dropped to his knees, squeezing between their legs. As he approached the edge, a loud squealing greeted him. He looked down into a great free-for-all: there was an enormous, roiling melee of beak and scale, tooth and claw, feather, fur and flying Spyrin parts. Suddenly, beyond the turbulence of bodies, he saw something else. He focused into the distance. Some great, striped beasts were having a field day.

"R-Razahs!" he pointed.

Adam studied them a moment. "There's another feeding frenzy out there, and they've got a lot of food. I'm sure they're not interested in *us*!"

"You're right," Tola grinned. "They're finishing off the fattest fare from the fringes of this frenzied flock!"

The men glanced down. "From the fringes…? Frenzied…?" They poked at him with their boots. "*Go* for it, round man!"

Laughing, Tola fended them off. "Hey!" He poked at the queen's body with his finger, grinning mischievously. "We got *more* ammunition! We've saved the best for last!"

They got the idea immediately. Sliding the bloated body to the edge of the opening, they counted to three and rolled the great sack over the edge. It hit the ground and ruptured, releasing a torrent of gooey, oval whitish eggs.

"There ya go!" he quipped. "Dunk for dessert, you delirious denizens!"

Squealing loudly over their heads, a new group joined the frenzy: aeronautas! Hundreds of them! The billowing cloud descended, hissing and letting out volumes of gas to lose altitude. "Pop, pop, pop…." As one of them brazenly scuttled by Adam's head, he snatched it by its coiled snout. "Gotcha!" It thrashed helplessly, it's squealing lost in the din. He plunked himself down on the edge and stuffed the creature between his legs to study it. The men crowded around him, kneeling for a closer look.

"Hmmm," he mumbled, "let's see what makes these babies tick." He squinted through the creature's thin, whitish membrane. "What in the world? Water?" He sloshed the bubble around. "Hey, Kron, got a portable air quality indicator on you?"

Startled, Kron checked his pockets. "Ah, yeah! Got one, sir!"

"I'm gonna give him a little squeeze. You check to see where the gas comes out." He applied a gentle pressure with his legs. The snout fluttered.

"Th-the nose?" Kron's eyes popped. "He farted out his *nose*?"

Hooting, they elbowed each other as Kron took the sample. "Huh? Y-you're not gonna believe this, sir!" He stuck the dial in front of Adam's face.

His eyes widened. "Hydrogen? That's…. Owww!" He jerked his hand away. "Hey! This little sucker just *shocked* me! He-he's got a *zapper*!" He pushed on the spot again and got the same response. "Ouch! Hey, what gives?"

"What *is* it, sir? A stinger? Spikes?"

"No, it feels like electricity! But-but how could *that* be?" As he mulled it over, a light dawned. "Of *course*, that explains the *water*! These little piglets must be able to break the water molecules down into their two basic components with…."

Kron cut in. "No! Come on, electrolysis?"

Adam continued. "Bingo! The hydrogen provides the lift and the oxygen's simply absorbed into his body through respiration!" He sloshed the squealing balloon creature around. "And look! The water acts like ballast to keep him upright! No wonder these guys need to be near water all the time! We're in the middle of a swamp here, right?"

He stood up and let the Aeronauta go. Just as he'd theorized, it released squirts of excess water as ballast, leaving a long trail of drops behind him. With a sudden, loud squealing, the enormous cloud of living bubbles followed his lead and began to climb, releasing their collective water ballast in a torrent. Each held a single, treasured, six-inch Spyrin egg coiled in their snout. As the cacophony rose to the jungle canopy, a loud slurping sound replaced it from base of the wall. They looked down. A lone, hungry straggler was noisily sucking up the contents of a broken egg.

"Well," Adam pointed, "that should mark the end of this Spyrin colony, except for the dead larvae down in the nest. Let's go finish the job."

"Wait." One of the men held out his hand, offering him a piece of smooth, leathery-looking paper. "What should we do about the nest itself, sir?"

"Hey, wow! This is a piece of nest?" He tried to tear it apart with his hands. "Tough stuff! We could just grind it up and spray it onto the forest floor. You know, like mulch?"

"Dust to dust," Tola mused, quietly. "Poetic justice again, sir."

Adam chuckled. "But we really should bring a chunk of it back to our lab and put some brains to work on it. There are hundreds of uses for cellulose!"

Peter's voice rose hesitantly from the back of the group. "What about the *gold*? What do we do with all the *gold* down in the dome?"

There was an instant silence.

Suddenly, Adam winced. Out of the blue, a powerful runic message flooded his mind. He found it hard to keep up with the string of glowing symbols.

"Adam, this is Duron. I have my feet planted firmly on the ground and am sending you this message through the planetary gridwork. I have been watching your progress through your telepathic eyes. Please give one of your crew this abandoned structure, as we have thousands more all over the planet. Consider it a reward for ridding our planet of this dangerous, mutant species. The Elders with me are in agreement that you and your men have taken enormous risks to accomplish this frightrning task. This is the least we can do."

He shook his head, blinked, and turned to Peter with a completely unexpected answer on his lips. "Ah, do you want it, Peter?"

Everyone swiveled toward him like he'd gone stark, raving mad.

Kron squeaked out a reply. "S-Sir, you're joking! You can't be serious!"

Adam laid it out. "No, I'm *not* joking. Duron, ah, told me to consider this first vault as a gift from the Elders. After that, they want each of us to get one as a reward for ridding the planet of Spyrins. Call it a little added incentive?"

Peter was sputtering. "But, but...."

"It's for real, men. The Bandors moved out of these vaults centuries ago to live in their bigger, more secure cities. This is just one of thousands of identical copies all over Aurona, and from what I'm figuring out, they're all over the universe!"

"Whaaat?" Tola interjected. "No *way*! They abandoned these gems? Why?"

He held up his hands. "Hey, t o Bandors, gold's just another metal. You know, it's decorative and useful, like the ultimate in rot-proof trash can liners, or something?" He thought a moment. "I don't know, guys. When you get your vault just use your imagination: live in it like a home, have a cool vacation retreat in the jungle, make it a research station, whatever! Strip the gold from the walls and melt it into computer connections! Personally, though, I want my vault to stay the same. I think it's beautiful."

Peter was still in shock. "C'mon ... *me*? Are you absolutely sure?"

He raised a brow, staring at him levelly. "I'm stark, raving positive!"

As the man let out a whoop and scampered down the ramp, Adam turned to the others and gestured toward the floor. "Sit a minute, guys. Let's give him some privacy. We've worked hard. Take a break and enjoy the cool breezes coming up out of the vault. Since you're my inner circle, I feel like this is a good time to pass on a bit of insight. Something important has been on my chest for quite a while."

Their eyes questioning, they settled to the floor at his feet.

"Gold," he began. "Our symbol 'Au' and number 79 in the periodic table. In fact, the symbol 'Au' is where the name 'Aurona' comes from: a gold planet with a corona around it? My grandfather thought up the name and the Bandors liked it."

"Hey," Tola chuckled, "he's cuttin' into *my* turf! Great name, though!"

Adam laughed along with the men. "So there you go. Anyway, in our periodic table, we squeezed gold between platinum and mercury. Since it's so rare on the Earth, we've given it a lot of value. All the gold we've ever mined would fit into a 60-foot cube. On the other hand, since it's so abundant on Aurona, it's just another metal. They don't use it as money. In fact, the Bandors have no need for any kind of hard currency here."

"But-but how do they *buy* anything?" a voice piped up.

"They don't," he shrugged. "Everything's bartered. *Everything*."

Tola raised a pudgy finger. "I just thought of something. Since gold is everywhere here, Aurona might have been bombarded with meteors during its formation."

Adam looked pleasantly surprised. "You've been *reading*, Tola!"

"Yeah, in the Dream Library. I was wondering what made this place tick."

He turned to the men. "Remember, guys. Take everything you read with a grain of salt; a lot of what we 'know' is just educated guessing. The scientists think, or guess, that tiny 60-foot cube of gold we've discovered, maybe 180 or 190 billion tons of it, came to Earth via meteorites very late in its history. That would put it just about 4 billion years ago, during the Late Heavy Bombardment period."

The small group elbowed and threw looks each other. Apparently, their young leader knew far more than he let on.

Adam homed in on his point. "Listen guys, and bear with me. Think about the concept of bartering. Think about all the things that bartering reflects and represents: motives can't be forced, nor can attitudes or heart, for that matter. Everybody here on Aurona works freely for the common good and everything's shared equally, even their thoughts! And no one goes hungry."

"Sounds too good to be true," Elke murmured.

"No, it sounds more like socialism," Tola corrected.

"Bees!" Adam slapped his leg, laughing. "They're all worker bees here! Seriously, you might think that lack of ownership might destroy every speck of initiative, but somewhere along the line a funny thing happened."

"What's *that* sir?"

He shrugged. "The greed disappeared. They totally forgot about it. Their real prize has turned out to be equally shared thoughts, their treasure fresh new ideas for the betterment of all! Here's the low-down: through their powers of telepathy, they've become an extremely closely-knit race. When one gets hurt they all feel the pain. On the other hand, when one gets a brilliant idea, he instantly beams it out over the entire planet. Think about this: telepathy is the Ultimate Internet! Telepathy is the sole reason they're so incredibly advanced, both materially and socially." He paused, contemplating. "But on the down side, now that we've arrived, there's something else I really worry about."

Kron cut in. "I think I know, sir." He shrugged, hesitantly. "It's *us*! Right?"

He turned to him, relieved. "Thanks, man. I-I was starting to feel like you guys might be hanging off the tip of my branch. Yes, it's us. We're a real danger to them."

"I'm with you all the way on *that* one, sir." Tola nodded.

He held up an admonishing finger. "We're *still* greedy. We're Neanderthals compared to them. We're still acting like stupid animals growling over our pitiful piles of bones. 'Survival of the fittest' is taking forever to die out in our backward civilization!"

"But-but the Bandors seem to *like* us...," one of the men offered.

"Yes," he interrupted, "but even *that* scares me! You've got to understand that in many ways they're like innocent children. They've been trusting each other so long they've forgotten about all the snaky human things like suspicion, dominance, greed, and stupid ego trips."

"Whooee!!" Kron expelled a breath of air. "*Go* for it! Tell it like it *is*!"

"*Preach* it, man!" Tola beamed. "I think you've missed your calling!"

Adam waved them off, laughing. "Listen, guys. Since I trust you, I want to ask each one of you a very important favor."

"What is it, sir?" Tola answered for the group.

"For the sake of these innocent Bandors, pass on this stuff to the rest of the crew? I know it'll be hard, but hopefully they'll come around. At least the ones with half a brain.... Oh, and speaking of Neanderthal thinking, you may be surprised that the Bandors have already spotted the, ah, negative people among us."

Kron interjected quickly. "Of course you're referring to Dexor and his goons?"

"Bingo! You noticed too? There's a serious flaw in their thought patterns. Telepathically speaking, they stand out like sore thumbs! Duron could actually see an aura around them! He simply couldn't understand their negativity and resistance."

"Well, *we* understand, sir," Kron affirmed. "You may not be aware of this, but some of us have had long talks about them. We got 'em locked in our sights!"

The morning sun was now streaming down brightly through the surrounding canopy of the rainforest, promising yet another perfect seventy-five degree day. Adam let out a long breath. A great weight had been lifted from his shoulders. The men were coming out of their shells and starting to know each other on a far deeper level.

"You know," he concluded quietly, "and I'm even more serious now, you've got to admire the way the Bandors have handled this planet. I mean, from zero: a barren, lifeless desert, to *this*?" He breathed deeply, filling his lungs with the pure air. "What a specimen, what a showpiece for the universe!" He stretched, looking around.

Tola grinned. "I'll tell you one thing, sir: if *we* were in control, the whole planet would've been zapped into a cinder by now!"

Chuckling, Adam started down the ramp. "Hey, gimme a minute, guys," he tossed over his shoulder. "I gotta talk to Peter."

As he descended the long spiral, he paused near the bottom of the stairs, rubbing his forehead. Someone was talking.

"Why me?"

Startled, he stood riveted to the spot, his hand resting on the alabaster wall. Cocking his head and listening intently, he stole a quick look around the corner. Peter was gazing intently over his head, but his mouth wasn't moving.

His voice came again in a disembodied whisper. *"I-I really don't need all this gold, but it's mine? Wow, once I get rid of that big nest up there, this would make a fantastic room for parties, for dancing.... Gee, I hope Ariel likes it and it's not too gloomy for her. Hmm, a few more ventilation holes up there might lighten this place up, and...."*

Adam had heard enough. Was this a breakthrough? Maybe now he could listen to Dexor's thoughts, too! He squared his shoulders and walked in, the picture of innocence. "Hey! Nice digs, Peter! A bit dismal, though, don'tcha think?" He swept his arm toward the glittering dome. "You might want to put in a skylight or two!"

He looked up, startled. "Wow! That's-that's exactly what I was thinking, sir! I can't speak for my *girl*, though. I-I haven't even asked her to marry me yet."

"Ariel, is it?" Adam chuckled.

Peter squinted at him suspiciously. "How'd *you* know?"

He shrugged, suddenly embarrassed. Had he *really* heard Peter's thoughts? Time to cover up. "Oh, we've all seen you," he bluffed. "It's obvious! The way you drool when she goes by? You know, the little things?"

The man grinned. "Oh. Sorry. I do slobber a bit."

He thumped him on the back. "Let's get the guys back down here to finish cleaning up. Hey, how about solar tubes? This vault could be a model for the others!"

"Wow! Even better! I was thinking, though, where'd I sleep, or eat? It-it just seems to be just one big, round room!" As he twirled around, his arms in the air, there was the sudden sound of thumping of feet.

The men filed in. They'd heard Peter on the way down. Lights flashing, they began to explore in earnest, their Asron torches reflecting brightly off the walls.

They paced off the perimeter, checked out the carvings, and poked their fingers into the crevices and elaborate designs carved into the heavily embossed gold. In a minute, Peter stopped short and swept his arm in an arc.

"Wait, guys! Do you see the way the big arches frame off these panels? Yeah, they're *definitely* some kind of doors! I wonder if…?" His sentence was left unfinished. Everyone began to jab and prod at them with renewed vigor.

Kron suddenly let out a shout. "Look! An *opening*!" They crowded behind him, their eyes following his fingertip and focusing on a tiny pinpoint of light beaming through the gold. "I was kinda' 'sniffing,' using my air quality indicator! It just registered a slight difference between the smoky air in here and a fresher breeze from … *there*!"

Peter put his nose up to the pinhole, sniffing. "Another room?"

"You'd think so," Kron answered, "but the air quality indicator reads differently. It says it's coming from the *outside*!"

Peter poked at the panel, enthusiastically massaging every nook of the elaborately embellished archway. Suddenly, as his finger brushed a small button in the middle of the grand center rosette, it gave a slight bounce. He paused, looked pointedly over his shoulder, and then pushed harder. There was a muffled clank. "Yes!" He grinned, his fist in the air. They backed away in excitement.

A huge, fifteen foot arched panel slid backward, and then smoothly changing direction, began to rise in total silence. Suddenly, a long bar of blinding sunlight stabbed into the gloom! Peter could contain himself no longer. Before anyone could react, he dove recklessly under the lifting door and scrambled into an incredibly bright, domed antechamber. He jumped to his feet, spinning around, his arms wide. "Holy cow, this is unbelievable!" His voice echoed hollowly. "Where's all this *light* coming from?"

They poked their heads inside, breathing deeply and inhaling the pure, filtered air. The walls were flawlessly polished white alabaster, buffed to a high gloss, precisely fit and amazingly reflective.

"Forget the light!" Kron exclaimed. "Where's all this cool, dry *air* coming from? We must be under a ventilation shaft or something!"

There was a hollow-sounding shout behind them. They spun on their heels to see Adam sprinting around the perimeter of the room like a madman, screeching to a halt in the floor litter and pressing the buttons in all the center rosettes. *More* light was pouring in! One by one, twenty brilliant antechambers slowly opened in sequence behind him! The magnificent carvings in the great central vault now gleamed brilliantly, shown in their real light for the first time in millennia!

Peter stumbled into the center of the great room. "No! All this is-is *mine*?"

"All this and *more*!" Kron poked his head out of the entrance of an antechamber, shaking his head in disbelief. "You're not going to believe this, but it goes on and on. I just opened a total of ten smaller chambers off *this* one!"

In a flash, they crowded in next to him. "Look at that long row of buttons on the left! C'mon, let's go inside!"

The antechambers were living quarters, every one of them, with bathrooms, small cooking areas and twenty hidden, paneled sleeping niches carved into their alabaster walls. There were more flush rows of buttons. They pushed them one by one, watching the sleeping niches open silently.

"Hey, I just added it all up, guys!" Kron held up his programmer. "Here goes: there are twenty antechambers around this huge main vault, with ten living areas per antechamber, then twenty sleeping niches in each one. You're not gonna believe it, but the numbers don't lie! There are a total of four *thousand* possible sleeping accommodations in here! This really *was* one of their early cities!"

Tola's jaw sagged. "Overload! Overload!" he twanged. "*Way* too many numbers! This small round unit will self-destruct in ten seconds! Overload! Overload...."

The crew guffawed, cutting him off.

"Hey, Peter!" someone shouted. "Looks like you could start a good-sized *family*!" They teased him, thumping him on the back. "Ariel might even have quadruplets!"

"C'mon, guys!" He blushed.

Working in the amazingly bright dome, they enthusiastically bent their backs into the last stages of cleanup. With a collective zap of their Stiflers, the great vestigial stump of the nest crashed to the floor and spilled its contents. As expected, the menagerie outside relished the dead, smoked larvae. Soon, not a trace of the Spyrins was left except clouds of black wings, drifting into glistening piles in the underbrush. By two o'clock the vault was totally empty, the debris swept into antigrav buckets and hauled away.

With the magnificent glass floor now clean and glistening, Adam was finally able to translate the runes that were revealed around the edges. They spoke of unknown sections of the universe and revealed yet another fabulous infrared star map. He sent the black holocamera aloft to record it in detail, figuring that Duron would be able to fill in the blanks and give them some answers.

They left in high spirits with chunks of nest material stowed behind their seats for the ship's researchers. Shields up, they switched to Amplified Autopilot: the onboard supercomputers crunched the numbers, reversing every compass, radar, gyroscope and altimeter reading they'd meticulously recorded on the way in. It was incredible: every twist, dip, and pause was flawlessly repeated in the opposite direction, but this time at quarter speed. As they gained confidence in their unfamiliar equipment, the men slowly relaxed as they sped home, exhausted after the morning's hard workout.

Chapter 21: METAMORPHOSIS

"Adam?"

"Umm?" He opened one eye groggily, then coming to his senses he sat bolt upright, grabbing for his covers. "Duron! How? Who...?"

The chuckling Bandor whisked in and plopped himself down on the foot of his bed. "Good evening and congratulations for a job well done this morning! I have been talking to Peter. He wants to install a force field over the entrance of his new home, and I think it is a splendid idea! We can produce what you call Solumbra domes in any shape and quite efficiently. Oh, I am sorry; did you have a pleasant rest?"

Just beyond the old one's oddly proportioned head, there was a new Auronian chronometer on the wall. The fine, downy fuzz of Duron's hair was backlit by a nearby fiberoptic sun-diffuser, and squinting, he could just about read the numbers. "Yeah," he mumbled, "I guess a four-hour nap does make a lot of difference. After that Spyrin chase this morning, I was pooped."

"Pooped?"

"Slang again, Duron. Tuckered out, frazzled, knocked for a loop... oh, forget it." He swung his legs over the edge of the bed. "Not to change the subject, but...."

"Y-yes?" The big head tilted way to the side, trying to keep up with the jargon.

"After we cleaned up the Spyrin nest, there was a star map on the floor showing a remote section of the universe. There was another system of galaxies I've never seen. I took some holo-photos of it, if you want to see them."

"Later, perhaps. I do remember as a child visiting the last of our ancestor's caves before we abandoned them for our new underground cities. There were also tales of a great coastal tomb, the very first to have ever been constructed, that was lost in a cataclysmic flood. Beyond that my memory seems to be incomplete."

"Wow, a coastal tomb, huh? Did it have infrared lines, too? Maps can't fully function as maps without directions, can they?"

Duron smiled. "I am afraid no one knows how to control their internal power sources anymore." At Adam's disappointed look he suddenly brightened. A slender finger rose in the air. "Except for, ah, maybe...," he mused. "No, no."

"Who? Adam prompted. "Someone still might have some answers?"

He looked distracted. "I am sorry, Adam. Could we talk about her later?"

"It's a *her*? Her who? Ah, is this Roson again?"

"Yes, yes, it is the old woman. But listen, it is really getting late. I am afraid I must change the subject and come directly to the real reason for my visit."

He shrugged in resignation. "Shoot." As a wispy brow rose, he fumbled, trying to amend his one-liner. "Oh. I-I meant, ah, dish it out, um, fill me in, ah...."

Both brows flew up. "Your idioms and word pictures are *extraordinary*," Duron slit-smiled. "Now. It is indeed getting quite late and I must come directly to the point." The timbre of is voice

241

changed, taking on a restrained exuberance, enticingly mysterious. "It is *time*, Adam! Please get ready, because darkness is approaching."

"Huh?" He groped excitedly for his clothes. "Whassup?"

The odd slit-smile stretched a bit wider. "*You*! You will be up, for one! The elders are waiting for us on top of the Motherlode!"

"What? On top of the…? What's it time *for*? What are you…?"

"Do not be nervous," he interrupted, gently. "You are ready, your body is relaxed, and your youthful mind is supple. It is time to take of the mind-fruit! The Rasheen! You *have* wanted to, haven't you?"

"Hey, I-I don't know about this, Duron! Only a lick, the tiniest taste, knocked me out, remember?"

The thin ribs heaved with a shallow sigh of exasperation. "All I can say is that you will never realize your true potential if you do not at least try."

"Well," he hedged, "I-I don't…."

"We have to prepare the mixture freshly, then it has to be ingested quickly because it spoils immediately. Only we elders have the full knowledge of this precise preparation; only with our methods can one reduce overt bodily distresses."

"Dis-distresses?" he paused freeze-frame, his arm halfway up a sleeve.

"Ah, there *is* a degree of discomfort involved," he hedged, "but it does go away quickly." As his voice trailed off, his dark eyes locked with Adam's own. "You simply *cannot* refuse us, Adam. We have never experienced anything near your potential of mind-power. Why, you surpass us all in your extensive base of knowledge and reasoning capacity! Telepathically you have already exceeded the skill level of our most advanced students, and they have been eating of the Rasheen for centuries! We simply cannot believe that you have already achieved this incredible level of awareness after only the smallest of tastes!"

"You mean I'm gonna be your guinea pig?"

Again, the big head tilted. "Guinea pig, Adam? What is…?"

"Test case, Duron, test case."

He sighed. "We merely wish to unleash the boundless reserves of your mind."

"I won't get hurt? I-I've got Elena and my crew to look after."

The old one lowered his voice, leaning toward him like a trusted confidant. "Your integrity is admirable. Listen closely now and trust me completely, my friend. Your eyes will truly be opened, your powers of observation and deductive reasoning will flower, your wisdom and discretion will grow exponentially, and your authority will stand unquestioned through the ages."

Adam switched to a quick Stooges imitation. "Hey! A *wise guy*, huh?"

His timing was perfect. Duron's great, mushroom shaped head tipped back and he let out a totally uncharacteristic whoop. "Adam, you are a total delight! Come, teach us your ways!"

Darkness was approaching. Shivering in the rising wind, Adam peered down into the distance through a notch in one of the Motherlode's leathery saw-toothed leaves. The low lights under the hull of the starship revealed some antlike figures joining a gathering throng. They looked like specks of dust under the edge of the immense saucer. "We're being watched," he growled. "Look! They're pointing at me!"

The old one shrugged. "It is only natural, Adam. You *are* their leader and we made no secret of our departure. But we are very high and they are at the foot of this tree. Therefore, their angle is not right to see over the top of this big leaf."

Adam scowled, then sighed resignedly. "I still don't like it." He peered through the notch in the leaf again, balancing on his knees. This, ah, 'thing' has got to be done in total privacy."

A murmur rose behind him. The other elders were starting to lose their patience. "Why, Adam?" Duron questioned again, speaking for the twelve. "This-this is an honorable ritual…."

"Why?" He spun around. "Because of people like Dexor, that's why! They'd completely run away with it! If he or his pals ever ate of the Rasheen, it'd be *curtains*!"

All the dark eyes closed, concentrating. "Curtains…ah, yes!" Duron murmured. "I think I am finally starting to see into your word-pictures! Alternatively speaking, you feel that if he were watching he would try to imitate our actions to gain power for himself, then it would be the end of your mission. Ah, let us see now…Zap City?"

A bright smile broke through Adam's scowl. "Hey, right on! I don't know where you got *that* from, Duron, but you nailed it! The mission would definitely be a washout! We'd be the underdogs in a lose-lose situation. And what would happen if our, um, activities 'leak' to Dexor's kind by some kind of unavoidable ah, shall we say, 'accident'? You know the old saying: 'Loose lips sink ships'?"

They'd totally lost him. The seniors were solemnly tapping and retapping their translator buttons, their dark eyes rolling at each other in confusion. Up to now they'd been listening respectfully, seated in a perfect circle in their immaculate, gold-trimmed robes and doing their best to keep up with Adam's breezy jargon. Duron glanced over his shoulder. "We-we do instinctively feel your wisdom … I guess…."

Adam joined the circle and let out a sigh. Looking pointedly at the other elders, he bobbed his head. In a chain reaction, twelve bald heads bobbed in a wave passing around the circle. As the crest surged back toward Adam, he did his level best to stifle his smile and put on his best 'sage' look. Nodding solemnly, profoundly, he bobbed his head in perfect synchronization. They were duly impressed.

"You *shall* have your privacy," Duron beamed. "Now please move into the center of the circle at once." Adam awkwardly scootched over the bumpy surface on his butt. Without another word, the elders turned their palms upward in their laps, tipped their heads back, and closed their eyes in deep concentration. The chattering and squawking of the animals fell to an eerie silence. Soon only sound of the rising wind remained.

There was a sizzle, followed by a loud crack. Something like a brightly lit fuse snapped to life behind Duron's elbow and started to move. Adam faced rigidly ahead, but his eyes warily watched the hissing point of light. Glittering clouds of vapor started to stream in from all directions to condense inside the invisible boundaries of the powerful, moving static charge. He blinked in disbelief. What was *this*? A visible shape was beginning to form, looking like a hard, curving *wall*? Like a potter's rope of clay, the gold vapor followed the energy field, building upward layer upon layer and constructing a shell of pure gold. It spiraled faster, gathering speed as it arched inward over their heads toward a central point. He braced himself. Suddenly, with a pop and blinding flash, it closed!

He rubbed his eyes. They were inside a gold igloo! Only he, the silent circle of elders, and a round disc of tough, green Motherlode leaf remained.

The jungle was getting darker by the minute. Squeezed together on a two-man SpeedSled, three impatient figures jostled awkwardly for room.

"Ouch! Hey! Watch where you put your foot, birdbrain!"

"That ain't a foot! It's a tripod!"

"Shut up, you boobs!" With a string of curses, Dexor lowered his nightscope into his lap. "Crud! Show's over!" he hissed. "The melon-heads have this round! We'll never get to see what Miss Smarty-pants is up to!" He threw up his hands in disgust.

Trennic cupped his hand over his wrist communicator to check a readout. There was a faint, momentary flash of blue.

"Douse that light, you idiot!" Dexor hissed.

"Ah, we gotta go real quick, Dex. Kron's PIL signal just entered my two hundred-yard radius, and it's speeding in this direction. He's in a big hurry."

Senn lifted his nightscope to his eyes once more. "Wow! What's that thing they're in? It looks like a–a gold pimple!"

"Don't you know a force field when you see one?" Dexor hissed. In silent fury, he cloaked their SpeedSled. The blue light flickered out and the trio disappeared.

Inside the metallic blister, once-familiar sounds were now reverberating strangely. With an amplified, starched-sounding rustle, Adam watched Duron reach under the folds of his cloak to carefully bring out a small golden chalice. "Nectar," he explained, simply. As he uncapped it, a strange, prolonged ringing started, like a high-pitched tuning fork. He flipped the cup's lid over to reveal a gleaming, slightly concave bowl of what looked like pure, shimmering energy. The ringing grew louder.

An elder carved off a miniscule section of freshly picked Rasheen and placed it on the vibrating lid. Nodding to each other, they reached ominously beneath their cloaks.

"We are ready," Duron breathed. "You must be restrained now."

Adam drew back, alarmed. "*Huh*? What gives? What are you guys…?"

"I am sorry," he interrupted, "but it *must* be done. You might hurt yourself in the ensuing struggle."

Adam stood up stiffly in the center of the dome, sighed, and dropped his arms resignedly to his sides. As if on signal, they surged inward to tie him up with seemingly endless loops of silken cords. After testing the bonds countless times, they stuffed his mummy-wrapped body into a white, quilted sack and laid him on his side.

Nodding in satisfaction, they returned solemnly to their seated positions. A soft, dirgelike chant began. Adam wriggled forlornly, casting a suspicious eye at the circle of bobbing heads. A strange vocalization rose, the beat reverberating with an incessant thrum inside the golden dome. Suddenly, from somewhere deep within their thin bodies, they broke out with loud, quavering wails, their wet tongues sticking out, their domed heads bobbing and dancing in the rhythm. Try as he might, he couldn't block out the awful sound. It worsened by the second, escalating steeply upward to an almost deafening level. His left and right ears were ringing way out of sync and the pain was becoming unbearable. Suddenly, the Elders diverged sharply into a cacophonous clash of upper registers. Overwhelmed, he yelled out at the top of his lungs into the discordant assembly.

"Stop! Stop!! *Stop*!!"

There was an immediate, shocked silence. Hanging suspended in the air, only the fading echoes of his voice remained. Ever so slowly, they closed their gaping slit-mouths and turned toward him. His heart was hammering. He stared back helplessly, suddenly wanting to disappear. With only his head sticking out, he felt like a fat, oval cocoon: he was the prey and they were the predators.

He grimaced awkwardly, his voice squeaking. "I-I feel like … *dinner*!"

They spun toward each other, their thin hands flying up over their mouths. After a fleeting moment of uncertainty, one of the elders let out a muffled snark. Hope glimmered in Adam's eyes. He craned his neck to see who it was. Another one picked up on the snicker, then another. Soon they were all elbowing and whacking each other on their backs, roaring at his one-liner. He breathed a sigh of relief. Yes, they'd finally seen the humor in his predicament.

Reluctantly, Duron raised his hands to call a halt. "Silence, please! I am sorry, Adam, but we must hurry now! The Rasheen lives only a few more minutes!"

Swiftly, he pressed a hidden button on the chalice. The small wedge of fruit started to spin, rapidly becoming a blur. He blinked: apparently, strong magnetic fields were emanating from somewhere within the lid, making the slice of Rasheen disintegrate instantly into a liquid. It roiled upward like a living cloud of contained plasma, shaped itself into a vertical column and then coalesced, dripping into a shallow, fizzing pool.

"Okay, this is *it*!" The old one leaned over urgently and held it under his nose. "When I combine this fragile liquid with the nectar in the chalice, drink the mixture very fast without stopping! Are you ready, Adam?"

Steeling himself, he nodded. The old one mixed feverishly and poured the mysterious potion down his throat.

As he swallowed the fiery liquid in convulsive spasms, his pupils constricted to tiny pinpoints. The world shrank and the crouching, anxious Bandors disappeared into a blank canvas of white.

Suddenly, he felt it deep in his body. Running in molten-hot rivers, the burning invader swiftly commandeered his nervous system and paralyzed his diaphragm. He began to struggle mightily. A terrifying, crippling pressure grabbed his chest, squeezing the last, reluctant breath from his lungs in a great gasp. His mouth gaped open. No air! In total panic, he thrashed around with his head. After several minutes it hit him. How could this be? He was still alive! Although he knew he wasn't breathing, he reasoned that the mysterious elixir must be super oxygenated and supplying his respiratory needs. He blinked hard, trying to see. Fading now, everything was fading. As his heart raced oddly in his chest, he lost consciousness.

His supple young arteries ballooned under a sudden, tremendous pressure, forcing the relentless, seeping invader through every thin capillary wall. As he slept, it penetrated swiftly, deeply into the very nucleus of his cells, unraveling and subtly altering the tightly woven structure of his genetic code. His mind, body, and very fabric of being started to transform. For the first time since the moment of his conception and birth, the sluggish, sleeping stem cells in his brain unfurled and awakened to an unprecedented spurt of new growth. The neurogenesis spread rapidly outward from his hypothalamus. Indeed, like a pupa encapsulated in a chrysalis, he was changing. Time itself seemed to slow to a crawl.

Bright, warm light shone redly through his eyelids. Adam shuddered and tried to move. His hands felt stiff. Forcing his clenched fists open, he stretched out weakly from a cramped fetal position, then with concerted effort opened his heavy lids to thin slits. He was *alive*! Flying animals and insects came into focus, lots of them, flitting about and hovering like great moths charmed to a flame. Beyond the blinding column of light over his head, there was nothing but pitch blackness. The silken bonds and mummy-sack were gone.

He blinked, uncomprehending. The top of his golden dome was gone, too, leaving a circular wall around him six feet high and twenty feet and diameter. As he struggled to sit, a thin blanket slid from his shoulders. He could only watch it fall; his helpless arms were too leaden to move. Well, it was a good thing they'd left the wall around him—he was totally naked now. Evidently, they respected the concept of modesty.

Suddenly, he felt alarming, snuffling movements on his hand. He jerked it away and turned to see. Perched on top of a strange-looking, colorful, yet neatly folded pile of clothing was a spotted ball of fluff. The creature watched his unsteady movements with intent, beady eyes. He whispered hoarsely, tentatively.

"F-Fandango? Is that you?"

Two ears shot up.

"Come over here, boy!" As he clapped his strangely stinging hands, Elena's favorite pet bounced eagerly toward him, wriggling and licking in ecstasy. He reached out and picked him up, astonished at the creature's seemingly complete acceptance. "Wow! You weigh almost *nothing*, don't you, boy?" Intensely curious, he parted the crinkled, wispy fur on the creature's back, turning the docile piece of fluff over and over to look for some kind of body structure. "Hey, what are you made of, *air*?"

"Adam!"

Suddenly, runic letters blazed to life in his mind, clearly outlined. "D-Duron?" He broke into a grin, looking around for his friend.

"Up here, Adam!"

Astonished, he turned his face skyward. His eyes ached as he attempted to squint into the dancing, scintillating brilliance of golden flakes.

"The creature in your hands is a Spotted WindRider! Throw him into the air!"

He beamed a runic reply. *"Duron? Where are you?"* He held Fandango at arm's length, studying him. "Of course," he whispered, "what else could you be, fella?"

The mind-voice came back. *"Adam! Set the creature free, then get into your WingSuit and follow him! We are all waiting up here!"*

He squeezed his eyes shut, yelling at no one in particular. "*Stop*! This is too much! How do you expect me to believe…?"

Duron's mind-message interrupted his tirade, calming him. *"You had better get dressed, Adam. The powerful wind-current lasts only one more hour. If you wish to complete your initiation ceremony, you must join us at once!"*

He groaned, shielding his eyes and squinting through the thick swarm of soaring creatures over his head. The light was way too intense. He gave up quickly and struggled to his feet, muttering to himself.

"C'mon now, this is too much! What did he just say, a-a WingSuit?" He bent over to pick up the strange, folded garment, then shook it out to study it. "Now this is what I call *weird*!"

Making a face, he slipped into the colorful apparel and flexed the elaborately scalloped, stiff-ribbed wings radiating from his armpits. "Wings? Now, really…." Fandango waited patiently at his feet as he snugly cinched the integral antigrav harness. A stiff, hollow tube, something like a channel, was running up his back. He pivoted on his heels to see it, his arms in the air. Like the wings of a bat, a supple elastic web stretched from his ankles to his wrists. Even the gloves on his hands were webbed in a similar fashion. "Rudders," he surmised, shrugging. His legs felt like they were tethered. Sighing, he looked down at his feet in exasperation. Another section fanned out between his legs as he spread them. "And a tail! Of *course*! I need a *tail*!" He shook his head and stooped to pick up Fandango. "What a goofy rig *this* is, right down to these dumb epaulets on my shoulders! What are they for? I feel like-like some kind of superhero cartoon character! Well, time to go, boy! Bon voyage!" With one arm, he tossed Fandango high into the air.

Immediately, the ball of fluff was caught in the powerful upward blast of air, ascending like a feather in a hurricane. Open-mouthed, he watched the creature shoot out of sight. As his hands gripped his wing-struts tensely, his exploring fingers suddenly found two hidden buttons. "Huh?" He pressed them. Something clicked. Twin booms shot out, stretching the rippling fabric to its limit.

Suddenly, the wall around him disintegrated into gold vapor and he was pummeled by a blast of wind. "Hey!" He braced his legs to steady himself. "Well, thanks for leaving the wall up, guys. My birthday suit would've raised a few brows!" As he tensed to jump, the antigrav harness sensed his movement and autoactivated. He spread his arms wide. Immediately, the powerful currents caught him and he shot upward, climbing in a tight, dizzying spiral.

"*Yowwww*! Heyyyy! I-I'm not readyyyy yet! This thing better worrrrrrk!!"

About seventy feet over the tree, he slowly folded his arms to his sides. Just as he thought: his ascent slowed dramatically! Grinning in delight, he hovered and made minute, fine-tuned attitude adjustments with his webbed fingers. Tilting his tail left and right, he practiced changing direction. In a few minutes he was turning, flipping end over end and just having fun. The ergonomically placed control surfaces of the WingSuit were performing brilliantly.

"Excellent, Adam! You fly extremely well! Now look up!"

He craned his neck, squinting. "Wow, what's *that* thing?" He let out gasp. Something resembling a gigantic flower was spinning over his head. As he drew nearer, his eyes widened in shock.

It was them! The elders! Like a formation of skydivers, their bodies all faced inward head to head. The scalloped blue-green fabric of their WingSuits fanned out into the shape of something resembling a giant carnation! In a burst of excitement, he spread his arms and tail wide to close the distance.

Duron was shouting through his translator button as he approached. "Your timing is perfect, Adam! In exactly fifteen Earth-minutes we will finalize your initiation rites! Be careful! Make sure to stay near the center of the column of light!"

They quickly created a wedge-shaped opening for him. He elbowed his way into the circle, squeezing between Duron and one of the elders. "Wow, what a *wind*!" he gasped, his heart pounding.

"Quickly! Link your SwivelGrip pads with us," the old one nodded with his head. "They push together and mechanically lock."

"Oh, *that's* what these things are!" He laughed. "I thought they were epaulets!"

As his shoulders locked tightly into the blue-green circle, they all released a hidden catch under their SwivelGrip pads. With a whir, they ratcheted out about a foot away from each other to make more room for their heads.

"Hey!" Adam glanced around the circle in surprise. "My *color* doesn't match!"

Duron plucked at his sleeve. "Yes, we see. This bright red-yellow WingSuit was the only one we could find in your size. It is on loan from a Bandor youth."

Another windblown, fuzzy head turned toward him. "Yes. Bright red, fading to yellow. Can you *believe* it? The young ones *like* that terrible color combination!"

He grinned. The vibrant wedge of color was indeed jarring.

Duron tapped his arm with a bony finger. "You will find thumb-release bars under the leading edges of your wings, Adam. They uncouple your wrist clamps to leave your forearms and web hands free, like mine. Try it!"

He released his wrists and flexed his arms from the elbows. "Ahhhh!"

"Oh, and perhaps most importantly, there is a sliding counterweight running up and down a hidden channel next to your backbone. It changes your center of gravity. Just tilt your head back to climb, forward to dive."

He nodded his head, rocking back and forth a bit. "Got it! Wow, these controls are almost an extension of myself! Brilliant engineering!"

Slit-smiles broke out all around. "Do not thank *us*," Duron beamed, "thank the *young ones*! They invented it! This new sport they call 'Light-Diving' is only a few hundred years old. Hence, this part of our ritual is but a recent extension."

"That's all? Only two hundred years? A mere fad!" Grinning, Adam pointed down into the jungle. "But haven't your youths been afraid of the, ah, Spyrins?"

Duron shook his head solemnly. "The youths have to cloak themselves to get out here to the

Motherlodes. We think they are very brave. Oddly, the Spyrins do not usually come near these intense beams of light. They seem to get blinded."

Another big head lifted, his downy fuzz rippling in the wind. "Greetings, Adam. I am Movon, Duron's third in command after Fendor."

He turned to gaze into a pair of great, dark eyes. "Well, I have a simple question for you. Why are we *up* here?"

"Duron has delegated me to explain," he offered eagerly.

"Okay, shoot. Why are we here? And why the suits?"

There was a slight, confused pause. "Indeed!" Movon's eyes ran distastefully over Adam's brilliant, fluttering red-orange misstatement of fashion. "I am at a loss to explain *that* terrible color."

Adam chuckled. "Hey! I-I *like* it! It's *radical!*"

Curling his thin lips, Movon continued. His bony hands waved toward the hundreds of floating specks below them. "Our youths took note of the Spotted Wind-rider's soaring techniques and factored in their existing knowledge of antigrav. Hence, the WingSuits. They have become extremely fond of their sport…."

"But if that's so," he interjected, "why don't I see any of their red-orange suits out there right now, diving inside all those other beams in the distance?"

Duron broke in. "They are fascinated but quite shy, Adam. They have never observed the likes of your crew."

"What? They're scared of *us*?"

"Yes, both of you and the great shields! They have only seen them go up once before in their lifetimes, and that was hundreds of years ago when your grandfather arrived." Duron paused, a troubled look shadowing his face. "By the way, he was also curious about telepathy."

Adam grimaced. "He tried it too?" he asked softly.

"Yes, Adam," he sighed. The other elders nodded in silent agreement. "Unfortunately, the effects of the Rasheen were extremely dangerous when initiated on older humans. Your grandfather suffered greatly. At several points we even feared for his life. Just before he disappeared he had become very sick."

"Do you think the Rasheen eventually, ah…?"

"Possibly, Adam," Duron shrugged, almost in a whisper. "We simply do not know. To this moment I refuse to believe that he is gone. To us he was far too young to die." As his voice trailed off, everyone reflected in painful silence, lost in reverie.

Somewhere deep inside, Adam realized that it was obvious that the twelve missed his grandfather tremendously. That same bond was now reaching out to envelop him as well.

After a moment, Duron summarized for the group. "We understand why you always seem to be searching, Adam, just like your grandfather. Yes, he mentioned the tragic loss of his wife, Annie, and then your parents, Ruben and Sophie." As the elders stole nervous glances, the old one stated the obvious conclusion. "We also understand that meant you grew up alone, with no family, no brothers or sisters."

Adam let out a long breath. "Hey," he sighed. 'Always look ahead; never dwell in the past.'

That's my motto! Well, I-I've got my crew now, right? *They're* my family." He turned to the twelve, grinning disarmingly. "And I'm their *role model*? Yikes!" Popping his eyes, he made a hurrying gesture with his webbed hands. "So let's get on with the show! Time's a-wastin'!"

Movon spoke up. "I am afraid to tell you that somehow it is even more dangerous tonight. Spyrin activity has been intense. They seem to be agitated by their loss this morning and therefore have become extremely aggressive."

"What? They're all riled up? I'm sure my men wiped out the whole kit and caboodle this morning! How could they have possibly ratted to the other bugs?"

There was an immediate tilting of bald heads. Hesitantly, Duron answered with a question. "Ah, maybe there were a few survivors? No matter, insect memories are extremely short. The youths are giving them a while to calm down. They are really anxious to get back to their beloved sport. To answer your previous question, perhaps as early as next week you might see them out by the hundreds. It is a beautiful sight...."

"It is time, Duron." One of the other elders interrupted. "Fifteen Earth minutes have nearly passed. We must move quickly with the final step."

The old one spun to Adam, smiling in a fatherly fashion. "So, my young protegé!" His dark eyes glowed mysteriously. "Are you ready?"

He swallowed hard, his heart starting to race. "I-I guess so."

"Good. Now three things, in this order: we all snap our wing struts firmly together at a pivot point near our wrists, turn our tail sections by lifting our right foot slightly behind us and finally, on my cue, we release our SwivelGrip pads."

"Why all that? And-and why only the right foot?"

"To start rotation! The resulting clockwise spin will stabilize our disk in the air like a gyroscope! Once this stabilization has been established, we will let go, spread our wings wide, and climb!"

"Oh," he whispered meekly. His heart was now hammering in his ears.

In an orderly fashion, they snapped their wings together to make a strong, swiveling socket at their wrists. As their leg movements synchronized, the circle started to spin, gathering speed like a giant pinwheel in the sky. Just when Adam thought they couldn't go any faster, Duron gave the signal.

They released their SwivelGrip pads. With the loud pop of suddenly taut fabric ringing in the air, the huge shape abruptly bloomed outward. Their once-folded wings flared, and overlapping at the wrists, they shot upward in a dizzying blur. Looking like a Day-Glo hand spinning maniacally around a flying abstract clock, Adam's wedge of red-orange whizzed around the blue-green circle.

It grew colder with the altitude. As the wind inside the column gradually diminished, their ascent slowed. Soon, they found themselves hovering in a lazy spin about six thousand feet above the tree.

"Owwwwch, my *ears-s-s-s*!" Adam moaned. "And I'm *freezing*, too! What about you guys?" He turned excitedly to Duron, then Movon and then to the rest of the elders. "What a *gas*! I didn't realize you dudes had it *in* you!"

The Bandors were pale as ghosts. Bug-eyed, staring downward, they hung rigidly. Their slit-mouths were working but no sound was coming out.

"Hey!" He nudged Duron. "Are you *sure* you've done this before?" He winced as a runic mind-message suddenly invaded his consciousness.

"We cannot speak, Adam, as we are all in greatest fear! Can you not see our paralyzed condition?"

Oops," he grimaced. "Sorry."

The old Bandor coughed, regaining his speech. "We…," he rasped, "we have not as yet tested our theory to this-this extreme limit. We never dreamed our expanded circle could c-climb so high and so fast," he whispered hoarsely. "However, we *did* want to take you up as high as possible in these first important minutes of teleconsciousness."

"Why?"

"The lessened gravity and barometric pressure helps immensely with your initial cranial and neurological expansion," he explained. "You should feel light-headed. The great centrifugal force has made the blood rush away from your brain to keep your newly increased circulation from overtaxing your fragile neural arteries. Now the Rasheen can simply invade your brain tissue more readily. Also, your white blood cells are fewer in number as they are pooling low in your body. They cannot attack the Rasheen in your brain. There is a combination of many other factors as well, Adam."

"Oh," he shrugged. "I see … I think."

Duron closed his eyes, wheezing laboriously from the lack of oxygen. "There is also one more aspect, a very important one. It-it is also hoped that by wearing these colorful WingSuits, the event will make an indelible impression on your memory. We have tried very hard to give you a visual, ceremonial symbolization of the phenomenon of metamorphosis. Figuratively speaking, you have just thrown off the dark, restraining cocoon of your old mind and have now begun to fully awaken. You can now spread your colorful, fragile neural wings into a bright, limitless future!"

Adam's throat constricted with emotion. These Bandors were incredible! They seemed to have instantly adopted him, opening up both their planet and their hearts. "I-I see," he choked. He bit his lip, trying to hold back the tears. It was no use; they came anyway, the cold night wind chilling them on his face. He turned to the group. "Yes, I *do* see your analogy very clearly, my friends. I must say that you've all been extremely brave and very patient to have taken me up here."

Duron was shivering uncontrollably. "T-this is quite unprecedented, Adam, this extreme altitude," he chattered. "W-we have *never* come this high. P-prepare yourself, b-because in a moment we will execute the final step. Only then will we see the real fruit of our efforts."

"You know, I do feel a bit strange."

Ominously, the elders closed their glazed-looking eyes and started to concentrate. From somewhere far below, a powerful, glowing electronic wave shot upward like a finger of light and started to surge around the spinning circle: as the charge passed through Adam, it cleaved into his gut like a sizzling wire.

"*Yow-w-w!*" His whole body jerked spasmodically. "Hey-y-y, what *gives*?" he wailed in sudden desperation.

"You can take it, Adam!" Duron retorted. "You have a strong body, much stronger than ours! The current you feel is borrowed directly from the Motherlode! It is stimulating the new expanding electrical circuitry of your electrochemical brain. As you may have guessed by now, the Rasheen was the missing chemical. It cannot work entirely on its own; it needs the electricity. Together, they form a synergy! Without our help, your newly found powers would have died within your body in these first important minutes!"

"In other words," he gasped, "you're giving me a jump start?"

Loud and long, they let out a wail of laughter. "Yes, Adam, yes!" they chorused, hooting and poking each other in delight. "A-a jump start!"

He steeled himself. "*Do* it." He hunkered down resolutely. "I can take it."

They fell silent, building up another massive charge.

The spark built slowly, gathering around the circle in a crackling aurora. As they cranked up the power into a spinning dynamo, his head started to vibrate and his ears began to ring. Slowly, red lines formed on the surface of his skin, intricately outlining the hidden, marvelously dovetailed fissures of his skull. Fully nurtured and prepared, his sleeping mind began to tingle and alter radically, as if awakening from a long sleep.

Chapter 22: THE STORM

Elena shivered in the cool night air. Pacing back and forth on the curved platform of the communications tower, she glanced repeatedly at the top of the Motherlode tree. "Where *is* he? The-the column of light's starting to *fade*!" She spun to the others. "What kind of 'meeting' could possibly have taken *this* long?"

Kron glanced away from his NightScope. "Sorry, Elena, I haven't seen anything up there all evening except those puffballs of yours and some weird bluish-green flying creatures," he shrugged. "Big moths, maybe?"

There was a low hum. An antigrav barge rose inside the large central opening, then Tola, Joelle, and Sahir hopped off and sprinted over to them.

"Any news?" The round man looked troubled.

"Not a thing, Tola," Elena answered nervously. "And you?"

"Well, I've been trying to monitor his PIL transmitter, but it seems to have gone whacko," he shrugged. "It keeps reading ten thousand feet, directly over the tree!"

"Technology!" Elena spat. "How could he be *that* high? The cold would be unbearable with his thin clothes! Besides, he was alone the last time Kron caught a glimpse of him with his NightScope, and that was over two *hours* ago! "

"Wait, wait!" Tola's eyes popped. "His signal's coming *down*, real *fast*!!"

Elena grabbed his arm. "What? Let me see!"

They crowded around Tola's tiny screen. The blip was indeed plummeting! Elena spun toward the tree, clutching her chest. "*There he is*!!" she pointed. "He-he's dropping like a *stone*!"

"Hit the lights!!" Kron yelled.

The area quickly became flooded with blinding, searching beams. In a moment, a fiery orange streak appeared in the distance, skittering down the side of the Motherlode and leaving a swirling wake of gold flakes sparkling behind it. Abruptly, the dot leveled out and headed directly toward them, hurtling at a tremendous speed.

Kron leaped to his feet, tipping his chair over. "What in the world? No *way*! That *can't* be him! How could anything move that fast?"

There was a loud whoosh. A strange form streaked over their heads, circled upward in a great arc, and flared to a stall directly over the tower. As it hovered in the brilliant searchlights, they stared in unbelief, their mouths gaping open.

Elena let out a tremulous breath. "You're kidding me. What in the...?"

Adam descended slowly, an incredible bat-winged shape. Gradually dialing down the power on his antigrav harness, he floated to the top of the tower and landed lightly on his toes. With a snap, he retracted the booms and waddled toward his friends.

There was an impossibly long, silent moment.

Tola finally spoke up. "Ah, nice threads," he ventured, lamely.

Elena had been studying his face. "Adam, you okay? And where have you *been*, flying around the *sun*? Your face is all swollen!"

A sharp pain stabbed at the base of Adam's skull, followed by a wave of nausea. He groped for balance, disoriented and confused.

"Yo!" Kron quickly offered him his chair. "Can you, ah, *sit*, sir?"

The wave passed. Grunting and twisting he sat, thought a minute, then released his wrist straps and flexed his webbed hands. "I-I feel like a beached whale."

"Better than you look," Elena quipped. An underlying quaver crept into her tone. "A-Adam, please listen. There's something really wrong with your face. Y-you've got weird red streaks under your hair, your lips are blue, and your eyes are all bloodshot."

"Well," he reasoned, "the Rasheen seems to be working more quickly than they expected! That is, I meant to say a whole lot faster...."

"You *didn't*!!"

"Yup. Nasty stuff. Down the hatch!"

Tola shook his head uncertainly. "We-we all thought you were a goner when you dropped from the sky like a bullet. What happened?"

He lifted his throbbing head. "Well, the column of light was fading quickly so I had to, ah, hurry. Truthfully, I thought I'd be flying back here in the dark and end up ramming into the tower. Thanks for crankin' up your headlights!"

Elena sighed, rolling her eyes. "Adam, please. You had us all scared to death!"

He slipped his icy hands around hers. "Yup. I'm back and I've got a very, *very* tall tale to tell! Come closer all of you. You're my trusted inner circle."

As the small group clustered tightly around him and listened intently, a spark of wonder kindled in their eyes and swiftly grew in intensity. Elena started to tremble. "You actually *did* it? A full dose? And now your *brain* is changing?"

"Yup. Oh, and the elders suggested that you five might make excellent first candidates. You know, to open up your minds and voluntarily share your thoughts?"

They pulled back, suddenly feeling vulnerable.

"Hey, don't worry: you can turn *off* your thoughts, too. Among other things, there's a defense mechanism you can learn called 'mind-shields.'"

They rolled their eyes at each other, thought a minute, and then shrugged.

"Okay. That's settled." He stood up decisively, clipped his forearms back onto the leading edge of his wings, and grabbed the booms. "Enough of this chit-chat," he grinned. "I've got things to do and places to go. We'll flesh all this out in more detail later, when we can talk more privately." With a rustle of fabric, he waddled his way toward the railing. "Hey, Kron, would you pull that chair over here?"

Elena gasped. "Adam! You *can't* be thinking what I think you're thinking!"

"Bingo!" He mounted the rail and teetered on the brink. "What's the diff, hon?" he shrugged, a mischievous gleam in his eye. "Two miles or three hundred feet?"

Tola glanced over his shoulder. "Pay no attention to him," he hissed in a loud stage whisper. "Why'd anyone want to listen to some nut in a Day-Glo jumpsuit, anyway? They're all the same!"

Adam laughed, peering over the edge. Far below, one of the crew had just noticed him. "There he *is*!" The voice wafted upward. "Turn up the spots!"

As the lights hit him full force, his suit blazed to life in a vibrant splash of color. Once more, he was the center of attention and made the most of the occasion. Theatrically snapping out his booms, he raised the broad wings over his head with a flourish. "Here goes," he quipped, tensing to jump, "one small step for man, one giant leap for…."

Elena groaned. "Adam, *please*!"

The simple WingSuit had almost turned into an extension of his body, an expression of pure instinctual joy. He cranked up his antigrav, leaped out into the air, and floated lightly away from the tower.

Two men nervously climbed out on top of the starship's slippery dome. One of them braced his feet unsteadily, dialed up the suction of his footgrippers, and pressed a NightScope to his eyes. An ominous, vertical wall of clouds was approaching in the distance. "Man! It looks like a bad one!" He studied the black clouds a moment, shaking his head in disbelief, then lowered his scope a bit to focus on the top of the tower. "Huh? What in heck's goin' on over there? Hey, man, check *this* out!" He knelt to scoot the instrument down his companion. "Incoming!"

The scope clattered on the polished surface and bumped into Nastix's back.

"Hey, what gives?" the man grumbled.

"Shut up and look!" Trennic hissed. "You're not gonna *believe* it!"

Nastix anchored his footgrippers firmly. As he lifted the beeping lenses to his eyes, two circles of blue light softly clicked on within the rims. Faster than he could blink, laser and sonar beams factored in the optical formula for the curvature of his corneas. With a faint whirring and clicking noise, the unforgettable view autofocused.

"Yike!" A giant foot kicked toward him in shocking clarity, starkly lit up from below. He quickly zoomed out. "*Whaaat*? Orange spandex? Where'd he dig up *that* rig?"

"I'm tellin' ya," Trennic repeated, "he's *lost* it! The geek's showin' off to his airhead friends!"

Suddenly, there was a derisive snort behind them. "Well, looky there!" Dexor clambered out of the open hatch, a NightScope in his hand. "I see a *party* goin' on! Looks like our resident lunatic's come out tonight, modeling her latest designer bat-suit!"

There was a muffled chorus of hoots. "Don' worry boss, the bat-freak's right at home," Nastix sniped, "buzzin' around his belfry!"

"What can I say," Dexor agreed. "They're all freaks! Every last brainwashed one of 'em! Just *look* at 'em!"

There was a long silence as the three watched the colorful spectacle. Suddenly, there was a deafening crash as another hatch slammed open right at their feet.

"*Nuttin' boss*!!" Senn bellowed into the darkness. "Da room's *whistle* clean!"

As the two attempted to recover their balance, Dexor gritted his teeth and bent over stiffly to glare at him, the veins in his neck standing out like ropes. "S-s-s-stifle yourself, you boob!" he hissed. "You'll wake the dead! And whaddaya mean, 'empty'? The keys *have* to be there!"

"Ah-ah, he musta' took 'em, boss!" the man stammered. "R-right? They were in da blue uniform, right? He wuz wearin' it when he disappeared … right?"

Dexor's ill-composed tone began to crack. "*Think*, mono-brow! Use that pea brain and be imaginative for once! Think, like me! The suit's gone, so what would I do?"

The beefy man bit his lip. "Ah, I dunno."

There was a measured pause. "Precisely," Dexor sighed. "Well, let's see. First of all, it's pretty obvious that everyone's quite, ah, *distracted* right now, right?"

Senn looked. They were. His ridged forehead furrowed deeper in concentration. Dexor waited for a sign, a spark, his patience nearly gone. He turned to the three. "Stay with me now, guys: this is critical, *very* critical!"

Nastix glanced at him questioningly. "Why, boss?"

"Tonight's the *night*!" Dexor hissed. "Our stowaway's *out*! His pod is open!"

Stunned, the three drew in their breath sharply. Nastix broke into a fit of coughing. "Ah, what time did he…?"

"This morning." Dexor interjected, putting on a scowl to mask his nervousness. "I was down there checking as usual when his light popped on. It read, 'Three hours to opening.' I grabbed all the notes and recordings we've been collecting and piled them in front of the pod. He'll *read* them of course, lose his temper, and then start looking for *us*!" He bent back to Senn. "So, this is *it*, big guy, the bottom line: we'll have to walk into that warehouse tonight with something tangible to offer, a plan in the works, something to show we been doin' our part! We really, *really* need those keys…."

"I-I know, boss," a nervous Senn cut in, nodding vehemently. "We gotta get da keys! We gotta *show* him sompin'!"

"Hallelujah!! It breathes!" Dexor threw up his hands. "Now watch my lips: go steal a SpeedSled."

"Steal a SpeedSled," he parroted.

"Go up to the top of the Motherlode and check it out. Most likely he left his uniform, and therefore his keys up there?" he prompted. "On top of… the…?"

A light came on, a dim bulb, but a light. "The *tree*! On top'a the *tree*!!"

Dexor's jaw clamped in frustration. "And use your cloaking device!"

Tucking in his chin, Senn stole a nervous glance at his boss and backed down the ladder. "G-g-got it! The cloakin,' ah, ah … cloakin' *what*?"

"Devissss-s-se!!" Dexor struggled to pull his clenched teeth apart, furiously rubbing his jaw muscle out of spasm. "And *no lights*, pinhead," he snarled, "they might *see* you! Remember to use your heat sensor for traces of…."

"*Hey, take a look at that*!!" Nastix shouted.

Dexor spun on his heel, teetering precariously on the edge of his open hatch. It seemed to be a night made for interruptions. Somehow, quite by itself, his jaw locked up. "How many timessss to I have to ssssay it? *Sssstifle yourselvesss*!"

His eyes wide, Nastix mutely nodded into the distance. They looked.

Far away, faintly backlit by the waning column of light, an oddly glowing silhouette was hurtling directly toward Adam. Like a cruise missile, its smooth flying form seemed to offer no resistance to the air.

Totally unaware, Adam turned up his antigrav to the max and shot upward. His timing couldn't have been better. Precisely where he'd been, the odd shape streaked under his feet, a blur of a glowing ultraviolet and indigo hurtling through the night. He felt the turbulence rocking him. "Hey, what was *that*?" Distracted, he glanced down, and then back up over his head. "And where are the stars? They were there a minute ago!"

His answer arrived with a chill slap in the face. Like a bullet through a marshmallow, his body punched through a low-flying rain cloud, drenching his skin. "A *c-cloud*?" he sputtered, shaking away ribbons of streaming moisture. "But-but the sky was *clear* a second ago!" He stopped at the zenith of his climb, floating at three thousand feet, motionless, weightless, breathless and dizzy.

"Aadam!"

He cocked his head to the side. Was that the crew shouting? He shivered and sneezed several times in succession. It was freezing at this altitude in his WingSuit's clinging, soaked fabric.

"Aaaadam!!"

He glanced around, startled. The searchlights found him and homed in; crossing their beams, they lit up his WingSuit like an orange Day Glo beacon.

"Aaaaadammm!!"

Something shot by his face, banking in a steep turn. "Yow!" He tried to follow the movement. "What's *that* thing?" he gasped. "A shuttlecock from hell??"

As a searchlight zeroed in on the new arrival, he could see it clearly. It had an odd, almost comical silhouette, bulbous on one end and tattered on the other. "Creepy," he intoned, his teeth chattering. It was barely fifty yards away and closing fast. Something like lightning was sparking out of the bulbous end and pulses of ultraviolet were flashing down the sides. Fear suddenly coursed through his veins. He plotted desperately, trying to focus, trying to gauge the distance and tensing to dive. "Oh, *no*! Too late! No time! No…."

The missile flared to a stop inches from his nose. Eyeball to eyeball, they stared at each other a long, tenuous moment. With a nervous cough, a young Bandor uncoupled a wrist clamp and raised a single, trembling finger. Adam winced and ducked away, then looked sheepish. The stranger was merely tapping his translator button.

"Adam, I came to *warn* you!"

"Ah, *w-warn* me?" he chattered. "W-what do you…."

His chilling message cut him off. "A great *storm* is on the way!"

"Huh? There's been no storms on Aurona for years!"

The Bandor's eyes grew wide. "Believe me, it is *coming*! This one will arrive in minutes! You must alert your crew *at once*!"

Adam peered into the darkness past the youth's taut, indigo-colored wings. A strange whirring sound was coming from the distance, like a thousand angry bees. The youth heard them too and spun around. If possible, his mushroom-colored face blanched even more pale under his dark helmet.

"There they are! We-we must dive *immediately*! The-the danger comes not from the storm itself, but what it carries in the winds ahead of it!"

Abruptly, a chopping sound beat the air. Adam jerked his head up in time to catch a glimpse of what looked like a whirling, upside-down *cone* thundering by a hundred feet over their heads. "What in God's name is *that*?" he pointed.

The youth quavered, speechless with horror. The distant hum was swelling into a mighty roar as more of the twirling cone shapes rode the wind toward them. The young Bandor had turned rigid with shock, his slit mouth gaping.

"What *are* those things?" Adam shouted. "*Tell me*!"

Silence. The youth's dark eyes were fixed on the gathering hoards with a blank, glazed expression. Adam looked down. The tower was a long way off. In a last-ditched effort, he abruptly changed his tactics. Concentrating hard, his mind translated the most elaborate, intricately shaped runes he could conjure up, and then formed them into a forceful wave.

"Last one down to the tower is a rotten egg!"

The youth's eyes snapped toward him. Adam's totally unexpected, yet more intimate mode of communication jolted him out of his paralyzed state.

"Rotten egg?" he beamed back. *"A spoiling embryo, Adam? Yes, Movon was right; you people use the strangest idioms."*

Adam rolled his eyes, grabbed the youth by his arm, and pointed downward emphatically. "Move it or lose it!" he shouted.

"What?"

"Dive, *dive*!!!"

Reversing their antigrav to a power-assisted pull, they tucked in their chins and somersaulted forward. The dancing spots attempted to follow the two brightly colored meteors as they streaked toward the top of the tower.

"Okay, that's it! There they *go*!!"

Falling over each other in haste, the four mutineers dove into the starship's open hatches and clanged loudly down a set of narrow metal steps. At the base of the holosphere, they burst out

The Storm

into the main hallway in a mad rush, with Senn splitting off toward an airlock to get a SpeedSled while the others piled into an open elevator.

The door slid shut and a bright overhead diffuser snapped on. His fists clenching, Dexor spun toward Trennic. "This had better be worth it, scumbag! How many Spyders did you plant on top of the tower anyway? Two? Three? And the codes, the codes! Did you write 'em all down like I asked?"

A shaking, rumpled list appeared, yanked unceremoniously out of a pocket. "Here ya go, boss," Trennic wheezed, "I parked *twelve* of 'em along the edge of the rail! *Good*, huh?" His eyes had a round, eager-to-please look.

There was no time to answer appropriately. A faint synthe-voice cut in to announce their location. *"Level R,"* it lulled. *"Center Storeroom."*

The elevator door slid open silently. A stooped, hooded figure stood with his back to them, brooding over a jumbled pile of e-helmets, his fingers drumming impatiently on top of an empty crate. Hearing the barely audible pop and squish of their footgrippers on the metal floor, he spun around in a snarling flourish. *"Yaahhhhhhh!"*

They stopped in a collection of squeaks, riveted in their tracks. The Scarred One's bloodshot eyes were wild and dribbles of froth were clinging to the corners of his mouth.

"What *took* you so long to open my pod?" he spit. "Me, down here, alone, a prisoner, while you flit around free as a bird? You forgot me! *Meeeee!*" He stomped his tooled leather boots hollowly in the cavernous hold. "I'm the originator! I'm the mentor! How *dare you* leave me down here?" he thundered.

Dexor croaked out a reply. "Ah, we got here a month ahead of schedule. Your pod wasn't connected to the mainframe because the plug was busted and the, ah, timing was off...." His voice was drowned out by the ventilation system as it came on with a roar. The crumpled paper fluttered in his hand. He made an effort, too late, to slip it behind his back.

The shadowed pig-eyes narrowed. "Give that to me at *once!*"

Quaking, Trennic and Nastix tried to hide behind each other's backs. This mysterious, mutilated being they'd been waiting for was definitely deranged; an unspeakable, pent-up fury was raging inside. The tense mood suddenly worsened. Without warning, a pair of small stilettos silently, mysteriously appeared from somewhere within voluminous folds of the black cloak. The Scarred One brandished them carelessly, seemingly oblivious to the numerous small cuts all over his hands.

"So the plug was busted, huh?" he sniped. "And you couldn't fix it? Nitwits!" He looked around the room. "And where's that *other* nitwit? The fat idiot? He'd better not be spilling the beans about us, had he? Well, *had he?*"

"H-he's, ah, g-gone," Dexor stammered.

"Wha-a-a-t???"

As the hold rang ominously, Dexor's face flushed crimson. "Ah, a-actually, I sent him out on a little reconnaissance mission. Senn's looking for Adam's uniform. You know, his captain's uniform? The blue one? He, Adam that is, he's not wearing it now, mind you. He's, ah, trying on something else with, um, a little different flavor. As soon as Senn finds them, the keys, that is, he'll bring them…."

Flames erupted. "*What* are you *babbling* about?" The darkly stained lips were frothing copiously around their edges. "Just *shoot* them!" he spat. "Didn't I tell you to just kill them? Get all the idiotic trash out of the way, *take* the keys, *grab* the discs, and *leave*! Simple? Well, *simple*? We should have loaded this starship to the hilt with *gold* by now!"

"But Senn might *have* the keys, even as we speak!"

The dark figure twirled around with lightning speed. "Don't mess with me, Dexor," he hissed, juggling the flashing pair of stilettos in a hypnotizing rhythm. "I happen to know the exact location of every major artery under your thin skin."

"But I've *tried*! That list contains…."

"*Enough*!" With an almost audible twang, the Scarred One's diseased nerves snapped. In a swift movement, he launched the two sinister messengers of death. Before Dexor had time to blink, they'd snickered through the air and buried themselves deeply into a crate behind him with soft, hollow thunks. A drop of crimson fell to the floor, then another. Precisely aimed, the two knives had scratched identical lines of blood as they flashed by his ears, one on either side of his head.

Dexor whirled to face his attacker. "Y-you *didn't*!"

A snaggle-toothed gape greeted his shocked gaze. "Oh, but I *did*!"

The three were thunderstruck. Was he a cyborg? No Earthly being could have possibly exercised such incredible control, such hair's-breadth precision and speed! This one had just sent a very pointed warning.

The grimace gaped into a full-blown sneer. "Now, as I said, don't mess with me," he rasped. His pig-eyes focused pointedly on the cowering group. Six knees were knocking, the hold echoing with their rapid breathing. "You see," he gloated, "I deal out death the old-fashioned way…. Behold!" He opened his cloak to reveal countless rows of neat, pocketed stilettos, every hilt exposed for quick deployment. Their eyes widened in astonishment at the incredible array.

"Let's see," he sang tauntingly, "do I have to take out all three of you at once, or one at a time? Will it be slow, or fast and painless? Six knives, or sixty? I've got plenty, you decide." For a long moment, his gaze trailed lovingly over the elaborately carved hilts, then with the swiftness of a cobra, he slid one out with a crooked finger. He held it up to the light, turning it over gingerly. "Yes, you're my favorite, aren't you," he cooed. A lone, beady eye was carefully gauging the cowed group from its slitted corner. "A rare DeathWatch! Poison-tipped, double-edged, and ready for action! There's no known antidote: one scratch and the uncertain vigil begins. A gradual paralysis of the diaphragm steals in on gossamer wings over a period of, say, a few hours, weeks, or maybe months. One never knows exactly when, but death is a certainty."

Suddenly, his rasp of a voice grated and whined into a higher pitch. "Oh, dear me," he teased, fumbling through the pockets. "Did just I throw one of my favorites? I see an empty slot here; maybe I mixed them up." The pig-eyes turned slowly toward the group. "Sorry, Dex." He shrugged. "Hard to keep track." Oh-so-carefully, he slid the DeathWatch back into its rightful place, then affecting the disdain of a true connoisseur, he waved off a few of the lesser brands in the bottom rows. "Of course I have the usual fillers. You know, the regulation VitaVetoes,

BloodBaths, VeinDrains, and AssassinAces. But they're so, shall we say, boring. Yes, that's it. So … uninteresting."

Twin rivulets of blood were running down Dexor's neck, blotting his collar with dark crimson stains. He was cornered and knew it. Time to switch tactics. He took a quick breath. "Hey, you're *right*," he shrugged, chuckling. "They're boring!" As the questioning pig-eyes met his own, he bared his teeth in a forced, uneasy grin. "You've been down here *way* too long! And flying? No contest! You're a *far* better StarPilot than Adam! Senn has the keys to the ship by now I'm *sure*!"

As the steely glint softened a bit under the overshadowing cowl, they dared to breathe a little easier. The Scarred One had almost gone over the edge.

"Does the fat nitwit have a Spyder? I want to keep tabs on him," he rasped. "I've read your notes about those odd surveillance tools. They're, ah, very interesting."

"Yes sir, Senn's all rigged out with one and Nastix planted a dozen more of the, ah, bugs around the top of the observation tower. So, waddaya say, let's put on these e-helmets and check out their plans, okay?"

The Scarred One crumpled the list of Spyder codes, dropped it to the floor, and shoved it toward Dexor with the toe of his boot. "Read me the numbers," he snapped, grabbing an e-helmet off the top of the pile.

As they madly tapped out the codes with their chins, the audio's surround-sound blasted on with a mighty roar and the top of the tower swam into view on their face shields. A glimpse of vibrant color streaked down the central shaft in a power dive, then closely on their heels, a floating utility barge immediately plugged the hole. Not a moment too soon. In the next breath, a massive, spinning object slammed into the railing and glanced off, tumbling end over end into the darkness.

A horrendous thud shook the tower as Adam and the stranger flared their wings and floated to a landing on the rubbery floor. The mighty, twisting cone had been hot on their heels. It was totally dark with the barge blocking the hole at the top, making the stranger's WingSuit glow spectacularly in the center of the room. Bouncing in staccato rhythms and bursts, its ultraviolet and indigo light bars bounced hypnotically off the curved walls.

Wide-eyed, the crew was sprinting in from the numerous side entrances, converging on the odd-looking duo. The bright neon reflected in Eric's dark eyes. "Wow! W-what's *happening* out there, sir? It's a nightmare! We all thought you were a goner!!"

Elke stumbled into the loose circle, looking especially pale. "And what're those huge chopper things? They're dive-bombing us!"

The tower vibrated with another earth-shaking thud, followed by a loud scream. Sahir ran in. "Help! Something just ricocheted off the tower and nearly *got* me, then screwed itself into the ground!" She spun around, pointing. "Look! There it *is*! It's right outside the door!!"

They squinted into the darkness through the sea of running people. The cone's menacing silhouette was still quivering from the force of impact, with clods of dirt raining down. As Adam spun toward the Bandor youth, his eyes questioning, Elena ducked under his wing and slipped her trembling arms around him.

The stranger turned to the crowd and raised the volume on his translator button. "I am *so* sorry for these unfortunate circumstances, people!" he began. "Speaking for all the youth of Aurona, I bring my sincerest apologies! I-I am Tavan... actually, Tavan 55477, to be historically accurate. Movon is my grandfather. As you can see, I have come entirely on my own to warn you and offer an explanation of these strange objects and unusual events."

Adam gestured mutely toward the cone. "Ah, that shouldn't be too difficult, Tavan," he prompted. "We have Exhibit A right outside the door!"

As the crowd glanced uneasily over their shoulders, the youth slit-smiled. "This may be odd, Adam, but in a way I feel I *know* you already? The elders have been speaking of you with utmost admiration. I-I must say, though, I had a difficult time getting to you and your crew tonight. Static charges are extremely painful because of all the gold in my system. You cannot imagine how much damage the lightning from this storm did to me. Thank you for providing this refuge." He turned back to the crowd. "Those cones are called AugerBlade seeds. When I saw them, I became rigid with shock! It was only by your Adam's untimely placing of an odd-sounding idiom that prodded me into action."

Elena glanced at Adam. "Ah, what'd you say?"

He shrugged. "What else *could* I say? I-I just told him, 'Last one down is....'"

The crew chorused the rest of the familiar phrase, "*A rotten egg*!!"

Tavan spun toward Adam, tilting his helmeted head. "What? Your crew heard us, too? I do not understand. Do they already have telepathy?"

Momentarily forgetting his or her panic, everyone was now straining to see this colorful new character. Inching closer, Joelle elbowed her way to the front, intently eyeing Tavan's glowing apparel. The phosphorescent fabric was almost alive in the dim light, pulsing with incredible indigoes and impossible ultraviolets. Finally, she couldn't hold back any longer. "Way *cool*, sky guy!" she bubbled. "Got any more of these rad suits down your hobbit hole?"

There was a stunned, dead silence.

She looked up, startled. "What?" Her eyes were round. "What'd I say?"

That did it. Any remaining ice floes were shattered. Even Tavan joined in the chorus of hoots. Encouraged, Joelle pointed at the remarkable helmet on his large head. It was seamless and glasslike, yet had a crackling aura about it. "And that bubble? Where's the opening? I mean, h-how do you breathe?"

The youth shrugged. "Oh, sorry," he apologized. "I will turn it off and explain." Slit-smiling mischievously, he reached for a narrow band around his smooth, pencil-thin neck. "Ready?" As he touched an inconspicuous button, the helmet dematerialized in a flash of light. "See? Gone!" He had the crew's rapt attention. "This collar around my neck generates a dome-shaped, aerodynamic windscreen."

Joelle squinted. "You're kidding. That little ringy-thingy?"

"Yes, it is a shield, employing the same technology as your SpeedSleds and starship, but on a much, much smaller scale. The shape is infinitely more refined and quite comfortable, actually."

His slit-smile widened. "*Nobody* flies without one! After all, you would not want to become windburned like Adam when you get your *own* WingSuits, would you?"

Joelle punched the air with her fist. "*Yess-s-s! Now* you're talkin'!"

The Storm

With sudden eager smiles, the crew packed tightly around Adam and Tavan. The stranger was now totally accepted, one of them.

It had been a long way to the top of the Motherlode. Senn floated uneasily through the darkness, jumping at every dark, scuttling shape and fluttering night creature. There was an odd chopping sound overhead and everything seemed to be in a panic, as if they were running for cover. Even the Aeronautas had expelled the last of their gas and were hanging tightly by their trunks under the shelter of the big leaves rolling their big eyes at each other in shriveled, nervous groups. Well, no matter. He shrugged and bent to his task, mimicking Dexor's gruff voice.

"'Use the heat sensor! No lights!' What does he think I am, an owl?"

Suddenly, his color-saturated monitor revealed an unmistakable circle of heat imprints where the elders had been sitting. In the center, fading fast in the cool night wind, was the glowing outline of a human form. Senn read the screen like a journal, piecing together the sequence of action: a few good-sized specimens had been by recently. Too recently. He glanced over his shoulder nervously, shuddered, and turned up his collar. The wind was getting stronger, too, causing the sled to drift.

As he activated the side thrusters, a deep buzzing sound startled him. His hand groped for the shield button. Abruptly, a brilliant searchlight hit him full in the face.

"A *Spyrin*?" he gasped. "Wha-what's that bug doin' way up...?"

There was no time to react. The heavy insect slammed into his sled full force, its jaws missing him by inches. Intent on its prey, the Spyrin scrambled on the slippery metal suface and reached out with a single hooked claw. It connected immediately, and became hopelessly tangled in the uniform's tough material. Screaming at the top of his lungs, Senn jumped off the sled, his sleeve stretched to the limit.

An odd shadow crossed the moon. Like a dancer in a sudden frenzied pirouette, an AugerBlade seed folded its great paddle-wings out of the way, dropped like a spinning missile, and hit its target with pinpoint accuracy. The Spyrin's head flopped as the colossal needlepoint pierced its body and skewered cleanly through its thorax. The spiral ridges continued to twist downward, and then with a rending squeal of sheet metal, reamed out through the bottom of the sled. With a shower of sparks, the small, lightweight vehicle began to spin.

Howling, the leading edge of the storm swept over the top of the Motherlode. Its mission complete, the half-plant's great wings folded downward and gale force winds quickly lofted the mighty cone and its cargo. In a roar, they were gone.

"*Nothingggggg*!!!!"

A long, hideous wail rang inside the cavernous hold of the starship, followed by a loud crash. An e-helmet ricocheted off the metal floor into a stack of crates. "*Yahhhhh*! Twits! You're all *twits*! We've been looking everywhere! Everyone's inside the tower, it's dark outside, and not a single Spyder can see a thing! You-you gave me *nothing*!"

Cowering, the three ducked out the way to watch him careen around the room, pushing over row upon row of boxes. "I've *had it*!" he screamed over the avalanche. "I can't wait any *longer*!"

He pointed at the trio, his bony finger shaking. "For your puny information, I have allies on this planet, awaiting my command!"

Their jaws dropped. What did he just say? They stared at each other in shock.

He stalked thunderously toward a dark corner of the room, waving a small electronic device over his head. "This little stealth transmitter worked just just fine after 700 years: I punched the button and they signaled their response! They know I'm here!" He spun around. "Now get *out*, the three of you! Remove this worthless pod tomorrow morning, and put it back in the pod room where it belongs! There's to be *no evidence*!"

They made a half-step toward the exit.

"Wait!"

They turned back to him, their frayed nerves on edge.

The gimlet eye narrowed, focusing razor-sharp on Dexor. "When you discovered that my pod wasn't plugged into the mainframe, why didn't you at least try rolling it back up to the pod room and reconnecting it? It might have recalibrated!"

Dexor drew in a sharp breath. "Ah, I don't know anything about electronics…."

"You *fool*!" he roared. "I was right! The blasted thing might have reset itself! You've all wasted nearly a month of my time! Now, get out! Get out!"

They beat a hasty retreat, relieved to just get away. The screeching voice echoed behing them out into the hallway. "They're he-e-e-r-r-re, waiting to move on my signal, the ones you knew nothing about! They'll all be arriving in less than a week, and then *nobody* will be able to hold us back!" As the warehouse door slid shut, the screams faded away. "Adam first, and then *everyone* dies…."

They ducked around a corner, leaning against a wall and shaking. Silence returned. Dexor sucked in a long tremulous breath, pondered a moment, and then feigned indignation to save face. "So he's bought his own ticket, huh? Why, that ungrateful bastard!"

Trennic was finally able to speak. "A week?" he gasped. "Less than a week?"

After all we've *done* for him!" Nastix fumed. "We've been duped!"

Dexor threw up his hands. "Ahh, don't listen to that creep! Good thing we didn't give him that last number, the one for Senn's *Spyder*! If our fat boy found bat-boy's keys, we should be able to pull this whole thing off ourselves!"

"W-what's the number?" Trennic quaked.

Dexor straightened out his crumpled paper. "M22-6492. Got it, pinhead?"

"Got it," the man sulked.

As they all tapped the last sequence, a puzzling view flashed onto their screens. It took a long, indecisive moment before they realized that Senn was actually in trouble. His Spyder transmission was weak and seemed to be rapidly approaching the limits of its range.

Tola gestured at the huge cone outside the wide cargo door. "C'mon, that monster is a *seed*? It-it was aiming for us! Does it have a brain?"

"Yes," Tavan grimaced, "it is a single seed on a mission. AugerBlades are a highly successful species and are taking over select areas of the planet." He turned back to the crowd. "And yes, they *do* have a brain, of sorts. Being immune to the Motherlode's enzymes and therefore the resulting root linking, they are stealing large chunks of surface area once productive in photosynthetic electricity. The elders are aware of this, but our group who flies regularly have seen large colonies of AugerBlade trees congregating by the hundreds, mostly near water. We call them Storm Makers because there seems to be a direct link: As more Motherlodes get crowded out, more storms appear; as more storms appear, more AugerBlade seeds can take to the air and germinate! They are very agile fliers. Some of my companions have seen how their wings work, right up close." His slender, demonstrative hands planed the air in stiff, angled, thrusting movements. "The three big, woody paddles can fold back or turn at will."

Tola ducked as an arm went by. "You mean they can *steer*?"

"Yes, very well." He pointed out the door. "But that one is not going anywhere now. In fact, it is going to die within a few days. Look, already the paddles are sagging."

"Die? Why?"

He turned back to the round man. "It simply failed in its mission. It needed blood. It happens to be a semi-intelligent creature, half plant and half animal. When it senses the strong updrafts and increased ozone levels from an approaching storm, it breaks free from the parent tree and falls, spinning away for hundreds of miles and following waterways and lakes, like this one."

The group edged away from the open archway, looking over their shoulders.

Tavan turned to Adam. "Oh, I almost forgot *this*," he apologized. He reached into his utility belt and handed him a small bundle. "Go ahead, open it!"

"What is it?" Adam mumbled, ripping at the thin paper. It was definitely fabric. He shook it out. "My uniform! Where'd you...?"

"Movon."

Adam immediately beamed out a mind-message. *"Did he find my...?"*

Tavan had anticipated his question and cut him off mid-sentence. *"Do not worry, Adam, the keys to your starship are still in the pocket."*

Adam smoothly switched back to audible speech. "Movon, huh? Well, thank him for me! Now, if you don't mind I'd like to ask you what happens *after* the storm tomorrow? You mentioned something else took place after the storm passed by."

"Oh, that!" He shrugged. "The DynaPods are ripening. I am talking about seeds again, but on a completely different scale. DynaPods may be small, but they're dangerous. When the sun comes out, the pods explode violently! The seeds can rip holes through WingSuits and sometimes even put out an eye."

Elena grimaced. "Please. I don't want to know any more. It's too much."

Miles away, Senn's Spyder video was playing out its last scenes: lit up by a continuous show of lightning, the turbulent sky whizzed by in streaks of pure madness. Here and there, stop-action glimpses of colossal, upside-down cones could be seen in the distance. A spatter, then a creeping smear of red began to obliterate the view.

Alarmed, Dexor commandeered Senn's Spyder to crawl out to the end of the sled for a better perspective. As he turned it around, its flat suction pads gripping firmly to the slippery metal, he heard a loud gasp beside him.

Nastix screeched into the audiodome of his helmet. "*Look boss, he's dead*!!"

For the third time that night Dexor's teeth clamped together entirely on their own, this time grinding off a bit of enamel. He whipped off his helmet, his bloodied ears ringing. "Are you *nuts*?" he bellowed. "Never, I repeat, *never* yell into this little round bump, understand?" His finger jabbed emphatically on the spot.

"Sorry, boss," he muttered.

"I can *see* him, you jerk, and he's *not* dead! His feet are still kicking! Nothing can be done about that fat fool right now, so shut your yaps and keep watching!"

They yanked down their helmets in hateful silence.

"Idiots!" he sputtered. "I get a crazed egomaniac, a fat fool, and two idiots. To top it off, I have to deal with a manic schizoid in a bat-butt suit having secret meetings on top of a *tree* with an army of hydrocephalic mushrooms!!"

Gingerly, he slipped his helmet over his sore ears. "And *now*? Killer Kones?"

Obviously being buffeted by the strong winds, the Spyder was gripping the slippery metal a few feet away from Senn. Yes, the man was alive, no question about it. His stubby legs were kicking and his head was thrown back by the tremendous centrifugal force. Although he appeared to be screaming at the top of his lungs, they couldn't hear him over the roar of the wind and chop of the great wooden paddles.

The Spyrin's body was nearly split in two by the colossal wedge shape, with dried, mahogany-colored blood liberally spattering everything. Tendrils—no, roots—seemed to be erupting from the cone's rough surface and entwining the insect's bloated body. They tunneled deeply to feed, distorting the insect's features and transforming the wasplike body into an unrecognizable, cracked lump.

Dexor's gut started to heave and it took a few breaths to come out of it. A movement caught his eye and he looked over his head. What was that? The trio of broad, woody paddles were angling around to catch the wind to a better advantage!

Dexor commandeered the Spyder to crawl back up the tough sleeve of Senn's uniform. As it reached his shoulder, the beefy man finally fainted from exertion and terror. His body flopping loosely he hung there, spinning.

Suddenly yellow light blazed to life in their e-helmets, followed by a prolonged, electronic buzz. Dexor quickly finished guiding the robotoid up to Senn's collar. As it latched on and hunkered down, their face shields went blank. The Spyder had just spun out of transmitting range.

"Show's over," Dexor muttered. His eyes glinted like steel as he nodded toward the exit. "Time to mingle, mutton-heads." He fingered his bloodied collar. "After I change into, ah, something more appropriate, we'll go crash the bat-party."

Shortly, they dashed through the rainy night and rendezvoused under one of the flaring overhangs outside the tower. Waiting for just the right moment, they slipped inconspicuously into the wet, noisy crowd one at a time. No one could possibly suspect a thing now; the trio had ironclad alibis.

Chapter 23: PRIMA

Everyone slept late the next morning, too exhausted to even think about exploding DynaPods. They'd been up until three in the morning waiting for the storm to abate and then, under very watchful eyes, had dashed through the lingering rain to the shelter and security of the starship. The AugerBlades' whirling cone shapes had filled the sky from horizon to horizon and lingered around the top of the tower in deafening hoards, almost as if they were waiting to catch someone out in the open. Maybe they had primitive pheromone sensors, perhaps it was the level of carbon dioxide seeping out of the hole on top, but everyone knew that they'd definitely sensed life inside.

By mid-afternoon, they'd taken a roll call and found that Senn was missing. The crew gathered for a full-fledged search party, and shortly, someone found an empty slot inside Cargo Bay F: he'd obviously gone somewhere on a small, one-man SpeedSled. The search immediately broadened to the nearby jungle and eventually to the top of the Motherlode tree, where metal sled fragments, woody shavings from an AugerBlade seed, a Spyrin's leg, and huge gashes in the leaves told it all. Only by a miracle could the man be alive, but they were helpless to trace him any further. His PIL was found in his room.

Adam wasted no time and called Dexor, Nastix, and Trennic up to his office, plying them with carefully phrased questions. As expected, he got nowhere and dismissed them. Totally frustrated, he summoned Tola.

The round man entered hesitantly. "Sir?"

Adam spun around, his hand on his chin, deep in thought. "You know, I-I was never one for funerals...." He studied Tola's face, taking a reading.

"Oh," he nodded, "I get it: bad experience, huh?"

Adam scowled. "Yup. One is enough. Ah, what's your take on all *this* mess?"

Tola threw up his hands. "It's obvious: Satan's lost one of his disciples! That Dexor could care less; the husky one was nothin' but roadkill. Hey, one down, two to go."

Adam groaned. "How'd I *ever* pick those creeps for my crew?"

Tola pondered a moment. "So their alibis were like a brick wall, huh?"

"You got it. I just wasted over an hour tail-chasing. I'm sure they rehearsed the whole thing," he scowled. "Anyway, let's get back to business: Senn's, ah, funeral?"

"Well," Tola murmured, "I say a man's a man, no matter who he follows or what he believes. I just wish I'd gotten through to at least *one* of those boneheads with the Truth. But for now, we'll just have to do the right thing. You know, for the sake of the crew? A memorial service isn't entirely out of the question...."

"That means you'll *do* it?" Adam prodded.

"Yeah, yeah, I'll do it," he conceded. "A simple ceremony in the Observatory Room is only right and fitting. It'll be short and to the point, pull the crew back together and give them closure. Hey, among other things, I'll have a great chance to blast those three knuckleheads with Proverbs. Catch my meaning? Spoon feed 'em?"

Adam brightened. "You'll have a captive audience! They'll *hate* you!"

"Oh, joy! I just love to be hated! Hey, it's my job, right?"

"No, *no*! It's *my* job!"

"No, It's *mine*!!"

"Fight you for it!"

They sparred, scuffling around the room.

Tola held up a chubby hand, puffing. "Wait, wait! I got way more ammo than you. I've memorized tons of Proverbs that fit the occasion. Here's an example: 'There is a way that seems right to a man, but in the end it leads to death.'"

"Perfect," Adam said, grinning. "Got more?"

"Yep! A zinger, custom-made for Dexor!"

"What is it? C'mon, hit me, oh mighty round one!"

Narrowing his eyes, Tola nodded sagely. "'Cast but a glance at riches and they are gone, for surely they will sprout wings and fly off into the skies like an eagle.'"

"Wow. Incredible. Say no more. Let's *do* this thing."

As the crew filed quietly into the Observatory Room for the evening's service, Adam whispered into Tola's ear. "Don't look now, but have you checked out Dexor and his clone-unit?"

"Yeah," he muttered. "They're stuck tighter'n a tattoo on each other's butt."

Kron spun toward them. "I *heard* that, preacher man! Hey, a guy never forgets his native language, right?" Chortling, he glanced at Adam. "I hate to ask, sir, but how'd it go this afternoon? The lies? The crocodile tears?"

Adam rolled his eyes and glanced at Tola. The round man rolled his eyes in the opposite direction.

"Okayyy-y-y, I see. *That* bad, huh?"

"Yep." Tola nodded. "Oh, don't look now, but when you get a chance, take a gander at those goons. They're pros! They should take their show on the road!"

Kron stole a look. Leaning stiffly against the back wall in their usual places near the exit, Dexor, Nastix, and Trennic were putting on a superb performance. As the crew passed by offering condolences, they put on long faces, thanking them profusely and somehow cranking out believable versions of 'empathetic' and 'gracious.'

Elena and Joelle joined Adam's group, watching the grief-show unfold, snatching bits and pieces of conversation wafting toward them. It seemed that Dexor and his men had been worried sick about their best buddy and had searched the rainforest all afternoon along with the rest of the crew. Why, Senn shouldn't have *dreamed* about going out there alone, especially on such an awful night. To them, the whole thing was way beyond comprehension.

Tola expelled a long breath and glanced at his watch. "Ready?"

Adam adjusted the round man's throat mike. "Sic 'em."

Tola's subject matter was dead on target. The crew sat delighted and open-mouthed as he fired off salvo after salvo of loaded, ticking time bombs into their laps, enraptured with this sudden, unexpected exercise in many-layered comprehension.

On the other extreme, Dexor and his men were turning green. Watching them from the corner of his eye, Tola monitored the wall-huggers for noticeable stages of 'sag' and 'droop.' Ah, there it was, his first sign: they were glancing at their watches and the door. Encouraged, he pulled out his Aces.

Dexor couldn't handle the onslaught. His cockiness flagged, his lips curled in revulsion, and he elbowed his men, rolling his eyes. The three fidgeted and squirmed along the wall toward the exit.

Tola kept up his barrage. Preaching boldly, masterfully, he timed his memorial to a close, waiting for the exact moment when Dexor's shaking hand was actually… on the door's… handle….

"Amen," he breathed.

Dexor let out a shallow gasp, dropping his hand.

With a monumental effort to stifle his laughter, Adam slowly stood and signaled for attention. "Well," he began, "it's time to get down to brass tacks." There was an almost audible vibe hanging thickly in the air. "We've just lost the first one of our crew and I know we've all been through a lot of other 'stuff' these past few days."

As the crew nodded in agreement, Dexor's lip returned to its curl.

"The danger out there is real. Razahs are real. Spyrins are real. And now, AugerBlades are real. Every day we're running into another piece of this big Aurona puzzle."

In the front row, Sahir had been doing her best to get more comfortable, squirming on a pile of pillows, her legs heavily bandaged. Elena slid another cushion toward her, propping it under her legs.

Adam watched the exchange. "You okay, girl?" he offered.

She glanced up, nodding. "Yes, thank you, sir. I'm healing fine, but…."

"Yes?"

"I had a question. My friends and I have been talking about this new guy, Tavan. We're all super, super thankful that he came to warn us about the storm and then explain what was going on. Could you tell us a bit more about him? You've been, ah, flitting around with him quite a lot lately."

There was a snicker, and then a few hesitant smiles. The mood escalated upward a few degrees, like a long-awaited spring after a harsh winter.

"Excellent question, Sahir. Well, first of all, Tavan's a whole new breed of Bandors. The older ones seem to be reaching out a bit, but otherwise they're bound by their traditions. Don't get me wrong: traditions are good, but they can become like a cork in a bottle. Sometimes you've got to let go of learned routines, do some reverse engineering, and figure out what's the *right* thing to do! Again, thanks. You've made it easier for me to segue into what I really wanted to talk about tonight…."

"Oh?" Sahir brightened. "What's that, sir?"

He shrugged. "Values." Monitoring Dexor's group out of the corner of his eye, he paraphrased a short snippet of the same pep talk he'd given to the men at the mouth of the Spyrin's nest. Stifling their groans, the three glanced at their watches again.

Ah, his litmus test worked. Brightening, Adam opened up, embellishing with extensive views on motives, attitudes and heart, then the intrinsic value of gold as opposed to greed and selfish ambition. Thirty minutes later, he extolled at length on the wonders of Bandor telepathy and bartering for the common good, then warned about the sometimes hidden and unintended side effects of technology.

The crew lapped it up: Adam was laying everything out into the open, uncovering their own hopes, fears and frustrations, and yanking their corks out of tradition-bound bottles! As he concluded, urging them to always look forward, broad smiles lit up the room.

His speech galvanized them into action. They gathered to talk in noisy groups about their future plans for Aurona, with his new Spyrin extermination project seeming to head their list. Adam's enthusiastic team of twenty jumped in, took the reins, and filled in a few gory details of their mission. As they finished and called out for more help, a sea of hands waved in the air. Kron appointed several groups to work in rotating shifts, each with leaders from the original fired-up crew. Their Spyrin plans now had teeth.

Sahir rose to her feet. "Guys, listen. What about the Augerblade trees? I think it's obvious that they should be exterminated too, right?"

As they looked at her injuries, they got the connection immediately. She was right: besides the obvious danger from their enormous seeds, the AugerBlade trees were putting the Motherlodes in danger. The entire planet's carefully balanced ecosystem was at risk.

Suddenly, Kron looked up with a start. "Hey! I just remembered something real important, guys! We have another Bitron invention aboard that'll be a perfect fit for this AugerBlade project … a large-scale LaserCutter! It's powerful enough to slice down AugerBlade trees like butter from the deck of our hovering starship!"

Dexor's ears tingled. He spun to his companions, raising his brows and making slicing motions with his hands. They threw him knowing looks, nodding vehemently. Quickly lifting his collar, he muttered a few words into his remote recorder.

"Wow, thanks Kron!" Adam smiled. "Honestly, I don't know about most of that Bitron stuff; they must have thrown it aboard our starship as a goodby present! So we got a large-scale Laser Cutter, huh? That's a real breakthrough!" He checked his wrist programmer. "Okay, one last question before you're dismissed … anyone?"

Joelle jumped to her feet. "Ah, this doesn't have anything to do with humongous flying seeds or laser cutters or giant bugs…."

"That's fine," Adam chuckled. "Go ahead, Joelle, we all need some diversion."

As the crew hooted, she pressed on, encouraged. "Speaking of bugs, this has been bugging me since we got here a month ago: why doesn't anyone have jet lag? We've all been feeling just fine from the minute we arrived, but we know there's a *huge* difference in the length of Earth's and Aurona's days."

Kron turned to her, grinning mischievously. "Yes, Joelle, there's yet *another* Bitron invention involved in…."

"I should'a guessed," she interjected, throwing up her hands. "Tell us, Kron."

"Our sleep pod's exercise tables were there, working behind the scenes! They took the entire length of our seven-year sleep to add four hours to our diurnal rhythm by warming our bodies and giving them exercise routines at regular intervals."

Joelle tilted her head. "Oh, so *that's* it! We've been reprogrammed! Along with a new planet and new chronometers, we've got a whole new life cycle!"

A new city, too. Early next morning, construction began in earnest on Adam's great, sprawling fifty-acre complex. The communications tower project had given the crew a bit of practice, but it had been built on a level, grassy plain. This time around they took a lot more time and thought it out, stacking and staging the equipment for the onslaught. Following Adam's plan, an army of Robodiggers carefully excavated and leveled the site, then poured out a solid slab foundation of epoxy polymer.

On signal, they went at it with gusto. It didn't take long to discover that they were actually having fun: his grandfather's AnchorPlank System slid and snapped together like a full-scale Lego toy. Working side by side, the Bandors and humans realized that far more than a city was being built: the joint venture was blossoming into a mutual admiration of cultures, a true meeting and melding of the powers of mind and body. While the tall, light-framed intellectual Bandors marveled at the human's brute strength, the rugged, impulsive Earthlings stood in awe of the Bandors' unsurpassed logic, attention to detail, and intuitive knowledge of construction technique. Hundreds of Bandors, old and young, were enthusiastically joining the effort. This city was to be a test for them, too. As the Bandors took over to finish the most technical details with nimble, flying fingers, the crew could only step back and watch in amazement.

Five days later, as it began to resemble some kind of final form, Adam suddenly, unexpectedly called a halt. They stopped dead in their tracks, shocked and puzzled.

Winking mysteriously, he informed them that the waterfront city was complete, and then scurried away with a mischievous glint in his eye.

Complete? It looked weird, unfinished! Was this some kind of a master plan? They stepped away, studying the vast, ring-shaped central form with its beautiful, yet seemingly haphazard shapes. *Complete*? Set at precise points along X, Y, and Z-axes, the intriguing, slant-fronted openings-to-nowhere jutted awkwardly toward an empty, windswept, central plaza. As they gathered in small groups, questions began to fly thickly. Was this his idea of a joke? Sure, it had been enjoyable work, but the results looked deranged. Was there more to it?

Suddenly, a loud beep sounded on everyone's wrist communicators. It was Adam! As they listened in surprise, he informed them it would be only a matter of minutes before the 'final union' took place. Union? What union? And where *was* he, anyhow?

A movement caught Joelle's eye. "Look, everyone!" She was pointing upward, her voice tinged with panic. "Our starship's *rising*!"

As the starship's great shadow dimmed the afternoon sun, they drew in a collective breath: Adam was hovering directly over the city! Why? With a distant whirr, the gel-pads began to angle around on the ends of their long booms and the craft slowly descended.

"What in the world?" Kron whispered to Tola. "He-he *can't* be thinking...."

The round man interrupted excitedly. "He *is*! He's gonna *do* it!"

Like a great eagle settling gently into her nest, the saucer hovered over the ring, rotated a few degrees, and then touched down. The rubbery ring of walls gave with a collection of squeaks as the ship squeezed tightly into place. Immediately, the circular, bowl-shaped form made sense: the 'final union' had taken place!

They all stood amazed at Adam's ingenuity: using a schematic of the starship and a HyperCAD program, he'd plotted out the whole thing to the fraction of an inch. The once-random, slanted openings now lined up precisely with every airlock and cargo bay under the hull. With sleeping quarters, dining hall, assembly rooms and holo-theater inside, the starship now served as both a focal point and nerve center.

Yes, the domed city was complete. The light-beige color of the saucer's hull even matched the surrounding ring of buildings; from afar, the seamless, curving roof melded gracefully with the continuous four-story ring around its perimeter. The avant-garde shapes of curving, covered walkways, soaring glass atriums, artfully sculpted commander's quarters, and even the looming Communications Tower near the rainforest formed a cleverly realized, eye-pleasing and functional unit.

Adam disembarked and stepped out into the brilliant, late afternoon sunshine. Officiating over a short, impromptu ceremony, he and Elena cracked a bottle of the lake's clear water on a floating, fan-shaped AnchorPlank pier. They christened the new city Prima. Number one. A new beginning.

Prima. The five-letter word pleased the Bandors greatly. The name hadn't been chosen by chance; Adam had put a lot of thought into its selection. As he'd toiled side by side with the Bandor workers, he'd listened attentively to all the great Auronian cities and powerful leaders they'd mentioned, faithfully recording the odd-sounding names into his wrist programmer's electronic notebook. It didn't take long to see phonetic patterns emerging: with very few exceptions both people and cities were strictly confined to five letters, things had six, and all rolled off the tongue nicely in two syllables. For eons, this clever letter-play, this inflaming name-game had been their custom, their tradition.

Glancing repeatedly at the sky and jungle, Dexor and his men watched the ceremony from an atrium's large, soaring window. They'd grown more and more apprehensive as the long, exhausting days of building had passed, expecting the Scarred One and his hordes of aliens to show up at any minute. Wordlessly they shrugged, rolled their eyes and left the bright, empty room to join the throngs below. The fateful time was nearly upon them.

As the last, fading columns of light winked out over the distant Motherlodes, Adam eased back in his luxurious new commander's quarters and let out a sigh of exhaustion. He'd secretly installed some tiny, remote stereo mikes and floating holo-cameras out in the jungle. With a series of voice commands, he began to watch and listen to the rainforest's nighttime symphony unfolding in three dimensions all around him, the pinpoint lights from the Arren Trees splashing over his curving walls.

"Elena?" he called, excitedly. No answer; she was busy in the bathroom.

He yawned and went back to his project, his finger running down a long list of cities he'd compiled. "Arrix, Belan," he muttered, "Felay, Hanor, Kezet…," he stopped short, his finger hovering over a particularly interesting name. "Meseo?" he sounded out the word. "Mes-e-o.

Hmm, *three* syllables, how untraditional." He suddenly remembered a short, intriguing statement from Duron. The old one had mentioned that Meseo was far beyond untraditional: breaking all the rules, it was constructed totally underwater. A relatively new project for the Bandors, it was top-secret and only about six hundred years old.

He leaned back, scheming. "Underwater? Yes, that's *it*, a perfect first venture! It's about time we explore a little and *enjoy* the planet; we've been working our butts off since we got here!" With visions of an ocean expedition filling his mind he closed his eyes, listening in awe to a chiming, bell-like sound in the distance. It was strange, dissonant, yet somehow melodious.

There was a faint rustle of fabric, and Elena poked her head out of the bathroom. "Ooh, that's *beautiful*, Adam! Dazzors? Where's the sound *coming* from?"

He opened his eyes and turned to her. She was wearing a gauzy number embroidered with delicate gold filigrees and entwining leaf motives. Amazing! Did one of the Bandor women give it to her? She blushed at his stares of admiration.

"Ah-ah-ah … yes, Dazzors," he stuttered. "They're ringing out the long day, oh apple of my eye!"

She batted her lashes. "You *noticed*!"

"Noticed? Noticed? I'd have to be a blind corpse *not* to!" He patted a spot on the bed next to him. She shimmied a few steps closer and then stopped abruptly.

"No. First tell me what I'm thinking."

"What? Aww, you said you didn't…."

"It's okay, I *want* you to this time! I have a feeling you'd *really* like to know," she teased. "You told me that you'd read my mind if I asked you."

"Well, truthfully, it might give you a headache," he cautioned.

She scowled. "Well, headaches go away! Besides, I think you'll find out that what I'm thinking is very, very interesting. In fact, *extremely* interesting!"

"I don't know…," he hedged.

"Aww, c'mon! Please, please, *please*!"

"Elena, I prom…."

"*Chicken*!" She plopped herself down and crossed her arms determinedly.

He sighed and rubbed his chin, his rock-solid resolve about mind-etiquette crumbling like sand on the shore. She'd piqued his curiosity with her air of mystery.

She glanced at him over her shoulder, one eye squinted shut. "I know it'll be a win-win if what I think will happen happens. Just read my thoughts and you'll see … see?"

He winced at her easy repartee; she could dish it out without even trying. "Okay, get ready." He concentrated gently, then pushed a little harder. She smiled enigmatically at him, her brows raised.

He sat back in shock. "*Three*?"

She tilted her head. "That's not what I'm thinking! What…?"

He held up his hand. "No, no. Three *signals*! I'm hearing three distinct thought waves!" His mouth dropped open, his eyes falling to her still-flat stomach. "Are you…."

"Pregnant? Yes, Adam. I know just by the way my body's been acting the last few days. But seriously, you can't be inferring that a little lump of cells can *think*, can you?"

"Not one lump, *two* lumps!" he corrected. "It's unmistakable, hon! I'm distinctly hearing three signals: A strong, clear one—yours—and then two weak, fuzzy ones! You're gonna have *twins*!"

It was Elena's turn to be astounded. "It's true!" she gasped. "All my life I've been wondering!"

Oh-so-gently he pulled her close, holding her like a piece of fragile crystal.

"Oh c'mon, h*u*g me, you big goober!" She shoved him hard, knocking him off balance. "I won't break!" She patted her hair back into place. "Twins really *do* run in my family; both of my grandmothers were fraternal twins!"

He pulled her closer and put his ear to her stomach. "In that case," he grinned mischievously, "you should be having *quadruplets*!"

She set her jaw. "You.... *Already* it starts! I think that deserves a *bite*!"

He drew back. "No! Not that! Anything but *that*!" She opened wide and lunged for his arm. As two perfect rows connected he thrashed around helplessly convulsed in spasms of laughter. "Lemme go, lemme go! Ouch! *Uncle*!"

She let go. "No more baby jokes?"

"No baby jokes."

"I don't believe you," she said levelly, watching him out of the corner of her eye. "We both know that's impossible, Adam. You can't *help* yourself. You're possessed."

He feigned shock, bordering on hopelessness. "I-I *am*? Well then," he grimaced, "I guess there's no saving me. In that case...." Solemnly contemplating his pillow, he commenced to stuff it into his mouth.

She crossed her arms, watching. "Go ahead...." A smile suddenly played across her lips. "Put the whole *thing* in. It'll fit."

He stopped, mid-stuff: There it was, another zinger. She'd done it again. With his shoulders shaking in muffled laughter, he pulled out a corner.

"Lemme *help* you!" She yanked it out with gusto. Her pinky immediately flew into the air. "*Yuck*! Now you'll be sleeping on a wet pillow!" As she gingerly put it aside, his list of Bandor names fluttered out onto the floor. "What's *this*, Adam?" She bent down to retrieve it, her voice trailing away.

Silence. He was sticking out a dry-looking tongue.

"Adam? Answer me. What's this list? It seems to be people, cities...."

"Meseo," he croaked.

"Huh?"

"Meseo. It's on the list. It's an undersea wonder! Ah, by the way, we're going there tomorrow, you and me. It's on the other side of the planet."

She sat bolt upright, her questions spewing out in a flurry. "Is it *safe*? What about my *condition*? Are there *pressures* under the ocean? Are...."

"Whoa!" He held up his hands. "You're barely pregnant and it'll be perfectly safe! After all, we slept on a Bandor starship hurtling through space for seven hundred years! That's *old* technology to them. *Millions* of years old!"

"Are you *sure* we'll...?"

"Absolutely!" He paused a moment, thinking, and then with a straight face, churned out a mighty effort. "Ah, Meseo's brand new, not a *sea*-quel! It's their most *current* city. Catch my, ah ... *drift*?" Grinning smugly, he coughed behind his hand, rightly proud.

She stiffened. "You can't help yourself, can you?" She scrambled for his wet pillow. "Catch *my* drift!" It swung through the air, catching him broadside.

Chapter 24: MESEO

The day dawned stormy and wet. Waking up in his new quarters, Adam gazed through the tall windows at the choppy waters of the lake. Rain again? The encroaching AugerBlade trees were definitely affecting the ecosystem. He studied the scuttling clouds, then shook Elena gently and went into his big closet to rummage around. Wanting to look his best for this first official outreach, he decided to switch to his commander's dress uniform. He put it on, studied himself approvingly in the mirror, then pulled the starship's discs and keys out of his old uniform's pocket. Staring at them in his hand he pondered a moment, and then shrugged. No, he didn't need to take them anymore: the starship was docked and lashed down securely into place as the hub of the new city. Shoving and prying, he inched a big jungle speaker away from the wall and hid them behind it.

While Elena was getting dressed, he sprinted through the rubbery, curving corridors to get Tola. He delighted in the little round man's company, especially his easy sense of humor and inventive knack with wordplay. Whispering excitedly, they walked back to his quarters to join Elena. As they waited, he tapped out a message on his wrist programmer: Kron would be in charge of Prima in their absence.

Shortly, the three slipped away in the morning downpour. As their SpeedSled hurtled toward the Solumbra portal on a preprogrammed AAP course, the rain danced and sputtered like butter on a hot skillet over their heads: The electrically charged shields burst the water into steam on contact, leaving a rocketlike contrail twisting through the rainforest.

Duron was waiting excitedly at the Solumbra with several elders at his side. They flew down into the bright underground vault of a city and then to the newest set of gleaming speed tubes. In minutes, the small party and their gear were being whisked through the center of the planet. A small bell chimed. They stared at each other in disbelief. They'd arrived already? It had only been minutes! As the doors opened, even in their wildest imaginations they weren't prepared for the sight.

A fantastic, floating city hung suspended before them in an interlocking series of bubbles. Although night was falling on this side of Aurona, the great city of Meseo glowed from within, alive with light.

They stepped warily out of the tube. The air was cool and dry, with a gentle breeze playing through the tops of tall palms lining the streets. Forever passionately curious, Adam edged up to the perimeter and poked at the glasslike wall. It was unexpectedly hard: some kind of unknown force field had to be keeping these bubbles rigidly in place and maintaining normal atmospheric pressures inside.

As they rounded a sprawling complex of buildings and stepped out into a great central park, they let out a gasp. Artfully arranged in varying sizes, huge bubbles of *water* were hovering in the air, suspended over the clearing! Evidently, that same mysterious force field could also contain water! Adam tapped Elena on the arm. In body language, he expressively cupped his hands to form three sphere-shapes within each other in succession.

"I see them!" she whispered. "Bubbles of water, within air, within water!"

Duron overheard her. "Yes, Adam's grandfather gave us a name for these bubbles before he left. Back then, our joint project was in its earliest planning stages. He called them 'Seaquariums': floating bubbles of varying sizes, the water pressurized inside each one to a specific, preset depth. The undersea specimens you see inside these Seaquariums come from all over our planet and range from tiny surface dwellers to the deepest ocean denizens."

Adam gestured at the ocean outside their huge bubble. "On the other hand, we might be seen by those sea creatures as if we were in their terrarium, right? They're probably looking at *us* right now, licking their chops!"

"Chops, Adam?" Duron was trying to keep up, baffled.

Bugging out his eyes, he pointed emphatically at his gaping mouth. Delighted, the elders let loose with a round of hoots and appreciative laughter.

Elena's nails dug into his arm. "Adam," she gasped. "Look, a sea serpent!"

Looming over their heads in the center of the grassy park, a mammoth bubble several hundred feet in diameter blotted out the overhead light. They peered up into it uneasily. Behind great rafts of seaweed, a great, paddle-footed torpedo shape with a snakelike neck was banking in a wide turn. A pair of alert-looking eyes had caught their movement and began to swim toward them.

She cringed, groaning in fear. "He *sees* us, Adam!"

"Oh, we'd be just a snack," he reassured. "An appetizer."

"Adam," she scowled. "There's a time and a place...."

He turned. "Hey, that's right, Duron, how *do* you feed them?"

The old one raised a skinny arm, nodding to a uniformed Bandor worker. "Actually, Matek is about show you right now." Standing behind a brightly lit console mounted on a podium, an attendant proceeded to punch in a sequence of commands. Duron turned, pointing silently into the distance with a slender finger.

A small bubble of water was disengaging from the far wall, looking almost like a tiny, dividing daughter cell. As it popped free and floated swiftly toward them, they could see life forms thrashing about inside.

"Food," Duron explained. "We locate and capture each creature's natural prey outside, in the open ocean. Animal, vegetable, or both."

They watched the feeding process in fascination. As the smaller bubble floated up to the larger one and paused, the great sea-beast commenced to lash about hungrily. His prey roiled in panic against the far wall of their tiny prison. Paddling furiously, the monster turned and surged toward his dinner at a tremendous velocity, crashing into the force field!

Grimacing, Adam pried Elena's fingernails from his arm. "Ah, hon?"

She opened one eye.

"Elena! It's okay; the shell didn't crack! *Look*!"

She squinted upward warily. "Oh, Adam! They're not...." Answering her half-formed question, the bubbles simply merged and the food was snapped up immediately.

The old Bandor continued, unhurried. "As you see, we are able to join bubbles as easily as we separate them." He held up a cautionary finger. "But before they merge as one, pre-equalization is necessary."

"How do you do that?" Adam prompted. "Some kind of pumps?"

Duron smiled. "No, it is far easier than that. I am sure you noticed that the smaller bubble paused. At that point, we were constricting its skin to increase the internal pressure and equalize it with the larger one. Unequal pressures invariably cause one bubble to rupture its contents into another, sometimes making them swell dangerously."

"Like a water balloon, right?"

Once more, the Elder's heads tilted questioningly.

Thinking quickly, Tola intervened. "Ah, try to understand the concept of a 'balloon,' guys. Here's an example: the creature we call an Aeronauta is essentially an air balloon, so filling him up with water could make him a *water* balloon, right?"

Behind them, the young Bandor worker was eavesdropping at his post, scratching his head and completely baffled. Duron chuckled. "Ah, yes, I think I understand, Tola. Water ... inside a balloon. Soon we will know more about your rich culture, but right now we can only imagine such delights." He turned to them, expounding on this new idea. "All over the planet, we form selectively pressurized water balloons around living sea creatures, in effect trapping them, and then transport whole clusters of these balloons through the oceans to Meseo. Gathering behind that ocean ridge over there, we are collecting a day's ration for each specimen in our underwater zoo."

Adam nodded enthusiastically. "Food pills!"

Duron hooted in delight, glancing over his shoulder at the other elders. "These, ah, food pills approach Meseo constantly, Adam," he chuckled, "from the furthest reaches of the planet."

Finally over her fright, Elena joined in. "How does it actually *work*, Duron," she interjected. "I mean, how do you *form* these bubbles?"

Duron smiled enigmatically. "I can only tell you this, Elena, in a way that you might understand. Eons ago, we conquered the force of gravity by using the opposing force of antigravity, of which you have seen only the elementary principles. Only after fully understanding antigravity could we begin to merge it with the dual phenomena of superconductive magnetism and surface tension. It was an extremely difficult balancing act combining the three, but as you can see, we have succeeded. This undersea city will soon be nearly eight hundred Earth-years old. Our next frontier is space, using similar methods."

Adam had become lost in a fog, uncharacteristically quiet and gazing into the distance. The old one noticed his faraway look. "What is it, Adam?" he probed, gently.

"Oh, nothing," he whispered, his voice barely audible. "It's just that all this talk about bubbles suddenly reminded me of a dream I had, long ago."

The elders spun toward Adam in rapt attention, their dark eyes wide in anticipation. "Please!" Movon urged. "Share this dream *immediately*! We *must* know!"

Adam shook out of reverie, his questioning eyes turning to Duron. He'd never seen such intense emotion coming from these passive Bandors!

The old one was equally excited. "Yes Adam, please tell us," he urged. "To us, *any* dream is rare. We view such unusual phenomena as prophecy."

"Prophecy? Really? Well, here goes," he began, warily. "Like I said, it all happened way back when I was a kid...."

As they crowded closer, Tola nudged him, discreetly shaking his head. "Keep it plain, man," he whispered. "These guys are dead serious!"

Adam paused, rethought his approach, and then started over. "Okay. I-I was only about twelve years old, during spring break in my senior year at Oxford." He held up a finger. "Oh. Wait, guys. I'm sorry, I just remembered this was really a-a *series* of dreams that happened over a two-week period. Are you sure you have time to...."

His voice trailed off. The elders' hands had flown up over their slit-mouths; whatever he'd said sure looked like it had tremendous significance. "A *series* of dreams?" they chorused. "Most *definitely* prophecy!" They urgently motioned for him to continue.

Shrugging, he took a deep breath and plunged in. "Okay, here goes: In the first night's dream, I was standing up on the roof of my grandfather's penthouse apartment, trying to get as high as I could. Something bad was happening down in the city. In the distance I could hear a loud wail of sirens. As I looked, I saw people running in panic for underground shelters. Evidently, the same thing was happening all over the world. How'd I know that?" He shrugged almost apologetically. "I-I dunno; you can just, ah, *tell* those things in dreams. You-you kinda sense it ... somehow." He looked up.

As Duron and the elders nodded at each other, great throngs of excited Bandors were appearing on the run with expressions of fascination and wonderment on their faces.

"*Hey*!" He looked Duron straight in the eye. "Is this being *simulcast*??"

The old one shrugged. "Why, all dreams of prophecy are shared, Adam."

"But this *isn't* prophecy! I-I've *always* had weird dreams!"

"Please continue," the elders urged, firmly. As the crowd settled to an expectant silence he scowled, suddenly nervous with all the attention.

"Well, all right. Here goes: As I looked down from my roof, I wasn't scared at all. The deafening sirens had stopped and there was this long, hollow-sounding silence. The people were all gone; no one dared to come out." He shaded his eyes with his hand. "I looked way into the distance...." As the faded memory unfolded, he started to get caught up in his own story, acting it out almost involuntarily and painting a vivid mind-picture with colorful narration. The Bandors appreciated it deeply; it was their style.

"There were these, ah, bubbles. Yes, clear bubbles just like the ones all around us, but different, enclosed by an outer, larger bell shape. Millions of them were swarming over the horizon in long 'V' formations like transparent, migrating birds. An-an alien invasion was beginning!" he paused, then lowered his voice to almost a whisper. "And they could see *me*," he continued. "They *knew* I was standing there, and that I was the only human on Earth who was curious about *them*! *How'd* they know?" Pausing for emphasis, he aimed his words directly at the assembled multitudes. "They could read my mind, just like *you*!"

As one living, mind-linked organism, the Bandors drew in a collective breath, their eyes wide and their slit mouths agape.

Adam was totally floored. Was this all true? Taking a chance, he broadcast a quick runic mind-message, his heart thudding loudly in his chest. *"This is scary to me! Are you really the ones? Are you Bandors the invisible aliens in my dreams?"*

The sea of eyes blinked, then motioned impatiently for him to continue.

As he tried his best to collect himself, he saw that Duron's hands were trembling. What was going on? Gathering his thoughts, he pressed on.

"Well, one of the bubbles spotted me and peeled off the formation, diving right at me at a tremendous speed! It was weird, but I wasn't afraid at all! I just stood there on the roof and watched it come! In seconds, it hovered in front of me, a ramp came down, and this voice ... this single, fragile-sounding voice beckoned from inside."

They were now hanging onto every word, every gesture. He squared his shoulders, then copying Elena's expressive ways, raised his arms over his head to form odd shapes with his hands. "The saucer was nearly invisible, like a ghost. The ball-shape in the center was constructed like a transparent orange with all the sections packed around a tapered core. In turn, the core had tiny, honeycombed tubes running up inside the center, wide at the bottom and drawn out extremely thin at the top. They looked like they might be some kind of a clear alloy of ceramic."

The elders were starting to fidget uncomfortably; the description of his mystery ship seemed to be striking a chord. Watching them out of the corner of his eye, he traced out another imaginary form in the air. "Where the sections joined in the outer seams, a clear fluid was trickling downward inside these channels, looking almost like blood inside capillaries." Fingers wriggling, he made sweeping, downward motions with his hands. "It circled underneath to the core and then turned upward at 90 degrees, shooting up inside the tapered honeycombed tubes at a tremendous velocity!" He watched Duron's face. "You know, thinking back on all this, that 'fluidic' propulsion system might have been just a pictorial representation of an abstract theoretical principle...." His eyes popped. "Hey, that's right! The antigrav ball must have been a supermagnetic ion driver with pulsed core resistance! Fusion-powered, of course, and-and omnidirectional!"

Wide-eyed, the elders exchanged looks of alarm.

"Yes, yes, omnidirectional!" He was breathing excitedly, now. "That's right! The orange-sectioned assembly fit snugly into the bell shape like-like a ball in a socket, almost like our starship but way, way different! It could rotate freely, directing the core's flow in opposition to gravity!" Strangely, he was becoming convinced that he, as a child, had indeed experienced a vision from the future, just as they'd surmised! After all, time travel, telepathy, and now concentric bubbles of water-within-air-within-water were all possible, so why not prophecy? He grew reflective, his voice becoming quieter, firmer.

"Listen to me carefully, all of you. I believe now, after seeing this city and these Seaquariums, that the aliens in my dream were indeed you Bandors. You were trying your best to represent to me in the simplest of pictures a very complex fusion-powered force of antigravity interacting with superconductive magnetism, resulting in the ultimate intergalactic starship of the future!"

Everyone, including Tola and Elena, stared at him in numbed silence. He continued, confidently. "And I believe that the translucent shapes were represented to me in a schematically visible form so I could understand how they moved and worked. As the ship accelerated through the atmosphere, the slow rotation of its outer hull correspondingly speeded up, too! That way, the bell-shaped exterior of the symmetrical lifting body could always present a cool leading edge to the airflow...."

Moving quickly, the old Bandor reached under Adam's chin and tapped down his translator button's volume. "That is *enough*," he whispered, his mind-shields up. "You may continue later, but only in utmost secrecy!"

"Why?" he stopped, exasperated and alarmed. "I-I was on a roll, Duron!"

The old one pulled him away from the group and leaned toward him confidentially. "I know you have not yet mentioned the way we can tip the whole ship on its side to become an air brake, or shoot at 90 degrees to the direction of travel! I know there is much, much more...." His voice fell to a hoarse whisper. "The others cannot hear us now, so listen to me. This entire city of Meseo was created as a research lab! It is five miles beneath the surface and safe from enemy eyes, but not *ears*!"

He paused a moment, pondered thoughtfully, and then sighed. "What I am trying to say is your dream-ship is real, Adam. Your grandfather initiated the concept and was instrumental in its complicated production. At this very moment it is sitting inside that building over there!"

"My-my grandfather?" Adam stuttered. His round eyes followed Duron's slender finger to an insignificant dark structure occupying an entire bubble on a distant ocean ridge. Yes, there was a definite air of secrecy about it; he could see armed guards everywhere.

"As to your dream," Duron continued, "there is now no doubt to me that another *being* has been present on Aurona. Somehow, the cloak of time has been torn open by this entity. You had this dream-series at approximately twelve years of age, right?"

"That's right! But how...?"

"Think, now. Your planet was in the rim of the Milky Way galaxy nearly seven hundred sleep-years from Aurona! Try to understand what I am saying: someone on Aurona beamed these visions to you in your past, taking the form of, as you say, a series of dreams."

His mind was racing. "M-messages from the *future* beamed into the *past*? And my grandfather was the one who thought up and directed this dream ship? You know, at one point in my life I would have disagreed with you, Duron, but now...." He sighed, shrugging his shoulders. "Hey, anything's possible, but one thing's certain: I have to *see* this dream ship. Only then can I believe all these fantastic hypotheses."

Duron was adamant. "Believe me, it is real, Adam. Your mystery starship will be ready for its maiden voyage very soon. I, for one, am aching for your brilliant and valued input into this project, but unfortunately, I still need to convince Movon and the rest of the elders to grant your wish."

"I understand what you're going through," Adam nodded, averting his eyes. "Although your vote carries more weight, you can still be vetoed, right?"

"Correct." Duron turned to join the elders. "Wait a moment, please."

The elders circled, threw up their mind-shields, and turned off their translator buttons. As they conferred, their tone became more and more argumentative. Their sibilant language crescendoed steadily in volume, rose to a peak, and then there was silence: the vote had been cast. Duron solemnly turned, tapping his translator button. A slow slit-smile spread over his face. "They like you, Adam. They agree that you are a man of great integrity, as was your amazing grandfather."

"Thanks, Duron." He bowed graciously to the elders. "And...?"

"And your prophetic dream has been received as a great sign. We feel you are indeed the one who will come from afar to change the direction of Aurona's history. You alone, with the aid of the Rasheen, have the intellectual potential to absorb every detail of our known past in our dream libraries and then chart our future with a firm hand. We have observed your unequalled qualities of trust and leadership, and are therefore prepared to grant your request."

He grimaced. "All *that*? I-I just wanted a peek!" As a roar of laughter went up from the Bandor multitude, Duron spun to face him, his face flushed.

"Adam!" he yelled over the tumult. "Just *look* at them! I have never seen such emotion in my life! What is it that you have that I ... ah, I mean *we* don't have?"

Adam traced his mouth, turned upward in a smile. "This," he shrugged. "I always tend to look for the humor in most situations." He pulled Elena closer. "I mean *we* do. We're a dream team, you know, and it's for life. Oh, by the way, we have two more in here...." As he patted her stomach, he was met with a quick slap.

"Adam!" she hissed. "You're embarrassing me!"

A stunned silence fell over the crowd. Duron spun to him, his eyes wide, his voice trembling. "*Twins*? So-so it is *definitely* true! You *are* the ones spoken about in our prophecy! It is genetically impossible for a Bandor woman to conceive twins, so the approaching birth of your fraternal twins.... Yes, Elena, a boy and a girl ... will be the final, conclusive link to our future! We are truly overwhelmed! It all seems to be happening, but it is much, much too soon! We are very confused...."

Suddenly, Duron stopped short. It looked like he'd just been shot! He rocked back on his heels, his great, dark eyes rolling back in his head. As he slumped, Adam grabbed for the edge of his cloak.

In moments, the old eyes fluttered open and he looked up uncomfortably into the concerned, trusting faces of his adopted family. "I-I am truly sorry to tell you this, but as you know, news travels fast on Aurona, literally at the speed of thought...."

"What *is* it, Duron?" Adam prompted.

"There are evil ones in our midst," he hedged. "They have been plotting against the unshakable course of our nation and the fulfillment of these prophecies for thousands of years. They will stop at *nothing* for the right opportunity to reshape history with their own hands!"

Adam's gut had started to quake. "W-what are you saying?"

Duron stood up decisively. "I am afraid I must be the bearer of bad news, Adam. Your new city, Prima, is under attack!"

He staggered backward. "No!!"

"Yes, right now, at this very moment! Some of your crew have been concealing an alien on your starship who has formed an alliance with these Bitron outlaws. They have extremely strong mind-shields!"

Turning on his heel, Duron began to issue telepathic orders, firing them off in rapid salvo to the other elders. One by one they sprinted away to perform their assigned duties. He spun to Adam. "You and Elena must leave at once. I am sending Tola and several regiments of armed guards behind you. They will follow a distance, shielded and cloaked."

Adam's brows lowered. "Why are we alone? Are we some kind of *targets*?"

"Frankly yes," he answered cryptically. "We are setting an ambush. I am sorry to tell you this, but once you are out in the open you will be both the hunters and the hunted. This outlaw group is crafty and may spot our trap, so you need to act as if you are alone!"

Elena pressed tightly against him. "Adam, I'm…."

"It's okay," he whispered, hugging her reassuringly. "I'll protect you."

Tola's voice was quavering. "T-timing is everything! As M-Movon said, you two gotta move on!"

Adam's brow raised questioningly. "Huh?"

The round man shrugged. "Vamoose! Skedaddle…. *Pronto*!"

Book Three:
WARPING TIME

Chapter 25: CRISIS

As serpentine ribbons of smoke writhed upward into the low flying clouds, the chill rain dissolved them into a watercolored blur. Out on the great semicircular wharf, the lights were blazing in Adam's new commander's quarters: clothes, furniture and equipment were flying through the air and his room was being thoroughly ransacked.

Abruptly, a darkly clad figure entered and walked purposefully to a far wall. He seemed to know precisely where to look: as he slid a heavy jungle speaker aside, Adam's holo-discs and glowing keys tumbled out. He punched the air in triumph, stuffed them into a valise, and glanced up at the ceiling: a stolen Spyder skittered across the surface and settled into a crevice, awaiting further reconnaissance commands. It had done its job well.

Looking around furtively, three figures stole out of the back of the cooling tower with their arms full of communications gear, threw it onto a utility barge, and sped toward the main compound. The disturbance in Adam's quarters brought Kron on the run. As he reached the door the mutineers poured out in a great wave, their sheer numbers overwhelming him. There were shouts, scuffles, then a loud retort of gunfire. Clutching his chest and bleeding profusely, he slumped to the floor unconscious.

In the starship's control center, there were maniacal cackles of glee. A stooped, hooded figure paused to study the instructions on the holodiscs for several minutes, then shoved the glowing keys into their slots. His hands trembling in excitement, he twisted them in a newly memorized sequence.

There was a loud crack and a dazzling shower of electrical sparks as the ship severed its moorings and slowly lifted away from its form-fitting nest. It rose silently to two hundred feet and paused, then another twist activated the cloaking device. The saucer dissolved out of the sky, just like the smoke in the rain.

Adam and Elena had finally reached the edge of the rainforest and peered uneasily into the clearing. There were signs of a great struggle. Off to the side, an antigrav barge lay toppled against a tree, its lone occupant twisted unnaturally under the smoking wreckage.

"Oh, no!" Elena turned away quickly, tears of recognition welling up in her eyes."It-It's *Jon*!!"

Adam hopped off and knelt next to him, glancing anxiously over his shoulder. "Where's Tola? Where are the guards? They're supposed to be right *behind* us!" Trembling, he groped for a pulse, then looked up grimly. "I'm afraid he's gone, hon. What in the world do you think happ...." His voice dropped off abruptly.

A twig snapped in the woods.

Elena cocked an ear. "Adam!" she hissed. "Did you hear *that*?"

A finger to his lips, he quickly retraced his steps back to the sled, slipped into his seat in a smooth, deliberate motion, and threw up the shields. With Elena pressed tightly against him, they watched through the shimmering curtain. It didn't take long to spot a fleeting, sinuous movement. She whispered the single, dreaded word.

"*Razah*!!"

The great beast was slinking stealthily through the underbrush, his steps short and quick. He paused, bobbing his head up and down, intently focusing on something. They looked in the direction of his gaze and quickly spotted his prey.

Elena let out a gasp."Oh, no! It's-it's…."

"Good *grief*, I see him!" Adam whispered, groping for his Stifler.

Barely fifty feet away, Jon's disembodied shadow was stumbling aimlessly through the thorny scrub palmettos. Todd looked beaten, dazed, and forlorn: easy prey. Crouching low and slinking noiselessly, the beast was now well within stun distance. Catlike, he set his claws into the dirt for the final dash, the tip of his long tail twitching in anticipation. Suddenly, in a most uncatlike manner, he poised his big head at an odd angle and aimed his frontal lobes for the blast that would send the child down.

Adam gritted his teeth. "No!" Propelled by impulse and adrenaline, he threw off the shields and leaped to his feet. "Hey, stupid! It's *me* you want!" he shouted. "I'm over *here*!" Setting his Stifler to 'kill,' he vaulted out of his seat and began to walk slowly toward the startled yellow eyes.

Elena sprang to her feet. The whole scene had quickly turned into a nightmare and events were spinning way out of control. "Adam!" she screamed. "Are you *crazy*??"

With a loud thump and crash, Todd tripped on a root and fell, crying out loudly in pain. As Adam turned his head for a split second, his sweaty palms felt the heavy Stifler slip. Suddenly he found himself grabbing at the air as it dropped, bounced off a root, and rolled somewhere into the underbrush. "Oh, no!" Adam's eyes widened in shock. The tables had abruptly turned and fear struck deeply with its icy sword.

Fear: the great beast's primal instincts sensed his age-old ally permeating the air; this tall one had succumbed to it and frozen in his tracks. An easy target. He spun toward Adam and aimed his bulbous forehead for a massive, pent-up neuron blast.

"Adam!" Elena screamed. "*Run*! The *sled*! The *shields*!"

Regaining his senses, he spun on his heels. "Get *ready*!! I'm gonna ju…."

With a guttural sound, his words were cut off at the throat. A visible, moving wave slammed into him from behind with tremendous force and threw his lanky body through the air to land facedown on the ground, inches from his goal. The blue lights of the sled's internal laser guidance flickered, played over his body, then shut off with a muffled click.

Enraged, Elena began to scream at the top of her lungs, throwing backpacks, shoes, anything that wasn't tied down. Hurtling through the air, a heavy specimen cage suddenly found its mark. The Razah bellowed loudly in pain, lashing at the air with his claws. Spinning toward her, he lowered his head to build up another massive neuron charge that would put this bothersome one away for good.

"Tola? *Anybody*?" she yelled, desperately scanning the rainforest for a sign of her friends. "Where *are* you??"

A small shout of acknowledgement came from the woods. Todd was limping toward her, his plump body covered with gashes, his slanted almond eyes streaked with tears. Her eyes quickly focused on his hand: dragging it awkwardly by the barrel, he was pulling a long Stifler behind him! She thought fast: if she threw up the shields to save herself, Todd would be stunned and she'd lose both him and Adam in the process. She had to take this last-ditch, calculated risk.

Keeping an eye on the Razah, she smiled reassuringly at the confused boy. Folding her hands together, she pointed a finger at the beast.

"*Pow*! *Zing*!!" she mimicked the sound of a Stifler.

The Razah was now thoroughly enraged. These loud creatures were annoying, far more annoying than his usual fare of quiet, passive jungle creatures. His neuron charge was ready. Lashing his tail, he angled his head for the easy stun.

A light suddenly dawned on Todd's round face. With a determined look, he turned the heavy gun around, aimed at the Razah, and squeezed the trigger. In rapid succession, two very different blasts cleaved the air and found their marks: As the Stifler's blazing arc of lightning slammed into the Razah's body and threw him off-balance, the beast released a hasty, badly aimed mind-stun. Winged, Elena fell unconscious into the sled.

It was over: shouting in anguish and milliseconds too late, Tola and his Bandor party sped into the clearing with their weapons drawn.

The cloaked starship skimmed over the treetops like a shimmering ghost. Down in a cavernous central hold, shouts of anger and defiance rang loudly. Locked up and held captive, about a hundred of the helpless crew were watching a monitor over their heads. As their beloved, smoking Prima slipped into the distance, the view turned into rolling jungle and then to flat, gray static. They turned to each other, their eyes wide and their jaws dropping in disbelief.

The mood was quite different up in the control room, almost a party atmosphere. Thirty odd--looking strangers were milling around Dexor and his two companions, gibbering in an unknown tongue as they squabbled over the starship's controls.

Trennic scowled, whispering. "Boy, they sure are *ugly*!"

Dexor's cold blue eyes shot him a look of alarm. "Quiet, you fool!" he hissed. "We don't know who we're dealing with!"

The man looked around. "Where'd these dudes *come* from, out of the woodwork?"

"You could say that," Dexor replied. "They're Bitron outlaws, all of 'em. The same race Kron lived with but renegades, like us. By the way, they're also plasmorphic."

"Plas-*what*-ic?"

Dexor leaned into him and twisted his arm painfully. "Like this, knucklehead: plastic! They've got changeable bodies! They can *disguise* themselves!"

Grimacing and rubbing his sore arm, Trennic studied the aliens in a new light. "You mean they've been here all the time, but d-disguised as...."

"You *got* it," Nastix cut in. "I saw one of 'em changing shape when he jumped off his SpeedSled. First he was a Bandor, then ... Poof! Ugly dude!"

"Lemme fill you in," Dexor snarled. "These aren't your run-of-the-mill outlaws. I overheard they've been banned from their planet for *life!* Sound familiar?"

The two elbowed each other in the ribs. "Sure does," Trennic nodded. "Those fake ID's cost a fortune, but they worked! Hey, that dumb bat-geek *fell* for 'em!"

Dexor lowered his voice to a barely audible whisper. "These ugly, scarred dudes have been waiting here on Aurona over seven hundred years for...." He jerked his thumb toward the commander's seat. "Their, ah, number one honcho over there."

As they turned to look, the hooded figure spun on his seat and glared directly at them, his lips curled into a snarl, the shadowed pig-eyes full of hate. Slowly, deliberately, he stood up, lowered his hood, and slithered toward them. With a shrug, the dark cloak slipped from his body, the stilettos glinting and hilts rattling.

The three drew in a collective breath. For the first time, they could plainly see his features: an impossibly wide gash ran across the top of his head, another deep scar connected a corner of his mouth to a mutilated ear and he was nearly bald, whitish tufts of hair scattered randomly over a deeply furrowed dome.

The Scarred One paused, raised his hairy, beetled brows, and struck an odd, almost awkward pose. The room fell silent. His features started to shift and bump around, as if someone were under his skin trying to get out. He was transforming. By the time he'd taken three steps his deep scars had smoothed out, two more steps and his pig-eyes protruded and became almost like glass. A final step closed the gap and he stood face to face with Dexor.

"So," he hissed, "we meet again ... *as strangers*!"

Gagging, Dexor shrank away form the putrid, rotten breath. The voice was still the same, with its snarling, grating whine.

"Of course, you should know by now that you've only been puppets in the big picture, a means to an end, all four of you.... Oops, sorry. One down, three to go."

Dexor flinched. This was now a life-or-death situation. His mind raced back to all the tactics he'd used before. The defiant stance never worked, nor the capable, independent leader-type. It narrowed quickly to boot-licker. He brightened, taking on a sadistically optimistic cheeriness. "Hey!" He smiled. "Did ya see the way your guys mowed 'em down? Blood was everywhere! Man! With these presto-chango disguises we can write our own ticket and *rule*!"

"We.... *We?*" The Bitron laughed uproariously, maniacally. Calming himself, he slowly shook his head. "No go, Dexo. Not *this* time.... However!" He poked a single, crooked finger in the air. "There still may be a few, shall we say, '*management*' positions open?" He raised a thin brow testily. "That's before we possibly say goodbye. That is, the *long* goodbye."

Trennic and Nastix eyed the exits, ready to bolt.

The Bitron caught on. "Of course, my allies will make sure that you don't change your minds." A few heads turned in their direction, nodding. "So go ahead! I know you're angry, but take out your aggression on your *own* kind! *Focus* it! '*Manage*' them!" He thought a minute, pursing his thin lips. "But of course we don't want to shoot *too* many; we need all the workers we can get. There's a lot of heavy lifting and digging ahead. We, ah, may end up having to ask *you* to do it!"

He walked slowly back to his seat, pondering, his eyes masklike and expressionless. He spun around. "Let's just say *this* for now: the better you are at controlling them, the better your chances for your *own* survival…. *Got* it?"

Dexor's mouth had turned into a tight, hard line. "Got it," he muttered.

As the last clinging curtains of pain parted, Elena opened her eyes. Several people were milling around the clearing, busily carting the Razah's rigid carcass away and pulling Jon's SpeedSled upright. She looked around in a daze, trying to remember what happened.

Sitting on a nearby SpeedSled, Joelle was consoling a terrified, whimpering Todd in her lap. She turned to Elena, relieved that she was finally awake. "Hey! Glad you're back with us, hon." She pulled the heavily bandaged boy to her chest, calming him down. "He's got nobody now and I've made up my mind: I want to adopt him."

Elena's eyes focused over Joelle's shoulder into the distance. "Is that a stretcher? Who's being loaded onto…. No!" Her memory suddenly rushed back. "*Adam*!!" She squeezed her eyes shut, her head and spinal cord throbbing in painful spasms.

Tola leaned toward her. "I'm sorry to say this, Elena, but it doesn't look good," he whispered, biting his lip. "He's beginning to, ah, draw up into a fetal position."

"What? That indicates *very* serious brain damage!"

He grimaced. "One of the Bandor guards mentioned that nobody could survive a major stun like that at such close range. Adam-Adam's heartbeat is … well, that's fading, too." The little round man bowed his head. "God help us."

Peter shuffled toward them, averting his eyes. "We saw it happen with our scope vision, Elena. There was nothing we could do. We were too far away."

Rico joined him. "There were no more SpeedSleds! We were running as fast as we could away from Prima! Some of us of could see the whole thing happening through that holocamera." He jerked his thumb toward a sphere hovering inconspicuously in the branches. "We felt helpless! We saw Adam fall and then you…."

Tola interrupted. "You guys sent a camera to 'SEEK' Jon?"

"Yes," he said. "It didn't take long to find him," he sighed, glancing at the blood-smeared barge. "Jon and his little brother fought well. They were part of the defensive ranks."

Elena opened one eye. "Defensive ranks?" Alarmed, she pulled herself upright, her pile of wet compresses falling to the ground. "Defensive ranks? What's going *on* here? Peter? Rico? The *truth*, now!"

Rico lowered his head. "Our saucer's gone, Elena. The very *heart* of Prima has been ripped out of its socket! I'm afraid to say that a lot of the crew have been taken hostage and, ah, some very good people have been … killed."

She fell back, stunned: this was *far* worse than she could have imagined!

Joelle tapped an earbud and shifted a pale-looking Todd in her arms. "Hey, I just got a call from Prima. Gotta get back there real quick."

Tola shrugged. "You're right. Go ahead, the four of you. Hop onto Adam's barge with him before it leaves. The rest of us'll follow." He patted Todd's arm, smiling reassuringly. The pale boy looked like he needed blood and some pretty serious stitches to pull him together. He turned back to Elena. "Now, as for you...."

She was sitting up on the edge of her stretcher. "I'm going too," she stated, matter-of-factly. "My place is with my husband."

He threw up his hands. "So! As I was saying, why don't we *all* go! What are we *waiting* for?"

Although Prima's waterfront was darkened with soot, its soaring shapes were dotted with strange, windblown puffs of white. Aeronautas had arrived, hundreds of them, poking among the rubble for anything edible. The blood-spattered walls were especially interesting. Their moist trunks uncoiled to taste the unfamiliar, rich, dried protein.

As the minutes ticked away, Adam's condition worsened alarmingly. Duron hovered closely at his side, his long fingers fluttering helplessly in the air, hissing commands to the elders in short, clipped phrases. It was obvious to everyone that the old Bandor loved his delightful young protégé; in a very short time this young human had become like a son, like his own flesh and blood.

Elena groaned, burying her face in her blanket. Within the space of an hour, everything had been turned completely upside down: the entire mission had gone from the loftiest pinnacles of security and success, then dashed to bloody despair on the ground. Several open graves lined the waterfront, ready for their young occupants. She turned away, touching Adam's face softly. As death began its relentless claim, his paralyzed fingers were growing steadily colder. She grasped his stiff hands, crying.

The elders quickly withdrew into a tight circle, pulling Duron with them. Although Prima's rubbery walls muffled the sound of their loud, sibilant language, in the midst, the anguished timbre of Duron's voice could easily be picked out.

"No! There is not enough *time*! He...."

Someone reached under his chin and tapped off his translator button. Although the English was cut short, his grief-stricken Bandorese lingered loudly in the air.

The confused, haggard remnant of the crew lay down their shovels, shook the dirt off their clothes, and walked out onto the pier. They cast furtive looks at their leader, appalled at his appearance: a humming respirator was crammed down his distended throat and his oddly contorted body seemed to be frozen in rigor mortis.

Elena suddenly felt violated by their prying eyes. "Please," she sobbed, covering him protectively with her blanket. "Please go *away*!! I understand how you feel, but there's nothing you can *do*!" As they backed away confused, she flicked her tangled hair away from her face and tried to regain her composure. "I'm sorry," she apologized. "I-I've heard rumors that Kron was hurt during the break-in. Does anyone know how he is?"

Tola answered. "Truthfully, he's, ah, really bad." He clenched his fists. "Joelle's with him right now, giving him a transfusion in Adam's quarters. Peter's the donor."

"Oh, no! What happened?"

"A bullet got him, next to his heart. A *bullet*, Elena! We're talking about semiautomatic weapons here, not electronic Stiflers! He was checking out a disturbance in your quarters when they cut him down. He had no time to react."

"In *our* room? We had nothing of value in there, except the keys…to…." She squeezed her eyes shut, a groan escaping from her lips.

Tola shook his head. "The starship was only a means to their end, Elena. They're after gold. *Gold*! Can you imagine?"

The circle of elders parted and Duron stepped out. His stride was quick, his voice steady, and his manner efficient. "Elena, you are to come with us," he ordered, quietly. "There is only one hope left for Adam and we have decided to pursue it. As there is insufficient time to unlock, power up, and dispatch another starship from our deep underground vaults, we are taking some SpeedSleds over that nearby ridge to the ocean's shore. There, transportation awaits to take us to…the island."

She gathered her blankets in haste. "Anything, Duron, anything. Take us anywhere. Do whatever it takes to save his life. We're in your hands, now."

The waves were rolling onto the shore with the sound of hollow thunder. The sea had a heavy chop and a stiff breeze was blowing in the morning's chill storm. Elena squinted into the biting wind. A great bubble of seawater was rising from the ocean's surface. Barely visible inside was a small, rectangular black box.

The elders stood shivering on the shore, rough blankets draped over their spotless ceremonial robes. Moving hastily, they unrolled a large, ten-foot metallic disc on the sand. As one, they picked up Adam's stretcher, positioned it carefully over the disc, and lowered it into the center. Gathering robes and blankets, they clustered tightly around it. As Elena joined them, she looked over her shoulder and stole another look at the enormous bubble.

"So how do we get inside that thing without getting wet?"

Duron pulled at her sleeve. "Patience, child. Sit down. We will be inside in moments." Turning, he motioned solemnly to the others. "Ready?"

As their palms turned silently upward, a snap, an electrical buzz, and the smell of ozone permeated her senses. A bright seam of light started to zip itself together around the perimeter of the disc and travel upward, drawing in long streams of the ever-present flecks of glittering gold foil from the air. A shield! In seconds, the gleaming golden shell shut with a loud retort above their heads. Rising swiftly from the waves, the bubble came ashore and settled over them, engulfing the brilliant orb. As one, the elders leaned their bodies toward the sea. Elena quickly followed suit. The bubble rose into the air, transformed into a horizontal teardrop, and swiveled toward the distant horizon.

"Ready?"

Elena nodded wordlessly, her eyes wide, her jaw hanging open.

The sleek shape plunged swiftly beneath the waves.

"What *is* this thing?" she whispered, awestruck.

"You are inside a large SeaSphere freight transporter, child."

"A what?"

"Just a minute. Please move aside."

As Movon reached down, he pulled the mysterious black box into his lap and began to tweak a few dials. "In our knowledge, there is nothing faster for traveling through the oceans. Since this vehicle consists of seawater itself, it moves without hindrance through its own medium."

She was puzzled. "Please explain. I-I don't understand."

"Several thousand years ago, we arrived at this ideal, streamlined shape by studying the bodily forms of the fastest sea creatures, but ironically, we took our clues for its unique locomotion by studying the slowest."

As Movon bent back to his navigational plotting, Duron explained. "I know it sounds like a paradox, Elena, but what Movon is saying is true. We know you are an expert in biology: most sea snails travel by sending a ripple, or pulsed wave, along their muscular stomach-foot, right? We have found a method of amplifying this same ripple along the surface of this liquid-capsule vehicle. The more powerful the pulse, the faster it goes and the more streamlined the shape becomes. Now with the aid of a newly discovered probe accelerator, some of our more advanced models have attained unheard-of speeds!"

For several minutes there was silence and a faint sensation of flying, then all went still. The bubble-within-bubble rose from the sea and settled on the shore, rupturing and trickling down into the dry sand. Once again, the golden shell simply became one with the atmosphere, the glittering droplets blowing away in the wind.

Elena was speechless. Within minutes, the sun was lower in the sky, it was definitely warmer, and they were sitting in a circle at the base of massive, white vertical cliffs. Incredibly, their SeaSphere had just crossed several time zones in its southwestward travel. Her eyes traveled slowly upward, searching for the clifftops lost somewhere in the ever-present atmospheric haze.

Chapter 26: **THE ISLAND**

Five miles long and a thousand feet high, the crescent-shaped landmass rose straight from the sea like an iceberg, the towering chalk cliffs an impenetrable fortress, a remote, almost dream-like castle. The fragile exterior was protected from the elements by a glowing force field that extended around the entire perimeter, both above and below sea level. Free from the threat of Razah and Spyrin, the island was secure in its splendid isolation.

The ancient one had lived here for most of her life, a long, eventful span now approaching an incredible ten thousand years. She coveted the unobstructed, windswept view and so manicured the flat-topped grounds every morning, pointedly yanking up every seedling that sprouted in the lush green carpet of grass that made her roof. The soil on top was rich, fertile loam, deposited eons after the limestone seafloor had thrust upward and separated from a larger landmass to the south. Gathering vegetation, it rode its continental plate into warmer climes.

By the time she'd discovered it in the wandering days of her youth, there was a rainforest on top. There was also a large, hollow chamber in the depths of the island. With an army of robodiggers, she'd carefully hollowed it out more and more through the ages, widening and reinforcing it as they descended. When the big atrium was ready, she lowered the jungle inside, piece by piece, into shelter. Eventually, she'd meticulously sculpted many terraced balconies opening into the vast, white-roofed central area. Solar pipes brilliantly lit the lush tropical garden and a young Motherlode now formed the focal point; with fruit in abundance, the perfumed air was now almost too rich to breathe. She was rightly proud.

Elena stared at the cliffs in a trance, then shook her head in confusion. Out of nowhere, a sudden, unbidden string of strange thoughts and scenes had been invading her consciousness. "Who is … *she*? A rainforest? What?"

Duron broke the spell with a chuckle. By the look on Elena's face, it was evident she was only partially understanding the telepathic mind-pictures and halting English narrative he was sending her. As he touched her gently on the elbow, she turned to him in shock.

"*You*? You're sending me…?"

"Yes, Elena," he finished in a whisper. "And our speed tubes are not quite operational out here as yet. SeaSpheres and saucers are presently our only access."

She shook her head in a daze. "Y-you just *showed* me all that? The history? The feelings? Memories and-and … robodiggers? You beamed all that into my *mind*?"

Before he could answer, Movon interrupted, urging both of them onward toward the cliffs. "Please explain all of this to her later, Duron? There is not a moment to lose!" He trotted a few steps further and called nervously over his shoulder. "She is waiting for us and y-you know how she gets!" His eyes rolled.

Casting knowing looks at each other, the elders tossed their blankets aside and ran after him. In their rippling gold-trimmed robes, they seemed to float over the white dunes like tall, elegant ghosts.

Elena puffed resolutely after the long-legged aliens, shading her eyes and squinting at the surreal scene in front of her. A tiny, greenish, vertical crevice had started to slit the shimmering force field, drawing back to reveal a blinding, sunlit section of wall as they approached.

The twelve arrived at the narrow electronic opening. Moving efficiently, they raised Adam's stretcher a bit higher to pull it through. She stumbled up after them, totally out of breath and throwing up clouds of powdery chalk with her feet. Her throat had never felt so dry. She raised her voice to speak, but no sound came out.

In a moment they were inside. Pausing to catch her breath, Elena began to grope along the walls, following the faint whisper of Bandorese voices in the distance. It was blissfully cool and some kind of strange, phosphorescent glow seemed to be lighting the tubular passageways. When her eyes finally adjusted to the darkness she began to see eerie movements up ahead with distorted, strangely lit shadows dancing over the walls. Spooked, she picked up her pace, winding through a bewildering labyrinth of greenish-white. Every wall looked the same, and passageway upon passageway seemed to stop in dead ends, turn blind corners or tunnel through endless chalk corridors. Her heart in her mouth, she rounded a last turn.

There they were! Green ghosts! Duron's head was bobbing in front of a long string of mushroom-topped, floating apparitions and they were in a dead run; evidently this section was quite familiar to them. Putting on a burst of speed, she caught up. Sprinting alongside Adam's bouncing stretcher, she slid the blanket off her shoulders and draped it over her husband's cold body. Suddenly, everyone bumped to a stop.

"Ah!" Duron's voice echoed. "The Western Wall!"

He made a smooth motion with something in his hand. An elevator was suddenly there, glowing chalk-white behind the greenish cast! As they bumped and squeezed into it, an insistent beeping sound rose over the rustle of starched robes and panting humanoids. Alarmed, Elena turned her focus to the battery of gauges and readouts monitoring Adam's vital signs. She let out a deep groan.

"Noo-o-o! He just stopped breathing! Look, his respirator's giving him plenty of air, but-but he's not *responding*! *Do* something quickly!"

A shaking hand covering his mouth, Duron checked and rechecked the gauges. "S-she is right," he hissed between his slender fingers, "He is leaving us! We have only moments!" He glanced nervously over his head as the proper floor approached on the control panel. "Let us all hope she is in her right mind tonight," he sighed, tapping on his chin nervously.

As the elevator stopped, Elena stumbled. "*She*? Who is this *she* person?"

The door slid open and they all looked into the room in silence. An enormous window had been carved in the outer wall and beyond the shimmering force field, the magnificent blue-green sea curved toward the darkening Western horizon. With a faint rustle, a lone, hunched figure suddenly appeared in silhouette.

"What *kept* you?" a raucous voice screeched out. "Couldn't you move your scrawny legs any faster??"

"It is Roson," Duron whispered. "Do not be afraid of her."

As the figure swept toward them into the greenish light of the elevator, Elena drew back, her heart pounding. This was a truly ancient Bandor woman with long, yellowed nails, small broken teeth and … something else. She tried to keep her eyes from traveling downward, but they did, quite by themselves. The crone's legs were evidently useless; she appeared to be floating in a seated position. Her strangely puffy robe was carefully spread out to conceal a small, round anti-grav chair. Yes, her eyes were dim and her hearing was faint, but her voice was *loud*.

"What *am* I, a *magician*?" she screeched. "Am I supposed to raise the dead?" She bumped rudely past them to examine Adam, jabbing his arm with a collection of strange instruments. "Why couldn't you bring him any *sooner*? You sent me your message an hour ago!! Tell your workers to hurry up and finish my speed tubes!"

Fighting an urge to scream, Elena scanned the room. Cluttered. Very cluttered. Definitely a bad sign. She clenched her fists uncertainly. There was a forked object on a nearby tray, just like the one Adam was being poked with. Quaking but curious, she picked it up. By its familiar deeply embossed logo, it was plainly of Bitron origin.

"Put that *down*!!" Roson roughly slapped the instrument of torture out of her hand and it fell to the floor with a clatter. "*I'm* the doctor in this house and don't *you* forget it!" As the ancient one waved a skinny arm in fury, a strange, shiny object suddenly protruded from the edge of her robe. Once more, Elena tried her best not to look. The crone jerked her head up suspiciously, her better eye traveling up and down her body, scrutinizing her in the minutest detail. Elena shrank back, trying to hide behind one of the elders.

"*Aliens!*" The A-word was spit out of the hag's mouth, like so much rubbish. "They're *all* the same!" She wheeled back to work, glancing repeatedly over her shoulder and muttering curses in Bandorese. Her gnarled hands flew, tweaking cryptically marked dials, poking long needles and prodding stiffened limbs. Finally, the prep finished, she wiped her hands.

"That's *it*! Now get him over *there*!" she shouted, pointing to the far wall.

The elders hesitated for a confused, split instant, trying to decide politely amongst themselves just who she meant.

"*N-n-now-w-w!!*" The instruments rattled in their trays.

They flew into action like cowed interns, all elbows and knees. Lifting Adam awkwardly, they shuffled in a tight, knotted group, strapped him to a table, and then leaped out of the way, falling over each other in haste.

A pair of arthritic-looking hands rested on a set of bony hips. "Could be better," the crone chided, shaking her head. "Amateurs! The *lot* of you!" She jabbed a button impatiently with her elbow. With a rumble, Adam's table slid down a pair of rails into what looked like a thick-walled decompression chamber. As the heavy door slammed shut with a loud bang, she floated to an oval window on the side to peer in. "I've given him a dose of my own medicine," she rasped, scowling darkly. The greenish glow from within lit up her face grotesquely. "A *concentrated* dose, mind you! If you fools hadn't respirated him, who knows how far the damage would have spread! Why, it's already paralyzed his motor neurons and speech center!" She seemed to be making herself angrier as she ranted. "Look," she screeched. "Just *look* at him! He can't move or talk! How's he going to rescue his crew now?"

Without warning, a strange look came over her face. "Oh, *blast* it! *Another* one!" As Duron and the elders exchanged knowing looks, she began to choke pitifully and fell backward, screaming maniacally and foaming at the mouth. Elena grimaced in recognition. She'd seen it many times before: with the disturbed electrical rhythms and convulsions, the grand-mal seizure had all the earmarks of advanced epilepsy. She took a step forward to help.

Just as suddenly, the convulsing stopped. Roson raised her head, muttering and smoothing out her robes. "*You*! All of you just *stand* there, *looking* at me! You're *all* in cahoots!" She spun around on her seat to point at Adam through the oval window. "It was *his* grandfather! That old man started it all! He sweet-talked his way into my life and then left! Poof!! Gone! Just like that! I never wanted to see another one of you aliens again as long as I live!" Suddenly, her eyes riveted on something. She scrambled off her barge and scrambled on her hands and knees to pick it up from the floor. Pulling up the hem of her robe, she determinedly repinned yet another piece of what looked like….

Elena discreetly leaned closer. Yes, it was: a piece of thin metallic gold foil, wrapped around scraps of a cardboardlike material. There was a sudden, sharp nudge to her ribs. Duron had caught her inquisitive gaze and was shaking his head in emphatic alarm. She pulled back.

The crone floated over to the windowsill, guzzled something from a decanter, coughed a moment and then raged on, sarcasm in her tone. "*Take* your medicine, *take* your medicine, they say! I *still* don't feel any different! I'm hurt, I tell you, I'm hurt. We were friends, or so … I thought." She was calming down. "The Rasheen will fix it. You won't die." She suddenly slumped, exhausted, and rolled off her small barge onto a sculpted contour chair. Sensing her weight it hummed to life, lowering her into a more horizontal plane.

Elena's knees had turned to jelly. She looked forlornly at Duron.

"She will be out for a while," he whispered, shrugging apologetically.

"Tell me," she muttered. "What in the world did this witch just *do* to Adam?"

"Oh, the, ah, *device* she put him into?"

"Yes. Everything. The iron lung, the needles, her decanter, the...."

"It is a Neuron Resuscitation Chamber. I believe it is one of her best efforts. She is an odd one, yes, but a genius. She knows that although your husband has suffered a severe neural shock, he is a mere infant by our Bandor standards and therefore his mind has extraordinary regenerative powers."

Elena narrowed her eyes. "I'm sorry, but all this just doesn't wash," she stated, flatly. "While we're just standing around, my husband is dying in that-that *thing* over there!" Her finger waved in the air. "And tell me!" She spun around to confront the group. "Speaking about *things*, what were all those things I saw pinned under the witch's robes, hmm?"

With a deep sigh, the tall Bandor crept up quietly to the old crone and unpinned one of her handmade contraptions. As he lifted it up to the fading light in the great Western window, the crinkled foil sent tiny, mirrored spots dancing around the room. "Shields? Reflectors? Maybe they ward off alien death rays or evil spirits? Who knows? We do not mention them around her anymore; she is definitely losing control. Her powers of reasoning have been damaged." He turned to Elena. "Please forgive her?"

She looked down, chagrined. "I-I'm sorry, Duron, I had no idea." A thought crossed her mind and she looked up brightly. "Her medicine seemed to work quickly! What was in it?"

"The concentrated Rasheen mixture *is* quick," he affirmed.

There was a loud sneeze behind them. As they turned, Roson stirred and lifted her head. "Ahhh, *there* you are!" she rasped, groggily. "Elena, you're finally here! They've kept me alive all these years to prophesy about you! You're the one who'll be taking my place!"

Elena's eyes grew round with shock. The ancient one's few words had hit powerfully. "W-what?" She stumbled. "P-prophesy about *me*? Are you...."

"Yes." The contour chair rose with a quiet hum. "I'm the prophetess who had the visions concerning you. I've waited for hundreds of years for you to arrive!"

"Hundreds? But, but...."

"Hush, child." The woman turn to glare at Duron and the elders, motioning impatiently with her head toward the exit. They nodded politely, backed up awkwardly as a unit into the elevator, and departed.

She leaned toward Elena. "I had my mind-shields up," she confided. "Now, I must explain something to you in a way you might understand. Listen closely." Her voice became barely audible. "I've found a way to conquer the relative concepts of time and distance. Understand? I've been able to watch both of you young people since childhood!" She leaned back, a pleased look on her face.

Elena's eyes widened. "Huh?" She glanced in the direction of the Neuron Resuscitator. "Both of us? You mean Adam and me? But, h-how?"

"You still haven't put it together, have you? You must know by now that your long sleep, a mere seven years to your suspended, frozen body, was in reality seven *hundred* actual years. As you hurtled through space toward us, you simply slept."

"Yes, but ... we slept? Now really."

"Oh well, hibernated. We extracted blood serum from a small mammal called the Orcan in the Forti Nebula. Orcans exist on an icy planet that travels in an extremely elliptical orbit around its sun, so they have evolved a spectacularly long period of hibernation. The Bitrons found a way to synthesize the serum in large volumes for their sleep pods. In truth, your long voyage was not what one would call 'time travel.' It actually took every one of those seven hundred years to get here!" She looked up. "Have you figured it out yet? Seven *hundred* years? Now think of what that means and all its implications!"

Elena gulped. "I know. I'm really seven hundred and twenty years old and all the people I knew back on Earth aren't even memories anymore. Right?"

The cloudy, ringed eyes closed to a slit. "Correct," she breathed. "Specifically relating to your case, memories just as soon forgotten. I've seen similar unfortunate memories and unnecessary melodramas being replayed every day, all over the universe. In countless other inhabited worlds out there, there are many variations on the theme of your life." As Elena stared at her open-mouthed, Roson locked level gazes with her. "This is woman to woman now. Straight talk. Don't be afraid, I'm in my right mind … for now." Smoothing out a crease in her robe, she began.

"At his grandfather's request, I began to monitor Adam's surprisingly efficient progress in forming this mission. He was sitting at his desk one day, reading your resume. As you walked in, my attention immediately turned to you and then to your mind. You seemed to be holding back most of your past as you answered him. You didn't want to tell him everything."

Elena started to interrupt. "No *way*! There's…."

Roson held up a finger. "Wait, let me finish. As he asked you routine questions about your history and schooling, you filled in a lot of missing gaps with your silent thoughts, right? Am I right?"

"Ah…." She was listening, but her mind was reeling. "Right."

"He asked you where you were born. Now listen and believe me as to what I'm about to say. At that very moment, through the eyes of your own memory, I watched your father abandon your mother in that tiny, dirt-floored shack in the woods. Why, it was nothing but a chicken coop! While he ran off to join the merchant marine, you slept in the top bureau drawer and your twin brother in the one below you. Your mother didn't have enough money to buy a crib, is that right?"

Elena was truly frightened. Her wide eyes answered mutely.

"When Adam asked you where you went to school, it triggered another thought. I saw your mother buying you secondhand clothes from that rich doctor up the street. When you went out to recess, the doctor's daughter sneered at you in front of all her friends, saying, 'I used to wear that dress and I *hated* it!'"

Elena was almost beyond words. "Y-you simply *couldn't* know that! You…."

"Ah, but I *do*," the ancient one nodded solemnly. "You know, Elena, I have to admire your mother; she was a clever woman. She saved every scrap, every coin laid across her palm and began to build: First, a real wooden floor for her shack, then a new window and then land. She bought a piece of land from one neighbor, then more land around that and then more. Always building, expanding, building."

Elena stood up indignantly, hot tears brimming in her eyes. "Stop it! You have no right!"

As she turned toward the elevator the crone clawed at her sleeve, catching it with her long fingernails.

"When Adam asked you about college, your mind played out another scene! Your mother had eventually amassed a small fortune in real estate along that old drainage canal, right? Land that nobody else wanted? She sold it all to that plastics company and netted enough money to send you through college! Had enough yet? Have I proven myself sufficiently?"

"Nobody, absolutely *nobody* knows about my past," she sniffed, pulling her arm away. "Especially not Adam! God knows I've tried to forget about it myself!"

"Ah, yes, you've had quite a troubled childhood, Elena. You came out of darkness and turmoil seeking peace, but the only peace and companionship you found was the simple, friendly one-to-one interaction with your video learning set. That's why you excelled in your schooling. Yes, you're exactly like your soul mate, Adam. You were a loner and knowledge became your only friend."

Her heart was pounding. In mere minutes, this woman seemed to have summarized her entire life, pinpointing that elusive common ground that had been there all along: her reason for loving Adam so deeply. Yes, it was true. They were both loners, both hurt and searching for someone to love. It was only by a miracle that they'd found each other. She slumped into a chair, all the fight leaving her. After a moment, she sat up and determinedly dried her eyes. "Sorry I mistrusted you, Roson. If you say Adam will live, I believe you."

"Good. Now while he's busy, ah, cooking, let's get right to the point. My ability to prophesy and how I actually *do* it? I know you're bursting to find out."

"Ah, yes, I guess. On to the point."

"Thoughts," Roson mused, absently tapping her small chin, "are simply stored electrical impulses in continually modified transit. These impulses are immeasurably small to be sure, but still electrical impulses and so *can* be detected. Electroencephalograms, right? You're a doctor, you should know about all those obsolete Earth contraptions."

"Trash." Elena nodded. "You have *far* superior methods."

"Good. Now I'll branch away for a moment and this gets tricky: whereas electrical impulses are indeed *real*, thoughts are supposedly *imagined*." She laid a bony finger across Elena's forehead. "Take that piece of equipment inside there, for example. It's nearly identical to mine, but somehow I've been able to cross mysterious, unknown boundaries with my so-called psychic ability." Suddenly, she paused to strike an unexpected profile in the window, her odd shape silhouetted against the darkening sky.

"Have you noticed our heads?" At Elena's stunned silence, Roson whooped it up delightedly, slapping her bony knees. "Oh, my! How could you have *helped* but to notice?" She snorted, drying the corners of her bloodshot eyes. "Yes, with the aid of the Rasheen, both our brains and bones...."

"Your *bones*, too??"

"Oh, yes. Our bones. They've both become radically altered into ultrasensitive receptors for electrical impulses."

Elena studied her head more closely. "Your brain's a receptor?"

"Yes." Roson glanced nervously in the direction of the elevator and then leaned forward conspiratorially. "They don't know this, but my so-called prophesy is mere trickery," she whispered. "I'm a *fake*, a *sham*!"

"But you told the *truth* about me; you knew my past...."

"Let me explain it this way," she interrupted. Turning in her recliner to face the window, she pointed to the ever-present golden haze on the dark horizon. "The gold shields around our planet are far, far older than I. Experimenting with them extensively, I've found them to be extremely flexible and sensitive to electrical impulses." The ancient one sighed, closing her eyes. "On clear, still nights like this, I still go up on my roof to control the gold particles with my mind. I can form them into an enormous, ultrasmooth parabolic depression over my island, maybe twenty miles across. By tweaking the shape of the curve, I can focus the incoming electrical impulses upward to a satellite parked in a geosynchronous orbit about two hundred Earth miles above my island. It amplifies the faint incoming signals by a nearly limitless factor."

She raised her sled and floated slowly toward the huge window. As the first evening stars blazed brilliantly in front of her, she breathed deeply of the cool evening air. "Your Earth is well within range of my secret receptor, child." A tired, faraway look came into her eyes as she gazed into the heavens.

"But how did you go *forward* in time for your, ah, prophecy?"

"I'm getting to that," she sighed. "That night it was more difficult. I'd decided to form a double parabola. It was the most complex receptor I'd ever put together, maybe a hundred miles across. A whopper."

Elena looked puzzled. "Wow, why a double parabola? You mean a small one inverted over a larger one, right?

"Yes," she agreed. "It greatly amplified the focus. It took over an hour to construct and sapped nearly every shred of my energy. The resulting secondary focus beamed down through a hole at the bottom, directly onto my head."

Elena gave a start. "No, *no*! Onto your head? What about your satellite?"

"Remember, girl, both my skull and brain contain gold, as a direct result of ingesting Rasheen! It makes an excellent conductor! As I probed, I saw something completely different. I-I struggled with my last ounces of strength to fine-tune the image...." She stopped to catch her breath and began to moan, swaying back and forth. "There was this burning, fiery agony! It felt like my mind was being ripped apart! I watched the very fabric of time beginning to tear like a gossamer cloth and dissipate into nothingness! I was gazing down what seemed to be a tunnel into Aurona's future! The vision lasted for only a few moments, then skipped like a stone over the water to about twenty years beyond that." Shaking uncontrollably, she grasped the windowsill for support.

"What I saw still frightens me beyond imagination," she whispered. "In that first, fleeting glimpse, I was looking into a mirror. I-I saw...*me*. I saw my own death, Elena, coming a few years after your arrival. This ancient body had passed away in its sleep." Her eyes slowly closed. "My lapses are becoming more severe, more uncontrollable and closer together, despite all the medicine they give me. In fact, I feel the effects beginning to wear off even as we speak! I guess my unthinkable age has finally caught up with me."

Elena's heart felt like it was about to burst. She quickly leaned forward to slip her arms around the frail shoulders and give her a long hug. "I think you're great, Roson. I'm amazed that I've had the privilege to meet you."

The old one opened her eyes and smiled wanly. "Thank you, my dear. So are you curious about the second part, the one about the skipping stone? This vision was about you, but a very different you, some twenty years from now. In that day, surprisingly, you will look very much like me in my youth. Your features will alter radically." She spun toward Elena. "Of course! My mind's playing tricks again! I've lived your life so long, I feel that you're me and I'm *you*!"

"Twins!" Elena laughed.

"Soul sisters!" the woman beamed.

"Soul sis…" Elena drew back, searching the dim eyes. "Where'd you get *that* from? And what did you mean a few minutes ago when you said you were hurt and you thought someone was your friend?"

"I said *that*?" Roson looked frightened for a moment. "Oh well, I guess out of the heart, the mouth speaks…."

"And *that*, too," Elena pointed, cutting her off abruptly. "That's *definitely* not a Bandor quotation!"

The old woman looked trapped. With one exception, no one had ever dared come this close. With a sigh of surrender, she sagged and released her clenched fists.

"Yes, child, my very thoughts and patterns of speech are quite new. They-They came from Adam's grandfather. I lived with him for many years. He arrived unexpectedly in a small starship that our ancestors had concealed on Earth. He had a holographic star map with him from one of our outposts."

"Yes, Adam told me all about the Galaxy Room."

"I sent out a telepathic mind-message to him when he arrived and just like Adam, we conversed in our runic language through opposite sides of our shields. The elders didn't want him in. They left him out there for nearly a month, can you imagine that? We became long-distance friends and soon began laughing together. I found him to be a brilliant, eloquent man and decided to smuggle him in because I grew to-to…."

"To what, Roson?" Elena pressed, gently.

"To love him." A sudden tic appeared in the corner of her eye and her countenance changed. She leaned dangerously far out of the window to shake her fist defiantly at the sky. "I *warped* those shields!" she screeched. "Ha, *ha*! I twisted a hole right through them with my mind! They couldn't figure it out! He was out there one minute and gone the next! Poof! He put on his cloaking device and landed upstairs on my roof."

"Wow." Elena patted her arm. "So Adam's grandfather lived down here?"

"With me," she affirmed, spinning around and calming herself. "No hanky-panky I assure you, just best friends," she grinned shyly. "Night after night we'd read our respective classics together, he from his Amorphous BubbleChips, me from my Memory Cubes. By the way, child, have you noticed that I'm *not* wearing a translator button? Ha! I don't *need* it! We wrote the Bandor-English translation together!"

Elena was grinning broadly. "You *did*? This is getting more interesting by the second! And classics, you say? Hmm, I assume that's why you know our idioms and quotations so well?"

"Yes," Roson answered absently. She was staring out the window. "Look, Elena!" She whispered excitedly. As Elena's gaze followed the ancient one's trembling, bony finger toward the horizon, the sight took her breath away.

Glowing like two orbs of molten fire and looking like dividing cells, twin moons parted from their dancing reflections in the dark, glassy sea and began to rise slowly, majestically into the starry vault.

"That one's Mazan," she whispered, "and the smaller one's Eonia. Adam's grandfather loved to stand right here," she sighed, "next to me. We stopped whatever project we were on and hurried over to this very window just to see our moons come up. Sometimes we'd wait for hours up on the roof to see who'd catch the first glimpse. We were together, always together, for years...." A look of pain suddenly shadowed her failing eyes. "And then it started. He expanded my lab downstairs and began tinkering on his inventions for months at a time with my Bitron friends. He astounded even *them*, Elena! A mind like his comes along only once in a million years! Well, with all the activity and with all the Bitron starships coming and going, my island began to be, ah, shall we say, *noticed*. The elders came into this very room to question me. I confessed that he was here and begged to let him stay. Well, we were right in the middle of arguing over him when he walked in, speaking perfect Bandorese and cracking jokes!"

Elena suddenly realized she'd stumbled onto a love affair that was never meant to be. This ancient creature was a loner, too. Either by chance or choice, she'd never allowed a living soul to approach her, let alone feel a man's embrace. She shook her head. So it had finally taken an alien, Adam's grandfather, to bridge this impossible chasm; his sparkling wit had evidently swept her off her feet. Roson had found someone in the closing chapters of her life and she'd meant to keep him. Elena understood. Woman to woman, she understood. She stared at the ancient one in a whole, new light.

Roson's shadow of pain was shading toward anger. "He's *gone*, now, child! Just vanished! No explanation, nothing! They tell me he's dead, but I don't believe them! They say Adam went to his funeral, but I don't believe them! They say...."

A loud chime sounded. She spun around, cowering. Her strained composure was now dissolving into confusion. "What? *What?*" The last, lingering effects of the medicine had worn off. She whisked over to the resuscitator and began struggling with the latches, banging her bony fists on the door and yanking the handle in frustration. "Don't just *stand* there, girl, help me get Adam *out* of this contraption," she shrilled. "Move it! I don't know why the Bitrons insisted on making the blasted door so heavy, I'm the only one on the planet that knows how to *use* it!"

Elena pulled with all her strength. There was a slight give, followed by a puff of air and the unmistakable odor of burnt hair. As the massive door swung open, she bent over hesitantly to look inside. Adam was sitting there, looking straight at her.

Taking a shallow breath, he gestured awkwardly in the air with his crippled hands. "Sweetpea?" he ventured softly. "Elena, I-I'm sorry."

The long ordeal had taken its toll. Breaking down, she wept openly.

Hand in hand, they stood together on top of the island's high plateau, taking in the sweeping vista. The morning breeze had brought thousands of long-tailed seabirds from the east and they fed noisily in the rich, upwelling currents. At Roson's insistence, Adam had remained in the Neuron Resuscitation Chamber at low power for the duration of the night to give him time to recover from his deep shock. She knew that as his strength returned, his memory would soon follow.

As he gazed at her in the sunlight, his eyes suddenly squeezed shut. "Oh, no!" he groaned, rocking back on his heels. True to Roson's word, the floodgates had burst open and recent memories were rushing back.

She grabbed his arm. "Adam, what is it?"

Unflinching, he stared straight ahead. His eyes were desperately trying to focus beyond the shimmering force field, beyond the great, wheeling, clamoring flocks to the uncluttered horizon. "So what happened, Elena?" he whispered haltingly. "To Jon? To Todd? To the crew and our beautiful city, Prima?"

She let out a long breath. She'd been expecting this moment and dreading it. As gently as she could, she filled him in and then stood patiently by his side.

He lowered his head, his eyes brimming with tears. In a moment he looked up decisively and smiled. Taking her by the hand, he nodded toward an elevator well near the edge of the cliff. After a short ride down, the door opened silently onto a small terrace near the top of the atrium. They stepped out to look over the smoothly sculpted chalk railing.

"There she is," Adam whispered. "She looks happy, doesn't she?"

Elena smiled distractedly, following his gaze. Way down below them, a tiny figure was digging in the soil, planting yet another bank of orchidlike flowers. She worked determinedly, steadily, pausing now and then to catch her breath.

"Adam?" She leaned against her husband, simply glad to have him back.

"Yes, hon?"

"I'm–I'm afraid. Don't get me wrong: I'm thrilled you're alive, but...."

"But what?"

She bit her lip. "What're we going to *do*?"

He sighed. "I've already done it," he muttered. "While we were up on the roof, I sent a mind-message to Duron. He and the Elders slept the whole night downstairs in one of the guest rooms. I-I just hope my range has improved to more than fifty feet. I asked him to come up and meet us on this balcony in a few minutes. We're going to leave with some Bandor security forces as soon as we can to go back and evacuate Prima. The remaining crew has to clear out of the city immediately."

She grabbed his sleeve. "No! You can't mean that!"

"Yes," he nodded, "I do, every word. Look, it's only logical: Prima is out in the open, and the crew members are sitting ducks! It's far safer for everyone to move underground into some kind of shelter, like one of the Bandor cities."

Her tears started to well up. "But we worked so hard to build that place, Adam, all of us! It was beautiful! It was an abstract sculpture! It was … *home*!"

"I know, I know! And we only got to sleep in our new quarters for *one night*! But all that stuff is just 'stuff' and can easily be replaced! Listen," he said firmly, turning to her. "When our crew actually *sees* us and knows we're alive, I'm positive it'll encourage them. They must be thinking I was dead after I was zapped at point blank by that Razah." His countenance darkened. "On the other hand, those stinkin' outlaws have taken a lot of our crew as hostage to God knows where. The shields and cloaking device on our starship are engaged and nobody has a clue where they are."

She was trembling. "Do you have a plan?"

He sighed deeply. "Don't worry, Elena, plans formulate and evolve on the fly. I'm a lot different now, hon, somehow extremely aware. It could be a synergy of the Razah's jolt and a lot of extra time baking in the Neuron Resuscitation Chamber…."

"Baking, Adam? Now really."

He grinned. "Hey, whatever happened inside that contraption, it seems to have accelerated the long-term effects of the Rasheen in my brain. Somehow I can see 'the big picture': it's kind of an aerial shot of the whole situation. So, looking down from this new perspective, there's something extremely important we have to do right now."

"What?" She wiped the tears from her face.

He lifted her chin and gazed deeply into her eyes. "After we encourage our crew, we gotta come right back here to this island and see Roson again. This whole unfortunate turn of events has put a huge dent in my plans. Now that I can, ah, 'see' things more clearly, there are some gut feelings and educated guesses I need to explore in depth. One of them is vital and a key to locating and rescuing the hostages. It just can't wait! Roson's our only hope, the only one with any real answers!"

Elena lowered her eyes. "I-I don't know how to tell you this…."

"Tell me," he interrupted. "I think I can take anything now."

"Roson's going to die, Adam. She told me. In only a few years."

He reflected a moment. "Well, we're *all* going to die someday…."

"No, she's just been waiting for us to *get* here!"

He squeezed his eyes shut, his fingernails biting into the chalk railing. After a moment, he lifted his head to look around. "Well, she just *can't* go! What's gonna happen to this island, to this beautiful atrium? The whole place is gonna go to pot real fast without *her* here! It's her life! It's her home! She…."

Elena cupped her small hand over his mouth. "Shh," she whispered, pointing discreetly over the edge of the railing, "those old ears are still pretty sharp. She'll hear you! And remember, all that stuff is just *stuff*." She motioned downward with her eyes. "They're almost done with her speed tubes, Adam. They're coming up right over there!" She stood on her toes to point to a spot near the base of the Motherlode tree.

"What are you trying to say?" He glanced at her out of the corner of his eye.

"You may have figured it out already, but I'll take a chance and give it to you straight: in a strange way, we're Roson's, ah, only children, so when she goes, this place, this island, will be...."

He caught his breath. "No *way*!"

Once more, she pressed her fingers to his lips. "Shh! Don't argue," she whispered, "it's all settled! It's in her will! She wrote it down five hundred years ago!"

There was a loud thump behind them. They spun around to see Duron stumble out of the elevator. His dark eyes widened in relief. "So *here* you are! I have been trying to figure out which balcony you were on," he slit-smiled. "By the way, Adam, your range has improved and dramatically so. I was down on the beach outside when you were up on the roof!" He beamed like a proud father. "As you have requested, we will now make all necessary arrangements to accompany you with our security forces to Prima. When you return, you and Roson can work together on the details of your upcoming mission...."

"Whoa, whoa!" Elena stopped them both short. "Ah, *what* 'mission,' Adam?"

"It's okay, hon," he reassured. "Our first stop is definitely Prima. Really."

"What *kind* of mission?" she persisted. "Are you sure you're up to this?"

He held up a hand. "Yes, I'm fine. And I won't be alone: You'll be with me."

She opened her mouth to speak, thought a moment, and then pressed against him. "Whatever you say, I'll do; I'm with you all the way. I-I'm not losing you again."

Duron was beaming. "The elders agree, Adam. I must admire your sound decisions: your people will indeed be safer underground with us; in fact, I will personally take charge of their evacuation and Prima's salvage operation." He looked up with a start. "I must hurry now! The Elders are waiting for us down on the beach. The security forces have been mobilized and the SeaSpheres are forming even as we speak!" Distractedly, he hustled into the elevator. "Come down as soon as you can, both of you. Maybe I can...." The sound of his voice was cut off as the elevator door closed.

Out of nowhere, a mind-message suddenly flooded Adam's consciousness with stunning visual scenes and a running, runic narrative. A continent away, near the edge of what was left of the once-vast desert of Arrix, a Bandor worker had just discovered an enormous, jumbled pile of goods that had been dumped out of the stolen starship. He threw aside the Motherlode sapling he'd been planting at edge of the expanding rainforest. Hastily taking off his coolant gloves and rebreather unit, he planted his feet firmly in the grass and pressed his fingers to his temples to announce his find.

Duron stumbled back off the elevator, wide-eyed. "So *soon*?"
Adam turned to him, equally excited. "Yes! *Incredible*, Duron!"
"They just dumped out everything?... Everything?"
"I guess anything that wasn't nailed down. The stuff took up too much room."
"But the pods, too?"

Elena pulled slowly away from them. Right out of the blue, they'd started talking in some sort of code. She glanced back and forth, trying to piece their cryptic conversation together.

"All but twenty!"

"Twenty sleep pods? But why?"

"Think a minute."

Duron pondered. A light dawned. "Ah, more room for the *gold*! *Then* they go!"

Adam smiled. "Correct. But then, there's…."

"Guys, guys! *Stop*!" She'd had enough. Inserting her small body between them, she tugged on Adam's sleeve. "Tell me, *what* gold? What're you talking about?"

Adam glanced at Duron, shrugged, then filled her in. As the story about the serendipitous find tumbled out, her mouth sagged.

"So *now* what?" she pressed.

Duron slit-smiled. "We simply amend our original plan, Elena. Even as we speak, my people have a large fleet of SpeedSleds and salvage barges on the way to the scene in Arrix to recover all the goods. I have given the order." He turned his eyes toward Adam. "Ah, when you finally come back to this island, do not forget to ask Roson for two of her newest models of the SeaSpheres. They have been greatly improved with some kind of probe accelerator. And please remember, she may not be in the best of condition."

"My wife knows her, Duron." Adam shrugged lamely. "They're, ah, friends. Elena can help me if things get out of hand. We'll just have to take the chance."

Chapter 27: EVACUATION

Down on Prima's fan-shaped wharf, some of the remaining crew had hastily transformed the entry foyer into a hospital. Several figures moved about quickly, purposefully, completely focused on the urgent task at hand. They'd modified bits and pieces of medical equipment that had been confiscated from Elena's research labs, and long tubes now stretched between Kron and Peter to connect their circulatory systems. Only with the aid of a direct transfusion could he hope to survive.

Shortly, Kron began to stir. As Joelle slid a respirator from his throat and propped his head up on a pillow, his eyes opened a slit. She bent bent over him to change his dressings, busily snipping and peeling away the dark, blood-encrusted wrappings and letting them fall in a stiff pile to the floor. Todd watched Joelle in fascination, his almond eyes following her movements, his small hands mirroring hers in the air. He was snipping too, adding his imaginary bandages to the pile.

"Hi, everyone," Kron whispered weakly. "Sorry about the mess."

As Tola pulled his chair closer, a very excited Todd hopped onto his lap. "Mess? What mess?" He thumped Kron on his arm. "The only mess I see is *you*, buddy!"

Kron reddened and quickly turned his face away to gaze out of the huge front window. "I-I'm sorry, but I just couldn't stop 'em!"

"C'mon, man. It's not your fault. You were ambushed and overpowered!"

Kron's disjointed memories suddenly fell into place. "So where's Adam?"

There it was: the question was out, and they glanced nervously at each other. Tola coughed. "Ah, well, the last time we saw him, he was still breathing."

Kron's eyes widened in alarm. "What happ…?"

"Whoa, settle down." Tola pushed him back against his pillow. "It was a Razah, not a bullet. We were following him and Elena back from Meseo, but he'd turned on his Advanced Autopilot and was way ahead of us. Then this Razah came out of nowhere. Adam was trying to save Todd when he dropped his Stifler and everything backfired. Your little Todd here blasted the Razah and threw him off-target just before the beast winged Elena with a stun, and…."

"Whoa, whoa," he interrupted. "So where are they now?"

Tola shrugged. "To tell you the truth, we don't know. Duron and the elders took them both away. They mentioned something about an island."

"Crud," Kron fretted. "So all our leaders are who knows where, and I'm knocked for a loop? This is great. You know, I suspected they were here all along…."

"They?" Peter interrupted. "There's someone else? Who do you mean?"

Joelle glanced over her shoulder. "Dexor and his three stooges, who else?"

Kron shook his head. "No, no! They're just small-time wannabes. I saw a lot of *other* weird faces, aliens that I'd never seen before! Their leader was really ugly, a scarred dude with this huge hood, griping and whining something about a 'long trip.'"

Peter pulled back, alarmed. "What? Nobody else came with us to Aurona, unless…."

"You're puttin' it together, man," Kron rasped. *"We had a stowaway!* That hooded guy was on the ship with us for seven hundred years! Believe it or not, I think Dexor and his gang may have brought him aboard."

"No *way*!" Peter sat up, yanking strips of tape from his arm.

"Yes way," he returned. "Remember all the confusion in that old warehouse on the morning we left Earth? I'm sure that's when those goons snuck him aboard!"

Peter swung his legs to the floor. "So what did you *see* this morning?"

Kron grimaced in pain as he pushed himself into a more upright position. "Well, I heard these banging noises coming from Adam's commander's quarters and started running down the East hall," he scowled. "Someone was boasting his head off, and when I came around the corner, they just started pouring out of the door and yelling. Before I could say a word, someone popped me! I-I must've had no pulse when they checked or they'd have finished me off right then and there!"

Joelle pointed out the window. "I heard this crackling noise and then saw our ship take off," she stated matter-of-factly. "They engaged the cloaking device, too."

"That's right," Peter affirmed. "Poof…. *Gone*!"

Kron clutched his chest. "But-but Adam and I are the only ones who know how to work those controls! Do you know what that means? They got the holodiscs, too! They know how to run everything! *Everything*!" As he lay there moaning, a concerned Todd reached out and laid his small hand on his arm.

Tola had been quietly contemplating. "The Bandors said the same thing down in Meseo, so our stories line up. Now let's be objective and think like Adam. He thinks differently… no, *way* differently than most of us. What would he do here?"

Joelle dropped her laser scissors with a clatter. "Well, I don't know what he'd *do*, but I'm sure how he'd *feel*! Hurt! Betrayed! *Deeply* betrayed, like all of us!"

"Amen to that," Tola nodded. "But he wouldn't let his feelings stand in the way of clear thinking, would he? Let's assume those creeps had no serious weapons aboard, just small stuff like rifles, handguns, and Stiflers." He tapped on Kron's chest. "They *did* commission a bullet for that job, right?"

"Yeah," Kron returned, hesitantly, "so what are you driving at?"

"We got one big thing in our favor: they dropped our only crate of Stifler rechargers in all the confusion. It was lying on its side near the communications tower, and it looked like it was still full!"

"Wow!" Kron brightened. "Hallelujah! They've got no juice!"

Tola shrugged. "But the creeps still have the big advantages, though: one, our cloaked starship, and two, about a hundred hostages! They can land completely undetected anywhere on the planet and force our friends into slave labor!"

Peter moaned. "And they took Ariel, too! They're unstoppable! If they're spotted, they can literally disappear!"

There were some banging sounds and a lot of rustling behind them. They turned to see Joelle off in a corner helping a few women sort through rumpled piles of clothing and debris. As they paused to peer out forlornly into the empty courtyard, Todd busily kept up the pace, randomly making piles of his own.

Tola hiked Kron's blankets back up over his chest. "The women are right: the best thing we can do is to follow Joelle's example and salvage what we've got left."

Joelle glanced up, scowling. "Just *look* at this mess! Why'd they have to pull everything out of Elena's closet and dump it out here? There are some lacy items a girl just ... *needs*!"

Kron raised a brow. "Well," he grinned, "don't give up, Joelle, we all may still get our, ah, things back. Anything's possible here, anything."

Todd raised his small voice. "*An-ting*!" he echoed.

Peter chuckled. "I'll vouch for *that*!"

Joelle stood on her toes, wiping the inside of a blackened window with a piece of torn clothing. "So what's next, guys? You three seem to be putting this puzzle together faster than any of us. It's up to you, and...."

"Hey, what's that sound?" Peter interrupted, cocking an ear. As a clamor of shouts arose from the pier, he ran over to the front window. "They're *here*! Adam and Elena are climbing out of ... huh? What kind of weird contraption is that? A bubble? This lake connects to the ocean? And- and look on the horizon! A whole lot of Bandors are coming toward us, and they've got a fleet of starships exactly like ours!"

Five titanic saucers were skimming toward them over the surface of the lake, their blue lasers fanning out and penetrating the surface of the water to the lakebed to establish their positions in the air. They stopped as a unit and hovered noiselessly, then one pulled away and touched down smoothly on the shoreline.

"Adam's back? Starships?" Kron reached out feebly. "Lemme see...." As Joelle wheeled his bed to the window, Todd excitedly hopped aboard.

Peter's focus returned to the bubble. "Wow, it's ... *gone*! What *was* that shiny thing?" he said, pointing. "The outside just dissolved and the gold blew away in the wind! All that's left is some kind of disc and a black box!"

As the group poised to run, Kron called out weakly, trying his best to appear controlled. "Keep me posted...." Forlornly, he watched them scoot out the door. Todd wasn't interested at all; he sat ensconced on the foot of Kron's bed, eyeing his bandages and comparing them to his own.

Kron held out his arms with a lopsided grin. "C'mere, you little squirt!"

"Who, *me*?" Peter twirled around, a finger poised on the face of his wrist programmer. "Just kidding, man," he said, laughing. "Hey, I'll shoot you a text!"

A sea of white-robed Bandors flowed out of the saucer into the city, mingling with the remaining slate blue-uniformed crewmembers. Side by side they poked as a team through the rubble, shooing away Aeronautas and stripping Prima of equipment and people. Soon it resembled a ghost town, gaunt and lifeless in the sun.

It didn't take long for Kron to get his text. Peter's dictated words scrolled by: "Hey, you! We've just been informed that we're going underground! Duron's in charge. See you shortly...." The message was hardly off his screen when the old one was at the door, slit-smiling. As he stepped aside and waved an arm, Adam and Elena entered right on his heels with the crew pouring in behind them.

The best of the Bandor physicians were waiting for Kron in one of their starship's hospital bays, instruments in hand and translator buttons activated. Wasting no time, they quickly lowered an arched rectangular frame of intricately woven gold wires over his chest. There was a large opening in the middle.

Kron raised his head off his pillow. "What's this?" he whispered, nervously eyeing the contraption. "You left room to, ah ... *cut*?" Seeing Joelle and Todd lingering outside the door, he leaned aside and gave her a subtle shooing motion.

Duron nervously turned to Joelle and repeated Kron's gesture. "Sorry, Joelle, it *is* best that the little one does not see."

A Bandor doctor activated the display. As he tapped a row of virtual buttons, ghostly, out-of-focus images began to float in the middle of the rectangle. In an odd way, they seemed almost abstract and organic in form, yet disturbingly familiar.

Kron bit his lip, watching the doctor's long, slender fingers play like an artist over the impossibly complex controls near his elbow. As the blurred forms slowly coalesced into solid shapes, his eyes riveted in shock on the moving mass of tissue that made up his inner body. "M-my guts!"

Peter's eyes widened. "Whoa! Gross, man!" he gagged. Pale as a ghost, he backed toward the curved wall, his hands feeling behind him for the open doorway.

Kron's organs floated in three dimensions inside the rectangle, gleaming wet, pulsing and stripped of flesh. The connecting veins and arteries rhythmically pushed their respective cargoes of bluish or reddish blood in sync with his heart, just visible under the ghostly edge of a translucent sternum.

Peter had finally found the door. "Pardon me, excuse me, excuse me, everyone, I...." Gagging, he flew into the hallway.

Elena was totally overwhelmed. She lifted a finger in the air and then let her hand drop back to her side. "That is... that's just... amazing. Wow. I wish we had this instrument back at Biozyne."

As the circle of bald heads nodded profoundly, the lead physician explained. "This is only the beginning, Elena. VitaView's main screen represents the overall picture. We can now isolate any organ and inspect it separately as well. Watch!" With a click, Kron's heart appeared, floating in space. It was robust, pumping powerfully.

Adam stepped forward, leaning first to one side and then the other. "Well, I'll be," he muttered, tongue-in-cheek. "They *missed*, Kron!"

The doctor slit-smiled, his finger poised over another button. "But not by much, Adam. Here is the metallic invader, in relation to his heart!" A gleaming cone appeared, mere millimeters to the right. The bullet!

Duron leaned into the circle with concern in his dark eyes. "Quickly, Ranod! Pulmonary and then circulatory. Fenet needs to assess the damage." He turned to the group and introduced the two as Ranod tapped the controls. "Fenet is our circulatory expert and Ranod our VitaView specialist. The best we have."

A fantastic web of blood vessels now surrounded the pumping heart and gleaming bullet. Like a star's exploding gaseous jet, a trail of plasmatic ooze clearly traced its path of entry, clouding the gel-like open spaces between. Obviously, several veins and one minor artery had been severed along the way.

As Peter poked his head in the door, his timing couldn't have been worse: a bloody, gory view now filled the screen. Choking, his cheeks puffing out, he spun on his heel and ran down the hallway. Todd hid behind Joelle, trying to block his ears from the awful retching sounds.

Fenet wasted no time. "I am ready. Prepare yourself, Kron; here is the anesthetic." As soon as he touched a probe gently against Kron's forehead, his eyes clouded and went blank. The Bandor was inside Kron's chest immediately, snaking a rubbery grasper along the cloudy path. In moments the bullet was out. He followed up immediately with a multi-tipped, nanorobotic manipulator arm, snipping, sucking, suturing and patching his way backward. He was indeed skilled at his profession; his slender fingers were a blur, the nanorobotic arm but a sensitive extension of his fingertips. The path of destruction slowly closed as the arm worked backward and then it, too, was out. He glued the surface of the wound together with a clear, flesh-colored dressing, then picked up a plain-looking applicator bottle and daubed it with the tip.

Adam rubbed his eyes. "What the...?" Incredibly, the puncture wound had already taken on a pinkish color, shading toward flesh tones around its perimeter. "It-it's already *healing*? No way! What's *in* that bottle anyway?"

Fenet tossed it to him. "Growth accelerator, Adam. Hyper Stemcells from living cultures of nuclei gathered inside Kron's own body. They were cloned in rapid acceleration in mini laboratory conditions right inside that bottle. Of course, the Rasheen was the stimulant."

Open-mouthed, Adam held the bottle up to the light, studying it. "No kidding!"

Hesitantly, Peter poked his head in the doorway. "You guys done yet?" He was shoved aside by an anxious-looking Todd towing a confused Joelle into the room.

Peter paused at the foot of the operating table. "Hey! W-where's the *hole*?"

They all gawked, their eyes popping. *Kron's chest was smooth, unblemished!*

It was incredibly hot in the depths of the equatorial rainforest, even in the shadow of the great saucer. Out here in the old-growth section, they'd found an incredibly rich vein: the gold was indeed thickest in the depths of the jungle, lying in long, filamentous ropes. Slightly below treetop level, the stolen starship was hovering over a circle of activity in its shadow. Cloaked in secrecy and under ever-watchful eyes, every port was open and bristling with cluttered arrays of sensors. Swiveling back and forth, the machines tracked the hostages as they made their way slowly through the soil, digging roots and flinging them onto utility barges, sweat pouring from their bodies. As man suddenly staggered and fell into the mud with heat prostration, someone bent to help.

"Back off!!" The butt of a rifle slammed down onto a log beside his hand, and the man jerked it away in alarm. "Leave him alone, scum! He'll come around!" Dexor picked up a gleaming section of roots, his mouth twisted in a cruel grimace. "And I won't be easy on you the next time," he snarled, "I'll just shoot! Hear me...." As a scream came from the perimeter of slate blue uniforms, he turned his head distractedly. "Oh, what *now*, another poison thorn?"

A sea of arms was pointing into the jungle. "*Razah!*" someone shouted.

Dexor threw up his hands in exasperation. "Oh, for … Trennic, Nastix! Go pop him! Target practice!"

A fusillade of bullets rained into the trees and the Razah dropped, riddled with holes. He spun around and shook his fist at the crew. "Whaddaya gawkin' at? Keep workin'!" He bellowed. "You, over there! Pull that smelter closer to that pile of roots!"

As ten men leaned their backs into a plaited golden rope, the belching machine moved a few yards. Dexor rubbed his hands together in satisfaction. "Now throw 'em in, *all* of 'em!" Bluish smoke wafted upward through the canopy, and in a few minutes the root's gleaming, fibrous netting melted in pops and whistles of steam. Out of the bottom of the glowing furnace, rivers of gold trickled into ceramic trays confiscated from the quarantine rooms. "That's right, keep it all moving!"

The crew was working in tight, fearful, sweating shifts. The close quarters combined with the trapped heat from the smelter were almost unbearable. Two women backed away from the others, untangling roots. Taking a chance, Shana whispered into her friend's ear. Her eyes darted around fearfully as she dropped another armload into the furnace. "Where *are* they? Why isn't anyone coming?"

Kalar wiped the sweat from her brow, leaving a long, black smudge. "I don't know," she breathed. "They turned off our PILs when they took our wrist communicators. Why'd they make us dump *everything* out there in the desert?"

"Whaddaya think? More room for this stupid gold!"

"And what're they gonna do with us? I mean when they're, ah, *done* with us?"

"I don't know; probably the same thing as the Razah."

"*Shoot* us? Why?"

"For sport, of course. They're twisted!"

With a loud clang, a bullet ricocheted off the smelter and plowed into the ground between them. Their faces drained of color. "*You!*" One of the odd-looking strangers screamed over their heads. "One more peep and you're Razah meat!"

Suddenly, as if to back up his tirade, a brilliant arc of electricity lit the air between them and sliced off a lock of Shana's hair. An unfamiliar, crazed-sounding figure screeched above them, brandishing a Stifler. "*No* interference will be tolerated! *No* whispering, *no* plans of escape! Until this ship is full, full, *full*, you will work, work, *work*! Only *then* I will decide what to do with you!"

Nastix turned and exchanged wide-eyed glances with his pals. This threat was obviously directed at them, too: It was becoming all too clear that this crazed Bitron had an agenda all his own. They groaned in frustration. The Scarred One had not been easy to deal with, especially in the last few days leading up to the coup. His mercurial temper had shown a new edge, and if possible, a widening crack of insanity was pulling him toward a dark, distant place. Those little pink pills, the ones he seemed to be eating like candy, should have given them a clue; it seemed the more he wolfed down, the more his mutilated hands shook.

Standing off to the side, Dexor fumed and cursed quietly to Nastix and Trennic. "Gaah! First, we let this jerk weasel his way into our plans with all his grandiose promises, and then he went berserk and started to bully us with threats of blackmail and exposure!"

"Yeah," Trennic agreed, vehemently. "We were duped!"

Dexor's lip curled. "And now he's pulled his ugly crowd of cronies out of nowhere! Without him, it would've been so … simple!" Disgusted, he fumbled for his last clip of ammo. He'd noticed that everyone's stash was getting precariously low, the Stifler rechargers were nowhere to be found, and there were still several more days of this hide-and-seek ahead before they could fill the ship and leave the planet.

"Hey," he shrugged, "ten percent of this stupendous take ain't chicken feed."

As Kron swung his legs over the edge of the table in the recovery room, Adam looked up in alarm. "Hey, you," he chuckled. "Lie back down. Fenet said no exertion!"

"Yeah, Kron!" Peter added. "You may *look* healed on the outside, but your inside's still all mooshed up!"

Slowly, determinedly, Kron stood and shuffled over to join them at the big viewing screen. "So hold me up, okay?" he whispered. "I gotta see, too!"

Adam draped Kron's arm over his shoulder. "Are you okay, buddy?"

"Mostly," he replied, smiling. "So, ah, where *are* we, anyway?"

"Underground," Tola shrugged. "We came in here through a big cave in the mountains. They had one of those gold force fields about a hundred yards inside the entrance. It opened and we passed through, and then the tunnel angled straight down. I mean, *way* down … in fact, we're *still* going down! It's a vertical shaft, kinda scary."

They stared at the big screen. Brightly lit with wide, horizontal bands of living phosphorescence, a seemingly endless tube swept up and over them in a colorful, hypnotizing pulse.

Tola shook his head. "Too much excitement, guys. I-I'm getting too old for this."

"Are any other ships with us?" Kron questioned.

Adam answered. "Yeah, four. We're leading the procession."

"But w-why so *many*?"

"Armed escorts," he shrugged. "Hey! All of Aurona's top leaders are in here!"

"Oh, right. Um, was there anyone else hurt besides me, sir?"

"Yes, unfortunately." Adam grimaced. "Several, ah, several died, too."

Tola turned to him, scowling. "I have the official guesstimate, sir, if you want to call it that. As far as I can figure, out of the original three hundred and fifty-one people, nine have died, if you include Senn. On this ship, I've counted two hundred and forty-two including you and your wife Elena. That leaves about a hundred that were taken hostage as far as we know.…"

Peter interrupted. "S'cuse me, guys! I think we're here.… Look!"

They had indeed stopped, and the viewing screen showed them joining ranks with hundreds of identical copies of their starships. They slipped into place along a vast, vertical wall, a tight, even pattern of saucers as far as the eye could see, parked and floating perpetually in space. Shuttlecraft emerged from cargo airlocks to whisk the armed Bandor guards and the remnant of the crew toward what looked like a hermetically sealed cliff building.

With a rustle of stiff fabric, some tall, white-robed Bandors swished purposely into the room. Movon stepped forward and flicked off the screen. "Time to go, gentlemen," he slit-smiled. "And Kron, you *must* remain quiet for now. I know that you long to be with your comrades but your internal sutures are fresh and unfortunately fragile. The microthreads that Fenet's nanorobotic arm deployed were soaked in a strong growth stimulant, but you only *look* like you are healed."

Kron sighed in resignation. "Gotcha."

Night had fallen. The hostages lay exhausted on the cool floor of one of the last empty quarantine rooms. Their captors had grown impatient with the incredibly slow progress and had decided to abandon the smelter: melting the gold roots into ingots was taking far too much time. Unfortunately, that meant the roots themselves had to be stuffed into every available space, so dirt was now smeared over nearly every floor of the starship and clods of weeds and mud were everywhere. In spite of further threats no one had yet been killed, but tomorrow might be a different story. Their quarantine room was completely sealed; all the latches had been fused into a twisted mass from the combined blasts of several Stiflers. They were alive, but despairing of the future and too afraid to sleep.

After about twenty minutes of numbed silence, they realized they were indeed alone for the night. One of the men staggered to his feet to open some drawers in a counter. "Boy, what I'd give for some water right now. A dry crust … anything!"

Another one answered. "Yeah! What could they be thinking? If they feed us, we'll have enough strength to dig all the gold they'd ever need."

Shana lifted her head from her knees. "Well, they do throw us a few scraps. And thank God they make us work in shifts or we'd be dead."

In stark contrast, a great feast was in progress up in the mess hall: The cafeteria tables were sagging with the weight of food of every description. Shouting raucously, the revelers were passing around plate after plate of the best fare from the cryotanks. As the plasmorphs chewed eagerly, their eyes glazed over in rapture.

"*Wow!*" one of them shouted. "What *is* this? You call it beef? It comes from an animal called a-a *cow*? We've never tasted anything like *this* on Aurona!" He passed a broiled rib eye to the scarred one, sitting at the head of the table. A pair of shaking hands eagerly reached out for it.

Dexor smiled to himself. Yes, he'd guessed right. The demented plasmorph was indeed bordering on a psychotic state. That lithium bicarbonate he'd been swallowing by the handful didn't seem to be working anymore. The fits of mania were nearly uncontrollable and the longer states of depression were becoming self-destructive. This fantastic Earth food seemed to fill the bill for now, calming his tormented mind and soothing the devils within. He leaned back, sipping his wine, biding his time.

Five miles beneath Aurona's surface, Duron and the elders had assembled in an improvised situation room. "Welcome, friends, old and new. Our team must now find answers. We cannot waste another moment." He nodded toward Adam.

Elena leaned wearily against her husband's shoulder. Although Adam was exhausted as he spoke, his young eyes glowed with a strange new awareness. He cautioned them that although they'd be safe under Duron's care, there was indeed no way to find the hostages with the stolen starship's superb cloaking capabilities. After a short pause, he revealed his immediate plans: he urgently needed to pursue a forgotten but vital power source in order to help them.

Kron lifted a finger, thought a moment, and then let his hand fall weakly back into his lap. "Adam's right, you know. We gotta seek answers wherever and whenever we find them. What else can we do right now?" He turned to Adam. "Go for it, man."

Joelle gathered a squirming Todd in her arms and turned to Adam. "Ah, you look good, sir, I mean considering what you've just gone through. We're so glad you *made* it!"

Adam raised his voice wearily. "Well, I'm glad I'm alive, for everyone's sake ... especially Elena's. Now that we're up to speed with each other, let's turn this meeting over to the Elders. I'm sure they have some clues to head us in the right direction."

Duron nodded and turned to his second in command. "Movon, if you will?"

Placing his palms on the surface of the featureless conference table, Movon closed his eyes in deep concentration. A hush fell on the large gathering as a hologram slowly formed in the center. Silently, majestically, it floated up to eye level.

Aurona! A breathtaking, translucent schematic shell of the planet revolved in the center of the room. Hundreds of neon-red lines were snaking through the depths and skirting the core. The speed tube's intricate patterns and threadlike, multiforked branches and intersections looked like a tangled spider's web.

The schematic began to change. As the red lines faded, a fine gridwork of green lit up, representing the land's surface. Placed precisely on the fifty-mile intersections, pinpoints of electric blue were glowing. Motherlodes! Slowly spreading underground, tan-colored openings represented the Bandor cities as vast, horizontal excavations, then in the ocean's depth, Meseo's cluster of ultraviolet spheres coalesced on a seafloor ridge. Finally, with a faint hum, wormholes of fluorescent orange tunneled down vertically under strategic mountain ranges to end in large, spherical chambers.

"Whoa," Adam breathed, "Duron, you don't need to explain a thing; this map is incredibly clear and self-evident. The *big* questions are, I believe, also self-evident and clearly on everyone's mind in this room: number one, are the crew's PIL signals audible, and number two, can Dexor and his gang be stopped?"

The old one sighed. "Unfortunately, Adam, the PIL frequencies are silent: The crew's wrist programmers have been confiscated by the Bitrons. You may not know this, but your starship's shields are far more powerful than you could ever imagine: they generate a large sphere and even penetrate underground. Yes, they completely envelop your crew, in effect making them invisible to our telepathic abilities."

"What? You can't pick up their mind signals?"

"No. I am sorry, Adam. We could have easily located them by now."

He exhaled a long breath. "I see. So things look hopeless at the moment, right?"

"Yes," he nodded. "Nothing can penetrate your ship's defensive shields. But we are working diligently; we are acting. There *is* a faint possibility that with all this heavy digging, the planetary system of linked, underground roots will register a feedback or disturbance into the Motherlode's gridwork. A bright blue ripple should radiate outward and pinpoint their location on the schematic's green gridwork."

Hope lit up in Adam's eyes. "Hey, *go* for it, Duron! That's the best option so far; I feel it in my gut! If you guys see that blue signal, send me a mind-message the minute it shows up. You'll have to bear with us on tomorrow's mission, though: Elena and I should be gone most of the...."

"I've been thinking, sir, Peter interrupted. "Why couldn't we just throw up those big gold shields around the planet so they can't get away?"

Duron intervened. "I am sorry Peter, but we would be blind. Those strong shields would definitely interfere with the delicate electrical root sensors."

Adam pulled Elena to his side and squeezed her protectively. "Well, right now my wife and I are going to get some much needed rest. We're totally exhausted. First thing in the morning, though, we're definitely onto Plan B. At first light, I'd like a quick lift back to the island on one of these starships. I just hope that Roson will go along with my harebrained scheme."

The ancient one had finished her gardening and was relaxing in front of the great window in her room. Adam noticed that her medicine bottle was empty, tipped over on its side. He stepped hesitantly off the elevator.

"Ah ... hello?"

She turned her head wearily. "Yes Adam. I've been waiting. I'm glad you went back and took some valuable time to comfort your remaining crew. I see that they dropped you and Elena off on my roof. You must be in a real hurry to get on with your Plan B, whatever that is."

Encouraged, he and Elena picked their way through the instrument-cluttered room toward her contour chair. "Well, ah, speaking of Plan B, you're the only one on the planet who can help us with it, Roson."

"How so? And why me?"

Adam came directly to the point. "We need two of your newest SeaSphere transporters and directions to the coastal tombs."

"*What*?" She sat up indignantly, her eyes flashing. "Those tombs have been underwater for millions of years! They're sacred! It's forbidden for any Bandor to...."

"For any *Bandor* to visit them," he interrupted politely. "That's precisely right! However, we," he winked, pointing to himself and Elena, "are not Bandors!"

She stopped short, pondering. In a moment she returned with a carefully phrased question. "What is it you seek?"

"Answers," he shrugged.

"How do you expect to find them *there*?"

"Intuition? It seems logical."

"Explain yourself."

He paused a moment to put it together. "Those tombs," he began, "are the earliest evidence of Bandor civilization on Aurona. If the pattern I've seen so far holds true, the earliest star maps should also be inscribed into their floors, showing your civilization's earliest journeys. But most of all, I believe one of the tombs is different."

"Different? How so?" She looked at him suspiciously.

"Among other things, it might have clues to obtaining a forgotten power source."

She raised a lone, wispy brow. "*You've* been listening to *Duron*!"

"So tell me," he insisted. "Is it true or not? If he's been lying, I'll forget the whole mission!"

She fell silent, mulling it over. The sound of Adam's excited breathing quickly found a rhythm, synchronizing with the breakers far beneath the open window. Finally, she looked up. "My boy," she sighed, "it appears that you've outfoxed an old fox. Yes, it is true, but I've been testing you."

The hint of a smile that had been playing across his face quickly disappeared. "Testing me? Why?"

"To see if my prophecy about you was genuine. I couldn't believe it myself and so have been trying to head you off with this conversation. Your future path seems set."

"Huh? My future? Tell me then, what did you see and why do I feel so driven to go to the tombs right *now* to find it? Especially at this really critical time?"

"Be assured, Adam. This is indeed the time. You will find two things: one of them is intangible but vital to this rescue. It will be for your people, our people and the very future of this planet. Oddly, you may not even recognize it when you find it!"

"Huh? Did you get any idea of…?"

"No," she interrupted, "I simply caught a glimpse of you becoming very excited as you discovered it. My visions are not as strong as they used to be."

"And the second thing?" he prompted.

She turned her head, pondering, staring out her great window. "Well, it was tangible, a tiny object. I couldn't get a clear view of it as you held it in your hand. I'm only guessing that as the tomb is so old, it might be some kind of a forgotten link to our distant past.…" She paused, scowling. "But!" She held up a scrawny finger.

"But?" His faint, hopeful smile faded.

"What Duron doesn't know is that I alone have *pinpointed* the location of the oldest tomb that you seek! Up to now, I'd intended to bring this knowledge with me to the grave!"

His smile returned. "*Yow!* Does that mean we get the new SeaSpheres?"

Elena intervened, her eyes pleading. "Adam, I still don't get *any* of this! Why that one particular tomb? Why now? It all sounds too risky, too dangerous!"

He exhaled a long breath, looking down at the floor. "We've just *got* to go, Elena, especially now that we know all this stuff! Every instinct I have is pulling me there! Remember that 'big picture' I told you about? Call it intuition, call it clairvoyance or prophecy, call it anything you want. As Roson just said, what I'm seeking will be a vital link to my ability to rescue our crew. My grandfather never gave up, especially when answers were so close!"

They both stared at him, deep in their own thoughts. Finally, Roson relented with a sigh. "So it is done," she mumbled. "Logic prevails. Yes, your grandfather never gave up; I trusted him and so must trust his progeny." She waved a scrawny arm and motioned behind them. "You'll probably need underwater foot propulsion, adjustable gravity belts, and breathing equipment. Be a dear and open that big drawer over there? Third from the bottom in the twenty-second row?"

"*Yes!*" He punched the air, hopping in a tight circle. "Thanks, Roson!" He sprinted to the far wall, counting. With a puzzled look on his face, he pulled out a handful of rubbery tentacles dangling from wide, spongy-looking, slitted bands. "What are these?" He squeezed and stretched them as he trotted back.

She reached out impatiently. "It's obvious, isn't it?" Shaking one of them free from the pile, she demonstrated, slipping it around her thin neck like a collar. "They're really quite simple to wear." Fumbling with her crooked fingers, she fastened it in the front. Raising her thin brows, she shrugged mutely in a very human gesture.

"That's it?" Adam was incredulous. "That's all?"

She chuckled. "They're gills. Artificial gills. Layers of semipermeable nano-membranes inside slits. They're just like a fish's lungs but far, *far* more effective at extracting oxygen and nitrogen from seawater. We invented them centuries ago. Oh, and they generate a force field over your heads, similar to Tavan's electronic helmet. The resulting bubble permits you to talk to each other underwater with your SeaPhones. We added that feature...."

"We?" Adam pressed. "You keep saying '*we*,' Roson. Who? My grandfather?"

"No," she shrugged, "this rush of creativity happened centuries before he arrived. I teamed up with the Bitrons, actually our ancestral cousins. They form a branch of our evolutionary tree that prefers *not* to eat of the mind-fruit. They believe it's a matter of matter over mind, and not...."

"Mind over matter?" he finished, chuckling. "Hey, I *like* those dudes! They're techno-geeks, just like me! But seriously, you guys are related to the Bitrons?"

"Yes. And there you have it, Adam, your first answer. Bandors and Bitrons share a common ancestor somewhere in the past."

"Wow! I knew you guys looked alike, except for the size of your heads!" As he studied her, his expression darkened momentarily. "So tell me, Roson, what's *really* going on? You know, Elena's kidnapping, and now this hostage-taking? I-I know our crew has evil ones in our midst and you Bandors have outlaws like those prophecy zealots who captured Elena, but-but now … the Bitrons, too?"

Roson's thin lips drew into a straight, hard line. "This is very difficult, Adam, as the Bitrons are my friends. Most are of superb character and excellent allies. As you've seen from Kron's holo-tape, our distant cousins have developed an offshoot of the cloaking and holographic technologies, coupled with rapid stem-cell generation. It's called plasmorphy, where another body image can be physically formed around their own to totally change their appearance. Yes, it's the ultimate in disguises but eventually it causes a lot of scarring on their original bodies. It's only inevitable that a few Bitron outlaws have capitalized on this technology and used to 'mix in' with resident alien populations. What am I saying?" She shrugged. "Just this: there are Bitron/Bandor plasmorphs living right here on this planet, Aurona, at this very moment. They're impossible to detect because they've learned the difficult art of mind-shielding."

Adam put it together quickly. "They mimic your mannerisms, too?"

She nodded. "Yes. One of these plasmorphs is particularly dangerous and has tricked some of your crew to join him in his treachery. I've only been able to catch glimpses of him in the past few hours, as he has momentarily let down his guard in the midst of all the action. Mind-shields are powerful defensive weapons."

Adam rolled his eyes and let out a low whistle. "Wow! So much for my idealistic view of this peaceful planet! Think of it: Plasmo-Wars!"

Elena tugged his arm and locked her eyes with his. "We've got to focus on your mission here, Adam. It's getting late and we need directions to the tomb."

"She's right," Roson agreed. "Once you employ your new SeaSphere's Phase II acceleration, it's precisely two and a half sea-hours away. If you'll pardon my trite but misplaced Earth-expression, you've got a lot of ground to cover!"

Chapter 28: THE TOMB

Hovering over the rolling waves in the predawn darkness, a pair of SeaSpheres flattened out into teardrop shapes and plunged quickly beneath the surface. Their supercharged skins danced like eager, spirited horses, chomping at the bit and raring to go.

Excitedly, Adam shouted into their new SeaPhones. "Hear me, hon?"

She flinched. "Ouch! Gotcha! *Very* loud and clear!"

"Oops, sorry," he apologized, "I'll crank it down a bit." He glanced at her through their shimmering walls. "Oh, Roson mentioned that these lap units fit down between our knees. She said it was very important."

Elena looked up, surprised. "Huh? Okay, lemme see.... Hey, they fit nicely! So *that's* why they have those soft u-shaped channels running down the sides."

"Aha! You're right! Form does follow function, right? Okay, I'm setting my stopwatch function for exactly two and a half hours now and I'll punch it when we're ready to start moving. About twenty miles from here, she said that the sea floor drops away from the island's continental shelf, and there's a huge pillar in the way, a big seamount of some sort. That's where we switch over to Phase II acceleration. It'll power us straight east for three thousand miles through unobstructed ocean parallel to the equator."

"Hey!" Elena blinked. "What happens if sea creatures get in the way?"

"Um, Roson also mentioned some kind of conical shock waves being generated about a half mile ahead of us. I hope that shoves anything out of the way."

"Good," she scowled uncertainly. "I feel *much* better... I think."

He studied her expression. "We'll be okay, hon. Really! I'm figuring on seven or eight hours for this whole mission, including five hours for traveling both ways. When we get there, it might take two or three hours just to find what we're looking for."

"Ah, what *are* we looking for, Adam? Please remind me; I still don't know."

He sighed. "I don't know either, but I'm positive it's there. Remember, she said it was, um, intangible. I just hope one of us recognizes it when we find it." Shrugging, he poised his finger over his stopwatch. "Ready?"

They departed in a rush of power. It seemed like mere minutes before the seamount was directly in front of them. They swiveled eastward, then nudged their throttles all the way forward to initiate the Phase II acceleration. Without losing a beat, a pair of long, thin probes began to extrude from the front of their lap units.

Elena looked down and yanked her feet away in alarm. "Good heavens!' She stared wide-eyed at the sharp points. "What are those little pricker things? If they stick out any further, they're gonna poke through the front of my bubble!"

"Let's wait and see," he whispered. "Maybe they're *supposed* to?"

As the probes reached the front walls of their bubbles, they simply flared out and attached themselves. A pair of long, sharp golden needles began to pierce the tensioned surface. They exchanged puzzled glances.

"What do you think is happening, Adam?"

He shrugged. "I honestly don't know; these new SeaSpheres seem to have a mind of their own. Again, I'd say let's just wait and…."

Without warning, two tremendous arcs of lightning sizzled out into the water! As the probes blazed open a huge gaseous chamber in front of the bubbles, a great wall of water immediately closed in behind them. Their SeaSpheres lurched forward into the openings, sliding and skittering under the surface like two bars of soap dropped into a bathtub.

"Holy Pokeymon!" Adam pried himself off the back wall. "Electrolysis!"

"Yeah!" she shouted back. "Seriously *big time!*"

The acceleration quickly leveled off: there was no detectable G-force, no sense of movement at all; the undersea world had simply turned into a blur. A display blinked to life on their lap units. "ARTIFICIAL GRAVITY-*ON*." Their eyes met questioningly and there was a short, numbed silence as they struggled to figure it out.

"Wow," Elena breathed, "how do they *do* all this stuff?"

He shrugged. "I have no idea; I-I guess we just have to trust the inventors!"

They blasted forward smoothly with ever-increasing speed, the continuous arcs of lightning shooting ahead of them like a torch. It was as if the SeaSpheres had sought and found a harmonious vibration within their own element, skittering alongside each other in perfect sync and leaving two long rooster tails of bubbles rising up to the surface. Their brightly lit probes gave the whole scene a dreamlike quality: in the dark ocean, they looked like enchanted, crystalline narwhals.

Adam settled into the back curve of his bubble, letting out a long breath. ""Whoeee, what a ride!" Slowly, page-by-page, he began to flip through the SeaSphere's on-screen manual. The low hum droned on, the blurry view remained unchanged, and in spite of himself, he drifted off. Suddenly a loud, insistent beep and a jarring buzz from his wrist programmer alerted him. His hands flew to the controls, his voice tense with excitement. "Whoa, whoa! Elena!"

She peered at him through her watery curtain, her eyelids heavy.

"Sorry, I-I fell asleep," he exclaimed nervously. "It's time! We've got less than a minute! Got your throttle ready?"

Nodding, she gave him a thumbs-up. On his signal, the SeaSpheres simultaneously withdrew their probes, their propulsion waves reversed, and they stopped dead in the water. Roson's timing had been precise: Two and a half hours to the second! They looked up.

Dead ahead of them was a vertical cliff!

They gasped, their jaws hanging open: Roson had figured out the timing *way* too closely! The wall appeared to be the edge of an ancient continental shelf, but oddly fractured and crumbling into the abyss beneath them. As they rose slowly through the dark waters toward the distant sunlight, a sudden warning beep alerted Adam: his lap unit's sonar had picked up a moving object below him. He spread his legs wide and looked straight down. His startled eyes riveted on a tremendous shape hurtling towards them from the depths.

"Holy cow!" he bellowed. "Elena! Pull a sharp right, *now*!"

As they snapped into opposite ninety-degree turns, a massive, blurred form shot between them, its jaws agape, its paddle feet lashing furiously.

"Yow, an Elasmosaurus! It's just like the one we saw back in Meseo!"

She pointed at the cliff. "Adam, look! There's a big crack in the wall!"

The sonar's warning beep intensified. The sea beast had turned and was diving directly at them, homing in for the kill. "He's locked onto us, Elena! Follow me inside and turn on your sonar! We'll have to use these lap units as our light source!"

They shot like crystal bullets into the opening. Their thumb steerers seemed to work intuitively, the AI assisting them as they skirted the ghostly 3D images of the walls. Suddenly, Elena felt a shove. She spun around, looking behind her. Its jaws agape, the great beast was snapping at the long whiptail of her SeaSphere.

"Eeek!" she squealed. "Faster, Adam, *faster*! He's gaining on me!"

Ahead of them, a blinding shaft of sunlight suddenly appeared and the walls fell away into a huge rift. As they accelerated into the open, Adam looked around desperately, blinking sweat out of his eyes. There was a tiny, dark spot on the surface of the far wall. He squinted at it, trying to focus. Could that be another opening?

There was a sharp cry from Elena: two more sea creatures were closing in! As they sped toward the wall, he improvised quickly.

"Quick! Flatten out your SeaSphere into a needle shape!"

"*How*?" she screamed in frustration. "How do I do *that*, Adam?"

He tried to keep his voice calm. "See that thin blue bar on the left? Hold it down, then lie on your stomach with the unit in front of you."

They contorted themselves like gymnasts inside their SeaSpheres, then changed their shape and shot into the tiny circular opening. With a series of loud thuds, the sea creatures crashed into the cliff behind them. Their nerves were on razor edge as they slipped through the unexplainably smooth, tubular passageway, threading through it like a pair of clear, flexible needles. As the tube rose in a short, vertical shaft, Adam's sonar let out a loud beep. Alarmed, he braked to a panic stop.

Elena bumped into him with a springy thud, her blunt needle shape colliding with his. "Ow-w-wch! What *is* it, Adam?" Her voice sounded hollow, pained.

He looked down at her. "The exit's blocked! Something's in the way!"

"Oh, no! What do we do now? It's too narrow to turn around and I really don't think I can back up all the way...."

"That's for sure!" he interjected. "Hey, what's your depth meter read? Mine says we're only eighty feet below the surface."

"Yeah, you're right: eighty feet! What're you thinking?"

"Well, we can't go any further with these things, so we'll have to swim from here. Slip on your fins and earphones, then activate your neck gills and head bubble. Tell me when you're ready, and then we'll dissolve the SeaSpheres."

"Dissolve them? How do you do that?"

"It's easy: You just turn up your pressure knob until the red lines match on your dial, then bingo: push that same blue bar again. Ready to roll?"

They scrambled into their gear. As the SeaSpheres dissolved, their once-encapsulated air escaped in a great bubble and rose to the top of the tunnel. The temperature dropped, their ears began to throb painfully, and as they floated up to the surface in the narrow rock tube, Adam began to hear a soft gurgle and hiss above him. "Huh?" He listened intently. "Elena, I think our air's escaping somewhere!"

He reached up into the darkness over his head, feeling for the tiny current As a probing finger found the hole and plugged it, the hissing stopped. "Huh? Something feels smooth, like metal!" Using his lap unit's screen as a light source, he tilted it upward. A large gold panel gleamed brightly near the top of the tube.

"Wow! An entrance, Elena!" His hands were shaking with excitement as he pressed on the heavily embossed surface, testing the resistance. It felt springy. Bracing himself inside the tube, he pushed with all his might. Something gave.

With a great belch, the trapped air escaped in a powerful, turbulent bubble. Their lap units were forcibly wrenched from their grasp as they were thrust into a great void, spinning head over heels. Helplessly, they watched them tumble down to the floor in slow motion, their sonar screens still glowing. The two tiny rectangles sent up a swirling, muddy cloud as they pierced a thick layer of sediment.

Light? They looked up, blinking in surprise. Yes, they could *see*! As their eyes adjusted to the low intensity, they spotted the source. Far over their heads, a tiny circlet of pinholes pierced the border of a great, barnacle-encrusted golden medallion. Intense shafts of light were streaming down through the ventilation shafts into the vault. They gave each other jubilant high fives and let out a whoop, their head bubbles jetting long streams of air.

They turned back to the floor. Glowing softly under the ooze on the bottom, their SeaSphere's lap units seemed to be beckoning them. There was no hesitation: they dove eagerly, breathing hard, their neck gills pulsing. Adam reached the bottom first. Gingerly picking up his lap unit, he brushed away the sediment and carefully inspected the rubbery surface for damage.

"Look, Elena, not a scratch! All the debris saved them!"

"Thank God for *that*, Adam," she agreed, turning hers over and over. "We wouldn't be able to get *home* without these things!"

Moving quickly, they opened a small compartment, pulled out a set of built-in straps, and slung them onto their backs like knapsacks. They began to shuffle about awkwardly on the floor, clearing away patches of debris with their flippered feet. Soon, just as Adam had predicted, they'd uncovered glimpses of a star-map, a big one, lying under the eons of silt.

"Hey, look!" Elena was pointing up excitedly. "Our air bubble's trapped under that medallion! We might be able to get a much better view from up there!"

They adjusted their antigrav belts and flippered upward. As Elena's head broke the surface, she turned off her neck gill's bubble. "Not bad," she puffed, sniffing the air. "A little musty, but breathable!" She glanced at Adam. His eyes looked huge, the edges red-rimmed from the saltwater.

"Yeah, it'll do," he said, grinning. "And thanks for your initiative; this is a *great* perspective! Think we can get a photo or two of the floor?"

"Maybe," she teased, "if we could *see* it!"

He looked down. She was right: the sediment was really thick. Suddenly, he brightened. "Hey, I just got an idea! We might be able to push it out of the way!"

Her brows rose. "We could? How's that possible?"

"Hopefully, this vault should be like the others and have a lot of antechambers around the bottom. Wait a sec... I'll check it out." He poked his head under the surface to study the carved decorations.

Yes, the panels were there, but these had very different motives: a collection of embossed, golden sea fans embellished the pendentives between the great circle of arches at the bottom. He lifted his head excitedly, shaking the water out of his hair. "I'm gonna dive again, Elena! Those arches look a bit crusty, but I'll try to open a panel or two. Watch what I do, and if it works, come down and help me."

He dove, his flippered feet thrashing exuberantly. In a few moments, he'd found a likely-looking rosette and pushed: sure enough, it moved! There was a crackling sound as a cloud of barnacles rained onto the floor, then a huge panel slowly pulled loose and began to raise smoothly, its alloy cables and counterweights still working flawlessly after untold eons of rest. As it reached ankle height, a long slit of light clicked on, glowing faintly through the murky sediment. Suddenly, Adam jumped: intense light was pouring in behind him. He turned to see Elena swimming around the perimeter of the great chamber, poking at sea fan rosettes.

Within minutes, the vault was flooded with light. Shielding their eyes in the brilliance, they swam toward one of the big antechambers. The domed marble room was on a far grander scale than the ones Adam had seen, and lying in darkness since the inundation, the lack of light had worked to its advantage: sea life had shunned the pitch-black cave and nothing could gain a foothold on the ultra-smooth, polished alabaster walls.

A row of buttons lined the wall near the entrance. As he pressed one, the nearest subchamber opened. They entered cautiously: sleeping niches lined all the walls, looking like catacombs in the eerie overhead light. A button was glowing next to one of the small, closed panels. As Elena pressed it, she jumped back in horror.

Bones! A disjointed torrent of skeletal fragments tumbled out onto the floor! Rising in wispy clouds, clumps of organic material began to gather speed as they circled upward, swept by some kind of a strong current exiting through the ceiling. In moments, the floor was scoured clean.

As she shuddered outside the entrance, Adam lingered, picking up the large, domed skull. He gave it a gentle squeeze, and it parted along the fissures and crumbled. He held a section up close to his face, his eyes widening.

"Let's go!" she squealed, jumping up and down. "This is too *creepy*!"

He glanced at her. She looked cold. She was right: it was time to move. In a moment, they broke the surface and deactivated their neck gills, breathing hard.

"That jawbone was laced with *gold*!" he panted.

She scowled. "I know all about the bones, Adam. Roson told me. The Bandor's entire skeletons are one b-big telepathic receiving unit, *especially* their s-skulls!"

He noticed that her teeth were chattering. "Of course," he grinned, draping his arm protectively around her shoulders. "There be gold in them thar Rasheens!"

She pressed closer to him for warmth. "I don't l-like it here, Adam," she chattered. "Are *all* those antechambers f-full of dead people ... ah, I mean Bandors?"

"They're mankind, Elena; there's no doubt. Our bone structure's identical, our smiles are, ah, *almost* the same and our emotions are *becoming* the same...."

"So what happened here? What kind of great c-catastrophe could've caused all these p-people to die in their beds? An earthquake? A tsunami?"

"Well, Roson's chalk island shows definite evidence of large-scale plate tectonics. If there *was* a quake, this place was probably inundated within minutes!"

She looked up. "So fast? B-but those holes in the ceiling are so s-small...."

"No," he corrected, "the ocean spilled down the big spiral staircase. It was the *air* that escaped through those little vents! The sleeping Bandors had no time to react. Most likely, the gold panels cranked down as a safety measure, but they move very slowly. The water was probably up to the top of their rooms by then."

"W-what a horrible way to g-go, Adam," she chattered. "This p-place is like the T-Titanic! No w-wonder the Bandors never w-wanted to c-come down here again!"

He suddenly realized that her lips were blue. "Holy cow! You gotta get warmed up, quick! Let's slip back into our SeaSpheres and talk through our headsets. I've got another plan hatching."

In a few minutes, they were leaning back against the soft inner walls, drying out and enjoying the higher oxygen content. Elena looked at him. "Your, ah, plan?"

He grinned. "Okay, this may sound kinda kooky, but here it is: First, think about that big, swirling current of water we saw in the antechamber and then think about a centrifuge. We're gonna make our SeaSpheres into an engine. We'll dive to the bottom and start circling and spinning around each other…"

"You're kidding," she interrupted, scowling. "Tell me you're kidding."

"Nope," he chuckled. "Last one down is a rotten egg!"

They dove to the center of the floor and started to spin around each other, spreading the debris toward the open antechambers. The powerful filters seemed oblivious to the fact that they were pulling seawater and the strong current began to vacuum fine, billowing clouds of debris upward through the tops. Soon, the glass floor was immaculate. They raced to the top and peered down excitedly.

Spread out in grandeur beneath them, a fantastically detailed, dustlike barred spiral galaxy was set into deep cobalt. The aggregation of stars seemed disturbingly familiar. Thinking a moment, Elena suddenly recognized it. A gasp escaped involuntarily from her lips.

"The Milky Way!" she blurted. "You're kidding! This was their very first *trip*?"

"It *had* to be," Adam reasoned. "This is supposed to be their oldest vault and the map in the glass floor was poured when they constructed it millions of years ago…." His heart pounding, his eyes skimmed along the runic border. "Okay, right over there! I'm reading their actual words, now. Listen to this: 'As this is the first and greatest of our underground dwellings, it will be a prototype for countless others to follow.'"

He glanced back at her. She was scanning the walls in confusion.

"Where'd you read *that,* Adam? I don't see…."

He bumped her bubble for attention. "Look down," he pointed. "See those runes around the border? I began at one o'clock and started to read around the dial."

"Oh," she shrugged. "Is there any info about the Earth or the Milky Way?"

"No, not yet. It's just, ah, well … I don't want to bore you, because it's just a lot of construction details. It's saying the outer shell was cast in one piece out of an impermeable alloy, a breakthrough in technology. The gold plates and alabaster walls were merely decorative fascia that slid into channels, overlapping each other…. Hey, wait! Do you know what that means? This thing *can't* rot! With impermeable alloys and solid gold, it's no wonder everything still works so well after so long!"

She bounced her bubble up and down, persisting with her question. "I'm so glad you cleared *that* up for me! I was just *dying* to know!"

"Huh?" He glanced at her, puzzled.

"The *Earth*, Adam! Does it say anything about the Earth?" She pointed to another spot on the border, her finger poking her bubble's taut membrane. "Try over *there*! Those runes look *much* more interesting … I think."

Stifling a grin, he swiveled his SeaSphere around and tipped it toward the floor to read. Suddenly, his eyes narrowed. "Wow! Sorry, Elena, there's nothing about the Earth yet, but it's saying something about the twin moons orbiting Aurona, and the distant future after the Bandors have finished the greening of their planet!"

She drew in a sharp breath. "The prophecy? The one Duron didn't have time to finish in Meseo? Quick! My babies!" Her arms encircled her stomach protectively. "Does it say anything about my babies?"

"Okay, here goes...." Collecting himself, he began to translate directly from the border. "'Just as our twin moons, Mazan and Eonia, are spun from the same slab of primordial rock and are mirror images of each other, so twins will be born one day to rule Aurona. They will mirror each other's moods, offering balanced judgment and a carefully planned future to our people. As it is genetically impossible for Bandor women to give birth to twins, we look to the heavens and await this gift with eager expectation. They and their parents will live for untold millennia, playing pivotal roles in the future of Aurona.'" He paused, breathing hard, contemplating. "Hon?" He waited a moment for an answer and then turned to her. She was staring blankly ahead, chanting something. Her voice sounded muffled, far away.

"Mazan, Eonia, Mazan, Eonia, Maz...." Sensing his silence, she looked at him. "Those names sound like a boy and girl to me, Adam. Duron did say fraternal twins, right?" Her eyes were round. "Those names are perfect!" she exclaimed. "Mazan is strong, masculine! And Eonia? C'mon, you simply couldn't refuse me *that* one; it's *incredibly* beautiful! I love both of those names and I want to keep them!" She crossed her arms with finality, glancing at him out of the corner of her eye. He was tapping furiously on his wrist programmer. "Honestly, Adam, what are you up to *now*?"

"Dictionary function," he muttered, his eyes focusing intently. "Ah, here it is; I thought it looked familiar. 'Eon': From the Greek word 'Aion,' meaning 'lasting for an immeasurably long time.'" He looked at her pointedly through his rippling wall. "Greeks? The Bandors got this name 'Eonia' from the Greeks? What's going on? A prophecy over two million years old, with Greek names?"

She shrugged indecisively.

"What are they, time-walkers, just picking out names from wherever and whenever it pleased them? It's downright spooky!"

"Maybe it's the other way around, Adam. Think: maybe the Greeks got the names from *them*! Open your imagination in new directions!"

"I-I don't *like* this direction; it's like a shotgun wedding or something!" he scowled. "I'd prefer to *choose* our kid's names like most parents-to-be!" As he caught her hurt look, he quickly tempered his rising tone. A mischievous grin began to tease at the corners of his mouth. "But on the other hand, you're right about one thing...."

Silence. Her bottom lip was teetering dangerously on the brink of a pout.

"Adam Junior *does* sound a bit dorky, doesn't it?"

She squinted at him with one eye. "Just read, please...."

He quickly tucked in his chin and scanned some more, paraphrasing on the fly. "Ah, I think this section of runes over here refers to holograms. It says the moving scenes can be controlled and changed several ways, one of which is by means of...," he stopped short, studying the great central medallion over his head: the embossed, heavily chased gold filigrees were standing out in deep bas-relief. "There's supposed to be a way to access some kind of main control panel up here, Elena. Help me look."

"So what are you looking for? A switch? A button?"

Suddenly, he pointed excitedly. "There it is! I see a tiny inscription, a code or something, carved into that six-foot leaf! C'mon! Let's go read it!" Their SeaSpheres bumped hollowly as they tapped along the ceiling.

The small hand-carved inscription was still gleaming as brightly as the hour it was painstakingly incised into the golden surface. Adam's eyes widened.

"Does it say to push somewhere, Adam? Does it have springs? Does the whole leaf swivel away from a concealed button?"

"Nope, nope and nope," he teased. "You'd never guess."

"What are you...." Her voice trailed off as he held a finger in the air.

He closed his eyes and began to imagine a delicately balanced mechanism; one that could be triggered by a mere nano-puff, a whispered breath of air. Duron had only hinted at such mind-controlled switches, yet here was one of them in the flesh, labeled with a numeric code and concealed from view only inches away. He focused on it mightily, pushing with his mind, concentrating on the coded runic numbers.

There was a muffled click, and the great medallion began to shudder. As eons of encrustation cracked loose, debris rained down into the clear water. The strong current from the antechambers swept it outward toward the brightly lit rooms.

A faint hum crescendoed into a loud rumble over their heads. With barely enough time to exchange wide-eyed glances, they scudded their bubbles out of the way. A gleaming, gold-railed viewing platform perhaps forty feet in diameter slowly descended: the enormous central medallion had concealed it all along! Open-mouthed, Elena turned slowly toward him.

"Y-you didn't touch a thing, Adam. I watched you. Your arms didn't move. You didn't budge. That means you opened this thing with your... with your...."

He tapped his forehead. "Telekinesis, Elena," he whispered. "Remember how the Razah's mind-stun slammed me onto the ground?"

She nodded slowly, hesitantly. "Yes, but ... *you*?"

"Listen. I don't want to scare you, but if a so-called dumb animal can do such an incredible thing, why couldn't I do something similar, on a much *smaller* scale?"

He was right. She relaxed, a softness returning to her eyes. In a moment, they grew round in wonder and admiration. "Wow," she whispered. "Just imagine all the new doors opening to you, Adam! This is definitely radical, cutting-edge stuff!"

He smiled. "Yup! Mind control is a *zillion* times faster than my body's mechanical responses! Duron told me I'm gonna have massive amounts of stored electronic output generated by my new neurons. All I gotta do is to learn how to regulate the output!"

She scowled and held up a finger. "Adam, look at me."

"Huh?"

She stared at him levelly. "I believe you already possess that power you're seeking. It's *inside* you! *This* is that invisible, intangible link that Roson mentioned!"

He was stunned: she was right! He fought hard to put it together, to find the right words. Finally, something gelled and he looked up. "I have a theory: It's my head! Why's my *head* always been such a target? I was whacked on my head and passed out on the Obelisk planet; I've eaten a powerful mind stimulant and then spun like a centrifuge thousands of feet over the top if a tree; I've been stunned at point-blank range by a Razah, and finally I've been the only living being who's ever been thrown into an experimental Neuron Resuscitation Chamber. My poor brain's been *kicked around*! He closed his eyes. "And now I've got … *telekinesis*? What's next?"

She stared at him, tears rolling down. "There's no limit, Adam. Believe it."

There was a faint click as the platform stopped. A multi-tiered control panel blazed to life around a massive central piston, sending sharp, prismatic rays across the ceiling. With another click, a ray of green fanned downward under the medallion, highlighting the runes around the perimeter of the floor. Suddenly, the symbols began to dance and jiggle in 3D a few feet above the surface of the floor.

Adam gawked at them, pointing. "Well, there they are, holograms, just like the runes said! I suspect we'll find more answers up on the viewing platform…."

"Wait!" she interrupted, a finger in the air. "First, let's make it darker in here! If we close all the antechambers, we might be able to see the holograms better."

"Wow! I'm impressed, girl! Great thinking!"

They wasted no time, bumping rosettes and closing doors. In a few minutes they'd skittered back up over the gold railing. Adam quickly dissolved his SeaSphere and rigged himself out with his SeaPhone, gills and head bubble. Gripping the rail tightly, he leaned way out to see. Yes, the holograms were indeed moving: rotating majestically and tilting slightly to one side, the Milky Way Galaxy was now ringed by the floating runic message, bathing the glittering walls in a spectacular light show. He pulled his SeaPhone tightly to his face and read some runes, his voice clear.

"It says they found this particular galaxy to be the home of countless planets, close to seven and a half billion of which were hospitable to life. Outposts were set up on only five of the most verdant: Erdma, Genoe, Aquan, Centis, and Simor."

He felt an insistent bump on his elbow. Elena's eyes reflected the trillion pinpoints of brilliance as she joined him at the rail. The Sagittarius arm slowly swept by under them, but there seemed to be an odd pulsing amidst the great aggregation of stars: a tiny blue *rectangle* was flashing, about a third of the way out on the arm. They spun back and forth in their bubbles. Just as they'd suspected: four more specks of blue were flashing on the other arms: The *outposts* that Adam had just named!

"Adam," she pointed, "can you can enlarge that little rectangle like you did in the Observatory Room?"

He grabbed the rail. "That's *right*! You're a *genius*! Wait, first I gotta go over to that big piston and find the controls!" Adjusting his gravity belt, he swam quickly toward the glare of the lights in the center. It was almost impossible to read the incised runes, and it took a while to even start making sense of anything.

"Um, what are you doing?" Elena's voice crackled in his headset.

He held up a finger. "Wait, wait! It says something here about railings. I can't see it very clearly in these bright lights. Lemme translate a bit more...."

"Railings?" Her face lit up with sudden inspiration. She dissolved her SeaSphere, landed lightly on her feet, and switched quickly to her alternate breathing mode. Kneeling on the spot, she examined the curved railing. Sure enough, a fine, threadlike horizontal seam bisected the foot-thick tube. As her sensitive fingertips traveled along the groove, she felt a small indentation. She shrugged, stuck in two fingers, and pulled up. A short section of rail lifted smoothly on its hinges, separating along its radial seam. She reached inside eagerly.

"*I got* it!" Adam shouted into his SeaPhone, spinning on his heel. "All you have to do is...," he stopped, midsentence.

Elena was already at the rail, her back to him, busily moving the blue rectangles around with the spinning trackball. Sensing his sudden silence, she glanced over her shoulder. "Hi!" She grinned sheepishly. "Ah, you mentioned 'railing'? Well, I thought about the way you opened the railing on our starship's loading dock to get at the controls. Our starship *did* come from this planet, right? So, ah ... there it is."

He nodded in silent admiration. "So there it is," he grinned. "My, you certainly *are* a woman of action!" He slipped up behind her and laid his chin on her shoulder. "Lemme guess. You're trying to zoom in on the Earth's outpost, right?"

"Ah...." She fiddled nervously with the controls. "Yes, I've been *trying* to, but-but I'm getting nowhere. I'm afraid I've made a mess of things."

He reached under her arm and tapped a button labeled with a single runic word: 'Outpost.' The five rectangles snapped back to their original positions and she stepped aside to let him concentrate. Studying the numeric keypad, he tapped on the runic number one. Sure enough, on the far side of the hologram, a rectangle began to flash. "Okay," he mumbled, "so if that's number one out of five, I think the one we're looking for should be in the middle of the list: number three." He tapped the button.

"Aquan!" Elena clapped her hands excitedly.

The Earth's blue rectangle was flashing. As Adam pressed 'MAGNIFY,' the entire Milky Way disappeared in a flash, replaced by a stark, floating schematic of the Earth's solar system, precise to the minutest detail: jostling asteroid belts, dustlike rings around Saturn and Neptune, the rocky asteroid-planetoids Pluto and Charon endlessly circling each other with their moons, *everything* was there.

"Yes!" He jabbed the water with his fist. "Hold onto the rail, baby, this next close-up should be a *whopper*!" He quickly slid the blue rectangle over the third planet from the blazing star at the center, then magnified the minuscule dot.

A great shape, nearly thirty feet in diameter, swelled beneath the platform. A crisp, minutely detailed, true-color hologram of the Earth began to rotate slowly on its axis. Gripping the rail in awe, they leaned way out to study the vast northern pole. Somehow, it was different: a sea of ice seemed to be blanketing all the continents, far below the Temperate Zone.

"Of course," he whispered. "Glaciers!"

"Wow, Adam! I'm-I-m getting cold just *looking* at them!"

"Well, get back into your bubble, girl!"

She quickly reformed her SeaSphere's comforting wall and floated up over the platform's rail, hovering a short distance away. "So how long ago *is* this, Adam?"

"Mid-Cenozoic, I'd say," he mumbled. "Probably early Pleistocene." He studied the formations carefully. "I'm no expert, but I'd say we're looking at the Earth approximately forty or fifty million years ago. No dinosaurs, just a few remaining reptiles, lots of birds, mammals, and the beginnings of...." As the truth hit him, his voice fell to a barely audible whisper. "The beginnings of *mankind*?" There was a long, uneasy silence. He spoke again, this time with an unknown fear tingeing the edges of his voice. "It-it just doesn't wash, Elena! The times don't jive! This supposedly two-million-year tomb we're standing in is a prototype for a *fifty*-million-year outpost on the Earth? No way!"

She dove impulsively and began to circle the planet, staring closely at the great ball of ice. "Maybe they discovered time travel, Adam? Maybe they found a way to move through time and turn either way, into the past or into the future?"

He puffed out his cheeks, thinking. "Two million.... Wait, wait, maybe it *wasn't* two million years! For all we know, it could've been a *hundred* million! Civilizations change. People change. This tomb's been sealed and avoided like the plague ever since that great cataclysm washed over it. I think the Bandors have totally forgotten their distant past and have been reciting what little they *do* remember simply as blind, oral tradition. It's been only recently that Roson accidentally rediscovered this time-window. As you say, she saw both ways, into the past and the future."

Elena stared blankly. "Her revelation was a prophecy that already existed?"

Adam's head had started to pound with the possibilities. As he bent over the railing to gawk, he accidentally bumped the trackball with his finger. Immediately there was a low hum, and the huge globe responded by rolling over several degrees on its axis. "Whoa, whoa! Look what I just did, Elena!"

She hovered closer to the phantom globe, only inches away. "I would've *never* guessed you could roll the whole Earth around like that, Adam! Go the other way!"

He was already twiddling at the trackball. As the globe rolled on its axis, the equator was suddenly beneath them, with South America on top. He gently nudged it to the right, and the Pacific slid majestically by: early French Polynesia, Fiji, the Solomon Islands and then...New Guinea. His heart started to pound as the big island rolled over the horizon.

"Look, Adam!" she pointed. "There's the blue rectangle! Why's it way over there on top of that island?"

He stopped New Guinea under him. Could it be? Yes, the rectangle was flashing over the center of a vaguely familiar ring of mountains! Impulsively, he pressed 'MAGNIFY.' In a flash, the entire, glacier-laden Earth disappeared, leaving Elena suspended in blackness.

"A-Adam?" Her voice sounded far away, lost. "W-what are *those* things?"

He glanced down. Small, clear glowing blocks were tumbling toward the center of the room through the dark watery void. A schematic of a translucent, vaulted structure was beginning to take shape, precise in every architectural detail, floating over the center of an excavated pit.

Spreading downward, a schematic shell formed around it, seeming to be poured from a giant, invisible ladle.

"You're kidding," he gasped. "The Galaxy Room? This is how it was *made*?" He jabbered into his SeaPhone, hanging precariously over the rail and pointing out details on the ghostly structure. "Hey, there's the ramp and the spiral staircase, and look, it had a moving medallion and antechambers, too! My grandpa and I never got to see them before…." His voice choked off.

The Galaxy Room's innermost secrets were finally revealed. The very last to form was the runic border, the golden symbols falling into place in precise order. Strangely, the ring looked as if it were a separate unit from the central floor. As he started to read the runes, the border abruptly dissolved. "Huh?" His heart started to pound as different runes began to form in their place. "Elena, Elena, look! The border runes changed! I'm *sure* the bottom layer had a record of the earliest explorations!"

"Well, see if you can *stop* them, Adam! There must be a way to…."

"You're right!" he shouted. He jabbed 'SEQUENCE,' then 'MINUS,' then 'HOLD.' Everything stopped midair; a whole squadron of runic letters suspended in their flight to finish the bottom layer. He jogged it forward a few stops until the message was complete. "Are you ready? These are the Bandor's very first writings on Earth…."

"Go ahead, Adam," she encouraged softly. "I'm listening."

He took a breath and began. "'We are here on Aquan, our small band of three hundred and fifty. Construction has not been easy, as our vast original numbers have been greatly decreased by strange diseases, short, hot days and relentless predation by forest creatures, particularly the one we called the Razah.'"

He looked up with a start. Elena was nudging on his elbow. She'd piloted her SeaSphere up over the rail to be next to him. "I-I know, hon," he reassured, "they're definitely sabertooth tigers. The geologic times are right, that's for sure."

She leaned forward nervously. "Read on, Sherlock."

"Okay, here goes … 'Although we were weak, we are starting to get stronger year by year as our immune systems adapt. Exploration parties are coming back from afar with strange-tasting foods and startling news. Memory cubes of these earliest journeys are available in the library module, Antechamber 6, Drawer 27. To view them press code ZZ-9799/ 'SEQUENCE.'"

His mouth flew open. "Hey, I remember seeing 'Antechamber 6' engraved on one of those doors down there!" Impulsively, he dove over the rail. At the bottom, he searched a minute, poked a button, then entered an antechamber. In a few minutes he emerged with something like a small, square bubble in his hand. He flippered excitedly toward her, grinning from ear to ear and whooping into his SeaPhone. "It's right where they *said* it would be! This cube just might *be* that tiny, forgotten link Roson mentioned! Wow, what a *system* they have down there!"

Suddenly, out of the blue, his eyes squeezed shut. "*Yeowwwch*!" He handed the cube to her and began to furiously rub on his neck and forehead.

"Adam, what *is* it? Did you get shocked? Was there a loose wire or something?"

He held up a shaky finger. "No, no," he choked. "Wait a sec…."

Duron's message had been amazingly clear, even over the thousands of miles of ocean that separated them. He tried to calm himself, tried to reason it out. "Well, Roson *did* say that after I baked in the Neuron Resuscitator, the neural paths in my brain would be vastly different, unobstructed, almost superconducting." Scowling, he looked Elena squarely in the eye and filled her in. "I've got some news."

She pulled away, looking at him fearfully. "O-okay...."

He shrugged. "Duron's in Meseo. He just, um, gave me an update."

"Duron? But that's impossible! He's thousands of miles away!"

Adam tapped on his head. "I guess I'm in the grid now."

She stared at him, shaking. "Well," she quavered, "w-what did he say?"

Slowly, objectively, he filled her in, then stowed the memory cube in his backpack. "Time to go," he whispered.

They exited the tomb through the same open hatch they'd entered. Adam turned, shut the small panel behind him, and quickly snaked out through the tubular passageway behind Elena. Their SeaSpheres blazing like torches, they sped in silence toward the undersea city of Meseo.

Duron's mind-message had been urgent: a large gap in the gridwork had just been detected in the old-growth rainforest on the Continent of Namet. There was absolutely no doubt about the reading: several acres of rainforest had just been toppled, possibly with the aid of a Bitron laser cutter. A great wound, an enormous gash had unraveled the knotted, chenille-like fabric of green.

Chapter 29: **THE POWER**

There was another deafening crash. Although they were locked up in the last empty Quarantine room, the two hundred captive crew members could hear and feel the vibrations from some kind of major destruction outside. An overriding note of wild, animalistic howling began to rise over the tumult.

The Scarred One had found a new toy. Drunk with power and screeching at the top of his lungs, he leaned out precariously over a railing. "There you go-o-o-o!" he bellowed, jabbing his fist into the air. "Fourrr-r-r miles, *gon-n-ne*!" The enormous Arren trees were toppling in the distance just like a shooting gallery. "Just *look* at 'em go down! This sucker has *incredible* range!!" He lurched almost drunkenly, swinging the barrel of the mighty Laser Cutter in a wide swath. As he swiveled around and purposefully wavered it at his nervous cronies, they jumped aside, shouting in alarm.

Stifling a smirk and ducking away from flying branches, Dexor sprinted into the airlock. A few more brilliant moves like that and the fool's credibility would be completely destroyed. He whispered to Trennic at his elbow. "An hour," he hissed. "I'll give him an hour, tops, before they jump him."

"Wow!" Nastix queried. "D'ya really think they'll…?"

"Definitely!" Dexor sneered. "He's losing it! This isn't just an ordinary breakdown, guys: those little pink pills aren't percolating his thick squash anymore."

There was a sudden lurch under their feet. The three glanced questioningly at each other as the starship began to rise, its mighty antigrav engines laboring with the weight of the booty. Dexor rolled his eyes. "Hold on," he whispered. "I'm sure there'll be more fireworks to come." The movement was different this time, however. All the loading docks slammed shut, the cloaking device engaged, and the colossal disc simply blotted out of the sky.

Movon gripped the edges of the table in the situation room, staring at the image in disbelief. Scowling, he sent a quick message to Duron: Aurona's schematic gridwork had suddenly stopped pulsing out its telltale ripples of blue.

The old one had been waiting patiently for Adam and Elena inside Meseo's darkened bubble, peering out nervously through the taut, curved windows. Finally, he could make out two slivers of luminescence in the distance, slicing through the gloomy sea like pencil-thin lasers. In seconds they were hovering just outside. As Movon's message came through, he groaned, then waved them nervously toward an airlock. Steeling himself, he relayed the bad news.

"Adam! I am so sorry, but we have just come up against an unfortunate development: a few minutes ago, the operators of your starship sensed our virtual presence and engaged their shields and cloaking device. They are gone! Although Namet is only a few thousand miles from here, you can be sure they may be anywhere on the planet by now. As you say, we are back to 'square one,' waiting for them to show up on the gridwork!"

Adam's teeth rattled. His brain was literally vibrating inside his skull at the extremely close range of Duron's transmission. He lost his balance, grasping at the walls for support as he entered.

As the airlock's inner panel slowly slid open, he stood there confused, disoriented and dizzy. In a moment, he saw Duron out in the middle of the room whispering urgently to a detachment of Bandor warriors. His hand shaking, he jabbed his translator button way too hard, raising the volume up to max.

"Yo! Duron!" it bellowed. His eyes flew open, his hands flew to his ears, and Elena ducked away from him in shock. Startled, the Bandor warriors dropped to their knees on full alert, leveling their menacingly glowing stun-weapons at him.

There was a long, nervous pause, then Duron's tensed shoulders relaxed a bit. He turned, a questioning look on his face. "Ah, yes, Adam?" Noting his confused condition, he made a discrert motion and the warriors lowered their weapons.

Totally embarrassed, Adam shuffled toward them, fumbling with his volume control, lap unit and flippers. "Ah, sorry. I-I didn't mean to…. Aaack!" Mid-stride, his foot caught on the airlock's raised sill. Totally off balance, he staggered out into the middle of the room and fell flat on his face. His lap unit hit the floor with a deafening clatter, skidding in a wild spin toward the warriors. He lay there in total shock, his face burning.

Thinking quickly, he leaped to his feet, hastily brushing the dirt off his knees. He ran his fingers nervously through his salt-caked hair. "So! Ahhh…." He rubbed his palms together, looking around brightly. "Where's this dream ship I'm gonna pilot?"

There was another shocked silence. This time, Duron broke into an uncharacteristic fit of coughing. Scarlet-faced, Adam turned to Elena, his eyes pleading for support. She grimaced at him, peering from behind the airlock's massive door. After a long, uncertain pause, one of the warriors tentatively reached out with a toe and pushed the lap unit toward Duron. The Old One stood there numbly, collecting his thoughts. With a sigh, he resolutely bent over and picked it up.

Adam attempted a smile, grinning a bit too much in the tooth. "Ah, w-what can I say? It-it's, um … it's just one of 'Life's Most Embarrassing Moments,' right?"

Averting his eyes, Duron handed him his equipment. "You are most correct, Adam." Suddenly a slit-smile teased at the corners of his mouth. "Yes, I *do* remember a similar instance involving Movon and his first attempt with a WingSuit! He…," the old one covered his mouth, the corners of his eyes crinkling with laughter. The spell was quickly broken and the warriors joined in heartily.

As Elena sidled up, he glanced at her sheepishly. "Smooth move, huh?"

"Right up there with your best," she nodded. "But don't worry, you're still my dashing hero-type."

Chortling, Duron led him carefully by the elbow toward a pair of enormous doors. "I think I understand what just went on, Adam. As you say, you still have not 'gotten it together' as yet. All of us here in Meseo are aware that your mind and body have just been through incredible torture….Actually, how *are* you feeling?"

Adam took a moment to reflect, assessing himself. "Hmm. Well, to tell you the truth, I don't feel like I'm *me* anymore? Does that make any sense? For one thing, physical sounds are much louder and clearer and your furthest remote mind-messages blast through like you're yelling into my ear. And to top it all off, I have this huge tenseness inside my head, like an enormous static buildup."

Duron exchanged knowing looks with the other Elders.

"Oh yeah, and speaking of that tenseness: when I was back in the tomb I actually got to use one of those mind-controlled switches you mentioned. Man, I never expected it could be so *easy!* There was this switch hidden behind a leaf with a code inscribed ... on the...." His voice trailed off as he noticed Duron's steps faltering.

"Adam!" the old one stopped short, spun around, and looked him squarely in the eye. "There are only twelve Bandors *alive* who have that capability!" He pulled his cloak tightly over his frail shoulders. "*That* is why we are *Elders*!"

He was stunned. "But I-I thought you said *anybody* who was proficient...."

"No, Adam," he interrupted. "Telekinesis is apex, the ultimate plateau. Many have studied this difficult offshoot of telepathy all their lives and have never come close to it. Now, without even trying, you have just entered a very elite group!"

Elena hesitantly joined the conversation. "Well, it's true, Duron. I saw him do it. He lowered the great central medallion without touching a thing!"

Their jaws dropping, the Bandor warriors stared at Adam in awed silence, seeing him in some kind of new light. Duron faltered, closed his eyes, and hurriedly joined into a mind-conversation with the other Elders. Shrugging, he sighed in resignation. Slowly, carefully, he pulled out a small, multifaceted sphere from the voluminous folds of his cloak and turned the object over in his hand, contemplating.

"Adam, this moment has come a lot sooner than we expected. We Elders have just reached a decision." He held out the odd-looking sphere. "This ... is the Zevox."

"Huh? The Zee-what? Come again?"

"The Zevox. None of us have reached its inmost compartments: it consists of seven spring-loaded spheres within spheres, each with a mind-code and nano-switch. They are progressively and exponentially harder as one exposes the spheres within. Only *one* Bandor, I myself, have entered through the first three to reach level four. Legend has it that the inmost sphere holds the key to 'the Power.'" He expelled a long, nervous breath. "Now. It is both my honor and privilege to offer you this unprecedented opportunity, my son."

Adam hefted the small, lightweight object, glancing questioningly at Duron. "This is all so sudden. But may I ask you a *far* more important question before I try?"

"Why, yes. Absolutely."

"I'm just curious: why'd you just call me 'son'?"

The old one raised a thin brow. "But I-I do not understand. By attaining such a level so quickly, you have indeed become the heir apparent, and our laws cannot be broken. If you open the Zevox even *one* more level than I, you will automatically become the Supreme Leader of Aurona, and...."

"The *what*?" Adam fumbled the sphere, nearly dropping it.

Duron shrugged. "We are comfortable with this concept, all twelve of us."

As Adam gripped the Zevox a bit tighter, it began to feel strangely warm in his hand.

Microscopic rows of lights began to light up, brilliantly outlining the perimeter and defining its shape. He raised it to eye level, watching it warily.

"What's this little, ah, gizmo doing?"

"It senses your ability, Adam. It is preparing itself."

"For what?"

"It is changing all the codes. It happens every time. No one can memorize them."

Suddenly, involuntarily, Adam's eyes squeezed shut quite by themselves. The tiny object had an enormous pull, a magnetism that locked his body in time and space as if he were in rigor mortis. No amount of struggling could change his position.

A long, twisting tunnel opened before him. With ever-increasing speed, his mind entered the tortuous pathway, blazing past first one, two, then three and more glowing inscriptions on the smooth walls. Ignoring the flashing codes, it burrowed relentlessly toward the center, homing in on the prize.... There it was! A runic 'CDX-4' blazed in front of his inner eye! He pushed mightily. There was a small click, then another and then more. As the outside sphere opened, all seven levels collapsed and lay flat in his hand. The Zevox had simply opened from within.

Just as quickly as it had come, the pull left him. Giving his head a quick shake, he opened his eyes. Duron had fainted and fallen into the arms of his shocked warriors. Everyone else lay prostrate on the floor, facedown and afraid to move. Imploringly, he caught Elena's eye.

"What's with *them*?" he breathed. "I-I just opened their little do-thingy!"

"I *saw*!" she whispered.

He turned toward her, sputtering. "But-but it was a cinch! A piece of cake!"

"Adam," she quavered, "you opened it from the *inside out*!"

"Oh, no! Maybe I did it *wrong*!" He turned the loose contraption over and over, studying it. The semicircular flaps hung limply from the center, looking like the petals of a wilted impressionistic flower. He tipped it upside down and shook it. "But-but there's no key inside," he shrugged. "It's empty!"

"Wait," she pointed. "Duron's coming around. Maybe he knows where it is."

As Adam bent to help the old one to his feet, the warriors let go, shrank back, and fell facedown next to their companions. Awkwardly, he folded the flaps together, trying to make it look round again.

"Ah, I'm afraid I gotta break the news to you, Duron: the Zevox is empty."

The Old One took a quavering breath. "Of course it is," he whispered.

"But you said...."

"Do not bother looking for the key, Adam: you already possess it. What you have effortlessly demonstrated is something we never realized: there has been only one path into the inmost sphere all along, and for millennia, we have been approaching it from the most obvious direction. How you instinctively knew, or could somehow 'see' inside to read the inmost code I do not know. But what I *do* know and therefore now all of Aurona knows, is that we have a new Supreme Leader. I happily and proudly step aside."

Adam let out a gasp. Hundreds of curious eyes were peering at him from behind the massive doors: as he turned to the left and then to the right, receding waves of Bandors fell facedown, unable to return his gaze.

"You know," he murmured, "this has *got* to be written down in some kind of record book as the most ultimate in extremes: First I'm a bumbling idiot, and then... a-a God?" He spun to Duron. "You guys *can't* be serious about this 'Supreme Leader' thing! Look at me! I'm just a dork, a dweeb, a hopelessly possessed techno-geek who's gotten *way* over his head into a lot of mind-bending phenomena!"

Duron gazed into the distance. "You are forgetting one important thing, Adam."

"Whazzat?"

"Your mind-body combination is a superior vessel, prepped and trained by the best your Earthly universities had to offer. When the new was added and tempered by extreme fire, the vessel proved resilient." He sighed, and then finally turned to meet Adam's eyes. "What has resulted is what your grandfather called a 'synergism.' You now have 'the Power,' and it is yours alone, my son. Do you know the scope of your new abilities?"

A slow, lopsided grin stole across his face. "Come on, Duron, this is *way* too hard to swallow. I might be able to move tiny things, but ... *bigger* objects? Nah." He paused, reconsidering. "I'm willing to try, though."

Elena grabbed his arm. "Listen, Adam, Duron really may be onto something here! Remember how you were *thrown* onto your face by the Razah's mind-wave? You might be able to do *far* more than...."

"Adam," Duron interjected, "please accept the fact that you are now indeed Aurona's Supreme Leader? As such, we can withhold no more secrets from you. At the moment, we are in a crisis and have urgent business to attend to. But most importantly, as promised, your dream-ship awaits you behind those big doors."

"*What*?" Adam's eyes suddenly lit up. "Now we're *gettin'* somewhere!"

"You will find the latest and best aboard. Your ship contains an experimental command center fitted out exclusively with mind-controlled devices. This, shall we say, 'flying bridge' occupies a raised frontal area directly over the conventional electromechanical bridge, and can override it at any time."

"I see," Adam nodded. "Redundant systems. I'll give you a few comparisons from Earth's history: when our old-fashioned sailing ships switched to the new steam power, a lot of them kept their sails for a while until the unreliable source proved itself. And-and when electric cars finally approached the mainstream, some still kept small gasoline generators to extend their range. You made a wise, conservative decision to incorporate the two control centers."

Duron slit-smiled. "Why, thank you. We constructed it with the hope that some day we might possess the telekinetic capacity approaching your ability, Adam. Thankfully, that day has arrived!" He waved an arm, and the lights came on in the cavernous room in front of them. "Behold! Your dream ship!"

The only sound was that of Adam's excited breathing. As he stared at it in a trance, a powerful wave of déjà vu washed over him ... yes, he'd *seen* this ship before! That familiar bell-shaped curve of the hull, that sphere within, the shapes burned anew in his memory from his childhood dream-series. He knew the exact location of every thruster jet, every hidden door, and every shape-shifting aileron. This ship had been constructed for him and him alone.

Suddenly, deep inside, he felt the now-familiar static charge building, channeling forward like quicksilver into his frontal lobes.

Was the ship calling to him? Was it alive?

Channeling this new extension of his being, he pushed forward gently with his mind. Silently, a hatch opened and a ramp extended to his feet. Excitedly, he bounded up to the top to look around. Yes, there it was; somehow he could see right through the airlock's door: the speed elevator to the flying bridge!

He quickly lost all connection with his open-mouthed companions. They scuttled up the ramp after him, their eyes wide, watching in wonder. He opened the airlock, then hands behind his back, he shifted his focus to the elevator door. A code appeared in his inner eye, flashing brightly. As he pushed forward, the doors opened on silent, rubbery rollers. They quickly crowded into the smooth capsule with him..

Duron broke the spell. "Ah … Adam," he coughed, "there were no mind-switches installed on the hatch, ramp, or elevator. They employ electromechanical devices, or use remotely operated codes such as those found in your explorer's…."

"I know," he shrugged. "You guys stashed my e-helmet in a locker down on level C. I used the helmet's menu codes and routed them up to the flying bridge."

Duron looked at him in shock. "W-what? Those codes up on the bridge can only be tapped into from *there*, but we're still way down *here*! H-how could you…."

"See them?" he finished. "I don't know, everything on this ship seems to be made of glass, just like in my dream. For instance, I just turned on the main computer in the flying bridge and read the menus. The mind-switches were a cinch to manipulate: they're totally electronic! There's nothing remotely mechanical about them, like that old-fashioned switch in the medallion's leaf!"

Duron was completely baffled. "But-but…," he stammered. "They were designed to be operated from a range of *six* feet, maximum, and as such, they were arranged in a precise semicircle around the pilot's head at eye level. He glanced at the elevator's readout. We are still *sixty* feet from the flying bridge!"

"Like I said," he shrugged, "I just don't know: six or sixty, walls, hulls, and even distances don't seem to be an issue anymore. Maybe it's a quantum electron chain reaction? Anyway, right now for instance, I'm reading the menu on the main screen just like it was in front of me." He closed his eyes. "I'll tell you what I see…."

Shrugging, they exchanged uncertain looks.

"The monitor's showing a schematic of the whole ship and we're almost to the top in this little red blip of an elevator. The room's matte black, and all the equipment's been stashed behind the walls except the huge main monitor. There's a chair in the middle of the semicircle, and it's fitted with mind-sensors for my head, galvanic pads for my fingertips, and a pair of biofeedback gloves. Artificial Gravity is off and the chair's suspended in a gimbaled linkage with a built-in gyroscope to keep it in the same plane no matter what the attitude of the ship is around it."

They gaped incredulously as he finished rattling off the specs. "The menus are responsive to my voice or mind-commands for the various forms of space, atmospheric or underwater travel, and…."

The elevator door silently slid open and the flying bridge blazed to life, almost as if it were welcoming him home. He entered, slid into the suspended chair and closed his eyes in satisfaction. "Now," he whispered, "let's get down to business."

It had been close: somehow, they'd been detected. The Scarred One had spotted the security light flashing urgently on a monitor, and letting out a string of curses, sprinted up to the control center. Pushing his cronies aside, he'd thrown up the shields and cloaking device, then flew the heavily laden starship to the other side of the planet to land in another old-growth section of rainforest. Every sensor on alert, they'd slipped silently into a two mile, grassy clearing on the continent of Benou, landing next to a particularly large Motherlode.

They'd been about ready to leave Aurona, but the only thing keeping them was greed. Nearly every available space had been stuffed with knotted, stinking, dirt-covered masses of roots. The Bitron outlaws had hollowed out only enough space in the Pod Room to disrobe and climb into the few remaining sleep transporters.

The crew was painfully aware of their fate. Sitting in darkness, they now faced stark reality and debated the three most obvious outcomes: either they'd be killed in the next few hours and dumped overboard, or they'd be killed in the jungle after they'd filled the last room with gold, or they'd continue to be used as bargaining chips until they were jettisoned into interstellar space. Groaning in frustration, they prayed as hard as they could for a miraculous, unseen Option Number Four.

Dexor was puzzled. He'd just been given orders to join a large, combined scouting party to check out the root supply. As the mixed group trudged toward the jungle, he began to scowl in suspicion…. Was this a setup? Nearly all of the Bitron outlaws had been dispatched to accompany him. They were eyeing his group, repeatedly checking their weapons. He set his jaw: something was definitely afoot.

He studied the landscape as they approached the jungle. It was beautiful, even serene. Some really strange plants surrounded the perimeter: hundreds of the short shrubs were flowering profusely, their hot-pink blossoms looking like an exotic carpet. He glanced into the clearing behind him. The Motherlode was by far the largest he'd ever seen, with a trunk at least two hundred feet in diameter.

Warily, he turned back to monitor the Bitrons out of the corner of his eye. He just couldn't shake off his suspicions. They were clumping into small, whispering groups, glancing repeatedly at him and loading their remaining ammo into their semiautomatics. A chill ran down his spine and he started to walk a little faster.

Trennic was clueless. Lingering a short distance away, he frowned. Something has been bothering him: only one of those weird shrubs seemed to be moving in the breeze. He wet a finger and held it up, testing. "Hmm, no wind…." Puzzled, he dropped to his knees to look closer.

His plant was moving animatedly, but the one right next to it was totally rigid. "Huh?" Intrigued, he ducked under the branches to get out of the starship's line of sight.

Dexor's voice wafted in from the distance. "What in blazes are you doing??"

Trennic raised a finger. "Wait, wait! Gimme a sec!"

As Dexor peered around a tree, several Bitrons spotted him and ducked. There was a staccato chorus of clicks as they released their safeties.

"Get over here, you goon!" he hissed. "*Now-w-w!*"

Nastix scowled determinedly. He was tired of being bossed around, and besides, this bush was far too interesting. Mumbling to himself, he twisted down a stem to look at it closer. Unexpectedly, a loud warning buzz greeted his ears. "*Huh?*" He jerked his hand away. The stem slowly reassembled itself, straightening and bending upward. "You're kidding!" he whispered.

He inched closer. As his warm breath hit the trunk's rough, overlapping surface, the evenly-spaced bark finally gave away the shrub's secret: a forest of antennae appeared, waved inquisitively, and then tucked away. His mouth flew open. As he tentatively poked the surface with his finger, the bark writhed and rearranged itself in response. "Ugh!" He stood up, totally disgusted, whacking the bush with the butt of his Stifler. "*Bugs*! They're all *bugs*! "

In an explosion of color and sound, the entire plant flew apart, then another, and then another. Suddenly, in an enormous chain reaction, three square miles of undergrowth erupted in a roar of of beating wings and flying insects!

The scouting party panicked. Stiflers and semiautomatics were fired at random, the bullets and beams of light stabbing through the dense, hot-pink cloud.

A chilling scream rose above the din, pumping the adrenaline of pure insanity into the air: a stray bullet had just hit the tripod of the mighty Laser Cutter! It began to topple slowly, cutting through the platform's railing like butter. Frothing at the mouth, the Scarred One clawed futilely at the heavy machine. He could only watch it fall, twisting and blazing great arcs of destruction. It hit the ground in a muffled explosion, disintegrating instantly.

The ultimate in damage had been done. As a great shadow darkened the forest, the scouting party felt a mighty wind at their backs. The air quickly cleared of flying insects. Alarmed, they spun around and looked up in horror: there was barely enough time to catch a glimpse of the massive, toppling Motherlode before it hit.

Adam's eyes popped. "*Yesss!!*" Both of his fists stabbed the air. Elena, Duron, and the three warriors backed away warily as he leaped out of his gimbaled chair and danced around the small room in unrestrained exuberance. He spun toward them, his voice jubilant, euphoric. "*I know where they are!*"

"What??" Elena grabbed him by the arms. "Are you *sure*?"

"I'm stark, raving positive!"

Duron tested him, guardedly. "Tell us how you, ah … 'know' this?"

It took a lot of effort to calm him down, but his breathing finally slowed to a more even tempo. He closed his eyes, took a breath, and explained slowly. "Don't ask me how, but in my mind's eye I found myself traveling along some kind of electronic pathways and then out through some schematic junctions and relays. Somehow, I-I was able to 'see' that green gridwork you've been monitoring! Just now, it flashed and sent out this *huge* blue ripple! They're on Benou, on the other side of the planet!"

Dexor drew back in shock, then nodded thoughtfully. "Well, I believe you, Adam. What is the best course of action? Remember, you are in command!"

Adam stopped short. "Yike, you're right. I forget that part." His mind spinning, he quickly formulated a plan. "Well, ah, here it is: first, we're standing in what I've decided to call the 'Phantom Cruiser.' At least that's what I always *wanted* to call this ship in my dreams. Ultimate stealth *is* one if this ship's greatest assets, right?"

Duron nodded hesitantly. "You are correct.... And?"

Glancing at the big monitor, Adam lit up a bright schematic of Aurona and rotated the planet on its axis. "They're right *there*, on that pulsing spot. I'm positive they're totally on the watch. Every sensor aboard is on high alert, scanning the sky for the slightest abnormalities. If they see a thing they'll be gone in a flash, so we've *got* to transition into this Cruiser's advanced stealth mode. It may take a bit longer to get there, but I've got a few things up my sleeve while we're on the way." He pointed at the schematic once more. "That starship has to be delayed long enough to give us a chance to get there, but most of all, they can't get suspicious. In other words, they shouldn't have a clue that *we're* the ones who are stopping them. I'll set my plan in motion as we start traveling. We've got no time to lose."

He slipped his arm around Elena's waist. "Ah, I'm really sorry, oh mother-to-be, there's only one chair. I-I've gotta sit up here in the flying bridge."

She shrugged. "I'm fine with that, Adam. It's okay."

"You sure?"

"Hey," she shrugged, "it's safer downstairs. We'll be connected by monitors."

Nodding, he gave her hand a squeeze and turned to the others. "Okay, here's the scoop: we'll use shape-shifting and travel atmospheric at Mach 8, just above the ocean's surface. Just before we reach their visual horizon, we'll drop to subsonic at a fifty-mile perimeter. Then, we'll slip in and snoop."

The Old One's head tilted. "What is...?"

"Spy," Elena interjected quickly. "We'll be right *next* to them and they won't suspect a thing, right Adam?"

He grinned. "Right in their lap, baby!"

A great bubble of seawater broke the surface above Meseo, releasing the Phantom Cruiser into a stormy ocean. Crackling and popping in a spectacular light show, it pierced the salty air with a tremendous aurora of static discharge. A vision from the future and built for speed, Adam's dream ship was far smaller and infinitely more agile than any of its predecessors. It hugged the surface of the ocean closely as it skimmed and danced like an acrobat between the crests of the waves, gathering speed in a runner's sprint toward the distant continent of Benou. The sound barrier's threshold proved to be no threshold at all: the Cruiser's enormous static discharge coupled with its ultimate shape-shifting capabilities seemed to open an atmosphere-free tunnel toward the bright, empty horizon.

The last of the dust was finally settling. As Dexor regained consciousness and began to move, he writhed in agony. Both of his legs were broken in several places, pinned under a massive Arren tree. With concerted effort, he lifted his head to look around. His gun was nowhere in sight and alien bodies were scattered everywhere, one hanging limply from a tree. He groaned, knowing that it would be just a matter of time before the jungle would claim them all. Suddenly, he heard a muttering and scraping sound. He gritted his teeth and pushed up on his elbow.

Cursing, Nastix and Trennic were pulling themselves up a steep slope. They'd missed death by inches, thrown through the air by a great tremor as the Motherlode's unthinkable mass buckled the planet's crust.

His memory was returning, and Dexor fell back shuddering. He'd caught a quick glimpse of the Laser Cutter as it zapped and sizzled through the Motherlode's dense wood: the angle of the cut couldn't have been more perfect. As the great tree's shadow outlined its area of impact, there'd been absolutely no time to cry out. The Bitrons probably never knew what hit them.

Summoning all his strength, he sat up. With the Motherlode gone, the starship was flashing brightly in the sunlight, hovering and spinning madly above the grassy plain. Debris was still flying off the hull. What was that? The sound of distant, maniacal laughter reached his ears. He rolled his eyes and groaned: yes, it *had* been a setup.

As the big saucer slowed down from its crazy spin, he could see the Scarred One's black robes flapping in the breeze as he hung precariously from a broken rail. A single, clawed hand was all that kept him from flying to the ground, but he was tenacious and wiry. Dexor watched him struggle against the centrifugal force, then regain his footing. As he climbed over the rail and disappeared into the depths of the starship, he gnashed his teeth in total, helpless frustration.

A drama of a different sort had taken place inside the starship. As a massive Arren branch had bashed into the resilient hull and set it spinning, the four remaining Bitrons in the control room couldn't crawl back against the tremendous centrifugal force. Down in the Quarantine room, the crew had been flung against the outer walls in a jumbled heap. As the spin slowed, they started to roll off onto the floor. The gold had been thrown outward too, tons of it. They could hear the muffled wrenching as it settled, crumbling through the storeroom walls in the distance. Although the hull was constructed of an impermeable alloy, the inner walls were not.

The spinning finally stopped. They crawled off each other, their hearts hammering. Miraculously, no one had been badly hurt; several had sprains and bruises but nobody had any broken bones, or worse, killed. They looked up, startled, as a great shudder passed through the starship. Quite evidently, someone was at the controls and they'd just turned the Artificial Gravity back on.

As the Scarred One lurched off the commander's bronze elevator and sprinted into the control room, three panicked Bitrons sat hunched over the displays, their fingers wildly jabbing at random buttons. Nearby, a fourth one laid limply, his neck broken. He drew in a long breath. "*Yaaa-a-ah*!!" As the monitors rattled, they spun around, pale and bruised. "How could this *be*?" he thundered. "What happened?"

A Bitron raised a hesitant finger. "We saw how it happened, sir. Some kind of plant-animal mimic started some kind of chain reaction!"

"*Wha-a-a-at*??"

Another one piped up. "Thousands of bushes just … *exploded*!"

The third one found his courage. "That's right! They actually…." As the beady eyes narrowed, his voice trailed off. The Scarred One wordlessly opened his cloak to reveal his countless rows of pocketed stilettos. They got the message.

"Strap in," he hissed. "We're *leaving*!"

They scrambled back into their chairs and initiated the liftoff sequence. The outer platforms closed with a bang, the external sensors retracted into the hull, and the great antigrav engines began to rev for the takeoff. Smiling smugly, the Scarred One bent to the controls. Yes, everything was going according to plan.

The jungles of Benou swept under them. As they drew closer, Adam zeroed in on the big clearing to assess the damage. "Holy smoke, guys! Someone just made a *major* goof," he whispered. "A *big time* goof!"

Duron's voice cut in. "Oh, no, one of our Motherlodes? It takes centuries to…. Wait! They are about to leave, Adam! Our sensors show it plainly!"

"Okay, okay," Adam mumbled. "I'm landing right next to them in the clearing at Level 4 Cloaking…." He quickly became lost in a trance. In his mind's eye, he entered his stolen starship and sped along its familiar pathways, burrowing inward toward his personal locker on level M. "Ah, *there* it is, my old, dented e-helmet!" As he pushed hard with his mind, it flickered to life. Narrow bars of light filtered out through the locker's louvers into the hallway.

The smirk suddenly disappeared from the Scarred One's face. Nothing was happening! Focusing intently, he carefully initiated the liftoff sequence once more, deliberately and precisely pushing and turning each button and bar. He leaned back and waited…. Nothing happened!

There was a long, pregnant pause, then a white-knuckled fist slammed down onto the control panel in total frustration. "*Yaaa-a-ah*!!" He leaped out of his chair, straps and buckles flying. The Bitrons scrambled to the far side of the room: they knew what was coming; they'd seen it far too often.

A shaking, scrawny finger slid out of its sleeve, pointing at them accusingly. "*You-u-u*!!" he hissed. "*You* broke my ship! You just *sat* here and let it happen!!"

There it was, the froth was dribbling from the corners of his mouth. The steam was rising, the momentum was building, and the flawed line of presumptive, accusatory reasoning was percolating. In their gut, the three Bitrons knew no amount of sound facts or legitimate excuses could calm him down. They tensed to run.

"*Where* do you think you're *going*?"

As they made a step toward the door, it slid shut quite by itself and locked with a decided click. They spun around in horror, raising their arms and fearing the worst. The Scarred One wasn't interested in them, however; his beady eyes were focusing on the control panel. A small, flashing light was scrolling by with an extremely unwelcome message.

"*Override ... Main Control Panel ... Override ... Main Control Panel....*"

His head jerked up. An external monitor showed the ground level slowly coming up, then all went blank as the big saucer settled onto its landing struts.

Adam let out a long, nervous breath and looked around. Now that this first order of business had been taken care of, he could plainly see how the mysterious, unfortunate chain of events had unfolded. Without question, it involved the Bitron's mighty Laser Cutter and resulted with an enormous fallen Motherlode.

Suddenly, the Phantom Cruiser's external sensors flashed: their infrared readings were showing three life forms stirring near a big Arren trunk! With a sinking feeling, he hoped and prayed they weren't all that was left of his crew. He checked the rest of the jungle. Nothing moved; the mighty crash had terrified all the life forms.

He quickly shifted his attention back to the interior of his starship. Concentrating intently, he scrolled through menu after submenu inside his old e-helmet, turning on lights in various storerooms, searching in earnest for someone, anyone. Each room's monitor showed pretty much the same thing, and he didn't like what he saw: buckled walls, clogged corridors, and caved-in floors. Finally, he detected a movement on the bottom level. Immediately, he hit the switches and flooded the big Quarantine room with light.

"*Yes!*" He jumped in his seat. "*Pay dirt!*" Excitedly, he patched the view through to Elena and Duron's monitors below. "There ya go," he whispered quietly, "we still have our crew! I can't crank up audio yet; someone might be lurking in the hallways."

In the storeroom, the hostages rose to their feet, shielding their eyes in the bright light and fearing the worst. Someone raised a shaking hand and pointed wordlessly. The top of an entire wall had been ripped open, the twenty-foot gash revealing the sawed-off stumps of an enormous pile of gold roots!

Chapter 30: MIND GAMES

The tension had become unbearable in the control room. Abandoning their efforts to pry open the massive bronze door, the three remaining Bitrons retreated into a corner, wide-eyed with fear. Suddenly behind them, the stench of putrid breath wafted into their nostrils. They recoiled, gagging and covering their mouths.

"Yes-s-s, we're trapped and someone *knows* it!" the Scarred One rasped.

"W-what?" one of them choked. "You mean *you* didn't close the door?"

"No I *didn't!*" he snapped. "Now, guess with me: That someone has a *name*...?"

A second Bitron uncovered his mouth. "A-Adam?" he squeaked.

The smirking face said it all. "Back from the dead," he whined. "Somehow, somewhere, he's caused a system override. Now listen: we're all in this together, so let's put our heads together and see if we can work as a cohesive group. We should be able to come up with some kind of an escape plan, right?"

They exchanged suspicious glances. Was this just another, even more treacherous side of this one's demented character? A ploy to worm his way back into their trust? Wavering with uncertainty, they waited in silence.

He continued smoothly, his voice like butter. "Now, let's see. We'll need a list of resources in the room, anything nonelectronic, purely mechanical." He gestured at the ceiling. "You could start poking around up there. Just a suggestion, mind you. Ventilation shafts, cable chases, any opening will be considered."

The last Bitron finally recovered. "Ah, hidden wall panels, sir?"

"Good *idea*!" There was the faintest hint of sarcastic, smirking derision, but it was reeled in quickly. "Oh, and while you're at it, check out the closets and cabinets and under the consoles." He turned away, rubbing his skinny palms together. "Now as for me, I'm going to pry a bit myself! This override can be overridden!"

Adam heard a faint ping and glanced up. A runic button was glowing on the bottom corner of his big screen, translating as 'Deep-X.'" He focused on it, pushed gently, and a short menu dropped. "Wow, what's *this*?" He leaned forward excitedly, scrolling through the options. You're kidding! It does all this stuff??"

He snapped on an external monitor to study the surface of his stolen starship. His system override had disabled the cloaking device, leaving it fully open to scrutiny. It sat quietly on the far side of the clearing, the shields up. Although debris was still sliding off its smooth, domed top, one of the cargo bays was hanging open and smoke was rising from an object under the hull, it looked relatively undamaged. He breathed a sigh of relief, turned on the first option, then leaned forward excitedly. "Good night! This is crazy, *crazy* stuff!" Impulsively, he channeled the mind-bending display to the monitors below, and there was an immediate response.

"Wow! Adam!" Elena gasped. "What's *this*, a giant x-ray of our ship?"

"You're close, hon. Let Duron explain while I check this out some more."

Duron eagerly joined into the conversation. "This is a High Density Scanner, Elena; a deeply penetrating schematic cross section of the starship. It also has an infrared overlay! Perhaps Adam can...."

"Hey! Look!" Adam interrupted. "There they *are*!"

He'd already found the link, and telltale heat signatures were now glowing: some were extremely bright like the mighty fusion reactor in the engine room, others were dull, like the freshly minted bullion cooling in the lower storerooms, but most importantly, a crowd of glowing human shapes were moving around in the bottom Quarantine room!

"Yes, thank God! I see them!" Elena gushed. "There's a *lot* of 'em, too!"

"Now look up in the control room, guys." Adam whispered. "There's only three ... no, *four* figures moving around."

Duron joined in again. "But Adam, why are there so few? And why have they not attempted to depart? They are just.... It appears that they are...."

"Searching." Adam finished. "They're in a temporary lockdown, something called a 'timed system override.' The bad news? We're at a stalemate: the shields are still up. I've tried and tried to disable them, but the mechanical relays must have been busted with all that heavy gold shifting around and buckling walls." He sighed, contemplating. "Well, the good news is that the shields aren't able to penetrate underground as far as they used to, only a foot or two." He studied his monitor. "Okay, while they're tryin' to figure out how to take off, I gotta move quickly! I've only been able to stretch out this override thing for maybe an hour, tops."

"But I don't remember that feature," Duron probed. "How did you...?"

"I tweaked," he shrugged. "I couldn't hack into your system to rewrite any code, because I don't know your language. I, ah, had to tweak a few things."

Duron was incredulous. "What did you actually do?"

"I created a bogus 'security alarm sequence.' You could call it a fake firewall. Monitors, flight controls, everything's timed except room lighting and the shields."

Shrugging, Elena and the warriors threw each other blank looks.

Adam continued. "Oh, and one more important thing: look around the ship. There are no more heat signatures, right?"

After a short silence, Elena answered. "You're right. There's just the two groups. Where's-where's everybody else? Outside?"

"Correct."

She scowled. "But ... *all* of them? Why?"

"That weird dude with the hood must have deliberately sent them out," Adam postulated. "Then he could slip away with all the booty, right? Gimme a sec, Duron, I gotta initiate a few more, ah, *details*!"

A slow slit-smile played across Duron's lips. "I know what you are doing, Adam. Tweaking your hidden e-helmet's controls once more, right?"

"Who, *me*?" Adam glanced up innocently at the monitor.

"Yes, you." Duron chuckled. "Tell us. What you are doing?"

"Wait, wait. First I have to initiate a few more sequences. Very different ones."

The Old One sighed and turned to Elena. "I guess we will just have to see."

They watched Adam on their monitors. He'd slipped on his biofeedback gloves and his eyes were dancing around as if he were looking at something in the distance. He began to make subtle opening motions with his hands, then shooing gestures.

Elena could contain herself no longer. "Um, Adam, what are you *doing*?"

"What? Oh, spying, among other things."

She caught on quickly. "You mean, with-with our little guys?"

"Yup. I just turned on a small light in a storage room a minute ago, and there was this pail of Spyders dumped over from the impact. When I switched on a bright corridor light, the little guys spotted a gash in the wall and started funneling out! They're all over the ship now, and I mean…. Wait! Hey, no kidding! Wow!!"

Duron was doing his level best to follow. "What, Adam? What?"

"I didn't expect *this*! About fifty of those little imps are jumping off a platform on Level E! The airlock's just hanging open. The railing looks like it's busted."

"You mean they are flying *outside*? How is that possible with the shields up?"

Adam stopped short. "Hey, you're right! They're just zipping through the shields as if they didn't exist! How can…. Wait, wait!!"

Elena was getting exasperated. "*What*, Adam? Please!"

"Their Spyder bodies are *glowing*! They're all lit up! Hold on, a whole flock of 'em just banked toward the woods! Quick, guys, grab your gloves and e-helmets and hop into a few of those Spyders! While I'm busy with the rest of my scheme, fly out there and see if there's any of our crew left! "

"Great idea!" Elena jumped. "Hey, Duron, where do you guys keep…." Her voice faded away as they all dashed out of the control room.

Mumbling to himself, Adam turned back to his tasks. "Wow! I gotta look into that shield-penetrating thing when I get a chance! That's *way* beyond amazing!" He closed his eyes to concentrate. "Okay, I've just wasted about fifteen precious minutes, yapping…. Gotta finish laying out the rest of my traps…"

The three Bitrons had searched everywhere, all with no luck. Eyeing the Scarred One, they retreated to the far side of the control room. Every trace of civility seemed to have vanished as quickly as it had been affected.

He turned slowly to them, opening his cloak once more to reveal his arsenal. "So here we are, one big dyssssfunctional family," he hissed. "Let's, ah, 'talk' about our next step." As a crooked finger slipped under his cloak, a loud loud warning buzzer sounded behind him. He spun around, the stilettos quickly forgotten. "Wha-a-a?"

In abrupt sequence, the control panel lit up, the massive bronze door skidded open, and a scrolling display flickered: "*Security Failure! Loading Platform Open on Level E! Security Failure! Loading Platform Open on….*"

A glimmer of hope washed across the Scarred One's face. "Saved by the bell!" He spun toward the cowed Bitrons. "So whaddaya waitin' for? Like it says, run down to Level E and secure that blasted exit!" He shooed them out, his cloak flapping. "We need all hatches closed for takeoff!"

A strangely-glowing cloud of Spyders was drifting toward the jungle. Angling their suction pads around to catch the strong breezes at the edge of the big clearing, Elena, Duron, and the three Bandor warriors were directing the floating specks. They gaped in awe as they flew over the trunk of the massive Motherlode. There were a few limp Bitron corpses flung out into the woods, and they could only guess how many bodies might have been crushed under the skyscraper-sized trunk.

Suddenly, Elena spotted a distant movement. She quickly flew closer. Dexor, Trennic, and Nastix huddled behind the trunk of a great, fallen Arren tree. They were obviously scared out of their wits, yelling and pointing into the distance. As her eyes followed their line of sight, she let out a gasp, her Spyder body hovering.

"Adam! A *Razah*!" she squealed. "A big one! He's about ready to stun some of our guys! What should I *do*?"

Distracted from his plotting, Adam looked up. "Huh? Oh, no!" He formed a quick, impromptu solution. "Um, um ... I know! Go land on the Razah's head!"

"*What*? You're kidding!"

"Just *do* it! Land on his *head*! Duron, you and your warriors fly over there, too! Land next to her! Please, I know Razahs! They move quickly!"

"Okay," they chorused. Landing on the rough, unkempt fur, they latched on tightly with their hooked feet. In moments, five Spyders were waiting for Adam's direction as he watched them through one of the Cruiser's external monitors.

The smell of blood hung thickly in the air. Momentarily swatting at the cloud of annoying insects flying around his head, the Razah quickly returned to concentrate on his slow, stealthy approach. His tail twitching, he focused intently on his prize. Barely thirty feet away, he raised his head high for a supercharged mega-stun that would put them all away.

"*Now!*" Adam shouted. "*Blast* that sucker! *Empty* those stink tanks!!"

A putrid cloud of vapor exploded, squirting directly into the Razah's face. Roaring in pain, he batted and writhed on the ground, then leaped to his feet and blindly wheeled toward the jungle, running at full tilt. In seconds, he crashed headlong into a tree, breaking his neck.

Dexor and his men winced at the crunch and snap of bones. His legs twitching, his great jaws stretching open, the Razah slowly stiffened into rigor mortis. They turned toward each other, their eyes wide.

"I-I don't *get* it," Nastix stuttered. "Our Spyders just put his lights out!"

"But ... *why*?" Trennic questioned. "Why'd anyone want to save *us*?"

Dexor was shaking his head in confusion. As he opened his mouth to speak, there was a sudden whirring sound. A lone Spyder floated down, landing on the back of his hand. "Guys, guys, look!" The three focused on it, staring in disbelief. The robotoid seemed to be gesturing in some kind of body language, jumping up and down and pointing to the far side of the clearing. In unison, they turned their heads.

Like a mirage, the mighty Phantom Cruiser dissolved a fifty-foot section of its cloaking device, spun a few degrees, and blinked its lights. Just as quickly, it disappeared. They turned back to each other, gaping in awed silence.

For the first time in his life, Dexor was thoroughly chastened. Uncontrollable tears welled up in his eyes, and he bit his lip. "Whoa, guys," he choked. "It's over. I'm done. I'm toast." He threw up his hands. "Two broken legs, no weapons and no reason left to fight." He turned to Trennic. "And I totally agree with you," he mumbled. "The *real* question is, '*Why*?'"

The hallways were thick with scurrying black shapes. Suddenly, there was a loud, rapping sound of leather boots approaching. The Spyders quickly defaulted into stealth mode and dashed for cover, squeezing into any crevice they could find.

Adam had been trailing the three Bitrons. As they paused to turn a corner, he quickly alerted Elena, Duron, and the warriors. Within minutes, they'd all found nearby Spyder frequencies and joined the chase. A small, furtive group now trailed along the ceiling over their heads.

The jittery, jumpy Bitrons carefully picked their way through the collapsed walls toward the bright, open airlock in the distance. In moments they edged carefully into the wide doorway. Flying debris had ripped off the metal railing and part of it had jammed the platform open. As they paused to adjust their eyes to the intense light, Adam's Spyder made a sudden, brazen move.

The group watched in fascination as his robotoid scurried down the doorframe behind the Bitrons and became a blur of motion. It seemed to be almost possessed, circling and recircling their legs, pausing only to do a weird squat and wiggle on their boots. Elena could contain herself no longer. "Um, Adam, what are you doing? I-I don't remember any of *those* moves."

"Yes, Adam," Duron added. "Your strange actions, could you be, ah…?"

Holding tightly to the door's frame, the Bitrons leaned way out to peer over the edge, some sixty feet off the ground.

"Okay, I'm ready." Adam answered cryptically. "My Spyder's gonna turn into some shiny bait to tantalize them. When I signal, lay down another mega stink cloud."

They nodded their Spyder bodies eagerly: they'd caught on.

Suddenly, right in front of three startled faces, Adam's Spyder leaped out through the shields and lit up with a strange glow! The bright dot spun and cartwheeled in a dazzling show, then carefully ruddered away until it was just out of reach.

The trio stood there uncertainly, fearful of the edge, yet studying the weird insect.

"*Now*!!" Adam shouted the signal.

The air turned purple. The Bitrons gagged as the horrendous stench enveloped them, backing away from it and flailing their arms. Suddenly, they realized they'd backed over the edge and looked down in horror. Screaming, they fell as a unit, their ankles entwined with a strange, glistening white thread. The small group of Spyders swiftly flew outside, angling their bodies around to see what had happened. What *was* that white stuff wrapped around their ankles? Could it be…? Their question went unanswered. They jumped as the hatch slammed shut behind them with a loud bang.

"That's *it,* guys!" Adam shouted. "Wow, we barely made it! That timed override just ran out, and there's only *one guy* left upstairs!"

The Spyders hovered upside down, studying the three Bitron bodies on the ground: yes, they were dead; there was no movement. Adam sighed, pulled off his helmet and gloves, then resolutely continued to lay out more bait. He needed to focus all his attention on his next trap. It would be pivotal, and a huge gamble.

A chime sounded. Glancing down at the main control panel, the Scarred One's pig eyes focused on a scrolling display. As he read it, he gaped in disbelief.

"Level E secure! Level E' secure! Ready for takeoff… Ready for takeoff…."

He leaped out of his chair with maniacal abandon and hopped in tight circles. "*Ha-a-a*!" His fists jabbed the air. "I don't know how, but those three idiots *did* it!! I'm back in business! It's all mine, *all* of it!" He yanked the glowing keys from his cloak, jabbed them into their slots, and twisted them in the memorized sequence. Sweating profusely, he impatiently rubbed his palms together. As the starship initiated its slow startup sequence, there was another small ping. A short, scrolling message caught his attention.

"Top Secret… Top Secret… Top Secret…"

He scowled, pondering. Was this *Adam* again? Was this just more of his *trickery*? Uncertainly, his hands drifted back toward the controls. Just as he was about to punch the button for takeoff, his eyes flew open: a stream of powerful, unbidden thoughts and wild ideas were surging through his mind. His heart racing, he clutched the arms of his chair. A schematic of Aurona lit up, dead center of his main display. Totally captivated, he let out a quavering breath, his pig eyes watching graphic arrows blinking and traveling around to the other side of the planet.

"Adam, you can't be *serious*!" Elena wailed. "You're letting him get *away*??"

Duron was beside himself. "*No,* Adam, *no!* We simply *cannot* let this deranged being escape with your starship and its telltale cargo of gold! They will all return in force one day, *thousands* of them, and…."

There was the sound of a door sliding open behind them. Adam was standing in the entrance with an odd, mischievous look on his face. "Hey, he shrugged, "don't worry, guys. I just beamed out a few tempting thoughts into his deranged mind. We just have to wait and see if he responds."

They spun back to their monitors. Yes, the starship was definitely moving. Gritting their teeth, they watched it retract its landing pods and rise heavily into the sky. In minutes, the cloaking device engaged and it was gone.

Tears brimmed Elena's eyes. "No, no-o-o!! Quick, Adam! Follow him! I know this Phantom thingy's *lightning* fast! Let's…."

He raised a finger. "It's okay hon, really. I know where he's going. I've given him a compelling reason to, ah, stay a while longer. Remember, he's got the shields up and two hundred of our crew aboard. We really *can't* do anything, right?"

Duron slumped into a chair, sputtering. "But-but…."

Adam turned his focus to the large central screen. It flickered, a few buttons lit up, and then a small, moving dot appeared, traveling over a schematic surface of Aurona. "Aha! There it *is*!" he whooped. "The Phantom Cruiser can '*see*' the starship! When all its available sensors combine, they become a synergy!"

Duron sat bolt upright. "But Adam, again, that function is not listed...."

He interrupted excitedly. "I know, I know! This stuff is *way* beyond what you guys dreamed up! I-I was just trying out one of my theories: when they're combined, all the sensors on the Phantom Cruiser can detect the molecular disturbance of a large object pushing through the atmosphere!"

They watched the big screen, hope returning to their eyes.

"Look. He's definitely *not* leaving. He took the bait."

Elena grabbed his hand. "Thanks, Adam," she sighed. "Now please fill us in? There have been way too many gaps for us to follow. We couldn't keep up with you."

"Okay," he shrugged. "First, I tripped the last three Bitrons with Spyder silk."

Duron's head snapped up. "I *thought* so! You used the other two...."

"The other two white canisters," Adam finished. "They contained an organic epoxy. Yes, we were both wondering what they were for. I figured it out a while ago, but I've been waiting for an ideal time to use the stuff. My plans kind of, ah, reorganize on the fly."

Elena prodded him. "Speaking of ... 'on the fly'?"

"Yes, you're right!." He zoomed the screen to the other side of Aurona, to the middle of the desert of Arrix. In moments they spotted the glowing dot once more. The room grew quiet as the wheels and gears of their minds began to turn, forming the inevitable 'big question.' One by one, they turned to Adam.

"Yes, I know what you're struggling with," he confessed. "It's true. I-I can beam out *thoughts* now. Powerful ones."

Elena's eyes widened. "Adam, you can't possibly be saying you 'compelled' that horrible, disgusting creature to land way out in the middle of a *desert*? He was inches away from freedom, and he still had our crew still aboard to barter with! How...?"

"Lies," he shrugged. "Alternate *facts*. Let's just say I let him in on a bogus 'top secret'!"

"Adam, please. Nobody has a *clue* where you're going with this."

"I made it all *up*! It's a total fabrication! I programmed a phony display on his main screen and then to back it up, I stepped inside his sick, warped mind with some trivial, random thoughts. You know, tiny, insignificant things like galactic domination, ultimate power, riches, and so on.... You know, typical ego fluff?"

Duron cut in, stifling his slit-smile. "Yes, Adam. Small details. Blips."

"Well, he grabbed the bait. With people like him, there's never enough, right? So, just like I thought, he's 'gotta do this one last thing' before he leaves Aurona."

As another flurry of questions began to fly, he held up a finger. "Listen, guys. I'll let you know what he's looking for...." He pulled them closer, whispering.

Their eyes widened, then snapped back to the screen. The starship's schematic dot indeed seemed to be slowing as it approached a small, red X.

"So," Adam shrugged. "Think it'll work?"

Duron was nodding with his whole body. "Yes, yes! What that crazed Bitron thinks he is getting will make his gold seem like ballast. You are correct, Adam, and an extremely keen observer of human nature I might add. Your bogus 'prize' is indeed *very* big, and you were very bold to have taken such a chance that he might respond. We now have this one last opportunity to rescue our crew."

Adam threw up his hands. "So let's take a break from all these mind games and let that dude *bake* awhile! Right now, we've got three bleeding men stranded out in the jungle. We gotta pull them inside before another Razah finds 'em!"

The starship shimmered like a mirage in the intense heat. His hands trembling, the Scarred One steered the craft over the glowing, triangulated spot on his main monitor, then deployed the landing struts. Indeed, the mountains of gold crammed into the holds now seemed trivial compared to what lay buried in the sands beneath him. He burst into the hallway, his mind racing. Yes, once again, the hostages would supply all the muscle he'd need, and then their room would be empty and available for his grand prize. He'd simply take off and leave the worthless scum to fry in the desert. He paused outside their dented, battered door and let loose with his portable laser cutter.

The crew stumbled out of cool darkness into the desert's blazing light and heat. Shielding their eyes in the overwhelming glare, they groped their way down a long, sloping ramp to the desert floor.

Suddenly, the madman thrust his cloaked body over the railing above them and let loose with a piercing shriek. "That's *it*!! Right over *there*!" He focused a laser pointer under the starship, and it glowed brightly in the shadows. "X marks the spot!" he shrilled. Now *dig, dig, dig* all of you! That's right, load all this sand onto those barges and haul it out! Don't get any bright ideas, though; I've got many cameras watching. If my weapons don't cut you down, there's open desert waiting for five hundred miles in all directions!"

The crew labored mightily, sweating profusely and keeping track of the deranged being out of the corners of their eyes. If possible, he was acting even stranger than usual: hopping in tight circles on the platform, he repeatedly jabbed the air with his fist. Whatever they were digging for seemed to have snared him in some kind of spell.

Back at the empty circular clearing, three mighty Bandor starships had joined the Phantom Cruiser. Stiflers drawn, a search party fanned out into the jungle and found Dexor and his men to be severely injured, with deep gashes and many broken bones. As their antigrav stretchers floated aboard a starship they remained subdued and contrite. With Elena and Duron watching discreetly from a doorway, Adam entered their hospital bay and walked directly to their beds.

They glanced up in astonishment, then totally embarrassed, quickly lowered their eyes. Speechless, Dexor turned his face to the wall.

Adam plunked himself down on the edge of his bed. "So?" He waited in silence.

On the spot, Dexor mumbled an answer. "So... I, ah, blew it."

Adam nodded. "Thanks. That's enough. We'll decide who's to blame for what later, but right now I gotta go chase my starship and get the rest of my crew back."

Dexor glanced at him for a brief, questioning moment. "They've left Aurona?"

He stood up. "No, not quite yet. We'll talk more, but I gotta go now."

"I-I…" Dexor raised his hand weakly, and then dropped it to his side.

Adam paused. "What's that?"

"Nothing," he mumbled. "I just wish I could help somehow, that's all."

Trennic stared at his boss open-mouthed, then turned to Adam. "We really hate how things turned out, sir. We didn't deserve to be rescued after…."

Dexor cut in. "After all we did to you," he finished. "We're sorry. Very sorry."

Trying his utmost to mask his emotions, Adam probed their inner thoughts. Why yes, they weren't lying! They *were* sincere, all three of them! As he probed for answers, his anger and resentment started to dissolve. So *that* was the real reason: the tables had been turned and they'd been deceived by the Scarred One. Totally defeated and humiliated, their consciences were being pierced by the disastrous results of their actions.

He faced the group, suddenly feeling a thousand years old. "I accept your apologies, the lot of you," he sighed, "but you still have to face the consequences: for one, there's a jury of your peers; for another, as guests on Aurona you'll be in front of a jury of our Bandor friends. The final decision…," he paused, mulling it over. "That's for me alone to decide." He walked to the door in silence, slipped his arms around Elena, and Duron and left.

The Cruiser raced toward Arrix, trailed by a distant squadron of Bandor starships. With its superior cloaking technology, it landed a few feet away from the stolen starship: not even a shadow revealed its location.

With two hundred of the crew digging for close to an hour, a great pit now yawned beneath the starship. They were extremely tired and many had crawled under the floating barges to get out of sight of both monitor and madman.

Adam activated a Spyder and flew it around the perimeter of the Cruiser, searching for the Scarred One. Spotting him on an open platform, he landed on the rail right behind him. Looking around, he checked his weapons: there was a portable laser cutter, three Stiflers, a semiautomatic, and countless rows of pocketed stilettos flashing from the folds of his cloak. This wasn't going to be easy.

He closed his eyes, manipulating his old e-helmet's controls aboard the starship. Traveling in his mind, he entered the commander's quarters, lit up the control panel, and turned on the external monitors. Good, the desert looked like a blank slate in every direction: every screen showed identical views, not a cloud or mountain range in sight. He'd picked this isolated spot very carefully.

The Scarred One kept glancing up, checking and rechecking the bank of monitors over his head. As quickly as he looked away, Adam commandeered them and froze their screens. Soon, no movement could be seen in any direction. He held his breath, waiting…. Good, he hadn't suspected a thing. There was a lone monitor under the starship. Fiddling with the video controls, he quickly recorded and patched in a ten-minute, recurring clip of his toiling crew, then transitioned it seamlessly through the break. There. It looked quite convincing. He breathed a sigh of relief. Now, Step Two….

Tweaking the ventilation controls, he simultaneously turned up the exhaust heat outside the Scarred One's platform and lowered the temperature inside his open hatch. It didn't take too long for the sweating madman to start edging backward into the cool airlock. Shortly, he was relying exclusively on all the phony monitors around him.

"Okay, guys," Adam whispered, "It's time for Step Three: Your Ultimate Spyder Mission. I've checked; we've got a ton of 'em on the Cruiser. You're gonna slip through the shields under the starship and, ah, 'talk' to our crew. Signal when you're ready."

Ariel felt a tug on her sleeve. As she glanced down into her lap, a river of sweat ran into her eyes, stinging and blurring her vision. She blinked it away, staring incredulously. Could it be…? She drew in a breath. Sure enough, it was a Spyder! It seemed to be urgently waving and pointing to the far side of the pit. She glanced up at the loading platform: had that horrible madman noticed? No, strangely, he seemed to have gone inside. She nudged Sahir with her elbow, pointing at the Spyder. Nearby, another small group had circled around another pair of Spyders. They were performing the same dance, jumping up and down and gesturing toward the far side of the pit. As they turned in the direction the Spyders were pointing, gasp went up.

A robodigger burst out of a hole in the ground, flinging away piles of sand! Right behind it, Adam and three Bandor warriors climbed out, emphatically cautioning them to be silent. Slowly, deliberately, he kneeled down and laid a small audio device on the sand, then turned up the volume. As the crew listened, the sounds of digging shovels and laboring utility barges filled the air, seamlessly blending in.

Whispering, he filled them in on his plan. "As you just saw, guys, sand was easy for that robodigger. I programmed the machine to install sections of duct as it went along. The tunnel's about thirty feet long and it curves downward under the shields. You'll have to crawl through on your hands and knees. So let's go! A fleet of SpeedSleds await!"

In single file, they madly scrambled through the duct, gathering outside the shimmering force field. Adam was right: a very different looking string of SpeedSleds was waiting. Where'd *they* come from? They boarded quickly, engaged their cloaking devices, and sped away in total silence, barely able to stifle their almost uncontainable and overwhelming joy. It had taken less than ten minutes to vacate the pit.

Adam lingered outside the opening, making sure everyone had left safely. Just as he was about to slip away, a faint sound stopped him dead in his tracks. What was *that*? He spun around, listening intently. There it was again, a faint whimper! Concerned, he beamed out a quick mind-message to Duron.

The Old One recoiled at the strength. Shaking, he turned to Elena. "Listen!" he gasped. "Adam needs our *help*! He said there is one person left under the starship, and asked us to go back into Spyder mode! Most of the crew is aboard, but there is no more room; about thirty remain outside and their cloaked SpeedSleds are forming a circle. We have to act very fast. The hooded Bitron may discover Adam at any moment!"

They yanked on their helmets and gloves, reactivating their small group of Spyders under the starship. The eager robotoids scurried to obey their new orders.

There was an urgent scraping sound coming from the inner airlock. The Scarred One jerked his head up, his senses on alert ... were the Bitrons sneaking up on him? Hastily checking his weapons, he spun the big wheel and waited for the door to open. Nothing. Scowling, he spun it again: still nothing! In a rage, he aimed his laser cutter and pulled the trigger. There was a click, a strange rattle, and then the big gun started to feel hot in his hands. As a curl of smoke wafted into his nostrils, he dropped it with a clatter.

Fire! The electrical circuits were burning, fusing together as they melted! Suddenly, a different kind of odor assailed his nostrils: burnt rubber, mixed with acrid, melting plastic. He looked down in alarm. Smoke was wafting from both of his Stiflers! He barely had time to unclip them from his belt before they burst into flame.

There was a subtle vibration against his leg, and then a metallic, scraping noise. Taking no chances, he yanked off his semiautomatic and held it out at arms length, eyeing it suspiciously. Just as he thought, something was inside the barrel! He rapped it hard, muzzle-down, on the floor. A Spyder tumbled out, then another, and then three more! The thing was *full* of bugs! Some kind of gooey, white *string* was surrounding the trigger mechanism, filling the magazine and oozing out of the barrel. Clogged solid! He unbuckled his now-useless ammo clip and heaved it over the rail into the desert. He peered over the edge. What was this, now? His landing ramp had been retracted and more of that same string had encased the controls with a white blob!

"*Yahhhh-h-h*!!!" His scream of rage rattled the metallic hull as he leaped over the railing. As he landed, he staggered to his feet and stared under the starship in shock. "What? The crew's ... *gone*? How can this *be*?" His robe flapping, he broke into a dead run, circling around to the other side of the big pit.

Elena, Duron, and the warriors had no problem disabling the Scarred One's weapons; it had almost seemed to be a natural movement to spin silk. Ruddering their suction cup feet in the breeze, their Spyders followed the Scarred One's fluttering black form around the starship. Suddenly, they stopped, hovering.

Adam! What was he doing just standing there? Duron winced as he received another powerful mind-message. He whispered urgently into everyone's headsets. "*Stop*, right now! Adam has chosen to face this one *alone*!" To a person, they stood down.

Adam focused intently on the moans wafting out of the duct: yes, there was one last crew member to rescue. As he walked slowly, resolutely toward the hole, he spotted a flutter of black in his peripheral vision. His heart began to race, and then with great effort, he calmed himself. So this was to be a battle royal, to the end. He stopped fifty feet away, waiting calmly.

Spotting Adam, the Scarred One skidded to a stop and stared at him incredulously. "Well, *well*! Back from the dead, I see," he puffed. His gnarled hands seemed to have a mind of their own, drifting down to the hilts of his last line of defense. "And why are there just *two* of us standing here? Could it be because your friends have *deserted* you? They've all run away from this worthless piece of equipment?"

Adam remained silent, letting his arms hang loosely at his sides. It was obvious that he was defenseless and bore no weapons.

The Scarred One's killer instincts kicked into gear: He began to approach in a swagger. "Nothing to say for yourself? You don't *care* about your friends? You don't *care* about your ruined city, your ruined mission?" He taunted Adam masterfully, pushing all the hurtful, confrontational buttons with laser precision. "What's the matter, are you *deaf*, too?"

Adam maintained his calm outward composure, but inwardly his blood was coursing powerfully, ballooning his arteries. He slowly turned his palms upward, his heart pumping strongly, his mind razor sharp.

The pig-eyes traveled uneasily up and down the lithe young form, searching intently for anything he might have missed. What was going on? What was this crafty one up to? He was becoming extremely nervous with Adam's stony, calm silence. He was well within range now, and stopped to open his cloak wide. The rows of elaborately carved hilts glinted brightly in the harsh sun.

Adam prepared himself: raising his arms wide, he tilted his head back and concentrated deeply. It felt as if he were becoming one with the elements around him.

The Scarred One's rage boiled over. Why, this was *unheard* of! This skinny kid was *inviting* him, even *encouraging* him for an easy kill! He wasn't used to this kind of treatment; people were always scrambling to do his bidding, cowed by his mere presence! His hands trembled in fury. This-this Adam character was *dissing* him, *ignoring* him! His gnarled fingers finding the hilts of a familiar pair of AssassinAces, he tensed for the big throw. Yes, he'd use *all* of them this time. No getting away.

"*Yah-h-h-h!*" He let loose with his great fusillade.

Adam had loosened up his body for the onslaught. As the slim flashes of metal began to float toward him, time itself seemed to slow to a crawl. He hopped, flinched, and contorted his lithe young body in a blur of motion. The messengers of death slowly slid by, mere fractions of an inch from his skin.

Almost as quickly as the onslaught began, it stopped. Feeling as if his arteries were about to burst, he forced his body to slow down, blinking sweat out of his eyes.

The Scarred One stood open-mouthed, his empty cloak hanging limply. A single word escaped involuntarily from his lips. "*No-o-o-o!*"

Never before had this happened to him; he'd *never* missed, ever, not a single time! Some kind of superbeing was facing him with incredible abilities, with moves like no one he'd ever seen.

Adam finally found his voice. "Are you done?" he rasped.

The mutilated jaw snapped shut. Furiously searching, the tiny pig eyes studied him intently, catching every nuance of movement. Wait! Could it be…? *Yes!* His *knees* were shaking, ever so slightly!

Adam was trying valiantly to keep his feet planted as the familiar, relentless blackness stole over him. Fear crept in: no, he couldn't waver, not even slightly! He had so much more to accomplish on Aurona, so much unfinished business! As the tunnel closed, his knees began to buckle.

The Scarred One wasted no time. Stooping, he pulled a long, hidden dagger from his tooled leather boot and poised himself for the final throw. Suddenly, right behind him, there was loud thud and rattle of heavy breathing. Startled, he spun around.

The last crewmember staggered out of the duct. Startled, he stared at the two of them in shock, looked back and forth, and then quickly assessed the situation. His finger shaking, he pointed at Adam. "You'd better duck," he rasped. "He's back!"

Drawing in a sharp breath, the Scarred One spun back around.

Adam stood there, his legs firmly planted, his hands on his hips. Far from fainting, it felt as if his mind had just entered into a whole new dimension of awareness. It was now the endgame, time to reveal the Big Aces up his sleeve: slowly shaking his head, he stepped aside and gestured behind him.

Stretching from horizon to horizon, a vast hoard of starships materialized in the shimmering desert, then the mighty Phantom Cruiser crackled to life, laser cannons protruding from its gun ports. Right up close, there was a string of staccato-sounding clicks: the crew released the safeties on their Stiflers and dropped their cloaking devices.

The Scarred One's face drained of color. How could *this* have happened? The entire crew had been watching him make a complete fool of himself, and this young human had been deliberately *toying* with him! Suddenly, in the electrically charged silence, he heard the faint sound of labored breathing behind him. His pig eyes widened: yes, he had one last chance! As swift as a cobra, he spun around and lunged behind the startled crewmember, pressing the long dagger to his throat.

He began to lash out at the vast assembly. "Yah-*haaah*! And your sorry excuse for a leader really thought that I'd believe this desert concealed your Great Guns? Well, he was *wrong*! I already *have* my prize, and I'm leaving right now! And yes, as you all fear, I'm returning one day with a great army of my own kind! I'll be master ... of the...." Suddenly, his voice choked off and his hands began to shake.

Ah, something finally gave. Encouraged, Adam pushed harder. He'd been concentrating mightily, tunneling inside the recesses of the Scarred One's diseased, deranged mind. There weren't many thoughts to work with except a few torn, scattered glimpses of self-centered reality confined inside a dark, tight little space. He tunneled deeper, pushing against a tangled web in the motor cortex area.

Involuntarily, the knife fell from the Scarred One's hand. Seizing his last chance at freedom, the hostage wrestled free and fled. Finding himself defenseless, the Scarred One wavered, desperately trying to reform his thoughts. As Adam pushed on his motor cortex with greater force, he staggered backward, groping for balance. Enraged, he jerked his head up defiantly.

"So this is *it*?" he screeched. "*This* is what it's come down to? You think I'm finished? Well, just *try* to stop me!! I'll be back with my great army, and...."

Suddenly, Adam felt no remorse. Absolutely none. It was time for this one to go. The Scarred

One had been a major stumbling block to his entire mission, a danger to the future of Aurona and a threat to the Bandor's civilization. He was a mutant species, a peril to everyone and everything in his path. Bracing his feet, Adam drew his head back, summoned all his strength, and blasted mightily toward his target.

In a rolling cloud of sand, a moving wave of energy smacked into the darkly clad figure and sent him flying head over heels. With a puff of smoke anpd the smell of burnt flesh and cotton, the demented creature crumpled, raised one arm weakly, and then succumbed to Adam's massive mind-stun. He was gone.

Chapter 31: THE UNEXPECTED

Adam lingered in the shadow of his starship for a long, silent moment, staring at the madman's crumpled body. He never dreamed his min-stun could be so powerful. Maybe it was because of his extreme frustration and anger, or from the deep resentment he felt at being duped by such a long-term, clandestine operation. No matter, he'd finally put this insane egotist out of the way and he could pick up where he left off. He was eager to get to a few remaining, tantalizing mysteries on Aurona.

As he turned on his heel to face his crew, he was met by a fearful, wary silence, like a stonewall. No one could return his gaze, not even Elena. He turned to Duron.

"A-Adam," the old Bandor stammered. "Do-do you realize what you just *did*?"

Elena's fearful eyes met his for a split second, and then turned away.

He clenched his fists. "That *thing* was insane and had *no* remorse; its diseased brain was *incapable* of such a concept! It-it was just plain *evil*, inside and out!"

"And evil begets evil," Duron agreed. "It brings out the worst in its companions."

As the crew murmured their agreement, Elena's bottom lip started to quiver.

Duron brightened. "Adam, do you have any concept of how you have forever changed Aurona's history? How you have become an *instant legend* among the Bandor people? We will be forever grateful; you are a good man, a hero!"

"What?" Adam recoiled in surprise. "Me? No way!"

"Yes, you *are*!" he insisted. "And the news of your ultimately powerful mind-stun has just spread over the entire planet! I myself still cannot grasp how far and how fast you have progressed! Your telepathic capabilities have gone way beyond our feeble attempts and you have pioneered a whole new mind-dimension! You have…."

"Wait, wait, hold *on* here!" Adam held up his hands. "Ah, actually *no*, Duron."

"No?" He blinked. "How can you say that?"

"This isn't new," he shrugged. "It's been done *many* times before. Razahs have been throwing mind-stuns for millennia, so why not humans?" He paused, reflecting. "But I was mad, and I put way *way* too much juice into that first stun…. Hey, to tell you the truth, I was just hoping I had enough energy left after my, ah, saber-dance."

His crew broke into hesitant smiles. "Oh, by the way, guys," he shrugged, "the shields are finally down. I must have zapped the remote in his pocket when I fried him."

With that news, the jubilant Bandor warriors couldn't wait another minute. A diamond-shaped phalanx of SpeedSleds swept toward the stolen starship in a tight military formation and rushed inside to search for any remaining mutineers.

Shouts and laughter arose behind them. Cheering at the top of their lungs, Tavan and a group of enthusiastic Bandor youths rushed past the crew and started to search the sand, remote metal detectors beeping in their hands. Shortly, they'd collected the entire array of the crazed Bitron's stilettos: the poison-tipped knives were physical proof of the momentous event, and would be displayed in a new national memorial. Donning gloves and facemasks, a few warriors lifted the madman's stinking black-robed body; gagging, they tossed it onto an antgrav barge to haul it off.

As the commotion died down, Elena reached out hesitantly and nudged Adam's arm. He glanced down into a pair of round, fearful eyes. "Adam?" She quavered. "I'm still scared of you. *Most* of us are. We-we don't understand what you just did."

He let out a long breath. "Well," he breathed, "I don't think I do either."

"Talk to them." She motioned with her head toward the gathering crowd. "They…. We *all* need some kind of explanation, some kind of reassurance."

Giving her hand a squeeze, he raised his translator button a notch and turned to the crew. "I was *protecting* you," he began. "Yes, all of you, our Bandor friends here included. I *had* to stop that crazed lunatic. Aurona is our *home*, hopefully forever. And yes, I did take a huge chance," he grimaced. "I-I do that. A lot."

Smiles of agreement riffled through the crowd: he'd nailed *that* one.

"But guys, things were totally different this time around; there was no chance involved. I knew *exactly* what to do when I probed inside his diseased mind…." His voice tapered off as he saw their eyes widening again. "Guys, guys! Hold on!" He waved disarmingly. "Hey, it was almost an empty shell up there! There really wasn't much to work with; the whacko was only workin' on *two cylinders!*"

A snark erupted, somewhere in the back of the crowd. Ah, they were almost his. Encouraged, he brightened. "Just think of that lunatic as a *rotten apple*, totally rotten to the *core*! You know, the kind of rot that spreads from the inside *out*? That guy…."

He stopped short as distant, powerful memory jolted him to his toes: another piece of the Aurona puzzle just shoved itself into place. A blurred connection to his past was suddenly becoming a lot clearer.

"A-Adam?" Elena hesitantly touched his arm. "Are you okay? What's going on?"

He mumbled in a daze. "A rotten *apple*, Elena. My-my grandfather warned me about this kind of guy before I ever *thought* about pulling a crew together!"

"Huh?… Apples?" She obviously didn't understand.

"Yeah, rotten ones. Listen, these are his exact words: He said, *'If a coupl'a bad apples sneak into your pile, don't worry about 'em; you can root 'em out when you get here. Don't ask me how, you wouldn't understand right now.'*"

He turned to the crew. "Whaddaya think, guys? We found out who the rotten apples were in our pile, and you just saw me, ah, root out the rottenest one."

Tola rolled his eyes. "Wow, you sure got *that* right!" He fanned the air with his hands. "Whooeee! That dude was stinko! Ready for the *compost* pile!"

Peter nodded vehemently. "And his rot was spreading into some of our guys!"

Adam held up a cautionary finger. "But wait, that's not all there is to it; there's far, far more involved in what my grandfather said, a whole, hidden dimension!"

Duron tilted his big domed head. "Dimension, Adam? What is…?"

He shrugged. "The timing, Duron. It's crazy. We're talking about seven hundred years here.

How could a regular guy like my grandpa know all this stuff was gonna happen *before* we left the Earth? This isn't prophecy. Could there be more to it?"

"Adam, I...." As Duron raised his voice to speak, the Elders suddenly, urgently pulled him aside. Shrugging apologetically to Adam, he joined into their mind-conversation. After a moment of thoughtful silence, the twelve nodded in unanimous agreement. The old Bandor caught Adam's eye and beamed him a hasty mind-message.

Adam listened carefully, and then straightened up with sudden purpose. "Of *course*! That's a long shot, Duron, but you know me: I tend to *go* for the long shots."

"Yes, Adam," he conceded, "we are well aware of your, ah, 'long shots.'"

Adam raised a hand. "Hey, you know what? This time around, I'd like *you* to present this crazy idea to my guys." He turned and glanced at the crew, grimacing. "I'm afraid they're startin' to think I'm the only nut in the bowl."

Duron looked startled. "But I-I...."

"It's okay, go ahead. I think it's high time that we *all* get a chance to bend our minds with some serious mental gymnastics."

Duron hesitated a moment, sighed, and then conceded. "You are correct, Adam. Now is the time; we have all become *one* today, every being on this planet." He turned to the crew and tapped up the volume on his translator button.

"Before I start, I need to give you an update and put things into proper perspective. You may not know this, but we have been monitoring your Adam for a long time. We have been astounded with his brilliant intellect and innate wisdom, and have found him to be a superior vessel. Therefore, abiding by our unshakeable Law of Mind-Superiority, your young leader has been chosen to be the one to decide the future of Aurona. In a unanimous vote, we have elected him as our Supreme Leader."

The crew was floored. Did they hear Duron correctly? Their Adam? They elected *him* as Supreme Leader of the *whole planet*?

The Old One waited patiently for the astonished clamor to settle down, and then continued smoothly. "Yes, it is true: we Elders have gladly and willingly stepped aside. I am sure Adam will, as he says, 'fill you in later' on the details of this unprecedented and historic transition of power."

Overwhelmed, Adam shrugged. "Yeah, later. We've been kinda ... *busy*."

"Busy?" Duron chuckled. "A few minor details, right?"

A large, diverse group broke into laughter: Bandors of all ages had been mingling into the crowd with the humans, listening in rapt attention.

Duron raised his skinny arms. "Now, right to the point: there has been a totally unexpected development and I have a thought of pure conjecture to share with you. I am hoping our combined intelligence may help solve this mystery." He glanced nervously over his shoulder. "But Adam, this may only be, as you say, a 'dead end'...."

Adam made a hurrying motion. "Mental gymnastics, Duron?" he prompted.

"Oh, right." The old Bandor resolutely took a breath and continued, forming his words carefully. "Thirty Earth-minutes ago, as our armed warriors swarmed aboard your starship and confirmed there were no more mutineers, they also took the time to assess the extent of the damage and report their findings." He paused to exchange glances with the Elders, then turned back to the crew.

"Now, let me try to phrase this correctly: your sleep pods are a *vital* component of these starships, and we carefully monitor and refresh them after long journeys such as yours. Our warriors counted twelve remaining pods on your starship. When we added this number to the great pile of pods that had been discarded in the desert, the resulting total was correct." He paused, holding a cautionary finger in the air, searching for the right words. "But just as our record keeper was closing his books, he discovered a disturbing mathematics problem: an entry had been altered at the bottom of the previous page! What am I saying?" He paused, waiting expectantly. "One pod, just *one pod* had been erased and the total had been changed!"

Tola shrugged. "So why's *that* such a big deal? One pod?"

Duron was adamant. "This tampering and erasure occurred over *six hundred* years ago. You may draw your own conclusions…." He coughed nervously, waiting.

There was a sea of blank stares. What in the world could he be inferring?

Duron studied their expressions. Yes, they were struggling mightily to piece this one together. After a long pause, he raised a finger. "Any guesses?"

"Let's see," Tola mused. "You might be thinking someone, ah, *stole* a pod?"

Adam couldn't wait another minute; this was taking far too long. He spun impatiently toward the old Bandor. "Duron, we gotta hurry this up! If this theory is *true*, there's a chance that he might be *alive* somewhere out there in the jungle, and…."

"What?" Elena interrupted. "He? Who's *he*? And what are you two talking about? Please cool your jets, you're going *way* too fast for us! *Who's* still alive?

He glanced at Duron. "Um, we're both guessing my, ah … grandfather?"

There was a collective gasp from the crew, and Tola quickly cut in. "But that's impossible, sir: you told everyone your grandfather was *dead*! You went to his funeral!"

Adam shook his head in exasperation. "I know, Tola, I know! But listen, all of you! I may have been just a kid, but right from the minute I arrived at that hokey funeral, I had my kid reservations: something wasn't goin' down right," he scowled. "That whole dopey production was awful, *worse* than Vegas: chintzy, gaudy, and *way* overdone! That weird body in the coffin looked like a *superficial* version *of* my grandfather…." He let out a long breath. "Listen guys, I'm being real here. I grew up with him; I knew the man inside and out. His real personality was the total opposite of that funeral: he was a quiet man with big ideas who loved to work from behind the scenes!"

Elena sighed, finally dropping her guard. Yes, this was her familiar Adam, back to his exciting, spontaneous ways. She grabbed his arms for attention, then stared him squarely in the eyes. "So *who*, or *what* do you think was in the coffin?" She prodded. "The, ah, body had to match medical and dental records close enough to fool everyone."

"Okay, okay." He let out a sigh. "Here's where I'm going with my crazy idea: Remember Kron's operation? Remember how quickly that Hyper Stemcell solution worked on him? I'm saying that the body in the coffin was a *clone* of my grandfather, but grown extremely fast in controlled lab conditions!"

The crew caught on immediately. A clamor of questions began to fly.

Adam raised his voice. "Hold on, guys! Think about the possibilities: If Kron healed from a bullet wound in less than 15 minutes, then a whole human body should take no more than a few *months* to grow, right?" He pushed his wild conjecture to the limit. "Of course, it would just be an empty *shell* of my grandfather, with no memories…."

"*Gross!*" Elena interrupted, scrunching up her face. "That's totally *disgusting!*" In a second, she reconsidered. "But very interesting!"

Tola's hand flew to his chin. "So what you're really saying is…. You think your grandfather's still alive, but sleeping in a pod and hidden somewhere on Aurona?"

"Yup."

Peter jumped in excitedly. "Well if he *is*, we gotta *find* him!"

Tola turned to him. "But *how*? It's a huge jungle out there!"

"You got *that* right," Adam agreed. "But knowing him like I do, he's probably holed up somewhere in one of his AnchorPlank surface dwellings, totally camouflaged with FlexNet. There'd be no way we could visually spot him from the air, unless…."

Elena pulled back. "Uh-oh, Adam. What are you hatching up *now*? Don't keep us all in suspense."

"Hey," he shrugged. "I'm keeping *myself* in suspense, too! Listen, this might be only a half-baked idea, but it might work. I'd need the Phantom Cruiser to pull it off." He spun toward the crew. "So who wants to come with me? We've got a lot of unfinished business to take care of, and I've only got room for fifty!"

The shouts of approval were unanimous. Once more, his self-depreciating humor and lame jokes had broken their final restraints of doubt. Young and resilient, they bounced back with him all the way.

"Whoa, whoa!" He held up his hands. "I appreciate your enthusiasm, but first we've got some *other* unfinished business to take care of." He motioned with his thumb behind him. "We all need to climb into that, ah, quite dinged starship of ours and salvage our personal stuff. Those rotten apples had bigger fish to fry; I know they were in too much of a hurry to pry open any of our lockers in the hallways."

Peter scowled suspiciously. "Ah, how do you 'know' *that*, sir?"

He shrugged, raising a brow. "My e-helmet's still in my locker. I used it to commandeer… the starship's controls…." Suddenly, his eyes clamped shut.

"*Eeeow-w-w-wch!*" He grimaced in pain, his hands flying to his head.

The crew made a half-step toward him in alarm: What was happening? Was he having a stroke? Had his mind-stun been too much of an ordeal? Had he been nicked by one of those poison daggers? Peter and Tola grabbed his elbows, steadying him.

"Whoa!" he choked. "That was *super* intense!" He blinked, shaking his head.

"What happened, sir?" Tola queried.

"Another unexpected development: I just got a very urgent mind-message. It-it kind of, um, *blasted* through. This long day of surprises is about to take on a new twist."

Confused, the crew waited, their heads spinning with the rapid clip of events.

Adam took a breath. "I just heard from *Roson*," he gushed. "She was eavesdropping! Believe me guys, her message popped *totally* out of the blue! She just offered us a vital ingredient to toss into my half-baked search-and-rescue mission!"

Too fast. Way too fast. Nobody could keep up with him.

"Well?" he exclaimed, waiting impatiently. "Guess what it *is*?"

Tola was game and gave it a stab. "An ingredient, huh? Some kind of radar?"

Peter took a breath and added his two cents. "A telescope? A camera?"

"You're gettin' real close, guys," he said, grinning. "When she heard that my grandfather still might be alive and we'd be looking for him, she suddenly remembered one of his *best* inventions, little satellites called 'MicroSats'! When he arrived centuries ago, he'd brought CAD drawings of the gizmos with him. He reprogrammed them with a lot of radical, updated features, and then repurposed the Spyder's nano-assembly lines to produce *hundreds* of 'em! And-and here's the *best* part," he gushed. "She's got *buckets* and buckets of these MicroSats stashed away, just waitin' for us to use 'em!"

He paused, studying the crew's faces in exasperation: They seemed to be made of stone. "So whaddaya *waitin'* for?" he urged. "Let's *go*! Who's coming?"

There it was: their old, familiar Adam was back, as brilliant and full of life as ever, perhaps even *more* so. A chuckling Tola and a very relieved Elena picked an enthusiastically waving team. They'd signed on for this wild ride and *loved* it.

After the crew had retrieved their personal belongings, everyone took off and rendezvoused inside the Bandor's mountain stronghold. With their arms full, they boarded an identical copy of their saucer, picked at random from the hundreds lining the walls in the enormous vault. They could only stare in amazement at the huge array: as wonderful and unique as their starship had seemed, it was just one of a vast fleet, ready to roam the universe.

Early the next morning the Phantom Cruiser and its handpicked crew of fifty flew to the Island. Roson was waving from the roof, circled by her robodiggers carrying heavy buckets of MicroSats. Thanking her profusely, they went right to work.

Circling in a low orbit over Aurona, they dumped out a great cloud of MicroSats and then sat back to watch in amazement. The tiny spheres quickly defaulted into a self-distributing, radar-distancing phase: with powerful, miniature ion propulsion thrusters, they shot away from each other at a tremendous speed to form an evenly seeded blanket of bright, metallic dots. Greatly encouraged, the crew prepped many Spyders to drop from the center hold: some objects of interest may be down on the planet's surface.

Adam settled into his gimbaled chair. Strapping his e-helmet on his head, he rested his fingertips on the galvanic pads and cranked up the Cruiser's sensors to the max. With his grandfather's MicroSats beaming out their extremely detailed 3D maps, it didn't take long to realize that he didn't need any of his big monitor's visual information: some kind of weird synergy was happening. He shook his head in confusion. Was his mind becoming *one* with the electronics?

As he turned off the bright screen in front of him, he let out a sigh of relief. The total darkness enabled him to focus clearly on the mental images and reams of amazing feedback pouring in.

He activated a mind-switch: Advanced Autopilot would have to take over the search in an auto-grid pattern.

Shortly, he began to hear a tiny, distant ping above all the electronic chatter. He recognized it immediately and shouted into his headset. "Listen everyone! I hear one of our little guys, ah, *talking* to us! Yeah, that's right, we have a Spyder signal, four hundred miles East of Prima! Turn up your audio! Help me scan for it!"

In minutes, a voice returned. "*Got* it, sir! Transmission code's on the way!"

As Adam locked onto the signal, a disturbing scene flashed into view on his face shield. A lone Spyder was high in a Motherlode, its hooked suction feet gripping tightly to a narrow band of dirty, slate blue fabric. There was a frantic breathing sound. Alarmed, he commandeered the robotoid to release its grip and fly a few feet away. As he swiveled it around to see what was going on, his eyes popped.

"W-what?" he sputtered. "You're kidding! It *can't* be! How could *anyone* survive, alone and unarmed in the middle of the jungle? I know it's been more than three weeks since the big guy disappeared, but…."

"Senn?" Kron interrupted. "You're saying that *Senn*'s still alive?"

"Yup, alive and kickin'! He looks really weak though, and he might fall. It's a long way to the ground from that Motherlode!"

The heavyset man had finally wormed his way through the tight web of Dazeen spikes on the trunk and was now inching his way upward on the rough bark. He'd obviously been through torture: he was definitely thinner, scrapes and scars covered his skin, and stains of blood were oozing through his uniform. He appeared to be extremely nervous and kept glancing downward into the big clearing below him.

Adam swiveled his Spyder to follow his line of sight. Sniffing around the trunk of a newly germinated AugerBlade seedling, a whole family of Razahs was on the prowl! Off to the side, Senn's one-man SpeedSled lay upside down. Tucking in his paddle feet, he dove. There was a large hole in the floor. The scenario knit itself together quickly.

"Okay guys, it's Spyder time: pour out about twenty of 'em! There's a family of Razahs down here and they've almost figured out where Senn is!"

Elena's voice shot back. "Okay, the Spyders are flying! Do you want us to…?"

"*Yes*!" he interrupted. "Land on all the Razah heads you see, just like you did before! Stink out the little ones, too, but don't empty your tanks. We only want to scare those nosey buggers away!"

It didn't take much of a purple cloud to send the Razahs careening back into the jungle. As Adam called off the swarm of black dots, they rose quickly on the upwelling currents toward Senn and surrounded him. He'd been climbing steadily and focusing all his attention upward, but looked startled and overjoyed as they landed on his arms. Adam directed his Spyder to point downward emphatically with its manipulator claw. Senn's ridged brow furrowed for a moment, and then he caught on. He looked down.

His SpeedSled was still *working*! With a loud clank and a great deal of sparks, it had somehow righted itself and was climbing rapidly toward him! His eyes wide, the big man crawled aboard the sputtering craft. Swiftly, the sled rose to the top of the Motherlode. He looked up. The Phantom Cruiser was descending silently, carefully, bit-by-bit, to within inches of his upraised arms. He cowered in terror, fearing he'd be squashed. A small, round center hatch opened and many strong arms pulled him inside.

Senn's amazing tale of survival spilled out as he was wheeled into sickbay. The man was severely dehydrated and covered with gashes, but full of gratitude. "I-I still can't believe it's *youse* guys! I wuz almost losin' my grip on da big tree! I wuz eatin' fruit off da ground an' hidin' under da SpeedSled every night.... Hey, the cloakin' part an' shields still worked; who knew? An'-an' whassup with *this* ship? Where'd it come from? How'd you *find* me? An' how's Dexor an' the guys? Are they still alive? An'...."

Joelle finished emptying her syringe into his arm. He'd be out for a while, long enough for Fenet's surgical team to glue him back together and give the Hyper Stemcell solution a chance to do its work. She rolled her eyes at Elena, shaking her head.

"Wow, hon, talk about a last-second intervention; we almost *lost* this guy! Those Razahs were so close! All they had to do was look up, and ... bam! Lunch!"

Adam smiled, turned off his sickbay monitor, and immediately defaulted back into his Cruiser's auto-grid pattern. He was really glad to have Senn back; he actually *liked* the simple man and had always been bothered that he'd been so easily duped by his companions. He sighed and closed his eyes to concentrate.

The Cruiser's sensors and MicroSats were now speaking to him in volumes: like DNA, their encrypted chatter was weaving into long threads of electronic information, streaming many-layered, extremely detailed 3D schematics of Aurona's surface directly into his mind. He sat there enthralled, surrounded by the sights, sounds, odors and textures. His galvanic finger pads could actually *feel* the surfaces of the leaves, rocks, and water!

Soon, just the anomalies started to pop out: the MicroSat's AI had easily adjusted to the *regular* pattern of life below, but now the *differences* were appearing! Startled, he focused on this new set of extreme, boldly colored graphics, trying hard to understand what he was seeing.

Yes, that was *it*! Highlighted in bright, glowing orange, the Cruiser's ground-penetrating, Deep-X radar was revealing the underground domes of long-abandoned Bandor dwellings! He turned his eyes and spotted a set of glowing, moving dots: a family of Razahs was on the prowl, standing out in bright infrared against the gridwork of green. Fluorescent purple identified large groves of AugerBlade trees clustering along some newly forming, pale green gaps in the planet's underground wiring. Yes, the invasive species was indeed spreading and proliferating rapidly, commandeering a lot of the Motherlode's former turf.

Astonished, he sank back into his chair. What a breakthrough! Now that he could see where the Razahs, Spyrins, and Augerblades lived, it would be a cinch for his capture and extermination crews to *find* them! A sudden thought flashed through his mind: his grandfather had figured out all this electronic wizardry before he disappeared, but had he *planted* the MicroSats with Roson, knowing that when his grandson finally arrived, he'd use this stuff to locate him in the jungle? His head beginning to spin off his shoulders with all the possibilities when *another* color suddenly showed up: a deep, vibrant blue, tinged with metallic gold edges.

"What's *that*?" He dropped like a stone out of the sky to get a closer look. The large, squashy central shape seemed to be deformed, like a caved-in oval. It had two wispy, curving passageways snaking out through the jungle that seemed to end in odd, domelike tips. Could it *be*? He dove to treetop level, hovering.

"Duron! Elena! *Everybody*!" he gasped. "I think I *found* him! Let's go *see*!"

With the Phantom Cruiser locked securely in a hover, Adam and a search party exited from several airlocks. It took a lot of tricky maneuvering to pilot their squadron of SpeedSleds down through the tangled canopy. They had to work their SpeedSleds through extremely tight spaces, using the strength of their shields to shove the heavy vegetation aside.

Duron nudged Adam with a bony finger. "Ah, you must be aware that Roson is watching everything through my telepathic eyes, Adam; I do not have to describe what I am seeing, as she is *here*! Just like you 'saw' Tola's early childhood on the plains of Oklahoma, she is reading my mind-pictures." The old one reflected quietly. "She is eager to know everything, Adam; she, ah, cared very deeply for your grandfather."

Elena turned to him. "That little lady's super excited her man might still be *alive*! We had a long, heart-to-heart talk."

"It's been a long time," Adam muttered. "I-I just hope that he's survived."

They landed in a small group, their runners crunching into forest litter. Fallen trees were everywhere and vigorous new growth was straining toward the few remaining openings overhead. On high alert they disembarked, walking in a tight, nervous knot. The dilapidated-looking structure appeared to have no entrances and was surrounded with a deteriorating force field: Clumps of bright gold particles were hovering in the depressions with a thin, blue haze wavering around them. As they walked a bit further around the perimeter, they stopped short.

"Oh, *no*!" Elena's hands flew to her mouth. "It sure doesn't look good, Adam!"

An enormous tree had caved in the roof. The force field may have resisted the great weight for a while, but as the trunk leaned further into it and more debris fell from overhead, the electrical shield had weakened. They noticed a small hole at the top. Thinking quickly, Adam tapped the shield with the toe of his boot: yes, there was a slight tingle, but he got used to it quickly. "Okay guys, we've got an entrance. I'm sure we can make it to the top, but we'll have to climb through some floppy FlexNet. Who's game?"

There was no hesitation: ten people joined him and picked their way carefully up the side, untangling their feet as they went. Bioluminescent lizards were everywhere, scampering out of their path like bright streaks of lightning. Evidently, these creatures had grown used to the weak electrical charge.

Adam reached the top first, and put his eye up to the small opening: there was an enormous oval room below him. "Wow," he mumbled. "It's really cluttered down there…," he pulled back, startled. "Huh? *Light*? Hey, he's got solar optics still working after all these centuries. Everything's *flooded* with daylight down there!" Excited, he tugged at a chunk of the rubbery FlexFoam, testing its resilience. "And this stuff is flat amazing; it's still just as strong as the day he sprayed it!" He stood up and fumbled around in his pockets, balancing on the springy surface. "Rats! Where's my portable laser cutter? I know I put it into my SpeedSled!"

The last man in line turned around and picked his way down the side to retrieve it. In moments, the group handed him the flashing instrument. Many nervous hands had passed it up to the top.

"Wait a sec...." Adam tested the power, setting the cutting distance to less than a foot. In seconds, chunks of foam fell inward and there was a hole big enough to squeeze through. Satisfied, he pocketed the cutter and glanced nervously over his shoulder. "I'm going *in*!" Twiddling with the strength of his antigrav belt, he floated halfway down and then hovered in place. "Okay, guys, set your Stiflers to stun, turn on your belts, and follow me. The rest of you down there, just guard the perimeter!"

They landed in the center of an instrument-cluttered room. Although the ceiling was lopsided and pushed in, the structure was still intact and in good shape. Someone let out a cry. A few scurrying and slithering forms had caught his eye. "*Rats*, sir! At-at least ... I *think* they're rats. And I saw a skinny snake, too!"

Tola focused his Asron torch down into a thin beam, then checked under a desk. Several sets of eyes blinked and turned away from the bright light. "Not rats, guys. No tails. Ears *way* too big! Snake's good sized, though. Maybe three feet."

Adam stood there, calculating. "Well, if there ever *was* food in here, it's long gone. These critters are using this place as a burrow or a den, and I'm sure the snake's in here after *them*."

Tola doused his torch. "Well, sorry, sir, it doesn't look like your grandfather's here; the room's totally empty. What a great collection of stuff, though!"

Adam scowled and pivoted on his heel. "C'mon, the pod's gotta be here *somewhere*!" Suddenly, he spotted a pencil-thin shaft of light filtering through a torn curtain. As he touched the fabric, it crumbled and dropped to the floor in a heap. "Aha!" he shouted. "A *tunnel*! I'm sure this is one of those long arms I saw twisting through the jungle!" He glanced over his shoulder at the crew and nodded toward the opening.

They followed eagerly. The passageway was quite long and completely lined with shelves and cabinets, the drawers brimming with odd instruments and yellowing stacks of papers. In a moment the passage widened, and then ended abruptly in a small, domed chamber. Adam stopped short in the doorway, quaking and speechless.

A pod stood in the center of the room!

As the crew circled the silent, oval shape, Adam's eyes filled with unbidden tears. A small table had been pushed up against the pod, a yellowing parchment note lying on top. Taking a breath, he read it aloud, his barely-restrained tears brimming over.

"*Adam,*" he choked, *"I'm sure many centuries will have passed by the time you read this note. I followed your journey as long as I could, until I had to sleep. Both my mind and body were giving out. Hopefully, my long rest will repair some damage. I'm so sorry about all my secrecy, sorry about my funeral deception, and especially sorry that we didn't have time to say our goodbyes. It was all my fault. When I went back to my saucer near the Galaxy Room, I made a huge mistake...."*

A mistake? Startled, Adam paused to wipe his eyes with his sleeve, took a breath and continued. *"I pushed the wrong button. My little TimeWarper got locked into a sequence and there was no turning around! To make matters worse, I had the keys to your starship in my pocket! It didn't take long to get here, but then I had to figure out a way to get your keys back to you and put them exclusively into your hands. It took a while to cobble my elaborate plan together. I'm sure that by the time you're reading this note, you'll have figured out a few details of my quite necessary trickery. As long as I'm apologizing, I'm really sorry about that scary-looking clone. Hey, it worked, didn't it? Well, I'm glad to see you're on your way. Gallons of love, G'pa.*

P.S. -Tell Roson I miss her terribly, more than she'll ever know."

Composing himself, Adam peered through the dark glass. A yellow light was pulsing with a disturbing message. *"Huh?"* He rubbed his eyes and focused, his face pressed tightly against the surface. "Hey guys! We gotta get this pod *outta* here, ASAP! There's no juice! The backup power's running *low*!"

Tola flashed his Asron torch under the pod. "Wow! Look, sir! The cord's been chewed by one of the critters!" Gritting his teeth, he yanked out the plug. They immediately put their backs to the heavy pod, levering, steering, and rolling it toward the long passageway. They burst into the big oval room, pulling away cabinets and bookcases, clearing a narrow path around the perimeter. It didn't take long; a particularly heavy wooden cabinet concealed the only exit: a wide door, bolted from the inside! As they released the catch, it creaked loudly and swung inward. The smells and sounds of the jungle poured in, and here and there, they caught glimpses of their SpeedSleds through the heavily overgrown FlexNet. Winking, Adam handed his laser cutter to Kron, and then stood aside to concentrate intently with his mind.

As the men heaved the pod outside, suddenly, quite by itself, a large utility barge pushed down through the treetops and landed next to them, crunching into the litter. Looking pointedly at Adam, they heaved the pod aboard. Bolting the dome's door from the inside and securing the hole in the roof with a makeshift patch, they jumped aboard their SpeedSleds. As they circled the oddly shaped structure, the rescue crew gave each other enthusiastic high fives: The whole operation had taken less than two hours.

Chapter 32: ZERAN

The cavernous Pod Room was echoing with a persistent rapping sound: several Bandor pod specialists were poring over the smooth surface, checking for cracks in the glass and making sure that none of the seals had been broken. Satisfied, they carefully spliced on a replacement cord. Adam had been anxiously monitoring the progress and held his breath as they plugged it into a simulated mainframe.

There was a faint ping, and a soft light turned on inside the darkened thermoglass. A technician turned to him, his faint slit-smile affirming the readings had snapped out of sleep mode. Taking a breath, he quickly bent back to reprogram the complicated opening sequence: there had to be plenty of time for his grandfather's aged body to adjust, as the old man would be quite fragile when he emerged.

Down the hall, an anxious group was waiting for the momentous event. Duron was on an eloquent roll: bright, lively and informative, he was demonstrating an extensive knowledge base with a solid grasp of facts, mixing everything liberally with prophecy and legend. The crew sat enraptured. Suddenly, there was a commotion in the hallway. As they turned toward the door, Elena gasped in disbelief.

"*Roson!*" She jumped up, her arms wide. "You *made* it!" The ancient crone swept proudly into the room on her antigrav chair, dressed in her finest ceremonial robes. Squealing in excitement, Elena rushed to her side with a warm, welcoming embrace.

Adam heard all the ruckus and sprinted down the hallway. As he poked his head into the doorway, a broad smile lit up his face. "Whaddaya know! Roson! Welcome to my grandfather's, ah, *rebirth*! I knew you wouldn't miss it for the world!" Taking note of her starched, pristine white robe with its heavily embossed gold borders, he raised a brow, nodding in approval. "By the way, nice threads, girl!"

Roson spun toward him in high spirits, cackling good-naturedly. "Oh, *this* old thing! Haven't worn it for *thousands* of years!" Her dark eyes gazed up into his. "Yes, you're quite right, my dear; I wouldn't miss the event for this or any other world! When your grandfather opens his eyes I want to be next in line, right behind *you*!"

Adam cautioned her. "They say there's still a bit of a wait. Did you, um…?"

"Yes," she interrupted, slit-smiling. "I brought plenty of antidote. And in case we're here for a spell, this thing I'm sitting on folds down flat into a bed! Your grandfather helped me … invent it…." Her words trailed off, her eyes rimmed with tears.

Elena gave her a reassuring hug. "It's okay, hon. He'll be back with us soon."

A technician suddenly appeared in the doorway. "The pod is starting to open!"

"*What?*" Roson jerked her head up with a start, grabbing Elena's hand. "Oh my goodness, this is *way* too soon! I-I barely made it in time!"

The technician reassured her. "Do not worry, sleep pods are programmed to respond only to the occupant's overall health and condition. If he were in poor health, it might have opened late tonight or even tomorrow, for that matter."

She pressed him. "That means he's in *better* condition than you thought?"

"Yes…." Noting the large crowd of humans, he slit-smiled and stepped into the room a bit further. "Ah, I need to tell you people that you have a hilarious leader," he chuckled. "Your Adam just called us specialists the 'Pod Squad'!"

Red-faced, Adam grimaced while the assembly hooted in laughter. The technician turned back to Roson. "Yes, we were quite surprised. Our best estimates had placed the opening sometime this evening, but the aged human is six hours *early*, indicating an extremely resilient recovery rate! You will still have to wait; the opening sequence involves nearly an hour of resuscitation before he starts to breathe on his own. But do not worry, he is being very closely monitored."

She slumped back. "Okay, false alarm…. Hey, I almost wigged out there!"

The crew shot each other surprised looks: where'd this ancient Bandor crone learn *those* Earthly idioms? They were quite dated, though, more than four generations before their own. In a moment, the association became crystal-clear.

Roson was sharp. "Hmm, do I detect puzzled looks, here?" She sat up ramrod straight in her chair, squaring her shoulders. Well, it's high time that I, ah, *confess* something, especially since I'm about to be reunited with my best friend ever, the love of my life. This is to be a day of truth; no more hiding…. We, ah, *lived* together on my Island for almost eighty years."

There it was, their nascent suspicions were confirmed. The crew nudged each other, winking and rolling their eyes.

And…!" She held up a scrawny, cautionary finger. "Before you young bucks and does get any *ideas*, we slept in our own *rooms*!" She paused, reconsidering. "No, that's not true: mostly, he slept on top of his papers and inventions. Awake three hours, sleep three hours, 'round the clock. He-he was *possessed*!"

Adam let out a snort. "You got *him* pegged! I couldn't keep up with him!"

She exhaled a short breath, her wrinkled cheeks puffing. "Nor could *I*!"

As the room rang with laughter, Adam bent low to her ear. "Roson, *eighty* years? Did he say much about me? Did he…?

She laid a bony hand across his arm. "Hush, my son. You will know soon enough. Ask him yourself when he awakens."

Several doors further down the long hallway, an entirely different scene was playing out: unconscious and lying flat on his back, Dexor was strapped tightly to a gurney in a recovery room. He'd nearly lost his legs. For several hours, Fenet and Ranod had worked feverishly, giving him extensive bone grafts, many yards of quickly grown arteries and veins, and finally a whole series of mega-injections with Hyper Stemcell solution. His lower body had turned into an extension of the lab in the bottle, rapidly accelerating massive tissue regeneration as it restored his major leg muscles and nerves.

The Bandor doctors were getting used to this type of traumatic surgery. Inexperienced youths were occasionally falling from great heights in their unfamiliar Wingsuits, and Speed Tube workers were getting their limbs crushed as they constructed massive force fields thousands of miles beneath Aurona's surface.

His head swimming with potent anesthesia, Dexor began to come out of his long, dark tunnel, his lower body throbbing powerfully as it knit back together. Behind him, wrapped tightly in casts and bandages, Trennic and Nastix kept glancing furtively over their shoulders.

"Are you sure?" Trennic whispered. "D'ya think he can hear us?"

"I dunno.... He sure ain't movin.'"

They studied their boss intently, making sure their conversation wouldn't be overheard. Shrugging, they leaned closer, their whispers barely audible. They began to marvel at how Adam and his crew had cared enough about them to rescue them, in *spite* of all they'd done to ruin their mission. Scowling, they vented in exasperation, contrasting the crazed, hooded Bitron's selfish motives and brutal actions: to him they were just pawns to be used, abused, and then dumped.

"Was it *worth* it?" Nastix quavered. "All our plottin' and plannin' and spyin'? Even if we had all gotten away, what would we be gettin' back to in *another* seven hundred years? The Earth was pretty messed up when we left!"

"Yeah," Trennic agreed. "No more unity. All the countries wuz breakin' away from each other an' thinkin' only about themselves, fightin' and fightin'...."

"Hey," Nastix scowled. "Would there even *be* an Earth left to spend our loot on?"

Overwhelmed, they sat back, quietly pondering the dire implications.

Finally out of anesthesia, Dexor had caught the tail end of their conversation. Struggling mightily, he rolled his head toward them and broke the silence. "Forget the Earth, guys," he rasped. "That planet was messed up because of people like us. Don't you *get* it yet? *We* were the problem!"

They spun toward him, their eyes suddenly wide and fearful.

"Ah, ah.... We didn't mean nuttin,' boss," Trennic stumbled. "We wuz...."

"It's okay," he breathed weakly. "And I'm *not* your boss anymore. You're free."

"Huh?" Nastix started to shake in his gut.

Dexor collected his thoughts. "You know, come to think of it, *I'm* free, too! The Bandor doctors were talking real loud out in the hallway before they put me out. They said Adam dropped that Bitron maniac with a super mega-stun. He-he *killed* him!"

The words stopped coming. Shocked to their core, the two men sat riveted in their beds with their mouths hanging open. So it really *was* over! After a long, uncertain moment, they glanced at Dexor again. Somehow, he looked completely different; his whole countenance was relaxed, his perpetually affected grimace was simply ... erased.

He caught their confused stares. "Yeah, you got it; I'm not *me* anymore. My mind feels weird, a lot clearer. I don't know what was in that stuff they shot me up with, but I've got no more reasons to fight anymore." He studied their faces. "And you shouldn't either. Take a look at this amazing planet and people, and then compare it to the chaotic, miserable lives we made for ourselves back on the Earth."

A great weight was lifting from Nastix's shoulders and he sat up a bit straighter. "You really mean it? We're...."

"Hey." Dexor attempted a shrug. "Forgive me? I was a real jerk."

Nastix agreed vehemently. "Yeah. Stinko. An arrogant bully. A real son of a...."

"Whoa!" Trennic jabbed him in the ribs. "He's tryin' to apologize, I think." He turned to Dexor uneasily. "Are you?"

The man's ribs were heaving in silent spasms of laughter. "You guys'll *never* change! Go ahead, pile it on, I deserve it," he chuckled. "I was all that and more!" He lay there quietly, contemplating. "And when you're done venting, I'd like us all to move on."

The pod had finished its opening sequence. As the throat insert withdrew and Adam's grandfather began to breathe fitfully on his own, several Bandor attendants lifted him out, removed the life-sustaining zippered suit from his limp body, and dried off the AmnioGel coating. Ever so carefully, they slipped a warm Bandor robe over his unconscious form and laid him in a contour bed. Checking their timepieces, they walked briskly down the hall toward the waiting room.

"*Twenty minutes*!" Fenet's loud translator button startled the crowd. The two doctors walked toward Adam, peeling off their gloves. "Your grandfather is out of the pod and breathing on his own," he smiled, "but he is still regaining consciousness."

"Yes," Ranod agreed. "And his vital signs are very good, even remarkable!"

Roson clutched her chest, tears welling up. "Whoa! This is *far* better news than I'd *ever* hoped for! I was starting to get *really* concerned about his deteriorating appearance during the months before he disappeared. He wouldn't talk about it and kept to himself." She threw up her bony hands in exasperation. "Typical male, a stuffer!"

Joelle threw knowing looks at her female friends: wow, this Roson chick was sharp, *definitely* on the same wavelength! Catching Elena's eye, she gave her an emphatic two thumbs-up.

Twenty minutes came and went. Checking his wrist programmer, Adam paced back and forth, sidling up to the doorway and glancing down the hall toward the recovery room. Suddenly, there was a distant sound of laughter, and Fenet's face appeared. Seeing Adam, he slit-smiled, beckoning.

"Yes!" Adam punched his fist in the air. Right on his heels, Roson and Elena bumped into him. As the three hurried down the hall and entered the room in a tight, nervous knot, none of them were prepared for the sight.

Someone resembling an extremely aged version of his grandfather's clone was lying on the contour bed, his head swollen grotesquely, his skin tissue thin and wrinkled. Hearing them enter, he rolled a pair of large, dark eyes and weakly stretched out a hand.

"A-Adam? Is that really ... *you*?"

The next morning, two very different-looking saucers emerged from the entrance of the long, bioluminescent tube and shot out into bright sunshine. They soared effortlessly, hovered a moment, and then banked toward the shore of the big lake in the distance. Prima was back, gleaming and restored to its original condition. The Bandor workers were proud of Adam's avant gard structure and had put in a mighty effort to get it ready. As the crew watched, Kron and a seasoned Bandor pilot slowly rotated the new starship a few, precise degrees and squeezed it into place in the big empty courtyard.

Totally on the other hand, Adam and his grandfather were like kids with a new toy. The Phantom Cruiser swooped, circled, and barrel-rolled around Prima before finally landing with a spin and flourish a short distance from the fan-shaped pier. Cheering, the crew stuffed themselves into the elevators and ran in a mob up the great spiral staircase toward the new Observatory Room. Once more, the saucer's main room had become their hub and was rapidly collecting an enthusiastic, mixed group of Bandors and humans. As Kron raised the stage, Tola directed some of the crew to bring up chairs from the cafeteria and set them into a semicircle.

Before they exited the Cruiser, Adam's grandfather slipped into a long white Bandor robe and donned a large pair of dark glasses. Adam watched for a moment as he adjusted and readjusted the large, floppy hood over his domed head.

"Ah, why all the getup, man? You goin' incognito on us?"

The old man shrugged. "Two reasons, my boy." He tied the sash and smoothed it out against his side. "First, the bright lights really bother my eyes, and second, I don't want to scare the crew. I think it's best to wait awhile before they see how radically I've changed. Hey, your features are already altering, and you've only been here a few months! I've been here for *centuries*!"

Adam thought a moment, and then shrugged. "Gotcha. You look just fine, Grandpa, even kind of elegant in a mysterious, cool way. The crew will get over it real fast; they've, ah, witnessed many strange sights since we got here…."

"Strange sights, huh?" he interrupted. "Strange sights?" Chuckling, the old man grabbed Adam's arm. "C'mere you little whippersnapper!" He threw him into a headlock. They tousled a moment, Adam helpless with laughter.

Pausing to compose themselves outside the big bronze doors, they walked in, waving and smiling broadly ay the party atmosphere. As they climbed the stage and sat next to the Elders, the crew settled onto their new cushions, eyeing the mysterious stranger. Just as Adam had predicted, they quickly adapted and accepted him as he was.

Their two incredible stories began to entwine: As they kept up a lively, running narrative for the crew, Adam, his grandfather, and the assembled Elders shared their memories and mind-pictures, effortlessly linking their minds in telepathy. Adam revealed how Joelle had accidentally 'discovered' the Spyders and how they'd proven to play the pivotal role in entering the shields, and then his grandfather recalled his amazing eighty years of life, inventions and peace on the island with Roson. Sighing, the ancient Bandor woman pressed tightly against him, listening in an enraptured daze. A big arm stole around her thin shoulders and pulled her closer.

Joelle spotted the not-so-subtle interaction. At a miniscule pause in the conversation, she jumped up quickly. "Hi! I'm Joelle, sir, and I've been wondering: ah, since you're Elena's grandfather-in-law, I guess that would make this pretty lady her…."

"Joelle, is it?" The old man chuckled. "Wow, somehow I get the feeling that you're slightly … *curious*?" As the room rang with laughter, he tucked Roson protectively under his arm. "This tiny, amazing lady has been waiting for me way too long, over six hundred *years*, in fact!" He held up a finger. "I think it's high time we make it *official*!"

"What?" Roson's eyes popped. "*Yes-s-s!*" Her bony fist jabbed the air.

As shouts, laughter, and congratulations flew through the air, the old man raised his hands to speak. "And so, our families are formed." He turned to look pointedly at Elena. "Speaking of families, I'm sensing new life within you," he mused. "In fact … *two* new lives? Could they be, ah, my great-grandchildren, perhaps?"

Elena reddened. "Yes," she shrugged. "Gee, it seems like everyone on Aurona knows about my babies! According to prophecy, my twins have been expected for *millions* of years!" She reflected a moment. "That's, ah, quite a *long* gestation!"

The old man roared with laughter. "No wonder Adam's *nuts* about you, girl! You're as sharp as a tack! C'mere!" He held out his white-robed arms and gave her a big bear hug. "And what's all this prophecy stuff?" he prodded. "Where'd you find out?"

She deferred to Adam, her eyes questioning. "Um, a few places…."

Adam shrugged. "It's okay hon, go ahead and tell him. He'd love to know."

She took a breath and continued. "Adam and I discovered the original runes when we explored the oldest Bandor dwelling. They called it The Tomb."

"*What*?" The old man blinked. "You *found* it? I've always wondered!"

Adam nudged his grandfather, sending him a strong blast of mind-pictures. In seconds, the old man had been informed of the entire, dangerous journey. He blinked behind his dark glasses, rubbing his broad forehead. "Holy cow! Duron's been bragging about your abilities, but I would've never guessed this degree of telepathy was possible!"

"Hey," Adam shrugged. "I'm a superconductor! I could'a beamed the info *much* faster, but I didn't know how quickly your mind could absorb it."

"Wow, my poor pea brain is overwhelmed." Grimacing, his grandfather made an attempt to return to the subject. "Can we get back to my great-grandchildren here?"

Encouraged, Elena brightened. "Adam and I decided to name our twins after your favorite moons! You know, Mazan and Eonia? Roson told me all about…."

"Hey," Adam cut in, his eyes sparkling mischievously. "I'm glad we we're not having *triplets*, because we'd have to name our third kid, ah…." he paused, thinking. Stumped, he turned to Duron. "Um, actually, what *did* you guys call that third moon? You never told us. I mean, you *did* give that nasty little orbit-wobbler a name, right?"

Suddenly on the spot, Duron caught the other elder's eyes. "Y-yes, Adam," he stumbled, "it *did* have a name. W-we called it Zeran. When our ancestors first landed on the planet, they found it had a thin atmosphere with mostly seas and aquatic life forms."

"Wow! A lottta wotta, huh?"

"Yes," Duron chuckled. "A lot of water. And for that very reason, a great debate arose: while Zeran had abundant seas, Aurona was mostly desert. After lengthy discussions, they decided that it was in our planet's best interest to drain Zeran's water and fill our own oceans. They pumped it through processing plants to remove all the salt. Then…," he paused, his voice swelling with pride, "they transported the entire ocean."

Adam let out a low whistle. "Whooee! How'd you guys manage to do pull *that* off? It must've been a *huge* project!"

Duron was on a roll now, positively beaming. "Yes, *yes*, it was! After removing the salt through micro-osmotic filters, breaking the hydrogen and oxygen's molecular bonds and isolating the two resulting gasses, they devised a unique and economical way to transport it. Reducing the volume under tremendous pressure and ultra low temperature, they formed small, solid pellets. Long chains of space barges transported them down to Aurona where they were reassembled back into fresh water. As it poured into our vast reservoirs, they mixed the salt back into it once again. It took hundreds of years to supplement our existing oceans and achieve the resulting greening of our planet."

"Wow! What an incredible feat," Adam exclaimed. "But … what about Zeran?"

Duron lowered his eyes. "Ah, yes: the small planet. This is very hard to say, Adam. Before the, ah, final parting, we were left with a small, silica-based sphere, a dried husk of its former self."

The crew suddenly caught their breath in alarm. Adam's eyes narrowed. "Come again? This story's startin' to have an awfully familiar *ring* to it...."

"How could *that* be possible?" Duron tilted his big head, puzzled. "I am positive we have not revealed any of Zeran's secrets to you!"

Adam glanced at his crew. Everyone's hands were spinning impatiently, making hurrying motions. He turned to Duron, his hands repeating the same gesture.

"Well, it appears that I really need to finish this story, and quickly!" Totally bewildered, Duron paused to gather his thoughts. "And so I will, in all honesty." He tuned to the assembly. "Ah, there was a dark side, a *very* dark side. As Adam knows, we had planned to blast the small planet out of orbit, but as we were completing the construction of our big guns, a far bigger problem had been developing...."

This story was starting to hit really close to home. The crew began to murmur, their eyes questioning. Adam subtly laid a finger across his lips to silence them.

"A group of shell creatures had discovered a gravesite containing some of our early workers...." The old Bandor paused, shuddering visibly. "And-and they *ate* the remains! It seems that by simply ingesting this decaying Bandor flesh and thus the elements of our Rasheen, their genetic codes quickly became unraveled: they evolved and started to grow at an exponential rate! Why, they were even developing a form of intelligence, just like our Razahs and Spyrins!"

There was absolutely no doubt now. As the crew stared at Duron open-mouthed and dumbfounded, the old Bandor turned quickly to his young protegé: Adam was shaking his head and sputtering, trying to form his jumbled thoughts into words. Like a concerned parent, the old Bandor laid a slender palm on his arm. "What is it, my son?"

"It-it just *can't* be," Adam stumbled, searching for the words. "I-I don't know how to tell you this, or how it's even *possible*...."

The Elders leaned toward him in alarm, sensing his emotional distress.

Adam blurted it out. "We were *there*!!"

Duron couldn't understand. "Yes, Adam? Where?"

"We were all on *Zeran*! We know where your third moon is!"

It was the Bandors turn to be shocked. Their eyes widened, pondering the impossibility, the tremendous odds of these young humans ever coming across their hurtling, arid white sphere. Suddenly, Adam's words and powerful mind-pictures burst into their minds, flowing like a raging torrent. They were helpless, and could do nothing but close their eyes to watch and listen as he babbled.

"Zeran's still alive! It's been caught in orbit inside a small solar system, halfway to the Earth. I called it the 'Obelisk Planet' because of the enormous shell monsters: they've gotten to be over a thousand feet high, guys, and they dig wide swaths through a white crystal surface to feed on millions of these, ah, seaweed-like fronds. And intelligence? *That's* an understatement! The oldest and biggest obelisks jammed my starship's controls by either telepathy or telekinesis or both and pulled us toward Zeran to force us to crash! Yes, guys, they wanted the starship to break up so they could... *eat us*!"

The crew was nodding vehemently in affirmation.

"They didn't count on the planet's soft surface, though; the starship just cut into it like butter and got buried. Honestly, guys, the ecosystem has evolved far beyond your wildest imaginations. I saw this crackling aura of electricity reaching out like tentacles for thousands of miles into space! Wait, wait, here's how we got away...."

As he beamed out a particularly vivid string of mind pictures, his grandfather and the Elders marveled at his sparkling ingenuity and creative problem solving, using only the materials at hand.

"*That's* how I finally figured out how to use the wind itself to uncover the starship," he concluded. "Oh, and by the way," he added, "when it rose out of its big crater, I noticed that you guys didn't get *all* the saltwater, some of it was left in the bottom of the hole...," he paused, making a rustling sound.

As the Elders opened their eyes, they saw him rummaging through his hip-pack and yanking out the contents. Shortly, he pulled out a sketchpad and a tiny holo-viewer, holding them up in triumph. "Ta-*daah*! Proof!"

Duron regained his tongue. "What-what is that small object, please?"

He smiled brightly. "A 3D camera!"

"You took pictures?"

"Lots of them! And I made some sketches, too! We brought back quarantine jars from the Obelisk Planet ... oops, I mean Zeran. The jars are real, guys: you can pull out the contents and examine them anytime. Hey, wait a sec! I'll back up this little gizmo a bit...." He excitedly pressed a few buttons. "There, take a look!"

As he passed the viewer and sketchpad around, their expressions changed from astonishment to wonder and then to fear. Duron shuddered. "Yes, those are definitely shell fragments from the monsters and your drawings are remarkable, but-but the question remains: how could it *be*? Zeran must be light-years away from us by now!" He pondered a moment, and then sat up straight in his chair. "Well, in view of all this indisputable evidence, I, for one, believe you. It *must* be so!" As he crossed his arms firmly, the Elders bobbed their heads.

His grandfather had been listening, conjecturing and putting his own thoughts together. "Adam," he interrupted quietly, laying his hand on his arm. "Believe it or not, I think I might have a way to help you figure out these mysteries."

"Huh?"

"Right before I put myself to sleep in the pod, I'd finally finished work on a huge project. I've retrieved the, ah, star of the show...," he paused, rethinking his wording. "I've got a tiny, pointy gizmo back in my lab. It should clear up this whole long, complicated sequence of events. We gotta be careful with it, though; it's very delicate and, ah, quite *radical*."

"Radical?" Adam's eyes glowed eagerly. "Let's *go*!"

He chuckled, pulling him back down onto his chair. "Whoa, slow down, boy!"

"Why?" He blinked. "You said...."

He stared at Adam pointedly. "First, pick a few people to come along as witnesses. We gotta fly in your new Phantom Cruiser," he added cryptically. "It's an integral part, and the only way to get where we're going."

Chapter 33: WARPING TIME

"Just a sec, almost got it…. There!!"

Maneuvering precisely with his thrusters, Adam lined the Phantom Cruiser up directly over his grandfather's surface dwelling. As he patched the dome's amazing gold-washed electric-blue image down to the crew's monitors, a gasp of astonishment erupted out of the surround sound.

"W-what?" Duron sputtered. "What instrument does *that*, Adam?"

He paused, thinking. "Actually, it's a group effort, kind of an AI-generated…."

"But Adam," he interrupted, "it took *decades* for us to construct this first working prototype. Hundreds of our brightest Bandor specialists were involved in the long, difficult task and they were working from extremely detailed technical drawings. That-that feature was *nowhere* in their plans!"

"You're right," Adam agreed, "it wasn't. But somehow, when I crank all the external sensors up high, the Cruiser's built-in AI weaves the schematics together into some kind of synergy, and then…. Oh, we'll talk more about it later." He parked the Cruiser in a rock-steady hover, and then popped open several landing platforms.

"Hey, Grandpa, you ready down there?"

There was an answering chuckle. "You bet, boy! Hey, come to think of it, I've been waiting for this moment for *hundreds* of years!"

Adam thought a moment. "Oh. Right, gotcha," he said, grinning. "So, let's skedaddle downstairs to your lab. I wanna take a look at your mysterious gizmo."

As the SpeedSled parted the last of the vine-covered branches, the old man's eyes widened. He stood up, lifting his dark glasses a moment to look around. "Good grief, Adam, you were right: the tree's enormous! That settles it. Before we go any further, the first thing we've *got* do is to pull that monster off my roof! My force field's strong, but not *that* strong!"

Adam looked up and raised his hands. "Wait guys, wait!" Above his head, the long chain of SpeedSleds sleds wobbled and then paused in their slow descent. "Here, Grandpa, take the controls for a minute. I just remembered that I've got three, ah, *helpers* in one of the cargo holds. I gotta call 'em out…" As he closed his eyes in deep concentration, the puzzled group landed, slid off their SpeedSleds, and began to walk slowly toward the damaged structure.

There was a sudden whoosh of thruster jets above them. The crew looked up to see three massive utility barges shoving their way through the tangled canopy. As the featureless rectangles descended and hovered next to the fallen tree, they could finally make out the cargo on top: two heavy-duty robots and a large laser cutter. They glanced back and forth and then at Adam, their eyes questioning.

"Hey," he motioned with his thumb. "Those badass dudes got the chops! They're *itchin'* to go to work!"

The mighty machines revved up. Locking their mechanical feet into matching brackets on their barges, the bots lined up on either side of the trunk. As the laser cutter adjusted its cutting length and shot out a blaze of light in the middle, they worked their way downward, slicing and flipping away huge sections of logs like matchsticks.

His grandfather could only shake his head. "You're *kidding* me, boy! Tell me you're not *directing* all this with your ... with your...."

Adam grinned, tapping on his forehead. "Yup! Just usin' the old noodle!"

As the last sections of logs flew away, the big, rubbery dome popped back up into shape as if it had never been damaged. Gathering strength, the force field returned in a crackling aura of light, haphazardly whipping off branches, forest litter, and brightly lit lizards. They ducked and flinched through the onslaught, holding their hands protectively over their heads. In a few minutes the big dome settled, alive and brimming with energy.

"Well, I'll be...," the old man breathed excitedly. "Home, sweet home."

Adam could contain himself no longer. "C'mon, c'mon, let's go take a look!"

His grandfather grabbed his arm. "Cool your jets, boy! That force field could *fry* you this time around! I gotta beam out my entry code!" As he waved his wrist programmer, the shimmering gold particles parted like a curtain. With his long robe fluttering behind him, the old man entered and walked briskly toward the far wall. He slid a tall bookcase aside smoothly to reveal another thin, twisting passageway winding through the jungle.

Kron peered over his shoulder. "Ah, another pod room, sir?"

The old man paused, thinking. "You're close. Let's just say there's a different form of suspended animation in there; more like the stuff dreams are made out of."

The long, twisting passageway ended in a large, brightly lit dome. The group filed in and stopped short, their feet squeaking on the rubbery floor. A large, mysterious object was sitting under a flimsy covering in the middle of the room. With no other entrances, how could something *that* big have gotten in? Their eyes turned to the old man.

"Okay, okay," he said, grinning. "This dome was my first sample, an actual, working prototype of my AnchorPlank system. It turned out so well that I lived in here while I expanded the rest of my complex."

Their eyes kept darting back to the mysterious object.

"Oh," he teased, "you wanna know what *this* is?" Ever so slowly, he reached for the edge of the covering, his fingers twitching tantalizingly.

Adam threw up his arms in exasperation. "Oh, for heaven's sake, lemme *help you*!"

As the group broke into laughter, they all grabbed the edge together. Yes, that was their Adam, back in the fast lane. They counted to three and gave a collective yank. The flimsy cloth disintegrated into a cloud of threads, drifting to the floor. Silence fell. The bare skeleton of a hollowed-out spacecraft sat propped up on triangular metal supports. Was this some kind of an experiment in progress? All around the perimeter, cluttered workbenches brimmed over with jumbled parts in various stages of disassembly.

The old man swept his arm in a big circle. "Well? Any guesses, boy?"

Adam grimaced. "No, Grandpa, you couldn't have! You *didn't*!"

"Yup," he shrugged. "This empty shell used to be my speedy little TimeWarper."

"But-but...."

"But what? How else could I have uncovered all its hidden secrets? And believe me, boy, there were a *lot* of 'em! Without this huge, long-term reverse-engineering project, I wouldn't have been able to dream up any CAD drawings for your…"

"No!" Adam interrupted. "*You* designed my amazing Phantom Cruiser!"

Nodding enthusiastically, Duron and the elders caught Adam's eye. The rest of the group could only stand there with their mouths hanging open, studying the old man in a new light.

"Hey," the old man shrugged, reached up under his hood, and tapped on his forehead. "Just usin' the old noodle!"

There was a long pause. "Wow," Adam whispered. "That's *really* usin' the old noodle! But not that I had any suspicions"; he winked, "the Cruiser has your name stamped all over it!" He paused again, searching for the right words. "But, um, I think I've got to dig deeper between the lines here, Grandpa. There's something *else* submerged under all this tech stuff: *s*omething huge, something *way* more important!"

"Oh? And that is…?"

"It's-it's kinda hard to explain."

"Go ahead, take a stab. I think I know where you're heading."

"Okay, here goes." He took a deep breath. "Is there a chance, a remote possibility that you *knew* the Elders would end up giving me the Phantom Cruiser, and once I got it you *knew* I'd be able to weave your enhanced AI sensors together to produce those new, hi-res color schematics?" He stood on his toes, leaning right up into to his face. "And here's the Big One: you *knew* I'd use those incredible graphics to find you sleeping here in your pod?"

He winced, grinning sheepishly. "Ya got me there, boy."

"But … *how*?"

"It wasn't hard. I had the missing piece."

"Huh?"

The old man pondered a moment and then answered Adam with a question. "You're familiar with an object's X, Y, and Z axes in space, right?"

"Ah, right. So…?"

"So I left a small gap in the command center's circuitry. It's hidden behind the main monitor in the flying bridge." He turned around and stared pointedly at Duron, looking over his glasses. "It's supposed to fit the, ah, missing piece…," he prompted.

The Elder reacted with a start. "W-why yes, you are correct! There *was* a strangely-shaped opening!" Duron stuttered. "Our engineers could not explain why it was left there, but they followed your plan to the most precise units of measure. What is it?"

The old man held up a finger. "Wait a sec." He walked over to a bench, rolled back the long sleeves of his robe, and slipped on a pair of heavily insulated gloves. Slowly, carefully, he slid a small object out of its protective box and held it high over his head for all to see. "This little gizmo," he explained, "is the missing piece. It generates something totally radical, a new force. I call it the 'W' axis."

"What?" Adam started. "There *is* a fourth axis?"

The old man nodded. "Yup. I pulled this tiny assembly directly out of the saucer, with no changes. It's the main ingredient, the ah, shall we say, *star* of the show. In honor of my little saucer, I'm calling it the 'Warper': it totally alters the perception of everything we know, changing the finite to infinite."

Tola's eyes popped. "Whooee! So now we've got *four* axes? W… XYZ? All those science fiction writers I debated when I was an editor weren't just *guessing*?"

"Nope. This is a large-scale Quantum Field Generator. It distorts both time and space." The old man turned the glowing object over in his gloved hand, contemplating. "So let's go plug this little sucker into the Cruiser and give it a spin, whaddaya say?"

The saucer rose swiftly through the atmosphere and pulled away from Aurona. Up in the flying bridge, Adam watched his grandfather punch a code on the main monitor's glassy surface to release a few hidden latches. As the huge, curved, floor-to-ceiling screen slid silently aside on hidden rollers, he took a short breath and stepped behind it. In moments he clicked on a small pin light and let out a loud whoop.

"Wow, come see this, boy! They did a *great* job following my plans!"

Adam squeezed in behind him and peered over his shoulder. Thousands of gold wires were reflecting brightly in the tiny pin light and a small, star-shaped opening gaped in the center of the great tangle of converging, printed circuitry. He squinted closer: there were five tiny pinholes punched into the perimeter.

"Ready?" With gloved hands trembling, the old man slid the Warper out of its protective sleeve, rotated it a few degrees, and snapped it securely into place.

There was a loud electrical snap. The floor vibrated and all the lights went out, even the tiny pin light clipped to the old man's sunglasses.

"Wow, Grandpa, what's going on?" In the pitch-blackness, Adam reached out and grabbed the walls for support.

"Shh, wait and *listen*, boy! You'll hear it coming any second!"

Stifling his eruption of questions, Adam closed his mouth. Soon, his excited breathing quieted until there was only the faint, muffled thump of his heart.

An elbow nudged his ribs. "There it *is*! *Hear* it?"

Adam bent his head, listening intently. Yes, far away, there was a distant rumble, almost as if a mighty locomotive were approaching. Abruptly, a great wave of energy passed through the Cruiser, wobbling the ship on its axis.

"Bingo!" his grandfather shouted, holding onto the walls. "We're in sync!"

As the lights came back on, their eyes met. His grandfather's hood had been thrown back and the fuzz on his domed head was standing straight out in a ball of powerful static discharge. Adam let out a snark. "Hey, you're a porcupine!

His grandfather silently pointed at Adam's reflection in the monitor: his hair was even wilder. "Yikes! And I'm a poodle!" He tried to slick it down, but the static persisted. With a shrug, his grandfather pulled his hood back up over his head, shut the big monitor, and fastened the latches.

Trying hard to stifle his persistent snickering, Adam settled into his gimbaled chair to watch his grandfather poke at more hidden switches. Another seat suddenly appeared from nowhere, smoothly unfolding and self-adjusting to the old man's lanky form. As he slipped into it, the room's surround sound returned with a roar, and with it, a cacophony of excited chatter rose from the crew below.

"Wow, what was *that*?" a voice quavered. "Some kind of dynamo revving up?"

"Yeah, it sucked all the energy out of the ship and made the lights go out!!"

A female voice cut in. "Eeww! My hair's all poofed out!"

Chuckling, the old man bent low to his headset. "Get used to it, girl. That hair thing's gonna happen every time we enter and leave the QDF!"

Adam scowled. "Ah … grandpa, the Q-what?"

"Oops, sorry. Too many acronyms. I mean the Quantum Distortion Field. By the way, guys, the whole Cruiser's now enveloped in a space-time bubble."

"Huh?" they chorused.

"In a way, we're not here," he shrugged. We don't exist. We sorta *disappeared*."

Adam slowly turned toward him. "What did you just say, Grandpa?"

"You named the Phantom Cruiser very aptly, my boy: it's invisible. We're ghosts, floating free from time and space. We can travel anywhere in the universe at any time, totally at our choosing."

Everyone was listening in awed silence, their minds reeling.

Tola posed a question. "Um, we're inside some kind of 'parallel universe'?"

"You got it. And in spite of all those brainy physicists who put up red flags when they discovered pear-shaped nuclei, time travel *is* real and the time-space continuum is still linear in its trajectory," he answered levelly. "While it might be a lot easier to go *back* in time than to go *forward*, the Cruiser's really tough and has a lot of redundant systems. It handles the 'forward' part effortlessly. By the way, guys, there's a lot more controls up here that I never had the time to figure out. The Cruiser may be able to step in and out of the QDF at will. You know, do weird things like appear, take some samples, and then disappear…," he paused, waiting for them to catch up.

Tola let out a long breath. "Wow, that means we can actually *see* history happening, *see* our stupid mistakes face to face, and then change the way things are going in our present time, right?"

"Excellent observation," the old man smiled. "This ship can be a tool to remodel our future. We'll witness the *real* scoop: no historian's research, no iffy legends, no second-hand guesses or intellectual opinions. But far more than that, we'll be able to go prehistory, way before anything mankind has ever observed or conjectured!"

After a long, thoughtful silence, a small voice arose. "Um, what actually happened when you used your TimeWarper to get to Aurona, sir?"

"Why do you ask?" he prompted. "Are you puzzled by the timing?"

"Yes, sir. This is Ariel. I'm sitting next to Peter. And yes, the timing's *way* off! You zipped to Aurona, and then after a few years, you zipped your weird body-clone back to Earth with the keys to our starship. In real time, those two trips would've taken our big starship fourteen hundred years! Your TimeWarper must'a really been *bookin'*!"

The old man let out a whoop. "You *got* it, girl! But, ah, 'bookin' isn't the term I'd use, here: it's more like the trips were instantaneous. All of you had to go into sleep mode for seven hundred Earth years, but I just stepped aboard the TimeWarper, pushed the wrong button, and found myself hovering outside Aurona's shields."

"Rats!" Peter groaned. "We wasted seven years of our lives sleeping?"

"To gain *thousands* more, living here on Aurona," the old man finished quietly. "Just ask Adam. He's already started his long journey. With guidance, you can, too."

Adam had been thinking, and turned to his grandfther. "Um, I have another big question. Get ready, 'cause this one's a doozey. I'm-I'm just gonna take a chance, here."

"Uh-oh, here we go again," he grimaced. "All right, I'll give it my best shot."

"Does this Cruiser have any way to plug in a holo-cube? I've got one right here in my hip pack." He patted his zippered pocket. "I took it outta the Tomb minutes before Elena and I left. I think it contains info from their earliest explorations of the Earth."

"Wow! You actually *found* one? I've heard of 'em, but I've never *seen* one!" He raised a finger. "You know, there *is* a holo-cube reader aboard, but I don't know how it works. I am guessing it locks onto the cube's space-time coordinates."

The crew had lost him. "Huh?" someone squeaked. "What are those?"

"They're really, really big numbers: long strings of numerical codes woven together and folded in on themselves, like DNA. Remember how your old Earth smartphones tagged photos with their GPS locations? Well, a similar kind of coordinates are recorded into Adam's holo-cube, but they're way more sophisticated. It doesn't create images because it doesn't *need* to. The Warper just … *takes* us there!"

Duron had been trying his hardest to catch up. "Adam, you found a holo-cube? You have actual *records*?" His voice wavered unsteadily over the surround sound. "Why, Aquan was our very first outreach! We modeled *all* our voyages from that one!"

The old man held out his hand. "Give me the cube, boy. I'll plug it in. The coordinates should bring our Cruiser right to the source. Wait, just lift your arm. The controls are hidden under your armrest. That's right, pull. It'll flip it open.…"

Adam whispered to his headset. "Um, could you give us a second here, Duron? This might take a bit of doing.…" As he opened his armrest, there was a small touch screen glowing; a square indentation was off to the side. "Holy cow, Grandpa," he scowled. "This stuff has been here all the time, right under my arm? We have a portal to another dimension?"

His grandfather turned red. "Um, ah, I gotta confess something here, boy: I pulled this whole chair, as is, out of the TimeWarper. I handed the assembly to the Elders as a package because it was way, way too complicated for me to reproduce. There are more buttons and gizmos under the other armrest, and I'm sure everything has some hidden mind switches, too. Anyway, here goes.…" His big fingers shaking, the old man dropped the tiny cube into the hole.

Immediately, everything faded to black. Somewhere in the distance, there was a faint gibberish: the hissing, sibilant cadence of a strangely familiar language.

"W-who's that, Adam?" Elena's voice drifted out of the surround sound. Where's all that talking coming from?"

"Let's find out, hon." Adam raised his mike a notch. "Everyone, turn on your translator buttons and listen!"

There were exclamations of surprise, followed by a flurry of tapping noises as they activated their buttons. As the whispering drifted closer, a blinding light suddenly enveloped them. Shading their eyes in the brilliance, they found themselves skimming across the surface of a phantom desert, right down at ground level.

Peter let out an exclamation of surprise. "Hey! I-I can't see my hands!"

"Me either," someone echoed. "Or my body! What's going on?"

Adam intervened. "We're not *here* guys, remember? Just wait and see...."

The Bandorese whispers had been growing steadily louder, more coherent. Over the din, a single, stronger voice started to narrate: *"Yes, that is right, Namron; I am now recording this onto one of the new holo-cubes.... What? Yes, I think this should be called 'Journey to Aquan, Trip Number 1.' Remember to return it to the library module in our new underground dwelling when we return to Aurona. That's right, Antechamber 6, Drawer 27. Let me see ... yes. To open the drawer, press code ZZ-9799/SEQUENCE."*

Adam whispered into his headset. "That's exactly where I found it, guys!"

The voice continued: *"Wait! Are those trees in the distance? Yes! In the midst of this vast, dry land there is actually a swath of green! Our mothership's cameras show the shape.... It looks like a large crescent."*

Suddenly, a forest was in front of them. The crew leaned forward excitedly. There seemed to be a tall spire towering over it. The Bandors quickened their pace.

"Amidst this extravagant vegetation there is an extremely tall tree growing in the center of large, circular clearing. It is spectacular. Our mothership's subsurface mining scanner shows that the roots of this amazing tree spread unbroken to the north, south, east, and west for hundreds of miles! But wait! What is this? Upon closer examination, our metal detectors are revealing something we have never before experienced: the sap of this great tree contains traces of the common substance, gold!

The crew nodded knowingly. Yes, there was no doubt about it; this enormous tree was indeed the Motherlode. It soared far above them, its branches lost in the clouds.

Suddenly, quite unexpectedly, the scene fast-forwarded. The operator of the new holo-cube didn't seem to be familiar with the controls. After a few minutes of thumping and rustling the sound came back on, but this time with a different narrating voice.

"We do not know what to do! A week ago, our leader accidentally ingested a small piece of the tree's mature fruit and went into a coma. We examined it and found it to contain a mind-expanding drug that was impossible for our labs to synthesize. Upon recovery, our leader discovered his cognitive powers had increased at an exponential rate, and strongly urged us to take a cutting of this interesting tree. We rooted it, then placed it in suspended animation with the other amazing specimens we have collected."

The narrating voice clicked off, the holo-cube's camera went dark, and another scene opened.

They crew found themselves outside a second, smaller clearing. Dark forest loomed in the background. As the Bandors entered cautiously, a blinding light suddenly enveloped them. A human ... no, not a human, an *apparition* formed out of hot, glowing coals was swinging a fiery, laser-like beam!

A frantic voice cut in. *"What is happening?? We can go no further! We are terrified! This-this great phantom creature is guarding what appears to be a second, smaller tree in the garden-forest."*

Amidst a lot of shouting, the scene went blank. As it reopened, the holo-cube recorder was rising off the ground. The operator seemed to have been in some kind of scuffle. *"I-I have just been attacked! Although we are approaching the tree with great caution and from many directions, the guardian will not let us get close enough to obtain a specimen! Our weapons are proving useless against it, passing right through its body! The creature is permitting us to record this beautiful tree on our holo-cube, however. We respect and hold in utmost admiration this superior being. Ensuing generations will indeed see and hear of this, our first and most remarkable encounter with another race on Aquan, for we are recording it for all time in the Great Book of Spirits."*

Apparently, the Bandors could look at the tree but not touch it. The crew watched in silence as the scene unfolded softly, like a flower. Perfectly symmetrical and deep, rich green in color, a small tree swayed in the breeze, its pendant lilylike blossoms a translucent, glowing white. The crew squinted, leaning toward it.

The branches seemed to be hollow: some kind of radiant light was pulsing from within, bathing the clearing in a shadowless brilliance. There was fruit in abundance, clinging close to the branches in soft, peach-colored hues. A gurgling sound emanated from somewhere under the dewy, small-bladed grass. They searched intently for the source, listening and turning in their seats. The clearing seemed to be swept clean and manicured to a velvetlike sheen. As the gurgling grew louder, they looked straight down.

Water! Clear, pure water flowed outward in all directions, *away* from the trunk! As they watched in shock and bewilderment, there was a swift, rushing sound somewhere behind them. They turned barely in time to see a blur of enveloping wings, then darkness.

In the long, awestruck silence, there was a subtle movement in their midst. A lanky Bandor warrior politely stood up, cleared his throat, and turned to face everyone. "I believe this is the point where I come in," he explained. Without another word, he removed his helmet and gloves, closed his eyes, and concentrated. As they watched him in total confusion, his features began to bump around.

Kron leaped to his feet. "Jaban? Could it be.... Is it actually you?"

The tall Bitron raised a finger. "Hello, Kron, my dear friend. Yes, it is. I have disguised myself as a warrior to join your group. I needed to see how this remarkable development unfolded. Now that you're all so close to getting some real answers, I believe that I have the extremely important missing pieces of your great Aurona puzzle. I'm sure they'll unravel any remaining mysteries."

He turned to Duron. "As your primary means of transportation, you Bandors used TimeWarpers in your early days of exploration. Wherever or whenever you traveled in time, you borrowed freely from your observations: languages, architecture, ideas or inventions, you absorbed them all and wove them into your daily life, establishing them as part of your great culture. It all stopped right after that great seaquake and tsunami destroyed the great underground structure you called the Tomb. All your leaders died in that disaster, and your people called an abrupt end to all planetary exploration. What's more, though, and quite troubling, is that they voted to erase all memory of those trips."

The elders pulled back in surprise and shock. "W-we did?" Duron stammered. "That must mean Adam's small holo-cube is the last remnant."

Jaban nodded. "It is, and that's why it's so priceless. But as to your real origins, where you actually came from, I believe Tola and Adam's grandfather have the answers." He turned to the little round man expectantly.

Tola stumbled and then began. "Well, Jaban's right. I'm going to attempt to put everybody's wild, racing thoughts into words. I-I don't know what to say here, guys, but I think we've just been given the Ultimate Privilege...," he paused, thinking. "I'm very familiar with this subject, so let me try to paraphrase the actual words for you: *'Then God planted a garden in Eden, in the East. He made all kinds of trees grow from the ground, trees beautiful to look at and good to eat....'*"

"You're kidding, Tola!" Adam interrupted. "All that stuff is just...."

"*Is* it?" Tola cut him off. "Let me finish, sir, and then you decide." He paused a moment to collect his thoughts and then continued. *"The Tree of The Knowledge of Good and Evil was in the middle of the garden, and also The Tree of Life. A river flows out of the garden, and then divides into four great rivers: The first is named Pishon. It flows through Havilah, where there is gold, and the gold in this land is good...."*

Tola paused. "Is that enough? Do I need to continue?"

Duron raised his voice haltingly. "But-but I do not understand. How is it possible that you humans have a written record of this encounter? Our ancestors did not mention they came across any of your race on Aquan; this was their very first outpost!"

Adam's grandfather had been listening quietly. With a sigh, he cleared his throat to speak. "Duron. Tola. Everyone. Think carefully now as you look at me." He switched on the big monitor's cameras, flipped back his hood, and removed his dark glasses to show his face. He raised a thin brow questioningly.

"Maybe everything was ... the other way around?"

They stared at him a minute, and then it sunk in.

They were looking at a Bandor.

CPSIA information can be obtained
at www.ICGtesting.com
Printed in the USA
LVHW060214150319
610713LV00001B/1/P